With love and many wishes
to Kate and Emma JH

For Alison W. and Ailie SY

Published 1992 by Thomasson-Grant, Inc.
First published 1992 by ABC (All Books for Children),
a division of The All Children's Company Ltd., London.
Text © 1992 Judy Hindley
Illustration © 1992 Selina Young

99 98 97 96 95 94 93 92   5 4 3 2 1

Library of Congress Cataloging-in-Publication Data
Hindley, Judy.
Maybe it's a pirate /
story by Judy Hindley : illustrations by Selina Young.
p. cm.
Summary: Just before she drifts off to sleep, a little girl imagines that
there are all sorts of fascinating things outside her bedroom door.
ISBN 1-56566-016-1
[1. Bedtime—Fiction. 2. Imagination—Fiction.
3. Stories in rhyme.] I. Young, Selina, ill.   II. Title.
PZ8.3.H5555May 1992
[E]—dc20   92-7261
CIP
AC

Thomasson-Grant, Inc.
One Morton Drive
Charlottesville, Virginia 22901
(804) 977-1780

Maybe It's a Pirate

Story by Judy Hindley   Illustrations by Selina Young

Thomasson-Grant
Charlottesville, Virginia

Bed is very nice sometimes.
And then,
sometimes it's not.
And I'm lying here and twitching
and I'm itching
and I'm hot—

and then I start to see things
that I didn't see before . . .
like a tiny little sparkle
just behind the closet door . . .
a tiny sort of shining
I can only barely see
where something very small
is sort of glittering at me . . .

maybe it's a fallen star!
Or maybe it's a key

with a map
to buried treasure

in a castle by the sea.

Maybe it's a wizard
playing hide-and-seek —

or a sad and lonely princess
with a tear upon her cheek.

Or the corner
of a magic window
with the moon behind it,
that takes you to a magic country
when you climb inside it.

Or maybe it's a witch's robe
that I could get to borrow —
Or maybe just some money,
that I could spend tomorrow!

WITCH'S MIRROR

But tomorrow must be nearly here—
and it's so warm in bed—
and I'm getting really sleepy . . .
But I'm
NOT
THERE
YET!

What if it's a pirate
with a diamond on his knee?

What if it's a tiger's eye?
A witch's smile of glee?

What if something
awful
is coming after me?
Well, I'm getting
tired of wondering.
I'm going to go and see.

I'll just slip
out my feet,

get my toes upon the floor—

just stand up—

I've done it!—

and slip behind this door—
I have to be so careful
—what if it should ROAR!
No!
It isn't going to frighten me!
Not Emily!
No more!
I'm going to take it
by surprise!
I'm going to tell it—
BOO!

Yummy Yummy Chocky COOKIES Eat as fast as you can

Oh!
I'm very sorry, Gladys.
And I'm very glad its you.
Don't be worried.
Don't be frightened.
It's all over, don't you see?
There's nothing to be frightened of—
it's really only me.
Just me.
Good old me . . .

. . . and
I'm really
glad
it's you.

THE Basics OF
Communication

2
EDITION

THE Basics OF
Communication
A Relational Perspective

2
EDITION

Includes Chapter on Histories of Communication

Steve Duck
David T. McMahan

SAGE

Los Angeles | London | New Delhi
Singapore | Washington DC

For information:

SAGE Publications, Inc.
2455 Teller Road
Thousand Oaks, California 91320
E-mail: order@sagepub.com

SAGE Publications Ltd.
1 Oliver's Yard
55 City Road
London EC1Y 1SP
United Kingdom

SAGE Publications India Pvt. Ltd.
B 1/I 1 Mohan Cooperative Industrial Area
Mathura Road, New Delhi 110 044
India

SAGE Publications Asia-Pacific Pte. Ltd.
33 Pekin Street #02–01
Far East Square
Singapore 048763

Printed in Canada

A catalog record of this book is available from the Library of Congress.

978-1-4522-0240-2

This book is printed on acid-free paper.

11   12   13   14   15   10   9   8   7   6   5   4   3   2   1

Executive Editor:	Diane McDaniel
Acquisitions Editor:	Todd Armstrong
Associate Editor:	Aja Baker
Editorial Assistant:	Nathan Davidson
Production Editor:	Eric Garner
Copy Editor:	Melinda Masson
Typesetter:	C&M Digitals (P) Ltd.
Proofreader:	Wendy Jo Dymond
Indexer:	Sheila Bodell
Cover Designer:	Bryan Fishman
Marketing Manager:	Helen Salmon
Permissions Editor:	Karen Ehrmann

Brief Contents

Detailed Contents

Focus Questions Revisited ■ Key Concepts ■ Questions to Ask Your Friends ■ Media Links ■ Ethical Issues ■ Answers to Photo Captions ■ References

CHAPTER 3 ■ Nonverbal Communication   49

CHAPTER 4 ■ Listening   77

CHAPTER 5 ■ Identities and Perceptions   101

CHAPTER 6 ▪ Talk and Interpersonal Relationships   133

CHAPTER 7 ■ Groups and Leaders   161

CHAPTER 8 ■ Culture and Communication 189

CHAPTER 9 ▪ Technology in Everyday Life   213

CHAPTER 10 ▪ Relational Uses and Understanding of Media   239

CHAPTER 11 ■ Preparing for a Public Presentation   265

CHAPTER 12 ■ Developing a Public Presentation   293

CHAPTER 13 ■ Relating Through Informative Speeches and Persuasive Speeches
319

CHAPTER 15 ■ **Interviewing** **367**

CHAPTER 16 ■ Histories of Communication   **407**

Preface

The Basics of Communication: A Relational Perspective was developed with the belief that basic communication courses play a central role in the discipline by attracting new majors, providing a foundation for upper-level courses, and supporting the entire academic community as important general education requirements and preparations for future life. The basic course is not just about training students in a discipline; it is about educating them more broadly for life beyond college and instilling within them an inquisitive curiosity that will serve them throughout their lives. It is one of the most important courses a student of any discipline will take.

Accordingly, we did not want to present students and the discipline with a cookie-cutter book that looked much like every other basic course textbook published in the past few decades—even though many publishers with whom we spoke encouraged us to do just that! Rather, if we were to develop a new textbook, it had to bring something fresh and meaningful to the study of communication. We believed that our relational perspective would provide students with a coherent structure to their study of communication and an opportunity to apply the material to their everyday personal and professional lives. We also believed that while some traditional material such as verbal communication, nonverbal communication, and listening should be included in any basic course, other material such as relational technology, social media, and culture was conspicuously absent from other books in spite of being an integral part of students' lives. We believed that pedagogical tools such as boxes and photos should be focused on learning. Finally, we believed that ancillary materials should be developed that would benefit students, new instructors, and experienced instructors alike.

In order to substantiate, challenge, and build upon these beliefs, we engaged in extensive discussions with our fellow basic course instructors and directors as well as students throughout the United States and other countries. We wanted to know what they needed in a basic course textbook, what worked and did not work with previous textbooks, and what innovations must be included. Primarily due to their input and encouragement during all facets of its development and production, the first edition of *The Basics of Communication* was met with an overwhelmingly positive response. These discussions continued once the first edition was published, and remained fundamental in the development and production of this edition.

New to This Edition

This second edition enabled us to advance the components that worked well in the first edition and to include additional features and modifications to enhance its use in communication classrooms. In general, we have streamlined much of the text in order to increase its readability for students. Forty-two tables have also been included to help students synthesize the material. Margin notes proved very popular with both instructors and students. Consequently, their numbers have been increased in this edition. The same holds true for the photographs included throughout the book, which also serve as learning tools for students. Most of the original photographs have been replaced, and many additional photographs have been included. Three new pedagogical boxes (Contrarian Challenge, Case in Point, and College Experience) have been included in each chapter. In response to reviewer and student comments, the coverage of some material has been rearranged, removed, increased, or added. Specific examples include an increased focus on perception when dealing with the development of identities and an entirely new chapter on interviewing. The latest research and findings have been incorporated throughout each of the chapters, as have updated discussions and examples.

We are thankful for the success of the first edition and are excited about the potential impact of the second edition. In what follows, we discuss the relational perspective, outline the pedagogical features of the book, and provide a final note about instructor support.

A Relational Perspective

This book allows all of these topics to cohere and coalesce by pointing out the *relational* basis of all communication as a major feature of students' everyday lives. By "relational basis" we mean the influences created by and upon relationships during the course of activities *other than* relational development, management, and intimacy creation—for example, the effects of a personal relationship on one's ability to persuade a person with health advice. In short, we deal not only with the creation of relationships but also with the way relationships flow into many other daily experiences. We then apply this perspective to basic issues in communication.

The Intersection of Communication and Relationships

The key feature of this text, then, is the idea that relationships make, are present in, modify, and create all communication. Our coverage of relationships is not as containers created by emotions; instead, we stress the importance and implications of the fact that they are perpetually *managed and enacted* daily experiences. In short, we emphasize the vital intersection of communication with relational contexts. We believe that this point provides both insight and coherence with reference to the topics normally covered in a basic text and simultaneously integrates such material with the increasingly popular and important, but previously independent, research on relationship communication, which is gradually refining or even replacing the traditional concept of "interpersonal communication." All of our coverage of traditional topics is extended and developed from this point of view.

The Social Context of Everyday Experience

The relational approach makes the importance and operation of communication more understandable through direct connections to student experience and therefore will facilitate classroom discussion while channeling and capitalizing on students' natural interests. We use this idea to illuminate the daily lives of students, and we offer the pedagogical purpose of showing how the students' experiences can be clarified through the principles of communication theory. Our goal is to help students understand their own daily lives by increasing the analytic awareness of their experiences and to show how communication theory and research can illuminate them. We further emphasize the social context of everyday experience, not only at the level of dyadic relationships and membership in networks but also by noting that people's interactions with one another create the location of society's influence on the individual: Social partners are the human face of such abstract notions as "society" and "culture." Our relational approach helps pedagogically by showing how much of life's experience (even of "society at large") is in fact perceived through direct social connections with other people. Only through our direct experience with others who represent "culture" and "society" do we feel these abstractions' influence at all.

A Way of Understanding the World

Given the variety of their educational backgrounds, demographic characteristics, and experiences, all students share the fact that their understanding of the world has been formed and influenced by relationships. Therefore, we focus not on the traditional approaches based on intimacy development but instead on the ways relationships create epistemics and rhetorical visions—that is, ways of understanding and (re)presenting the world—and we interweave this claim into traditional topics in interpersonal communication and media to show how much of life's apparently personal experience is in fact processed through social connections. By adopting an overall coherence of approach, it is possible to prevent segmentation of topics by use of the guiding overarching theme and hence to tie together several previously—but to us always artificially—separate aspects of communication, which will help communication majors develop further as their courses proceed and allow them to see connections between presently disparate areas of communication study. This basic hybrid text will therefore lay the groundwork for a lifetime of learning, as well as present a strong overview of communication for those whose only exposure to the work of communication scholars will be this book. In this way, we hope to make the book relevant to business majors, to those in training for the health professions, and to many other students with an interest in communication studies.

Pedagogical Features

We view the pedagogical features within textbooks as fundamental elements in the comprehension and incorporation of the material being presented. Unfortunately, chapter boxes and other pedagogical elements, often sidebar features, are frankly overlooked by students and instructors alike. Accordingly, we have included pedagogical features with a fundamentally integrative and summational force, which will give students an immediate and visible structure for what they study in the text. These pedagogical tools are located throughout, as well as at the end of, each chapter.

Overview

To help guide the students, each chapter begins with a pedagogical overview: "These are the key things you need to know about this topic. Now let's look at them in more detail and go on to extrapolate and develop the complexities." Focus Questions are then posed to further direct students through the chapter. These questions are positioned *after* an opening narrative rather than at the very beginning to increase the likelihood that students will use them.

Chapter Boxes

The main body of the chapters includes the following pedagogical boxes: (1) Make Your Case, (2) Strategic Communication, (3) Listen In On Your Life, (4) Contrarian Challenge, (5) Case in Point, and (6) College Experience. Make Your Case boxes provide students with opportunities to develop their own positions or to perform an exercise about the material, which then can be used as a basis for class discussion. Within the nonverbal communication chapter, for example, students are asked to consider a situation where they felt uncomfortable in the presence of another person. Strategic Communication boxes present students with guides to integrate the material into their lives when influencing others. For instance, the technology chapter asks students to consider how the purpose of their messages and the technological preferences of the person they are contacting will determine the appropriateness of face-to-face, telephone, or computer-mediated interaction. Listen in on Your Life boxes ask students to consider the material in relation to their lives and lived experiences. Specifically, this feature will sensitize students to issues and encourage them to become careful observers of the activities and events going on in their lives, compelling them to examine and apply the material. For example, the listening chapter asks students to consider friends, family, classmates, or coworkers they would label as *good* and *bad* listeners. Students are then asked to consider what behaviors led them to these evaluations and then to determine measures to enhance others' listening skills. Contrarian Challenge boxes encourage critical thinking by asking students to consider positions that counter or contest those presented in the text or commonly held in society. For instance, in the "delivering a public presentation" chapter, we encourage students to use manuscript delivery only when careful wording is required and maintain that novice speakers, especially, should avoid this delivery style. However, we ask students to develop an argument for why novice speakers would benefit from manuscript delivery. Though students may agree with what is presented in many instances, we want to encourage the critical examination of all material discussed in the book. Case in Point boxes encourage students to apply what they have learned in the analysis of everyday life situations. For instance, the culture chapter asks them to find a public space where members of a unique cultural group are gathered and observe the ways they communicate. Finally, College Experience boxes encourage students to apply the material discussed to better understand and perhaps manage situations encountered in academic contexts. A major factor in the retention of students is their development of relationships with classmates, instructors, advisors, and others on campus. These boxes have been developed to help students evaluate and handle academic life and relationships. Chapter 1, for example, asks students to consider how academic-based relationships such as those between instructors and students frame interactions, influencing what is said and how communication is interpreted.

Margin Notes

Margin notes are also included in each chapter to provide students with additional information or open-ended questions to ponder as they study the material. Accordingly, some margin notes serve to enhance student interest in the material by providing unique information, such as who invented the Internet. Other margin notes urge students to reflect upon the material by posing such questions as whether families would be considered groups.

Photographs

Photographs included in each chapter also serve as pedagogical tools. Each photo caption is stated in the form of a question that corresponds with material being discussed. Students will be asked to examine the photograph and answer the accompanying question based on their understanding of the material. Rather than being open-ended, these questions have specific answers that appear at the end of each chapter.

End-of-Chapter Pedagogical Materials

Each chapter also ends with pedagogical materials that bring the overview and focus questions full-circle. Focus Questions Revisited is implemented as a way of summarizing chapter material via pedagogical structure rather than as a simple (and usually ignored) chapter summary. Also, instead of including review questions, which often serve only to establish lower levels of comprehension, each chapter includes (a) Ethical Issues, (b) Media Links, and (c) Questions to Ask Your Friends. These features enable students to further examine how the chapter material fits within their communicative lives as a whole. Ethical Issues urge students to contemplate and develop a position regarding ethical quandaries that arise in communication. For example, the technology chapter asks students to consider whether employers should use material on social networking sites, such as Facebook or Twitter, when making hiring decisions. Media Links lead students to draw from media in order to further explore the issues discussed in each chapter. For example, the relationships chapter instructs students to examine the Sunday newspaper section of marriages, engagements, and commitment ceremonies for similarities in attractiveness. Finally, Questions to Ask Your Friends provide students with questions to ask their friends in order to further increase their awareness of the material and integrate it into their lives. In the culture chapter, for example, students are urged to ask their friends about themes in their favorite children's stories and to connect those themes to cultural ideals and norms.

Conversational Tone

To further assist student learning, we have adopted an informal tone in our writing. This is intended primarily to invite students into the conversation about the issues that we present as basics of communication. We also want to engage their capacities to reflect about a problem and work through it with us, leaving them with a greater sense of having mastered the material. We continually refer to everyday issues that students may have encountered or heard about from others, and we challenge them from time to time to reflect on and apply to their own lives what they have been reading about here.

Instructor Support

Although a fundamental feature of the book is, of course, to update discussion of topics by integrating the latest research while providing a new relationally based perspective on the material normally included in traditional texts, this is a two-edged sword. A challenge associated with developing a new textbook—especially one offering an original approach and addressing more up-to-date issues of communication—is that many instructors already have their courses in good shape and do not need the extra burden of rewriting those courses to fit a completely new text. We have therefore sought to add material in a way that supplements and develops rather than replaces traditional material. By this means, we seek to support those teachers who have developed courses on the basis of older material and who want to add some spice from the newer research without having to completely revise their existing lectures and notes. Thus, although the present text updates much of the theory and research included in older-style texts, we have constructed this book to reflect the traditional, basic text design. A host of ancillary materials are also available that would benefit both new and experienced instructors of the basic course.

In sum, we see the advantages of this book as fourfold:

1. It presents a coherent reformulation of communication around the theme of relational and everyday experience.

2. It recognizes transformations within the discipline of communication and covers material increasingly relevant to students' lives.

3. It has strong self-reflective pedagogical features applied to students' own personal experiences and is thus different from many older texts.

4. It can be readily adopted without major restructuring of existing courses because it adds, we think, a more interesting approach to existing topics rather than entirely redrawing the map.

See if you agree.

***

The Basics of Communication: A Relational Perspective (Second Edition) is accompanied by the following supplements, tailored to match the content of the book.

Ancillaries

Student Study Site

www.sagepub.com/boc2e

An open-access student study site provides a variety of additional resources to build on students' understanding of the book content and extend their learning beyond the classroom. The following resources are featured for each chapter:

- **Self quizzes** with multiple-choice and true/false questions for every chapter allow students to independently assess their progress in learning course material.
- **E-Flashcards** reinforce student understanding and learning of key terms and concepts that are outlined in the book.
- **Web resources** to various sites on the web for further research related to the chapter topic.
- A "**Learning From SAGE Journal Articles**" feature provides access to recent, relevant full-text articles from SAGE's leading research journals. Each article supports and expands on the concepts presented in the chapter. Discussion questions are also provided to focus and guide student interpretation.
- Carefully selected, web-based **video** and **audio link** resources feature relevant content for use in independent and classroom-based exploration of key topics.
- **Web exercises** direct students to various sites on the web and ask them to apply their knowledge to a particular topic.

Instructor Teaching Site

www.sagepub.com/boc2e

A password-protected instructor teaching site provides one integrated source for all instructor materials, including the following key components for each chapter:

- An updated **electronic test bank**, available to PCs and Macs through Diploma software, offers a diverse set of test questions and answers to aid instructors in assessing students' progress and understanding. The software allows for test creation and customization and each chapter includes multiple choice, true/false, and essay questions. The test bank is also available in Microsoft Word.
- **PowerPoint presentations** designed to assist with lecture and review, highlighting essential content, features, and artwork from the book.
- **Chapter outlines** and **key terms** have been provided for each chapter that can be used to structure daily lesson plans.
- **Classroom activities**, **discussion questions** and **course projects** are provided to reinforce active learning.
- **Web resources** to various sites on the web for further research related to the chapter topic.
- Carefully selected, web-based **video** and **audio link** resources feature relevant content for use in independent and classroom-based exploration of key topics.
- **Sample syllabi** provide suggested models for creating the syllabus for your course.
- **Speech evaluation** and **format guidelines** assist in grading student speeches and provide the "how to" of putting a speech together.

Acknowledgments

A book such as this is a far larger undertaking than we realized when proposing the first edition. Although our two names appear on the front cover of both editions, many other people have contributed to their development. Chief among these and to whom we owe the largest debt is our editor, the inestimable Todd Armstrong. Working with Todd has been a genuine pleasure, and this project benefited enormously from his experience and wise guidance. Like many authors, we signed with SAGE specifically because of Todd's professionalism, enthusiasm, keen intellect, and appreciation for both the discipline and the written word. His pioneering vision and commitment to knowledge further position him without equal among those in the publishing industry. Plus, he has great taste in ties.

We are grateful to those colleagues and friends who took the time to read drafts and redrafts of manuscripts at all stages of development—from initial outlines to re-revised "final" versions—for their wisdom and suggestions. We would also like to thank our students, both graduate and undergraduate, who knowingly or unknowingly provided observations, examples, and thoughtful discussion of the ideas presented here.

We are also thankful to the instructors and students who used the first edition of the book for allowing us into their classrooms. Many of them enabled us to live out the relational perspective through personal contact by phone and e-mail and through visits on campuses and at conferences. Their feedback and encouragement are greatly appreciated and have enhanced this second edition in immeasurable ways.

Involvement in books such as this takes an enormous toll on family life. We are grateful to our respective spouses and families that we have managed to complete another project and still remain married. Their forbearance provides a supportive atmosphere for us to manage the long hours and extended absences required to bring such projects to completion.

Finally, we would like to thank all of our parents, siblings, nieces and nephews, extended families, friends outside academics, acquaintances, strangers we have encountered, people we like, people we do not like, detested colleagues, and despised enemies, all of whom have provided us with ideas for a relational perspective on communication and an awareness of the importance of everyday life relating.

We are also indebted to the following for their unstinting generosity in commenting on the textbook in spite of their incredibly busy schedules and for making many brilliant suggestions that we were all too happy to borrow or appropriate without acknowledgement other than here. They generously contributed to whatever this book in its turn contributes to the growth and development of the field. We could not have developed the relational perspective without their professionalism and thoughtfulness.

Matt Abrahams
De Anza College

Brent E. Adrian
*Central Community College–
Grand Island*

Allison Ainsworth
Gainesville State College

Elizabeth R. Alcock
Bristol Community College

Carlos Alemán
James Madison University

Melissa W. Alemán
James Madison University

Alicia Alexander
*Southern Illinois
University–Edwardsville*

Karen Anderson
University of North Texas

Alice Araujo
Mary Baldwin College

Christine Armstrong
*Northampton Community
College*

Kevin Backstrom
University of Wisconsin–Oshkosh

Bryan H. Barrows III
Lone Star College–North Harris

Douglas Battema
Western New England College

Sally Bennett Bell
University of Montevallo

Keith Berry
University of Wisconsin–Superior

Robert Betts
Rock Valley College

Robert Bodle
College of Mount St. Joseph

David M. Bollinger
*University of North
Carolina–Wilmington*

Deborah Borisoff
New York University

Jay Bower
*Southern Illinois
University–Carbondale*

Kathy Brady
*University of
Wisconsin–Whitewater*

Michele Bresso
Bakersfield College

Paulette Brinka
*Suffolk County Community
College*

Pamela Brooks
*Arizona State University
Polytechnic*

Stefne Lenzmeier Broz
Wittenberg University

Nancy J. Brule
Bethel University

Dale Burke
Hawai'i Pacific University

Linda Cardillo
College of Mount St. Joseph

Sheena M. Carey
Marquette University

Anna Carmon
*North Dakota State
University*

Laura Cashmer
Joliet Junior College

Mindy Chang
Western New England College

Yvonne Yanrong Chang
*University of Texas–Pan
American*

April Chatham-Carpenter
University of Northern Iowa

Denise M. Chaytor
East Stroudsburg University

John Chetro-Szivos
Fitchburg State College

Daniel Chornet-Roses
Saint Louis University–Madrid

Carolyn Clark
Salt Lake Community College

Brian Cogan
Molloy College

Sarah Cole
Framingham State College

Janet W. Colvin
Utah Valley University

Anna Conway
*Des Moines Area Community
College*

Erica Cooper
Roanoke College

Gil Cooper
Pittsburg State University

Lisa Coutu
University of Washington

Miki Crawford
*Ohio University Southern
Campus*

Alice L. Crume
*Kent State
University–Tuscarawas*

Kevin Cummings
Mercer University

Kimberly M. Cuny
*University of North
Carolina–Greensboro*

David D'Angelo
*Kent State
University–Tuscarawas*

Roberta A. Davilla
Western Illinois University

Quinton D. Davis
*University of Texas–
San Antonio*

Jean Dewitt
*University of
Houston–Downtown*

Linda B. Dickmeyer
*University of
Wisconsin–LaCrosse*

Aaron Dimock
*University of Nebraska–
Kearney*

Marcia D. Dixson
*Indiana-Purdue University–
Fort Wayne*

Shirley K. Drew
Pittsburg State University

Michele Rees Edwards
Robert Morris University

Michael Elkins
Indiana State University

Larry A. Erbert
University of Colorado–Denver

Suzanne Stangl-Erkens
St. Cloud State University

Billie Evans
Graceland University

Lisa Falvey
Emmanuel College

Jeanine Fassl
*University of
Wisconsin–Whitewater*

Sarah Bonewits Feldner
Marquette University

Diane Ferrero-Paluzzi
Iona College

Jerry E. Fliger
Toccoa Falls College

Sherry Ford
University of Montevallo

Jil M. Freeman
Portland State University

John French
Cape Cod Community College

Tammy French
University of Wisconsin–Whitewater

Todd S. Frobish
Fayetteville State University

Jodi Gaete
Suffolk County Community College

Beverly Graham
Georgia Southern University

Darlene Graves
Liberty University

Dawn Gully
University of South Dakota

Suzanne Hagen
University of Wisconsin–River Falls

Donna L. Halper
*University of
Massachusetts–Amherst*

Thomas Edwards Harkins
New York University

Martin L. Hatton
Mississippi University for Women

Patrick J. Hebert
University of Louisiana–Monroe

Susan Hellweg
San Diego State University

Valerie Hennen
Gateway Technical College

Deborah Hermach
Lane Community College

Annette Holba
Plymouth State University

Lucy Holsonbake
*Northern Virginia Community
College*

Sallyanne Holtz
*University of Texas–
San Antonio*

David Hopcroft
*Quinebaug Valley Community
College*

Alec R. Hosterman
*Indiana University–
South Bend*

Gayle E. Houser
Ball State University

Bill Husson
University at Albany—SUNY

Rebecca Imes
Carroll University

Ann Marie Jablonowski
Owens Community College

Amir H. Jafri
Davis and Elkins College

Lori Johnson
University of Northern Iowa

Michelle Johnson
The College of Wooster

Bernadette Kapocias
*Southwestern Oregon
Community College*

Jim Katt
University of Central Florida

William M. Keith
University of Wisconsin–Milwaukee

Doug Kelley
Arizona State University

Elizabeth Kindermann
*Mid Michigan Community
College*

Branislav Kovacic
University of Hartford

Shelley D. Lane
University of Texas–Dallas

Rachel Lapp
Goshen College

B. J. Lawrence
Bradley University

Kathe Lehman-Meyer
St. Mary's University

Amy Lenoce
*Naugatuck Valley Community
College*

Nancy R. Levin
Palm Beach Community College

Kurt Lindemann
San Diego State University

Judith Litterst
St. Cloud State University

Deborah K. London
Merrimack College

Karen Lovaas
San Francisco State University

Louis A. Lucca
*F. H. LaGuardia Community
College (CUNY)*

Julie Lynch
St. Cloud State University

Valerie Manusov
University of Washington

Lawrence M. Massey
*Spokane Falls Community
College*

Masahiro Masuda
Kochi University

Marie A. Mater
Houston Baptist University

Nelya McKenzie
*Auburn University–
Montgomery*

Bruce McKinney
University of North Carolina–Wilmington

Donald S. McPherson
Indiana University of Pennsylvania

Shawn Miklaucic
DeSales University

Jean Costanza Miller
George Washington

Yolanda F. Mitchell
Pulaski Tech

Thomas Morra
Northern Virginia Community College

Kay E. Neal
University of Wisconsin–Oshkosh

Vicki Nelson
Curry College

John Nicholson
Mississippi State University

Michael E. Nitz
Augustana College

Carey Noland
Northeastern University

Kristen Norwood
Trinity University–Texas

Laura Oliver
University of Texas–San Antonio

Rick Olsen
University of North Carolina–Wilmington

Susan Opt
Salem College

Miri Pardo
St. John Fisher College

Nan Peck
Northern Virginia Community College–Annandale

Lynette Sharp Penya
Abilene Christian University

Frank G. Perez
University of Texas–El Paso

Jeffrey Pierson
Bridgewater College

Jon Radwan
Seton Hall University

Rita L. Rahoi-Gilchrest
Winona State University

Pravin Rodrigues
Ashland University

Tracy Routsong
Washburn University

M. Sallyanne Ryan
Fairfield University

Erin Sahlstein
University of Nevada–Las Vegas

Jim Schnell
Ohio Dominican University

David P. Schultz
Trinity Lutheran College

Pamela Schultz
Alfred University

Pam L. Secklin
St. Cloud State University

Marilyn Shaw
University of Northern Iowa

Tami Spry
St. Cloud State University

Gina Stahl-Ricco
College of Marin

Suzanne Stangl-Erkens
St. Cloud State University

John Stone
James Madison University

John Tapia
Missouri Western State University

Jason J. Teven
California State University–Fullerton

Avinash Thombre
University of Arkansas–Little Rock

Amy Torkelson Miller
North Dakota State University

April R. Trees
Saint Louis University

David Tschida
St. Cloud State University

Stephen Thompson
College of DuPage

Jennifer Tudor
St. Cloud State University

Jill Tyler
University of South Dakota

Ben Tyson
Central Connecticut State University

Michelle T. Violanti
University of Tennessee–Knoxville

Catherine E. Waggoner
Wittenberg University

John T. Warren
Southern Illinois University–Carbondale

Sara C. Weintraub
Regis College

Scott Wells
St. Cloud State University

Richard West
Emerson College

Joel Whittemore
McMurry University

Bruce Wickelgren
Suffolk University

Sarah M. Wilde
University of North Carolina–Greensboro

Daniel Wildeson
St. Cloud State University

Richard Wilkins
Baruch College

Bobette Wolensenky
Palm Beach Community College South

Denise Woolsey
Yavapai College

Sarah Wolter
Gustavus Adolphus University

Yinjiao Ye
University of Rhode Island

Lance Brendan Young
Iowa City VA Medical Center

Mei Zhang
Missouri Western State University

We would also like to extend our deep appreciation to the following student reviewers of the published first edition for their keen insight as those for whom this book is truly intended.

Fayetteville State University: Katrina Faison, Kristy Mitchell, Jourdan Scruggs, Elvia Stangle, and Desiree Thomas; *University of Iowa:* Daniel Usera; *Lone Star College–North Harris:* Lyndi Bryson and Beverley Church; *Molloy College:* Karenlyn Barone; *University of Nevada, Las Vegas:* Jenny Farrell; *McNeese State University:* Scott Backstrom, Dontae Cannon, Halie Cooper, Hunter Duhon, Jordan Gandy, Ilias Khidhr, Jeremie Mitchell, Brandon Regis, Chad Robertson, Rae Williams; *Owens Community College:* Stephen Traxel; *University of Tennessee, Knoxville:* Kathleen Adgent, Holly Albright, Sarah Arnold, Mary Ashritz, Noel Austin, Joseph Barnes, Alyson Bauer, Flora Katherine Bell, Amanda Betts, Jessica Bishop, Tanya Bishop, Erica Boozer, David Bottoms, Ciarra Bragg, Mary Brandon, Krysta Elise Brown, Sayers B. Burgess, Kyle Cantrell, Preston Chandler, Elizabeth Darnell, John Daunais, Andrea Davis, Jasmine Davis, Krista Davis, Timothy Dembek, Tyrone Dowell, David Drew, Weston Duke, Katherine Duncan, Ashley Dupree, Jay Faris, Matthew Farris, Darren Flanery, Joseph Franklin, Russell Garner, Allison Goo, Richard Graves, Andrew Hamilton, Shani Hammonds, Myosha Hardnett, Ashley Harris, Carrie Hatcher, Robert Hayes, Max Healy, Brad Hernandez, Jonathan Hill, Charles Hodges, Cara Holloway, Brian Hopson, Cathleen Hosfield, Jessica Howell, Sara Horne, Morgan Hutcheson, Lacie Hyder, Lauren Kedrow, Caroline Johnston, Allison Kelly, Traci Kerr, Alyssa Knight, Jennifer Lea, Patrick Lees, Kijeka Lewis, William Lewis, Senwhaa Lim, Rachel Mathis, Ashley McClusky, Elizabeth McPherson, Brooke Mooney, Manika Moore, Rachel Moore, Lara Ann Muldowny, Cori Mullaney, Emmanuel Negedu, Jessica Newsom, Joseph Ohman, Kelly Paley, Kensey Parker, Jessica Pensinger, Rebecca Perkins, Devin Phillips, Jessica Pinkston, Chasen Plunkett, Sarah Polston, Andrew Puryear, Cary Queen, Cara Rains, Rachel Robinson, Adriana Rodriguez, Christian Ross, Carrie Rowland, Brent Russell, Ian Salter, Gina Sarli, Courtney Schiller, Hannah Schwartz, Richard Sharp, Sharina Sheehan, Jessica Shipp, Lindsey Sowders, Ben Sproul, Robyn Steffen, Hannah Strickland, Charles Treadway, Victoria Treece, Ellis Turner, Brittany Vaughn, Mark Vick, Marie Waller, Phil Walters, Samantha Weinschreider, Madi Weller, Eric White, Chris Williams, Krisgianna Woods, Michael Young; *Washburn University:* Lisa Bellanga, Garrett Bendure, Adam Forbes, Andrew Foxhoven, Blaine Grooms, Kari Hadl, Janelle Hill, Kaitlin Marsh, Tessa Okruhlik, Elise Richardson, Carmen Romero-Galvan, Lindsey Scott, Talia Van Anne, Cassandra Wall Gaddis, and Shannon Ware; *Winona State University:* Jana Heydon, Chris Johnsen, Jennifer Lamont, McKenzie Larson, Kate Perardi, Amanda Peters, Brad Reiter, Erin Rieckenberg, Paul Rohde, Emily A. Schultz, Katrina Theis, Danielle Topka, and Brent Vyvyan; *University of Wisconsin–Milwaukee:* Angela McGowan.

About the Authors

Steve Duck taught at two universities in the United Kingdom before taking up the Daniel and Amy Starch Distinguished Research Chair in the Department of Communication Studies at the University of Iowa in 1986, where he is also an adjunct professor of psychology. He was recently promoted to Collegiate Administrative Fellow and works with the deans' caucus in the College of Liberal Arts and Sciences, and as an extension of this position for 2010–2011 he has been appointed interim chair of the Rhetoric Department. He has taught several interpersonal communication courses, mostly on interpersonal communication and relationships but also on nonverbal communication, communication in everyday life, construction of identity, communication theory, organizational leadership, and procedures and practices for leaders. Always, by training, an interdisciplinary thinker, Steve has focused on the development and decline of relationships from many different perspectives, although he has also done research on the dynamics of television production techniques and persuasive messages in health contexts. Steve has written or edited 50 books on relationships and other matters and was the founder and, for the first 15 years, the editor of the *Journal of Social and Personal Relationships.* His 1994 book *Meaningful Relationships: Talking, Sense, and Relating* won the G. R. Miller Book Award from the Interpersonal Communication Division of the National Communication Association. Steve cofounded a series of international conferences on personal relationships that began in 1982. He won the University of Iowa's first Outstanding Faculty Mentor Award in 2001 and the National Communication Association's Robert J. Kibler Memorial Award in 2004 for "dedication to excellence, commitment to the profession, concern for others, vision of what could be, acceptance of diversity, and forthrightness." He was the 2010 recipient of the UI College of Liberal Arts and Sciences Helen Kechriotis Nelson Teaching Award for a lifetime of excellence in teaching. He was elected in 2010 as one of the National Communication Association's elite Distinguished Scholars. He hopes to someday appear on *The X Factor* and be famous.

David T. McMahan has taught courses that span the discipline of communication, including numerous courses in interpersonal communication, media, communication education, theory, and criticism. David's research interests also engage multiple areas of the discipline with much of his research devoted to bridging the study of relationships and media. This work includes examining the discussion of media and the incorporation of catchphrases and media references in everyday communication. A great deal of research has been derived from his experiences in the classroom and his commitment to education. His early work in this area focused on communication competence, self-conception, and assessment. His focus has since shifted toward topics that include both media and relationships, such as contradictions within advisor–advisee relationships and discussions of media in the classroom. His diverse research experiences include studies on symbolic displays of masculinity and violence in rural America, media-based political transformations of the world's nation-states, *The New York Times*' reporting of mass-murder suicide, and primetime animated series. His work has appeared in such journals as *Review of Communication, Communication Education,* and *Communication Quarterly,* as well as edited volumes. A member of the Central States Communication Association, Eastern Communication Association, Iowa Communication Association, National Communication Association, Southern States Communication Association, Speech Communication Association of Puerto Rico, and Western States Communication Association, David has served numerous roles within these organizations. He has received multiple awards for his work in the classroom and has been the recipient of a number of public service and academic distinctions, most recently being named a Centennial Scholar by the Eastern Communication Association. He hopes to someday appear on an updated version of *Tic Tac Dough* and beat the dragon.

1

An Overview of Communication

If you think there is anything important in your life that does not involve communication, leaf idly through this book and see if it makes you challenge your first thought. It will take only a couple of minutes, and then you can put the book back on the shelf. In reality we do not think you will be able to come up with any aspect of life that does not involve communication and that would not be made better by your ability to understand communication more thoroughly. We are passionate about the study of communication, and we believe very strongly that you can benefit from knowing more about how communication works. We wrote this book partly because we believe that everyone needs to know something about communication. *The Basics of Communication: A Relational Perspective* will help you better understand—and even improve—your life through better understanding communication.

The Relational Perspective and Everyday Communication

What makes this book different from other communication textbooks is the *relational perspective* taken when considering communication. The constant guide in understanding communication will be the relationships that you have with other people. The relational perspective is based on the belief that communication and relationships are intertwined processes. Any type of communication you ever participate in has a relationship assumed underneath it.

The relationship shared by people will influence what is communicated, how it is shared, and the meanings that develop. People generally talk with friends in a different way than with their parents. Coworkers generally talk with one another in a different way than with their supervisor. The meanings of communication also change depending on the relationships. For instance, saying "I love you" will take on different meaning if said to a romantic partner, a friend, a family member, a supervisor, or someone you just met. In turn, communication creates, reinforces, and modifies all relationships.

Saying "I love you" can do many things. It can lead to the creation of a new relationship, strengthen a relationship, maintain a relationship, or result in the realization that people do not view a relationship in the same way. Ultimately, the link between relationships and communication is undeniable, and it can be used to study all communicative activity.

Something else that sets this book apart from other basic course textbooks is its focus on *everyday communication.* The discipline of communication has traditionally focused on the "big" moments or seemingly extraordinary events of human interaction. These instances include initial encounters, betrayals, disclosure of secret information, family upheavals, and other dramatic experiences you may occasionally encounter during your lifetime. These events may be memorable, but they do not make up much of a person's lived experiences. For instance, romantic relationships only rarely feature moments in which partners hold hands, gaze into one another's eyes, and share their deepest darkest secrets and declarations of unending love.

Most interactions of romantic partners include brief conversations as they get ready for work or school, a quick phone call or text between classes or during a break, talking in the car while in traffic, or chatting while watching television. The content of these conversations is seemingly mundane and may include topics such as schedules, weather, what to eat, what to watch on television, what bills need paying, or the source of a foul odor.

Everyday communication may not always be memorable, but it does *constitute* (i.e., compose) a person's life, and it happens to be incredibly important. It is through routine, seemingly mundane everyday communication (more than through extraordinary events) that major portions of a person's life take shape.

Everyday communication creates, maintains, challenges, and alters relationships and identities as well as culture, gender, sexuality, ethnicity, meaning, and even reality. When discussing all types of communication, we will continuously interconnect them with your everyday life and experiences.

We sincerely believe that your life as a student, friend, romantic partner, colleague, and family member can be improved through the study of communication from a relational perspective.

Whatever your purpose in reading this book, and whatever your ultimate goal in life, we hope that it will

- enrich your experience,
- sharpen your abilities to observe and analyze communication activity,
- make your life a little bit more interesting, and
- help you understand the processes going on around you.

Before fully jumping into our exploration of communication, let's take a look at some of the features of this book.

Features to Guide Your Learning

Because we are convinced of the importance of the topic and because we are passionate about helping people learn about it, we have used some special features designed to make it particularly interesting and relevant to you.

First of all, the tone of this book is somewhat different from that of other textbooks you may have come across. We have deliberately adopted an informal and conversational tone in our writing, and we even throw in a few jokes. We are not attempting to be hip or cool: Trust us; we are far from either, so much so that we are not even sure if the words *hip* and *cool* are used anymore. Instead, we use a conversational voice because we believe that it makes this book more engaging to read. Plus, we genuinely enjoy talking about this material. We want to share our enthusiasm in a way that we hope is infectious. We have become used to seeing the significance of communication as if it speaks for itself, but we realize that not everybody sees communication that way. Because we are also deeply committed to the importance of studying communication, we want to discuss it all in such a way that is clear, understandable, and applicable to your life. We hope that this will make it as exciting to you as it is to us.

Everything that appears in this book—even every picture—does so for a reason. That reason centers on increasing your understanding, your application, and even your enjoyment of the material. For example, the pictures do not have standard captions, but each asks a question that you can answer for yourself (although we provide a possible answer at the end of each chapter). The pictures are here not just to make the book look pretty, but they serve the purpose of teaching you something and *making you think for yourself.*

Instead of beginning each chapter with questions to focus on before you know what the chapter is about, our **Focus Questions** follow an opening narrative for each chapter. They are so positioned because we want to ensure that you read them *after* you have seen the basic issues with which the chapter deals. We personally skipped Focus Questions when we were in school because they were not any help to our learning: They appeared at the very beginning of the chapter, and we did not yet know what they were about.

For this book, we strongly encourage you to read them. Because they come after the narrative that sets up the questions in each chapter, they will guide you through the chapter and provide you with insight as to what you should focus on as you read. Because they are important, we will also revisit and answer them at the end of each chapter so that you can see if your answers match ours. In fact, we do this instead of summarizing the chapter in the conventional way. The end of every chapter is therefore directly connected to the beginning.

We did not want to include boxes in support of material just to break up the text or just because they are generally included in other textbooks. We thought very carefully about what types of boxes would be most beneficial to your understanding of the material and to applying the material in your life. Ultimately, each chapter includes the following six types of boxes: (1) Make Your Case, (2) Strategic Communication, (3) Listen in on Your Life, (4) Contrarian Challenge, (5) Case in Point, and (6) College Experience.

Make Your Case boxes provide you with opportunities to develop your own positions or to perform an exercise about the material that might be used during class discussion. In the verbal chapter, for example, you are asked to find out the secret languages that you and your friends speak without realizing it.

Strategic Communication boxes help you integrate the material into your life when influencing others. For instance, the technology chapter asks you to consider how the purpose of a message and the technological preferences of the person you are contacting will determine the appropriateness of face-to-face, telephone, or computer-mediated interaction.

Listen in on Your Life boxes ask you to consider the material in relation to your own life and lived experiences. We want you to start recognizing communication in your life and how the material addressed within this book applies. For example, the listening chapter asks you to consider friends, family members, classmates, or coworkers you would label as *good* and *bad* listeners. You are then asked to analyze what behaviors led to these evaluations and to determine measures to enhance the listening skills of others. These exercises, therefore, will also serve to further your understanding and comprehension of the material.

Contrarian Challenge boxes invite you to think more carefully about what you have read and see if we have persuaded you or if you can see another side to what we have written. For example, in the chapter on delivering a public presentation, we encourage you to use manuscript delivery only when careful wording is required and maintain that novice speakers, especially, should avoid this delivery style. However, through the Contrarian Challenge box, we ask if you can make an argument for why a novice speaker would benefit from manuscript delivery. In many instances, such as that one, we think you will come to agree with us. However, we want to encourage you to critically examine all that is discussed in the book and not just take what we say without evaluation.

Case in Point boxes encourage you to apply what you have learned in the analysis of everyday life situations. For instance, the culture chapter asks you to find a public space where members of a unique cultural group are gathered and observe the ways they communicate. Doing so and answering questions posed within the box will help you better understand the ways in which culture and communication are connected.

College Experience boxes encourage you to apply the material discussed to better understand and perhaps manage situations encountered in academic contexts. The majority of people reading this book are students (or our relatives). Whether you are navigating your first-year experiences or still figuring things out after a few semesters or terms, these boxes will help you evaluate and handle academic life and relationships. For example, this chapter will ask you to consider the ways in which academic-based relationships such as those between instructors and students frame interactions, influencing what is said and how communication is interpreted.

Also included in each chapter are **margin notes,** which provide additional information about the material or open-ended questions to ponder as you study it. Accordingly, some margin notes provide unique information, such as when the first "smiley face" emoticon was sent, who invented the Internet, or what percentage of people believe that they are shy enough to need treatment. Other margin notes urge you to reflect on the material by posing questions, such as whether or not families would be considered "groups."

The very end of each chapter includes features to further enhance your mastery and comprehension of the material. Once again, we thought very carefully about what to include here. We did not want questions that ask you to merely memorize and repeat what you read in this book. Parrots can do that; rather we wanted you to *think* about the material outside of class as you carry out the rest of your life. We wanted to include features that ask you to go beyond each chapter's content and engage in higher levels of thinking.

Accordingly, each chapter also includes the following features: (a) Ethical Issues, (b) Media Links, and (c) Questions to Ask Your Friends.

Ethical Issues urge you to contemplate and develop a position regarding ethical quandaries that arise in communication. For example, the technology chapter asks you to consider whether employers should use material on social networking sites, such as Facebook, when making hiring decisions, and the relationships chapter asks if it is ever ethical to have two romantic relationships going on at the same time and why (or why not).

Media Links ask you to draw from media in order to further explore the issues discussed in each chapter. You are asked to watch a TV newscast and discover ways in which the newscasters establish a relationship with the audience, for example, and to read a newspaper article looking for examples of logical fallacies. The relationships chapter invites you to examine the Sunday newspaper section of marriages, engagements, and commitment ceremonies for similarities in attractiveness. Believe it or not, romantic partners often look alike!

Questions to Ask Your Friends provide you with questions to ask your friends in order to further increase your awareness of the material and integrate it into your life. In the chapter on preparing for a public presentation, for example, you are urged to ask your friends about two people whom they consider to be very different. If they wanted to try to convince each person of the same idea, how would they have to adjust their strategy with each one? Examining this issue will help you—and your friends—better understand the need to adapt presentations to particular audiences. Plus, these activities will help underscore the significance of relationships in your life. As with the boxes, we are serious about having you try out these instructional tools to improve your study of the material.

A **Student Study Site** is also available to improve your study of the material. It includes electronic flash cards to check your knowledge of key terms and concepts, study quizzes, Internet activities and resources, links to video and audio clips, and a link to the Facebook group created for the book. You can access the site for free at **www.sagepub.com/boc2e**.

Ultimately, we want to invite you into the conversation about the issues we present as basics of communication. As part of that, we are trying to stretch your capacity to think about a problem and work through it with us, leaving you with a greater sense of having mastered the material by thinking through it for yourself, under guidance.

Within this initial chapter, we invite you to start thinking more carefully about communication and how it works. In doing so, we will examine what makes communication more complex than many people may believe. We will also explore what communication entails by discussing a few of its key characteristics. So, with that in mind, let's get started with those focus questions we mentioned above.

Focus Questions

1. What are symbols?
2. How is meaning established?
3. Why should communication be considered cultural?
4. Why should communication be considered relational?
5. What are communication frames?
6. What does it mean to view communication as both representational and presentational?
7. What does it mean to view communication as a transaction?

What Is Communication Anyway?

In introductory chapters such as this one, you might expect the primary subject to be defined. In this case, you might be looking for an authoritative definition of *communication* that may very well show up on an examination you will take in the near future. Well, here is one you might like: *Communication is the transactional use of symbols, influenced, guided, and understood in the context of relationships.* Actually, that definition is not half bad, but it does not really do justice to what communication really entails. Your instructor may provide you with a better one.

There are a number of definitions of communication out there, and many of those definitions are very acceptable. Communication scholars Frank Dance and Carl Larson (1976) once compiled a list of 126 definitions of communication appearing in communication scholarship. Imagine the number of definitions that must have emerged in the four decades since then! Of course, education should go beyond memorizing a definition and rather should explore deeper issues or characteristics of an issue or a topic, so that is exactly what will be done in this chapter.

One fact that makes the study of communication unique, as opposed to, say, chemistry, is that you have been communicating your entire life. Previous experience with this topic can be very beneficial, since you will be able to draw from relationships and events in your own life when studying the material. You will even be able to apply the material, hopefully improving your communication abilities and life in general along the way.

You will notice that when we refer to someone else's work or ideas, we will list the surname of the author(s), a date, and a page number when quoting the author(s) directly. The date gives the year in which the original paper or book was published, and the page number is where the original quote can be located. This format is used in most social science textbooks and professional writing, with the full reference at the end of each chapter or at the end of the book. You may also be asked to use this format when you write your own papers or speeches.

The drawback to previous experience is that people may not see the value in studying something that is such a common part of life. You may even be asking the "big deal" questions: What is so problematic about everyday communication? Why bother to explain it? Don't people know what it is about and how it works? Communication is just about sending messages, right?

True: Most of the time, people communicate without thinking, and it is not usually awkward. But if communicating is so easy, why do people have misunderstandings, conflicts, arguments, disputes, and disagreements? Why do people get embarrassed because they have said something thoughtless? Why are people misunderstood, and why do people misunderstand others?

If communication is simple, how do people know when others are lying (if all that matters is listening to their words as a straightforward representation of a situation)? Why would anyone be agitated or anxious about giving a public talk if talk is just saying what you think? Why is communication via e-mail or text message so easy to misinterpret?

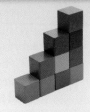

Make Your Case

If you are not already convinced, the importance of communication will hopefully become increasingly clear as you continue reading this chapter and finish the entire book. You may be using this book for a required course in your major, a required general studies course, or an elective course. Make the case for a basic communication course being required for all graduates at your school. To get you started, people in the professional world consistently rank effective communication a vital trait for new hires and necessary for advancement. What are some other reasons a communication course should be required?

People would never disagree about what happened in a conversation if the students who asked the above "big deal" questions were right. Why, then, are allegations of sexual harassment sometimes denied vigorously, and how can there ever be doubt whether one person intentionally touched another person inappropriately? Why are coworkers so often a problem for many people, and what is it about their communication that makes them difficult?

When first coming to the study of communication, many students assume that communication simply involves the sending of messages from one person to another through e-mails, phone calls, gestures, instant messages, text messages, or spoken word. That basic view has some truth to it, but communication involves a lot more than merely transmitting information from Person A to Person B.

As you read this chapter, you will likely start to recognize that communication is more complex than it initially appears. Let's begin by examining a common situation, a restaurant server speaking to customers:

"Hi! My name is Alice, and I'll be your server today. Our special is witchety grub stewed in yak fat with broccoli sautéed in mushroom sauce for $24.95. If you have any questions about the menu, let me know."

Photo 1.1 Is communication simply the exchange of messages? (See page 21.)

What you may already suppose about communication before studying it formally may be somewhat obvious in this example. Words are being used to convey information from one person to another person. Upon closer inspection, however, much more activity is taking place in this basic exchange.

The message is made up of words or symbols, which are used to allow one idea or representation to stand for something else. Taken-for-granted cultural assumptions are being made when these symbols are selected. "Menu" rather than "a list of all the food that we prepare, cook, and serve in this restaurant for you to choose for your meal" is said because it is assumed the customer will know the code word *menu* and its meaning in a restaurant as opposed to its meaning on a computer screen. If you do not recognize "witchety grub," it may be because you are not an Australian for whom this is a food delicacy, but the rest probably makes sense even if you do not know that a yak is a species of livestock cattle in China.

The server's message may also make sense because you know how to "perform/speak/do restaurant." The comments are appropriate only in some places and at some times. If Alice was standing in the middle of a park screaming them at everyone who passed by, you would likely think she was nuts. They also make sense only at the beginning of the interaction, not during the meal or when the customer is leaving the restaurant.

Notice also how the message makes the interaction work in a particular way, setting up one person (server) in a particular kind of relationship with the other person (customer) while setting that relationship up as friendly and casual ("Hi," not "A thousand welcomes, my royal masters. Command me as you will, and I shall obey").

You have built-in expectations about the relationship between a server and a customer. You already know and take for granted that these relational differences exist in restaurants and that restaurants have "servers" who generally carry out instructions of "customers." Therefore, you expect the customer will be greeted, treated with some respect by the server, told what "the special" is, and asked to make choices. You know the customer will eventually pay for the food and that the server is there not only to bring food, water, the check, and change but also to help resolve any difficulties understanding the menu. Alice will answer any questions about the way the food is prepared or help if you need to find the restrooms. Both the customer and the server take this for granted; it is a cultural as well as relational element of communication.

This relatively brief encounter also demonstrates that communication is more than just the exchange of messages. It may appear as though a simple message involving the greeting, the speaker's name and job, her relationship to you, and the nature of the special on the menu is being sent to the customer. Beyond the transmission of a simple message, however, something will take place as a result of the message exchange. Further, worlds of meaning are being created, and personal perspectives are being displayed.

Additional issues such as gender, status, power, and politeness are being negotiated. All of these things and much more are taking place within this simple exchange.

In the remainder of this chapter, we will introduce and begin our initial discussion of seven key characteristics of communication: (a) Communication involves symbols, (b) communication requires meaning, (c) communication is cultural, (d) communication is relational, (e) communication involves frames, (f) communication is both presentational and representational, and (g) communication is a transaction. Examining these characteristics will provide a better understanding of what communication and its study really entail.

Communication Involves Symbols

All communication is characterized by the use of symbols. A **symbol** is an arbitrary representation of something else. This may be an object, an idea, a place, a person, or a relationship—to name only a few. As we discuss in the upcoming chapters, symbols are either verbal or nonverbal. Verbal communication involves language, while nonverbal communication involves all other symbols. Accordingly, a symbol can be a word, a movement, a sound, a picture, a logo, a gesture, a mark, or anything else that represents something other than itself. For example, the shape of a heart is a symbol of love; a star on the shoulder is a symbol of rank and power; a touch on the arm could be a symbol of sympathy or love; a large car could be a symbol of wealth, power, and status.

The exact meaning of the representation or the best way to represent what we mean can be something that we can change or that a society (or partners in a relationship) can argue about, or it can be something where different cultures make different arbitrary choices.

To fully understand symbols, we can begin by discussing what they are not. Although the terms *symbol* and *sign* are sometimes used interchangeably, they do not represent the same thing. **Signs** are consequences or indicators of something specific, which human beings cannot change by their arbitrary actions or labels. For example, a weather vane is a sign of the direction of the wind; wet streets are a sign that it has rained; smoke is a sign of fire. However, we argue about it, we cannot make smoke *not* happen when there is a fire or make streets *not* get wet when it rains. There is a direct causal connection between smoke and fire and between wet streets and rain.

Symbols can be split into those that are iconic and those that are not. Both are representations of other things, but icons look like what they represent—for example, the stick figures used to indicate men's and women's restrooms or the airplane sign used to indicate the way to the airport. Other symbols do not have the pictorial connection to what they represent. The dollar sign does not look like a dollar; the heart shape symbolizes love but is not a picture of love.

Symbols, on the other hand, have no direct connection with that which they represent. They have been arbitrarily selected. For instance, the word *chair* has been arbitrarily chosen to represent the objects on which we sit, and other languages present the same item in different symbolic ways (i.e., *sella, chaise, stoel,* and *zetel*). We call a chair a *chair* simply because the symbol made up of the letters *c, h, a, i,* and *r* has been chosen to represent that object. There is nothing inherent within that object that connects it to

Photo 1.2 As close to a cow placed on a large pole as we are going to get, this particular traffic sign is actually warning motorists of a cattle crossing rather than instructing them to stop. Are traffic signs really signs, or are they symbols? (See page 21.)

the symbol *chair*. There is nothing about the symbol *chair* that connects it to that object. Once again, a symbol is an arbitrary representation.

It is sometimes difficult to recognize that symbols are just arbitrary representations. For English speakers, it is difficult to think of an object you sit on as anything but a *chair*. It seems as though there is a natural connection rather than an arbitrary connection. A stop sign—or more appropriately stop *symbol*—is another example of how people tend to see symbols as naturally linked to what they represent. It may seem natural that a red octagon with the capital letters *S*, *T*, *O*, and *P* written in the middle would compel you to cease forward movement when driving an automobile. However, there is no direct connection between that symbol and that particular behavior. A cow placed on a large pole could arbitrarily represent that same course of action just as naturally as the symbol people call a *stop sign* arbitrarily represents that action. There is no direct causal connection between a symbol and what it represents.

Because symbols are arbitrary, made-up conventions for representing something, they can be different in different cultures, and strangers need extra help. When Steve's mother first came to the United States, for example, she could find directions not to "toilets" but only to "restrooms," and she did not want a rest. Eventually, she had to ask someone. The euphemism *restroom* is not immediately obvious to cultural outsiders as a reference to toilet facilities. In other cultures—for example, in England—they may be referred to as "conveniences" or by a sign saying "WC" (meaning water closet). Even some indicators for restrooms within U.S. culture are quite confusing, as they very clearly require a shared understanding of cultural reference points (for example, we have seen indicators for "Does and Bucks," "Pointers and Setters," "Lads and Lasses," and "Knights in Need and Damsels in Distress").

The word (symbol) *set* has the most definitions of any English word, with some unabridged dictionaries including over 400 meanings.

Making things even more difficult is the fact that the same symbol can mean a variety of different things even in the same culture. We talk more about meaning in the next section, but for now consider how the symbolic act of waving to someone can have multiple meanings (e.g., a greeting, a farewell gesture, or an attempt to gain attention). The word *mouse* can mean an animal scurrying across your kitchen floor or something attached to your computer. A police officer's uniform is a symbol for "power," "official," "law and order," or "corruption" depending upon a person's perspective. The complexity of symbols is further evidence of the complexity of communication, but recognizing such complexities will enable you to begin constructing a more advanced understanding and appreciation of communication.

Communication Requires Meaning

Communication requires that symbols convey **meaning**. What a symbol represents is said to be its meaning. Particular meanings, however, are not tied to only one symbol but can be conveyed in multiple ways using different symbols. For example, happiness can be conveyed by saying "I'm happy," by giving a thumbs-up sign, or by jumping up and down when your team scores. A friend may indicate "I'm happy" just by talking more frequently than otherwise. Over the course of the relationship, you have learned that frequency of talk is a meaningful indicator of his or her emotional state. Furthermore, because they are completely arbitrary, symbols have the potential for multiple meanings subject to change.

Social Construction of Meaning

Social construction involves the way in which symbols take on meaning in a social context or society as they are used over time. Communication scholars Hopper, Knapp, and Scott (1981) pointed out this context in personal relationships, such as when romantic couples develop code words and phrases ("personal idioms"). These are secret ways to refer to other people or to discreetly tell each other that, say, it is time to leave a party early. You could quite easily say openly to your partner, "My left foot itches" as a code phrase for "I'm very bored; let's get out of here," but the second phrase would be very impolite to say in front of others.

The meaning of symbols within a society or a relationship does not develop overnight but instead results from continued use and negotiation of meaning within that society or relationship, as shown by the yellow ribbon example in Figure 1.1. If such a change can occur, any meaning attached to a symbol has been arbitrarily constituted and socially constructed.

Meaning and Context

A single symbol or message can also have multiple meanings when used in different contexts. For example, the *physical context*, or the actual location in which a symbol is used, will impact its meaning. If you said, "There is a fire" while in a campground, it would mean something entirely different than if you said those exact same words while in a crowded movie theater.

The same symbols will also differ in meaning according to the *relational context*, or the relationship shared by the people interacting. Look again at the earlier example of saying "I love you." It means something vastly different said to you by your mother, your brother, your friend, your priest, your instructor, the president of the United States, your physician, someone you have been dating for more than a year, or someone you have just met on a blind date.

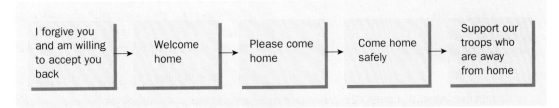

| I forgive you and am willing to accept you back | → | Welcome home | → | Please come home | → | Come home safely | → | Support our troops who are away from home |

Figure 1.1   Symbols such as the yellow ribbon tied around a tree have held multiple meanings over time.

Source: Griffin, E. (2009). *Communication: A first look at communication theory* (7th ed.). New York: McGraw-Hill.

Photo 1.3 What type of communication context involves physical locations? (See page 21.)

The *situational context* will also impact the meaning of a symbol. Consider the phrase "I love you" said by the same person (e.g., your mother) on your birthday, after a fight with her, as you leave home for school, on her deathbed, at Thanksgiving, or at the end of a phone call.

Verbal and Nonverbal Influence on Meaning

Accompanying verbal and nonverbal symbols will also impact meaning. For instance, the same words send different messages depending on how they are delivered. Officially beating the example to death, consider "I love you" said by your romantic partner in a short, sharp way; in a long, lingering way; with a frown; with a smile; with a hand on your arm as you get up to leave; or with a hesitant and questioning tone of voice.

Further, you know when someone is being sarcastic—and accordingly how to interpret his or her verbal message—based on nonverbal behavior such as tone of voice and facial expression. We discuss the interaction between verbal and nonverbal communication in greater detail in Chapter 3, but for now just recognize how determining meaning is more complex than it may originally seem.

Meaning and the Medium

The **medium**, or the means through which a message is conveyed, will also impact meanings of a message. A medium might include sound waves or sight—especially when interacting face-to-face with someone. It can also include cell phones, text messages, e-mail, instant messaging, chat rooms, social networking sites, a note placed on someone's windshield, smoke signals, or many other methods of communication.

The topic is especially important in cases involving a medium. For instance, breaking up with a romantic partner can be accomplished using any of the means listed above, but some may be deemed more appropriate than others. Breaking up with someone face-to-face may be considered more appropriate than sending him or her a text message or changing your relational status on Facebook from "In a relationship" to "Single." Beyond the message of wanting to break up, additional messages including how you viewed the romantic partner, the

Contrarian Challenge

Try to come up with a word, a phrase, or nonverbal behavior that has the same meaning regardless of changes in context. Honestly, this task is probably impossible. Are there any symbols that come close to always having the same meaning?

relationship itself, and yourself are conveyed based on the medium used. We address relational technologies such as cell phones and the Internet in more detail in Chapter 9, but for now just recognize their potential impact on meaning.

Communication Is Cultural

Another characteristic of communication is that it is cultural. Different cultures make different assumptions and take different knowledge for granted. Each time you talk to someone, from your culture or another, you are taking knowledge for granted, doing what your culture expects, and treating people in ways the culture acknowledges. You are doing, performing, and enacting your culture through communication.

Ultimately, culture influences communication while communication creates and reinforces these cultural influences. Consider what took place during your most recent face-to-face conversation with someone. Did you greet this person with a kiss or a handshake? Was there additional touch or no touch at all? How far were you standing from one another? Did you maintain eye contact? What were you wearing? Did you take turns talking, or did you talk at the same time? How did you refer to one another? What did you talk about? Did the physical setting impact what was discussed? How was the conversation brought to a close? What happened at the end? Your answers to these questions are based in part on cultural expectations.

When you follow these cultural expectations, you are also reinforcing them. Their position as the "proper" way to do things has been strengthened. Cultural expectations are also reinforced when someone violates them. Consider the most recent experience when you or someone else did something embarrassing. It was probably embarrassing because cultural expectations had been violated. Or, if there was no touch in your most recent face-to-face conversation, what would have happened if you had touched the other person? If touching would have been inappropriate, then the other person may have responded in a negative manner—enforcing cultural expectations.

Strategic Communication

Communicating in a manner consistent with cultural expectations increases a person's ability to influence others. Consider how you might adapt or adhere to cultural expectations when planning to speak with another person, a group or people, or a large audience.

Communication Is Relational

As mentioned previously, communication and relationships are intertwined. Communication impacts relationships, and relationships impact communication. The ways in which communication and relationships are interconnected are fully explored throughout the

In Japanese, there are more than 200 ways for one person to address another according to protocols of respect and status differences recognized by the participants.

book. For now, it is important to recognize that relationships are assumed each time you communicate with someone.

Paul Watzlawick and his colleagues (Watzlawick, Beavin, & Jackson, 1967) put it a little differently, suggesting that whenever you communicate with someone, you relate to him or her at the same time. All communication contains both a content (message) level and a relational level, which means that, as well as conveying information, every message indicates how the sender of a message and the receiver of that message are socially and personally related.

Sometimes the relational connection between sender and receiver is obvious, such as when formal relational terms (e.g., *dad*) or terms unique to a relationship (e.g., *sweetie* or *stinky*) are included. Even when addressing a stranger, people are more likely to say "Excuse me" than "Hey, jerk."

Sometimes the relational connection between sender and receiver is less obvious, but relational cues within communication would still enable you to determine, for instance, who is the boss and who is the employee, who is the professor and who is the student, who is the parent and who is the child, or who is the server and who is the customer. For example, yelling "Come into my office! Now!" indicates a status difference just through the *style* of the communication. Because the relationships between people most often are not openly expressed but subtly indicated or taken for granted in most communication, the content and relational components of messages are not always easy to separate.

Exploring the relational characteristic of communication a bit further, it can be maintained that relationships create worlds of meaning for people through communication, and communication produces the same result for people through relationships. Group decision making, for example, is accomplished not just by the logic of arguments, agenda setting, and solution evaluations but also by group members' relationships with one another outside the group setting. Groups that meet to make decisions almost never come from nowhere, communicate, make a decision, and then go home. The members know one another, talk informally outside the group setting, and have personal likes and dislikes for one another that will affect their discussions about certain matters. Many decisions that appear to be made during an open discussion are actually sometimes tied up before the communication begins. Words have been dropped in ears, promises made, factions formed, and relationships displayed well in advance of any discussion.

Consider examples from your life. Is everyone equal in your family? How are your interactions with friends different from your interactions with enemies? When watching television, does it make a difference whether you like the newscaster? Have you ever felt a connection to a character in a movie? On your last job interview, did the employer treat you like a potential valued colleague or an interchangeable worker? Are you more likely to contact some people through text messages and less likely to contact other people through text messages? When you listen to a speech, what difference does it make feeling as if the speaker understands and cares about you? We examine these questions and more throughout the remainder of the book.

Communication Involves Frames

Communication is very complex, but the use of frames helps people make sense of things. **Frames** are basic forms of knowledge that provide a definition of a scenario, either because both people agree on the nature of the situation or because the cultural assumptions built into the interaction and the previous relational context of talk give them a clue (Wood & Duck, 2006). Think of the frame on a picture and how it pulls your attention into some elements (the picture) and excludes all the rest (the wall, the gallery, the furniture). In similar fashion, a communication frame draws a boundary around the conversation and pulls our attention toward certain things and away from others.

Frames help people understand their role in a conversation and what is expected of them. If you are being interviewed, for instance, your understanding of the interview frame lets you know that the interviewer will be asking questions and you will be expected to answer them. Likewise, your understanding of the restaurant frame helps you understand why one person is talking about "specials" and insisting that you make decisions based on a piece of laminated cardboard that lists costs of food. Your understanding of the classroom frame will inform you of what you should do as a student and how you should interact with your instructor and with your classmates. A shared understanding of these frames is what enables people to make sense of what is taking place to coordinate their symbolic activities.

People also use framing assumptions to make decisions about what symbols are used and how these symbols should be interpreted. Your relationship with someone and your knowledge of that person, for instance, influence what can be taken for granted or left unsaid and what must be explained. Having both taught at the University of Iowa, when your authors talk with one another, we can include words or terms that presume knowledge of the university (such as *Hawkeyes*, *Pentacrest*, and *LR1-VAN*). These terms require a background of knowledge built into the interpretation of the words themselves, some of which depends specifically on knowing about the University of Iowa (e.g., that University of Iowa students are nicknamed "Hawkeyes," that the Pentacrest is the administration

College Experience

Consider the different relationships that create your life as a college student. Examples might include relationships with instructors, classmates, advisors, and roommates, just to name a few. How do these relationships frame your interactions? For instance, how does the instructor–student relationship influence what is said and how communication is interpreted? How do your interactions with instructors differ from those with classmates or others with whom you share an academic-based relationship?

Listen in on Your Life

After your next conversation with someone, take note of two or three key things that were said by this person. What was taken for granted? What did you need to know in order to understand these things? Do the same thing with someone with whom you share a different relationship. In what ways were the taken-for-granted assumptions the same, and in what ways were they different?

Photo 1.4 Many conversations between close friends are "framed" by previous experiences and conversations—hence, the phrase *frame of reference*. In what ways can you work out that these two women are friends and that they therefore share some history together that frames their interaction? (See page 21.)

center, and that LR1-VAN is a particular lecture hall). Each term would not need to be explained in our conversation because both of us know that the other one understands what those words, or symbols, mean. We talk more about how friends often talk in special codes, or conversational hypertext, in Chapter 2.

Communication Is Both Presentational and Representational

Communication is both representational and presentational. Accordingly, although it normally describes facts or conveys information (**representation**), it also presents your particular version of the facts or events (**presentation**). Communication is never neutral. It always conveys the perspective or worldview of the person sending a message. Your communication with other people *presents* them with a way of looking at the world that is based on how you prefer them to see it. Communication is not a neutral descriptive representation; it is always presentational and potentially persuasive (Hauser, 1986).

At first glance, the notion of communication being both presentational and representational is difficult to grasp. Consider the following way of looking at this issue. When you speak to someone, you have a number of words—your entire vocabulary—that can be used to construct your message. You will choose some words to construct the message and not choose other words. You will arrange those words chosen in certain ways and not in other ways. Your selection of words and the arrangement of those words are meaningful acts. What you do not say is often as important as what you do say. Your use of words and your construction of messages do not just *represent* ideas and information; these acts *present* your view of the world to others.

On some occasions, the presentation of these views is carefully developed. For example, imagine or recall a situation in which a friend has questioned something you have done, but you believe your actions were justified and want to explain this justification to your friend. In such cases you would likely select your words very carefully and thoughtfully, wanting your friend to view the situation from your perspective. Your message is conveying information (representational) while at the same time providing a glimpse into your perspective and how you want your friend to view the situation (presentational).

On other occasions, the selection of words may not be carefully planned but nevertheless presents your perspective to others. In fact, each time someone communicates, a worldview is being shared through the selection of terms, regardless of how much thought has gone into the construction of a message. Someone saying, "I suppose I should probably go to work now," in a gloomy manner provides a glimpse into how that person views his or her job, presumably not favorably. Someone saying, "I get to go to my communication class now," in an understandably excited manner provides a glimpse into how that person views the course, presumably very favorably.

The representational and presentational nature of communication is not limited to interactions between people but includes all types of communication. Consider the communication class example above. Our use of the descriptor *understandably excited* provides a glimpse into the worldview of your authors. When you give a persuasive speech, you do not just give the facts (representation); instead, you carefully select those facts that will make your presentation more persuasive. When the two sides in a court case tell their stories, they are not representing reality but presenting two different ways to think about an event. When a conservative news channel reports political events, it picks up on different aspects of the news than a liberal news channel does. Both channels explain, analyze, and evaluate events differently. Each channel presents reality in the way it wants you to understand it. In this sense, you might want to think of representation as "facts" and presentation as "spin."

Communication Is a Transaction

The transactional nature of communication is the final characteristic we will address in this chapter. When addressing communication as a transaction, though, we first must address two other common ways of thinking about communication: communication as action and communication as interaction. Each way of thinking about communication assumes something different about how communication works, with communication as transaction being the more sophisticated and more fruitful way of thinking about communication.

Communication as Action

Communication as action is simply the act of a sender sending a message to a receiver. Communication as *action* occurs when someone leaves a message on your voice mail, posts a message on your desk, or puts a message in a bottle in the ocean—that is, when someone transmits a message. So if Carlos sends an e-mail to Melissa, communication has occurred. It is pretty simple, really. However, it is not too interesting. If action was all there was to communication, we would be studying something else and not writing books about it. Communication as action could be developed slightly by questioning whether someone must *receive* a message for it to be communication. What if Melissa does not read her e-mail? Has communication truly occurred? According to the definition of communication as action, the answer is yes, but really all you know is that there has been an attempt to communicate. If communication was only an action, this book would end here, and you would likely not be studying communication in a class.

Photo 1.5 Would sending a text message be considered an act, an interaction, or a transaction? (See page 21.)

Communication as Interaction

Communication as interaction counts something as communication only if there is an exchange of information between two (or more) individuals. Using the previous example, communication exists between Carlos and Melissa if Carlos sends Melissa an e-mail and Melissa replies. This exchange represents a much more typical perception of communication. Someone sends a message, which is received by someone who in turn sends a message back to the original receiver. While this view of communication is slightly more advanced than communication as action, it remains limited in its scope and fails to capture what truly happens when people communicate.

Communication as Transaction

An even more sophisticated way to see communication is **communication as transaction**, or the construction of shared meanings or understandings between two (or more) individuals. For example, communication exists between Carlos and Melissa if, through their e-mail messages, they both arrive at the shared realization that they understand/love/know/need each other. It is also transactive communication if an exchange of messages results in a deal, an agreement, or a contract. In other words, communication in this sense is more than the exchange of literal messages. The speakers get more out of it, and extra meanings (e.g., about the relationships between the people) are communicated above and beyond the content of the messages exchanged.

Communication is interesting and worthy of study not because it merely involves the exchange of messages but because something magical and extra happens in this process. Two people speak and trust is built (transacted); two people touch one another and love is realized (transacted); two people argue and power is exerted (transacted); someone calls a grown man "boy" and racial bigotry is transacted; a man holds the door open for a woman and either sexist stereotyping or politeness is transacted. In all cases, the communication message transacts or constitutes something above and beyond the symbols (words or nonverbal actions) being exchanged.

Communication does not just create meaning; it creates the stuff of life. This **constitutive approach to communication** maintains that communication creates or brings into existence something that has not been there before. From the transactional/constitutive point of view, communication does not just construct meaning. It is through communication that relationships are created, that culture is created, that gender is created, that ethnicity is created, that sexuality is created, and even that reality is created. These are not only created through communication but also maintained, negotiated, challenged, and altered through communication.

Case in Point

We have begun to introduce new ways to analyze situations in your everyday life. The next time you go for a meal in a restaurant, take notes about the server–customer relationship. How does the relationship get accomplished? For example, what is communicated/transacted by a server's uniform, style of speech (bubbly or bored), or manner (friendly or aloof)? What impressions do you form about the server and his or her view of you?

For instance, relationships are not locations that we suddenly jump into—even though people refer to being *in* a relationship. Instead, relationships are quite literally talked into existence. It is through communication—especially talk, but also nonverbal communication—that relationships are brought into being, and it is through communication that the maintenance, negotiation, challenges, and alterations of relationships occur.

FOCUS QUESTIONS REVISITED

1. What are symbols?

Symbols are arbitrarily selected representations of something with no direct connection to that which they represent. Though sometimes used interchangeably, the terms *symbol* and *sign* do not describe the same thing. Signs are consequences or indicators of something specific, which human beings cannot change by their arbitrary actions or labels.

2. How is meaning established?

Because they are completely arbitrary, symbols have the potential for multiple meanings subject to change. The meaning assigned to a symbol has been socially constructed and is contingent on the contexts (physical, relational, situational) in which the symbol is used and other symbolic activity (verbal and nonverbal), as well as the medium used to transmit it.

3. Why should communication be considered cultural?

Culture influences communication while communication creates and reinforces these cultural influences. Each time someone communicates, he or she is taking knowledge for granted, doing what his or her culture expects, and treating people in ways the culture acknowledges. Culture is accomplished, performed, and enacted through communication.

4. Why should communication be considered relational?

All communication contains both a content (message) level and a relational level, which means that, as well as conveying information, every message indicates how the sender of a message and the receiver of that message are socially and personally related. Communication and relationships are intertwined. Communication impacts relationships, and relationships impact communication.

5. What are communication frames?

Communication frames are basic forms of knowledge that provide a definition of a scenario, either because both people agree on the nature of the situation or because the cultural assumptions built into the interaction and the previous relational context of talk give them a clue. A communication frame draws a boundary around the conversation and pulls our attention toward certain things and away from others. Frames help people understand their role in a conversation and what is expected of them. People also use framing assumptions to make decisions about what symbols are used and how these symbols should be interpreted.

6. What does it mean to view communication as both representational and presentational?

Communication describes facts or conveys information (representation) while conveying the perspective or worldview or slant of the person sending a message (presentation). Communication gives other people and audiences a way of looking at the world that is based on how the source of a message prefers them to see it.

7. What does it mean to view communication as a transaction?

Viewing communication as a transaction means understanding that communication is more than just the simple exchange of messages. Rather, communication involves the construction of shared meanings or understandings between two (or more) individuals. Moreover, communication constitutes, or creates, aspects of life such as relationships, culture, gender, and even reality.

KEY CONCEPTS

communication as action   17
communication as interaction   18
communication as transaction   18
constitutive approach to
    communication   18
frames   15
meaning   11

medium   12
presentation   16
representation   16
signs   9
social construction   11
symbols   9

QUESTIONS TO ASK YOUR FRIENDS

1. Ask your friends to define communication. In what ways do their definitions align with the characteristics of communication discussed in this chapter? In what ways do their definitions counter these characteristics?

2. Ask your friends to consider the difference between signs and symbols. Do they find it difficult to view some symbols as being completely arbitrary?

3. Ask your friends whether a message must be received in order for communication to occur. What do their answers tell you about viewing communication as an action?

MEDIA LINKS

1. In what ways do song lyrics not merely entertain but also *present* particular ways of living, particular attitudes, and particular styles? Find examples that present relationships differently (e.g., from The Killers, Lady Gaga, Otis Redding, Toby Keith, Mel Tormé, The Beatles).

2. Watch a political discussion on C-SPAN, on a television news channel, or online. How are opposing positions being *presented?* Is the distinction between representation and presentation obvious or hidden?

3. Watch the audio and visual coverage of a live event on television or online. Then read about the same event in a newspaper the next day. How does the medium impact your understanding of the event and the meanings you assign to the event?

ETHICAL ISSUES

1. What assumptions appear to be built into people's speech concerning race, gender, sexuality, and age? Are such assumptions justified, or should no assumptions be made concerning these aspects of a person?

2. Is communicating in a manner consistent with someone's cultural expectations but inconsistent with your normal communication style unethical?

3. Your communication with someone may appeal to certain relational obligations. For instance, friends may be expected to do certain things (give someone a ride) if they are truly friends. Is it ethical to appeal to such obligations, or is it simply part of being a friend? Are there any limits to what a person may ask someone else to do based on their relationship?

ANSWERS TO PHOTO CAPTIONS

Photo 1.1 ■ No. Communication is actually quite complex.

Photo 1.2 ■ Traffic signs are really symbols rather than signs.

Photo 1.3 ■ Physical context entails the actual location in which a symbol is used.

Photo 1.4 ■ The women are probably close friends as demonstrated by obvious enjoyment of the conversation as well as their physical closeness and touch, which are signs of intimacy.

Photo 1.5 ■ Though it could result in an interaction or in the occurrence of a transaction, simply sending a text message would be considered an act.

STUDENT STUDY SITE

Visit the study site at **www.sagepub.com/boc2e** for e-flashcards, practice quizzes, journal articles and additional study resources.

REFERENCES

Dance, F. E. X., & Larson, C. E. (1976). *The functions of human communication: A theoretical approach.* New York: Holt, Rinehart & Winston.

Hauser, G. (1986). *Introduction to rhetorical theory.* New York: Harper & Row.

Hopper, R., Knapp, M. L., & Scott, L. (1981). Couples' personal idioms: Exploring intimate talk. *Journal of Communication, 31,* 23–33.

Watzlawick, P., Beavin, J., & Jackson, D. (1967). *Pragmatics of human communication: A study of interactional patterns, pathologies and paradoxes.* New York: Norton.

Wood, J. T., & Duck, S. W. (Eds.). (2006). *Composing relationships: Communication in everyday life.* Belmont, CA: Thomson Wadsworth.

2

Verbal Communication

A man walked into a bar. A second man walked into a bar. A third one didn't, because he ducked. You know the word *bar*, and you know that in our culture jokes and stories often start with the phrase "A man walked into a bar." Such cultural knowledge frames your expectations about the story you are being told. A *frame*, you recall, is a context that influences the interpretation of communication. However, the word *bar* has different meanings. If you were faintly amused by the opening sentences here, it is partly because the word is used in the first sentence differently than you expected on the basis of the frame of the story. The punch line works only because you are misled—twice—into thinking of a different kind of "bar." Familiarity with the story's cultural form frames your expectations in a way that pulls the last sentence right out from under you.

As we mentioned in Chapter 1, *verbal communication* involves the use of language. Whenever you speak, you *use* language in ways that take much for granted, and the study of *language use in talk* is the subject of this chapter. Language has a grammatical structure, but when used conversationally, it uses cultural and relational assumptions. These are represented by symbols, frames, and meanings. In this chapter you will learn more about the workings of these aspects of the spoken language of everyday life and how they serve to build and sustain relationships.

In everyday talk, words weave together seamlessly within a context that includes nonverbal communication. Examples of nonverbal communication include facial expressions, hand gestures, movements, changes in posture, and pacing or timing of speech. In practice, nonverbal aspects of communication help frame your expectations and interpretation of what someone means. For convenience, though, we have to separate verbal and nonverbal communication into two parts: verbal, or language, in Chapter 2 and nonverbal in Chapter 3. Keep in mind, however, that this split is artificial when it comes to understanding everyday life.

Focus Questions

1. What are the differences between grammatical language (*langue*) and talk in everyday use (*parole*)?
2. What frames your understanding of talk and gives it meaning?
3. What values are hidden in the speech you use?
4. How does everyday talk make use of relationships to frame meanings?
5. How do different types of talk work, and how do they connect to relationships?
6. What is talk style, and how does it frame meaning?
7. What are the key elements of stories?

How Do You Know What Talk Means?

When you use the word *cat*, everyone assumes you are referring to an animal. You know what animals are and, specifically, what a cat looks like. When you started to learn to read, "The cat sat on the mat" may have been one of the first sentences you ever came across. In everyday life talk, however, if you say to a person, "You really are catty" (Norwood, 2007), you are speaking not literally but relationally or metaphorically. A listener would understand what you mean, even though the words are literally not true: He or she is not a cat. This example emphasizes an important point: The formal grammar of a language is different from use of that language in everyday talk.

Linguists like Ferdinand de Saussure (Komatsu, 1993) therefore draw a distinction between *langue* (pronounced "longg") and *parole* (pronounced "pa-rull"). **Langue** is the formal grammatical structure of language that you will read about in books on grammar. **Parole** is how people actually use language, with informal and ungrammatical phrases that carry meaning to us all the same. "Git 'er done!" is an example of parole but would earn you bad grades in an English grammar course (langue). When people feel relaxed in a close relationship, they are much more likely to use parole. People in a formal setting are more likely to use langue. Communication is used loosely in close personal relationships because they are quite informal, but formal relationships are more uptight. Relationships frame both what gets said and how it gets understood.

Language and your use of talk are also based on other frames. One is familiarity with the other person: The friendlier you are with the other person, the more you use relaxed, informal language. Other influences on your speech affect the words you choose or the relational messages sent by the words you pick out ("Hey, you!" is different from "Excuse me, sir").

Other frames for talk depend on the times that you live in and the items that are familiar to you. Your great-grandparents may have called their father "sir" whereas you probably call yours "Dad" or something less formal.

A final frame requires that you know how the strict rules of grammar may be bent when you speak language out loud. We are sure that our readers normally speak in perfectly polished grammatical sentences; after all, you are educated people. However, quite probably you also know that in everyday talk you can speak in ungrammatical ways that everyone else understands. For example, "Ain't no way I'm gonna do that!" does not make a lot of sense from a strictly grammatical point of view. All the same it sends messages of defiant resistance to anyone who speaks a current modern form of English. "A pox on you, knave" means something when you are reading Shakespeare, but you would be unlikely to say it in everyday life today.

Multiple Meanings: Polysemy

Words, gestures, and symbols can have different meanings on different occasions/ circumstances according to the particular frame for talk. Communication scholars and philosophers call this **polysemy**, multiple meanings for the same word (Ogden & Richards, 1946). Even though you already knew that the same word could carry multiple meanings, knowing the academic term for it becomes important for deepening your insights into the way that everyday conversation actually works. You need to know how, in a particular sentence, you work out which meaning a person is using. If every communication—whether words, facial expressions, or gestures—can have several different meanings, then each time you speak or hear a word, you must determine which meaning applies.

Ambiguity   다의성

Polysemy exists as a feature of all communication, and you must always deal with the ambiguities that it creates. Ability to deal with this ambiguity is very important in everyday communication because that talk consists of many types of utterance (both formal and informal). Some examples of everyday talk are technical jargon, ordinary slang, put-downs, boasting, euphemisms, and even occasional cursing.

In the course of a single conversation, the partners can switch between styles and vocabularies. So they need to be sure that the context/frame clarifies what is going on when these switches occur. If a friend moves from informal to formal talk, suddenly curses, or switches from slang to technical talk, is he or she angry with you, or is there another explanation? Look at it the other way, too. If an acquaintance switches from formal to informal talk, this might mean that he or she wants to develop a friendly relationship in place of a previously more formal one. The most important point in this chapter, then, is that *relationships frame the meaning of talk*. So a strong and close connection exists among language, talk, and relationships.

Uncertainty

Uncertainty about meaning decreases as your understanding of frames that relationships and other contexts give you increases. The best and most helpful guide to a person's meaning is the personal knowledge you have from a close relationship with him or her. People tend

Did you know that a "cat" is not only an animal but a kind of whip (cat-o'-nine-tails), a movable penthouse to protect soldiers besieging a medieval castle, a jazz fan (a "cool cat"), and a brand of tractor (Cat, short for Caterpillar)?

to hang around with others who share their general system for understanding meanings (Duck, 2007). That familiarity helps narrow down the uncertainty in meaning.

You are better able to communicate with another person when both of you can assume you are in the same frame and know what you are talking about. You make assumptions about the best choice of meaning based on what you know about the frame you are in. You signal the frames you are using by means of various relational, cultural, and personal cues. For example, "Let's not be so formal" is a direct way of saying that you are in the "friendly frame," but "Take a seat and make yourself comfortable" has the same effect. More subtly, the fact that therapists have cozy offices with comfortable furniture, rather than hard benches, sends the same framing message in a different (nonverbal) way. Such cues place an interaction into a frame of informal relaxation rather than emphasizing toughness, distance, business, or threat.

Reading Conversational Frames

People can work out what you mean on a given occasion by reading these broad cues. The more familiar you are with the meanings available in a culture, the easier it is to read them. But the key to deeper understanding—the crucial guide to interpreting what someone means—is your relationship to others and how well you know them and their thinking styles. Talk is more than just language: It is the *use* of language, and the use of language can be personalized. In fact, the more closely two people get to know each other—what they know, how they think, how they talk—the more personal their talk becomes.

Photo 2.1 Why might this pairing of street signs be amusing to a citizen of the United States, and what is taken for granted by those people who understand the joke? (See page 46.)

Conversational Yellow Pages: Categories That Frame Talk

Having culture or relationships is like having the Yellow Pages for conversation in a particular language. There are lots of phone number categories, so it helps if you know you are looking for a plumber and can find the page with the plumber numbers listed. So, too, with talk: It helps if you know that when your partner talks about love, you are on the "romance" page, not the "tennis" page. Probably the strongest clue in language is provided by naming.

Naming and Defining

You already learned in Chapter 1 that language splits our world in many ways, dividing it into those items for which there are names. **Naming** is important because it seems both *arbitrary* ("It doesn't matter if you call it salad or dessert; it's still just Jell-O") and *natural* ("What do you mean, 'What's Jell-O?' It's Jell-O. Everybody knows Jell-O"). Naming involves another process, too: distinguishing items from other items for which we also have (different) words.

Several thinkers from both rhetorical studies (Burke, 1966) and psychology (Kelly, 1969) have observed that definition involves negation or contrasting. That is, whenever you say what something is, you also say either explicitly or implicitly what it is not. When a behavior is named as "sexual harassment," it is not "a joke" or "flirting." Some thinkers even suggest that you cannot know some concepts without knowing their opposites (for example, the concept of light makes no sense without the concept of darkness).

An even stronger version of this idea was proposed by Edward Sapir and Benjamin Whorf (Sapir, 1949; Whorf, 1956). The **Sapir/Whorf hypothesis** proposes that "you think what you can say." In other words, the names that make verbal distinctions also help you make conceptual distinctions rather than the other way around.

Contrarian Challenge

English speakers have a word for the front of the hand (*palm*), but no single word for the back. According to the Sapir/Whorf hypothesis, does this mean that English speakers should not be able to tell the difference?

Naming and Understanding the World

The words that a person or culture uses will have a direct influence on how the person or culture understands the world: The words make the world rather than the opposite, as you might typically think. You have no doubt heard the urban myth that the Eskimos have some different words for snow because people in that part of the world want to be able to differentiate between sorts of snow that "mean" or carry different implications for their activities in life. For example, assume that *snow1* indicates a kind of snow that means the coming of a storm, and *snow2* indicates a kind of snow that means the coming of spring. Using different words (*snow1, snow2*) helps the Eskimos make this and other important distinctions that matter in their lives.

Naming something not only sticks a label on it but also differentiates it from the rest of the world; your name tag, for example, goes on only *your* stuff. So a major function of language is to separate the world into different categories of objects and concepts (chairs, dogs, ideas, papers, professors, students, taxes, death, justice, freedom).

Phrased in a more academic way, language—and, in particular, the names we use in talk—will classify our world by giving things separate identities and properties. These serve to structure our worlds into *thought units* or items that we consider quite different from each other. Naming is incredibly powerful, and it makes a huge difference, for example, whether you name someone "an insurgent" or "a freedom fighter." Because there are two subtypes of meaning, we can connect them to the distinction we made in Chapter 1 concerning representation and presentation.

Types of Meaning

Communication studies draw a distinction between *denotative* and *connotative* meaning as a way of splitting the world into finer thought units. **Denotative meaning** refers to the identification of something by pointing it out. If you point at a cat and say, "Cat," everyone will know that the sound denotes the object that is furry and whiskered and currently eating your homework. **Connotative meaning** refers to the overtones, implications, or additional meanings associated with a word or an object. For example, cats are seen as independent, cuddly, hunters, companions, irritations, allergens, stalkers, stealthy, and incredibly lucky both in landing on their feet all the time and in having nine lives. If you talk about someone as a "pussycat," you are most likely referring to the connotative meaning and implying that he is soft and cuddly and perhaps stealthy, companionable, and lucky. You are unlikely to be referring to the denotative meaning and warning people that he is actually, secretly a cat and has fur and eats homework.

A handy way of thinking about this distinction is that "denotative meaning" basically identifies something, and "connotative meaning" gives you its overtones. Connecting these meanings with the ideas in Chapter 1, you can see that denotative meaning roughly corresponds with representation/facts and connotative meaning roughly corresponds with presentation/spin.

Denoting

Once you understand this distinction, you can see its importance in everyday talk. Conversation works only when both people can assume that they split the world by using the same words to denote and connote items. Denoting the same object or idea by the same words is an obviously fundamental requirement for communicating. If you point to something and use the applicable word (*bar, cat, food, witchety grub*), but the other person does not understand what you're pointing to, the communication is not effective. As we phrased this idea in Chapter 1, what occurs is action, not interaction; that is, the message is sent but not received.

When parents teach their children to communicate, they spend lots of time pointing out objects and repeating the correct words (communication as action) so the child learns to connect the object with the label ("Look at the cat." "Yes, that's a cat"). At the moment when the child gets what is going on, communication as interaction begins (message sent and received). Something even more magical begins to happen as the child starts to understand his or her world more effectively and to see connections and meaning and learns to *go beyond*. "That's a fire. It's hot. Don't touch it, or you will hurt yourself" turns the communication into transaction. Constitutive activity occurs as the child learns to associate fire as an object with the possibility of heat and therefore pain.

Connoting

On the other hand, connoting is about the implications and background behind the same words. For example, some words carry baggage that makes you feel good, and some do not. Consider the different emotions stirred up by the words *patriot* and *traitor*. The first connotes many good feelings of loyalty, duty, and faithfulness. The second connotes bad qualities like deceit, two-facedness, untrustworthiness, and disloyalty. These connotations are extra layers of meaning atop the denotation of a person as one kind of citizen or the other. You would feel proud to be called a patriot but ashamed to be called a traitor.

What are the connotations of the term *black-eyed peas*? Does it matter whether you first hear the word *cooking* or the word *hip-hop*?

Words carry strong connotations in your particular culture, but connotations can be personal and complex the better you know someone. A consequence of this association is that your ability to understand people improves as you know more about their minds and helps you to understand their specific intentions on a particular occasion. If you know where someone's "buttons" are, you know whether he or she responds irritably to an exclamation ("Go, Hawks!") because he or she is feeling defensive, just tired, or not particularly playful.

Intentionality

As we noted in Chapter 1, communication scholars have spent considerable time discussing the notion of **intentionality.** A basic assumption in communication studies is that messages indicate somebody's intentions or that they are produced intentionally or in a way that gives insight, at the very least, into the sender's mental processes. For example, if someone says something apparently insulting ("You dork!"), it makes a great deal of difference whether you believe he or she did it intending to be funny and didn't mean it to be hurtful (for example, if he or she said it with a smile or a joking tone of voice).

People usually assume that communication cannot happen unless someone sends an intentional message. However, the issue of intentionality is not whether it was actually present but more accurately depends on whether you *assume* that it was (for example, whether you believe that someone was really joking or is just saying that he or she was). Intentionality matters, then, not as an objective issue about what is really on the other person's mind but as a subjective judgment. What does an observer attribute to and project onto the other person? To interpret messages more accurately, you must develop a good feel for the speaker's intentions.

Culture, context, past history, and your relationship to the other person in a conversation help you know what meanings are listed on the relevant "Yellow Page." Otherwise, you'd end up having constant arguments and conflicts about what was going on. One person might assume that the other person meant something other than intended. That would create confusion, ill will, and suspicion, which would threaten the relationship.

Suspicion and Mistrust of Intent

Interactions between enemies and rivals or conversations based on mistrust show exactly this characteristic. Rivals are always looking for, or suspecting, a hidden meaning or agenda. Communication scholar Dan Kirkpatrick and colleagues (Kirkpatrick, Duck, & Foley, 2006) noted that enemies do not trust each other to mean what they say, always suspecting a lie or a "setup." This suspicion makes the conversation unproductive and very difficult to handle.

On the other hand, the deeper and more trusting your relationship with someone, the more likely you are to understand his or her intentions. Once again, the close connection among relationships, communication, and meaning solves social dilemmas for you and helps you understand what is going on.

Larry and a friend share a running joke about "tiramisu." Once something funny happened in a restaurant when one of them ordered tiramisu for dessert. Mentioning the word *tiramisu* is now a shorthand way of saying, "This person has made a very weird response in an odd way." Larry knows that; his friend knows that; but other people are not in on the joke and would be completely unable to interpret it.

Relationships and Connotation

The more personal your relationship with them, the more you are able to understand people's intentions and meanings. Part of becoming closer to other people is learning how they tick—an informal way of saying that you understand their worlds of meaning. When you know people better, you also know better than strangers what they mean when they make certain comments.

Relationships and the Taken-for-Granted

In a relationship context, your assumptions, shared understandings, and forms of speech encode/transact the relationship by means of shared understanding. The understandings shared by you and your friends represent not only common understanding but also your relationship. No one else shares the exact understandings, common history, experiences, knowledge of the same people, or assumptions that you take for granted in that relationship.

Think for a minute about what happens when a friend from out of town comes to visit, and you go out with your in-town friends. You probably notice that the conversation is a bit more awkward even if it is still friendly: You do a bit more explaining, for example. Instead of saying, "So, De'Janee, how was the hot date?" and waiting for an answer, you throw in a conversational bracket that helps your friend from out of town understand the question. For example, you may say, "So, De'Janee, how was the hot date?" and follow it with an aside comment to the out-of-towner ("De'Janee has this hot new love interest she has a *real* crush on, and they finally went out last night").

When you talk to people, you use words that refer to your shared history and common understandings that represent your relationship or shared culture. As you talk, you monitor that knowledge and occasionally must explain to outsiders, but the very need for explanation—particularly important when you are giving a speech to an audience that does not know what you know—indicates a level of relationship, not just a level of knowledge. Relationships presume common, shared knowledge.

> **Listen in on Your Life**
>
>
> You and your friends probably have several examples of shorthand terms and phrases for reminding one another of events, feelings, or people who populate your relational history. You may also have special nicknames for people known only to you and your partner or close friends. Come up with some examples, and bring them to class.

Words and Relationships

Words differentiate the world into objects and thought units and then name them. Talk does this relationally, too: With friends, we draw on words differently than we do in work relationships, family relationships, enemy relationships, and competitive relationships. It is very important to recognize that there is more to talk than just use of language (enshrouded in nonverbal communication) to denote something in the world.

You do not just do things with words when you talk. You do things with *relationships*, too, and the words you use in conversation transact your relationships. As well as the naming that *language* does, people adopt different styles of *speaking* according to their relationship. Restaurant servers, for example, identify items strictly relevant to their task, such as broccoli, witchety grub, and prices. Friends can refer to their previous experience together, their common history, their knowledge of particular places and times, and other experiences they likewise understand ("Remember when we went to Jimmie's?"). Because both friends know what is being referred to, neither of them needs to explain.

Words and Hidden Values

Let's take this a little further: Words make value judgments and these judgments are built into talk in relationships, and vice versa. A society or culture not only uses different words from those current in another language (obviously!) but also prefers some subjects to others. For example, how do you react to the words *spider, ice cream, class test, Porsche, sour, Republican, liberty, death*, and *justice?*

Photo 2.2 Two people's conversation may be affected by the context, their relationship, and their age, culture, and experience, among other things noted so far. What might these friends be talking about? (See page 46.)

God Terms and Devil Terms

Communication philosopher Kenneth Burke (1966) made a distinction between **God terms** and **Devil terms** in a particular culture. God terms are powerful terms that are viewed positively in a society, and Devil terms are equally strong terms that are viewed negatively. The obvious difference is that both are powerful, but each in a different way; terms like *justice* and *liberty*, for example, are seen very positively in U.S. society (God terms), whereas *Osama bin Laden* may be a Devil term (see Table 2.1 for some other examples).

Table 2.1 God and Devil Terms	
God terms in the United States	Liberty, Freedom, Justice, American Dream
Devil terms in the United States	Communism, Torture, Inequality, Prejudice, King George III

Depending on your political point of view, such words as *Bush* or *Clinton* or *Obama* may be one or the other, so you can see that God and Devil terms are not absolutes for everyone in the same society. The terms apply in relationships, too, because the partners in a relationship will have special references for people and events. Both of you will know what topics may not be mentioned or topics that you know your partner is sensitive about—his or her Devil terms—and that you steer away from. Sometimes your partner may act on behalf of society: "Oh! You shouldn't say such things! You're bad!"

Make Your Case

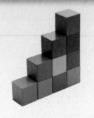

Which of the words below would you consider God terms, and which would you consider Devil terms? Make your case for each of your answers.

Abortion   Facebook
Banker   Natural
C (course grade) Politician
Cigarettes   Raw Food
Exercise   Twitter

In such a statement, he or she is reminding you about the norms of society and its God and Devil terms.

Other Values in Words

We noted previously that symbols indicate not only what is true but also what you would like people to think, and we used the terms *presentation* and *representation* to describe this difference. At times, your speech is persuasive or preferential; it makes distinctions that you want your audience to accept as valid.

Kenneth Burke's (1966) point about the value judgments built into words is very similar—namely, that your words encode your values and you see some concepts as good (communication studies) and some as bad (pedophilia). Every time you talk, you are essentially using words to argue and present your personal preferences and judgments, as well as simply describing your world. Your culture has preferences, as do you and your friends. Your communications express values in both obvious and hidden ways. Start paying more attention to those expressions of the values embedded in the words that you use to talk in your everyday lives. If you tell your instructor about your grade and say, "I think I deserved a B−, but you gave me a C+," both you and the instructor recognize that a B− is "better than" a C+ in the framework of meaning taken for granted in school. Your words are going beyond what they seem to be saying and are taking for granted the context, the relationship, and the culture in which the conversation occurs.

Keep in mind that nonverbal communication is a constant context for all talk. Not only the words themselves but also how you choose to utter them will differ and serve as frames. Frames can also be created by the style in which something is said. If talk is friendly, chances are that an ambiguous comment is friendly and not hostile, so previous context helps you make the decision about its meaning.

Everyday Life Talk and the Relationships Context

Duck and Pond (1989), apart from being our favorite combination of authors' names, came up with some ideas about the way relationships connect with talk in everyday life. They pointed out that talk can serve three functions for relationships: It can make something happen in relationships (instrumental function), indicate something about the relationship (indexical function), or amount to the relationship and make it what it is, creating its essence (essential function). Although these functions might sound complicated at first, you practice each of them every day without knowing it. Let's take a closer look.

Instrumental Functions

Whenever you ask someone out for a date, to a party, to meet you for a chat or a coffee, to be your friend, or to be just a little bit more sensitive and caring, you are performing an **instrumental function of talk** in relationships. What you say reveals a goal that you have in mind for the relationship, and talk is the means or instrument by which you reveal it. Anything you say that serves the purpose of bringing something new to or changing anything about the relationship is an instrumental function of talk in relationships.

College Experience

When people are in college—especially when they first enter college—they sometimes experience difficulties when talking with friends off campus or friends back home. The reason for these difficulties is that they get used to talking in certain ways with friends on campus. Have you experienced these challenges? What does this tell you about talk and relationships?

Indexical Functions

An **indexical function of talk** demonstrates or indicates the nature of the relationship between speakers. You index your relationship in the *way* that you talk to somebody. If you say in a sharp tone, "Come into my office; I want to see you!" you are not only being discourteous, but you are indicating that you are superior to the other person and have the relational right to order him or her around. The content and relational elements of the talk occur together. In your talk with other people, you constantly weave in clues about your relationships.

Conversational Hypertext and Hyperlinks

We have already slipped in one form of indexical function in talk: *hyperlinks.* Duck (2002) noticed that lots of talk involves a kind of **conversational hypertext.**

You know what hypertext is from your use of computers and the Internet, and how you talk to people works the same way. In conversation, we often use a word that suggests more about a topic and would therefore show up on a computer screen in blue, pointing you to a hyperlink. For example, you might say, "I was reading Duck and McMahan, and I learned that there are many more extra messages that friends pick up in talk than I had realized before." This sentence makes perfect sense to somebody who knows what "Duck and McMahan" is, but others may not understand. On a computer, they would use their mouse to find out more about Duck and McMahan by going to www.sagepub.com/bocstudy, but in a conversation, they would "click" on the hypertext by asking a direct question: "What's Duck and McMahan?"

Conversational hypertext, therefore, is the idea that all of our conversation contains coded messages that an informed listener will effortlessly understand. In relationships, the shared worlds of meaning and the overlap of perception make communication special and closer. Uninformed listeners, however, can always request that the hypertext be unpacked, expanded, or addressed directly.

How Friends Understand One Another

You and your friends talk in coded, hypertextual language all the time. Only when you encounter someone who does not understand the code do you need to further explain. In the previous example, "De'Janee" is hypertext until you have been introduced to her, and the "hot date" is hypertext until you learn that De'Janee has a new love interest. After that initial explanation, the term *hot date* might become a shared reference. Even the friend from out of town now knows what it means. If, later in the conversation, someone starts to talk about "De'Janee's hottie," the out-of-town friend will be included in the shared knowledge. At that point, the group of friends will have created a new hypertext to the conversation and the relationship that even the out-of-town friend understands.

Research shows how you can tell, just from their talk, whether people know one another because of the way they treat conversational hypertext as needing no further explanation. Planalp and Garvin-Doxas (1994) reported studies where they played tapes of talk to an audience and asked the listeners to say whether the people on the tape were friends. Listeners were very skilled at making this identification. They could easily tell whether two conversational partners were acquainted or merely strangers. What made the difference was whether the talkers took information for granted or whether they explained the terms used. Said without explanation, "Jim was worried about his foot again" identified the two conversers as friends. On the other hand, the following showed them to be unacquainted: "Jim—that's my friend from high school—was worried about his foot again. He has gout and has to be careful about setting it off. It is a problem that keeps coming back. It worries him a lot, so he usually calls me when it flares up, and I help him deal with it."

Essential Functions

People very easily underestimate the extent to which talk and its nonverbal wrapping *are* a relationship. Of course, even when you are in a relationship, you and your partner do not spend every moment with each other. You experience absences, breaks, and separations: They may be relatively short (one person goes shopping), longer (a child goes to school for the day), or extended (two lovers get jobs in different parts of the country, go on vacation separately, or are involved in a commuter relationship).

Because these breaks occur, there are ways to indicate that, although the interaction may be over, the relationship itself continues. For example, you might say, "See you next week," "Talk to you later," or "Next week we will be discussing the chapter on informative and persuasive speeches." All of these phrases are examples of the **essential function**

> Think about a situation where you overheard two people talking and you could tell—you just *knew*—that they were not close but that one of them was trying to impress the other and get into a relationship with him or her. What did you notice that made you sure you were right about the person doing the "impressing"? How did you know whether or not the other person was impressed?

of talk. Talk makes the relationship real and talks it into being by simply assuming that it exists. The above examples, talking about the continuance of the relationship beyond an upcoming absence, demonstrate that the relationship will outlast the separation.

Most of the time, however, talk creates and embodies relationships in other ways, both implicitly ("I've got you, babe") and explicitly ("You're my friend"). There can be direct talk that embodies the relationship ("I love you") or indirect talk ("What shall we do this Friday night?") that recognizes the relationship's existence but does not mention it explicitly. The essential function of talk operates in hidden ways as simple as more frequent references to "we" and "us" or inclusion in talk where joint planning is carried out or nicknames are used. Linguistic inclusion (*let's, we, us*), also known as **immediacy**, is a seemingly small but powerful way to essentialize the relationship in talk. Nicknames, even as obvious as *honey* or *Jimbo* rather than *James*, clearly show familiarity. Inclusion in planning ("Let's do something really special tonight") signals the essentializing of the relationship as a taken-for-granted part of the speaker's life.

Case in Point

Spend some time listening for different types of talk that occur in everyday life. Listen for the ways in which relationships are essentialized and transacted. Up to this point, we have not said a lot about how "talk" can be divided into different categories. We have treated "talk" as a unitary and consistent "thing." But it is not. How many different types of "talk" can you identify?

Politeness and Facework

Different kinds of talk essentialize relationships in different ways. For example, a polite conversation is different in style from an impolite one and essentializes a different type of relationship. Of course, other frames may indicate whether the impoliteness results from dislike or the informality that characterizes close friendship.

Politeness

Let's start with politeness, since in one way or another, most of our everyday talk is polite even with strangers. Communication scholars Bill Cupach and Sandra Metts (Cupach & Metts, 1994; Metts, 2000) speak of **facework**, a term that refers to the management of people's "face," meaning dignity or self-respect. When people are ashamed or humiliated, you might talk of them "losing face." Although that is a metaphor, it is worth noticing how often people who are embarrassed or who feel foolish cover their faces with their hands. An almost automatic reaction to shame or to the recognition that we have done something foolish, it makes our point that "face" is connected to moral appearance in the social world as a composed and centered social being. You might also see that the term *boldfaced lie,* used for a particularly daring falsehood, refers to the same idea. Doing facework or presenting a strongly favorable image of yourself, a particularly important aspect of giving talks, speeches, or interviews, is even more basic to daily conversation.

Photo 2.3 Talk in friendships or relationships can be described in terms of three functions: instrumental, indexical, and essential. Which function of talk would you use to describe the two men in this photo? (See page 46.)

Saving Face

Sociologist Erving Goffman (1971) promoted the notion that "face" is something managed by people in social interactions, noting that you "save face" for yourself and other people. Many times, for example, you try to save someone else's face by trivializing an embarrassing mistake ("Oh, don't worry about it; I do that all the time"; "Think nothing of it"; "No big deal"). In effect, you are saying that you don't see the person's behavior truly as an indication of who he or she really is: You are trying to let him or her off the hook as a person and are distinguishing his or her momentary *actions* from his or her deep, true *self*.

Face Wants

People have positive face wants and negative face wants: **Positive face wants** refer to the need to be seen and accepted as a worthwhile and reasonable person; **negative face wants** refer to the desire not to be imposed upon or treated as inferior. The management of this last type of face want is perhaps the most familiar: "I don't mean to trouble you, but would you . . ."; "I hope this is not too inconvenient, but would you mind . . ."; "Sorry to be a nuisance, but . . ."; and our personal favorite from students, "I have a *quick* question" (implying that it will not be a lot of trouble or a big imposition to answer it).

Although this management of people's negative face wants is quite common, positive face wants are also dealt with quite frequently, and you often hear people pay compliments like "You are doing a great job!"; "How very nice of you"; or "You're too kind."

Use of either type of behavior allows you to manage your relationships by paying attention to the ways people need to be seen in the social world. The behaviors are therefore a subtle kind of relational management done in talk. It may not have been obvious—or at least not obviously connecting talk to relationships—but it is a basic feature of communication.

Ways of Speaking

In everyday conversation with people you know, other aspects of talk are worth noticing as ways to transact relationships. The form of language through which you choose to express your thoughts carries important relational messages. You sometimes use that knowledge as part of what you choose to say on a particular occasion.

Codes of Speech

When people talk to very young children, they tend to adopt baby language; when students or employees talk with professors or supervisors, they try to sound "professional." When talking with friends, you use informal language, but in class or in conversation with your boss, your language may be a bit more complicated.

High Code/Low Code

Think about the difference between saying, when you're hungry, "I'm so hungry I could eat a horse" and "My state of famishment is of such a proportion that I would gladly consume the complete corporeality of a member of the species *Equus przewalski poliakov*." The first example is written in what communication scholars call **low code**, and the second is written in **high code** (Giles, Taylor, & Bourhis, 1973). Low code is an informal and often ungrammatical way of talking; high code is a formal, grammatical, and very correct—often "official"—way of talking. You might be able to look around your lecture hall and see a sign that says something like "Consumption of food and beverages on these premises is prohibited." That is a high-code way of saying the low-code message "Do not eat or drink here."

Polysemy and Speech Style

By now, then, you can see that not just individual words are polysemic. The whole structure of language and the *way in which* you speak can be polysemic. Let's spend some time elaborating on this so that you come to understand how it plays out in relationships with an audience, whether public or intimate.

The language you use contains more than one way of saying the same thing—a sort of stylistic polysemy. Although this may not have struck you as particularly important yet, the form of language you use to express essentially the same idea conveys its own messages about something other than the topic you're talking about.

In fact, it connotes and essentializes the relationship between you and your audience, as well as conveys something about you as a person. A high form is formal, pompous, and professional; a low form is casual, welcoming, friendly, and relaxed. By choosing one form over another at a particular point, you are not just sending a message but

1. delivering *content* about a particular topic,

2. *presenting* yourself as a particular sort of person (projecting identity), and

3. *indexing* a particular sort of relationship to the audience.

Part of your connotative meaning at a given time is always an essentializing commentary about "the state of the relationship" between the speaker and the audience, whether a large or small group or an individual. Just as public speakers adopt particular ways of talking depending on the group with which they strive to identify, so too a person can choose a friendly, informal style or a more distant, formal style with a stranger.

Accommodation: Convergence and Divergence

Just as you can set the frame, you can change it. You can choose a particular way to say something. You may change or adapt it either to suit an audience or to see changes in feelings or in the relationship that occurs during the course of the interaction.

Giles and his colleagues (1973) have shown that people will change their accent, their rate of speech, and even the words they use to indicate a relational connection with the person to whom they are talking. They called this process **accommodation** and identified two types: convergence and divergence. In **convergence**, a person moves toward the style of talk used by the other speaker. For example, an adult converges when he or she uses baby talk to communicate with a child, or a brownnosing employee converges when he or she uses the boss's company lingo style of talk. In **divergence**, exactly the opposite happens: One talker moves away from another's style of speech to make a relational point, such as establishing dislike or superiority. A good example is how computer geeks and car mechanics insist on using a lot of technical language with customers, instead of giving simple explanations that the nonexpert could understand. This form of divergence keeps the customer in a lower relational place.

The different ways of sending the same content in a message are another instance of how meaning and relationships are inextricably tied together. Talking conveys content and something about your identity. It conveys even more about your sense of the ongoing changes in your relationship with others and how it may be altered by the course of an interaction.

Photo 2.4 People tell stories every day, whether about the crazy commute that made them late to work or a funny interaction with a bank teller. How do you know that one of the people in this photo is telling a story, and what role does storytelling seem to play in their relationship? (See page 46.)

Narration: Telling Stories

The multilayered framing aspect of talk is quite noticeable when people tell stories. Communication scholars use the term *narrative* to cover what is involved when you say *what* people are doing and *why* they are doing it. This applies whether talk includes funny events, tragic events, significant emotional experiences, or relational stories (meeting new people, falling in love, breaking up). You may not always notice that talk has the features of a story. You have heard many examples—"How We Met," "How My Day Was," and even "I Couldn't Do the Assignment," which may not at first strike you as a story. A **narrative** is any organized story, report, or prepared talk that has a plot, an argument, or a theme, or can be interpreted as having one. In a narrative, speakers do not just relate facts but also arrange the story in a way that provides an account, an explanation, or a conclusion. Often stories make the speakers look good or are told from their own particular point of view (i.e., their talk appears representational when it is really presentational). Some remarks do not appear story-like but follow the same pattern all the same: for example, "I couldn't do the assignment; it was way too hard." This relates a fact and presents a conclusion. You said you couldn't do it because it was too hard. Your instructor may have thought you did not do enough work. Different stories!

Strategic Communication

Kenneth Burke's (1969) pentad can help you analyze the stories of others. However, it can also be used as you develop your own stories. Consider when it might be more appropriate to emphasize scene, agent, act, agency, and purpose when sharing particular stories with others.

Everyday Stories: Part of Human Nature

Much of everyday life is spent telling stories about yourself and other people, whether or not they walk into bars. For example, you may tell a story about when you went into a shop and something funny or unexpected happened. Or you may tell your friends how when you were, like, working in the pizza parlor, some guy came in and couldn't, like, make his mind up about whether he wanted, like, double cheese or pepperoni, and you, like, stood there for, like, 5 minutes while he made up his mind.

Communication scholar Walter Fisher (1985) pointed out that much more of human life than we suspect is spent telling stories. He even coined the term *homo narrans* (Latin for "the person as a storyteller or narrator") to describe this human tendency. Indeed, he suggested that storytelling is one of the most important human activities. Stories are also a large part of relating, so we need to spend some time exploring how people narrate and justify their action in stories.

Everyday talk can be "a story." Narratives often appear to be special kinds of talk, but they are hidden in straightforward talk. They are elaborate frames, too, that provide excuses for your actions. For example, in the cheese and pepperoni case, the end of your story might be "I was so mad." The details about the person failing to make up his mind are used to justify (frame) the fact that you felt irritated.

People often give excuses and tell stories that help explain their actions within a set of existing frames. This section looks at how stories use, and provide, frames for your talk to present you incidentally as a relationally responsible and attractive person (facework).

Burke's Pentad

All stories have particular common elements that were identified by Kenneth Burke (1969) as a **pentad**; *pentad* is a word derived from the Greek for "five" (see Table 2.2 for a listing of the elements).

Table 2.2 Common Elements of Stories That Make Up Burke's Pentad	
1. Scene (setting)	*Where* it happened
2. Agent (character)	*Who* was involved
3. Act (single event or sequences of events)	*What* (facts) unfolded in time
4. Agency (plotline)	*How* (the way in which) acts happened
5. Purpose (outcome)	*Why* (What was the result or goal?)

The outcome usually offers a moral result (the moral of the story). The next time you hear people telling stories in everyday life communication, you can check how far their reports fit this framework for justifying and explaining their actions.

Elements of the Pentad

Stories start out with a *scene* in which something happened (*act*) ("I was working in a pizza parlor last night, and this guy came in . . ."; "My professor told me yesterday during office hours that . . ."; "My mom was driving home from work last night and realized . . ."; "I was talking with my boyfriend yesterday, and we decided to break up because . . ."). These elements of talk introduce the main characters (*agents*), often yourself and someone you know ("I was working . . . this guy came in"). Stories involve the interaction and intersection of characters (*agency*)—"He couldn't make up his mind"; "I stood there for 5 minutes waiting"—and their plotlines are based on a sequence of events that result in an *outcome* ("I was so mad").

The simple pizza story now looks quite different. For one thing it is organized and structured in the way Burke (1969) proposed. Although you may not previously have been able to name the terms this story encompasses, you now know more about stories than you did before.

Burke's Pentad as Frame

The important point is how the story is used to frame its outcome as reasonable and inevitable. Table 2.3 shows how the punch lines of stories—even news stories and scientific reports or tales of

Table 2.3 How a Story Is Used to Frame Its Outcome as Reasonable or Inevitable	
Agent:act ratio	• Uses a person's character to explain actions • For example, "He's the kind of guy who does that"; "Friends don't let friends drive drunk."
Scene:act ratio	• Uses a situation or circumstances to justify action • For example, "Desperate times call for desperate measures"; "This is war and we need to use harsh methods to obtain the truth from prisoners."
Scene:agent ratio	• Uses a situation to explain the kinds of characters who are found there • For example, "Politics makes strange bedfellows"; "Miami is a sunny place for shady people."
Scene:agent:act ratio	• Uses a situation or circumstances (e.g., a disintegrating parental marriage) to explain a person's actions • For example, "Children of divorced parents are more likely to be insecure in relationships and get divorced themselves later in life."

people walking into bars—are seen as reasonable and acceptable. It all depends on how they are set up in such ratios of justification and presentation.

Stories and People's Frames

The elements of the pentad that show up in a person's typical accounts of everyday life experience give insight into how the person thinks. The terms of the pentad used by a narrator present selected aspects of the world. When a person highlights an element of the pentad, that gives insight into the way he or she thinks about the world. From this point of view, stories are not simply narrations of events but personalized ways of telling: The narration indicates presentation of a perspective or personal frame.

One significant frame that sets the scene for all narratives comes from

Photo 2.5 The woman on the left is telling her friends about the series of events that she encountered that day. Which pentadic element is most likely being highlighted? (See page 46.)

1. the character of the agent telling the story, making the speech, giving a toast, reporting the gossip, or talking the talk, and

2. the relationship between the speaker and the audience (a latent agent-to-agent ratio).

In formal settings a toastmaster may wear a uniform, a priest who is speaking may wear the clothes of office, or speakers may wear business clothes to clarify their importance, professionalism, and seriousness. However, even in informal settings all speakers invite you to accept the important frame that they *matter* whether or not they are giving a formal presentation.

The bottom line of many stories really comes down to "I'm a decent person, and what I'm telling you is essentially a good idea/I did the right thing, didn't I?" Outside of therapy, you rarely meet anyone who does not, at root, like to think he or she is a good person, essentially decent and OK. Now you may recognize that these story "bottom lines" are offering justifications and accounts for acts. Also the features in this chapter relate the speaker and the audience. Speaking to any audience is always an act set in a relational scene.

Character as Frame

A speaker's character frames what he or she says and justifies his or her attempts to persuade an audience. It is the same whether the speaker addresses a formally seated audience at a political rally or gives a business speech or is just talking with a friend.

All speakers want to make relational partners, potential friends, and other audiences appreciate or even like them. In most everyday life conversations, the chances are

Formal speakers are often introduced in ways that frame them as important for their audience by listing their rank, their accomplishments, or the reasons the audience should pay attention to them. For example, "I am pleased to present the president of the corporation"; "We are very honored to have with us today the Secretary of State"; "Today's speaker has for a long time been a leading member of our community."

that you are already speaking to friends, family, and people who like you quite a bit to begin with. Your relationship then frames, or sets the scene for, what you are going to say, just as much as your argument and your words do.

Scenes as Frames

Other scenes also exist. Narratives, stories, and all daily talk are framed by assumptions about the culture and what works within it. They may be framed by assumptions about justice, responsibility, free will, personality, "speaker truth," and audience.

When you talk with your friends, you most likely do not find it necessary to keep convincing them that you are speaking the truth. You assume that *they* assume that you speak the truth. In other circumstances, it may be more important for you to tell stories in a way that reflects assumptions based on your own particular reasons. For example, if you are talking about the terrible character of a person who just broke off a relationship with you, the frame is that you are a decent person while the other person is a jerk.

At other times, you may want to describe yourself in a way that helps other people understand how you "tick." You may want to reveal personal information that helps them understand you better. Again, remember that you do this very much from your own point of view and personal motives. Don't ever believe that when someone tells you a story, it is a neutral and simply representational view of the world.

All stories and speech are presentational. When listening to politicians, you can expect them to present events in a way that suits their personal interests best. You have to learn to recognize that *everyone* is a politician for his or her own party: the "vote for me because I am a good person" party.

Giving Accounts

Although narratives appear on the surface just to report (represent) events, they frequently account for (present) the behaviors. **Accounts** are forms of communication that offer *justifications* ("I was so mad"), *excuses* ("I was really tired"), *exonerations* ("It wasn't my fault"), *explanations* ("And that's how we fell in love"), *accusations* ("But he started it!"), and *apologies* ("I'm an idiot"). Accounts "go beyond the facts."

Presentation, Representation, and Frames

Psychologists, communication scholars, and sociologists would talk about the above pizza parlor story as "giving an account" (Scott & Lyman, 1968): telling a story in a way that justifies, blames someone for, or calls for someone to account for what happened. Even the "facts" in reports can turn out to be presentational. Your description of something contains "spin" that explains the "facts" you are reporting. For example, you tell your friend, "I just failed a math test. It was way too hard." Both statements appear to be facts. One is actually an explanation for why you failed (the test was too hard). It is also a *presentational* account—a personal view about the reason for your failure (the test was too hard). Your teacher may think you failed because you did not do the homework.

Listen with fresh ears to everyday conversation, and you will start to hear framing justifications much more often. Think about their structure and what it tells you about communication and the implied relationship between the speaker and the audience. For example, you don't bother to justify yourself to people whose opinions you do not care about. You would not justify yourself to an enemy in the same way you would to a friend. You expect the friend to know more about your background and to cut you some slack. This familiarity influences the style of your report, once again connecting talk to relationships.

Remember what we wrote at the start of this chapter: that a whole system of nonverbal communication frames what we say, too. If I say "I love you" but wince when I say it, that frames the words in a different way than if I smile and look all gooey when I say it. The next chapter covers nonverbal communication on its own and then reconnects it as a frame for interpreting talk. Although we have separated talk from its real behavioral context so that you can understand features of talk itself, talk never happens in life in a way that is separated from nonverbal behavior. The next chapter shows you how nonverbal behavior works and how it is used not only to send messages on its own but also to affect how the messages in talk are modified or understood.

FOCUS QUESTIONS REVISITED

1. What are the differences between grammatical language (*langue*) and talk in everyday use *(parole)*?

Grammatical language has a formal structure (*langue*), whereas talk in everyday use tends quite frequently to disregard the rules of grammar (*parole*). Langue is used in formal settings, and parole, often a mark of the fact that the people know one another well, tends to be used in less formal settings.

2. What frames your understanding of talk and gives it meaning?

Context, situation, language structure, culture, and the task at hand all give you clues about the frame you are in for a given conversation. The previous talk also gives lots of clues. Likewise, you draw clues about relationships and appropriateness of talk directly from context: In restaurants, you talk to servers about food; in a romance, you talk about love, but at work, you do not—unless you are a therapist or are giving a colleague some personal advice.

3. What values are hidden in the speech you use?

Many cultural and personal values are hidden in the speech used between persons in everyday life. Cultures recognize certain kinds of relationships but not others, and manage the degree of respect shown by one person to another in different ways. Other values may be hidden in a particular society's use of God and Devil terms. Your speech often also contains codes that indicate the depth of relationship you have with the person to whom you are speaking.

4. How does everyday talk make use of relationships to frame meanings?

Everyday talk draws on the relationship that exists between two people in a conversation to indicate what is appropriate or inappropriate for them to do and say to one another. Friends who know one another well may talk in ways that are inappropriate between strangers.

5. How do different types of talk work, and how do they connect to relationships?

We already pointed out politeness, conflict, and rudeness, but other types of talk could include information, questions, argument/persuasion, jargon, euphemism, instructions, assignments, profanity, rituals, catch-up talk, hostility, harassment, bullying, comforting, social support, advice, small talk, planning, speechmaking, confession, and forgiveness. Many of these forms of talk represent ways to keep a relationship together; others are ways of keeping people away.

6. What is talk style, and how does it frame meaning?

The style of talk can be carried out in high code or low code. High code is appropriate for formal settings, and low code is appropriate for informal settings. The choice to use one or the other frames the meaning of the interaction, and switching between the two types of code is a way of creating greater closeness or distance, depending on which direction the switching takes place in. Convergence is when two people speak in the same style and indicates closeness or liking, but divergence is when they speak in different styles and indicates distance or disliking.

7. What are the key elements of stories?

According to Burke's pentad, the key elements of stories are scene, agent, act, agency, and purpose/outcome. The act is what is done, the scene is where it takes place, the agent is the person performing the act, the agency is how the act is done, and the purpose or outcome is basically the result or endpoint of the story, often tinged with moral judgment.

KEY CONCEPTS

QUESTIONS TO ASK YOUR FRIENDS

1. Try conducting a conversation with one of your friends where you use only high code. Afterward, ask your friend how long it took to notice something wrong or inappropriate in the situation.

2. Ask your friends if they ever find it hard to know when you are kidding and what makes it hard.

3. Have your friends report an occasion when they caught someone in a boldfaced lie and how they knew. How did they handle it (thinking of facework)?

MEDIA LINKS

1. Find news stories that are structured in ways that illustrate the pentad.

2. How do news anchors introduce stories intended to be seen as "not serious" as compared to those regarded as serious and important?

3. What techniques do news anchors use on television in order to relate with their audience and seem friendly, likeable, and credible?

ETHICAL ISSUES

1. Note how sexist, racist, and heterosexual (marking) language is relational and always places one group of people in an inferior position relative to another group of people. Is it ever ethical to use this kind of language?

2. Should the stories you tell always be true? Why or why not?

3. Should you always be polite and save people's face when they do something embarrassing?

ANSWERS TO PHOTO CAPTIONS

Photo 2.1 ▪ The U.S. Constitution stipulates the separation of church and state, but this pair of street signs indicates that this is the point where Church and State intersect. Someone who finds it amusing would have to know about the U.S. Constitution and the fact that Americans do not say the word *street* when talking about the intersection of two roads.

Photo 2.2 ▪ Clearly these two women are close friends (context cues about their personal familiarity are their physical closeness and the whispering). The subject matter of their conversation is both secretive and funny. One has her hand up "to stop other people from hearing," so we know that the conversation is private and personal. This and their shared laughter indicate that they both share some of the same common knowledge about people and events and have a similar sense of humor.

Photo 2.3 ▪ Indexical or essential function. They seem very at ease and familiar in speaking with each other; the talk is occurring in a kitchen at night, which suggests that they are friends and must be relaxed by the atmosphere because the chairs certainly wouldn't help.

Photo 2.4 ▪ The individuals are relaxed, indicating a friendship and shared bond. Everyone is looking at the person who is gesturing and telling the story (actually it is Sir Lancelot). The story presumably confirms him as a hero and those around him as sharing the same heroic values and seeking the same results, affirming their bonds of loyalty to one another.

Photo 2.5 ▪ Scene is most likely being featured in this person's story.

STUDENT STUDY SITE

Visit the study site at **www.sagepub.com/boc2e** for e-flashcards, practice quizzes, journal articles and additional study resources.

REFERENCES

Burke, K. (1966). *Language as symbolic action: Essays on life, literature and method.* Berkeley: University of California Press.

Burke, K. (1969). *A grammar of motives.* Berkeley: University of California Press.

Cupach, W. R., & Metts, S. (1994). *Facework*. Thousand Oaks, CA: Sage.

Duck, S. W. (2002). Hypertext in the key of G: Three types of "history" as influences on conversational structure and flow. *Communication Theory, 12*(1), 41–62.

Duck, S. W. (2007). *Human relationships* (4th ed.). London: Sage.

Duck, S. W., & Pond, K. (1989). Friends, Romans, Countrymen; lend me your retrospective data: Rhetoric and reality in personal relationships. In C. Hendrick (Ed.), *Review of social psychology and personality: Close relationships* (Vol. 10, pp. 17–38). Newbury Park, CA: Sage.

Fisher, W. R. (1985). The narrative paradigm: An elaboration. *Communication Monographs, 52,* 347–367.

Giles, H., Taylor, D. M., & Bourhis, R. Y. (1973). Towards a theory of interpersonal accommodation through language use. *Language in Society, 2,* 177–192.

Goffman, E. (1971). *Relations in public: Microstudies of the public order.* New York: Harper & Row.

Kelly, G. A. (1969). Ontological acceleration. In B. Mather (Ed.), *Clinical psychology and personality: The collected papers of George Kelly* (pp. 7–45). New York: Wiley.

Kirkpatrick, C. D., Duck, S. W., & Foley, M. K. (Eds.). (2006). *Relating difficulty: The processes of constructing and managing difficult interaction.* LEA Series on Personal Relationships. Mahwah, NJ: Lawrence Erlbaum.

Komatsu, E. (Ed.). (1993). *Saussure's third course of lectures on general linguistics (1910–1911)* (R. Harris, Trans.). London: Pergamon.

Metts, S. (2000). Face and facework: Implications for the study of personal relationships. In K. Dindia & S. W. Duck (Eds.), *Communication and personal relationships* (pp. 72–94). Chichester, UK: Wiley.

Norwood, K. M. (2007). *Gendered conflict? The "cattiness" of women on "Flavor of Love."* Paper presented at the Organization for the Study of Communication, Language, and Gender, Omaha, NE.

Ogden, C. K., & Richards, I. A. (1946). *The meaning of meaning* (8th ed.). New York: Harcourt Brace Jovanovich.

Planalp, S., & Garvin-Doxas, K. (1994). Using mutual knowledge in conversation: Friends as experts in each other. In S. W. Duck (Ed.), *Dynamics of relationships* (Understanding relationship processes 4, pp. 1–26). Newbury Park, CA: Sage.

Sapir, E. (1949). *Selected writings in language, culture and personality* (D. Mandelbaum, Ed.). Berkeley: University of California Press.

Scott, M. B., & Lyman, S. M. (1968). Accounts. *American Sociological Review, 33,* 46–62.

Whorf, B. (1956). *Language, thought, and reality: Selected writings of Benjamin Lee Whorf* (J. Carroll, Ed.). Boston: MIT Press.

3

Nonverbal Communication

Nonverbal communication is always present in talk in normal interaction and carries messages over and above the words you speak. For example, a smile makes your words seem friendly, but a sneer makes the same words seem sarcastic. Nonverbal communication most often goes along with and supports talk, although not always. You might say, "I'm *not* angry" but look as if you are really angry. Or you might say, "I love you" and only have to exchange a glance with your partner for him or her to see that you really mean it. Nonverbal communication frames talk, but it can also frame other people's assessments and judgments of you before you even speak. It also indicates how you feel about other people. The way you move, look, and sound (the speed and pitch of your voice) conveys relational messages to others. These others can be friends chatting in a lounge or an interviewer considering you for a job or patients as you tell them bad news. All nonverbal communication conveys something about your sense of relaxation and comfort with the person(s) with whom you're speaking. Nonverbal communication also indicates your *evaluation or assessment* of that person. In short, nonverbal communication is an essential *relational* element of all interaction, and you cannot have interactions without nonverbal communication; nor can you have interactions without the *relational messages* that nonverbal communication sends.

Classic research claims that about 80% of the meaning of a message is conveyed nonverbally.

Nonverbal communication, or NVC, has been tied up with your communication all of your life. That can make it difficult for you to appreciate its importance because it is so "obvious." But is NVC something worth understanding and learning about? You bet!

Focus Questions

1. What is nonverbal communication?
2. How does nonverbal communication work, and what work does it do in communication?
3. How does nonverbal communication regulate (e.g., begin and end) interactions?
4. What are the elements of nonverbal communication, and how do they interconnect?
5. How can you improve your use of nonverbal communication?

What Is Nonverbal Communication?

Nonverbal communication is everything that communicates a message but does not include words. This definition covers a very wide range of topics: facial expression, hand movements, dress, tattoos, jewelry, physical attractiveness, timing of what happens, position in the interaction (for example, instructors generally stand at the front of the class), tone of voice, eye movements, the positioning of furniture to create atmosphere, touch, and smell—and that is not an exhaustive list.

The Two Sides of Nonverbal Communication: Decoding Versus Encoding

It is important to distinguish between **decoding** and **encoding** of NVC. Decoding a nonverbal message is exactly like decoding anything else: You draw meaning from something you observe. For example, if somebody blushes unexpectedly, you might decode that as meaning he or she is embarrassed. On the other hand, when you encode a nonverbal message, you put your feelings into behavior through NVC. For example, if you are feeling happy, you *look* truly happy. A good *de*coder can work out sensitively what is going on inside another person, but if you're a good *en*coder, you put your feelings "out there" well and help other people "get" what is going on inside you. Skillful actors, teachers, and public speakers are good encoders; effective therapists, advisors, and interrogators are good decoders. Good encoding helps your listeners understand what you feel about your subject; good decoding helps you figure out what the speaker is trying to tell you.

Encoding is important when you go on a job interview, give speeches, or go on a first date because you need to display confidence rather than anxiety, and the more confident you are, the more people will attend to what you say. Decoding is important when you're chatting with a friend: You need to be able to notice if your friend is anxious or having a hard time but not telling you directly, for example, or even lying.

The Two Modes of Nonverbal Communication: Static Versus Dynamic

Communication scholars traditionally divide the many kinds of NVC into two aspects (Manusov & Patterson, 2006): **static** (fixed) and **dynamic** (changeable).

The color of someone's eyes is static NVC; a change in the size of his or her pupils is dynamic NVC.

Static NVC refers to those elements of an interaction that do not change during its course. For example, the arrangement of furniture in a particular room can send non-verbal messages about status and power or about comfort and informality; it is unlikely that the furniture itself will be moved around during the course of the interaction. A judge's power in the courtroom is symbolized by the fact that the judge sits higher than all the other people in the court. A shop assistant going behind the cash register to complete your purchase is using a static aspect of the design of the shop that separates out "customer areas" from "shop assistant areas." Customers can go into one part of the shop but not into the other part without permission. If you follow the assistant behind the cash register, you might be suspected of intending a robbery.

The room in which you interact counts as a static nonverbal cue (Duck, 2007). An interaction in a friend's bedroom is conducted in a different static environment than one in a public lounge. The space frames the interaction with a different context. How you interact at home may be influenced by the lighting and décor (static nonverbal cues) that make the environment relaxing. When you're speaking in the static environment of a large lecture hall it is not relaxing.

Other examples of static nonverbal cues are body piercings, military uniforms, the clothes you wear into an interaction, the color of your hair, your sex, your age, your tattoos, your height and build, your ethnicity, or whether you are wearing sunglasses, pajamas, a sexy outfit, or jewelry. Although some of these things *may* change during the course of an interaction, most often they don't; they can, however, send signals about your relationship to other people. For example, Seiter and Sandry (2003) showed people photographs of job applicants with different body piercings. They found that reviewers did not give different *physical attractiveness ratings* according to the type of jewelry the applicants wore. The applicants' *credibility,* though, was rated much lower when they were wearing jewelry. Applicants were significantly less likely to be hired if they were wearing a nose ring.

Dynamic NVC involves movement and change during the course of the interaction—behaviors closely watched by poker players. Most dynamic NVC relates to bodily movement or position—for example, facial expressions, gestures, postures, the pitch and tone of the speaker's voice as she relates a story, the way someone's eyes move, and the amount of touching that takes place during the course of a conversation. Dynamic NVC can be broken down into several different parts. Don't forget as we explain all these parts that each of them can convey emotional and relational messages separately and together. As you will see later in the chapter, NVC also serves a second, extremely important relational function: It regulates (e.g., starts and stops) interaction.

Photo 3.1 What features of nonverbal communication can you use to draw inferences about this person, and what is your impression? (See page 74.)

How Nonverbal Communication Works

Having discussed the two sides and modes of NVC, we can now discuss the operation of nonverbal symbols in your everyday experiences. Both verbal and nonverbal communication are symbolic and share many of the same characteristics, such as being personal, ambiguous, guided by rules, and linked to culture. As we discuss the nature of NVC, we address the characteristics it shares with verbal communication as well as how they materialize. We also discuss characteristics unique to NVC, such as its continuous nature and that it is often beyond your full control. This comparison will help you understand the workings of NVC and should also add to your understanding of verbal communication, with which it often occurs (Knapp & Hall, 2002; Remland, 2004).

Symbolic

Both nonverbal and verbal communication are symbolic. The key difference between them is that verbal communication involves the use of language and NVC involves the use of all other symbolic activity.

Like verbal symbols, nonverbal symbols can be described as polysemic; that is, a single nonverbal symbol can have multiple meanings. The ambiguity of nonverbal symbols often makes it difficult to decide their intended meanings. For example, what does a stare mean: affection, anger, hostility, interest, longing, or "Be quiet!"?

Guided by Rules

Nonverbal communication is guided by rules. Rules guide the choice of nonverbal symbols that should be used in specific situations and with certain people. You would probably shake his or her hand rather than give your instructor a high five. The appropriateness of greeting someone with a kiss depends on whether he or she is your romantic partner, an attendant behind the counter at a gas station, or someone from a culture where a kiss on the cheek is an accepted greeting even between persons of the same sex (Russia or Italy, for example).

Rules also guide evaluation of nonverbal behavior. For instance, you know that nonverbal expressions of gratitude include shaking a person's hand, smiling, and talking in an appreciative tone of voice as opposed to avoiding eye contact, pouting, and talking in a surly tone of voice. A brisk handshake is evaluated differently than a hearty handshake; a slight smile is evaluated differently than a broad smile. You can even gauge the extent of a person's degree of appreciation through slight alterations in his or her tone of voice.

As opposed to those guiding verbal communication, the rules guiding NVC are learned indirectly and primarily through your interactions with others (Remland, 2004). This course may be the first time you have ever formally studied NVC, but you have been studying verbal language in school for years. In your English classes, for example, you learned the difference between nouns, verbs, adjectives, and adverbs and about proper sentence structure. In grade school, you learned vocabulary skills and the meanings of certain words. With NVC, you have learned nearly everything, from the meaning of particular nonverbal symbols to the structure of their use, informally throughout your lifetime as you have interacted with other people, though when you were a kid, your parents may have said directly, "Don't stare. It's rude," or "Look at me when I'm talking to you."

Cultural

Nonverbal communication is linked to cultural appropriateness (Knapp & Hall, 2002). In the United States, eye contact is often viewed as a display of courtesy, honesty, and respect. In other countries, making eye contact, especially with a superior, is considered improper and highly disrespectful. Meanings of nonverbal messages also depend on culture, including use of space, touch, and time. Dialect and accent can also indicate that a person comes from a particular country or region, and particular cues may be associated with stereotypes—for example, sexiness (French accent), slowness (Southern drawl), or cheeky friendliness (Irish accent). Also, many gestures are acceptable in some cultures but impolite or offensive in others (although in our culture the forefinger-to-thumb "O" means "perfect," in other cultures it is an offensive sexual suggestion). Many nonverbal behaviors and symbols are perhaps universally recognized (the smile, for example), but they do not necessarily have universal meaning in the same contexts (Remland, 2004).

Personal

Nonverbal communication can be very personal (Guerrero & Floyd, 2006). Similar to verbal communication, you develop your own personal meanings and use of nonverbal symbols. A person's use of some nonverbal symbols may even become idiosyncratic over time. Some people may not like to hug or be hugged, for example. One person may view the peace sign (shown in Figure 3.1) as cliché and may look at celebrities flashing the peace sign at cameras with disdain. Another person may view this sign as still having great meaning and value and may regard its use with admiration. Others still may cover themselves with tattoos.

A disability called NLD (nonverbal learning disorder) exists (http://www.nldline.com/) where people fail to understand NVC. They may stand too close to you, get in your way when you try to get past them, fail to read your tone of voice correctly, or be unable to distinguish anger from nonanger. Several otherwise high-functioning intelligent people (including Albert Einstein, some believe) suffered from this particular disorder, showing that it is possible to be both extremely intelligent and nonverbally disabled.

Photo 3.2 How does static NVC work, and what work does it do in communication? (See page 74.)

Figure 3.1 The Sign for Peace. Note that as presented it means "peace" in the United States but "victory" for Winston Churchill. If reversed so that the back of the hand is shown to someone, it is the UK equivalent of "the finger."

Ambiguous

NVC is highly ambiguous, even more than the meaning of verbal communication. You are often uncertain what another person's NVC actually means, unless you have clear signals from context. The physical or situational context, along with your relationship with that person, helps you assign meaning to NVC.

The ambiguity of NVC is valuable when flirting with someone. Nonverbal behaviors associated with flirting can mean so many different things. You could use eye contact, a quick or sustained glance, a smile, or even a wink either to flirt with someone or just to be friendly. Here, ambiguity is useful because it releases the pressure of not receiving the desired response. If the other person is interested, the response transacts your ambiguous message (for example, a long and perhaps longing stare) as a come-on. If the other person is not interested, the response transacts your ambiguous behavior as "just friendly." Always remember the ambiguous nature of NVC and heed this piece of advice: Another person may perceive your friendly glance as a sexual provocation.

Less Controlled

Nonverbal communication is less subject to your control than is verbal communication. You might be able to keep from calling someone you dislike a jerk, but nonverbally you may be expressing your displeasure unknowingly through dirty looks or changes in pupil size.

Nonverbal behaviors often occur without your full awareness and reveal how you really feel. This betrayal of your internal feelings is known as **leakage**. Because your spontaneous NVC is more difficult to control than your verbal communication, people are more likely to believe your nonverbal over your verbal messages—especially when the two are contradictory. Audiences rely more on what you do than on what you say.

Continuous

Nonverbal communication is continuous and ongoing. You will always be communicating nonverbally through your physical appearance; furthermore, in face-to-face speaking, you begin communicating nonverbally before you start talking and will continue communicating after you stop. For example, if you do not want to give a speech, you may convey this message nonverbally by having a look of dread on your face before

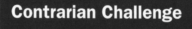

Contrarian Challenge

We maintain that nonverbal communication is less controlled than verbal communication. However, some people (such as con artists and actors) can train themselves to appear certain ways and even control their heart rates and other physical features. Does this mean that nonverbal communication is actually easy to control with enough practice?

you begin speaking. Afterward, this look of dread may be replaced by a look of relief as you say your final words.

The Functions of Nonverbal Communication

Nonverbal communication, whether static or dynamic, has many functions in everyday life, some of which reinforce verbal behavior, some of which regulate interactions, and some of which serve to identify people. Nonverbal communication also registers people's emotional states or displays their attitudes about themselves, the other person in the interaction, or their comfort level. One of the clearest indicators of liking and disliking, for example, is registered by NVC: Pupil size, an uncontrollable activity, indicates the degree to which someone likes the person or idea that he or she is considering. If you look at a person you like very much, your pupil size will increase, whereas if you look at someone you dislike, your pupil size will decrease. You just can't help it.

Interconnects With Verbal Communication

One function of NVC involves its interconnection with verbal communication. Your interpretation of verbal meaning is often framed by accompanying nonverbal elements, such as tone of voice, facial expression, and gestures.

Your NVC might *repeat* your verbal communication, sending a corresponding nonverbal message. For example, when you say hello to someone from across the room, you might wave at the same time.

Alternatively, nonverbal messages can *substitute*, or be used in place of, verbal messages. For example, you might just wave to acknowledge someone and not say anything.

Nonverbal communication is often used to *emphasize* or highlight the verbal message. If you have ever gone fishing and described "the one that got away" to your friends, you have no doubt used NVC to emphasize just how big that fish really was by holding your arms out wide to indicate its gargantuan length. A verbal message can also be emphasized through your tone of voice. When you tell someone a secret, for example, you may use a hushed voice to emphasize its private nature.

When NVC is used to *moderate* verbal communication, it plays down a verbal message. For instance, a doubtful tone of voice and the slight scrunching of your face and shoulders could indicate uncertainty. If your supervisor did this while saying, "I may be able to give you a raise this year," you would probably not expect a raise. By moderating the verbal message nonverbally, your boss is letting you know there is uncertainty in that statement.

Your NVC can also *contradict* your verbal communication—sometimes intentionally, such as when you are being sarcastic ("Oh, nice job!" said angrily when someone spills coffee on you). Contradiction may occur unintentionally as well: for instance, when someone charges into a room, slams the door, sits down on the couch in a huff, and says, "Oh, nothing" when you ask what is wrong. Contradiction is not always obvious, but you are generally skilled at detecting it—especially when you share a close, personal relationship with the speaker. Faced with contradiction, you will be more likely to believe the person's nonverbal over verbal communication. Why? (Hint: Spontaneous NVC is less subject to your control than is verbal communication.)

Regulates Interactions

NVC also helps regulate your interactions. Nonverbal communication aids in starting or ending interactions. Used to determine whether you should actually engage in interactions with another person, NVC helps you know when to send and when to receive verbal messages.

Regulators are nonverbal actions that indicate to others how you want them to behave or what you want them to do. One familiar regulator occurs at the end of most college classes: Students begin closing their books and gathering their belongings to signal to the instructor that it is time to end class. Other regulators include shivering when you want someone to close the window or turn up the heat, a look of frustration or confusion when you need help with a problem, and a closed-off posture (arms folded, legs crossed) when you want to be left alone.

Nonverbal communication can indicate whether you will actually engage in conversation. If one of your friends walks past you at a rapid pace with an intense look on his or her face, it shows that he or she is in a hurry or not in the mood to talk. In this case, you might avoid interacting with your friend at this time. If someone looks frustrated or confused, however, you may decide to interact with him or her because the nonverbal behavior signals a need for help.

Nonverbal communication also serves to *punctuate* how you talk to other people; it starts and ends interactions and keeps them flowing. Specifically, NVC creates a framework within which interaction happens in proper sequence. Most of the time it is perfectly effortless and unconscious, but you must *act* to get in and out of conversations: For example, you must "catch the server's eye" to start ordering in a restaurant.

You follow elaborate nonverbal rules to begin and to break off interactions. Consider what happens when you see someone walking toward you in the distance and wish to engage in conversation. Kendon and Ferber (1973) identified five basic stages in such a greeting ritual, as shown in Table 3.1.

Nonverbal communication also signals the end to an interaction. You may, for example, stop talking, start to edge away, or show other signs of departure, such as looking away from the other person more often or checking your watch. You might also step

Photo 3.3 How does NVC regulate (begin, maintain, and end) interactions? (See page 74.)

a little farther back or turn to the side. When the interaction is coming to an end, speakers join in rituals of ending, such as stepping back, offering a handshake, or stating directly that it's time to go.

Table 3.1 Kendon and Ferber's (1973) Five Basic Stages of a Greeting Ritual

1. Sighting and recognition	Occurs when you and another person first see each other
2. Distant salutation	Used to say hello with a wave, a flash of recognition, a smile, or a nod of acknowledgement
3. Lowering your head and averting your gaze (to avoid staring)	As you approach the other person you break off your visual connection till you get close enough to talk and be heard
4. Close salutation	Most likely involves some type of physical contact: a handshake, a kiss, or a hug, which brings you too close for a comfortable conversation
5. Backing off	Taking a step back or turning to the side to create a slightly larger space, the actual size of which is dictated by the type of relationship you share with the other person

Identifies Others

Nonverbal communication also functions to identify specific individuals. Just as dogs know each other individually by smell, humans recognize one another specifically from facial appearance. You also use physical cues like muscles, beards, skin color, breasts, and the whiteness of a person's hair to identify him or her as a particular sex, age, race, or athletic ability.

Clothing is an identifying signal for someone's sex (men rarely wear dresses), personality (whether a person wears loud colors, sedate business attire, or punk clothing), favorite sports team, and job (police, military, security). Clothing can also identify changes in people, such as whether they have a special role today (prom outfits, wedding wear, gardening clothes), or indicate specific differences about their lives (casual Friday).

People can also distinguish others' scents: What perfume or cologne do they wear? Do they smoke? Are they drinkers? People often do not comment on these kinds of clues, but if your physician smells of alcohol, you may well identify him or her as professionally incompetent to deal with your health concerns.

Make Your Case

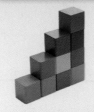

Note the date (1973) of Kendon and Ferber's greeting ritual research. When discussing touch later in this chapter, we reference works by Heslin and Jourard, which were conducted at around the same time (1974 and 1971, respectively). In a later chapter, we encourage you to be cautious when using references that are dated. However, some material may stand the test of time. There are two cases for you to make here. First, has Kendon and Ferber's greeting ritual research stood the test of time, or have changes in greetings occurred since it was conducted? Second, will the meanings of some nonverbal behaviors never change, or is all communication and meaning open to change?

Transmits Emotional Information

An additional function of NVC is to convey emotional information. When you are angry, you scowl; when you are in love, you look gooey; when you feel happy, you smile. Nonverbal communication actually allows you to convey three different kinds of emotional information as follows.

Attitude Toward the Other

NVC conveys your *attitude toward the other person.* If your facial expression conveys anxiety, viewers assume you are frightened. If your face looks relaxed and warm, viewers assume you are comfortable. If you care about what your instructor has to say, you fall silent when a lecture begins; talking in class (instructors' biggest complaint about students) makes it difficult for people to hear but also shows lack of respect. So there!

Attitude Toward the Situation

NVC conveys your *attitude toward the situation:* Rapidly moving about while talking conveys a message of anxiety. Police officers often see fidgeting and an inability to maintain eye contact as indicators of a person's guilt.

Attitude Toward Yourself

NVC conveys information about your *attitude toward yourself.* If a person is arrogant, confident, or low in self-esteem, it is expressed through nonverbal behaviors. Arrogance shows up in nonverbal actions, such as facial expression, tone of voice, eye contact, and body posture. If someone stands up to her full height and faces you directly, you might assume that she is confident. Conversely, if she slouches and stares at the ground, you might assume that she is shy, lacks confidence, and is insecure.

Establishes Relational Meaning and Understanding

Your relationships with others inform your everyday communication, and your everyday communication develops relationships. Nonverbal communication is a silent *relational* regulator. Regulation of interactions serves to regulate engagement,

College Experience

Instructors often try to establish a sense of immediacy or closeness with their students.

Such behavior frequently results in positive learning outcomes. Verbally, immediacy can be established by using words like *we* and *us.* Nonverbally, it can be established through such behavior as eye contact, tone of voice, arrangement of classrooms/offices, physical closeness to students, and touch. Consider how your instructors attempt to create immediacy with students. Do some instructors seem more immediate than others? Do some instructors attempt to establish a "wall" between themselves and students? Can instructors exhibit too much immediacy?

politeness, coordination of action, and sense of pleasure in the interaction—all of which are ultimately relational in effect. The appearance of others enables you to distinguish and make judgments about them. Appearance also forms the basis of relational attraction. In fact, you often are attracted to people with facial and bodily features very similar to your own.

The Elements of Nonverbal Communication

So far we have discussed NVC as if it is a single thing. Actually NVC has many different elements used collectively in the construction and interpretation of meaning, the development of identity, and the enactment of relationships. We discuss them individually to provide a more detailed explanation, but keep in mind that NVC works as a whole system comprising all these elements. Accordingly, we put them back together again at the end of this section.

Proxemics: Space and Distance

Proxemics is the study of space and distance in communication. Space used in different ways conveys different meanings: You lay it out as living rooms, bedrooms, offices, or bus shelters, and you decorate, rearrange, and occupy it. You often mark and establish it as your own even when you do not have exclusive control over it: sitting in your favorite chair at school or laying your books on a table to indicate its occupation. Countries possess space and usually mark it with a flag to indicate ownership and control. Both countries and people get upset if their space is invaded in some way. If somebody sits in your favorite chair or moves the books you placed on a table, you will probably be irritated. If a person you have just met stands mere inches away and stares at your face, you may feel uncomfortable. By contrast, a romantic partner standing that close to you may be more than welcome. The occupation of space and the distance you maintain from others conveys messages about control, acceptance, and relationships.

Territoriality is the establishment and maintenance of space that you claim for your personal use. Knapp and Hall (2002) point out three types of territory that you may establish: primary, secondary, and public. *Primary territory* is space that you own or have principal control over; it is central to your life, such as your house, room, apartment, office, or car. How you maintain and control this space communicates a great deal to those around you. Decorating your home in a particular fashion not only provides you with a sense of comfort but also informs others about the type of person you may be or the types

Strategic Communication

Your arrangement of the space in your interaction can make another person feel more comfortable or less comfortable and make that person feel more in control or less in control. Consider ways in which the arrangement of space that you control can be adjusted according to the types of relationships you wish to achieve when people enter your space.

of interests you may have. Even in dorm rooms, though they are generally less than spacious, roommates find a decorative way to assert ownership of "their" areas.

You establish *secondary territory as your own through repeated use,* even if it is space that is not central to your life or exclusive to you. A good example of secondary territory is the room where your class is held. Chances are pretty good that you and your fellow students sit in the exact same seats that you sat in on the first day of class. Even though this space does not belong to you, others associate it with you because of repeated use. Accordingly, if you came to class one day and someone was sitting in "your" seat, you would probably get irritated or uncomfortable during class if you were forced to sit elsewhere.

Public territory is space open to everyone but available for your sole temporary occupancy, such as park benches or seats in a movie theater. Secondary and public territory can involve the same type of physical space, such as a table at a restaurant, so consider this: If you go to the same restaurant every day for lunch and always sit at the same table, eventually it will become your secondary territory. Although it is open to everyone, once you claim that space for your temporary use, you assume exclusive control over it for the time being and would not expect anyone to violate that.

There are cultural variations in the use of public territory. In the United States, for example, if you and your date went to a restaurant and were seated at a table for four, the two additional seats would remain empty regardless of whether other people were waiting to be seated. In many European countries, however, it would not be surprising if another couple you do not know were eventually seated at your table.

Markers, used to establish and announce your territory, are surprisingly effective. People mark space by putting their "stuff" on it. Markers are common when using public territory that is open and unrestricted. For example, when you lay a jacket over the back of a chair, you have claimed that chair. Should someone want to move the chair, he or she would probably ask your permission rather than simply removing the jacket and taking the chair. Markers are often used to indicate privacy and control; you feel uncomfortable if someone else enters the space without permission. People meet this "invasion" with varying degrees of disapproval, but blood pressure frequently goes up (Guerrero & Floyd, 2006).

A friend of ours was traveling home on a plane. The woman in front of him kept grabbing the top of her seat and draping her fingers down his movie screen. In those tight seats, her wiggly fingers were just 14 to 16 inches from his face and distracting him from the movie. At one point, he coughed. She must have felt the air on her hand because she quickly jerked it back and never placed it on his movie screen again. This is a great example of "spoiling the space" for her and reclaiming it as his.

Personal Space and Distance

You carry around with you an idea of how much actual space you should have during an interaction. This idea will be affected by your status, your sex, and your liking for the person with whom you are talking. It also will be affected by the situations in which you find yourself.

Personal space refers to that space legitimately claimed or occupied by a person for the time being. Close friends are literally closer to you—people generally stand closer to people they like. In fact, if you look around, you can tell whether people are friends or strangers according to the amount of space between them.

All of us have a **body buffer zone**, a kind of imaginary aura around people that they regard as part of themselves. People differ in the size of their body buffer zone. If you step into the body buffer zone that someone feels is "his space," even if it is beyond what you would normally expect, you may be in for trouble. Your friends and family can enter your body buffer zone more freely than other people. You react to space and its use depending on the kind of situation in which you find yourself. An early pioneer of personal space research, E. T. Hall (1966) distinguished among intimate distance (contact to 18 inches), personal distance (18–48 inches), social distance (48–144 inches), and public distance (12–25 feet) (see Figure 3.2). Although valuable, this early research does not explain cultural differences. It has become accepted that people from Latino and Arab cultures require less space for each type of encounter than do Northern Europeans and North Americans.

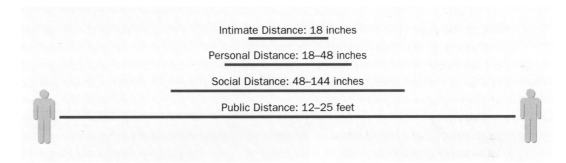

Figure 3.2   Hall's (1966) four types of personal space

Proxemics and Everyday Life

The meaning of space or distance is framed by your relationships with others. What it means for someone to stand mere inches away from you will differ depending on whether he or she is a friend, an adversary, or a complete stranger. A friend moving the backpack you placed on a table in order to sit near you would mean something entirely different than a complete stranger doing the same thing.

Your use of space and distance enacts these relationships. Subordinate individuals tend to give more space to individuals in leadership positions. An employee, for example, would stand at a greater distance when talking with an employer than with a coworker, indicating the superior–subordinate nature of that relationship and enabling both interactants to perform their respective roles.

Physical space is often laid out to indicate and perform leadership or power roles. A formal chair of a meeting sits at one end of the table, usually in a special seat, and everyone else lines up along the length of the table at right angles to the chair. In contrast, a more secure or less formal leader might sit anywhere at the table. From seemingly minor physical facts about the distribution and use of space, then, you can determine relational information about the people in a setting—who is in charge and who is not—as well as the leader's preferred style of interaction, formal or informal.

Space and distance also allow relational negotiation to take place. For instance, a friend who desires a more intimate relationship with you may begin standing a bit closer to gauge your reaction. Similarly, a subordinate decreasing the amount of space granted to a superior may be indicating a desire for a more equal relationship. Either attempt could be accepted or rejected depending on the other person's view of the relationship. Such relational negotiation frequently takes place in families once adolescent sons or daughters start to claim bedrooms as their own space that is now private from invasive parents.

Space and distance also guide interactions with others. If your friend has books, papers, and other material spread out over a large space, it could indicate that he or she prefers to be alone. In this case, you might ask your friend before you move these items to the side, or you might avoid going over altogether. Your instructor working in his or her office with the door wide open could be indicating that he or she is available to see students. Still, you would probably attempt to knock or at least announce yourself before entering the office, because you are essentially invading the instructor's primary space. The reactions of your friend sitting at a table or your instructor working in the office—looking up and smiling or expressing annoyance—will probably dictate what you do next, which brings us to the next element of NVC.

Photo 3.4A and B Notice the difference between these two photos. The first photo is a scene from a Western city in which people are noticeably uncomfortable by their lack of personal space. The second photo captures Japanese train pushers, whose job is to cram as many people onto a subway car as possible. Little consideration is given to lack of personal space in this Eastern city. What imaginary aura around people that they regard as part of themselves is obviously more restricted in the latter photo? (See page 74.)

Kinesics: Movement

Kinesics refers to the movement that takes place during the course of an interaction. While interacting, you may move around quite a bit, shift position, walk around as you talk, cross and uncross your legs, lean forward on a table, or sit back in a chair. Kinesics can be broken down into posture, gesture, and eye contact/gaze. In every case, whether separately or in combination, these cues convey messages about your relationship to the speaker or your audience, about the subject you are discussing (discomfort or relative ease), or about the situation as a whole. Movement can be either very intimate or very aggressive, especially if you move into somebody's space.

Posture

The position of your body during an interaction may be relaxed and welcoming or tense and off-putting. For example, someone draping him- or herself over a chair will look very relaxed, and someone sitting up straight or standing to attention will not. You can probably look around the room now and see people with different postures. Even during class, you likely draw conclusions about whether people are interested just from the posture they adopt.

In an open posture, the front of the body is observable, and in a closed posture, the front of the body is essentially shut off, usually because the arms are folded across the chest or the person is hunched over. Both types of posture convey the three attitudes noted before: (1) attitude about self (confidence, anxiety, shyness, a feeling of authority), (2) attitude about others (liking, respect, attention), and (3) attitude about the situation (comfort, ease). An open posture conveys positive messages, and a closed posture conveys negative messages. When someone feels "down," he or she tends to look "down," slumping over, slouching, and generally being depressed ("depressed" means pressed down). These postures send messages about a person's relaxation, attention, confidence, comfort, and willingness to communicate.

Gesture

Gesture can be defined as a movement of the body or any of its parts in a way that conveys an idea or intention or displays a feeling or an assessment of the situation. Suppose you were in a foreign country, one of your friends suffered heatstroke, and no one knew the word for *dehydrated* in that country's language. You would likely indicate your need for water by making a "drinking" gesture.

When people think of gestures, hand or arm movements most often come to mind, but facial expressions also count as gestures for our purposes. Quite frequently, your face and the rest of your body work together to express meaning. For instance, when a person is expressing an emotion, the face will provide information about the exact emotion being expressed, and the body will provide information about its extent. You could, for example, be angry and scowling while your body is fairly loose and fluid, indicating low-intensity anger. However, you could be scowling, holding your body tight and rigid, and almost shaking, which would indicate great anger and tell others to use their knowledge of proxemics to give you plenty of space!

Richard Nixon and Winston Churchill each used a version of the emblematic "V is for victory" to denote a different political message. Nixon's use indicated his personal victories, and Churchill's use related to the British people's fight against Germany in World War II. Can you think of a female historical figure who used an emblematic gesture?

Gestures can be split broadly into two sorts: those that signal a feeling not expressed in words (emblems) and those that signal something said in words (illustrations). Emblematic gestures are not related to speech in the sense that they do not help illustrate what is being said, although they may clarify what a person means. Consider conductors directing bands and orchestras, police officers directing traffic, and coaches signaling plays. Emblems can nevertheless be translated into verbal expressions; for example, you recognize that bouncing the palm of your hand off your forehead means "How stupid of me! Why didn't I think of it before?"

Illustrators

Illustrators are directly related to speech as it is being spoken and are used to visualize or emphasize its content. For example, turning your palm down and then rotating it as you describe how to unscrew a bottle cap is an illustrator, and scrunching up your face while saying "This tastes disgusting" is an illustrator using facial expression. Like other NVC, gestures can also regulate interaction. While making a speech, you might raise a finger to draw attention to the fact that you wish to make a key point.

Eye Contact Versus Gaze

Eye contact refers to the extent to which you look directly into the eyes of another person. Someone who "looks you in the eye" while talking is generally seen as reliable and honest; someone with shifty eyes is treated as suspicious and untrustworthy.

Gaze—distinguished from eye contact, where both interactants look at each other—describes one person looking at another and, most of the time, is seen as rewarding. Most people generally like to be looked at when they are talking to someone else. In fact, if you gaze at a speaker and smile or nod approvingly, you will probably find that the speaker pays more attention to you, looks toward you more often, and engages in eye contact with you. Try this with your instructor the next time you are in class, and see if he or she responds to you personally in this way.

Starting with the broad generalization that gaze and eye contact convey mostly positive messages, note that eye contact indicates engagement in interactions, and eye contact and orientation can start conversations or establish the likelihood of interaction. A continued positive pattern of eye contact shows that you are paying attention to someone and are interested in what he or she is saying.

Although most eye contact is positive, it can also convey negative messages. A wide-eyed stare can mean a disbelieving "Excuse me?!" or be a threat. Years ago, Ellsworth and her colleagues (Ellsworth, Carlsmith, & Henson, 1972) stood at the intersections of roads and stared at some drivers and not others. Those who were stared at tended to drive away more speedily, suggesting that a stare is a threatening stimulus for flight. Gaze can therefore be threatening and negative as much as it can be enticing and positive. Something for you to think about, then, is how this particular element of NVC helps you determine whether a positive or negative message is being sent (hint: NVC is a system of different parts that interrelate).

Eye contact or gaze is often used to gather information or acquire feedback from the speaker as you are listening and

A recent television show, *Lie to Me,* is based on the idea that expert observers of nonverbal communication can tell whether people are lying and help solve crimes.

from the listener when you are talking. If you are looking at someone, you can see how he or she is doing and get a better idea of what is going on. If you are talking, this allows you to assess whether another person is paying attention, how he or she responds to what you are saying, and how he or she evaluates you.

Some people (shy people, for example), afraid that others will evaluate them negatively, tend to decrease eye contact (Bradshaw, 2006), which cuts out negative inputs from other people. For shy people, this is a distinct advantage, but it also reduces the amount of information they can gather about a listener's reaction to what they say. Many outsiders assume that decreased eye contact is evidence of other social flaws, such as deception, so a shy person who avoids eye contact through fear of feedback may eventually create an impression of being shifty and unreliable. Burgoon and colleagues (Burgoon, Coker, & Coker, 1986) found that gaze aversion produces consistently negative evaluations of interviewees. Typically, unconfident behavior (as in shy people) involves not only low eye contact but also nervous speech, poor posture, tendency for long silences in conversation, and lack of initiative in discussion.

Eye contact is also used to regulate interactions. Some characteristic patterns of eye movements go along with talk in conversations to regulate its flow. The speaker tends to look at the listener at the start and end of sentences (or paragraphs, if the speaker is telling a longer tale) but may look away during the middle parts. A listener who wishes to speak will tend to look hard at the present speaker, and a person asking a question will look right at the person to whom it is directed, maintaining his or her gaze while awaiting a reply. Listeners look at speakers more consistently than speakers look at listeners. When giving a speech to a group or large audience, it is important that you not only look at your audience (rather than at your notes) most of the time but also distribute your gaze around the room, looking both left and right.

Interaction is further regulated through use of eye contact to manage the turn taking noted earlier, a kind of eye-based "over and out." In cultures where simultaneous speech is taken as a sign of impoliteness, rather than of active and desirable involvement in the interaction, eye contact is used to end or yield a turn (a speaker looks longer toward the audience at the end of sentences), as well as to request a turn (a listener establishes longer eye contact with a speaker in order to signal willingness to enter conversation). You leave conversation by breaking off eye contact (typically 45 seconds before departure) and then, when the talking stops, turning toward an exit.

Vocalics: Voice

Vocalics, sometimes called paralanguage, refers to vocal characteristics that provide information about *how verbal communication should be interpreted* and how you are feeling. For example, the tone of your voice can be strained when you are angry or high-pitched when you are anxious, and your talking speed may be fast when you are excited. Vocalics indicate your degree of comfort and whether you like the person to whom you are talking or feel upset by him or her. You can also signal how you feel about what you are saying. You must manage your paralanguage when giving a speech, for example, to let people know you're interested in your topic.

A main element of vocalics involves the sound of your voice (voice quality) and how it can change during the course of an interaction or a speech, referring not to what you say but to how you say it. Sometimes you can tell who is calling on the phone just by the way a call begins; some people do not need to identify themselves directly to you since you just know how their voices sound. Even people who do not know you can tell something about you from your accent and tone of voice. For example, your accent can give people information about where you come from (the Deep South as opposed to Minnesota). The sound of your voice alone can indicate your age and sex. Also, some people make decisions about your attractiveness on the basis of the sound of your voice, with some accents preferred over others.

You often use the tone or pitch of your voice to emphasize the parts of a sentence that you think are the most important. A loud scream or a shout of "Fire!" or of "Help!" conveys the situation as urgent in a way that a simple conversational tone would not. These aspects of vocalics are used to emphasize elements of an interaction to which an audience must pay more attention. You can make a speech more interesting, for example, by varying vocalic pitch and tone in a way that keeps the audience attentive and helps the audience identify the most important parts of the speech. Tone of voice also enables you to determine what someone really means and is especially important when trying to determine whether or not a person is being sarcastic.

What do you think when you hear a person with a Southern accent, a New York accent, or a British accent? How do you think people perceive you based on your accent?

Another aspect of vocalics is speech rate, or the speed at which someone talks. When a teacher wants you to pay special attention to what is being said, he or she will sometimes slow down so you realize the importance of the point. Someone who speaks too fast is likely to be treated as nervous or possibly shy. In everyday life, where people are relaxed among friends, their speech rate tends to be lively and fluent rather than stilted or halting. In stressful circumstances, however, their speech rate may be hesitant or uneven.

One surprising part of vocalics is silence. You have likely heard the seemingly contradictory phrases "Silence is golden" and "Silence is deadly." Tending to differ on the extent to which they view silence as one or the other, people evaluate silence depending on contextual and relational factors surrounding its use. Most people in the United States—especially on a date or in an interview—meet silence or a prolonged break in conversation with discomfort. Silence could indicate embarrassment, anxiety, or lack of preparation as well as shyness, confusion, or disrespect. Silence can also be used to show anger or frustration, such as when you are mad at someone and give him or her the "silent treatment," or relational comfort, in that people do not feel pressured to keep the conversation going. "Shared inactivity" can be an indication of the absolute comfort in one another's presences as when you and a partner just veg out in front of the TV.

Giles (2008) shows that people can indicate their membership in a particular group by the way they use vocalic nonverbal behavior. For instance, if you are from the South, you might use a heavier accent in your conversation with others from your state or region, but you might tone down your accent when talking to people from the Northeast. Where people wish to maintain a distance from the person they are talking to, they will diverge, or hang on to differences in accent. When they want to become closer to the other person, they will tend to converge, or match their way of talking to the other person's. You may notice yourself copying the speech styles of people you like.

Vocalics and Regulation

In addition to sending relational messages, people use vocalics to regulate their interactions. A sharp intake of breath indicates shock, pain, or surprise; *uh-huh* or *um*, known as **backchannel communication** (vocalizations by a listener that give feedback to the speaker to show interest, attention, and/ or a willingness to keep listening), may be used either to encourage someone else to keep talking or to indicate that a speaker does not want to yield the floor because he still has something to say but has not yet decided what.

The most common use of vocalics in regulating your interaction is with **turn taking**, which is when you hand over speaking to another person. This handover happens much less obviously than does a radio form of communication, where an airline pilot or a trucker, for example, says "over" or "comeback" to indicate that he or she has finished speaking and wants another person to respond.

Case in Point

People often find that they unconsciously adopt a similar posture to another person in an interaction (for example, they fold their arms when the other person does). Go to a public space on campus and observe whether people's nonverbal behavior mirrors that of people they are with.

In your normal interactions, you don't need to say "over" because you can tell from the speaker's tone of voice or eye movements (referring back to kinesics) that he or she wants you to begin speaking, but you still need to signal a handover. For example, when someone asks a question, raising the pitch of his or her voice afterward serves to prompt you that the questioner now expects an answer. You also know when people are coming to the end of what they want to say because they will generally slow down somewhat and drop the pitch of their voice. That is how students know when a lecture is coming to an end and that they should start closing their books!

Chronemics: Time

Chronemics encompasses use and evaluation of time in your interactions, including the location of events in time. For example, the significance of a romantic encounter can often be determined by when it occurs. You might see a lunch date as less meaning-ful than a late-night candlelit dinner. Whether you are meeting for lunch or dinner, however, your meal will have a time structure and pattern. You probably have the salad before the ice cream.

Chronemics also involves the duration of events. Boring lectures seem to last forever. You may also have had the experience that people often end their college romances after about 18 months or during the spring semester, when one partner might be graduating or going away for the summer. You are quite likely to comment if you run into some-one whom you have not seen for "a-a-a-ges." Also, you would probably feel the need to apologize if you left an e-mail unanswered for too long, did not answer a text message, or were late for an appointment. Cultural differences in attitudes toward time also exist; some cultures especially value timely completion of tasks over atten-tion to relationships, respect, or status, while others place the priorities exactly in reverse, feeling that it is discourteous to get down to the task before taking plenty of time to create a good relational atmos-phere first.

The meaning of nonverbal behavior depends on the *context* of the interaction and the relationship of the interactants. Is your arriving 20 minutes late to class acceptable? What if your instructor does it?

Chronemics and Regulation of Interaction

Chronemics can affect the structure of interactions. You all have an expectation about the number of milliseconds that are supposed to elapse between one person finishing speaking and the other joining in. When this timing gets disrupted, interaction becomes uncomfortable for everybody—one reason why people who stammer or who are shy create difficulty for others in interaction by not picking up the conversational baton when they are expected to (Bradshaw, 2006). You also recognize that when someone is really paying attention to you and is interested in what you are saying, he or she will tend to be engaged and maintain "synchrony." He or she will not allow too much time to elapse between utterances and try to synchronize his or her interaction and behavior with yours. In addition, you can indicate interest in somebody else by answering his or her questions promptly, a chronemic activity. You also convey information about your knowledge and expertise by keeping your talk flowing freely and by not allowing your-self too many hesitations. Both fluency and the absence of hesitation count as chrone-mic elements of nonverbal communication since they are about the timing of speech.

Haptics: Touch

Haptics is the study of the specific nonverbal behaviors involving touch. When people get into your personal space, they will likely make actual physical contact with your most personal possession, your body. Touch is used not only as a greeting to start an interaction (a handshake or a kiss) but also in ceremonies, whether baptism, the con-firming laying on of hands, holding a partner's hands while making wedding vows, or as a means of congratulation from a simple handshake to a pat on the back to those piles of players who form on top of the goal scorer in sports.

Psychologist Sidney Jourard (1971) observed and recorded how many times couples in cafés casually touched each other in an hour. The highest rates were in Puerto Rico (180 times per hour) and Paris (110 times per hour). Guess how many times per hour couples touched each other in the mainland United States? Twice! (In London, it was zero. They never touched.) Jourard also found that French parents and children touched each other three times more frequently than did American parents and children.

Heslin (1974) noted that touch, of which there are many different types, has many different functions, as shown in Table 3.2. These forms of touch show positive feelings, but each could also produce negative feelings: Someone you feel close to shakes your hand instead of hugging you, or someone you are not close to tries to hug you. Touch can also indicate influence. Have you ever seen a politician who places one arm on the back of a visiting foreign dignitary to indicate a place to which the person should move? The two actions together serve to indicate politely to the other person where the next stage of a discussion or proceedings will take place. Touch can also serve as a physiological stimulus, for example, in sexual touch or from a reassuring back rub.

Table 3.2 Heslin's (1974) Functions of Touch	
Functional/ professional	Touch is permitted by the context—for example, during a medical exam, someone you hardly know may touch parts of your body that even your best friend has never seen.
Social/polite	Touch is formal—for example, a handshake.
Friendship/ warmth	Touch is an expression of regard.
Love/intimacy	Touch is special, permitted only with those with whom you are close.

As with all other NVC, touch can play a role in interaction management. For example, you can touch someone on the arm to interrupt the flow of conversation. Also you both begin and end encounters with handshakes on many occasions, indicating that the beginning and ending of the interaction have essentially relational consequences because you imply, through touch, continuance of the relationship beyond the specific interaction.

The Interacting System of Nonverbal Communication

In the last few pages, we have split NVC into separate parts to give a better understanding of the complicated system that makes it work, but we promised to reassemble them at the end. It has probably struck you that elements of NVC carry double messages or, at least, that they can be "read" in more than one way. A stare can be a threat or a sign of longing; a touch can be an intimate caress or a sexual harassment violation; a move toward someone can be loving or aggressive. Same behavior, different meaning! How do you know what to make of the behavior and how it should be understood?

Essentially, you can interpret the meaning of NVC in four ways that recognize that it occurs as part of a system and is related to other parts of an interaction:

Photo 3.5 From how many types of NVC can you tell that these two people like each other? (See page 74.)

1. Nonverbal communication has a relationship to the words used with it. It can affect how words are understood, and words can affect how NVC is understood. Someone caressing your thigh and saying "I love you" is doing something different from someone touching your thigh and saying "Is this where it hurts?"

2. Any NVC has a relationship to other NVC that happens simultaneously. If someone is staring at you with a scowl and clenched fists, you can assume that the stare is intended as a threat; if the stare is accompanied by a smile and a soft expression, it is intended as friendly. Likewise, a smile accompanied by agitated gestures, sweating, or blushing probably means the person is nervous, but someone smiling and looking relaxed with an open posture is probably feeling friendly and confident.

3. The interpretation of NVC depends on its context. If someone stares at you in class, it feels different from a stare across a crowded singles bar; a scream at a sports match probably means your team just scored, but a scream in your apartment could indicate the discovery of a spider.

4. How NVC is interpreted is also affected by your relationship to another person. If the person caressing your thigh is a nurse, you're probably right to assume that the touch is part of a treatment or medical exam, so stay there and get well. If the person is your instructor, it's time to leave—and leave quickly.

We have referenced a few of the errors and violations that can occur in NVC (such as sitting in someone else's special chair or touching someone when he or she does not want to be touched), but we have not given you direct guidance for how it can be improved. The preceding four guidelines should generally help you avoid serious errors, but we can go further and address specific ways to improve NVC overall.

Improving Your Use of Nonverbal Communication

Let's start with what you already know. People can be poor at encoding their intentions or at decoding others' meanings. The goal of improving NVC suggests immediately that you can identify errors that need to be improved or avoided.

A violation is a serious breach of NVC rules, such as invading someone's territory or personal space in ways discussed earlier. In general, a violation openly breaks a rule that ignores the four guidelines in the previous section that help interpret the interacting system of NVC. All the negative interpretations that follow violations of NVC rules derive from the fact that the violations are taken to *indicate a negative attitude or relationship* toward the other person, usually of dislike or disrespect. Although any NVC rule can be violated, the most fateful are violations of touch since the body is the most personal and primary area of space. Invasion of someone's body or personal space is a deeply disrespectful or extremely intimate act.

Successful conversation and use of NVC depend in large part on how people tune in to one another and respond appropriately. Recall the earlier distinctions between encoding and decoding. Someone who is socially skilled is a good encoder *and* a good decoder. You tend to notice, though, when someone is bad at encoding and continually producing inappropriate NVC. For example, some very young children do not yet understand the rules and often need to be told directly, "Don't stare; it's rude," or "Look at me when I am talking to you." It is harder to notice when someone is a poor decoder and just "doesn't get it."

One way to become a better decoder is to make sure that you *attend* to whether other people pay attention to NVC and seem to understand it. A good decoder also *bonds* with the speaker and watches out for the signals that the speaker sends about comfort in the situation. A good decoder will notice when the speaker is anxious and will smile more often or reward the speaker with head nods and encouraging NVC to put him or her at ease. A good listener also *coordinates* with the speaker and responds to his or her cues so the interaction runs smoothly with no awkward silences. Skilled listeners should also *detect/decode* the undercurrents of a speaker's talk by attending carefully to eye movements and gestures that "leak" what the speaker truly feels. Finally, a good listener is *encouraging* and invites the speaker to continue, shows interest, looks at the speaker directly, is focused, and makes the speaker the center of attention in the conversation.

Listen in on Your Life

Think about a situation where you felt uncomfortable in the presence of another person. Inside, you may have been filled with anxiety. How do you think the other person could have known that you were anxious? Were you sweating, blushing, agitated, speaking too fast, or jumpy? What did you do to try to conceal your nerves? Have you ever seen other people trying to appear calm, but you weren't fooled? What were they doing? What were their bodies saying to you in these languages of NVC? What behaviors gave away their anxiety?

Table 3.3 Encoding and Decoding Skills	
Speaker/encoder	**Listener/decoder**
Affirming	Attending
Blending	Bonding
Consistency	Coordinating
Directness	Detecting/decoding
Emotional clarity	Encouraging

What about skilled encoding? A good speaker will *affirm* the listener by encoding approval and liking while talking—that is, by smiling or good eye contact. Good speakers also *blend* their NVC with the talk to allow for *consistency* between what is said and what is delivered in the NVC channels. *Directness* is achieved by making sure that NVC is done clearly and unambiguously, and *emotional* clarity is presented by good signaling of what is felt. Good speakers and good actors are able to convey the emotions of their words by matching their nonverbal expression of emotion to the meaning of the words.

The skills listed in Table 3.3 can be broadly summarized by saying that two people in an interaction should not disrupt the usual patterns of normative interaction. They show the importance of NVC in regulating interaction while also sending positive messages about the other person and yourself—in short, about the relationship between the two people.

FOCUS QUESTIONS REVISITED

1. What is nonverbal communication?

Nonverbal communication (NVC) is everything that communicates a message but does not include words. Among other things space and distance, movement, vocal tone and pitch, time, gestures, touch, eye movements, and posture are NVC.

2. How does nonverbal communication work, and what work does it do in communication?

NVC conveys attitudes about self, others, and interaction and regulates interaction.

3. How does nonverbal communication regulate (e.g., begin and end) interactions?

Nonverbal communication regulates interaction by initiating conversation, regulating the turns with which people speak, and defining when interactions have reached their end. It does this through eye movements, vocalics, and gestures, among other things.

4. What are the elements of nonverbal communication, and how do they interconnect?

Elements of NVC are proxemics, kinesics, vocalics, chronemics, and haptics. They work as an interacting system so a particular cue (e.g., a stare) can be interpreted in the context of other cues (e.g., a grim or friendly expression). The overall meaning is determined by the combination within the system and by the frame of the relationship in which it happens.

5. How can you improve your use of nonverbal communication?

There are two sides of NVC that can be improved: encoding and decoding. Improvement of encoding involves better projection of your emotions and feelings; improvement of decoding involves paying more attention to the other person in an interaction and fully understanding what he or she means.

KEY CONCEPTS

QUESTIONS TO ASK YOUR FRIENDS

1. Ask your friends how good they believe themselves to be at determining when other people are not telling the truth.

2. Ask your friends whether they can tell when you are embarrassed or uncomfortable even though you might not tell them. What nonverbal behaviors inform them of your embarrassment or discomfort?

3. Ask your friends whether they think they could get away with telling you a lie.

MEDIA LINKS

1. Look for television news stories involving police putting people into cars. What percentage of police touch the person's head? In what other circumstances, if any, do people open the car door for someone else and then touch the head of the person getting in? What do you think is being conveyed?

2. How many news stories can you find where a fight got started because someone felt another person was "looking at him in a funny way" or infringing upon his personal space?

3. How do television shows use the placement of furniture to add something to the story?

ETHICAL ISSUES

1. Now that you know more thoroughly some of the behaviors involved in nonverbal communication, would it be ethical for you to use this information to deceive other people?

2. Would it be unethical for you to use your knowledge to reveal when other people are being deceptive?

3. If a member of another culture is breaking a rule of nonverbal communication in your culture, should you tell him or her? Why or why not?

ANSWERS TO PHOTO CAPTIONS

Photo 3.1 ▪ There are static cues and dynamic cues: Static cues include the hairstyle, wristband, chain, and necklace, all identifying him as a "punk." Although this is a still photo, he has taken a posture that in everyday conversation would be part of a dynamic system of movement. His posture is aggressive, threatening, or hinting at menace.

Photo 3.2 ▪ Bodily adornment can create images of power and intimidation in enemies. People sometimes adopt body modifications in order to raise their status or inspire fear.

Photo 3.3 ▪ First, nonverbal communication regulates interaction through recognition (we recognize someone as the individual he or she is by sight, by touch, or in the case of animals and human beings by smell/fragrance), and then there are various rituals of behavior that begin interactions (catching someone's eye, shaking hands, bowing, or sniffing) and behaviors that are used to end interactions, such as a handshake, a bow, a wave, or a wag of the tail.

Photo 3.4 ▪ The body buffer zone is more restricted.

Photo 3.5 ▪ You can tell they like each other from at least the following: physical closeness, touching together parts of the body not normally touched with strangers (thighs and calves), and smiling at an intimate distance. Their similar dress codes and open postures indicate comfort with each other; the woman's body (her left shoulder) and head lean toward the man. There are also static cues: Where they are sitting is an intimate place.

STUDENT STUDY SITE

Visit the study site at **www.sagepub.com/boc2e** for e-flashcards, practice quizzes, journal articles and additional study resources.

REFERENCES

Bradshaw, S. (2006). Shyness and difficult relationships: Formation is just the beginning. In C. D. Kirkpatrick, S. W. Duck, & M. K. Foley (Eds.), *Relating difficulty: The processes of constructing and managing difficult interaction* (pp. 15–41). Mahwah, NJ: Lawrence Erlbaum.

Burgoon, J. K., Coker, D. A., & Coker, R. A. (1986). Communicative effects of gaze behavior: A test of two contrasting explanations. *Human Communication Research, 12,* 495–524.

Duck, S. W. (2007). *Human relationships* (4th ed.). London: Sage.

Ellsworth, P. C., Carlsmith, J. M., & Henson, A. (1972). The stare as a stimulus to flight in human subjects: A series of field experiments. *Journal* of Personality and Social Psychology, 21, 302–311.

Giles, H. (2008). Communication accommodation theory. In L. A. Baxter & D. O. Braithwaite (Eds.), *Engaging theories in interpersonal communication* (pp. 161–173). Thousand Oaks, CA: Sage.

Guerrero, L. K., & Floyd, K. (2006). *Nonverbal communication in relationships.* Mahwah, NJ: Lawrence Erlbaum.

Hall, E. T. (1966). *The hidden dimension.* New York: Doubleday/Anchor.

Heslin, R. (1974). *Steps toward a taxonomy of touching.* Paper presented at the meeting of the Midwestern Psychological Association, Chicago.

Jourard, S. M. (1971). *Self-disclosure.* New York: Wiley.

Kendon, A., & Ferber, A. (1973). A description of some human greetings. In R. P. Michael & J. H. Crook (Eds.), *Comparative ecology and behavior of primates* (pp. 591–668). New York: Academic Press.

Knapp, M. L., & Hall, J. A. (2002). *Nonverbal communication in human interaction* (5th ed.). New York: Holt, Rinehart & Winston.

Manusov, V., & Patterson, M. L. (2006). *Handbook of nonverbal communication.* Thousand Oaks, CA: Sage.

Remland, M. S. (2004). *Nonverbal communication in everyday life* (2nd ed.). New York: Houghton Mifflin.

Seiter, J. S., & Sandry, A. (2003). Pierced for success? The effects of ear and nose piercing on perceptions of job candidates' credibility, attractiveness, and hirability. *Communication Research Reports, 20*(4), 287–298.

4

Listening

What if we told you that we could provide you with the secret to academic success, career advancement, and improved relationships? It does not involve giving copies of this book to your instructors, employers, friends, and family—although that is a tremendous idea! Imagine the look of joy on their faces when they open the package and see their very own copy of Duck and McMahan, the perfect gift for the young and young at heart! OK . . . sorry for the shameless self-promotion. The truth is, though, that we can tell you the secret to these things, and it is something many people rarely consider: listening.

Effective listening entails more than merely going through the motions of the listening process. Effective listening means being an active, engaged, critical, and relationally aware listener who recognizes and overcomes the many obstacles to listening encountered in everyday communication.

In this chapter, we discuss the objectives for listening, such as relational development, gaining and comprehending information, critical evaluation, enjoyment, and therapeutic goals. We also address the process of active listening and discuss how listening and hearing are not the same thing, even though the terms *listening* and *hearing* are often used interchangeably. Discussions of listening frequently do not go beyond the active listening process, but communication involves more than simply listening carefully and intently. We specifically examine engaged listening and relational listening as we discuss how people may go beyond active listening in the communication process.

You do not have to read this book to realize that people listen more effectively on some occasions than on others; however, you may not be fully aware of the many obstacles that people actually face when listening. Accordingly, we address these obstacles and discuss how you might overcome them. You may very well be a listening champion once you finish studying this chapter! Even if you do not receive an award for listening, your listening skills will significantly improve, assisting you in school, your career, and your relationships.

Focus Questions

1. Why is listening important enough to have an entire chapter devoted to it?
2. What are the objectives of listening?
3. What does it mean to listen actively?
4. What are engaged and relational listening?
5. Why do people sometimes struggle when listening?
6. What is critical listening, and why is it so important?
7. What are fallacious arguments?

The final part of this chapter is dedicated to critical listening. Being critical does not necessarily entail finding fault or disagreeing with messages, but it does involve determining their accuracy, legitimacy, and value. This process may lead just as often to a positive evaluation of a message as to a negative evaluation of a message. We discuss the prevalence of critical evaluation in everyday life and examine the four elements of critical evaluation. We also explore the use of fallacious arguments, those that seem legitimate but are in reality based on faulty reasoning or insufficient evidence. Fallacious arguments, actually quite evident in everyday communication, appear in many of the commercials and advertisements you come across each day. After reading this chapter, you will be better equipped to recognize—and not be fooled by—these arguments.

Why Is Listening Important?

Listening is the communication activity in which people engage most frequently. In fact, studies conducted over the past 80 years have consistently ranked listening as the most frequent communication activity (Barker, Edwards, Gaines, Gladney, & Holley, 1980; Janusik & Wolvin, 2009; Rankin, 1928; Weinrauch & Swanda, 1975). One of the most recent studies examining the amount of time spent listening found that people dedicate nearly 12 hours daily to listening-related activities, such as talking with friends, attending class, participating in a business meeting, or listening to music on an iPod (Janusik & Wolvin, 2009). In other words, you probably spend half of each day listening!

As frequently as people engage in listening, its significance in daily life is not always given a lot of consideration. Since listening is so pervasive, people may tend to take this essential communication activity for granted. Perhaps the most mundane activity of everyday life (Halone & Pechioni, 2001), listening is nevertheless crucial to everyday interactions in a number of important contexts.

Listening and Education

Listening—often the primary channel of instruction at all levels of education—is a fundamental element in instruction and key to academic success. Listening is also a critical component in the relationships that develop between students and their instructors and between students and their academic advisors. Both instructor–student and advisor–advisee relationships demand effective listening by everyone involved. Ironically, while listening is the primary method of instruction and is so fundamental to academic achievement, it remains the least-taught type of communication skill (see Beall, Gill-Rosier, Tate, & Matten, 2008).

Listening and Career

Effective listening skills are also crucial to career success and advancement. Employers frequently rank listening as one of the most sought-after skills. Furthermore, most success and achievement from both organizational and personal career standpoints can be connected in large measure to effective listening (see Flynn, Valikoski, & Grau, 2008). Surveying the importance of listening in all professions and its significance in developing occupational areas, one listening scholar concluded "job success and development of all employees, regardless of title, position, or task will continue to be directly related to the employees' attitudes toward, skills in, and knowledge about listening" (Steil, 1997, p. 214).

Listening and Religion and Spirituality

Although in this context it has received less attention from researchers, listening is also an important component in religion and spirituality. Surveying this context, it was noted that listening in this area includes intrapersonal listening when engaged in meditation and prayer. Interpersonal listening occurs in such instances as listening to sermons or music and studying sacred and holy texts. Finally, interfaith listening occurs when one is attempting to understand the beliefs and perspectives of other religions (Schnapp, 2008).

Listening and Health Care

Listening is also a fundamental element of health care. The extent to which both patients and providers listen effectively has a tremendous impact on whether correct diagnoses are established and on whether patients accurately follow provider instructions. Listening is also vital to successful communication among health care workers such as when nurses receive instructions from doctors or when nurses update doctors on patient information (Davis, Thompson, Foley, Bond, & DeWitt, 2008).

Strategic Communication

We will remind you to do so when examining obstacles to effective listening, but as you read this chapter, consider the ways in which your listening in the classroom can be enhanced. Also, consider how interactions with your instructors, your classmates, your advisors, and others with whom you share an academic-based relationship can be improved through engaged and relational listening.

Photo 4.1 Enabling someone to talk about a problem or concern is known as what type of listening? (See page 80.)

Listening and Relationships

Listening also plays a fundamental role in relationship development and maintenance. Those relationships in which both partners engage in effective listening tend to be successful, long lasting, and positive, while relationships in which one or both partners fail to engage in effective listening tend to struggle and provide less satisfaction and enjoyment. Effective listening is an essential component of every action that takes place within relationships at all stages of development.

Listening Objectives

People generally have reasons for listening in most situations and contexts. While they may have a primary objective for listening, a single communicative exchange can have multiple listening goals. Table 4.1 presents these listening goals in isolation, but keep in mind that all listening situations may entail more than one objective.

Table 4.1 Listening Objectives	
Relational development and enhancement	People may engage in listening for the development and enhancement of relationships. Through listening, you can gain a greater understanding of yourself, your partner, and the relationship—even when these are not being discussed directly.
Gaining and comprehending information	People also listen to gain and comprehend information. As a student, you are likely well aware of this listening objective as you listen to lectures during class or to a classmate during a class discussion.
Critical listening	The goals of critical listening include evaluating the accuracy of a message as well as its value in a given situation. For example, you may listen critically during a class lecture or when listening to a salesperson discussing a product. Critical listening may lead to negative or positive evaluations of the message.
Enjoyment and appreciation	People also listen for enjoyment or appreciation: listening to a friend tell a story about a recent trip, listening to music on an iPod, or listening to crickets chirp and birds sing while you walk through a wooded area. The objective of these listening experiences is to gain pleasure.
Therapeutic listening	Therapeutic listening enables someone to talk through a problem or concern. Examples of therapeutic listening include listening to a coworker complain about a customer or client or listening to a neighbor talk about financial difficulties. In these situations, the person might simply be needing to express certain anxieties or frustrations, might be seeking approval or justification for feelings, or might be seeking advice and counsel about appropriate actions.

The Process of Active Listening

Many people use the terms *hearing* and *listening* interchangeably. Although connected, they are not the same. **Hearing** is the passive physiological act of receiving sound that takes place when sound waves hit your eardrums. If someone starts beating on a desk, the resulting sound waves will travel through the air and hit your eardrum, the act of which is an example of hearing. As a passive act, hearing does not require much work or energy to occur; you can hear without really having to think about it. **Listening** is the active process of receiving, attending to, interpreting, and responding to symbolic activity. As opposed to hearing, listening is active because it requires a great deal of work and energy to accomplish. It is also referred to as a process rather than an act, since multiple steps or stages are involved.

Receiving

The first step in the listening process is the act of **receiving** sensory stimuli as sound waves travel from the source of the sound to your eardrums. As mentioned above, listening and hearing are connected, and receiving is the point at which that connection is established. As you continue reading, keep in mind that the entire listening process is not limited to aural stimuli. Multiple sensory channels, including taste, touch, smell, and sight, can be used to make sense of a message you have received.

Attending

Attending to stimuli, the second step in the listening process, occurs when you perceive and focus on stimuli. You are constantly being inundated with competing stimuli, only some of which you pick up. The stimuli that receive your attention are generally those you deem most necessary to accomplish the task at hand. In a conversation with your boss about an important project that must be completed by the end of the day, for example, you will probably attempt to concentrate on what he or she is saying rather than on competing stimuli, such as other conversations taking place nearby or music playing in the background. Although you may attempt to focus primarily on those stimuli that enable you to complete your task, it is sometimes challenging to maintain your focus. There is a reason it is referred to as an active process!

Interpreting

The third step in the listening process, known as **interpreting**, is when you assign meaning to sounds and symbolic activity. You use multiple sensory channels and accompanying stimuli when listening, especially sight and visual stimuli. Returning to the earlier example of a person beating on a desk, if you see his or her hand hitting the desk each time that sound is received, this cue will assist you in making sense of what you hear. Likewise, visually perceiving a smile or a scowl when a person is speaking to you will help determine whether he or she intended a caustic remark as a sarcastic joke or as a serious retort.

Responding

An additional step in the listening process, **responding** is essentially your reaction to the message or communication of another person. Your response, or feedback, to messages occurs throughout the entire communication process. Even though you may not express yourself verbally while another person is speaking, you may express yourself nonverbally as you react to a message being received. Responding to a message while it is being received shows another person you are indeed listening to what he or she is saying. In addition to letting someone know you are listening, responding

Traditional positive feedback or response to a message includes leaning forward, smiling, and nodding your head in agreement, while negative feedback or response includes leaning away from the source, frowning, and shaking your head in disagreement. Feedback can also include looks of shock, excitement, boredom, and confusion.

while a message is being received enables the sender to know how you feel about the message.

After receiving a message, you may respond with verbal feedback in which you explain your interpretation of the message. **Reflecting**, sometimes referred to as paraphrasing, involves summarizing what another person has said in your own words to convey your understanding of the message ("I understand you to mean that our team has until the end of the week to finish the project"). Sometimes these reflections or paraphrases are accompanied by requests for clarification or approval ("Do you mean it will be impossible to receive my order by the first of the month?"). Reflecting primarily assists in ensuring accurate understanding of the message, but it serves the secondary function of exhibiting attentiveness to the message and concern about its accurate interpretation.

Engaged and Relational Listening

For quite some time, the process of active listening described above has been viewed as the ideal method of listening. It has been included in many communication textbooks and corporate training sessions throughout the years. Acknowledging the responsibilities of both the source and the listener in the communication process, active listening demands that the listener fully take part in the communication process by attempting to accurately interpret a message as it was intended and by responding to the message source. This description is correct for the most part; however, participating in the communication process involves more than listening carefully to what is said, even if you listen intently and can repeat it. A tape recorder can accomplish both of these things! We are not saying that active listening is wrong; we are saying that it is not enough. Two other types of listening are necessary for truly effective communication to take place: engaged listening and relational listening.

Engaged Listening

Engaged listening entails making a personal relational connection with the source of a message that results from the source and the receiver actively working together to create shared meaning and understanding. Not just listening actively, engaged listening involves caring, trusting, wanting to know more, and feeling excited, enlightened, attached, and concerned.

Disengaged Listening

Perhaps the best way to explain what we mean by engaged listening is by first demonstrating what it is *not*. Examples of disengaged listening include standard attempts to be friendly and positive in boilerplate responses to technical support questions and apologies from the bank/airline/hotel after receiving a complaint. Most of these responses start off saying how important you are while the rest of the message in both form and content conveys a contrasting meaning.

Perhaps the most obvious example of being actively involved but not engaged emerges in the nonverbal attentiveness that managers and other customer service providers learn during training courses. Taught many of the active listening response behaviors, such as eye contact and displays of warmth and understanding, the really bad managers and customer service providers learn to do this without ever learning engagement. They simply go through the motions, with no real meaning underlying their behaviors.

Photo 4.2 Customer service representatives often appear to be listening actively, but they do not really understand the point of view of the customer. If they attempted to make a personal connection with the customer and actively worked to create shared understanding, what type of listening would they be doing? (See page 80.)

Engaged Listening for a Transactional World

Engaged listening accompanies the view of communication as a transaction rather than a mere action or interaction. If communication were merely an action or interaction, active listening would be more than sufficient. However, communication involves more than the sending or exchanging of symbols. It involves the construction and negotiation of shared meaning between people and the personal connections that they subsequently develop. Communication is a transactional process that demands engaged listening to be effective.

Engaged listening enables you to grasp a deeper understanding of the message that goes beyond what can be achieved through mere active listening. Take reflection, the routine approach to active listening described earlier. While you may be able to paraphrase or repeat what you hear, this ability does not guarantee you will actually understand the overtones of what is said. For example, active listeners may be able to understand and "reflect" that when someone says, "As a father, I am against the occupation of Iraq," he is stating opposition to the situation in a foreign country. Active yet disengaged listeners,

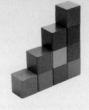

Make Your Case

Recall an experience with a customer service representative in which you felt that you were not listened to. What about the customer service representative's responses made you feel this way? If you were training customer service providers, how would you prepare them to be good listeners?

Photo 4.3 What must be considered when engaging in relational listening? (See page 80.)

however, may miss the deeper significance of the first three words. Apparently irrelevant to the rest of the sentiment expressed, they were probably uttered because they are central to *the speaker's view of self* and to *the speaker's view of his relationship with others* and therefore constitute a major part of what he wants to tell the world. Engaged listeners would be able to pick up on this additional meaning.

Relational Listening

Relational listening involves recognizing, understanding, and addressing the interconnection of relationships and communication. Vital to understanding how your personal and social relationships are intrinsically connected with communication, listening relationally will also enhance your understanding of your personal relationships and the meaning of communication taking place. When engaging in relational listening, you must address two features of communication and relationships: how communication impacts the relationship and how the relationship impacts communication.

All communication between people in a relationship will impact that relationship somehow. Some exchanges may have a greater impact than others, but all communication will exert influence on the relationship. Relational listening entails recognizing this salient feature of communication, considering how a given message impacts the relationship, and addressing this impact in an appropriate manner. The relationship people share will also influence what is (or is not) communicated, how it is communicated, and its meaning. Relational listening when receiving a message would thus entail addressing the questions listed in Table 4.2.

Table 4.2 Questions to Consider When Receiving a Message

1. What impact does this message have on my understanding of this relationship?

2. What impact may this message have on the other person's understanding of this relationship?

3. Does this message correspond with my understanding of this relationship?

4. Is something absent from this message that would correspond with my understanding of this relationship?

5. Is this message being communicated in a manner that corresponds with my understanding of this relationship?

6. What does this message mean based on my understanding of this relationship?

7. What does this message tell me about the other person's understanding of this relationship?

How you answer these questions will determine the actions that result from the message you receive. First, these questions will guide your actual response to the message, given your relational understanding of its meaning and its impact on your relationship. Second, your answers to these questions will change your perception and understanding of the relationship. Sometimes these changes in perception and understanding will be quite profound, while other times your perception and understanding will be only slightly modified. All communication will change your relationship, once again underscoring the importance of listening.

Recognizing and Overcoming Listening Obstacles

Effective listening is fundamental in the development of shared meaning and understanding, allowing you to comprehend and appreciate the perspectives of others and providing others with insight about you. It accounts for many of the positive attributes derived from our interactions with others. Yet, while effective listening can lead to many positive outcomes, ineffective listening (frequently resulting from obstacles inherent in and associated with listening) can lead to equally negative outcomes and cause problems in your relationships. In this section of the chapter, we discuss listening obstacles along with suggestions for overcoming them. Recognizing these obstacles and the detrimental impact they have on everyday communication is the first step in overcoming them.

Environmental Distractions

Environmental distractions result from the physical location where listening takes place (Wood, 2009). If you have ever tried listening to a friend when loud music is playing at a bar or restaurant, for example, or if people are whispering in class or texting while you are attempting to focus on

College Experience

Listening has a profound impact on classroom performance. As you explore obstacles to effective listening, consider how you can enhance your listening abilities in the classroom by recognizing and overcoming these obstacles. Which of these obstacles do you find most common in the classroom? What can you do to manage them?

your instructor, you already know well that the environment can hinder effective listening. However, a host of environmental distractions can obstruct listening, and these distractions go beyond competing sounds that make it difficult to hear and pay attention. The temperature of a room can distract you from fully listening if it happens to be uncomfortably warm or cool. Activity and movements of people not involved in a conversation can also distract you from focusing on a message being received.

Medium Distractions

Medium distractions result from limitations or problems inherent in certain media and technology, such as mobile phones or Internet connections. You have probably needed to include the phrases "Are you still there?" and "Can you hear me now?" in a conversation with someone when at least one of you was using a cell phone. You also likely have continued talking long after a call has been disconnected only to realize the disconnection when your phone starts ringing in your ear. Such distractions make it very difficult not only to pick up on the words being spoken but also to fully concentrate on the message. Similar to problems encountered with cell phones, problems involving poor connections and delays also occur when using instant and text messaging, making it very difficult to concentrate on the messages being exchanged.

Source Distractions

Source distractions result from auditory and visual characteristics of the message source. Vocal characteristics—for example, an unfamiliar or uncharacteristic tone and quality of voice, extended pauses, and such repeated nonfluencies as *um, uh,* or *you know*—can distract you from listening to someone's message. A person's physical appearance, proxemics, haptics, and artifacts may also serve as distractions. For instance, someone may be standing too close to you or touching you more than you find appropriate or comfortable.

Factual Diversion

Often a problem students experience when taking notes while listening to a lecture in class, **factual diversion** occurs when so much emphasis is placed on attending to every detail of a message that the main point becomes lost. Students become so intent on documenting every single detail that they lose the main point of the discussion. Imagine you are in a history course studying the American Revolution. The instructor is discussing Paul Revere's "midnight ride," which just so happens to be her area of expertise. As a result, throughout the discussion she offers multiple details about this infamous ride, including the type of buttons on Revere's jacket, the color and name of his horse, the temperature, and even what he ate for breakfast that morning. You begin to furiously write them all down in your notes. In fact, you note every single detail but one—the purpose of his ride! You know the color and name of his horse but not what he was doing on top of it. When you focus too much on every detail of a message, you very likely will miss the main idea.

Semantic Diversion

Semantic diversion takes place when people are distracted by words or phrases used in a message through negative response or unfamiliarity. People tend to respond positively or negatively to words they encounter. The intensity of this response will vary, with some words eliciting a strong or weak response in one direction or the other (Osgood, Suci, & Tannenbaum, 1957). Semantic diversion occurs when your response to a certain word used during a message causes you to focus unnecessary attention on that word or prevents you from listening to the rest of the message. For example, you may hear a word that elicits a strong negative response, such as a racial or sexual slur, and focus on your feelings about that word rather than fully attend to the message. Semantic diversion also involves letting unfamiliar words or phrases cause us to stop listening to or shift our attention away from the message. People often encounter unrecognizable words in a message; for instance, during a lecture your instructors may occasionally use a word with which you are unfamiliar.

Content (Representational) Listening

Content (representational) listening occurs when people focus on the content level of meaning, or literal meaning, rather than the social or relational levels of meaning. Content listening occurs when you focus solely on the surface level of meaning and fail to recognize or engage in determining deeper levels of meaning. A classmate may remark, "This project I have been working on is more difficult than I anticipated." If you listen only at the content level, you may see this statement as a mere observation; however, it may very well have a deeper meaning: Listening at a deeper level may uncover that this classmate needs your assistance, is seeking words of motivation, or is determining if your relationship is one that would provide such support. Content listening does not engage in seeking the deeper levels of meaning inherent in most messages and only focuses on surface-level meaning.

Selective Listening

Selective listening occurs when people focus on the points of a message that correspond with their views and interests and pay less attention to those that do not. Essentially, people pick up on the parts of a message that correspond with their views or that they find most interesting and disregard the rest. Imagine meeting a friend for lunch when you are particularly hungry. Upon meeting your friend, she begins telling you about her morning. You drift in and out of the conversation until she asks what restaurant you prefer. At that moment, you become very interested in the conversation and focus on what is being discussed.

Egocentric Listening

Egocentric listening occurs when people focus more on their message and self-presentation than on the message of the other person involved in an interaction. This type of listening is frequently observed during disagreements or arguments when people concentrate so much on what they are going to say next that they fail to listen to others. Perhaps you are in the middle of a heated discussion with a rival coworker and have just come up with a brilliant sarcastic remark. You cannot wait until your coworker's lips stop moving so that you may use this line. The problem is that you have stopped listening to your coworker. You are so absorbed in developing and presenting your own message that you have failed to listen to his or hers.

> ## Listen in on Your Life
>
>
>
> Which of your friends, family members, classmates, or coworkers would you consider *good* listeners? What behaviors do these people enact when interacting with others? In what ways could their listening still improve?
>
> Which of your friends, family members, classmates, or coworkers would you consider *poor* listeners? What behaviors do these people enact when interacting with others? In what ways could their listening improve?

Photo 4.4 Why are wandering thoughts so common? (See page 80.)

Wandering Thoughts

Wandering thoughts occur when you daydream or think about things other than the message being presented. This lack of attention happens to everyone from time to time. No matter how intent you are on focusing on a message, your mind wanders, and you start thinking about other things. Consider listening to a lecture in class when your mind starts to wander. You think about a high school classmate, the great parking space you found last week, where you will eat after class, or a YouTube video that you have seen at least 20 times. Wandering thoughts are caused not necessarily by lack of interest in the topic but rather by the connection between the rate of speech and the ability to process information, which can directly impact listening comprehension (Preiss & Gayle, 2006). People speak on average between 100 and 150 words per minute, but listeners process information at a rate of between 400 and 500 words per minute. An effective way to overcome this obstacle is to take advantage of the extra time by mentally summarizing what the speaker is saying. This strategy will enable you to remain focused, as well as increase your understanding of the message.

Experiential Superiority

Experiential superiority takes place when people fail to fully listen to someone else because they believe that they possess more or superior knowledge and experience than the other person (Pearson & Nelson, 2000). If you have worked at the same job for a number of years, you might choose not to listen to a recently hired employee's suggestion about your work. You might feel that because you have more experience in the position, you do not need to listen because you will not hear anything new. Unfortunately, the new hire's suggestion might be good, but you will never know because you did not listen.

Message Complexity

Message complexity becomes an obstacle to listening when a person finds a message so complex or confusing that he or she stops listening (Wood, 2009). At times, you may listen to a person discussing a topic that you feel is beyond your grasp. You may try to listen intently to comprehend what is being discussed, but you just find it too confusing and difficult to understand. In this situation, you feel tempted to stop listening because you believe you cannot glean anything valuable from paying further attention. You might, however, actually gain some understanding from continuing to listen, and the discussion might actually start making sense. Unfortunately, you will lose this understanding if you continue to ignore the remainder of the message.

Past Experience With the Source

Past experience with the source becomes an obstacle to listening when previous encounters with the message source lead people to ignore the message. You may know people who habitually lie or who seem to be wrong about nearly everything they say, and your past experience with these individuals may compel you to not listen to them. Although they may have something worthwhile to say, you will never know because you decided not to listen. Of course, just because you should listen to that person does not mean that you should believe what he or she tells you. We talk more about the need to critically examine messages in the next section.

Critical Listening

Critical listening involves analyzing and evaluating the accuracy, legitimacy, and value of messages and is part of the more general process of critical evaluation of everything in life. Being critical does not necessarily mean being negative or finding fault with a message. Students often see the term *critical* and initially believe that critical listening entails disagreement or disapproval. However, critical listening can just as easily result in a positive evaluation of a message. Much like movie critic Roger Ebert, who rates movies with either a "thumbs down" or a "thumbs up," as a critical listener, you may evaluate messages positively or negatively. In addition, a message will likely have both positive and negative qualities, in which case you must decide whether the positive attributes outweigh the negative ones or vice versa. Few messages can be evaluated as entirely negative or entirely positive, with the actual evaluation ranking somewhere in between. Rather than "thumbs up" and "thumbs down," perhaps "thumbs slightly askew upward" and "thumbs slightly askew downward" are more appropriate.

Critical Evaluation in Everyday Life

Critical evaluation encompasses every aspect of daily life and all symbolic activity. People are constantly being called to make critical evaluations and judgments as they encounter others' messages and general life experiences. Your critical choices can range from major life-altering decisions, such as deciding to attend college, to seemingly less important but still significant decisions, such as which television program to watch or where to meet a friend for lunch. The need for critical listening pervades your daily life.

Elements of Critical Listening

Now that we have introduced critical listening we can examine the four elements that compose it.

Evaluation of Plausibility

Some messages seem legitimate and valid whenever you first listen to them. When encountering other messages, however, you immediately get the feeling that something is just not right. Even if you cannot immediately pinpoint the problem with these messages, you feel as if something is amiss. When you experience these feelings, you are evaluating the **plausibility** of the message, or the extent to which it seems legitimate (Gouran, Wiethoff, & Doelger,

1994). You might not believe that diaper-wearing winged monkeys were spotted flying over campus because this event is implausible. The plausibility of other messages might not be as obvious, but something might still strike you as problematic. For example, an automobile dealership guaranteeing "free maintenance for life on all new cars sold this month" may strike you as plausible but problematic. You may feel that the message does not provide sufficient information or is not entirely genuine. When you are unsure of a message's legitimacy, it is best to follow your instincts. The evaluation of plausibility is your first line of defense as a critical listener, and often your first impression of a message is accurate.

Evaluation of Source

When critically examining a message, you must evaluate its source. As mentioned when discussing listening obstacles, you may know people who never provide you with good advice or who always seem to be wrong about everything. While you should still listen to these people in case they offer a worthwhile message, your past experiences with them may dictate the degree of belief and value that you place on their messages. The **status of the source** will also impact the extent to which you critically engage a message. People tend to be more critical of messages from individuals of equal status than of those from higher-status individuals. For instance, you may not critically evaluate a message from your instructor because you assume he or she will be correct (Pearson & Nelson, 2000).

Photo 4.5 Are there some types of relationships or areas of life that do not require critical evaluation? (See page 80.)

Evaluation of Consistency

Consistency concerns whether the message is free of internal contradiction and in harmony with information you already know is true (Gouran et al., 1994). Earlier in this chapter, we mention the importance of listening. If we contend later in the chapter that listening is not very important in your everyday life, this contradiction should strike you as problematic. One of these two statements is obviously wrong or misrepresented, and this contradiction might lead you to question the information being provided. (Incidentally, you do not need to search for that statement later in the chapter. We have a great editor who would prevent such a situation, and we really do believe in the importance of listening.) Consistency also entails whether the information provided agrees with information you already know as true. If someone is describing the best route to travel through the South and mentions that "once you enter Mississippi, just keep driving south until you reach Tennessee," you might question the message given your previous knowledge that Tennessee is actually located north of Mississippi. The information being offered is not consistent with previous information you know to be true.

Evaluation of Evidence

As a critical listener, you must also evaluate the evidence by considering the following criteria: verifiability, quantity, and quality. **Verifiability** indicates that the material being provided can be confirmed by other sources or means (Gouran et al., 1994). If someone tells you during the day that the sky is blue, you can verify this by going outside and looking for yourself. If someone tells you Alexander Hamilton was shot in a duel with Aaron Burr, you can verify this by confirming the information in a book about these historic figures. Some material may be more difficult to verify, in which case you must evaluate other aspects of the message. When it comes to the quantity of evidence, there is no magic number to indicate a well-supported argument or claim. Such judgment is based on other evaluations of a message as well as the quality of evidence that is included. Evaluations of quality include determining such issues as a lack of bias, sufficient expertise, and recency. The evaluation of evidence and sources will be discussed further in Chapter 11.

Critical Listening and Fallacious Arguments

Engaging in critical listening requires the recognition of **fallacious arguments**, or those that appear legitimate but are actually based on faulty reasoning or insufficient evidence.

Argument Against the Source

Argument against the source occurs when the source of a message, rather than the message itself, is attacked. This fallacy is traditionally known as *argument against the person* or *ad hominem (to the human being) argument,* but we prefer to call it *argument against the source* to recognize the growing trend in attacking not only people but also media sources. Political analysts are often guilty of this fallacy. For instance, you might hear a political analyst say, "The senator's latest proposal is not acceptable because she is nothing but a pathological liar." Rather than critically evaluating the actual proposal, the analyst attacks the source of the proposal. Challenging the source of a message instead of the message itself may indicate the message as sound; otherwise, the flaws of the message would be challenged. Sometimes actual media sources or systems are challenged. For instance, when discussing a television news segment you just watched with a friend, he might say, "That cannot be right because television news is biased against the current administration," challenging not the information within the segment but the media source of the information.

Appeal to Authority

Appeal to authority happens when a person's authority or credibility in one area is used to support another. Sports heroes and actors, for example, have been used to sell

Contrarian Challenge

Arguing against the source rather than the message is considered a fallacious argument. However, are there times when it would be appropriate to question the source of the message?

everything from magazine subscriptions to underwear. However, just because a person has particular knowledge or talent in one area does not mean he or she is knowledgeable or talented in all areas. Ask most college administrators to change the oil in an automobile and see what happens!

Appeal to People (Bandwagon Appeal)

Appeal to people (bandwagon appeal) claims that something is good or beneficial because everyone else agrees with this evaluation. Consider the many products that boast their own popularity in advertisements: "Squeaky Clean is the nation's top-selling brand of dish soap" or "See *British and Redneck Professors Go to Vegas,* the movie that audiences have made the number one comedy for 2 weeks in a row." No mention is made of dexterity in removing grease from pans or of wonderful acting. These products' popularity is offered instead, and you are asked to join the crowd. As a critical listener, you should recognize when the appeal to people fallacy is being used and question why other evidence was not provided.

> Sometimes it is not the messages of others that make people susceptible to the appeal-to-people fallacy but rather their own intrapersonal communication, or communication with the self. They convince themselves of the value of an object or a behavior because of the actions of other people. Making a decision based on what you perceive others to be doing is referred to as social proof (Cialdini, 1993).

Appeal to Relationships

Appeal to relationships occurs when relationships are used to justify certain behaviors and to convince others of their appropriateness. Communication scholar Erin Sahlstein (2000) has noted that people often refer to the relationship they share with another person in an interaction when attempting to convince him or her to behave a certain way. When someone says, "Could you be a friend and give me a ride to the library?" the inclusion of the relational term *friend* underscores the existence of the relationship and reminds the other person of behaviors and duties associated with that sort of relationship. You might expect a "friend" to provide transportation when requested, but not an "acquaintance." The use of relational terms also justifies requests being made. A "friend" *could make* and *be asked to make* this sort of request without great loss of face by either interactant. Appealing to a relationship may be somewhat legitimate but also fallacious. Asking a friend for a ride to the library is one thing; asking a friend to drive the getaway car while you rob a convenience store is another. Certain obligations are associated with each type of relationship, but each responsibility also has limitations. As a critical listener, you must determine when the use of relational terms is legitimate and when it is unreasonable.

Post Hoc Ergo Propter Hoc *and* Cum Hoc Ergo Propter Hoc

Latin for "after this; therefore, because of this," **post hoc ergo propter hoc** argues that something is caused by whatever happens before it. According to this logic, the following statement is true: A man kissed a woman, and 2 weeks later she was pregnant; therefore, the kiss was responsible for her pregnancy. You likely see the inherent problem with this statement. Admittedly, the above example may seem a bit obvious. However, the use of this sort of reasoning is actually quite common and frequently evident in advertising.

Cum hoc ergo propter hoc argues that if one thing happens at the same time as another, it was caused by the thing with which it coincides. Once again, we are dealing with a Latin phrase. *Cum hoc ergo propter hoc* translates into "With this; therefore, because of this." As with its *post hoc* companion, this fallacy argues that one event causes another due to their association in time. While *post hoc* argues that something occurring *before* something else is the cause, *cum hoc* argues that something occurring *at the same time* as something else is the cause. Someone might remark, "I wore a new pair of socks on the day of my communication midterm and earned an A on the test. Wearing new socks must have been the reason I scored so high. From now on, I'm going to wear a new pair of socks each time I take a test." If this were all it took to score well on an examination, life would be pretty sweet! Wearing new socks at the same time you ace an examination, however, will not guarantee you a high score on your next exam. If you really want to improve your exam scores, try visiting **www.sagepub.com/boc2e**. Although quite common and often very convincing, these fallacies are difficult to prove when challenged.

Upon recognizing them, as a critical listener, you may question and expect the speaker to prove two things: First, does a direct link actually exist between what is deemed the cause and what is deemed its effect? Second, if a link between the cause and its effect exists, did any additional variables work to produce the effect?

> ## Case in Point
>
>
>
> Watch television and analyze the commercials being aired. What fallacious arguments are evident in these commercials? Are some forms of fallacious arguments more prevalent than others?

Hasty Generalization

Hasty generalization arises when a conclusion is based on a single occurrence or insufficient data or sample size. Asked about where to purchase a new car, someone might remark, "My coworker bought a car at that dealership east of town, and it broke down a week later. If you buy a car at that dealership, it will probably be a lemon." Just because the dealership sold a faulty car once does not mean it will sell another defective car. Sometimes, the hasty generalization is based on a small sample size. In other words, the people involved or questioned are not significantly representative of a given population. When defending a new policy on campus, someone might say, "I asked people in my algebra class, and they all agreed that a campus-wide attendance policy is a good idea. So I guess the policy is a good one that the students like." Simply because a few people agreed with this policy in one class does not mean it is good or that the majority of students agree with the policy.

Red Herring

Red herring describes the use of another issue to divert attention away from the real issue. This fallacy is especially common when someone wishes to avoid a particular topic. When talking about the cost of higher education, you might hear "I find it difficult to fathom that you insist on addressing higher-education funding when the spotted pygmy squirrel is on the verge of extinction" or "Sure, the cost of higher education is staggering, but so is the cost of health care, which has become a major burden on millions of people." During an argument between romantic partners, you might hear the following use of a red herring: "Why are we talking about me going out with my friends when we should be talking about your inability to commit to this relationship?" This example contains a strategic attempt to divert attention away from the issue of going out with friends by dragging commitment to the relationship across the conversational trail.

The name "red herring" comes from the phrase "draw a red herring across the trail," derived from the practice of 17th-century dog trainers. They would drag a smoked herring across the trail of a fox to determine how well dogs could remain focused on the original scent (Urdang, Hunsinger, & LaRouche, 1991).

False Alternatives

False alternatives occur when only two options are provided, one of which is generally presented as the poor choice or one that should be avoided (Pearson & Nelson, 2000). One flaw in this reasoning is that there are usually more options than the two provided. Traveling by plane, for example, comes with the likelihood of delays caused by mechanical problems and the always kind and supportive airline personnel who have been known to use false alternatives by explaining, "You can either endure a delay while we find a plane that is functional, or you can leave as scheduled and travel in a plane that is not working correctly." Waiting for a functional plane seems much better than facing possible mechanical problems after takeoff; however, this overlooks the other equally probable option: having a functional plane available to begin with by ensuring proper maintenance is accomplished well before the flight is scheduled to depart. As a note of caution, pointing out this option to airline personnel at the gate will severely decrease your chances of receiving a seat upgrade on that particular flight!

In addition, quite possibly the option deemed less favorable is not as negative as it is portrayed, and the preferred option is not as beneficial. Likewise, an auto mechanic may explain, "You can either replace the serpentine belt in your car now or face being stranded should it end up breaking at one of those cracks." It is possible that the serpentine belt does not need immediate repair, as well as that you would not be stranded somewhere should it actually break. Such claims and options often go unchallenged unless a person recognizes this fallacy is being utilized and critically examines the statements being made.

Composition and Division Fallacies

Composition fallacy argues that the parts are the same as the whole (Pearson & Nelson, 2000, p. 118). According to this fallacy, any student at your school could be picked at random to represent all students at your school. Common sense tells you that one person cannot accurately represent an entire group of people, but this fallacy nevertheless remains quite common. Consider how often entire populations are represented in newspaper articles by one person or perhaps a few people. An article might say, "Students on campus are in favor of the tuition increase to pay for the new sports complex. When asked about the increase in tuition, sophomore Emalyn Taylor noted, 'If it takes an increase in tuition to replace the old sports complex, that's what needs to be done.'" This report essentially says that if one student (part) is in favor of the tuition increase, all students (whole) are in favor of it as well.

Division fallacy argues the whole is the same as its parts (Pearson & Nelson, 2000, p. 118). For instance, when being set up on a date by a friend, you might argue, "Everyone you have ever set me up with has been a loser, so this person is going to be a loser too." This statement essentially reasons that if previous dates have been losers (whole), this date (part) will also be one.

Equivocation

Equivocation relies on the ambiguousness of language to make an argument. The equivocation tactic is frequently used in commercials. You might hear an announcer proclaim, "Squeaky Clean dish soap is *better!*" This sounds good, but you cannot be certain what Squeaky Clean is actually better than. Is it better than using no dish soap at all or washing dishes by dropping rocks into the sink? Is it better than other brands of dish soap? The use of equivocation leaves such questions unanswered, often the point of this fallacy. When ambiguous words and phrases, such as *improved, bargain, good value, delicious,* or *soothing,* are used, listeners must fill in the context on their own, which often results in a product or an idea being received in a much more positive manner than warranted. The makers of Squeaky Clean dish soap could say, "We never said *it was better than all other brands;* we just said it was *better.*" While this tactic is tricky, this statement would be absolutely true. The good news is now that you are able to recognize the use of equivocation, you will be well equipped to find the best dish soap—whatever *best* means!

FOCUS QUESTIONS REVISITED

1. Why is listening important enough to have an entire chapter devoted to it?
Listening is not only the communication activity in which you engage most frequently but is also fundamental to success in education, careers, and relationships. Often the most common activity in classrooms, listening has been directly linked to academic achievement, is one of the most sought-after skills by employers, and is critical to success and advancement in the workplace. Effective listening in relationships leads to greater satisfaction and is essential for successful relational development.

2. What are the objectives of listening?

There are five objectives of listening:

- Relational development and enhancement
- Gaining and comprehending information
- Critical listening
- Enjoyment and appreciation
- Therapeutic listening

Even though these objectives were discussed in isolation, remember that a single communicative exchange can involve multiple listening goals.

3. What does it mean to listen actively?

Active listening is a process of receiving, attending to, interpreting, and responding to symbolic activity. Receiving auditory stimuli is the first step in the listening process. Attending occurs when you perceive and focus on stimuli. Interpreting involves assigning meaning to sounds and symbolic activity. Responding, the final step in the active listening process, entails reacting to this symbolic activity.

4. What are engaged and relational listening?

Engaged listening and relational listening are advanced types of listening that demand more of the listener than active listening. The engaged listening process entails making a personal relational connection with the source of a message that results from the source and the receiver actively working together to create shared meaning and understanding. Relational listening involves recognizing, understanding, and addressing the interconnection of relationships and communication.

5. Why do people sometimes struggle when listening?

You may encounter a number of obstacles to listening. Recognizing and overcoming these obstacles are crucial to effective listening.

6. What is critical listening, and why is it so important?

Critical listening is the process of analyzing and evaluating the accuracy, legitimacy, and value of messages. Involving the evaluation of a message's plausibility, source, argument, and evidence, critical listening has a profound impact on personal relationships, learning, and the evaluation of persuasive messages.

7. What are fallacious arguments?

Fallacious arguments are those that appear legitimate but are actually based on faulty reasoning or insufficient evidence. The ability to recognize fallacious arguments will enable you to become a more critical listener.

KEY CONCEPTS

QUESTIONS TO ASK YOUR FRIENDS

1. Ask a friend to recall a time when he or she misunderstood someone else. Have your friend describe the situation and determine if problems with listening had anything to do with the misunderstanding. If so, how could the misunderstanding have been prevented through effective listening behaviors?

2. Evaluating your listening, in what ways do your friends consider you a good listener? What suggestions do they have for improving your listening?

3. Ask a friend to describe a time when he or she made a purchase based on the recommendation of a salesperson that he or she later regretted. Was a lack of critical listening partially responsible? What suggestions could you offer your friend when making future purchases?

MEDIA LINKS

1. Find videos of two people talking. These videos could include actual interactions or fictionalized interactions such as a television program or movie. Select one video

in which one or both of the interactants are listening effectively, and select another video in which one or both of the interactants are listening ineffectively. What made you characterize them as effective or ineffective respectively?

2. Watch a political talk show, such as *Fox News Sunday, Meet the Press,* or *The O'Reilly Factor.* What obstacles to listening are evident during interviews and panel discussions on these programs?

3. Concurrent media exposure occurs when two or more media systems are used simultaneously. For example, you may be using the Internet while listening to the radio or reading a newspaper at the same time you are watching a movie on television. What impact might concurrent media exposure have on listening to media?

ETHICAL ISSUES

1. When would you consider the appeal-to-relationships fallacy *appropriate?* When would you consider this fallacy *inappropriate?*

2. We mentioned that you should be aware of your limitations when engaged in therapeutic listening. When would you consider it appropriate to suggest that a friend seek professional assistance?

3. Consider a situation in which you were engaged in therapeutic listening and a friend told you in confidence that he or she was doing something harmful or dangerous. Would it be appropriate to tell someone else if you believed it would prevent your friend from being harmed or harming others? If you believe it would be proper to tell someone else, in what circumstances would this behavior be appropriate?

ANSWERS TO PHOTO CAPTIONS

Photo 4.1 ▪ Therapeutic listening enables someone to talk through a problem or concern.

Photo 4.2 ▪ Engaged listening entails making a personal relational connection with the source of a message that results from the source and the receiver actively working together to create shared meaning and understanding.

Photo 4.3 ▪ When listening relationally, a person must consider (a) how communication impacts the relationship and (b) how the relationship impacts communication.

Photo 4.4 ▪ Listeners are able to process information at a faster rate than people generally speak.

Photo 4.5 ▪ No. All relationships and even the most mundane parts of life require critical evaluation.

STUDENT STUDY SITE

Visit the study site at **www.sagepub.com/boc2e** for e-flashcards, practice quizzes, journal articles and additional study resources.

REFERENCES

Barker, L., Edwards, R., Gaines, C., Gladney, K., & Holley, F. (1980). An investigation of proportional time spent in various communication activities by college students. *Journal of Applied Communication Research, 8,* 101–109.

Beall, M. L., Gill-Rosier, J., Tate, J., & Matten, A. (2008). State of the context: Listening in education. *International Journal of Listening, 22,* 123–132.

Cialdini, R. B. (1993). *Influence: The psychology of persuasion.* New York: Morrow.

Davis, J., Thompson, C. R., Foley, A., Bond, C. D., & DeWitt, J. (2008). An examination of listening concepts in the healthcare context: Difference among nurses, physicians, and administrators. *The International Journal of Listening, 22,* 152–167.

Flynn, J., Valikoski, T.-R., & Grau, J. (2008). Listening in the business context: Reviewing the state of research. *The International Journal of Listening, 22,* 141–151.

Gouran, D. S., Wiethoff, W. E., & Doelger, J. A. (1994). *Mastering communication* (2nd ed.). Boston: Allyn & Bacon.

Halone, K. K., & Pechioni, L. L. (2001). Relational listening: A grounded theoretical model. *Communication Reports, 14,* 59–71.

Janusik, L. A., & Wolvin, A. D. (2009). 24 hours in a day: A listening update to the time studies. *The International Journal of Listening, 23,* 104–120.

Osgood, C. E., Suci, G. J., & Tannenbaum, P. H. (1957). *The measurement of meaning.* Urbana: University of Illinois Press.

Pearson, J. C., & Nelson, P. E. (2000). *An introduction to human communication* (8th ed.). New York: McGraw-Hill.

Preiss, R. W., & Gayle, B. M. (2006). Exploring the relationship between listening comprehension and rate of speech. In B. M. Gayle, R. W. Preiss, N. Burell, & M. Allen (Eds.), *Classroom communication and instructional processes* (pp. 315–327). Mahwah, NJ: Lawrence Erlbaum.

Rankin, P. T. (1928). The importance of listening ability. *English Journal, 17,* 623–630.

Sahlstein, E. M. (2000). *Relational rhetorics and RRTs (Relational Rhetorical Terms).* Unpublished manuscript. Iowa City, IA.

Schnapp, D. C. (2008). Listening in context: Religion and spirituality. *The International Journal of Listening, 22,* 133–140.

Steil, L. K. (1997). Listening training: The key to success in today's organizations. In M. Purdy & D. Borisoff (Eds.), *Listening in everyday life: A personal and professional approach* (pp. 213–237). Lanham, MD: University Press of America.

Urdang, L., Hunsinger, W. W., & LaRouche, N. (1991). *A fine kettle of fish and other figurative phrases.* Detroit: Invisible Ink.

Weinrauch, J. D., & Swanda, R., Jr. (1975). Examining the significance of listening: An exploratory study of contemporary management. *Journal of Business Communication, 13,* 25–32.

Wood, J. T. (2009). *Communication in our lives* (5th ed.). Boston: Wadsworth Cengage Learning.

5

Identities and Perceptions

We don't know you, and you don't know us. From reading this book you might have some impressions of us. You know who *you* are, though—not just name and address but the kind of person you are. You have an **identity**, and we don't just mean an ID that you show people to prove your age. You are an individual who is friends with other individuals, each perhaps quirky with a unique personality and identity. You might see these individuals and yourself as persons with a history deep inside, a childhood set of experiences that made them who they are and you who you are. You know things about yourself that no one else knows. You are you, you-nique!

This chapter will teach you that you have multiple identities and that these identities are transacted through communication. Some are created by the situation in which you find yourself or in the company of certain people but not others. (Do you really behave the same way with your mother as you do with your best friend?) Others are the result of cultural symbols attached to "being gay or lesbian" or "being a go-getter or a team player." Some are performed for an audience. In intimate relationships, you can perform and express most of your true self. In a police interview, you may want to conceal some of what you are. In a hospice at the end of your life, you may want to hang onto a little *dignity*. You lose control over the skills, performances, and parts of your body and self that used to compose your identity, and you become physically more dependent on others. Those old folks who look a lot older than you now could be how you will be someday. Think about it.

Identity is partly a *characteristic* (something that you possess), partly a *performance* (something that you do), and partly a *construction of society*. For example, society tells you how to be "masculine" and "feminine" and indicates that "guys can't say that to guys" (Burleson, Holmstrom, & Gilstrap, 2005). This restricts the way in which men can give one another emotional support. Society also provides you with ways to describe a personality;

Focus Questions

1. Some textbooks picture a person's identity like an onion, built layer by layer and communicated slowly as intimacy increases. Does this really make any sense?
2. How do daily interactions with other people form or sustain your identity?
3. How much of your "self" is a performance of social roles where you have to act out "who I am" for other people?
4. What is meant by a symbolic self, and why do we have to account to other people for who we are?
5. What is the role of culture in your identity experiences?

the media focus you on some traits more than others. Categories like *gluttonous, sexy, short, slim, paranoid,* and *kind* are all available to you, but they are not all equally valued.

The ways you express yourself and the ways you respond to other people in your social context *transact* part of your identity. Your identity is partly constructed through your interactions with other people. Have you had the experience of being with someone who makes you nervous when you normally aren't nervous or who helps you relax when you feel tense? In these instances, your identity is molded by the person, situation, or communication. You'll get used to a rather odd phrase in communication studies: "*doing* an identity," used instead of "*having* an identity." Communication scholars now pay close attention to the ways in which people's behavior carries out, enacts, transacts, or *does* an identity in talk with other people.

The transaction of identities is guided in part through perceptions of yourself, others, and various components of an interaction. In other words, your internal views of yourself and others influence the external construction of identities. This notion may be somewhat difficult to comprehend, and we discuss this matter in more detail later in the chapter.

Up front, though, this is a very significant consideration and sets the discipline of communication and this textbook apart from others. Identities, relationships, cultural membership, and the like are not located within people or embedded within their minds waiting to be discovered. These things are instead created symbolically through interactions with others. At the same time, how a person views the world, organizes what is seen, and evaluates this information will influence the symbolic activity that does take place, and ultimately how that symbolic activity is viewed, organized, and evaluated. It is therefore important that these activities are also taken into account when exploring the transaction of identities.

Who Are You?

Bob is a really nice guy. He is a good friend, loyal, trusting, open, honest, comforting, seriously devoted to his kids, caring, charitable, active in his religious community organizing charitable events (especially for mentally challenged kids), giving, respectful, a fabulous cook (he specializes in the cuisines of other cultures), and very caring to his aging parents (he never misses a visit and takes them on a short trip each weekend even though his father does not remember any longer who he is and his mother is seriously arthritic). Bob is the kind of guy who would give you one of his kidneys if he matched and you needed it. Everyone in the neighborhood knows and loves Bob; at some time or another everyone in Baxter Close has experienced his stellar generosity, whether the single-parent family that found groceries on their doorstep the week they ran out of food stamps or the feisty senior lesbian who just lost her lifetime partner and needed someone to talk to. He is active in the PTA, does long Saturdays coaching and refereeing the blossoming mixed-sex soccer group that he started, and does a spectacular comedic turn as George W the Orangutan.

Dr. Harold "Fred" Shipman was a respected family practitioner in England, working in two practices in the 1980s and 1990s and even appearing on TV in a discussion about the way to treat mentally ill patients. He was a quiet but well-respected pillar of the community. He was also England's most prolific mass murderer and in January 2000 was convicted of murdering 15 patients. Subsequent inquiries revealed that he was directly responsible for the murders of at least 215 people, and that figure is probably a serious underestimate.

At work Bob is the most hated SOB in the Border Security branch of Homeland Security. There is no one who is such a completely ruthless, nasty, dogged, suspicious, awkward cuss. He is an officious, pettifogging a-hole, and there is no one better at interrogation. He nails people who make illegal applications for a green card and has the highest record in the whole border area for catching cheats. People lie to him, and he gets them every time (he read Chapter 3); people fudge, and he owns them; people say things that do not match up with what they wrote on their forms, and he gets it right away without even looking. Nobody gets past Bob. He asks all the right probing questions, uncovers the half truth and the full-out lie, trusts no one, and never accepts at face value anything on an application form (he even caught the fact that one person could not spell his own name the same way in two different places on the same form). He regularly has grown men breaking down in tears in his office. If you get interviewed for immigration by Bob and are not 100% straight up, then he will get you. Believe it.

We all know a version of Bob. We all know a supervisor who is a pain in the buttermilk plant where he rules without mercy, gives no one any breaks, and cuts no slack, but in the rest of his life he is a beacon: a leading member of his church community, a giving and generous community member, and a social delight as long as there is no one there from the workplace.

Other examples surround us everywhere in everyday life. The same person may be unfriendly and distant on one occasion but funny and sociable on another. You may know someone whom you consider to be kind, yet one of your friends sees the person as nasty. In both cases you're talking about the same person, but people can have mood swings as a result of periodic hormonal imbalances, drinking too much, gluten intolerance, or just having had a series of really unfortunate events happen to them on a bad hair day.

College Experience

Consider the situation of nontraditional students and identities, which may apply to you personally or to other students in your classes. Nontraditional students have the same concerns as all students such as getting their work done on time and receiving good grades at the end of the semester or term. However, they view themselves differently. Nontraditional students frequently return to school after working for a number of years, perhaps the result of deciding their line of work was not satisfying or the result of losing their job in a rough economy. Many of these students have been quite successful, and yet they are very apprehensive about entering the classroom. Such students are used to being obeyed, someone to whom people turn for advice, a leader, a mentor, and an example. Which is the *real* person: the successful professional and authoritative leader or the obviously older student in a classroom where previous experience counts for very little?

Now consider the situation of traditional students, which again may apply to you personally or to other students in your classes. These students most likely experienced some success in high school. Many entering students graduated with honors, participated in many activities, received a number of awards and distinctions, were well known in their school, and were looked upon with admiration by others. Now, these students may view themselves as isolated in a sea of people who were equally or even more successful in high school. Which is the *real* person: the standout high school student who excelled at everything or the awkward first-year student seeking some sort of recognition?

Return to these questions once you have read the entire chapter and see if your perspective has changed.

That is perhaps not terribly surprising since many changes in mood are temporary, relatively unimportant, and reversible. Get the hormones back into balance, let them sleep off the hangover, and let the sun shine in, and then they will be back to their same old self.

What is much more complicated for communication scholars is the question of why different people disagree about whether someone is *essentially* good or bad. Why might two professors argue about whether a particular student is (a) intelligent or (b) someone who stands no chance of improving? Why might the bosses in an organization argue about whether someone should be promoted or passed over? If every person had just one identity at the core of his or her multilayered onion of personality, then these kinds of questions would make no sense.

If people had a stable core inside a set of layers we could peel away to reach "the truth," then we would never be able to change our mind about someone. If someone were a good and loyal friend, he would never turn into an enemy unless he had a personality transplant. Yet you've most likely had the experience of seeing someone in a different light over time. This is a real problem for scholars of communication thinking about the nature of identity and self and why some people do not include "self" in their courses: far too mushy.

When a stranger does something unkind, your first thought may be to blame personality: This is an evil person, perhaps with psychopathic tendencies. Or you could put it down to the identity that had been constructed during childhood when there were some bad experiences. Lawyers often explain their clients' bad behavior in such terms. On the other hand, the "unkind stranger" probably saw identity in personality terms, too, but more favorable ones—as a good decent person who was being irritated by an annoying stranger (you!) and walked away thinking, "What a jerk [or some other non-specific and dehumanizing term]!"

Of course, *you* (and your friends) have never done anything that dehumanizes, stereotypes, or depersonalizes others, have you? You have never called anyone "an illegal" or "a frat boy" or lumped someone together with all other "college kids" or chanted, "Oh, how I hate the team from State."

Framing Identity

Earlier chapters talked about frames for situations and thinking. Shotter (1984) sees identity as a frame for interpreting other people's actions: Your beliefs about other people set the stage for your understanding of how they act. Burke (1969) also saw motives and personality language as helpful frames for interpretation (see Chapter 2). In short, your identity will be revealed in a language that reflects the priorities of a particular culture or relationship and its frames for thinking about how humans should act and describe themselves.

Human beings talk about their identities in ways that are steered by social norms and conventions in their society. In return you expect other people to present such narratives and behaviors. Your culture frames identity as a stable inner self; it therefore feels quite normal for you to think in those terms, so you can easily understand the idea that someone would reveal a private self layer by layer. However, you would be thought crazy if you said, "My identity is blue with an elephant spirit inside." You'd soon be locked up.

You have to use terms and phrases that your audiences recognize as symbolically meaningful in the culture: "I'm a go-getter but quite private, ambitious yet introverted." In other words, you *frame* your talk about yourself and your identity in the language that your culture has taught you to use.

Perceiving Encounters and Transacting Identities

Your framing of an encounter is based, in part, on the perceptions you develop. **Perception** is a process of actively selecting, organizing, and evaluating information, activities, situations, people, and essentially all the things that make up your world. In what follows, we explore this process and its influence on identity construction.

Selecting

In Chapter 4, we discussed how receiving stimuli does not necessarily mean you will recognize their presence or direct your attention to them. Imagine going up to a friend whose concentration is focused on a book (or a newspaper, a television program, a computer screen, a ball game, or any number of objects or activities). You greet her by saying hello or by saying her name, but she does not seem to recognize you are speaking. This person continues to focus solely on the book. You speak again, a little louder this time, and still receive no response. You may have to tap her on the shoulder, hit her over the head, or practically scream to get her attention away from that book. You are not being ignored; this person is simply not attending to, or selecting, the sound of your voice.

You select and focus more on some things going on around you and less on other things. Certain factors influence exactly to what extent you focus. If something stands

In Chapter 10, we discuss how you are more likely to select and attend to particular media that support your beliefs, attitudes, and values using the principle of selective exposure.

out for whatever reason, you are more likely to focus your attention on that. For instance, if you scan a room of people wearing similar clothing, you will likely focus on a person whose clothing is dissimilar to that of the others. Another factor influencing focus is *selective exposure,* which means you are more likely to focus on and expose yourself to that which supports your beliefs, values, and attitudes. During your interactions with others, you will be more likely to pick up on activities that support your views of the world and pay less attention to those that do not. If you view yourself as a competent person, you will be more likely to pick up on the behaviors of others that uphold this view such as compliments and less likely to focus on behaviors that counter this view such as criticism. The opposite, of course, would happen if you viewed yourself as an incompetent person.

Organizing and Evaluating

Observations of the world are not floating randomly around in your head. Instead, they are organized in ways that allow you to retrieve them when necessary, and new information is connected to previous information that is already organized and stored. **Schemata** are mental structures that are used to organize information in part by clustering or linking associated material. For example, information about relationships can be stored and connected in "relationship" schemata and drawn from when needed. Since this information is stored in a relatively accessible manner, it can be used to make sense of what you are experiencing and to anticipate what might happen in a given situation.

This particular approach is based on the work of George Kelly (1955), who saw people as scientists making hypotheses about everyday life and then testing their effectiveness. When researchers conduct experiments, they make calculated guesses about what will happen and then decide if what they anticipated actually occurred once the experiment has been completed. Kelly maintained that people do the same thing in their everyday lives. For instance, upon meeting you may greet someone in a particular way because—based on past experience and observations—you believe doing so will lead to approval from the other person and a proper relational connection. If your expectations are proved *correct,* your existing way of viewing the world will be strengthened, and you will be more likely to perform the same action in the future. If your expectations are proved *incorrect,* you will likely revise your way of viewing the world, and you will be less likely to perform the same action in the future.

Your organizational system is constantly being updated and modified based on new experiences and as a result of evaluating its accuracy and usefulness. This system seems pretty efficient and beneficial. However, it is not without its disadvantages. Kelly (1955) maintained that a person's processes are "channelized" by the ways in which events are anticipated. As a result, certain ways of acting and viewing the world become more deeply ingrained in your thinking. Imagine running the end of a stick in a straight line over and over in the same spot on the ground. Eventually, an indentation begins to develop and becomes deeper and deeper as you continue to run the end of that stick in the same place. The same thing can be imagined with certain ways of behaving and viewing the world. The more you behave in a certain way and the more often you view the world in the same way, the deeper and more ingrained it becomes in your thinking. After a while, it becomes difficult to imagine behaving in another way or viewing the world in a different way.

Consequently, Kelly (1955) urged people to imagine a table as being soft. When touching a table, you probably anticipate that it will be hard, and most of the time you will be correct. However, you should always consider the possibility that the table will be soft. Always consider the opposite, and always consider other possibilities. When done consistently, a person's behaviors and views frequently become seen as correct and natural rather than things that should be constantly evaluated and reassessed. Alternatives may or may not be better, but they should always be considered.

Kelly's (1955) work has resulted in a better understanding of the ways in which people think and relate to others. It can also be used to better understand how our perceptions influence the transaction of identities through prototypes, personal constructs, and scripts.

Prototypes

A **prototype** is the best-case example of something (Fehr, 1993). You may have a prototype of an ideal romantic partner, for instance. This prototype could be a composite of different people or an actual person. Accordingly, your romantic partner prototype could be compiled from characteristics of past romantic partners, or it could be a single romantic partner. It could be made up of people you actually know, people you have observed, and media representations. All prototypes are influenced culturally.

When identities are transacted they are broadly measured using prototypes as standards. Someone attempting to construct the identity of a romantic partner would use his or her prototype as a model, and other people would use their respective prototypes of a romantic partner in order to evaluate and make sense of this person.

Personal Constructs

Personal constructs are bipolar dimensions used to measure and evaluate things. Whereas prototypes tend to be broad categories, personal constructs are narrow and more specific characteristics. These personal constructs can be used in the development of a prototype and to determine how close someone may come to meeting all the criteria. Using romantic partners again as an example, the following personal constructs could be used:

Attractive–Unattractive

Kind–Mean

Passive–Aggressive

Intelligent–Ignorant

Humorous–Dull

Employed–Unemployed

Like prototypes, personal constructs are used to make sense of the world and to evaluate what is taking place. Personal constructs, though, are more specific and detailed. They can be used to determine just how well a person measures up according to certain categories.

Scripts

Scripts are guides for behavior developed from our system of knowledge. A movie or television script informs actors what they should be doing and saying. Such scripts assist actors in performing a character. Likewise, you use scripts when performing social roles and enacting identities in everyday life. For example, you know what to say and how to act when performing the role or identity of a student. You are following the script of a student. Using the running example of romantic partners, you know what you should do and say as a romantic partner through scripts developed from personal experience and observations of others. You know when the other "actors" are following a script correctly and performing an identity accurately. You also know when they have forgotten their lines and are giving a horrible performance.

While following scripts is important, most actors are required to improvise their performance from time to time. They also explore the creation of a character by saying different things and behaving in different ways. You must do the same thing when you are performing particular identities. You develop your own spin on an identity. Furthermore, you must improvise and edit scripts when scenes or contexts change.

Listen in on Your Life

How would you describe yourself? Would you give your national identity, ethnic identity, gender identity, sexual identity, age identity, social class identity, religious identity, or anything else?

Now check the categories that you can use to personalize your profile on Facebook or another social networking site. People are generally asked to identify themselves by association with particular categories and such items as favorite videos and music, hobbies, and sexual orientation. Are these the categories you would use to describe yourself to a child, an employer, or a new neighbor? How would you feel if your instructor composed a slide show of all the Facebook profiles of the people in your class and showed it to everyone?

Scripts are subject to change and revision through experience and assessment. Sometimes a person discovers the table is soft! Beyond careful evaluation, however, scripts change with the passing of time. This change is especially noticeable with scripts involving identities associated with close personal relationships. For instance, the script of a friend in elementary school is different from the script of a friend in high school. Both scripts are different from the script of a middle-aged friend. Returning yet again to the example of romantic partners, the script of a romantic partner early in the relationship will likely be different from the script of a romantic partner after a number of years in the same relationship.

Ultimately, scripts focus our attention on the mutual influence of perception and the transaction of identities. Identities are performed though interactions with others, and perceptions guide our understanding of what should be done and the evaluation of symbolic performance. In what follows, we examine how people may view themselves as having an established inner core or identities to be revealed, but in actuality identities are performed though communication and personal relationships.

Identity as Inner Core: The Self-Concept

We start with the "commonsense" idea that you have a true inner self. By the end of the chapter, however, we will show that there is more to learn about personal identity built by relationships with other people. The chapter connects identity to language; to other people; to the norms, rules, and categories in society/culture; and to narratives of origin and belonging to other relationships. This identity may be represented by such statements as "I'm an African American" or, on a bumper sticker, "Proud parent of an Honor Roll student at City High." These examples make statements of identity that claim it through relationships with other people or membership in groups, not just as a person with an inner core.

Psychic/Reflective Self

When you think about persons as having some true personal, private, and essential core, covered with layers of secrecy, privacy, and convention, this is known as a **self-concept**. Because everyone is assumed to have this core, you are alarmed by people who have multiple personalities or are bipolar. Someone should have only one consistent personality; people who have more parts are disturbed or irrational. Your identity may be hard for other people to reach, but according to many self-help books and celebrity biographies, it is reachable. Communication serves to help people *talk about* or *express* what is inside, perhaps in greater depth as they get to know one another better. Communication scholars can teach you the skill of expressing yourself well or help you be open and honest and let "the real you" be heard.

Photo 5.1 How do daily interactions with other people form or sustain your identity? What is being communicated here about gender, identity, and culture? (See page 129.)

The Weirdness of Consistent Expectations

A consistent inner self would be made up of the person's broad habits of thought (e.g., someone is kind, outward-looking, introverted, or self-centered). You might see that self revealed communicatively in styles of behavior (e.g., someone is aggressive, calm, ambitious, reliable, hardworking, or manipulative) or in characteristic styles of perception (e.g., someone is paranoid, trusting, insightful, or obstinate). *Personality* is the label that you would first use to describe someone's *identity* if you were asked about it casually in a conversation by someone who wanted to know what that person was like.

But it's a very odd idea indeed. People are too complex. A person can *simultaneously* be many identities. For example, a person can simultaneously be a loving parent, a vegetarian, a conservative, quick-tempered, a good dancer, a bad cook, business savvy, and a team player. You also have a choice in the identity you describe: a relational identity (friend/parent), an interactional identity (worker/customer/server), a sex or gender identity (male/female/masculine/feminine/GLBT), a racial/ethnic identity (the boxes to check on government forms), or a behavioral identity (extrovert/introvert). It's a choice, then, to describe your identity.

Unstable Behaviors

Another key point about identity comes from everyday experience. People are multi-layered and can have different moods, being good company on one day and bad on another. People can fluctuate during the course of the day, and events may happen to them that cause them to act "out of character." These fluctuations help demonstrate that it's a peculiar idea that somebody could have a *fixed* inner identity if it can also be so variable and complex over time.

The best you can hope for, then, is that the more you get to know someone through talk, the more you can understand the person's usual self. You can learn about what triggers a tailspin or a rant.

The upshot, though (and we are sorry to spoil it for you), is that all the magazine articles that offer to tell you about "the real [Lady Gaga/Beyoncé/Ashton Kutcher/

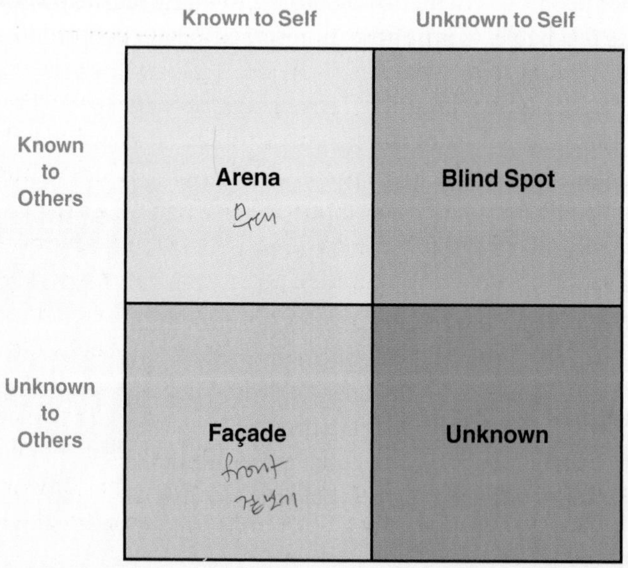

	Known to Self	Unknown to Self
Known to Others	**Arena**	**Blind Spot**
Unknown to Others	**Façade**	**Unknown**

Figure 5.1 The Johari Window

Source: From "The Johari Window: A Graphic Model of Interpersonal Awareness," by J. Luft and H. Ingham, 1955, in *Proceedings of the Western Training Laboratory in Group Development* (Los Angeles: University of California, Los Angeles).

Joseph Stalin/Sarah Palin]" are always going to be nonsense. The notion that someone has a real single inner core is suspect for communication scholars from the get-go. Also, if identities could not be changed or reviewed, there would be no therapists or communication textbooks with advice on how to develop your communication and presentation skills (i.e., how to present your "true self" more effectively).

The Johari window, developed in 1955 by two guys called Joe (Luft) and Harry (Ingham)—and we're not kidding—distinguishes between what a person knows about self and what others know about the person. As you can see in Figure 5.1, people have *blind spots:* Everyone but the person in question can see something obvious (for example, that Bob is "a pain"). In other cases we pretend (*façade*), concealing from people something that we know about ourselves (guilty secrets and so forth). The *arena* is basically where we openly act out a public identity that everyone else knows and recognizes.

Describing a Self

Ask people to tell you who they are. They will tell you their name and start revealing information about themselves, usually with a narrative that places their self in various contexts. *Steve Duck* indicates to someone in your culture that the person is male and has to put up with many very unoriginal jokes about his name. Although he has lived in the United States of America for more than 25 years, he is a Brit, or English as he prefers to think of it. His family comes from Whitby in North Yorkshire, England, where the first recorded Duck (John Duck) lived in 1288. John Duck and Steve Duck share the same skeptical attitude toward authority figures. John is in the historical record because he sued the Abbot of Whitby over ownership of a piece of land. John was descended from the Vikings who sacked and then colonized Whitby in about 800 A.D. *Duck* is a Viking nickname–based surname for a hunchback. (Have you ever ducked out of the way of anything? If so, you have crouched like a hunchback.)

Steve Duck is also relatively short for a man, is bald but bearded, likes watching people but is quite shy, and can read Latin, which is how he found out about John Duck while researching his family tree. Steve likes the music of Ralph Vaughan Williams, enjoys doing cryptic crosswords, knows about half the words that Shakespeare knew, and has occasionally lied. He resents his mother's controlling behavior, was an Oxford college rowing coxswain (cox'n), loves reading Roman history, and is gluten intolerant. He thinks he is a good driver and is proud of his dad, who was a Quaker pacifist (that antiauthority thing again) who won three medals for bravery in World War II for driving an unarmed ambulance into the front line of a war zone in order to rescue two seriously wounded (armed) comrades. Steve has lived in Iowa for 26 years. He has had two marriages and four children, carries a Swiss Army knife (and as many other gadgets as will fit onto one leather belt), and always wears two watches. He is wondering whether to get the new Swiss Army knife that has a data storage capacity, a laser pointer, and a fingerprint password. Sweet.

Self-Description and Stereotypes

Notice that some of this information about Steve's identity is *self-description.* That is, these words describe him in much the same way that anyone else could without knowing him personally (e.g., male, bearded, short, bald, two watches, magnetic sex appeal).

Self-description usually involves information about self that is obvious in *public* (or on your résumé). If you wear your college T-shirt, talk with a French accent, or are short, this evidence about you is available even to strangers who can see your physical appearance or hear how you sound. "Identity" in this sense is communicated publicly and physically. It parks the individual in categories (national, racial, or ethnic groups) or else lumps him or her into stereotypes. It isn't really an individual identity but is more about group membership.

Case in Point

Analyze recent interaction with people you would consider a friend, an acquaintance, and a stranger. What, if any, disclosure took place? What does this tell you about disclosure and relationships?

Self-Disclosure

Some points in Steve's description of himself count as **self-disclosure**: the revelation of information that people could not know unless Steve *made* it known. In the above example, these are the points that describe particular feelings and emotions that other people would not know unless Steve specifically disclosed them. The *resents, is proud of, enjoys, thinks,* and *is wondering* parts give you a view of his identity that you could not directly obtain any other way, though you might work it out from what Steve says or does.

These parts, since they are spoken as insights, are self-disclosure, not self-description. The term *self-disclosure* is limited to revelation of private, sensitive, and confidential information relevant to identity. Values, fears, secrets, assessments, evaluations, and preferences all count as such confidences that you share with only a few people.

The Importance of Being Open

Jourard (1964, 1971) wrote about self-disclosure as making your identity "transparent" to others. People who make the most disclosures are acting in the most psychologically healthy manner. Early research also connected self-disclosure with growth in intimacy. Classic reports (e.g., Derlega, Metts, Petronio, & Margulis, 1993) found that the more people become intimate, the more they disclose to each other information that is both broad and deep. Also, the more you get to know someone's inner knowledge structures, the closer you feel to him or her.

Closeness generally develops only if the information is revealed in a way that indicates it is privileged information that other people do not know. For example, if a man lets you (and only you) know the secret that he has a serious invisible illness (such as diabetes, lupus, or prostate cancer), an unusually strong fear of spiders, or a significantly distressed marriage, you feel valued and trusted, because he let you into his inner life.

Openness and Closeness

There is an important relational process going on here: When someone tells you about inner identity, you feel honored and valued by someone's revelation of the inner self, or you may actually not care for what you are hearing. The important point is that disclosure itself does not make a difference to a relationship; the relationship makes a difference to the value of disclosure. If you feel the relationship is enhanced by self-disclosure, it is. If you don't, no matter how intimate the disclosure, the relationship does not grow in intimacy.

Later research has refined this idea (Dindia, 2000; Petronio, 2002). For example, too much disclosure of identity is not necessarily a good thing at all times. You've probably been bored by somebody telling you more than you wanted to know—TMI! By contrast, people who are closed and don't tell anything about themselves are regarded as psychologically *un*healthy.

Communication scholar Kathryn Dindia (2000) points out that the revelation of identity is rarely a simple progression and is certainly not just the declaration of facts and then—*bam!*—intimacy. Self-disclosure is a dynamic process tied to other social processes that relate to your identity and how you disclose yourself over time. It continues through the life of relationships and is not a single onetime choice about whether to disclose or not. Part of your identity is the skill with which you reveal or conceal information about yourself and your feelings, as any good poker player knows.

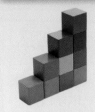

Make Your Case

Consider the following example: José learns more about Juanita's identity when she discloses something about herself that makes him feel positive about their relationship. It also makes him nervous because, in the past, he did something that her disclosure shows she would not like. So he tells her what he did and how sorry he is about it. Juanita likes the fact that he confides in her and feels better about the relationship as a result. She wonders if José is still the same person he was when he did the bad thing or if he is genuinely sorry and has changed.

Using this example, make the case that identity, self-disclosure, and relationships are mutually connected *transactions*, not just simply the peeling away of layers.

Dynamics of Revelation

In fact, the revelation of your identity, like identity itself, is an open-ended process that continues indefinitely in relationships even after they have become deeply intimate. It is dynamic, continuous, and circular so that it is hard to say where self-disclosure or identity begins or ends. It is also influenced by the behavior and communication of the other person(s)—the audience. Both self-disclosure and identity occur in the context of a relationship that has ups and downs.

Dialectic Tensions

Everyone places a limit on the amount of information that he or she reveals to others, and some choose to remain private, even in intimate relationships. Baxter and Montgomery (1996) identify a push-pull **dialectic tension** of relationships. These tensions occur whenever you are in two minds about something or feel a simultaneous pull in two directions. Some communication scholars (e.g., Baxter, 2004, 2011; Baxter & Braithwaite, 2008) suggest that there simply is no singular core of identity but a dialogue

Photo 5.2 How do you explain the fact that a person can experience different sides of self and hold different views simultaneously? (See page 129.)

between different "voices" in your head. For example, in relationships, you want to feel connected to someone else, but you do not want to give up all of your independence. You can see how you—and your identity—can grow by being in a relationship, but you can also see that this comes at a simultaneous cost or threat to your identity, independence, and autonomy.

The autonomy–connectedness dialectic is one dialectic tension, but another is openness–closedness, where people feel social pressure to be open yet also want to retain control over private information. This tension leads to people sometimes giving out and sometimes holding back information about themselves. Even in the same relationship, a person can feel willing to reveal information sometimes but crowded and guarded at other times. A personal relationship is not a consistent or a simple experience any more than identity is. Each affects the other over time. Also you may tell different versions of your identity to different audiences on different occasions.

Identity and Its Boundaries

In fact, people in relationships negotiate boundaries of privacy (Petronio, 2002). Part of the difference between friendship and mere acquaintance is that you have stronger boundaries around your identity for acquaintances than you do for friends.

As Jon Hess (2000) notes, you simply don't like some people. You don't want them to know "personal stuff" and may actively limit what they find out. Caughlin and Afifi (2004) have shown that even intimate partners sometimes prefer to completely avoid topics that may annoy or provoke the other person.

Petronio (2002) deals with the inconsistencies in the revelation of information by pointing to the importance of boundary management of the topics within different relational settings. People experience a tension between a desire for privacy and a demand for openness differently in different relationships. Couples make up their own rules for controlling the boundaries of privacy. So, for example, two people may define, between themselves, the nature of topics that they will mention in front of other people and what they will keep to themselves. A married couple may decide what topics it can discuss in front of the children, for instance, and these topics may change as the children grow older. In other words, people show, employ, and work within different parts of their identity with different audiences at different times.

Self-Disclosure and Boundaries: Who Am I, for Whom?

One of Petronio's (2002) key points is that the suitability of something for disclosure is itself affected by relational context and by agreement between the partners. There are no absolutes.

She also draws attention to the ways in which a couple can decide how much to disclose. Amount, type, or subject of self-disclosure can be a topic for discussion (often called *metacommunication* or communication about communication). In contrast to Jourard's (1964, 1971) idea that there are absolute rules about self-disclosure of identity, Petronio (2002) demonstrates that it is a matter of personal preference, worked out explicitly between the partners in a relationship through communication.

The upshot of this discussion of self-disclosure questions identity as a straightforward, layered possession of your own inner being. Your self-disclosure and your identity are jointly owned by you and a partner. There is more to identity than just *having* or *revealing* one, then. The norms of appropriateness for reciprocity, the rules about amount of revealed information (especially negative information) show that there is a social context for communication about identity. Identity is revealed within that set of social rules, cultural norms, and contexts.

Self-disclosure reacts to a **norm of reciprocity** (an unspoken rule about fairness and giving back about as much as you receive). If you say something self-disclosing to someone, that person should tell you something about himself or herself in return. If one person keeps telling information but gets nothing back, the person will stop doing it. Oddly enough, the norm of reciprocity can actually be used to interrogate people or find out information about them indirectly. If you say something personal about yourself, that loads an obligation on the other people to respond by saying something equally personal about themselves.

Identity and Other People

Saying that there is a social context for identity is basically making two points:

1. Society as a whole broadly influences the way you think about identity in the first place.

2. The other people who meet a person may influence the way that person's identity is expressed.

When you reveal your identity, you often use stories to tell the audience something about yourself and help its members shape their sense of who you are. As with self-disclosure, so too with stories: They are influenced by both society/culture and the specific persons or audience to which you do the telling.

Narrative Self and Altercasting

People tell stories about themselves and other people all the time and pay special care to what they will say, particularly for occasions like job interviews, sales pitches, and strategic communication of all sorts. You may have noticed that you adapt stories of your identity for consumption by other people in a social context (see Chapter 2).

Stories We Tell

A report about your identity characterizes you by means of a memory or history in its narrative or a typical or an amusing instance that involves character (your identity), plot, motives, scenes, and other actors (see Chapter 2). Even when you reveal an internal model of self, this story organizes your identity in ways other people understand in terms of the rules that govern accounts, narratives, and other social reports. As Kellas (2008) has pointed out, narratives can be an *ontology* (how I came to be who I am), an *epistemology* (how I think about the world), an *individual construction,* or a *relational process,* such as when romantic partners tell the story about how they first met.

Origin Stories

Reports about an identity have a narrative structure that builds off both the sense of origin derived from early life and a sense of continuity. The self comes from somewhere and has roots—"I'm Hispanic," "I'm a true Southerner," "I'm a genuine Irish McMahan."

Identity comes in part from narratives of origin. These can be personal, cultural, or species ("What was my great-grandfather like?" "Where did I come from?" "Where did our culture come from?" "How did humans get started?"). A sense of origin leads, for most people, straight back to their family, the first little society that they ever experienced (Huisman, 2008). The specific context of family experience is the first influence on a person's sense of origin and identity. It gives the person a sense of connection to a larger network of others. Indeed, in African American cultures, "the family" can be seen as a whole *community* that goes beyond the direct blood ties that define "family" in other cultures. The earliest memories give you a sense of origin as represented by your experiences in a family-like environment.

Origin, Memory, and the Telling of Your Self

However, early memories are not neutral facts. They are loaded, like dice, by the experiences you think you had in your family. A childhood seen as terrible can make you absorb an identity that gives you low self-esteem, for example (Duck, 2011), and could lead you to treat later relational opportunities with great caution. People treated respectfully by parents end up confident and secure about themselves, whereas those treated by their parents as nuisances come to see themselves that way. They also become anxious in relationships or avoid them altogether.

Table 5.1 Early Experiences and Influences on Your Later Life

Early experiences affect your thought worlds/worlds of meaning.

They influence your sense of identity.

They create identity narratives about you and your history.

They influence feelings about self, the goals that you set for life, the levels of ability you feel you have, the ways you relate to other people, the dark fears that you hoard all your life, your beliefs about the way to behave properly (religious beliefs, rituals about birthdays, who cares for people emotionally, whether sports "matter"), and whether you see life as peacefully cozy or violently conflicted.

A key point, then, is that by both direct and indirect means, your interactions and communication with other people shape your views of yourself. This happens even when you don't realize it or necessarily want it to happen—and this influence is not automatically something you just grow out of. Therapists get paid to put clients' childhood into better perspective! Early experiences in "the family" lay down many of the tracks upon which your later life will run.

Stories about you must fit with what your audience believes to be coherent and acceptable. It is not just that you *have* a self but that you shape the *telling* of your identity in a way that your audience (culture, friends) will accept.

Photo 5.3 How is your sense of identity represented by connections to the past? (See page 129.)

This distinction is like the difference between the words in a joke and the way someone tells it: The telling adds something performative to the words, and a person can spoil a joke by telling it badly. Likewise with identity, it has to be performed or told in appropriate ways. When Bob, the nontraditional student, the Purdue fan, or the frat boy brags about his achievements to friends, he probably tells his identity differently than he would to former workmates, the police, Indiana University fans, or the dean of students.

Labeling

Identity is also made by **labeling** the characteristics that you want to stand out. One of our faculty colleagues refers to himself as "Dr. Dave," which creates a certain kind of image, a mixture of professionalism and accessibility that is also an amusing cross-reference to the cultural icon Dr. Phil. Such nicknames and labels can be used for reinforcement of a type of identity. In the case of *other people,* a technical term used in discussion of communication and identity is **altercasting**. Altercasting refers to how language can give people an identity and then force them to live up to the description, whether positive or negative (Marwell & Schmitt, 1967). For example, you are altercasting when you say, "As a good friend, you will want to help me here" or "Only a fool would . . ." These label the listener as a certain kind of person (or not), by positioning the person to respond appropriately (as a friend or not as a fool). Even such small elements of communication transact your identity and the identities of those people around you.

When you communicate about yourself, therefore, you assume that the audience will understand you, so you assume a shared basis for understanding other people. On top of that, you assume that special people—friends, for example—not only understand your "self" but also do reality checks for you. When people talk about identity, then, they assume their audience will be able to comprehend, interpret, and probably support it.

The earlier description of Steve, for example, mentions a Swiss Army knife because that particular item is well known in the culture. Any description of an identity is therefore steered by beliefs about the criteria, categories, and descriptions that will matter to, or even impress, the audience. For example, people project a professional identity by wearing smart business clothes to a job interview. People also communicate their cultural identity through their accent and behavior. Thus "who you are" is a *relational* point.

Symbolic Identity

Your sense of self is influenced by language frames, culture, origin, membership, and other people's thoughts about you. But don't you actually *do* a lot of your identity for specific people, such as your priest, your neighbor, your best friend, and your coworkers and customers?

The Many Yous

Most people have a range of identities that they can turn on as necessary according to where they are and who is there with them. In that case, identity is not so much something that you *have* as it is something that you *do* in ways that people recognize as suitable.

Do you ever feel like a different person when you are with your friends compared to when you're talking to your mother? Are you the same person all the time, or do you have good and bad days? Do you ever do things you regret or regard as not typical? Ever say things you regret?

Most people have protested that someone has misrepresented them. Until now you would not have called that resistance to an altercasting by refusing to accept it, but that is what it is. A hostile or negative person can make you feel very bad about yourself. Have you ever met anyone who didn't really "get" what you are about?

On the other hand, you may have had a close relationship with a partner that felt good because you were able to be your *true self* around the other person or because the person helped bring out sides of you that other people could not. Did you struggle to assert an identity independent from your parents when you were a teenager?

You must already be wondering how any of that is possible if "you" are one identity. You may also have started to think about how advertising, religion, and social fashions influence the ways you dress and act. Other people can affect your values, the choices you make, and how these feed into your sense of identity. Your culture and your identity at the very least interact with one another. At most, culture and its icons (pop stars, fashion models, celebrities) account for quite a lot of your identity, by showing you how to dress and how to behave and what standards of belief are "OK."

Contrarian Challenge

If you do not have a central core that is "you," then how come people who know you well can apparently predict what you will do and know how you should be dealt with?

Symbolic Self

The lesson is simple: Your identity is shaped by culture and the people you interact with. This is because you can reflect that your "self" is an object of other people's perceptions and that they can do critical thinking or listening about you as well. In short, your identity is a **symbolic self**, a self that exists for other people and goes beyond what it means to you; it arises from social interaction with other people. As a result, you fit identity descriptions into the form of narratives that your society and your particular acquaintances know about and accept. Hence, any identity that you offer to other people is based on the fact that you all share meanings about what is important in defining a person's identity.

Symbols and Identity: Reflection

Another way of thinking about identity, then, is in terms of how broad social forces affect or even transact an individual's view of who he or she is. This set of ideas is referred to as **symbolic interactionism**. In particular, George Herbert Mead (1934) suggested that people get their sense of self from other people and from being aware that others observe, judge, and evaluate one's behavior. How many times have you done or not done something because of how you would look to your friends if you did it? Has your family ever said, "What will the neighbors think?"

Mead (1934) called this phenomenon the human ability to adopt an **attitude of reflection**. You think about how you look in other people's eyes or reflect on the fact that other people can see you as a social object from their point of view. Guided by these reflections, you do not always do what you want to do but what you think people will accept. You may end up doing something you don't want to do because you cannot think how to say no to another person in a reasonable way. You cannot just stamp your foot and shout "SHAN'T!"

Your identity, then, is not yours alone. Indeed, Mead (1934) also saw self as a transacted result of communicating with other people: You learn how to be an individual by recognizing the way that people treat you. You come to see your identity through the eyes of other people, for whom you are a meaningful object. People recognize you and treat you differently from everyone else, as distinct in their eyes and so in your own.

Self as Others Treat You

Relationships connect through communication to the formation of your identity. If other people treat you with respect, you come to see yourself as respected, and self-respect becomes part of your identity. If your parents treated you like a child even after you had grown older, they drew out from you some sense that you were still a child, which may have caused you to feel resentment. If you are intelligent and people treat you as interesting, you may come to see yourself as having different value to other people than does someone

Physically attractive people often act confidently because they are aware of the fact that other people find them attractive. On the other hand, unattractive people have learned that they cannot rely on their looks to make a good impression. They need other ways of impressing other people (e.g., by developing a great sense of humor; Berscheid & Reis, 1998). In a phrase, you come to see yourself as others see you.

who is not treated as intelligent. You get so used to the idea that it gets inside your "identity" and becomes part of who you are, but it originated from other people, not from you.

If you are tall, tough, and muscular (not short, bald, and carrying a Swiss Army knife), perhaps people habitually treat you with respect and caution. Over time, you get used to the idea, and identity is enacted and transacted in communication as a person who expects respect and a little caution from other people (Duck, 2011). Eventually, you will not have to act in a generally intimidating way in order to make people respectful. Your manner of communicating comes to reflect expected reactions to you. Although your identity began in the way you were treated by other people, it eventually becomes transacted in communication.

Society as Other Individuals: Society's Secret Agents

Another way of thinking about this is to see how "society" gets your friends to do its work for it. You have never met a society or a culture, and you never will. You will only ever meet people who (re)present some of a society's key values to you. This contact with other folks puts them in the role of *Society's Secret Agents*. These people you meet and talk with are doing your society's work by enacting ways that culture represents the values that are desirable within it.

When you communicate with other people in your culture, you get information about what works and what doesn't, what is acceptable and what isn't, and how much you count in that society—what your identity is "worth." For example, the dominant culture in the United States typically values ambition, good looks, hard work, demonstration of material success, and a strong code of individuality. People stress those values in their talk ("The American Dream"/"Winners") or else feel inadequate because they don't stack up against these values ("Losers").

Of course, you are forced to interact with some people whether you like them or not (coworkers, professors, or relatives, for example). The principle is the same even though you most often think of the influence

Photo 5.4 What is meant by a symbolic self, and why do we have to account to other people for who we are? (See page 129.)

of your friends and relatives or key teachers on your identity. Nonfriends may challenge aspects of your sense of identity and make you reflect on the question, "Who am I?" Sometimes this reflection results in reinforced confidence in your opinions, but sometimes it undermines, modifies, or even challenges them. Either way, discussions of everyday communication transact some effect on your view of self, your identity. Your sense of self/identity comes from interactions with other people representing society as a whole.

Individuals acquire their individuality through the social practices in which they carry out their lives. Accordingly, they encounter powerful forces of society that are enacted by Society's Secret Agents in ordinary interactions. That "raised eyebrow" from your neighbor/instructor/team fan was actually society at work! Your "self" is structured and enacted in relation to those people who have power over you in formal ways, like the police, but most often you encounter the institutions within a society through its secret agents: public opinion. The people you know who express opinions about moral issues of the day and give you their judgments—they are Society's Secret Agents, guiding what other people do and thinking just as they do. And for that matter, your talk with other people makes you an agent also. Every time you comment on someone else's behavior, dress, relationships, or speech, you (yes, you) are helping to enforce social norms and practices.

Transacting a Self in Interactions With Others

In keeping with this book's theme, you can't have a self without also having relationships with other people—both the personal relationships you choose and the social relationships you reject. A person cannot have a concept of self without reflection on identity via the views of other people with whom he or she has relationships. Your identity is *transacted* or constituted in part from two things: First, you take into yourself the beliefs and prevailing norms of the society in which you live. Second, you are *held to account* for the identity that you project. As a football fan, you lose face if you don't know the score during a game or cannot name your own team's quarterback. As a student, you are expected to know answers about the book you are reading for your class.

Banality of Life as an Identity Maker

Again, your identity is a complex result not only of your own thinking, history, and experience but also of your interaction with other people and their influence on you, both as individuals and as Society's Secret Agents. Behind all those things that you think of as abstract social structures, like "the law," are real individuals acting in relation to one another (you and the police officer). These social relations get internalized into yourself. You slow down at speed-limit signs not because you want to but because you saw the police car and don't need another ticket.

Strategic Communication

People develop impressions of others through social networking profiles. Consider what your profile says about you. Does your profile convey the identity or identities you desire? If not, what might be changed to help construct the desired identities? If your profile is working, how can it be enhanced?

The routine ordinary banality of everyday life talk with friends who share the same values and talk about them day by day (a) actually does something for society and (b) helps make you who you are. Daily routines like meeting at 11 A.M. for coffee in the coffee room put events in a predictable framework of meaning through trivial and pedestrian communication (Wood & Duck, 2006). But—here's the point of this section, so remember it well—you *do* your identity in front of the audiences, and they might evaluate and comment on whether you're doing it right.

The same kinds of processes occur in interaction when you profess your undying allegiance to one football team and your supposed hatred of the opposing team, or say that murder is wrong or that bankers are gouging customers. The people around you do not resent it but actually encourage you and reinforce your expression of ideas that make up your identity. They share it and support it. Just as Bob and his colleagues dehumanize "illegals" as targets for his most diligent attention and scrutiny—and his colleagues admire him for it—so do you when you categorize the opposing team as some kind of enemy. The underlying idea—that a group of people can be treated as nothing more than depersonalized, dehumanized others with no appreciable individuality—runs through team loyalty and rivalry, town versus college kids, treating older students as aliens, and any other kind of stereotyping.

Performative Self

Other people influence who you are and how you are treated. Other people use labels and judge your behavior. You are not just an inner core but part of a heritage. You are not just you; you are a symbol in a cultural and social structure.

On top of that, add the curious idea that you don't just *have* an identity; you actually *do* one. Identity is not just *having* a symbolic sense of self but *doing* it in the presence of other people and doing it well in their eyes. This is an extremely interesting and provocative fact about communication: Everyone *does* his or her identity for an audience, like an actor in a play. **Performative self** means that selves are creative performances based on the social demands and norms of a given situation. As we will now discuss, you try to present the right face to people you are with and do your identity differently in front and back regions.

Mock put-downs are a common form of intimate banter in English-speaking countries but not in Eastern cultures. This suggests that face is culturally influenced on top of everything else that influences it. For instance, direct challenges to a person's competence ("You are a failure!") are openly offensive. Friends, though, may have a running joke between them that allows them to say it to one another.

Facework Revisited

Facework is part of what happens in everyday life communication (Chapter 2), and people have a sense of their own dignity. This gets transacted in everyday communication by polite protection of the person's "face."

This idea is about the performance of one's identity in public, the presentation of the self to people in a way that is intended to make the self look good.

Erving Goffman (1959) indicated the way in which momentary social forces affect identity portrayal. Goffman was interested in how identity is performed in everyday life so that people manage their image to make everyone "look good" (Cupach & Metts, 1994). The concept of "looking good" of course means "looking good *to other people*." It is therefore essentially a relational concept. (Table 5.2 provides challenges to a person's face.)

Table 5.2 Embarrassments and Predicaments

Embarrassment is when you perform a behavior that is inconsistent with the identity you want to present (Cupach & Metts, 1994; Metts, 2000). Someone who wants to impress an interviewer but instead spills coffee on his or her lap undercuts "face" of professional competence by being clumsy. Someone who wants to present a "face" of calmness and confidence but who suddenly blushes or twitches allows nonverbal behavior to contradict the identity of being cool and composed. The *performance* of an identity (face) is undercut by a specific behavior that does not fit.

Predicaments present a longer challenge to the performative self (think of predicaments as extended embarrassment). If you go to a job interview and your very first answer makes you look stupid, you still have to carry on, with the interviewers all thinking you are a hopeless, worthless, and unemployable idiot. You cannot leave; you have to sit it out watching their polite smiles and feeling terrible.

It takes you one step closer to looking at the interpersonal interaction that occurs on the ground every day. Rather than looking at society in an abstract way, Goffman (1959) focused on what you actually *do* in interactions. In part, your portrayal of yourself is shaped by the social needs at the time, the social situation, the social frame, and the circumstances surrounding your performance. Remember the server from Chapter 1? She does not introduce herself that way to her *friends* ("Hi, I'm Alice, and I'll be your server tonight") except as a joke, so her performance of the server identity is restricted to those times and places where it is appropriate.

Front and Back Regions

Goffman (1959) differentiated a **front region** and **back region** to social performance: The front region/front stage is *not a place* but *an occasion* where your professional, proper self is performed. For example, a server is all smiles and civility in the front stage of the restaurant when talking to customers. This behavior might be different from how he or she performs in the back region/backstage (say, the restaurant kitchen) when talking with the cooks or other servers and making jokes about the customers or about being disrespectful to them. But again, the back region is not just a place: If all servers are standing around in the restaurant before the customers come in and they are just chatting informally among themselves, the instant the first customer comes through the door, their demeanor will change to "professional" and they will switch to a front-region performance.

That means the performance of your identity is not sprung into action by your own free wishes but by social cues that this is the time to perform your "self" in that way. An identity is a performance. It shows how a person makes sense of the world not just alone but within a context provided by others.

Any identity connects to other identities. You can be friendly when you are with your friends, but you are expected to be professional when on the job and to do student identity when in class. So is this what allows Bob to be "two people," one at work and one in the social community? Is he just doing a front-region SOB performance at work?

Individuals inevitably draw on knowledge shared in any community, so any person draws on information that is both personal and communal. If you change from thinking of identity as about "self as character" and instead see it as "self as performer," you also must consider the importance of changes in performance to suit different audiences and transactive situations.

Self Constituted/Transacted in Everyday Practices

We have seen that identity is not just a personal inner core but a communicative performance molded by surrounding cultural influences, the way that you *do* your identity and how you are recognized as having one. Your practical performance of "being yourself" is affected by the social norms that are in place to guide communication in a given society. People judge your identity performance in a practical world and expect you to explain or account for yourself.

Practical Self

Your identity is performed in a material world that affects who you are. For example, the fact that you can communicate with other people more or less instantaneously across huge distances by mobile telephone materially affects your sense of connection to other people. This practical self is born from the ability to do practical things and is illustrated by the importance to many young people of learning to drive a car. When you can drive, not only do you go through the transformation of self as "more of a grown-up," but when you have a car you also can do what you cannot do when you do not have one. The ability to drive and obtain access to a car expands your identity in a practical way.

Part of your *performance* of self is connected to the practical artifacts, accompaniments, and "stuff" that you use in your performance. If you have the right "stuff" (professional suit, bling, or a sports car), the self that you project is different from the self you perform without it.

Accountable Self

An important element of doing an identity in front of an audience is that you become an **accountable self**, which essentially allows your identity to be morally judged by other people. What you do can be assessed by other people as right or wrong according to existing habits of society. Any performance of identity turns identity into a moral action. That is, identity becomes a way of living, based on choices made about actions that a person sees as available or relevant. Others will judge and hold the performance to account. The social construction of identity is influenced by societal value systems. Society as a whole encourages you to take certain actions (do not park next to fire hydrants, protect the elderly and the weak, be a good neighbor, recycle!).

Moral accountability is a fancy way of saying that society as a whole makes judgments about your actions and choices. It holds you to account for the actions and choices that you make, but it also forcefully encourages you to act in particular ways and to see specific types of identity as "good" (patriot is good, traitor is bad; loyalty is good, thief is bad; open self-disclosure is good, passive aggression is bad, for example). As noted before, "society" does this through everyday performances and communications by Society's Secret Agents—including you.

Photo 5.5 What can you say about a transgender person who has had reassignment surgery? What problems might a transgender person encounter in relation to identity as discussed in this chapter? (See page 129.)

Improvisational Performance

The identity that you thought of as your own personality, then, is not made up of your own desires and impulses but is formed, performed, and expressed within a set of social patterns and judgments. These are reinforced by the practices in a community through the relationships that people have with one another. The Indiana University fan is not asked why she is cheering for Indiana University by other Indiana University fans; Bob is not asked by his colleagues why he is so tough on "illegals."

A person's identity is a complex and compound concept that is partly based on history, memory, experiences, and interpretations by the individual, partly evoked by momentary aspects of talk (its context, the people you are with, your stage in life, your goals at the time), and partly a social creation directed by other people, society and its categories, and your relationship objectives in those contexts. Your performance of the self is guided by your relationships with other people, as well as your social goals. Even your embodiment of this knowledge or your sense of self is shaped by your social practices with other people. Your self-consciousness in their presence influences the presentation of yourself to other people. Although a sense of self/identity is experienced in your practical interactions with other people, you get trapped by language into reporting it abstractly as some sort of disembodied "identity," a *symbolic* representation of the routine practices and communication styles that you experience in your daily interactions with other people. Once again, then, another apparently simple idea (identity, personality, self) runs into the relational influences that make the basics of communication so valuable to study.

Table 5.3 summarizes what you've learned in this chapter about identity and relationships.

Table 5.3 Some Ways to See Identity Communication and Relationships	
Psychic/ reflective self	*Habits of thought/of behavior/of perception identify a person's "personality."*
	What you normally think of as identity a priori: Your communicative behavior just expresses the inner self.
Symbolic self	*Broad social forces affect self differentiation/characterization.*
	Self arises out of social interaction and not vice versa; hence, it does not "belong to me." You are who you are because of the people you hang out with, interact with, and communicate with; you can be a different identity in different circumstances.
Performative self	*Present social situation affects self-portrayal.*
	Selves are acted out in a network of social demands and norms; you do your identity differently in front and back regions and try to present the right "face" to the people you are with.
Practical self	*Material world affects self/how you think of self.*
	Practical aspects of materiality transform the concept of self. Your identity is represented by objects that symbolically make claims about the sort of person you are.
Accountable self	*Social context influences broad forms of portrayal.*
	Personality is just an abstract concept. People act within a set of social ideas and habitual styles of thinking, allowing other people to comment and steer how they behave.
Improvisational performance	*There is a rhetorical spin to this and how "self" is presented.*
	Ideology affects the manner of presentation of terms, characteristics, and so on. We try to narrate ourselves in the way that our society expects us to represent identity.

FOCUS QUESTIONS REVISITED

1. Some textbooks picture a person's identity like an onion, built layer by layer and communicated slowly as intimacy increases. Does this really make any sense?

For some reasons and purposes, it makes sense for us to see identity this way, but it really is not the only way that "identity" actually works in the everyday encounters of relationship life.

2. How do daily interactions with other people form or sustain your identity?

In at least two ways: Their responses to us affect the way we feel about ourselves; also, they act as Society's Secret Agents by innocently enforcing society's norms and beliefs through their comments on our own styles of behavior and identity performance.

3. How much of your "self" is a performance of social roles where you have to act out "who I am" for other people?

Much of what you do in everyday life is steered by your awareness of yourself as a social object for other people. Hence, you perform roles and styles of behavior that are appropriate in the circumstances. Your "inner self" may be constrained by this awareness.

4. What is meant by a symbolic self, and why do we have to account to other people for who we are?

Your "self" is presented to other people as a symbol, and you have to describe yourself in terms and phrases that your audiences recognize as symbolically meaningful in the culture. You are also able to take an attitude of reflection that recognizes that you are an object of other people's perceptions and judgment. You will remember from Chapter 1 that people can observe your behavior and "go beyond" it to its symbolic meaning.

5. What is the role of culture in your identity experiences?

Culture has multiple roles in identity experience. For one, cultures regard "individuality" differently; for another, your origin from a particular culture steers the way you think about people and their styles of behavior; for still another thing, your culture is part of your identity, and people proudly claim their cultural heritage as part of "who they are."

KEY CONCEPTS

accountable self   124
altercasting   117
attitude of reflection   119
back region   123
dialectic tension   113
front region   123
identity   101
labeling   117
moral accountability   125
norm of reciprocity   115

perception   105
performative self   122
personal constructs   107
prototype   107
schemata   106
scripts   108
self-concept   109
self-disclosure   112
symbolic interactionism   119
symbolic self   119

QUESTIONS TO ASK YOUR FRIENDS

- Discuss with your friends or classmates the most embarrassing moment that you feel comfortable talking about, and try to find out what about the experience threatened your identity. What identity were you projecting at the time, and what went wrong with the performance?

- Have your friends look at how advertisers sell the *image* of particular cars in terms of what they will make the owner look like to other people; the advertisers recognize that identity is tied up in material possessions. Discuss with your friends the following topics: How is your identity affected by your preferences in music, the Web, fashion magazines, resources, or wealth?

- Get a group of friends together and ask them each to write down what sort of vegetable, fish, dessert, book, piece of furniture, style of music, meal, car, game, or building best represents their identity. Read the responses out loud and have everyone guess which person is described.

MEDIA LINKS

- Watch the movie *Sideways* (Payne, 2004) and fast-forward to the veranda scene during which Miles talks to Maya about his preference for wine and it becomes apparent that he is using wine as a metaphor about himself. He projects his identity through his knowledge about the subtleties of wines. Basically he uses it to describe himself, and his hope is that Maya will learn to understand him.

Maya: You know, can I ask you a personal question, Miles?

Miles: Sure.

Maya: Why are you so into Pinot?

Miles: [laughs softly]

Maya: I mean, it's like a thing with you.

Miles: [continues laughing softly] Uh, I don't know, I don't know. Um, it's a hard grape to grow, as you know. Right? It's, uh, it's thin-skinned, temperamental, ripens early. It's, you know, it's not a survivor like Cabernet, which can just grow anywhere and, uh, thrive even when it's neglected. No, Pinot needs constant care and attention. You know? And in fact it can only grow in these really specific, little, tucked away corners of the world. And, and only the most patient and nurturing of growers can do it, really. Only somebody who really takes the time to understand Pinot's potential can then coax it into its fullest expression. Then, I mean, oh its flavors, they're just the most haunting and brilliant and thrilling and subtle and . . . ancient on the planet.

- Collect examples that demonstrate how media representations of ideal selves (especially demands on women to be a particular kind of shape, but try to be more imaginative than just these images) are constantly thrown in our path.
- How do television talk shows encourage us to be open, honest, and real? Do these programs teach us anything about the "right" ways to be ourselves?

ETHICAL ISSUES

- If your identity is partly constructed by other people, how does this play out in relation to diversity, cultural sensitivity, and political correctness versus speaking the truth?

- Analyze the difficulties for someone "coming out" in terms of performance, social expectations, norms, and relationships with those around the person.

- If you have a guilty secret and are getting into a deep romantic relationship with someone, should you tell him or her early on or later? Or should you not tell him or her at all?

ANSWERS TO PHOTO CAPTIONS

Photo 5.1 ■ There are messages about identity both "inside" the picture and "outside" it: The performance of femininity and womanhood is being communicated to the girl, a sense of the importance of looks and the enhancement of natural appearance in private. The picture also communicates to outsiders the role of personal hygiene in personal identity.

Photo 5.2 ■ Baxter (2011) points out that people have different dialogues available to them at each moment to draw them one way or another. Dialectical tensions are a constant part of daily life, and you may often feel pulled in two directions at once, whether in expressing what you feel or in enacting your identity.

Photo 5.3 ■ Interactions and experiences with older people give us a sense of our own identity and where we came from. This boy is learning how to connect himself to the past of his family.

Photo 5.4 ■ Symbolic self means that your identities represent something to other people and not just yourself. Furthermore, identities are transacted symbolically through your interactions with others. Many of the roles that you enact in everyday life are drawn from cultural expectations about the kind of person you "should" be. Part of your identity is therefore always an act. Identity can be "performed," and the performance takes over the identity. We all know who the impersonator is *trying* to be, but . . . he's not that person. We actually just saw the real guy working at a truck stop in Omaha and going by the name *Barry!*

Photo 5.5 ■ Sometimes physical self needs to be aligned with inner self through sex reassignment surgery. The transgender person still has to perform (dress, behave) in a way that convinces others that the correct sex has now been assigned. Family members need to learn new labels for the person: Who was once a son is now a daughter; an aunt is now an uncle; a sister is now a brother (Norwood, 2010).

STUDENT STUDY SITE

Visit the study site at **www.sagepub.com/boc2e** for e-flashcards, practice quizzes, journal articles and additional study resources.

REFERENCES

Baxter, L. A. (2004). Distinguished scholar article: Relationships as dialogues. *Personal Relationships, 11*(1), 1–22.

Baxter, L. A. (2011). *Voicing relationships: A dialogic perspective.* Thousand Oaks, CA: Sage.

Baxter, L. A., & Braithwaite, D. O. (2008). Relational dialectics theory: Crafting meaning from competing discourses. In L. A. Baxter & D. O. Braithwaite (Eds.), *Engaging theories in interpersonal communication* (pp. 349–361). Thousand Oaks, CA: Sage.

Baxter, L. A., & Montgomery, B. M. (1996). *Relating: Dialogs and dialectics.* New York: Guilford Press.

Berscheid, E., & Reis, H. T. (1998). Attraction and close relationships. In D. T. Gilbert, S. F. Fiske, & G. Lindzey (Eds.), *The handbook of social psychology* (4th ed., pp. 139–281). Boston: McGraw-Hill.

Burke, K. (1969). *A grammar of motives.* Berkeley: University of California Press.

Burleson, B. R., Holmstrom, A. J., & Gilstrap, C. M. (2005). "Guys can't say that to guys": Four experiments assessing the normative motivation account for deficiencies in the emotional support provided by men. *Communication Monographs, 72*(4), 468–501.

Caughlin, J. P., & Afifi, T. D. (2004). When is topic avoidance unsatisfying? Examining the moderators of the association between avoidance and dissatisfaction. *Human Communication Research, 30*(4), 479–513.

Cupach, W. R., & Metts, S. (1994). *Facework.* Thousand Oaks, CA: Sage.

Derlega, V. J., Metts, S., Petronio, S., & Margulis, S. T. (1993). *Self-disclosure.* Newbury Park, CA: Sage.

Dindia, K. (2000). Self-disclosure, identity, and relationship development: A dialectical perspective. In K. Dindia & S. W. Duck (Eds.), *Communication and personal relationships* (pp. 147–162). Chichester, UK: Wiley.

Duck, S. W. (2011). *Rethinking relationships: A new approach to relationship research.* Thousand Oaks, CA: Sage.

Fehr, B. (1993). How do I love thee: Let me consult my prototype. In S. W. Duck (Ed.), *Understanding relationship processes* (Vol. 1, pp. 87–120). Newbury Park, CA: Sage.

Goffman, E. (1959). *Behaviour in public places.* Harmondsworth, UK: Penguin Books.

Hess, J. A. (2000). Maintaining a nonvoluntary relationship with disliked partners: An investigation into the use of distancing behaviors. *Human Communication Research, 26,* 458–488.

Huisman, D. (2008). *Intergenerational family storytelling.* Iowa City: University of Iowa Department of Communication Studies.

Jourard, S. M. (1964). *The transparent self.* New York: Van Nostrand Reinhold.

Jourard, S. M. (1971). *Self-disclosure.* New York: Wiley.

Kellas, J. K. (2008). Narrative theories: Making sense of interpersonal communication. In L. A. Baxter & D. O. Braithwaite (Eds.), *Engaging theories in interpersonal communication* (pp. 241–254). Thousand Oaks, CA: Sage.

Kelly, G. A. (1955). *The psychology of personal constructs.* New York: Norton.

Luft, J., & Ingham, H. (1955). The Johari window: A graphic model of interpersonal awareness. *Proceedings of the Western Training Laboratory in Group Development.* Los Angeles: University of California.

Marwell, G., & Schmitt, D. R. (1967). Dimensions of compliance-gaining behavior: An empirical analysis. *Sociometry, 30,* 350–364.

Mead, G. H. (1934). *Mind, self, and society.* Chicago: University of Chicago Press.

Metts, S. (2000). Face and facework: Implications for the study of personal relationships. In K. Dindia & S. W. Duck (Eds.), *Communication and personal relationships* (pp. 74–92). Chichester, UK: Wiley.

Norwood, K. M. (2010, April 26). *Here and gone: Competing discourses in the communication of families with a transgender member.* Unpublished PhD thesis, Department of Communication Studies, University of Iowa.

Payne, A. (Director). (2004). *Sideways* [Motion picture]. United States: Fox Searchlight Pictures.

Petronio, S. (2002). *Boundaries of privacy.* Albany: State University of New York Press.

Shotter, J. (1984). *Social accountability and selfhood.* Oxford, UK: Basil Blackwell.

Wood, J. T., & Duck, S. W. (Eds.). (2006). *Composing relationships: Communication in everyday life.* Belmont, CA: Thomson Wadsworth.

6

Talk and Interpersonal Relationships

We want you to rethink relationships: They're not just about emotion. Instead, they are about knowledge, ways of understanding the world (Duck, 2011) and connecting symbolically to people. Communication helps you make connections between people and knowledge, and you really cannot have one process without the other, of course. Communication and relationships, as well as what you know and how you know it, are directly connected.

Everyday talk occurs in an evaluative context involving critical thinking and (moral) judgment. Critical thinking applies not only to big stories told in politics or persuasive appeals but also to small talk. Critical thinking about relationships can be based on the internal coherence of a breakup story, for example—whether it all seems to hang together—or the plausibility of the talk. You have heard friends tell a story about how they acted well in a romance and, while listening politely and smiling pleasantly, privately thought skeptically to yourself, "Yeah, right!"

This chapter covers four topics:

1. how communication in relationships supports your knowledge,

2. how everyday communication increases intimacy levels,

3. how everyday communication decreases intimacy levels, and

4. critical evaluation of the concept of relational stages.

Focus Questions

1. How does your everyday communication with other people transact your relationships?
2. How does your talk compose your relationships during everyday conversation?
3. How do relationships grow or change, and how does this show up in speech?
4. What are the different types of communication that take place when a relationship is coming apart?
5. Do relationships develop and break down in a linear fashion?

What Is the Best Way to Connect Talk, Relationships, and Knowledge?

How many of your present beliefs do you discuss with friends and family? How much of *what* you know depends on *whom* you know? You may discuss your life, current news, the nature of the outside world, and how to interpret the events that happen in it with people at work. Researchers have shown that you typically prefer to hang out with people who share similar attitudes and beliefs (Byrne, 1997; Kerckhoff, 1974; Sunnafrank, 1983; Sunnafrank & Ramirez, 2004). Who knew? You tend to respect their judgments and enjoy talking to them because they often reinforce what you believe (Weiss, 1998)! Of course, you will occasionally disagree, but mostly your friends let you talk about yourself in ways you like. In turn, they talk about themselves in ways you like, adopt the attitudes and beliefs you like, and see the world in broadly the same way you do.

Also very likely to have similar social, religious, racial, economic, and educational backgrounds, your friends live in worlds very like your own. When you communicate with them, you feel broadly supported—as a person who lives in a similar world of meaning (Duck, 2011).

How much of your daily talk involves comparison of ideas with someone else ("What do you think of the way she's dressed?" "I didn't like that lecture, did you?" "I forgot to check Facebook this morning. What's new?")? Even casual chatter serves to compose your experience of life and your relationships (Wood & Duck, 2006). Your interactions with friends may often seem light and unimportant—not, in fact, very productive. On the contrary, even small talk serves to reestablish the relationship, provide you with reality checks, give you information, transmit news, bring you up to date, and, most important of all, make you feel included. That is a relational outcome: *Inclusion* is a relational term; any talk, however small, that acknowledges and includes you serves a relational purpose.

Relationships and What You Know

Everyday communication reinforces both your relationships and what you know. All forms of communication show how you rely on your connections with other people to filter your knowledge and help you critically evaluate events, people, and situations. Because communication involves information, the people you know and with whom you spend your time affect your knowledge. They influence/steer/select the messages you send or attend to, the information you believe, the type of critical thinking you do, and how you evaluate the outcomes. So, not just a *result* of communication, relationships are also significant in the opposite process, the formation and transaction of knowledge—the creation of the world of meaning you inhabit.

Relationships also exert influence on the distribution of information. You tell secrets to your friends that you would not tell to strangers, and news travels through networks of folks who know one another (Bergmann, 1993;

> ## Make Your Case
>
>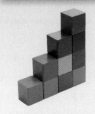
>
> Pay careful attention to media discussions of whatever happens to be the romance of the month, the breakup of the month, or the cheater of the month. How do such stories set ideals for society about romance and at the same time reinforce moral values about the ways in which relationships should be conducted? Watch out for words like *perfect couple, betrayal, lie, cheat, stand by your (wo)man,* and *ashamed,* all of which are secretly telling you what are the right and wrong ways to do romantic relationships.

Duck, 2007). Relationships also affect what you believe or challenge about the world in general, how you think about other people, and how you evaluate their behavior (whom you gossip about and why, for example). The marketing world knows about the power of the connection among relationships, information flow, critical thinking, and "knowledge." Marketers use WOM (word of mouth) campaigns that exploit the fact that we respect our friends' opinions about the right purchases to make and what is "cool." In the latest marketing fad, "buzz agents" are paid to tell their friends about particular products, thereby creating "buzz" and influencing people to buy them (Carl, 2006).

Building and Supporting Relationships

Robert Weiss (1974) identified six specific areas where relationships provide us with something special, needed, or valued. These six **provisions of relationships** are as follows.

Belonging and a Sense of Reliable Alliance

The major benefit that people desire from relationships is *belonging and a sense of reliable alliance:* You like to feel that someone is "there" for you. Quite often, you state this desire explicitly, but more often you just learn from daily interaction that someone looks after your interests, cares for you, inquires about your state of mind/health, and can usually be relied upon to help when asked—and sometimes even without being asked. That's what Weiss (1974) meant by "reliable alliance." It comes over in talk not only directly ("I'm here for you") but also indirectly as you listen to another person and realize (transact) from the talk that he or she really is reliable and interested in your welfare (Leatham & Duck, 1990).

Emotional Integration and Stability

Other people provide you with emotional support in the form of a shoulder to cry on. In daily communication, friends often offer comfort and support in gender-specific ways (Burleson, Holmstrom, & Gilstrap, 2005). They also, however, support your knowledge base. Carl and Duck (2004) indicated how much people rely on each other to verify, support, or do reality checks on the world in their everyday communication. Drawing on the previous work by Weiss (1974), they indicated the importance of using other people as sounding boards for emotions or responses to situations. For example, people often ask friends, "Did I do the right thing?" "Do you think I should believe what this person says?" or even "Should I take this job?" Friends also give you information about the rules for conducting relationships (Baxter, Dun, & Sahlstein, 2001) and offer you advice about other problems in life (Goldsmith & Fitch, 1997).

Opportunity to Talk About Yourself

Opportunity to talk about yourself not only is enjoyable but subtly gives you extra chances to derive the above provisions from other interactions. People like to put themselves into their talk, offer their opinions and views, be important in stories they tell, and otherwise be part of a narrative of their own lives that makes them appear valuable and good. Indeed, one of the main things that makes a relationship more rewarding to people, according to Robert Weiss (1974), is a sense of being known, so it is hardly surprising that self-disclosure largely comprises what happens in relationship growth and maintenance.

Opportunity to Help Others

Humans also like the feeling of being there for others, which is Weiss's (1974) fourth provision. A request for advice is flattering and implicitly recognizes the value of your world of meaning. It also allows you to talk about yourself and thus simultaneously fulfills another provision noted above. Manusov, Kellas, and Trees (2004) examined how friends told and listened to one another's stories about a failure in their life and explored the facework (making someone "look good") done in the accounts. People who asked about the event and then received a very long and complex explanation felt more burdened, despite the fact that the speakers imagined such accounts were more acceptable from the listeners' points of view. So, those who took the opportunity to help others ended up feeling burdened by an overly lengthy response, but at least the speakers appreciated the chance to talk about themselves!

Provision of Physical Support/Reassurance of Worth and Value

Relationships ratify and gratify your world by providing support when you need it. Weiss (1974) divided this support into two provisions: the *provision of physical support* and the *reassurance of worth and value.*

Physical support is offered by friends and relatives: If you have to move a heavy piano, you need other people; or you might need someone to drive you to the airport or look after your pet rat while you are on vacation. These are the favors that friends do for one another as part of the role of friendship.

You may find a subtle reassurance of your worth when someone gives up time for you in this way, but you certainly find it confirming when someone says, "Good job!" "Sure! Drop that jerk. You deserve better anyway," or "I'd love to help solve that with you." More important, relationships show you how other people see the world, how they represent/present it, what they value in it, what matters to them, and how your own way of thinking fits in with theirs. In such talk and action, they reassure your worth and value as a human being (Duck, 2011).

Everyday communication provides reassurance and other provisions seamlessly. People advise, seek advice, help, seek help, encourage, reveal things about themselves, and talk to one another in ways that offer the above provisions all the time, often without being obvious. In the course of everyday life, you communicate with people who offer you ways to check your knowledge of the world, and you share knowledge about other people in return.

Suppose someone praises you ("Great job!" "I love your outfit!" "You did well on the test—and you are making great comments in class. You are obviously a good learner"). What subtle processes are going on? The speaker not only claims the relational right to make comments about you but also shows a desire to connect positively and make you feel good. Organizing, reaffirming, correcting, or otherwise presenting a view of you that affects your knowledge of self and how you appear to other people, the person emphasizes those parts of the world in which you do things right and perform commendably.

Support for an area of your knowledge about yourself transacts validation for that part of your identity. In contrast, criticism undermines confidence about your performances. Criticism also claims the other person's relational rights to comment on you (or else you resent that the person claims such a right: "Who does s/he think s/he is?"). Validation of your world, as well as what challenges or undermines it, demonstrates the tight connection between relationships and what you know and believe about yourself.

Photo 6.1 How does your end-of-day communication with other people transact your relationships? How are the relationships between the people here conveyed and transacted in talk? (See page 156.)

Composing Relationships Through Talk

Talk transacts knowledge and relationships. Part of what is composed during the tight connections among talk, relationships, and knowledge is a range of different relationships. These relationships are recognized by different styles of talk. Every culture has its own way of thinking about relationships, so the transactions of culture and relationships connect very directly in this chapter. For example, Japanese language differentiates more than 200 ways of indicating a speaker and a listener's relationship, and whenever two Japanese speakers converse, they inevitably and directly signal their status relationship at very complex levels. By contrast, American culture often splits up relationships into a very basic distinction between "formal" and "informal." This broad differentiation includes important subtleties (e.g., hookups, cross-sex nonromantic relationships, speed dates, nonresidential parents, in-laws, buddies, "the 'rents").

Types of Relationships Recognized in Talk

People in Western culture differentiate among strangers, neighbors, friends, family, and romantic partners, sometimes within categories. For example, among romantic partners, you can differentiate between dates, affairs, and spouses. Aware of the overtones, you might decide to think carefully about how you sign off on an e-mail, a job application, or a postinterview thank-you letter, recognizing that *yours, love, see ya,* and *cordially* connote different relational messages. When denoting different relationship types, some types are given more value in a given culture than other types. Table 6.1 reviews the assessment of status in Confucian philosophy and in the United States.

Table 6.1 Status and Types of Relationships
Confucian philosophy in Chinese culture represents six basic types of relationships (all of which center on men and five of which are essentially structured as superior–subordinate relationships): emperor–subject; father–son; husband–wife; elder brother–younger brother; teacher–student; and one of equality, friend–friend.
In the United States, titles used in talk, such as *Professor, sis, pal,* and *Mom,* that directly indicate the status relationship of one speaker to another.

Western scholars make a distinction between social and personal relationships. **Social relationships** involve essentially interchangeable people. For example, your relationships with Alice the witchety grub server, store assistants, bus drivers, and prison guards are not truly personal. Any of them could change shifts with other individuals who continue to perform the same tasks and functions. Only specified and irreplaceable individuals (e.g., your mother, father, brother, sister, or very best friend), on the other hand, may engage in **personal relationships** with you. You can't just pick a random person off the street and make him or her instantly into your best friend—and certainly not into your father or sister. You could in time attempt to turn servers, bus drivers, or checkout clerks into acquaintances, dates, or lovers. You cannot, however, just switch people around in personal relationship roles in the way that you could pick one cashier over another and still be served politely in an interchangeable social relationship.

One of the authors was out to lunch with two deans. At the end of the meal one said to the other, "I see you don't like the way they do potatoes here," and the other replied, "Sure, have them if you want." That struck us as a terrific example of the assumptions and taken-for-granted information that give away the fact that two people know one another very well and that each of them can interpret what is said in that light.

Keeping Relationships Going in Talk

Communication theorist Stuart Sigman (1991) considered how even small talk can keep relationships going by acknowledging that the relationship still continues even when the partners are *not* face-to-face and may be apart from one another. Technically this type of communication is called **relational continuity constructional units (RCCUs)**. In less complex and more memorable terms these are simple conversational symbols that indicate that you expect relationships to exist through time even when the partners are physically distant. You can anticipate an absence, acknowledge that you are apart but the relationship still exists, or recognize that you have just met up again and reaffirm the relationship. Sigman divided these symbols into *prospective, introspective,* and *retrospective* types, and they are not as frightening as the names suggest: In fact they are so obvious that you probably overlook them or take them for granted.

Listen in on Your Life

Listen to how you talk with friends differently than you do with strangers during a chosen day. Note the kinds of differences in the relationships involved. How many relationships are with intimate strangers or, more accurately, with familiar acquaintances (people you talk to and whom you know well enough not to ignore but do not feel close to)? Look at the lists you have created in this exercise, and identify the differences between communication with friends and communication with strangers. What topics do you talk about with friends but not strangers? What range of topics do you talk about in each type of relationship? Does the topic, style, or range of topics make a difference between the relationships, or is it something else?

Prospective Units

Prospective units provide recognition that an interaction is about to end but the relationship continues. In essence, prospective units refer to a coming absence, and they create a conversational leapfrog that gets you over it. Prospective units include "Let's set the agenda for next time" and "When shall we three meet again, in thunder, lightning, or in rain?" Other examples are "See you later" and "Talk soon."

Any other form of communication—even nonverbal communication—that suggests the likelihood of the partner's return is also a prospective unit. For example, if one partner leaves a toothbrush in the other's apartment, the toothbrush indicates the missing partner will likely return. It offers recognition that the absence is temporary but the relationship remains intact. Sigman (1991) referred to such nonverbal evidence as "spoors," like the track marks made by deer in snow, that indicate the partner's previous physical presence (and expected return). Grieving parents often keep a dead child's room just the way it was the day the child died, as if they expect a return. Queen Victoria kept Prince Albert's desk and dressing room spick and span for 40 years with a new shirt laid out each day. As noted in the previous chapter, parents of transgender people often experience "ambiguous loss" (Norwood, 2010) because they are not sure whether, during any gender reassignment surgery, they have lost a daughter or gained a son. It takes time for them to adjust.

College Experience

For those of you who recently graduated high school, we have what may be some surprising news. For those of you who have been out of high school for a while, you are well aware of this news but will still learn something about recent research.

Regardless of how many times "B[est] F[riends] F[orever]" has been written in high school yearbooks, very few relationships last after graduation. In fact, you will never again see many of the people with whom you graduated, and most will become nothing but a faded memory. If you are suddenly worried about losing your friends, do not worry too much. You will soon make new even closer friends in college. Also, some high school friendships do last long after graduation. Those that do survive are those in which regular contact is maintained. Cummings, Lee, and Kraut (2006) discovered that high school relationships maintained through e-mail and instant messaging declined less rapidly than those primarily maintained by phone and even face-to-face contact. The authors speculate that these findings resulted more from increased contact through online communication than from any other factor.

Introspective Units

By contrast, *introspective units* are direct indications of a relationship's existence during the physical absence of one partner. The difference between introspective units and prospective units is that prospective units note that the absence is *about to happen* whereas introspective units acknowledge it already has. Examples include wedding rings worn when away from the spouse, greetings cards, phone calls, mediated contact, and, of course, e-mail messages, as well as photos of family on your desk at work.

Retrospective Units

Retrospective units directly recognize the end of an absence and the reestablishment of the relationship through actual interaction. The most familiar nonverbal example is a hug or handshake or kiss upon greeting. The most common forms of conversation that fit this category are catch-up conversations and talk about the day (Vangelisti & Banski, 1993) but also counted are "Hi!" "What's up?" "How ya doin'?" and "Long time, no see."

By reporting on their experiences during the day, partners emphasize their psychological togetherness, as well as a shared interest in one another's lives and the events that happened in those lives during their physical separation. Hence, in these communicative moments, or "end-of-the-day talks," with your partner or friends, you are relating to each other as well as simply reporting what happened. The talk reestablishes the relationship.

Even little bits of small talk often serve relational purposes, and such phrases as *talk soon* do something to compose relationships in everyday life: They reinforce your relationships and establish you as connected with other people. They demonstrate conversationally that the people are important to you and that you want them to know about your life experiences. This connection is the essential function of talk (Chapter 2). People's favorite complaint when they miss someone is that they cannot talk to that person as often as they wish. If you have ever been in a long-distance relationship, you

to progression in the relationship. As feelings intensify, they are just worked out unproblematically and translated into behavior. The relationship develops more or less straightforwardly from emotions without the involvement of—and certainly not with any particular behavioral effort from—the individuals concerned.

How the relationship actually develops in behavioral or communicative terms is often not explained but merely measured as an increase in intimacy assessed by means of scales and self-reports. If people report steadily increasing "intimacy," they must have a steadily deepening relationship. The relationship must have become progressively deeper as their intimacy grew. This theory is often called "the evolutionary course of personal relationships." Think, though: Is it all that realistic? Not at all for those shy, awkward, or inept people who desperately want to relate to others but cannot summon the courage to develop their relationships.

Hess (2000) indicated that people have an extensive range of communicative strategies for keeping disliked people at a distance, from simply ignoring them to treating them as objects to direct and open hostility and antagonism. In normal life people know that unwanted relationships happen and have strategies to deal with them, so the rosy assumption that all relationships develop positively is too simplistic.

The theory represented in this research is, of course, an invention of researchers (Duck, 2011) and is not really real in other ways, either. As Jesse Delia (1980) pointed out long ago, most of our relationships are shallow and do not really develop at all, even with frequent contact. How much deeper is your "relationship" with your regular supermarket checkout clerk than it was the first time you went to the grocery store?

Also, many relationships are deliberately kept at a careful distance, and there are many people you don't ever want to get to know in great and intimate depth (such as your defense attorney, your boss, your professor, or even, in some cases, your roommate).

Weak Ties

By far, the majority of your relationships in everyday life are weak ties of this loose and distant nature (Granovetter, 1973). Can you generalize about the development of relationships, then? The next section explores a different model for relationship progression.

Photo 6.3 How do relationships grow or change, and how does this show up in speech? (See page 156.)

The Relationship Filtering Model

Duck's (1998, 1999) Relationship Filtering Model suggests that people pay attention to different cues in sequence as they get to know someone. Basically you use whatever evidence is available in order to form an impression of another person's underlying thought structure. The sequence in which you pay attention to characteristics of other people is basically the sequence in which you encounter them: physical appearance, behavior/nonverbal communication, roles, and attitudes/personality. At each point in the sequence, some people are filtered out as people you do not want as partners. Only those who pass all filters become friends or lovers. The model follows the intuitive process through which you get to know people layer by layer. It assumes your basic goal is to understand others on the basis of whatever cues are available at the time. At each deeper level, you get a better understanding of how they tick, and you let them deeper into your world (see Figure 6.1).

Basic Facts About Others

Think about meeting and getting to know strangers. When you meet obvious members of your culture, it is reasonable to assume you share common language and probably a set of beliefs about your culture's workings. Typically careful of strangers, however, newly acquainted people engage in safely noncontroversial small talk. You never know if someone is an ax murderer and just hasn't told you yet. The conversation normally stays on safe topics unless you meet in a singles' bar, on a speed date, or in a context clearly intended to promote relational growth (such as "welcome to the neighborhood" events or orientation weeks).

When you meet strangers, all you have to go on initially is how they look and sound. In everyday life when basic personal information is missing, you seek it out by asking questions. Interactions with strangers focus on information gathering, and providing information about yourself. This small stuff covers where you come from, your general background, and perhaps some of your personal views. Mostly, this information appears inconsequential: Who really cares which high school you attended, where you work, or whether you have grandchildren?

Well, the answer is that this sort of trivial information provides evidence about your background—even your religion, socioeconomic class, or style of thinking—that can be useful to your "audience." If you go on to make evaluative remarks about your school, you could give your audience helpful insights into your general attitudes,

Strategic Communication

An interview is a special situation where the interviewer has more personal information about you than you have about him or her. How do you think this inequality affects your ability to build a relationship with this person? What could you do to gain knowledge about the interviewer? Check out Chapter 15 for more information about interviews!

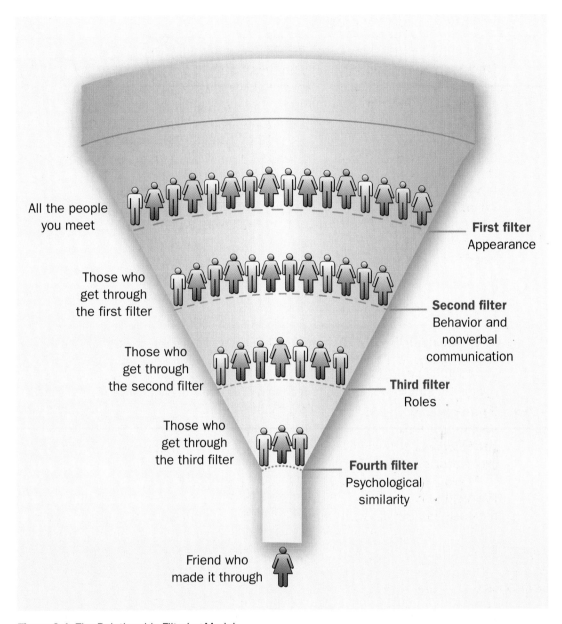

All the people
you meet

First filter
Appearance

Those who
get through
the first filter

Second filter
Behavior and
nonverbal
communication

Those who
get through
the second filter

Third filter
Roles

Those who
get through
the third filter

Fourth filter
Psychological
similarity

Friend who
made it through

Figure 6.1 The Relationship Filtering Model

ways of thinking, and values. These pieces of information might be important in building a picture of yourself that will help other people make a decision. Are they interested in allowing you through to the next filter to become their acquaintance or friend? You can even make some deductions about strangers' looks that might help you judge their values and personality so you know how to talk to them. If someone is young, he or she probably won't have much to say about arthritis, and if someone is wearing a suit and carrying a Bible, you might not start a conversation about Darwinism.

Information and Inference

The more you get to know people—whether colleagues at work or people in your classes—the better your map of their world of meaning. Most of your classmates are, at best, little-known acquaintances. Yet you share some experiences and knowledge that would create some common topics to talk about if you happened to get stuck in an elevator or had to sit together on a long bus journey. You'd have some common topics of knowledge and an idea of each other's position on issues—though perhaps not the depth of understanding that talk with a friend has established.

As Duck (2007, p. 80) notes, however, "The development of relationships is not simplistically equivalent to the revelation of information nor to the decrease of uncertainty. The process of relationship development is created by the *interpretation* of such things by the partners, not by the acts themselves."

In other words, the relationship grows not from the information that you learn about the other person but from how you "go beyond" it. Physical appearance, nonverbal communication, roles, and attitudes are *information-loaded nuggets*. You can "go beyond" them to make inferences about a person's worlds of meaning.

Similarity Begins Near Home

You are much more likely to meet people of the same race, educational background, socioeconomic status, and religion as you. This leads to a tendency to assume, when you meet such people, that you share common values at some level. Later interaction may prove that you share fewer values than you first thought, but at least you began the relationship with a good working hypothesis.

When you first meet people, therefore, the Relationship Filtering Model asserts that you will *assume,* unless they demonstrate otherwise, they are similar to you. Your goal is ultimately to understand them, so the assumptions that you make initially may need to be modified with time. The same principle applies to all other "stages" of the Relationship Filtering Model. Your goal is to understand more accurately how the other person thinks—and sees the world.

The Assumption of Similarity and Difference

When you first see people, even from a distance, you may make assumptions about them just on the basis of their appearance. You can observe their age, race, sex, dress, number of tattoos and body piercings, height, and physical attractiveness. You can also see any marked social stigmas, such as extremely unusual hairstyles or disfigurements, visible disabilities, or physical peculiarities.

Although these cues do not necessarily provide accurate information, people make inferences from such things to the inner world of meaning. The Relationship Filtering Model assumes that you filter out people who do not appear to support your ways of seeing the world or confirming self and thus that they are not prospects for the kind of relationship you like or are seeking.

As you begin to interact more, you can adjust your perceptions in order to make more accurate judgments about whether people are like-able or unlikeable and whether they support your worldviews. If they pass the filter, you may begin to make extra efforts to include them in your social circle.

In all of your filtering interactions, you are really trying to find out what people are like at the level of their deeper worlds of meaning, so you aim all the questions you ask and all the communication strategies you adopt toward finding these deeper selves. The more fully you understand somebody, the more you understand how he or she thinks.

The Relationship Filtering Model proposes this ultimate goal of understanding people's thinking as the goal of all communicative activity in relationship development. The more you understand someone and the more he or she appears to support your world of meaning, the more you want to hang out with him or her and, accordingly, the more you use emotional labels like *friendship* and *love* to represent this connection.

Photo 6.4 As relationships come apart, people, especially couples, find it harder to interact and tend to become more hostile and unsympathetic in their behaviors toward each other. What are the signs that these partners are in distress about their relationship? (See page 156.)

Coming Apart

Unfortunately, not all relationships work, and some come apart at the seams. Duck (1982) and Rollie and Duck (2006) have proposed a basic model to explain the workings of relational breakup—in particular, the conversational changes that take place at different points in the process.

Models of Breakup

The original model (Duck, 1982) proposed five stages, moving from the negative thoughts inside an individual's head to how the broader social network eventually becomes involved with the final story about ending a relationship. This old model focused on the uncertainties surrounding the end of relationships, which involve the partners and others in the network.

In the **intrapsychic process**, an individual simply reflects on the strengths and weaknesses of a relationship. Should it be ended? The person highlights the advantages of leaving over the disadvantages, as well as the disadvantages of staying over the advantages. Next, the **dyadic process** involves confronting the partner and openly discussing a problem with the relationship. This confrontation may be unpleasant or lead to greater understanding and forgiveness. If not, the process goes on to the third phase, the **social process**. Here, the person tells other people in the network about the relationship problem, seeking either their help to keep the relationship together or their support for his or her version of why it has come apart. You would like people to hear your side of things. What's more, you would like them to agree with your presentation! Fourthly, the **grave dressing process** involves creating the story of why a relationship died and erecting a metaphorical tombstone that summarizes its main points from birth to death.

Communication and Breakup

More recently, Rollie and Duck (2006) added a further **resurrection process**, which deals with the ways people prepare themselves for new relationships after ending an old one. The end of a particular relationship is not the end of all relational life, and one of people's major tasks once any single particular relationship has finished is to begin seeking a replacement. The Rollie and Duck model is strongly focused on the types of communication that occur during each process.

Rollie and Duck (2006) discuss the talk *topics* and *patterns* of communication that go with each process. For example, in the intrapsychic process, the person withdraws, reflects alone, and pulls back from the partner. In the dyadic process, the person speaks specifically with the partner and focuses on the relationship itself ("Our Relationship Talks"). Because these discussions take time from other activities, friends may notice they do not see as much of the person as before. In the social process, the person actively seeks greater contact and communication with third parties—not with the partner—to get advice, to cry on someone's shoulder, to get supportive commentary, or even to have his or her evaluation of the partner confirmed ("I always told you he was a jerk!").

The grave dressing process involves storytelling, and you've probably heard a lot of breakup stories yourself. The most usual form of breakup story follows a narrative structure that portrays the speaker as a dedicated but alert relater who went into the relationship realizing it was not perfect and needed work. After all, the speaker wants to look like a good person, not a fool! The speaker then tells of the work that went into the relationship. The partner was unresponsive or unhelpful, or perhaps both partners were mature enough to realize their relationship was not going to work out, so they made the tough but realistic decision to break it off. Such a narrative is advantageous in its presentation of the person. Not as "damaged goods" but as perfectly reasonable, this good relational worker is ripe and ready for a resurrection in a new healthy relationship. So this kind of breakup story projects a person's identity as attractive to other people looking for relationships.

Other sorts of relationship breakup stories normally indicate how a partner betrayed the speaker, but all these accounts follow a basic narrative form (Chapter 2) and make the speaker look OK, if somewhat shocked. Listen for such stories. You can learn a lot about human nature and about particular people by listening to the stories they tell about relationships. Figure 6.2 shows the breakdown process model.

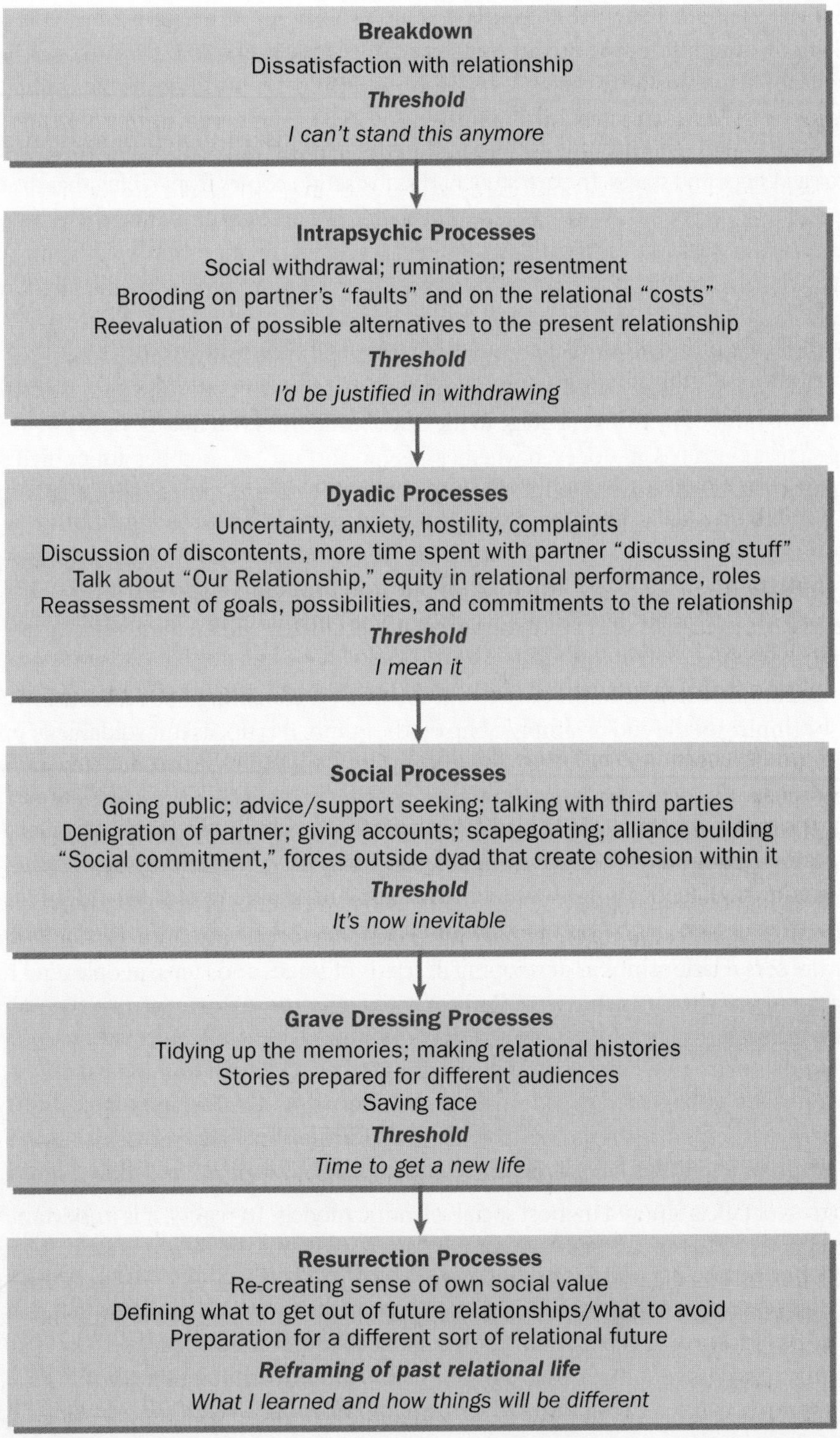

Breakdown

Dissatisfaction with relationship

Threshold

I can't stand this anymore

Intrapsychic Processes

Social withdrawal; rumination; resentment
Brooding on partner's "faults" and on the relational "costs"
Reevaluation of possible alternatives to the present relationship

Threshold

I'd be justified in withdrawing

Dyadic Processes

Uncertainty, anxiety, hostility, complaints
Discussion of discontents, more time spent with partner "discussing stuff"
Talk about "Our Relationship," equity in relational performance, roles
Reassessment of goals, possibilities, and commitments to the relationship

Threshold

I mean it

Social Processes

Going public; advice/support seeking; talking with third parties
Denigration of partner; giving accounts; scapegoating; alliance building
"Social commitment," forces outside dyad that create cohesion within it

Threshold

It's now inevitable

Grave Dressing Processes

Tidying up the memories; making relational histories
Stories prepared for different audiences
Saving face

Threshold

Time to get a new life

Resurrection Processes

Re-creating sense of own social value
Defining what to get out of future relationships/what to avoid
Preparation for a different sort of relational future

Reframing of past relational life

What I learned and how things will be different

Figure 6.2   Breakdown Process Model

So Are There Stages in Relationship Development or Not?

In our experience, students find the linear progression idea built into "stages" both informative and frustrating. Although familiar with the idea that relationships take steps, grow, or pass from one stage to another, they recognize the messiness of life. Relationships do not easily fall into rigid steps and stages. In part, student dissatisfaction comes from seeing that the different types of relationships are not so similar. One date is not necessarily like another, every engagement has unique features, and all personal relationships are importantly different. Life is just too complex to fit into simple boxes, categories, stages, and progressions, but all the same the idea of stages is appealing. How do we reconcile this? Easy! Stages are not literally what happens, but they help us to see how relationships ebb and flow or grow and decline.

That is why it makes sense that you have probably also experienced relationships that have not moved smoothly from one stage to the next. Sometimes you may be hard put to say what stage a relationship is at—or even whether it is "on" or "off" (remember junior high school?). In particular, stage models tend to underestimate the extent of individuals' resistance to progression. In the case of a declining relationship, people very often try hard to stop the decline and do not want it to happen. It hurts! So they often propose to reconcile or make up and stop things from falling apart. Much of their activity seems to suggest that they do not—as the stage models might suggest—see a breakup as inevitable. However, like a map, a stage model is only a guide to the terrain but does not actually look like what you see out of the car window.

Not always obvious to the partners at the time, the breakup of a relationship could be the beginning of the end or simply a blip on the graph. It is not as unavoidable or programmatic as researchers assume. You may already have seen one reason why: Researchers tend to ask people to report on what has happened to them, which of course focuses them on reports of the past ("retrospective reports"). When people give retrospective reports, they fit everything into a narrative structure in the form discussed in Chapter 2. Because they already know what happened, people can shape their reports in a way that makes sense of events—even those that may have been messy or uncertain at the time. Because our culture sees relationships as developing in terms of stages and steps, people tend to report relational activity in such terms. Retrospective reports also accentuate the notion that relationships are plainly goal oriented even when life is less clear cut.

The Accidental/Confused Breakup

The possibility that relationships are redefined quietly and almost thoughtlessly during the progress of talk is ignored in most social scientific models. In reality, it is important to focus on relational change as a whole—not just big changes but the little ones too. Relationship development is not always strategic or conscious or directed in linear fashion. Most often it is based on the uncertainty that surrounds the future outcome of relationships and the different ways they are essentialized in the talk of everyday life.

These bits of talk can lead to questions about the nature and form of the relationships, which is how change occurs. Is dissolution a special case of human processing or just an extension of these processes? It is one more example of how talk changes relationships in the context of uncertainty about the future.

People talk, things happen, and relationship consequences arise. In short, your talk reflects cultural expectations and can lead to self-fulfilling prophecy. Processes of change may be connected to everyday experiences in complex ways and are not necessarily different just because researchers (and particularly researchers' methods) treat them as such. If you listen critically to how talk makes relationships work, we hope you will agree.

You have probably noticed that every relationship that benefits you also brings you difficulties, what Jackie Wiseman (1986) elegantly referred to as the bond/bind dilemma. To be in a successful relationship with someone, you must give something up or be prepared to make sacrifices. If you want to benefit from a bond with another person, you must also be prepared to put up with the binds, such as driving him or her to the airport, and to supply the other provisions of relationships that we discussed at the beginning of the chapter. We humans do not simply *need* these provisions for ourselves but also *supply* them for others, so the provisions of relationships are a two-way street.

Photo 6.5 Do relationships develop and break down in a linear fashion? (See page 156.)

A more complicated illustration of this idea by Baxter and Montgomery (1996) pays attention to the dialectic tensions present in relationships that people have to manage day-to-day. A dialectic tension is essentially a built-in contradiction between two aspects of the same dimension, such as **autonomy–connectedness** or **openness– privacy**. Everyone wants to be autonomous and independent; everyone simultaneously wants to connect with someone else. For that reason, from time to time you experience the tension between autonomy and connectedness and must make choices about how to handle it. In the same way, you recognize that you must be open and honest with your partners in relationships, but you also need some privacy and do not always wish to tell them everything. The operation of these two dialectics, demonstrated in the talk that individuals have with one another, is often very significant in relationships. The simultaneous push/pull that individuals experience in negotiating their relational activities tends to show through in their talk. Once again, it seems that stages are not clearly laid out in relationships but rather that you experience ups and downs, pushes and pulls, and tensions and countertensions in almost all of your relational experiences. If your talk reflects a degree of ambivalence about what is happening in a relationship, that is because relationships are very complicated to conduct successfully.

When searching for a "breakup" photo for this page, the only photos we could find featured women who were brokenhearted rather than men. Even though the picture we finally selected includes a man who appears to be upset, a woman is clearly at the forefront. What does this tell you about cultural views of relationships?

Given all these pieces of evidence, then, it is not surprising that relationships are often turbulent and that stage models of relationship growth and decline can be viewed as too simplistic in the real world. Certainly, as we indicated at the beginning of the chapter, relationships are not simply driven by emotions but are the result of complex management of competing forces handled in both direct and indirect talk.

FOCUS QUESTIONS REVISITED

1. How does your everyday communication with other people *transact* your relationships?
Everyday communication with other people transacts your relationships by supporting your knowledge base and providing some of the psychological and other needs for support and understanding. Several forms of communication serve to include people in relationships, thus transacting the intimacy between them. There are several forms of communication that build support and sustain relationships, ranging from direct intimacy talk to indirect discovery of similarity.

2. How does your talk compose your relationships during everyday conversation?
Talk composes your relationships both directly (for example, through requests for friendship and connection or requests to end a relationship) and indirectly by demonstrating social and personal relationships in the kind of talk two persons engage in. Everyday chit-chat can show that a relationship still exists between two people, and friends as compared to acquaintances tend to take much more for granted and do less explaining in their conversations. Relationships are also sustained by relational continuity constructional units, or small-talk ways of demonstrating that a relationship persists through absence.

3. How do relationships grow or change, and how does this show up in speech?
Relationships grow and change in several ways, as people become more knowledgeable about one another and more relaxed in each other's company. In the early stages of a relationship's development, conversation tends to be about broad and uncontroversial topics, where people need to fill in details about themselves and their past history so the other person can understand. As the relationship becomes more developed, individuals need to fill in less background information and are able to take much more for granted.

4. What are the different types of communication that take place when a relationship is coming apart?
The breakdown of relationships is marked by changes in both the topic of conversation and the audience to which the person communicates. In the early parts of a breakup when an individual is simply contemplating ending a relationship, he or she tends to withdraw from social contact and become very brooding. The second phase of a breakup is characterized by confrontation with a relational partner and less time spent with other friends. A third phase develops where the person decides to tell friends and associates about the breakup and to enlist their support. In the fourth phase, the person develops and tells a story to the world at large, explaining how the breakup occurred and making himself or herself "look good." The final (resurrection) phase is characterized by communication aimed at developing new relationships and letting go of the past.

5. Do relationships develop and break down in a linear fashion?
No. There are many cultural reasons why people would like to believe that there are stages in relationships, but these cultural beliefs tend to force their narratives of relationship into a pattern that conforms with their beliefs and therefore creates a self-fulfilling prophecy. People can make sense of both the development and the breakup of relationships, often a messy process, only retrospectively, and it is easy to make a relationship look as if it moved in linear fashion even when it did not.

KEY CONCEPTS

autonomy–connectedness   153
dyadic process   150
grave dressing process   150
intrapsychic process   150
openness–privacy   153
personal relationships   138

provisions of relationships   135
relational continuity constructional units
  (RCCUs)   139
resurrection process   150
social process   150
social relationships   138

QUESTIONS TO ASK YOUR FRIENDS

1. Write the story of your most recent breakup. Does it follow a neat progression? Have a friend read it and ask you questions about particular details. Does this questioning make you want to revise your narrative in any way?

2. What turning points are there in relationship growth or decline that you and your friends believe you can identify through talk?

3. The next time your friends ask, "How was your day?" ask what they think they are accomplishing. Enter into a broad and fulfilling discussion on retrospective RCCUs and how even small talk serves to maintain relationships during absence.

MEDIA LINKS

1. Look at several Sunday paper sections on marriages and engagements. Check for similarities in attractiveness level between the people involved. Next take these pictures and cut them down the middle. How easy is it to reconnect the right people?

2. Take any movie where a romance develops between two main characters. Does it either develop or dissolve according to the proposal made in this chapter, and if not, how?

3. What models of "true romance" are presented in different kinds of movies? Is the romance depicted in action films, if any, the same as or different from that presented in romantic comedies? In what ways?

ETHICAL ISSUES

1. Do you think that someone who is ending a relationship with someone else has an ethical duty to explain to the other person why?

2. What is unethical about having two romantic relationships at the same time?

3. Can you think of a time when the autonomy–connectedness dialectic presented you with an ethical dilemma (e.g., made you think about lying in order to maintain your freedom without losing a relationship)? Don't use that example, but try to find others.

ANSWERS TO PHOTO CAPTIONS

Photo 6.1 ▪ A husband and wife talking about the books they are reading at the end of the day might compare notes about their reactions to their reading and share their enjoyment. Reading to one another is also a great pleasure to many couples. The activity reaffirms connection and also highlights the parts of the reading that each person values, thus reaffirming the connection of their worlds of meaning.

Photo 6.2 ▪ It is an example of prospective units, providing recognition that an interaction is about to end but the relationship continues.

Photo 6.3 ▪ People self-disclose their inner thoughts, secrets, worries, and concerns as they become closer. This conversation between friends (look at the distance between them, the place where the talk is happening, and their postures) is obviously very intense and deep, not shallow and uninvolving.

Photo 6.4 ▪ The expressions—hostile resentment and dejected resignation—on the two people's faces are clear, and the woman has literally turned her back on the man and is looking upward, as if for help from the skies, while close to tears. The man's closed posture shows difficulty, but the surroundings are comfortable and the man and woman are sitting close to one another, suggesting that they are either at home or in counseling.

Photo 6.5 ▪ No. Relationships do not break down linearly, though people often report as if they do.

STUDENT STUDY SITE

Visit the study site at **www.sagepub.com/boc2e** for e-flashcards, practice quizzes, journal articles and additional study resources.

REFERENCES

Acitelli, L. K. (1988). When spouses talk to each other about their relationship. *Journal of Social and Personal Relationships, 5,* 185–199.

Baxter, L. A., Dun, T. D., & Sahlstein, E. M. (2001). Rules for relating communicated among social network members. *Journal of Social and Personal Relationships, 18,* 173–200.

Baxter, L. A., & Montgomery, B. M. (1996). *Relating: Dialogs and dialectics.* New York: Guilford Press.

Baxter, L. A., & Wilmot, W. (1985). Taboo topics in close relationships. *Journal of Social and Personal Relationships, 2,* 253–269.

Bergmann, J. R. (1993). *Discreet indiscretions: The social organization of gossip.* New York: Aldine de Gruyter.

Burleson, B. R., Holmstrom, A. J., & Gilstrap, C. M. (2005). "Guys can't say that to guys": Four experiments assessing the normative motivation account for deficiencies in the emotional support provided by men. *Communication Monographs, 72*(4), 468–501.

Byrne, D. (1997). An overview (and underview) of research and theory within the attraction paradigm. *Journal of Social and Personal Relationships, 14,* 417–431.

Carl, W. J. (2006). What's all the buzz about? Everyday communication and the relational basis of word-of-mouth and buzz marketing practices. *Management Communication Quarterly, 19*(4), 601–634.

Carl, W. J., & Duck, S. W. (2004). How to do things with relationships. In P. Kalbfleisch (Ed.), *Communication yearbook* (Vol. 28, pp. 1–35). Thousand Oaks, CA: Sage.

Cummings, J. N., Lee, J. B., & Kraut, R. (2006). Communication technology and friendship during the transition from high school to college. In R. Kraut, M. Brynin, & S. Kiesler (Eds.), *Computers, phones, and the Internet: Domesticating information technology* (pp. 265–278). New York: Oxford University Press.

Delia, J. G. (1980). Some tentative thoughts concerning the study of interpersonal relationships and their development. *Western Journal of Speech Communication, 44,* 97–103.

Duck, S. W. (1982). A topography of relationship disengagement and dissolution. In S. W. Duck (Ed.), *Personal relationships 4: Dissolving personal relationships* (pp. 1–30). London: Academic Press.

Duck, S. W. (1998). *Human relationships* (3rd ed.). London: Sage.

Duck, S. W. (1999). *Relating to others* (2nd ed.). Milton Keynes, UK: Open University Press.

Duck, S. W. (2007). *Human relationships* (4th ed.). London: Sage.

Duck, S. W. (2011). *Rethinking relationships.* Thousand Oaks, CA: Sage.

Goldsmith, D. J., & Fitch, K. (1997). The normative context of advice as social support. *Human Communication Research, 23,* 454.

Granovetter, M. S. (1973). The strength of weak ties. *American Journal of Sociology, 78,* 1360–1380.

Hess, J. A. (2000). Maintaining a nonvoluntary relationship with disliked partners: An investigation into the use of distancing behaviors. *Human Communication Research, 26,* 458–488.

Honeycutt, J. M. (1993). Memory structures for the rise and fall of personal relationships. In S. W. Duck (Ed.), *Individuals in relationships* (Understanding relationship processes 1, pp. 60–86). Newbury Park, CA: Sage.

Kerckhoff, A. C. (1974). The social context of interpersonal attraction. In T. L. Huston (Ed.), *Foundations of interpersonal attraction* (pp. 61–77). New York: Academic Press.

Leatham, G. B., & Duck, S. W. (1990). Conversations with friends and the dynamics of social support. In S. W. Duck with R. C. Silver (Eds.), *Personal relationships and social support* (pp. 1–29). London: Sage.

Manusov, V. K., Kellas, J. K., & Trees, A. R. (2004). Do unto others? Conversational moves and perceptions of attentiveness toward other's face in accounting sequences between friends. *Human Communication Research, 30*(4), 514–539.

Norwood, K. M. (2010, April 26). *Here and gone: Competing discourses in the communication of families with a transgender member.* Unpublished PhD thesis, Department of Communication Studies, University of Iowa.

Parks, M. (2006). *Communication and social networks.* Mahwah, NJ: Lawrence Erlbaum.

Paul, E. L. (2006). Beer goggles, catching feelings and the walk of shame: The myths and realities of the hookup experience. In C. D. Kirkpatrick, S. W. Duck, & M. K. Foley (Eds.), *Relating difficulty: Processes of constructing and managing difficult interaction* (pp. 141–160). Mahwah, NJ: Lawrence Erlbaum.

Planalp, S., & Garvin-Doxas, K. (1994). Using mutual knowledge in conversation: Friends as experts in each other. In S. W. Duck (Ed.), *Dynamics of relationships: Understanding relationship processes* (Vol. 4, pp. 1–26). Newbury Park, CA: Sage.

Rollie, S. S., & Duck, S. W. (2006). Stage theories of marital breakdown. In J. H. Harvey & M. A. Fine (Eds.), *Handbook of divorce and dissolution of romantic relationships* (pp. 176–193). Mahwah, NJ: Lawrence Erlbaum.

Sahlstein, E. M. (2004). Relating at a distance: Negotiating being together and being apart in long-distance relationships. *Journal of Social and Personal Relationships, 21*(5), 689–710.

Sahlstein, E. M. (2006). The trouble with distance. In C. D. Kirkpatrick, S. W. Duck, & M. K. Foley (Eds.), *Relating difficulty: Processes of constructing and managing difficult interaction* (pp. 119–140). Mahwah, NJ: Lawrence Erlbaum.

Sigman, S. J. (1991). Handling the discontinuous aspects of continuous social relationships: Toward research on the persistence of social forms. *Communication Theory, 1,* 106–127.

Sunnafrank, M. (1983). Attitude similarity and interpersonal attraction in communication processes: In pursuit of an ephemeral influence. *Communication Monographs, 50,* 273–284.

Sunnafrank, M., & Ramirez, A. (2004). At first sight: Persistent relational effects of get-acquainted conversations. *Journal of Social and Personal Relationships, 21*(3), 361–379.

Vangelisti, A., & Banski, M. (1993). Couples' debriefing conversations: The impact of gender, occupation and demographic characteristics. *Family Relations, 42,* 149–157.

Weiss, R. S. (1974). The provisions of social relationships. In Z. Rubin (Ed.), *Doing unto others* (pp. 17–26). Englewood Cliffs, NJ: Prentice Hall.

Weiss, R. S. (1998). A taxonomy of relationships. *Journal of Social and Personal Relationships, 15,* 671–683.

Wiseman, J. P. (1986). Friendship: Bonds and binds in a voluntary relationship. *Journal of Social and Personal Relationships, 3,* 191–211.

Wood, J. T., & Duck, S. W. (Eds.). (2006). *Composing relationships: Communication in everyday life.* Belmont, CA: Thomson Wadsworth.

7

Groups and Leaders

Researchers have been writing about small groups for years and years and years. Small groups (say, fewer than 15 people)—from committees in Congress to juries to college admissions committees to job interview panels—can affect our lives in multiple ways. Juries, for example, can deprive us of life, liberty, and the pursuit of happiness.

Obviously you want to be sure that groups make good decisions—or at least do not make bad ones. Many questions arise about how group members communicate with one another when they are making decisions and what communicative mistakes they make. Feminist scholars have recently drawn attention beyond the different communicative styles of men and women in groups to marginalization in groups and the effects of group composition on group communication and behavior.

Communication scholars focus on a number of questions about groups. For example, why do groups sometimes make bad decisions even though they have talked about all the issues very thoroughly? Why is group conflict such a common experience? What makes most group meetings so tedious and boring? Does a group leader communicate, or relate, differently than other members of a group (and, if so, in what ways)? How can a good leader influence a group ethically and directly? What sorts of leadership communication styles help a group reach good decisions or complete tasks on time and well? How much difference do leaders make to whether groups get along?

There are many different theories about these questions (Poole & Hollingshead, 2005), including psychodynamic perspectives seeking to understand the psychological forces that lead group members and leaders to act how they do (McLeod & Kettner-Polley, 2005). Others deal with social identity and how groups (try to) make themselves coherent and at the same time distinctive from other groups (Abrams, Hogg, Hinkle, &

Otten, 2005). Some look at a network perspective on groups and explore the connection of one group to another (especially in a larger organization—say, "sales" in relation to "marketing") and of the relationship of one group member to another, whether familiar with each other or not (Katz, Lazer, Arrow, & Contractor, 2005). Others look at how groups form, develop, and change and how communication among members changes in style and form during these processes (Arrow, Bouas Henry, Poole, Wheelan, & Moreland, 2005).

A growing style now is to stress that both group membership and leadership are kinds of *relationships* that exist behind communication in groups (Northouse, 2009). For one thing, a leader needs good relationships with group members, and groups that are cohesive and get along well are usually more successful. By contrast, conflict that happens in groups should be seen not simply as a battle of *ideas* but as a battle between *people who have ideas.* This again makes group activity relational. If you have ever been involved in group conflict in class or with people in your friendship network, you know how painful and difficult it is to deal with. Not really about ideas, arguments, and abstractions, group conflict is about emotions, feelings, and relationships—and the *people* who *hold* the ideas and *make* the arguments.

Focus Questions

1. What exactly is a group, and what makes it different from an assembly, a collective, or a team?

2. Can you define groups only in terms of the kinds of communication that take place between members, or must you look at the relationships that lie behind the communication? Does communication transact the existence and nature of the group?

3. How do groups form, and what changes in their communication?

4. What communicative and relational skills make a leader into a good leader?

5. In what ways are discussions of team-based organizing and communication different from traditional approaches to small-group communication?

6. How can a group promote its own decision-making capacities in more effective ways?

What Makes a Group?

We first must decide what a group is and is not. Is a group just one more person than a dyad and one person short of a crowd? Or is it less a matter of numbers than the activities that groups carry out? In this section, we give you some pointers about how groups communicate or transact their "groupness." Think of any group you belong to, and you have already answered the question "What is a group?" by referencing your sense of *membership.* The key point is that essentially a collective becomes a group once it recognizes itself as one and its members identify themselves as such.

Defining a Group

Beyond the recognition of membership a simple assembly or collection of people is not really a group unless it has a **common purpose.** That is, people are working toward the same goal, or are collected as a group to achieve a particular result (such as a sales group wanting to find ways to increase sales). Beyond that minimum requirement, however, people in groups are *organized,* have *awareness* of one another as *members* of the same group, and carry out *communication* among themselves.

Different groups communicate differently (some formally, some casually), and everyone in a group does not necessarily have to talk to everyone else for it to count as a group. For example, in a college discussion section, the students may all talk to the discussion leader but not to one another. A discussion section still counts as a group rather than a random collection of students because there are a common purpose, a set time to meet, some rules, and a leader (i.e., an implied organizational structure). Most important, the people see themselves as more than just a bunch of folks and as members of something shared.

There are many types of small groups that might be part of your experience: Bible study groups, board meetings, sorority/fraternity committees, friends deciding what kind of pizza to order on Friday night, chat rooms, focus groups, or sets of roommates working out a cooking schedule. In each of these groups, when decisions are made, someone essentially persuades someone else, in the context of the rules that govern the relationship. Everyday life relating involves informal persuasion of people in a group just as persuasive speeches to large audiences have an underlying set of assumptions about the relationship of speaker to audience (Chapter 14). Here, we look only at the processes by which decisions get made by small interactive groups. By and large the principles—the transactive principles of communication now familiar to you—are broadly similar in all of these cases: They depend on relationships.

A collection of cancer patients visiting a hospital for chemotherapy is not a group. The stay-at-home dads waiting outside to pick up their children from school are not a group, although they arrive at the same place at the same time with the same goal (to pick up their kids). If they get to know one another and start to talk routinely, *then* they become a group transacted by talk (their talk creates an interchange of information and creates a sense of belonging). So now they have a recognized, organized, social, or even personal relationship with each other. They shared a purpose all along, but communication and sense of knowledge makes them more than just a collection of bodies waiting for something else to happen.

Photo 7.1 What exactly is a group, and what makes it different from an assembly, a collective, or a team? How many of each of these can you see in this picture? (See page 185.)

Communication and Transaction of Groups

Scholars have most often looked at group decision making in terms of quality of information and message transmission. Much information transfer and decision making takes place relationally. You listen to complaints, give advice, carry out tasks, and do favors for friends without really giving the prospect much thought. It's what friends do for one another, offering advice, knowledge, information, help, and support. The *kind* of communication and how it is carried out makes the group the sort that it is (see Table 7.1).

Table 7.1 Types of Groups			
Type of group	**Primary/fundamental purposes**	**Features**	**Examples**
Formal groups	Task oriented, general management oversight, outcome focused, often legislative or formally structured to run an organization	Membership is restricted or delegated; attendance is expected. There is a clear structure; power is vested in the chair; there is an agenda. There may be formal rules for speaking/turn taking; there may be voting.	Congress, congressional committees, debate clubs, shareholder meetings, annual general meetings of organized bodies, executive committees of unions, student government organizations, legislative assemblies
Advisory	Task specific, usually evidentiary or evaluative, with the intention of producing an outcome that is a focused "best solution" to a specific problem or arrangement of an event	Membership is specific and restricted; there may be a chair, there may be structure, and there may be an agenda. Discussion is usually open, informal, and focused on the weighing of evidence or alternatives. Critical and evaluative argument of different proposals is encouraged.	Sorority and fraternity social affairs committees, homecoming committees, juries, accident investigation boards, review boards for awards and prizes
Creative	Evaluation of concepts or creation of new products or approaches to complex problems	Membership is usually invited. There is a lack of structure; individuals are discouraged from critical comment on the ideas generated by others. The point is to generate as many ideas as possible and evaluate them later.	Brainstorming; consciousness raising; creativity groups; focus groups; test-bed groups for developing specifications and criteria for complex projects, such as the beta versions of new software, advertising logo development teams
Support	Advising, comforting, sharing knowledge, spreading information, and raising consciousness about specific issues	Membership is loosely defined; members come and go as needed; participation is voluntary as and when desired.	Alcoholics Anonymous, breast cancer survivors, grief support groups, study groups, PFLAG (Parents, Families and Friends of Lesbians and Gays)
Networking	Obtaining, building, or sustaining relationships, usually online	Membership is not defined; members join and leave as desired.	Chat rooms, social networking groups, MySpace, Facebook

Many communication courses focus exclusively on deliberate and purposive persuasion, especially in groups that make formal decisions or in public presentations and speeches. There is a relational basis to this kind of communication, too, founded on immediate trust or liking for a speaker with whom the listener is unacquainted.

In contrast, discussion in real-life groups involves interaction with people you know over time. We live in groups, at work, in school, and in the local community, and the effective forms of communication that help such groups reach decisions are focused on set tasks and objectives (such as a team responsible for deciding whether to launch a space shuttle, business associates meeting to decide a sales plan, or a jury deciding on guilt or innocence).

You may not have been in such important decision-making groups or meetings yet, but you may have taken part in a dorm meeting or class discussion about whether or not to do a particular class exercise. You will certainly be familiar with group decision making that does *not* occur in formal groups: for example, family discussion about chores, friends' discussions about pizza toppings to order, and other group decision making that happens between people in longer-term relationships.

College Experience

Students who are unhappy and those who quit school often indicate that they do not feel "connected" to the school or that they feel out of place. What they are actually saying is that they do not feel relationally connected. Relationships with a school are not those between students and a bunch of buildings, sidewalks, and landscaping. Rather, students' relationships with a school are represented in their relationships with faculty, staff, administrators, and one another. If you are feeling disconnected with your school or you just want to enhance your college experience, we encourage you to seek out groups on campus. Doing so will increase your sense of connection as well as bring about a host of other benefits and opportunities.

Formation of Groups

Groups created for experimental purposes and those in real organizational settings develop their own ways to conduct business. Bruce Tuckman (1965), a psychologist, proposed five stages of group development, and another similar phase model was proposed by communication scholar Aubrey Fisher (1970).

Tuckman's Five Stages of Group Development

1. *Forming:* The group comes into existence and seeks direction from a leader about the nature of its task and procedures.

2. *Storming:* The group gets creative. Focusing on its goals, it may become entangled in socioemotional and relationship storms and interpersonal conflict between individuals.

3. *Norming:* The group defines its purposes, roles, and procedures, moving more formally toward a solution.

4. *Performing:* Having established *how* it will perform its task, the group now does so. Members seek solutions to their problems but are careful about one another's feelings.

5. *Adjourning:* The group reflects on its achievements, underlines its performative accomplishments, and closes itself down. A good leader will summarize what has been done, repeat who has been assigned tasks to be done before the next meeting (or by a date certain), and then thank everyone and, if truly appropriate, do some congratulation: "Good job, everyone."

Fisher's Model of Group Progression

- *Orientation:* Group members get to know one another and come to grips with the problems they have convened to deal with.
- *Conflict:* The group argues about possible ways of approaching the problem and begins to seek solutions.
- *Emergence:* This occurs when some daylight of consensus begins to dawn. The group sees the emergence of possible agreement.
- *Reinforcement:* The group explicitly consolidates consensus to complete the task.

Communication and Relationships in Groups

Fisher (1970) supposed that the types of communication in a group would identify, as well as promote, the particular stage. For example, if someone says, "That's a really good idea. I think we're getting somewhere," and others mutter, "Yeah," or just nod, then that would count as emergence as well as moving people to the general sense that they are moving from conflict to consensus. His model helps researchers who watch a decision-making group to see where it is headed or to help it through toward the final conclusive stage. He assumed that the stage of the group produces certain identifying types of communication, whereas we would say it is vice versa.

Speech Style Differences

We have emphasized the importance of everyday communication throughout this book, and you can immediately recognize that groups, whether or not they change their speech styles in the exact stages proposed by Fisher (1970), certainly speak differently than when friends chat.

One feature that makes formal groups feel different is that they affect everyday

Listen in on Your Life

Regular "friendship groups" or "social networks" are not included in Table 7.1. Why do you think researchers would see a friendship group as different from the other types of groups, and does it matter? One obvious point is that friendships have very little structure and are based on the notion of equality, whereas many other groups have a formal structure that gives people different rank or powers. What other differences do you notice between the "groups" you belong to and the "friendships" you have?

speech by adopting rules that alter the patterns of speaking from those of everyday speech. "Will the senator yield?" and "If it pleases the court" are not remarks you often hear outside of formal decision-making groups!

What are the effects of the differences between everyday communication and the confining formal speech that happens in group decision making? For one thing, you must know the right language to belong to a group: The Speaker of the House of Representatives does not begin the business of the day by announcing, "Yo, dogs, wassup?"

Is your family a group? If so, is it the same as or different from the other groups you belong to? Which parts of it make up the group, and how far do you extend membership (e.g., do you count cousins, stepsiblings, or neighbors who are "just like family")? Where are your boundaries?

There is a prescribed formula, not widely known to outsiders: After the Pledge of Allegiance, the chair asks, "Shall the Journal stand approved to date?"

One element of group membership, then, is created by *knowledge of the styles and rules governing talk* in the group. They will differ from everyday life conversation.

A Key Point About Groups and Communication

For this reason—the nature of assumptions in communication and its styles—seeing "the composition" of groups as just a counting of heads is a mistake. Groups are not structures but communicatively related membership systems. It only makes sense to identify the composition of a *collective* in terms of names, ranks, sex, age, and other general demographic information. *Groups* interact not because of their "composition" (numbers of females or males, old or young) but because of *communicative relationships* and the kinds of talk shared between specific people involved.

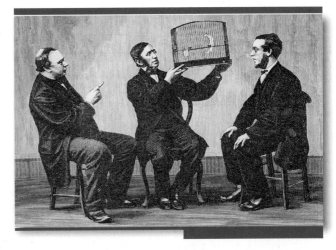

Photo 7.2 Three Scotsmen in 1877 judge a prize canary, their equivalent of a beauty pageant. Which of Fisher's stages do they portray? (See page 185.)

A "group" can be those attending a business meeting or just a set of friends talking to one another to decide where to go for dinner. *All* groups are not simple structures but dynamic, communicative, relationally transacted entities.

Features of Groups

Many different sorts of researchers study groups, ranging from management studies to jury decision making to military mission control. We repeat our emphasis on

Strategic Communication

Recognizing the relational elements of groups will greatly assist you when promoting a particular agenda or decision. Groups are not structured as bodies, numbers, and depersonalized decision makers. Within a general structure sit real human beings who have relationships with one another. Review the following example and consider how it can apply to groups to which you already belong and groups to which you may belong in the future.

The "board of executives'" decision may be influenced by the friendship between Alina and Sangeet. Distrust of six members for the chair makes the group less effective. An agreement made before the meeting by Kristen, Bianca, and Brendan to "stick together on this one" may cause the good arguments against a proposition to fail all the same. A board meeting can be seen as a formal structure in an organization tasked with making top-level decisions, but the specific people put into it will develop personal relationships with one another that can influence their decisions. Within the board, Jim may be friends with Sarah; Sarah trusts Chitra; Juanita resents Jamaal . . . and formal and informal relationships can clash. For example, Sarah trusts Chitra interpersonally, but in a board setting, they both have to act not on their personal feelings but in the service of their own department goals. Success of the group is more important than Sarah's personal trust for Chitra. Anyway, in service of the company Sarah and Chitra may have to carry out tasks that strain their personal trust: For example, they may be asked to decide which of their personal employees to fire so the business can cut costs.

relationships in all cases. Groups are necessarily dynamic interpersonal relationships between members.

Togetherness: Cohesiveness and Relationships in Groups

The members of a group are first defined by their common motives and goals (Thibaut & Kelley, 1959). For example, a city council advisory committee shares the task of coming up with a thoughtful report. A homecoming committee shares the goal of making this the best homecoming ever, with the smartest ideas and themes.

Interdependence

A related feature of groups is that they divide the labor in a way that leads to **interdependence**. That is, everyone relies on everyone else to do his or her part of the job well. The team cannot function properly if its members do not work interdependently. For example, members of a football team are interdependent because the performance of the whole team depends on the coherent yet distinct performance of each of its members.

Interdependence involves the division of labor into particular jobs so the members can achieve their goals. Interdependence works as a transacted outcome of the communication between team players. The coaches and the captain have the job of communicating and coordinating the other members' performances in a way that hangs it all together.

Commitment

Group members usually show *commitment* to each other and to their group's goals when a group is working well (Harden Fritz & Omdahl, 2006). One transactive feature that makes a group "a group" is that individual members share a commitment to the overall group goals. They want to be team players, and communicate that desire in talk and behavior.

The members may also show commitment to one another, watch each other's backs, and look out for one another, particularly in effective groups. The more people share commitment to one another as members of a group, the more they help the whole group move forward toward its goals. The group may show commitment to individual members through caring for their welfare, as well as aiming to achieve the goals of the group.

Cohesiveness

Cohesiveness, essentially another word for *teamwork*, describes people working in unison (Hogg, 1992). You may have seen a motivational poster of a team of rowers all pulling their oars together. They are synchronized and cohesive: They work in time together with one another. If they pulled their oars whenever they felt like it rather than all at the same time, they would show low cohesiveness and keep getting in each other's way. Their oars would clash, and the boat would go nowhere (take it from an Oxford rowing coxswain!).

Another goal of many groups is to maintain high morale and civility by making sure that members do not disrespect each other. Maintaining good relationships between members, another example of cohesiveness, is a goal of any group that seeks to be effective. Cohesiveness, however, or the degree to which members are attracted and committed to one another, is a primary output of groups' social emotional exchanges in talk and thus is a transactional and relational consequence of communication.

Avoiding Out-Groups

In any small group there can develop a power cell of disgruntled folks who feel undervalued, mistreated, disrespected, not included, or overlooked. Often dubbed "out-groups" such people can be either disruptive or constructive, and a

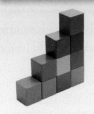

Make Your Case

Consider whether these count as groups: a family; an audience of people watching a football game in a sports bar; an audience at a public lecture on campus; the people watching a movie at the cinema; witnesses to a car accident talking to one another as they watch the police take notes. You might also reflect on whether or not you are in a group when you use the speakerphone feature on a mobile/cell phone in a public place. Who is in the group, and who is out? What communicative features are different in the above cases?

In football, not everyone can be a quarterback; people in the offense have different jobs than those in the defense. The work is divided because the team as a whole shares a purpose: namely, winning the game. The ultimate success of the whole team will depend on whether every member does an assigned job. If everyone tried to do the same task (all tried to throw the ball, all tried to block the other team, all tried to catch passes), it would be ineffective because the other jobs would not get done.

good leader can use them in the better role to challenge and question group assumptions by listening carefully to their concerns.

Disruptive out-groups will tend to prevent the rest of the group from completing its business. Out-groups can, however, serve a useful purpose by making the majority members of the group discuss more options, reflect more carefully on their opinions, answer challenges, and rethink their arguments.

Expectations About Performance

Groups usually expect particular behavior from members. This is a specialized, localized version of the larger society as it makes assumptions and enforces behaviors as a whole on identity (Chapter 5). We saw that others' expectations work as Society's Secret Agents to influence our own behaviors and the performance of our identity. Small groups have more specific expectations about behavior and influence the group itself. Correct behavior elicits a reinforcing response, which then influences further expectations of and for other people. This is another example of the constitutive and transactive way in which communication sustains behavior.

Group Norms

Group norms involve established status relationships, values, and sanctions. They are informal rules and procedures that occur in a group but not outside it. A group norm may be that everyone should speak in turn and that all voices should be heard, as is common in meetings in the Netherlands, for example. Another group norm could be that everyone should speak in order of seniority, follow the leader, or speak creatively without fear of being criticized. Some group norms may require that "nobody rocks the boat and everyone should be a team player." Most groups have a norm that requires mutual respect.

How do various groups to which you belong show their commitment to membership? Don't just list your college "fight song" but report on specific examples of communication that transact commitment.

Negative Norms

Some therapy groups try to break down people's defensiveness about their egos. This is intended to lead to a norm of making honest, even if negative, comments about each other with no attempt to dress them up politely (sensitivity groups and encounter groups; Weigel, 2002).

A stronger version of this norm is found in military training groups. The purpose here, in part, is to break down the recruits' individuality. This can involve insulting them and getting them used to the idea of doing whatever they are told without objecting or answering back. In all of these cases, though, the group sets its own norms and ways of ensuring their enforcement.

Enforcing the Norms

Most groups have their own **group sanctions**, or punishments for "stepping out of line," speaking out of turn, or failing to accept the ruling of the chair or leader. For example, an unruly member—one who persistently violates the norms—may be thrown out of a meeting. This has the effect of silencing his or her participation in, and influence on, the group.

More subtly, everyone else in the group may shun a dissenter and classify him or her as to be avoided outside and ignored inside the meetings. "Shunning," or excluding people from participation in the group, or not even acknowledging their presence, is a very powerful social, relational, and communicative punishment used by such religious communities as the Amish and the Jehovah's Witnesses.

Member Roles

Other expectations about performance concern roles. You know about roles from movies: A role is when someone acts out a part that fits in with parts other people play in "the drama."

Erving Goffman (1959) pointed out that people perform a lot of life as if it were drama, and in Chapter 5, we discussed the *performance* of identity. In many groups the role of leader is key, but groups with a continuous existence tend to mark out other roles as well.

In formal organizations, these roles have titles, like *sales director* or *manager*. If you have ever bought a car, you know that one dealer will often play the role of "the friendly guy" while another one will play the role of "hardnose." That way they can soften you up first and then play hardball in the negotiations over price.

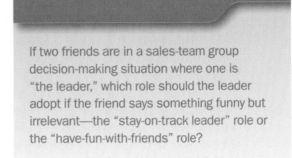

Photo 7.3 Sidelining a player for an offense during a soccer game is a good example of a particular group behavior. What is that? (See page 185.)

Informal Roles

Groups that meet more than once and interact frequently with an expectation of continued future existence also develop roles. In groups of coworkers, "the sales team," or a college discussion section, roles evolve for several people involved. Patterns of interaction that repeat themselves and reinforce these roles evolve as well. People in that group likely will be categorized and informally assigned particular roles ("the joker," "the grinch," "the loose cannon," or "the rising star," for example).

If two friends are in a sales-team group decision-making situation where one is "the leader," which role should the leader adopt if the friend says something funny but irrelevant—the "stay-on-track leader" role or the "have-fun-with-friends" role?

Roles and Traits

The identification of members' roles was based at first on the idea that certain people are better suited to some roles than others or have the personality traits that make them better than other people in certain roles. In particular, leadership in groups was regarded as a role for which some people may show early evidence in traits.

An early hope of research in group processes (e.g., Hollander, 1958) largely grew from research done in World War II. The military wanted to identify future leaders early in their careers and give them fast-track promotion to leadership roles. Even today, the military identifies individuals as "flyers" and places them on the fast track as a result of tests during the first few weeks of their enlistment.

This style of research assumes that leadership is an inborn trait and has run into the objection that it takes too little account of how people adapt to situations and circumstances. Communication in group interaction can generate unexpected skills or adaptations in people, especially since situations are constantly changing and need adaptive techniques. Usually groups have a culture that steers their decisions in particular ways.

Group Culture

A **group culture** is another form of expectation set that affects groups. Group culture is evident in how members talk to one another, the clothes they wear while working as a group, or the special terms and language or jokes they use. For example, an organization may have a formal dress code in the workplace except on "casual Friday," or group members may talk in ways that reflect an organizational hypertext language specific to their particular organization.

Workers on a construction site may have a group culture that particularly values physical strength rather than managerial thinking. Such workers tend to play down any evidence of thoughtfulness. Dennis Mumby (2006) illustrates this kind of group culture when he writes about his experiences as a college student working in a manual labor job. The other workers mocked the fact that, with all his "college boy" intelligence, he could not drive some of the machinery as well as they could. The very use of the term *college boy* to describe him represents, in talk, the group culture that "book learning" is less important than practical skills.

All of these expectations in groups (norms, roles, culture) are important ways of stressing communicatively that a person belongs to a group and must play particular parts in its performances. They all transact the relationships between people, and that communication makes groups what they are (revisit Table 7.1).

In the cult film *Office Space*, one element of group culture in the restaurant where the Jennifer Aniston character ("Joanna") works is the wearing of "flair" (badges and decorations on the servers' uniforms). In one scene, a manager points out that Joanna is wearing only the *minimum* amount of flair and therefore is not demonstrating adequate commitment to the group culture. By the way, the manager in that scene is actually writer and director Mike Judge!

Leadership

In real life, groups usually have an appointed leader. Your first thought is likely that **leadership** is the formal position where a specific person has power over the others in the group: a boss in the workplace, a team leader in a task group, a chair of any committee, or an elder of a religious community. Indeed, such people are required to communicate authoritatively, to run the agenda, and to move the group forward in particular ways that others should follow.

Case in Point

Listen for the norms, roles, and culture of two or three of the groups to which you belong. Identify their differences in terms of each kind of respective group.

Leadership Styles

The classic discussion of leadership, since Bales (1950), has divided leaders into those who are focused on the **task** and those who focus on the **socioemotional** well-being of the members of the group. As discussed below, more recently leaders have been regarded as group stewards or *team* leaders (Northouse, 2009).

Task Leaders

A task leader

- stresses the activity of the group,
- keeps members on topic,
- follows the agenda,
- makes sure decisions get made,
- is responsible for defining the group's intended accomplishment,
- is charged with directing what happens to fulfill the set tasks of the group,
- makes sure the group reaches a conclusion at the end of its allotted meeting time,
- summarizes what got done in a meeting, and
- sets the agenda for the next meeting.

This kind of leader also is responsible for ensuring that proper procedures are followed during the course of discussion. The chair of a committee of Congress, for example, must know the proper rules of parliamentary procedure encoded in Robert's Rules of Order. These procedures may involve such matters as who may propose a motion, the form in which a motion may be proposed, how amendments may be discussed, and the order in which motions must be debated.

Socioemotional Leaders

A socioemotional leader

- pays attention to how everyone feels in the group,
- ensures that members feel comfortable with the decision-making process,

- allows everyone to get a turn in the discussion,
- makes members happy with the outcome,
- keeps the personal relationships between group members on an even keel, and
- manages people's "face" and handles their feelings.

Of course, the task leader and the socioemotional leader can be one and the same. For example, in *Apollo 13*, "Flight" manages to rally his team members by recognizing their anxieties, providing firm authority and so calming them down, inviting their input and inclusion in the discussion, and then forcing them to be realistic.

Different forms of communication are involved in the two tasks (Parsons & Bales, 1955), and a person may be good at one element of the group process (task) but poor at the other (keeping everyone happy). When the two roles are performed by separate people, most often the formal leader focuses on goals at the expense of the feelings of the people involved.

Types of Leadership Power

Talk sometimes creates conflicts between formal power and informal power, making power itself a transactive result of communication. A leader is said to have **formal power** when power has been formally allocated by a system or a group. However, a group may communicate in a way that this power doesn't mean much. For example, the chair may be ineffective, and another member may be better at communicating or more respected than the chair. **Informal power** is based on liking, relationships, and communication competence. This type of leadership power has not been formally granted but rather has been developed through the group's interactions.

Informal Power

John Hepburn and Ann Crepin (1984) studied the relationships between prisoners and guards in a state penitentiary. The formal structure of power seems obvious: The guards are in control, and the prisoners are not. But think again. The system cannot work if only formal power is taken into account. Informal power must also be taken into account within this system.

First, the prisoners outnumber the guards. At any time, if they acted together, they could overpower a single guard, whether or not the guard is carrying weaponry.

There is one obvious example from your own life where a person who appears powerful over you might find things turning around unexpectedly. Your instructors appear to have power over you, but you get to rate them at the end of their courses in a way that may influence their careers or pay status.

Second, the guards' superiors take note of how they handle prisoners. Particular guards get a reputation for being good with prisoners, while other guards are seen as incompetent. The good ones receive bigger pay raises than the others. Once again the prisoners can influence the outcomes for the guards in unexpected ways.

If the prisoners choose to communicate cooperatively with a particular guard, the superiors will see that guard as doing the job well. If the prisoners decide to make a particular guard's life difficult by disobeying orders or showing disrespect in their talk, he or she will be frequently pulled into conflicts. The superiors will eventually see this as evidence of inability to get the job done well.

So the guards need to play along, communicating with prisoners in a constructive and amiable way that helps them develop decent working relationships so they can do their job at all. So who *really* has the power?

An informal system of power also exists among the prisoners: Some prisoners are top dogs while others are not. The guards must pay attention to this informal hierarchy and not treat them all equally. Otherwise, the prisoners will stir up trouble for the guards. Again, power is transacted into being by how two parties relate and communicate.

Power in groups, then, is not always as clear as it seems from group structure. As you can tell, power is always a transactional concept and is always related to relationship dynamics. It depends on acceptance by followers as well as on its execution by a leader.

More Types of Power

French and Raven (1959) went further and distinguished five types of power (see Table 7.2), and indeed the exercise of power is more complicated than it may appear at first.

Table 7.2 French and Raven's Five Types of Power

Type of power	Features of the type	Examples
Legitimate	Conferred by a person's office rank or official status	Police officer, judge, CEO, two-star general, elected political official
Expert	Created through special knowledge of a particular topic	Mechanical engineer, electrician, automotive expert, nurse, lawyer
Referent	Created by the allegiance of one group of people to another person or group	Singers, popular politicians, celebrities, star actors (for as long as they are popular)
Reward	Created by the power to give benefits to other people, or to manage or withhold them	Paymasters; instructors who can give or withhold good grades; lobbyists who can corrupt politicians with bribes, gifts, free lunches, and the usual political trough
Coercive	Having the power to punish (as distinct from withholding of rewards, this means actual applicant of punishment)	Executioners, prison guards, instructors who penalize students for absences from class

Note that a single person can often have more than one of these types of power. For example, a police officer has legitimate power, some expert power (knowledge of traffic law, for instance), and coercive power (the power to write tickets, to deprive you of liberty through arrest, and to restrain you from going where you want to go if it would involve crossing "Police: Do Not Cross" tape). In a group it is more of a problem if the "legitimate power-holder" is not also the expert. If one other member of the team knows more than the boss and so can legitimately contradict some of the boss's ideas, then that can make

Most research on group decision making assumes that the structure and the style of communication are more important than the personal relationships among members. Which do you think is more important?

Photo 7.4 Which communicative and relational skills make a leader a good leader? (See page 186.)

relational life difficult in the group. The assumption that "the leader" has all of the power is not always justified.

Leadership Is Transacted

The preceding discussion really means that leadership is not a trait and that there are complicated social influences from other people in a group. These influence how a leader behaves—and relationships between group members are part of that. This really means that leadership is an *interpersonal process,* not a trait.

Leadership is a communicative relationship between one person and others such that when one gives a direction and another gladly carries it out, leadership has been successfully *transacted* in the interchange. Leadership is not *in a person* but *between people.*

It is true that a leader, manager, director, or department head has real control over resources that other team members need. But French and Raven (1959) teach us that these apparent powers can be undermined by the existence and use of other kinds of relational power. Sometimes, particular members of decision-making groups come up with consistently better ideas than the designated leader, and eventually people start to see those members as the true influencers. Or sometimes followers just refuse to obey.

Recent work on leadership (Northouse, 2009, 2010) has emphasized leaders' roles as "stewards" of either people or resources during their tenure at the helm. This emphasizes that the rest of the group should still be coherent and effective as a team once a new steward takes over.

Of course the term *team* has a rhetorical spin that presents interdependence, cooperation, effective division of labor, common goals, coordination, and mutual respect. Relational communicative terms, no? Relational aspects of an effective team are at least as important as the group's task outcomes. Hence, research on teams places emphasis on making people feel valued as well as getting the job done (Clampitt, 2005).

Any nasty despot can force slaves to build pyramids, but very few leaders can make their underlings feel important afterward. Julius Caesar's leadership qualities included making a point of knowing the names of as many of his men as humanly possible—he had a staggering memory—and addressing each one personally as often as he could. By paying attention to their feelings as people, he built his legions into formidable teams that would do for him what they would do for no one else (Dando-Collins, 2004).

Effective teams and their leaders are therefore interdependent. They all attend to personal relationships and carry out the friendly and respectful communication necessary for truly "personal" relationships. Personal communication transacts a collaborative climate, strong personal commitment, high regard for other team members, and a unified commitment to excellence. This enables the group to achieve its goals as clearly articulated by a good leader (Northouse, 2009). Clarity and purposefulness, two extra features of a leader's communication, thus help the team once interpersonal trust and mutual respect have been built.

Group Decision Making

In the movies, decisions are always important, are always made in futuristic glass-paneled executive suites, and usually have the subplot that one of the group decision makers is an inside traitor (*The Negotiator, V for Vendetta, Michael Clayton, Avatar,* and *Rendition,* to name a few).

In research on group decision making, random strangers are pulled together to make up a group and then given weird problems like deciding how to get back from the moon, using only a few pieces of special equipment.

Real life resembles neither of these scenarios, and for that reason much research on group decision making is remote from your experience. You experience the fact daily that groups of different types make decisions all the time in ways that this formal, stilted, and illusory way does not adequately represent. Most everyday life groups are not made up of extremely powerful people, and most decisions are not based on the availability of unlimited resources. Most important, the most familiar groups that make decisions are composed of people who already know one another both inside and outside the group decision-making scenario. When you and a group of friends decide which movie to see, the stakes are a lot lower than in the earlier examples, but you have to live with the result in your future dealings with these friends.

Even formal groups can come to conclusions and make decisions in a

Many people, including leaders, naively assume that groups are immediately inspired and immediately willing to adapt themselves when a leader proposes a new vision. For at least 100 years it has been documented that this is a stupid assumption, and whole volumes have been dedicated to "resistance to change in organizations."

Cornford (1908) noted that *organizations are motivated to oppose change* and presents their resistance to change in arguments that we can still recognize as opposing any suggestions for novelty. Among these were *the principle of unripe time* (this is not the right time to make this move; let's wait . . . until it's too late to do it); *the principle of the wedge* (if we do this now, then we will be facing a larger problem in the future); and *the dangerous precedent:*

The Principle of the Dangerous Precedent is that you should not now do an admittedly right action for fear you, or your equally timid successors, should not have the courage to do right in some future case, which, ex hypothesi, is essentially different, but superficially resembles the present one. Every public action which is not customary, either is wrong, or, if it is right, is a dangerous precedent. *It follows that nothing should ever be done for the first time.* (Cornford, 1908, p. 17) variety of ways, such as voting, consensus, straw polls, or mandates from the boss. They usually do this when formally in session "as a group." When the people meet informally, business can still be conducted, but in different ways. Informal discussions could still influence the outcome of a group deliberation. For example, a formal committee session may be influenced by a private discussion between the chair and a committee member before the meeting. Likewise, faculty members' votes on a particular issue may be influenced by concerns about tenure, promotion, and fear of future retaliation. Informal meetings and the personal concerns about later consequences are significant and meaningful.

Group Goals and Functions

Leaders are supposed to keep a group on track, but the group often strays onto other stuff because groups are boring and the people want to take account of one another's face and emotionality as well as the task. Formal groups work better when they have a number of objectives very clearly worked out beforehand, but the leader may not be able to hold group members to the agenda.

Much research in communication studies has looked at the best way groups can be sure to make "effective decisions," but since the effectiveness of a real-life decision cannot be known until its results play out, most of this research involves 20/20 hindsight analysis to identify where the group went wrong. Given that reservation, a particularly influential approach to this question is the functional theory of group decision making (Gouran & Hirokawa, 1996). This approach suggests that the "most effective sequence" in group decision making is rather obvious: to define the problem, analyze the issues, establish the criteria, generate solutions, evaluate solutions, choose and implement the best solution, and then develop an action plan to monitor the solution.

It is most important for a group to start with problem analysis. The group must first decide what requires improvement or change in a situation, and to do so, the members must analyze the problem carefully and thoughtfully to ensure that they understand it fully before trying to solve it, making sure they have a good grasp of what is at stake.

Having understood the nature of the problem, the group's next task is goal setting, or what it needs to do to solve the problem. The group must establish criteria by which it can work out whether the problem has been solved and then effectively evaluate whether its solution is better than other possibilities. To do this evaluation, the group must identify and discuss alternative ways to solve the problem and then evaluate effectively whether each will work. Assessing and evaluating the positive and negative consequences of each possibility are important in order to see whether the solution is better than the problem. For example, a medical team that decides to cut off a patient's hand because his or her palm constantly itches has probably not thought the problem through properly or evaluated alternative solutions effectively.

Communication That Helps Group Decision Making

There are three forms of communication that can help a decision-making group achieve its goals, divert from its goals, and get back on track, respectively: (1) **promotive communication,** (2) **disruptive communication,** and (3) **counteractive communication,** as described in Table 7.3.

Table 7.3 Three Forms of Communication in Decision-Making Groups	
Promotive communication	• Helps a decision-making group achieve its goals by specifying them • Works toward moving the agenda along and keeping people on track (i.e., serves their objectives in effective ways) • For example, a person may help the group focus by telling a story about how he or she solved a similar problem (Glidewell, Tucker, Todt, & Cox, 1982)
Disruptive communication	• Diverts the group from its goals and takes it down side alleys • Does not push the group forward toward achieving its goals • Does not help the group toward goals but may raise morale or lower tension • Somebody who tells an amusing story from his or her own life that has very little connection to the group's goals would be a disruptive communicator
Counteractive communication	• Gets the group back on track by reminding its members of its purposes • For example, in *Apollo 13*, Flight reminds the team members that they are telling him *what they need* to solve the problem of how to return the space capsule safely to Earth, and he is telling them what they have to work with. In short, he uses counteractive communication to bring them back to reality and to tell them that resources are limited and unalterable—they simply must work within the available means.

Leadership and Group Decision Making Are About Relationships

In discussing the group decision-making process, we have pointed out that group culture, group history, group future, group norms, and cohesiveness or conformity are all in their own way relationship concepts (see Table 7.4).

Bad Group Decisions

An attempt to be cohesive at the expense of anything else, however, can sometimes get in the way of a group's effective functioning. If everyone wants to keep everyone else happy rather than make tough decisions, this leads to a special kind of *conformity*. Sometimes, people would rather preserve good relationships than make good decisions.

Irving Janis (1972) famously referred to this negative kind of consensus-seeking cohesiveness as "groupthink." In groupthink, members place a higher priority on keeping the process running smoothly and agreeably than they do on voicing opinions that contradict the majority opinion. The group prefers the well-being of its members, morale, and teamwork at the expense of proper critical evaluation of ideas. Groupthink can result in faulty decision making because a group prefers to be a *happy* ship rather

Table 7.4 Relationship Concepts in Group Decision Making	
Group culture	The relationships that exist between the people in a group
Group history	A sense of collectivity and common origin, which, as you recall from Chapter 5 on identity, is important in how people and groups enact themselves. Groups are often aware that they have to live up to their own history and not let down those who have gone before them
Group future	Indicates that the members of a group feel they will still be connected and committed in the future (many lab research groups lack this sense)
Group norms	Defined ways of behaving that set the standard for that behavior
Cohesiveness	How people treat one another and regard the group as an important relational component of their common life irrespective of the achievement of other goals
Conformity	Going along with the group even if you disagree; adopting a style of dress, behavior, or language that makes you fit in through a strong desire to be accepted or liked
Groupthink	A type of conformity based on the desire to have a happy consensus in the group rather than a real debate about the issues; unwillingness to disagree caused by desire not to upset others in the group

Photo 7.5 What (usually undesirable) characteristic of groups is depicted in this photograph? (See page 186.)

than a ship going in the right direction. Although usually a good thing, cohesiveness can lead to negative consequences.

Group Decision Making and Persuasion

Persuasion is based on relationships, even in groups. Your friends persuade you and you persuade them, but people in groups reach decisions in a more formal way than friends do day-to-day. The question is really whether the formality of groups changes how persuasion works or whether relationships lie at the bottom of it all.

Because power in groups is manifold (see Table 7.2), leaders do not always get their own way. Your relational standing in the group will influence whether people do what you want. Bosses control resources (such as pay), agenda, policy, and other norms to do with dress code and organizational expectations, so they are supposed to have power in an organization. Incompetent, bullying, and authoritarian bosses can rule with a stick, but everyone still hates them and often takes any quiet chance to undermine them in everyday chatter around the water cooler and in privately circulated e-mail exchanges. By contrast, popular and inclusive or supportive bosses and leaders can get people to do more than absolutely required and encourage greater efforts without force. In these cases, people do what their bosses ask because they like them and do not resent the request (referent power).

Group Decisions Are Influenced by Outside Relationships and Interactions

Formal group decision making is normally presented in textbooks as if it were a rational type of interaction, where groups sit around and work through decisions smartly and thoughtfully. This just seems to be wrong, and if you have ever sat in on a group making a decision, you will know that.

The type of decision making that gets overlooked in all the books is the everyday persuasion that is often masked or unnoticed. When you separate decision making into the activities of groups in meetings, you tend to overlook just how much persuasion of group members actually occurs in other settings for other reasons. Sometimes, people vote for a proposal not because it is compelling but because they like the person who proposed it or dislike the person who opposed it, for instance. Groups are made up of *people.* Members (e.g., members of a work team) have relationships with one another *outside* as well as *inside* their meetings. After the formal discussion, when the group splits up, the members go on with the rest of their lives, which can mean chatting to other group members in places outside the group. Real-life groups exist continuously both as groups (e.g., "The work team meets every Friday," "Bible study group is Wednesday night," "The book club meets every Thursday") and as individuals whose lives may be connected outside the group (e.g., two members of the same work team may be friends, Bible study group members may also be neighbors, book club members could be in the same family).

All your lives, you are embedded in various groups: families, workplace groups, friends, servers/diners, salespeople/shoppers. Our point is that these outside-world processes of interpersonal communication can apply even to formal, small-group decision making. Instead of isolating group decision making like a big animal in a zoo that needs its own diet and treatment, it makes more sense to see all human communication as part of the same interdependent ecosphere where creatures (like family communication or persuasive speeches) roam in different spaces but, as it were, essentially share about 99.9% of the common communication DNA.

In real life, people *do* sit down and make actual decisions about what to do, but often the banal routine of everyday life does it for them. If you know it is your job to clean up the dishes after a meal on Wednesday night, the group does not have to keep deciding it. Sometimes you may need reminding about an existing decision still in force ("It's Wednesday, your day for the dishes"). A group can also, of course, sit down and make a decision again and change the roster. Most of the time, however, previous decisions are assumed to still be in force and have power, unless they are explicitly brought up for reconsideration.

It is a mistake to overlook the influence on groups and leaders defined by preexisting decisions. If your group has a ritual way of "doing Friday night," few decisions are needed on any particular Friday. Everything just follows the regular path. People show up at the expected time and place without being reminded, and then the Friday runs the

Contrarian Challenge

The research literature in interpersonal communication concerning group decision making is most often attentive to formal groups that have power and resources. Although the studies that have been done to test theories of group decision making were often based on more limited types of groups with few resources, the intention was always for the results to apply to those groups in the outside world that are more fully endowed with importance and possibility. To what extent does this literature on group decision making actually apply to real life as you know it? Is it legitimate to make broad generalizations using limited types of groups?

same course as always. Everyone is happy and does not sit down to decide to change the ritual.

You are influenced by your groups whether you notice it or not, just as your interaction with specific people (as we saw in Chapter 5 when thinking about symbolic interactionism) brings out your identity in interesting ways.

What we have written about decision making draws on the existing research literature about it with skepticism. A tension exists between treating group decision making as a special case of human behavior and seeing it as a species of behavior that has more in common with the rest of life. In this textbook, we emphasize the relational underpinnings of every aspect of life. We see this underpinning as the core of most behavior that happens during communication episodes—whether or not they happen in groups.

FOCUS QUESTIONS REVISITED

1. **What exactly is a group, and what makes it different from an assembly, a collective, or a team?**

A group may be regarded as an organized structure composed of individuals having a common purpose, interdependence, and division of labor. The key elements that make a group different from a random collection of people, however, are that group members are aware of one another as such and communicate it through their talk. Groups are different from teams in that teams are more concerned with the strength of the relationships among members and involve mutual respect and concern among members. Team members want to avoid anyone in the group feeling bad about a particular outcome or decision.

2. **Can you define groups only in terms of the kinds of communication that take place between members, or must you look at the relationships that lie behind the communication? Does communication transact the existence and nature of the group?**

Group communication is all about everyday talk and relationships, especially the relationships between people who have, hold, and use different sorts of information in the group. Indeed, it is not so much that groups transact communication but that, when communication and relationships are seen as interconnected, the very notion of a group is a transacted and symbolic concept. Through communication, the group members see themselves as belonging to a group, and the group sees itself as an entity with meaning sustained and created by its own symbolic actions. Groups are not structures or composites but dynamic human relationships and processes transacted within and by means of norms and roles.

3. How do groups form, and what changes in their communication?

The formation of groups has most often been studied in experimental settings, and how they form in normal life has been less clearly understood. Where formation of groups has been studied, it appears that changes in the nature of talk occur, with the first stages being general orientation toward one another and the later stages representing discussion or conflict, which resolves itself in the solution of a task and is followed by mutual congratulation. In longer-term groups, not simply focused on the completion of a particular task in a specific time frame, people will more likely move from formal and superficial talk toward deeper and more meaningful personal talk, much in the way that self-disclosure occurs, though they will also focus their talk on any tasks or objectives the group has in front of it.

4. What communicative and relational skills make a leader into a good leader?

Leaders need to focus on the task and have knowledge that allows them to direct and guide other people toward its completion. A good leader is also able to handle the socioemotional activity in a group and make people feel they are valued members of a team. A really good leader has a combination of communicative skills that help solve problems and present judgment clearly, listens carefully to understand other people's perspectives, and is able to reflect the value of members' contribution to the team. Frequent communication with team members and openness of communication that lets people know what is going on help sustain members' sense of value to the group. Clarity and purposefulness are also communicative features of a good leader.

5. In what ways are discussions of team-based organizing and communication different from traditional approaches to small-group communication?

Team-based organization and communication differ from traditional approaches to small-group communication in that they place much more emphasis on the value, personal feelings, mutual respect, and internal cohesiveness of the members of the team. The division of labor, and the interdependence of team members specifically, builds bonding among them that can outlast the tenure of a particular steward of the team. The team, therefore, does not fall apart once the leader is changed, and the emphasis of team-based organization is to sustain the team as a coherent, self-respecting, and mutually respecting unit, irrespective of the specific problems it is dealing with at a particular time and of the leader nominally in charge for the moment.

6. How can a group promote its own decision-making capacities in more effective ways?

A group can promote its own decision-making capacities by setting a definitive agenda, doing a thorough problem analysis, assessing its goals, and thoroughly assessing alternative possibilities. The group should establish its goals explicitly and realistically, setting goals that are attainable within a specified timeline, and have clear criteria by which it can evaluate the outcomes. Promotive communication and counteractive communication are ways to keep groups on task.

KEY CONCEPTS

cohesiveness   169

common purpose   163

counteractive communication   179

disruptive communication   179

formal power   174

group culture   172

group norms   170

group sanctions   171

informal power   174

interdependence   168

leadership   173

promotive communication   179

socioemotional   173

task   173

QUESTIONS TO ASK YOUR FRIENDS

1. How does your group of friends decide what to do on Friday night? Ask your friends this question to determine their perspective. Which processes discussed in this chapter can you see at work there?

2. Who do your friends think is a good leader, and what makes a person so?

3. What group norms and rituals can you identify in the small groups and organizations to which you belong? Ask your friends in these groups this question and then compare answers.

MEDIA LINKS

1. The following three movies offer good instances of groups in action and cover some of the concepts discussed in this chapter: *Office Space, Apollo 13,* and *12 Angry Men* (the original Henry Fonda black-and-white version). Each movie demonstrates something different about groups: The opening sequence of *Office Space,* for example, gives you a good idea of a group culture, and some of the characters represent different leadership styles (analyze Lumbergh's—ugh!—power and leadership style). *12 Angry Men* demonstrates how a task leader can bring emotionally led individuals back on track by using promotive communication but also handle the socioemotional concerns of different members. What aspects of leadership and group norms can you identify in the group communication that takes place in *Apollo 13?*

2. The next time you are in a group, pay attention to any discussions about media. For instance, someone might bring up a television program viewed the previous evening or a newly discovered website. In what ways could such discussions be considered

disruptive communication? In what ways could such discussions actually enhance group relationships?

3. In any reality shows you watch, how do groups form, what are their dynamics and transactions, and what are their weaknesses?

ETHICAL ISSUES

1. Some say that leaders must use authority to mobilize people to face tough decisions when the followers are struggling with change and personal growth. Others stress that leaders should take care of and nurture their followers. What do you think?

2. Should groups and organizations do what is right even if it results in lower dividends to stakeholders to help finance their operations? For example, should oil companies make more real and substantial contributions to environmental protection even if it means that shareholders receive no dividend in a particular year? Should tobacco companies stop selling cigarettes?

3. What conditions would make it wrong, and what conditions would make it right, to blow the whistle on your group irrespective of the consequences to you personally?

ANSWERS TO PHOTO CAPTIONS

Photo 7.1 ■ A group has a common purpose, and members are aware of each other, have organization, and communicate with one another. A collective may have a common purpose but lack organization, so the audience (which has to be imagined in this picture, as is so often the case in English cricket, an exceptionally tedious game to watch) is a collective. Each side in the game is a team as well as a group, since the members (presumably) care for one another's welfare and play together more effectively by creating chances for each other or not trying to do it all on their own. It is hard to tell one from the other in cricket, where both sides wear all white, but the one with the bat is on one side and the others are on the other side. The man in black trousers is the umpire. The people sitting in chairs are most likely players on the batsman's side waiting their turn to bat. Contact the authors on Facebook for an explanation of the rules.

Photo 7.2 ■ Orientation. They are sizing up the problem before they begin to offer their competing views.

Photo 7.3 ■ The use of group sanctions to enforce norms. People who break the rules are not allowed to stay in the group until they have repented, apologized, or served a fixed amount of penalty time. The "silent treatment" is another example of this group sanctioning, where people refuse to speak to a group member who disobeys norms or does not support the group. In England the term *sending someone to Coventry* is used to describe the refusal of trade union members to speak to another member who has not backed a strike. It can last from a few days to several years.

Photo 7.4 ▪ The ability to identify with the audience shows understanding of their concerns, a sharing of their feelings, and having answers that will work. A good leader focuses people on issues, motivates people to address solutions, and helps them to achieve their goals. Leadership is not in a person but is transacted between people, as the leader acts as steward of their interests, for the moment.

Photo 7.5 ▪ Conformity. They all look exactly alike, and in humans this can indicate an undesirable overruling of independence by the desire to be accepted. Look around you and observe that conformity can often be paradoxical: All students look alike in *not* looking the same (sweatshirt, jeans, possibly a baseball cap).

STUDENT STUDY SITE

Visit the study site at **www.sagepub.com/boc2e** for e-flashcards, practice quizzes, journal articles and additional study resources.

REFERENCES

Abrams, D. B., Hogg, M. A., Hinkle, S., & Otten, S. (2005). The social identity perspective on small groups. In M. S. Poole & A. B. Hollingshead (Eds.), *Theories of small groups: Interdisciplinary perspectives* (pp. 99–137). Thousand Oaks, CA: Sage.

Arrow, H., Bouas Henry, K., Poole, M. S., Wheelan, S., & Moreland, R. (2005). Traces, trajectories and timing: The temporal perspective on groups. In M. S. Poole & A. B. Hollingshead (Eds.), *Theories of small groups: Interdisciplinary perspectives* (pp. 313–367). Thousand Oaks, CA: Sage.

Bales, R. F. (1950). *Interaction process analysis.* Cambridge, MA: Addison-Wesley.

Clampitt, P. G. (2005). *Communicating for managerial effectiveness.* Thousand Oaks, CA: Sage.

Cornford, F. M. (1908). *Microcosmographia academica: Being a guide for the young academic politician.* Cambridge, UK: Bowes & Bowes Publishers.

Dando-Collins, S. (2004). *Caesar's legion: The epic saga of Julius Caesar's elite tenth legion and the armies of Rome.* Chichester, UK: Wiley.

Fisher, B. A. (1970). Decision emergence: Phases in group decision making. *Speech Monographs, 37,* 53–66.

French, J. R. P., Jr., & Raven, B. (1959). The bases of social power. In D. Cartwright (Ed.), *Studies in social power* (pp. 48–67). Ann Arbor: University of Michigan Institute for Social Research.

Glidewell, J. C., Tucker, S., Todt, M., & Cox, S. (1982). Professional support systems—The teaching profession. In A. Nadler, J. D. Fisher, & B. M. DePaulo (Eds.), *New directions in helping 3: Applied research in help-seeking and reactions to aid* (pp. 163–184). New York: Academic Press.

Goffman, E. (1959). *Behaviour in public places.* Harmondsworth, UK: Penguin.

Gouran, D. S., & Hirokawa, R. Y. (1996). Functional theory and communication in decision-making and problem-solving groups. In R. Y. Hirokawa & M. S. Poole (Eds.), *Communication and group decision making* (2nd ed., pp. 55–80). Thousand Oaks, CA: Sage.

Harden Fritz, J. M., & Omdahl, B. L. (2006). Reduced job satisfaction, diminished commitment, and workplace cynicism as outcomes of negative work relationships. In J. M. Harden Fritz & B. L. Omdahl (Eds.), *Problematic relationships in the workplace* (pp. 131–151). New York: Peter Lang.

Hepburn, J. R., & Crepin, A. E. (1984). Relationship strategies in a coercive institution: A study of dependence among prison guards. *Journal of Social and Personal Relationships, 1,* 139–158.

Hogg, M. A. (1992). *The social psychology of group cohesiveness: From attraction to social identity.* London: Harvester Wheatsheaf.

Hollander, E. P. (1958). Conformity, status and idiosyncrasy credit. *Psychological Review, 65,* 117–27.

Janis, I. (1972). *Victims of groupthink.* Boston: Houghton Mifflin.

Katz, N., Lazer, D., Arrow, H., & Contractor, N. (2005). The network perspective on small groups: Theory and research. In M. S. Poole & A. B. Hollingshead (Eds.), *Theories of small groups: Interdisciplinary perspectives* (pp. 277–312). Thousand Oaks, CA: Sage.

McLeod, P. L., & Kettner-Polley, R. (2005). Psychodynamic perspectives on small groups. In M. S. Poole & A. B. Hollingshead (Eds.), *Theories of small groups: Interdisciplinary perspectives* (pp. 63–97). Thousand Oaks, CA: Sage.

Mumby, D. K. (2006). Constructing working-class masculinity in the workplace. In J. T. Wood & S. W. Duck (Eds.), *Composing relationships: Communication in everyday life* (pp. 166–174). Belmont, CA: Wadsworth.

Northouse, P. G. (2009). *Introduction to leadership concepts and practices.* Thousand Oaks, CA: Sage.

Northouse, P. G. (2010). *Leadership: Theory and practice* (5th ed.). Thousand Oaks, CA: Sage.

Parsons, T., & Bales, R. F. (1955). *Family, socialization and interaction process.* Glencoe, IL: Free Press.

Poole, M. S., & Hollingshead, A. B. (2005). *Theories of small groups: Interdisciplinary perspectives.* Thousand Oaks, CA: Sage.

Thibaut, J. W., & Kelley, H. H. (1959). *The social psychology of groups.* New York: Wiley.

Tuckman, B. W. (1965). Developmental sequence in small groups. *Psychological Bulletin, 63,* 384–399.

Weigel, R. G. (2002). The marathon encounter group—vision and reality: Exhuming the body for a last look. *Consulting Psychology Journal: Practice and Research, 54,* 186–198.

8

Culture and Communication

As we begin our exploration of culture, we want to address two issues involving the ways in which people often think about culture. First, when most people think of culture, they tend to think of it as something involving *other* people—wearing unusual clothes, eating strange foods, participating in odd customs, living in unique structures (bamboo huts, Roman temples, Chinese pagodas), and doing strange things with coconuts and tulips.

However, what is considered abnormal by one culture is considered perfectly normal by another. In fact, *you* perform cultural practices and communicate in ways that those from another culture might regard as odd, even though these practices and ways of communicating may seem to you to be natural and right. For instance, if you follow a traditional U.S. approach to time, many cultures would view arriving at a very specific time quite strange, utterly obsessive, absurd, and valueless. After all, you should stop to the smell the roses, or the tulips. In short, it seems just as normal and natural and right to the Japanese, the Italians, the Serbo Croatians, and the Tutsi to act the way they do as it does to you to do what you do.

Believing that your culture is the benchmark for all others is called **ethnocentric bias**: Your own cultural way of acting is right and normal, and all other ways of acting are only variants of the only really good way to act (yours!). If

As you study the material in this chapter, it will be important to be as detached as possible and to treat your own culture as objectively as you treat others—as far as that can be achieved. Cultural influences run so deep within your routine talk and relational performance that you do not recognize them at first, but this chapter shows you how.

this manner of thinking seems familiar, you are not alone, and it does not necessarily make you a bad person. However, appreciating and recognizing the value of other cultures will assist you personally and professionally, especially given an ever-expanding multicultural world. Doing so will also increase your appreciation for and understanding of your own cultural behaviors.

The second issue to address is that many people think of culture as something that is possessed or something to which a person belongs. Actually, you do not just have or belong to a culture; you *transact* and *perform* culture. This notion is similar to that discussed in Chapter 5 when examining identities. Identities and cultures are transacted (or constructed) symbolically and performed when interacting (or relating) with other people.

Accordingly, cultures do not create different communication; rather, different communication creates cultures. Thus, cultural groups are distinct not because they live in different places but because they communicate in different ways. Culture is created symbolically, not through positioning in a physical location.

Of course, relationships remain fundamental to the actual creation and maintenance of culture. Using the relational perspective to examine identities in Chapter 5, we noted that the only way you ever meet *society* is through other people you meet. Similarly, your exposure to *culture,* whether your own or another, is not exposure to an abstraction. You meet culture when you encounter people performing that culture; you perform your own culture when you communicate with other people. Society's (and Culture's) Secret Agents are the very friends you meet, other people on the streets, human beings you observe, and everyone who communicates with you.

In what follows, we examine the two primary approaches to identifying and studying culture: structured and transacted. From a structural approach, we discuss cultural differences concerning context, individualism/collectivism, time, and conflict. Examining culture as a transaction, we further explore the connection between culture and communication using a relational perspective. Specifically, we examine how culture is embedded in communication and how cultural membership is enacted or denied through communication.

Focus Questions

1. What does it mean to view culture as structured?
2. What does it mean to view culture as transacted?
3. How is communication organized to reflect cultural beliefs about context, collectivism/individualism, time, and conflict?
4. What does it mean to say culture is coded into communication?
5. What does it mean to say that cultural groups are created through communication?
6. How do people enact cultural membership through communication?

How Can Culture Be Identified and Studied?

We begin our exploration by examining how culture has been identified and studied. As mentioned above, the two primary ways in which culture has been examined are as a structure and as a transaction. The most common approach to studying culture has been to view it as structural. Increasingly, however, the limitations of this perspective have become more obvious. Nevertheless, using this approach has provided a wealth of information about culture and should not be shoved aside without full consideration.

Culture as Structured

Viewing *culture* from a structural standpoint has a long history in the communication discipline. This way of seeing culture focuses on large-scale differences in values, beliefs, goals, and preferred ways of acting among nations, regions, ethnicities, and religions. We could therefore differentiate Australian, Indian, Japanese, Dutch, and Canadian cultures. Clear distinctions could be made between Eastern and Western cultures and the communication styles displayed among people of these areas.

Cross-Cultural Communication and Intercultural Communication

A great deal of valuable research has been conducted from a structural standpoint, examining communication within and among nations or physical regions. This research is usually referred to as cross-cultural communication or intercultural communication.

Cross-cultural communication compares the communication styles and patterns of people from very different cultural/social structures, such as nation-states. For example, Seki, Matsumoto, and Imahori (2002) looked at the differences in intimacy expression in the United States and Japan. They found that the Japanese tended to think of intimacy with same-sex friends in relation to such expressive concepts as "consideration/ love" and "expressiveness" *more* than did the Americans. The Japanese placed *more* stress than the Americans on *directly* verbalizing their feelings when considering intimacy with mother, father, and same-sex best friend. On the other hand, Americans placed more value than the Japanese on *indirectly* verbalizing their feelings for others.

Examining the influence of social networks on romantic relationships, Jin and Oh (2010) discovered that Americans tend to involve their friends and family in romantic relationships more often than Koreans. Social networks among Americans also provide more support for romantic relationships.

As Nakayama, Martin, and Flores (2002) point out, White adults and especially "white children do not need to attend to the norms and values of minority groups unless they have direct exposure in their neighborhoods and schools. Minority children, however, are exposed to and compare themselves to [the dominant] white cultural norms through television, books, and other media" (p. 103). Whereas White people can act without knowledge or sensitivity to other cultures' customs in a White society, minority groups are rapidly disciplined for failing to observe White cultural norms.

Listen in on Your Life

Consider the television programs and fairy tales you enjoyed as a child and their accompanying cultural themes. For example, many children's programs in the United States stress the importance of a person's individuality and his or her ability to achieve everything he or she desires through hard work and determination. This belief accompanies the U.S. beliefs in rugged individualism and achievement. What was your favorite program as a child? What themes were reinforced?

Intercultural communication deals with how people from these cultural/social structures speak to one another and what difficulties or differences they encounter, over and above the different languages they speak (Gudykunst & Kim, 1984). Chiang (2009), for instance, examined office-hour interactions involving international teaching assistants and American college students. Potential linguistic and cultural issues were isolated, and strategies for improving communication among these groups were offered.

Examining cultural metaphors related to health care, Le and Chiu (2009) examined Asian views of health care in Australia. The purpose of their research was to assist health care providers and patients in understanding respective views of medicine and the implications of health care.

Limitations and Benefits

While this view of culture has provided a better understanding of different groups and has improved interactions among people, it is not without its limitations. For example, when you start looking at cultures as identifiable national or regional groups, you rapidly notice some important points: First, multiple "cultures" exist in one national or regional group. Second, multiple *social communities* coexist in a single culture and talk amongst themselves as part of their conduct of *membership* (for example, bikers, car mechanics, vegetarians, and ballet dancers).

Nevertheless, from a communication point of view, we can study how all members of a nation partake of the customs or beliefs of the nation and its communication patterns and styles. Although broad, such distinctions nevertheless seep down to a person's way of thinking, and they are structured into meaning systems used in everyday communication. Accordingly, while a social community of construction workers (or any other group) may communicate in unique ways, members' styles of communication are still impacted by those of the larger social structure in which they are embedded.

Culture as Transacted

As we have maintained throughout this book, it is through communication (or symbolically) that relationships, identities, meanings, and realities are created or transacted. Culture is no exception. As we have also maintained, relationships are key to realizing and understanding how it all happens. Culture is an ideal example. You belong to sets of people who share meanings and styles of speaking, systems of beliefs, and customs. In other words, you live your life in the context of communicating sets of individuals who transact universes of thought and behavior, which emerge and are supported through unique cultural styles of communication.

Cultural ways of communicating, beliefs, and values are established and imposed through everyday communication. You are constantly reminded of them by your contacts with other people (Society's/Culture's Secret Agents). Your conformity to culture is constantly and almost invisibly reinforced in the daily talk that happens informally in the interactions with such agents as your friends, your family members, your coworkers, and even strangers. The nature of culture and your connection to society is conducted through the specific relationships you have with other individuals whom you meet fairly frequently and with whom you interact daily.

Photo 8.1 The Harajuku area of Tokyo is a popular destination for teenagers, many of whom dress in such cultural styles as gothic lolita, visual kei, and decora. Are artifacts such as clothing the primary distinction between cultural groups? (See page 209.)

Cultural groups are recognized and labeled as such when some consistency and distinctiveness is observed in their behavior and communication. For example, the *shared relational* use by goths, punks, and emos of symbols like hairstyles, body piercing, cutting, and self-harm along with a relevant music genre and vocabulary transacts their identity and collectively forms the goth, punk, or emo culture. Similarly, rednecks and redneck culture have been identified and caricatured through particular stories and jokes (for example, by Jeff Foxworthy and Larry the Cable Guy).

You may or may not be a goth, a punk, an emo, a redneck, or a goth-redneck. If you are, you may be able to relate to the above examples. If not, we can try another angle. Even if you belong to a strict nudist culture, we are going to go out on a limb and assume you generally wear clothing in public. Aside from the possibility of breaking a handful of laws (which themselves uphold social norms) and aside from protecting yourself from the weather, why do you wear clothes? After all, you probably would be much more comfortable without them. Well, you wear clothes because you have been convinced that it is the culturally proper and right thing to do. It was not some abstract notion of culture that convinced you. Rather, it was developed and maintained from observing the behavior of people around you. It was developed and maintained from being taught to wear clothes by your parents or guardians, who were taught the same thing by their parents or guardians. It was developed and maintained from knowing that negative evaluations or consequences could arise through friends, family, and other people in your life. Once again, Society's/Culture's Secret Agents are on the case!

Coded Systems of Meaning

What makes this approach to studying culture different from a structural approach is that culture is seen as a **coded system of meaning**. Culture is not just a structured bureaucratic machine but a set of beliefs, a heritage, and a way of being that is *transacted* in communication. From this point of view, then, you can think of culture as a meaning system.

If you think of culture as a system of norms, rituals, and beliefs, any group with a system of shared meaning is a culture. Farmers, athletes, gamers, members of business organizations, comic book fans, health professionals, truckers, fast-food employees, and musicians could all be considered members of a unique culture. The list of unique cultural groups is virtually unending.

Viewing societies and cultures as unique meaning systems provides an opportunity to go beyond a traditional structural view of cultures. Although these conventional views can still provide a great deal of valuable information, they tend to overlook numerous, distinct meaning systems within larger structure-based labels such as *nation-state*. You cannot legitimately maintain that everyone in the United States communicates the same way, that everyone in Lithuania communicates the same way, that everyone in India communicates the same way, or that everyone in any other nation-state or region communicates the same way. There are many different cultures within the United States (and other nation-states) communicating in very unique ways.

Studying how culture is symbolically transacted enables us to examine how styles of communication serve to include people in or exclude people from cultural communities and groups. We can focus on how people "speak themselves into culture" and how membership in a particular culture is done through communication.

Case in Point

Go to a public space where members of a unique cultural group are gathered and observe the ways they communicate. (Naturally avoid dangerous places and situations. We do not want you injured and cannot afford to bail you out of jail.) There are many groups from which you may choose, but based on some of those mentioned here, you might observe farmers at a cattle auction barn, comic book fans at a comic book store, or truckers at a truck stop. What is unique about their communication? What does their communication tell you about their cultural beliefs and values?

Structure-Based Cultural Characteristics

Although we have indicated that it is far too simplistic to equate culture *exclusively* with nation-states or regions, some very broad differences between such groups have been observed and should be taken into account. As we mentioned earlier, all members of a nation or citizens of a country are impacted in some way by the most general communication styles and patterns.

Children learn to view the world in culturally appropriate ways as they learn to communicate and interact with others. For example, small children may be rushed from the store by embarrassed parents who have just been asked loudly, "Why is that man so ugly?" and they will certainly be taught a culture's nonverbal rules: "Look at me when I'm talking to you" and "Don't interrupt when someone is talking." "Remember to say thank you" is another way children are taught culture's rules about respect and politeness as they learn to talk.

During your childhood and introduction to culture (socialization), you learned how to behave, interact, and live with other people as you learned to communicate. These styles of behavior readily became more and more automatic—and hence were automatically included in your later communication—as you grew up. If this did not happen, you could not communicate with other people in your society. Thus, learning to communicate includes learning the habits of your particular culture or society.

It makes sense to look at the rich list of differences uncovered among cultures—even if these sometimes amount to stereotypes that you hold about other nations when representing how people there *typically* act. In what follows, we examine the following cross-cultural characteristics: (a) context, (b) collectivism/individualism, (c) time, and (d) conflict. As these communication styles and meanings are discussed, keep in mind how they are learned and reinforced through interactions with friends, families, and others with whom relationships are shared.

Strategic Communication

When attempting to persuade someone or to develop a positive relationship with someone, communicating in a manner consistent with his or her culture will increase your chances of success. However, check out the Ethical Issues at the end of this chapter for more on this matter.

Context

Context involves the emphasis placed on the environment, the situation, or relationships when communicating. Some cultures tend to leave much unsaid, with the assumption that others will understand what is meant based on such influences as circumstances encompassing the interaction and relationships among those communicating. Other cultures tend to be more explicit and straightforward when communicating, rather than relying on contextual factors. Cultures are accordingly categorized as being either high-context or low-context.

High-Context Cultures

Some societies, known as **high-context cultures** (Samovar, Porter, & McDaniel, 2010), place a great deal of emphasis on the total environment or context where speech and interaction take place. In a high-context society, spoken words are much less important than the rest of the context—for example, the relationships between the people communicating. It is much more important for people to indicate respect for one another in various verbal and nonverbal ways than it is for them to pay close attention to the exact words spoken.

In such countries as China and Iraq, for example, a person's status in society is extremely important, and people tend to rely on their history and their relationship to the speaker or the audience. In Iraq and some African countries, additional importance may be attached to a person's religious or tribal group to assign meanings to conversation. Such cultures greatly emphasize and give major priority to relationships among

There often exist contextual-based differences between the marketing or sales force in a business and the technicians or engineers who actually make the product. For marketing team members and salespeople, it is very important to have good relationships with their customers and with a network of other sales personnel. For the technicians who actually make and service products, it is more important that accurate information be conveyed to customers than that the customers be made to feel good interpersonally. This difference of emphasis sometimes leads to conflict between the same organization's marketing and technical personnel.

family members, friends, and associates. Therefore, it is regarded as ethical to favor one's relatives or as fair to give contracts to friends rather than to the highest bidder. Everything is connected to this background context of relationships and other personal contexts of status, influence, and personal knowledge.

Low-Context Cultures

By contrast, when communicating in a **low-context culture**, the message itself means everything, and it is much more important to have a well-structured argument or a well-delivered presentation than it is to be a member of the royal family or a cousin of the person listening (Samovar et al., 2010).

In a low-context society, therefore, people try to separate their relationships from the messages and to focus on the details and the logic. Detailed information must be given to provide the relevant context, and only the information presented that way counts as relevant to the message. In low-context societies, people may remove themselves from decision-making roles if a friend or family member is involved. Nepotism, or favoritism shown to a family member or friend, is evaluated negatively in low-context cultures.

Collectivism/Individualism

An entire chapter of this book is dedicated to identity (Chapter 5), but the very notion of a personal identity is more of a Western than an Eastern idea. Some cultures stress collectivism/togetherness, and some stress individualism/individuality.

Collectivist Cultures

As traditionally noted (Gudykunst, 2000; Morsbach, 2004), Eastern societies, such as Japan, tend to be **collectivist**—that is, to stress group benefit and the overriding value of working harmoniously rather than individual personal advancement. Collectivist cultures place greater importance on the whole group, stressing common concerns and the value of acting not merely for oneself but for the common good. Accordingly, in a collectivist culture, your value is based on your place in a system—portraying you as just a single bee in a beehive—more than your special and unique qualities as an individual.

These characteristics are developed and reinforced through personal relationships and interactions with others. Within a collectivist society, an individual who acts to achieve personal rather than collective goals would be viewed as simply selfish and disrespectful. He or she would be brought back into line and made to understand and accept the value of community and collectivity. Such reprimands, especially made by someone with whom a close relationship is shared, would bolster the prevailing view of society.

Individualist Cultures

Western societies, such as the United States, are generally characterized as **individualist**, or focusing on the individual person and his or her personal dreams, goals and achievements, and right to make choices (Gudykunst, 2000; Morsbach, 2004). Individual desires and freedoms are emphasized, and your value is measured according to your personal accomplishments.

As with collectivist cultures, these characteristics are constructed and strengthened through relationships. Contrary to collectivist cultures, within individualistic cultures, personal achievement is lauded and reinforced through conversations with others. For instance, supervisors may talk with employees about the development of personal goals and post "employee of the month" placards to single out individual achievements. Next time you see such a placard, think of it as an example of American cultural ideals being transacted before your very eyes!

Time

Cultures are also categorized and differentiated according to their views of time. Consider how time is perceived in the United States, where the phrase *time is money* is quite common. Time is valuable, and so it is important to not waste it. Therefore, showing up on time helps create a positive impression. Many employees are required to punch in on a time clock or log into a computer system when arriving and leaving work, so precise time can be measured. And, if a person consistently arrives late for work, he or she will likely lose the job.

Contrarian Challenge

Some research presents a sharp distinction between individualist and collectivist cultures. Can you think of contrary examples in U.S. culture where the individual is required to subordinate personal goals to the collective good? If you can, does this undercut the whole idea of the great distinction between collectivism and individualism?

Because cultures differ in how they view time, the importance of brisk punctuality, as opposed to that of leisurely relationship building, is also given different weight. This broad difference of emphasis on activity or relationships in time is labeled as a distinction between monochronic and polychronic cultures.

Monochronic Culture

If you think of time as a straight line from beginning to end, you are thinking in terms of *monochronic time,* where people do one thing at a time or multitask only because it helps them work toward particular goals with tasks in sequence and communication fitting into a particular order.

Photo 8.2 This man seems very concerned about time. Would his perception of time be considered monochronic or polychronic? (See page 209.)

Monochronic cultures, such as the United States, the United Kingdom, and Germany, view time as a valuable commodity and punctuality as very important. People with a monochronic view of time will usually arrive at an appointment a few minutes early as a symbol of respect for the person they are meeting. In the United States, after first establishing a pleasant atmosphere with a few brief courtesies, people will more likely bring up the matter of business fairly early in the conversation.

Polychronic Culture

If you think of time as the ever-rolling cycle of the seasons or something more open-ended, you are thinking in terms of *polychronic time,* where independent and unconnected tasks can be done simultaneously and also where people may carry out multiple conversations with different people at the same time.

Polychronic cultures have a relaxed attitude toward time. Indeed, as Calero (2005) noted, the predominant U.S. notion of time translates as "childishly impatient" to polychronic cultures. This notion of time is true even in relation to food, specifically in, say, Italy or France where two-course meals can take 3 hours. In polychronic societies, "promptness" is not particularly important, and as long as the person shows up sometime during the right day, that will count as doing what was required. Some Mediterranean and Arab countries do not regard as impolite being late to an appointment or taking a very long time to get down to business. Indeed, placing so much emphasis on time that people's relationships are ignored is regarded as rude and pushy; instead, time should be taken to build the relationships. In the same way, it is important in some countries not to get to the point too quickly, and a lot of time is spent talking about relational issues or other matters before it is polite to bring up a business question.

Future and Past Orientations

Cultures also differ in the way they pay attention to the past, the present, and the

Make Your Case

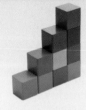

The United States is generally regarded as monochronic. However, the increased use of cell phones has tended to alter our perception of time. For instance, schedules are frequently loosened as a result of being able to contact someone immediately and alter plans. Make your case for one of the following:

The United States will remain a monochronic culture.

The United States will become a polychronic culture.

future. Different cultures tend to assume that the present is influenced either by one's goals and the future or by past events, and fatalism and preordained destiny tend to control to a greater extent what happens in the present. In the United States, many groups place much greater emphasis on future orientation, particularly in the short term, than on their control over present and distant

> Polychronic views of time are more likely to be connected with high-context cultures, while monochronic views of time are more likely to be connected with low-context cultures.

future events. Some Asian societies, on the other hand, pay more attention to the distant future and, like South American and Mediterranean cultures, tend to assume a greater influence of the past on the present and that destiny or karma affects what happens to us in the present moment (Martin & Nakayama, 2007).

Conflict

Cultures can also be compared according to their understanding of and approach to **conflict**, which involves real or perceived incompatibilities of processes, understandings, and viewpoints between people. Communication scholars Judith Martin and Thomas Nakayama (2007)—drawing from the work of Augsburger (1992)—differentiate two cultural approaches to conflict: conflict as opportunity and conflict as destructive (pp. 404–413).

Conflict-as-Opportunity Cultures

Conflict-as-opportunity cultures tend to be individualist, such as the United States. This approach to conflict is based on the four assumptions listed in Table 8.1 (Martin & Nakayama, 2007, p. 404).

Table 8.1 The Four Assumptions of Conflict-as-Opportunity Cultures
1. Conflict is a normal, useful process.
2. All issues are subject to change through negotiation.
3. Direct confrontation and conciliation are valued.
4. Conflict is a necessary renegotiation of an implied contract—a redistribution of opportunity, a release of tensions, and a renewal of relationships.

Source: Martin & Nakayama, 2007, p. 404.

Members of these cultures view conflict as a normal and useful process, an inherent part of everyday life. Naturally experienced when interacting with people, conflict will lead, if handled constructively, to the enhancement of personal and relational life. This cultural view of conflict also understands all issues as subject to change, meaning that all personal or relational processes, goals, or outcomes can be altered. When a person wants to make changes in his or her relationships or personal life, he or she is expected to fully express and work with others to achieve these desires. Finally, members of these cultures view conflict as not only normal and useful but also a necessary requirement for renewing relationships and for achieving personal goals and overall well-being.

Individualist cultures tend to view conflict as opportunity, while collectivist cultures tend to view conflict as destructive.

Conflict-as-Destructive Cultures

Stressing group and relational harmony above individual needs and desires, **conflict-as-destructive cultures** tend to be collectivist or community-oriented such as many Asian cultures. Religious groups, such as the Amish and Quakers, also view conflict as destructive. David's dad attended Quaker meetings as a child and adhered to pacifist ideals even on the playground. He has told stories of other children hitting him, knowing he would not fight back. As instructed in the Bible, he would literally turn the other cheek, and the other children would promptly hit that cheek as well. Nevertheless, David's dad remained steadfast in his culturally based belief in the destructive nature of conflict. As with conflict-as-opportunity cultures, four assumptions guide this approach to conflict, as listed in Table 8.2 (Martin & Nakayama, 2007, p. 406).

Table 8.2 The Four Assumptions of Conflict-as-Destructive Cultures
1. Conflict is a destructive disturbance of the peace.
2. The social system should not be adjusted to meet the needs of members; rather, members should adapt to established values.
3. Confrontations are destructive and ineffective.
4. Disputants should be disciplined.

Source: Martin & Nakayama, 2007, p. 406.

Contrary to conflict-as-opportunity cultures, this cultural approach views conflict not as a natural part of everyday experience but rather as unnecessary, detrimental, and to be avoided. Also contrary to conflict-as-opportunity cultures and reflective of collectivist cultures in general, members of conflict-as-destructive cultures do not view individual needs and desires as more important than group needs and established norms. Furthermore, rather than valuing direct confrontation, members consider confrontations futile and harmful to relationships and the group as a whole. Accordingly, those who engage in confrontation should be disciplined to discourage such destructive behaviors since they undo relationships and solidarity.

Managing Conflict

Of course, conflict occurs in all relationships and among all groups, even those viewing conflict as destructive. However, the management of conflict will also differ among cultural groups. When conflict occurs, people generally engage in one of five styles of conflict management: (1) dominating, (2) integrating, (3) compromising, (4) obliging, and (5) avoiding (Rahim, 1983; Ting-Toomey, 2004).

Dominating. Dominating styles involve forcing one's will on another to satisfy individual desires regardless of negative relational consequences. For example, you and a friend decide to order a pizza, and as you call in the order, your friend mentions a desire for pepperoni. You would rather have sausage and reply, "Too bad. I'm making the call, and we are having sausage."

Photo 8.3 The person on the left did not want to engage in conflict, so he did not say anything when his friend wanted to order a pizza topping he did not like. What cultural orientation to conflict do his actions represent, and what style did he use to manage the conflict? (See page 209.)

Integrating. Integrating styles necessitate a great deal of open discussion about the conflict at hand to reach a solution that completely satisfies everyone involved. You and your friend differ on what pizza topping you would like, so you openly discuss your positions and the options available until you reach a solution that fulfils both of your desires—perhaps getting both toppings or half sausage and half pepperoni.

Compromising. Compromising styles are often confused with integrating styles because a solution is reached following discussion of the conflict. However, making a compromise demands that everyone must give something up to reach the solution, and, as a result, people never feel fully satisfied. Returning to the pizza quagmire, you and your friend discuss the conflict and decide to get mushrooms instead of sausage or pepperoni.

Obliging. Obliging styles of conflict management involve giving up one's position to satisfy another's. This style generally emphasizes areas of agreement and deemphasizes areas of disagreement. Using this style of conflict management, as you and your friend discuss what topping to include on your pizza, you probably mention that the important thing is you both want pizza and then agree to order pepperoni instead of sausage.

Avoiding. Finally, avoiding styles of conflict are just that: People avoid the

Cultural beliefs and values are first learned in childhood and then reinforced by relationships throughout your entire life. In this way, you do your culture by using the filters you learned in your early years without even realizing it, rather like wearing glasses. The lenses, for example, affect what you see to make perception more effective. Most of the time, people are not aware of wearing glasses because of their lenses' "transparency," but nevertheless, they affect what the wearer sees and how he sees it. So too with culture: Though it shapes and to some extent distorts perceptions and focus, people are largely unaware of culture and how it affects them.

conflict entirely either by failing to acknowledge its existence or by withdrawing from a situation when it arises. So, your friend expresses a desire for pepperoni on that pizza, and even though you really want sausage, you indicate that pepperoni is fine and place the order.

Transacting Culture

The preceding section emphasized a set of broad and general differences resulting from seeing culture in structural or geographical terms. Structural discussions of cultural characteristics treat culture very broadly and categorically: If you are a Westerner, you will behave and communicate in the Western way. Although such broad-brush ideas are very helpful in many circumstances, especially when traveling to other countries, dealing with international relationships, or discussing the clash of cultures and/or diversity, it is important to go beyond the broad ideas and add some finer detail.

Indeed, a lot of *who you are* depends on *where you are*, or at least on *where you come from*, as well as on the groups you belong to and how they expect people to behave. You are not alone: You *belong* and do not always have a choice. You belong to many groups, some small (groups of friends or neighbors), some large (your citizenship or your ethnic group), some central to your life (family, friends), and some probably peripheral (your tax group, your shoe size). Somewhere in there, somewhere in your sense of yourself, however, is the culture (are the cultures) that you see as yours.

Studying culture as a transaction requires you to consider how your membership in cultural groups goes beyond such structural categories as nation-state, ethnicity, or religion. Instead, you must focus on how culture is created symbolically through communication and is reinforced through your relationships with others and your everyday experiences. Cultural codes are embedded within your communication, and you "speak" culture each time you communicate. Accordingly, it is through communication that cultural groups are established and cultural membership is achieved.

In a sense, people create culture symbolically and then are bound by that which they create. For example, standing a certain distance from a particular person might be considered the norm among members of a cultural group, because proper distances have been socially constructed over time. Yet, members of this group are constrained and must adhere to what they have created, because there may be repercussions if cultural norms involving distance are violated.

Culture Is Embedded Within Your Communication

Your culture is coded in your communication not only in the language you speak but also in the thoughts you express and the assumptions you make. Obviously, talk accomplishes this in the straightforward sense: French men and women speak French. But they also speak "*being* French." Accordingly, every time a person communicates, other people know something about his or her culture. When someone is seen wearing "cultural clothes," difference is assumed, but that person actually *wears* his or her culture in talk and behavior, too.

Your two authors, Steve and David, are different. Steve is English; David is American. When we travel in the United States, people say to Steve, "I love your accent," but when we travel in the United Kingdom, they say it to David. So which of us has an accent? No one in either place ever says with marvel to us, "You speak good English," though when we go to France, people might say, "You speak good French" (if we did). In the United Kingdom, people can tell that Steve is from "the West country," and in the United States, they know David is *not* from "the South." All of them can tell, even on the phone, that we are not ethnic Dutch or Indonesian. They also know we are not women or 5 years old. This is not only a result of vocalic differences but also a result of what we say and how we say it.

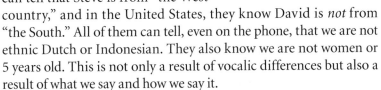

Photo 8.4 Would someone studying biker culture within the United States be more likely to take a structural approach to culture or a transacted approach to culture? (See page 209.)

When Steve first met a new colleague (an Eastern European), the conversation lasted only briefly before the colleague said, "You're not American." Steve said, "Oh, the old accent gives me away yet again!" but the colleague said, "No, actually. I'm not a native English speaker, and I can't tell the difference between English and American accents. It was something in your *style* that announced you as 'other.'"

David grew up on a farm in rural Indiana, and like everyone, his communication styles and assumptions about the world were influenced and informed by people around him. He views the world differently and communicates differently than someone who was raised in the city, someone who grew up wealthy, or someone who has never worked the land. His rural Indiana cultural beliefs and values are displayed by what he says and how he says it. Rural Indiana communication styles and patterns are embedded in his talk.

Culture Goes Beyond Physical Location

Notwithstanding the importance of a person's place of origin, Steve is not just "West country," and David is not just "rural Indiana." Steve is a coxswain. David is a radio announcer. Steve is a father. David is a bartender/bouncer. Steve is a genealogist. David is a singer. Both of us are academics. These cultural activities and roles—past and present—have influenced our views of the world and our communication styles. Furthermore, each is cultural in its own right. Steve communicates coxswain culture, father culture, genealogy culture, and academic culture. David communicates radio announcer culture, bartender/bouncer culture, singer culture, and academic culture. At times one may be more pronounced than others. Also at times it may be more important to enact membership into one culture than another. For instance, at academic conferences, we tend to communicate academic culture rather than coxswain or bartender/bouncer culture—although doing the latter may be a way to liven up future conferences!

What ultimately becomes clear—other than we have just spent too much time talking about ourselves—is that people belong to multiple cultures and that cultural membership is enacted through communication.

Cultural Groups Are Created Through Communication

As we have discussed in great detail, a structural understanding of culture as being encompassed by a nation-state, a region, an ethnicity, or a religion is restrictive. It does not give an entirely accurate depiction of culture in everyday life. For instance, several cultures may exist within one country (Houston & Wood, 1996). These cultural groups are recognized and differentiated through their unique communication and meaning systems.

Co-cultures

Co-cultures are smaller groups of culture within a larger cultural mass. For instance, most countries have regions regarded as different and distinctive (the South, the Midwest, Yorkshire, the Valley). The belief systems in these small and diverse groups are often recognized as somewhat different and distinct from those within the larger society or nation. A large group like "Americans" can be broken down into smaller groups ("Northern Americans" and "Southern Americans") containing smaller sets of both nations and societies, such as Irish Americans, Southerners, Sioux, African Americans, Iowans, or Republicans.

Sociologically and demographically, discussions of co-cultures are significant because they underscore the vast number of cultures that can be explored and that encompass a person's life. However, there is still the tendency to take on a structural approach to their study. Accordingly, someone might say, "Republicans communicate this way, while Democrats communicate that way."

Speech Communities

A more communication-based view labels these cultures as speech communities (Hymes, 1972; Philipsen, 1975, 1997). **Speech communities** are cultures defining membership in terms of speaking patterns and styles that reinforce beliefs and values of the group. Essentially, cultural groups are set apart based on their unique communication styles. In this way, various **speech (communication) codes**, or a culture's verbalizations of meaning and symbols, tend to have built into them certain ways of understanding the world that guide the particular talk patterns people use in conversation with one another.

In a male offenders' prison, Julia Wood (2004) uncovered a special kind of talk, based on physical strength and the assumed right to control other people, in spouse abusers.

One characteristic of any culture is what it takes for granted. For example, in a particular culture, certain topics can be talked about and certain ideas are taken for granted, even during persuasion. Kristine Muñoz (Fitch, 2003) has written about these taken-for-granted assumptions as **cultural persuadables**, certain topics that people in a society never bother to persuade anyone else about because their arguments are always raised against a background of common understanding and shared beliefs. For instance, some speech communities adhere to very traditional notions of gender roles. Accordingly, it is unnecessary to say anything directly about these gender roles because they are implicit in everything that is communicated.

Teamsterville and Nacirema

So, multiple cultures exist based on the unique ways in which they communicate and what is taken for granted in communication. As mentioned earlier, we can therefore pinpoint and study an essentially limitless number of cultures throughout the world. Two classic studies examining the cultures of "Teamsterville" and "Nacirema" exemplify this approach and laid the groundwork for subsequent research.

Communication scholar Gerry Philipsen (1975) explored the talk in Teamsterville, a pseudonym for a working-class community in Chicago showing a "man's communication style." For members of this community, the style of speech occasionally prefers action to words and is based on talking only when power is equal or symmetrical. In this community, a man demonstrates power by punching someone rather than arguing about a problem. Speech is regarded as an inappropriate and ineffective way of communicating in situations when demonstrating power. For example, if a man were insulted by a stranger, the culturally appropriate way to deal with the insult would be to inflict physical damage rather than discuss the issue. In Teamsterville, speech in such a situation would be characterized as weak. On the other hand, when a man in Teamsterville is among friends, his speech is permitted to establish his manliness. If a man's friend made a derogatory remark about the man's girlfriend, the man would either take the remark as a tease or simply tell the friend not to say such things, and violence would not result as it would in the case of strangers saying the same thing.

Photo 8.5 How might break time at a factory be an opportunity to learn about and enact cultural membership within this culture? (See page 210.)

In addition to his identification of the cultural Code of Honor carried out by the men of Teamsterville as they "do manliness," Philipsen (1997) identified a cultural Code of Dignity, which he identified as characteristic of the "Nacirema" (*American* spelled backward). This communication code emphasizes relationships, work, communication, and individual/self and is quite easily discovered on TV talk shows and in the broader context of speech in large parts of America. The work by Philipsen and others (e.g., Fitch, 1998) helps us see that speech (communication) codes create membership within a given culture.

College Experience

Contemplate how members of an academic community can be considered a unique cultural group. This approach to academic communities can be applied to people in academics in general, and it can also be applied to your very own school.

1. What unique communication styles and accompanying meaning systems are performed at your school? In other words, how is membership into that particular academic community enacted and displayed?

2. Do you consider yourself a member of this cultural group? If so, how does your communication when on campus reflect that of others in the group? If you consider yourself a member of this group, you probably feel more connected than when you first arrived on campus. How did this sense of connectedness develop? (Warning: If you do not include interactions and relationships in your answer, your authors may shed many tears!)

3. If you do not consider yourself a member of your school community, why do you think that might be? Do you choose not to perform membership into this group? Is it possible that you display cultural membership more than you realize?

4. Finally, how many different cultural groups do you observe while on campus? What is unique about the communication of these groups? Are some groups more exclusive or separate than others?

Cultural Membership Is Enacted Through Communication

Enacting membership in a cultural group means communicating and assigning meaning in ways similar to other members of that group. For instance, musicians enact membership into a musician culture by communicating like members of that culture. It can be broken down further, and we can distinguish musician cultures related to jazz, blues, death metal, hip-hop, rhythm and blues, country, bluegrass, rockabilly, and barbershop just to name a few. Once again, each cultural group communicates in unique ways, and enacting membership requires communicating as such.

However, enacting membership into a cultural group is more complicated and restrictive than it may initially appear. If you want to be a rapper, you cannot just talk like a rapper and suddenly become one. It is not just the act of communicating that establishes membership into a cultural group; it is also, and more important, knowing the meaning of that communication that does so. A cultural understanding is required. If you do not know how to perform membership in a particular community, you are excluded from it. Membership in a culture can be represented in and restricted by one's knowledge of speech (communication) codes.

The unique ways of communication and the underlying meaning of that communication create a sense of otherness or separateness. Some cultural groups may rejoice in their exclusivity. For instance, certain clubs or organizations may have secret ways of communicating concealed from everyone but their members. When "outsiders" attempt to enact membership into certain cultural groups, they may be referred to as "fakes" or "wannabes." Members of rural communities often view people who move into the area with suspicion. These new people may be living in the same area, but they do not automatically become members of the culture.

Cultural speech (communication) codes must be learned and understood before a person can fully enact membership into a group. Doing so requires interacting and forming relationships with members of that cultural group. It is through relating that cultural understanding is transferred and maintained. Cultural understanding is fundamental to enacting cultural membership, and it is through relationships that this understanding is learned.

FOCUS QUESTIONS REVISITED

1. What does it mean to view culture as structured?

Viewing *culture* from a structural standpoint has a long history in the communication discipline. This way of seeing culture focuses on large-scale differences in values, beliefs, goals, and preferred ways of acting among nations, regions, ethnicities, and religions. Research using this perspective is often referred to as either cross-cultural communication or intercultural communication.

2. What does it mean to view culture as transacted?

When viewing culture from a transactional standpoint, culture is seen as a coded system of meaning. Culture is a set of beliefs, a heritage, and a way of being that is *transacted* in communication. When viewing culture as a system of norms, rituals, and beliefs, any group with a system of shared meaning can be considered a culture.

3. How is communication organized to reflect cultural beliefs about context, collectivism/individualism, time, and conflict?

Cultures can be categorized as either high context or low context. High-context cultures place a great deal of emphasis on the total environment or context where speech and interaction take place. In a low-context culture, people try to separate their relationships from the messages and to focus on the details and the logic.

Cultures can be categorized as either individualist or collectivist. Collectivist cultures place greater importance on the whole group, stressing common concerns and the value of acting not merely for oneself but for the common good. Individualist cultures focus on the individual person and his or her personal dreams, goals and achievements, and right to make choices.

Cultures can be categorized as either monochronic or polychronic. Monochronic cultures view time as valuable and adhere to schedules. Polychronic cultures view time more holistically and have a much more relaxed attitude toward schedules. Cultures also differ in their orientation to past, present, and future events.

Cultures can be categorized as viewing conflict as either opportunity or destructive. Cultures viewing conflict as opportunity perceive conflict as a normal and useful process, an inherent part of everyday life. Cultures viewing conflict as destructive perceive conflict as unnecessary, detrimental, and something to be avoided.

4. What does it mean to say culture is coded into communication?

Culture is coded in communication not only in the language spoken but also in thoughts expressed and assumptions made. Every time a person communicates, other people know something about his or her culture. Cultural beliefs and values are displayed by a person's communication.

5. What does it mean to say that cultural groups are created through communication?

Multiple cultural groups are recognized and differentiated through their unique communication and meaning systems. Speech communities are cultures defining membership in terms of speaking patterns and styles that reinforce beliefs and values of the group. Essentially, cultural groups are set apart based on their unique communication styles.

6. How do people enact cultural membership through communication?

Enacting membership in a cultural group means communicating and assigning meaning in ways similar to other members of that group. However, it is not just the act of communicating that establishes membership into a cultural group; it is also, and more important, knowing the meaning of that communication that does so. Membership in a culture can be represented in and restricted by one's knowledge of speech (communication) codes.

KEY CONCEPTS

co-culture   204
coded system of meaning   193
collectivist   196
conflict   199
conflict-as-destructive culture   200
conflict-as-opportunity culture   199
cross-cultural communication   191
cultural persuadables   205
ethnocentric bias   189

high-context culture   195
individualist   197
intercultural communication   192
low-context culture   196
monochronic culture   198
polychronic culture   198
speech (communication) codes   204
speech communities   204

QUESTIONS TO ASK YOUR FRIENDS

1. Have your friends tell you about their favorite children's stories, and then discuss the themes demonstrated by those stories and connect them to the cultural ideals.

2. Ask your friends in how many cultures they view themselves as having established membership. In what ways do they establish these memberships?

3. Ask your friends to describe a recent intercultural experience. What did they find most challenging? What did they find most rewarding?

MEDIA LINKS

1. Select and analyze a movie with intercultural themes (i.e., *The Namesake*) to show how individuals from different cultures build relationships and develop understanding. Describe how culturally relevant concepts and ideas from this chapter are shown in the movie's characters, plot, setting, script, and acting styles.

2. How are different cultures represented on television and in movies? Compare current with 30- or 40-year-old shows and movies. What differences do you see?

3. How are other cultures represented by newspapers, television news, or online news sources? Can you identify any ethnocentric bias in these reports?

ETHICAL ISSUES

1. As mentioned in the Strategic Communication box, communicating in a manner consistent with another person's culture will generally make you more persuasive. If this counters your own cultural perspectives, are you being deceitful? Is there a difference between adapting a message and being disingenuous?

2. Evaluate a problem currently being discussed in this society that grows out of cultural dynamics. Explore at least two possible solutions to, for example, immigration or racial/ethnic/religious profiling.

3. Should people of the world be accepting of all cultural behaviors? For instance, in some cultures, women are forced into subservient roles. Children of some cultures must endure rites of passage that might be viewed as disgraceful or dangerous in other cultures. Some cultural groups disfigure their bodies in certain ways. Should other cultures intervene in some circumstances?

ANSWERS TO PHOTO CAPTIONS

Photo 8.1 ■ No. While clothing is part of a person's cultural identity and perhaps one of the first things people of other cultures notice, it is just one of many symbolic behaviors through which culture is transacted.

Photo 8.2 ■ He seems to view time as a valuable commodity and punctuality as very important, which means he has a monochronic view of time.

Photo 8.3 ■ He likely views conflict as destructive rather than as opportunity. He used the avoiding strategy to manage the conflict.

Photo 8.4 ■ Someone studying biker culture or other speech communities would likely be taking a transacted approach to culture rather than a structural approach.

Photo 8.5 ▪ Break time at a factory would provide an opportunity to interact with coworkers and establish relationships with them. It is through interaction and relationships that cultural meaning is truly recognized and understood.

STUDENT STUDY SITE

Visit the study site at **www.sagepub.com/boc2e** for e-flashcards, practice quizzes, journal articles and additional study resources.

REFERENCES

Augsburger, D. W. (1992). *Conflict mediation across cultures: Pathways and patterns.* Louisville, KY: Westminster/John Knox.

Calero, H. (2005). *The power of nonverbal communication: What you do is more important than what you say.* Los Angeles: Silver Lake.

Chiang, S.-U. (2009). Dealing with communication problems in the instructional interactions between international teaching assistants and American college students. *Language and Education, 23,* 461–478.

Fitch, K. L. (1998). *Speaking relationally: Culture, communication, and interpersonal connection.* New York: Guilford Press.

Fitch, K. L. (2003). Cultural persuadables. *Communication Theory, 13*(1), 100–123.

Gudykunst, W. (2000). *Asian American ethnicity and communication.* Thousand Oaks, CA: Sage.

Gudykunst, W. B., & Kim, Y. Y. (1984). *Communicating with strangers: An approach to intercultural communication.* New York: Random House.

Houston, M., & Wood, J. T. (1996). *Gendered relationships.* Mountain View, CA: Mayfield.

Hymes, D. (1972). Models of the interaction of language and social life. In J. Gumperz & D. Hymes (Eds.), *Directions in sociolinguistics: The ethnography of communication* (pp. 35–71). New York: Holt, Rinehart & Winston.

Jin, B., & Oh, S. (2010). Cultural differences of social network influence on romantic relationships: A comparison of the United States and South Korea. *Communication Studies, 61,* 156–171.

Le, Q., & Chiu, C. (2009). Culturally-informed health metaphors on health service delivery. *International Journal of Social Health Information Management, 2,* 48–59.

Martin, J. N., & Nakayama, T. K. (2007). *Intercultural communication in context* (4th ed.). New York: McGraw-Hill.

Morsbach, H. (2004). *Customs and etiquette of Japan.* London: Global Books.

Nakayama, T. K., Martin, J. N., & Flores, L. A. (Eds.). (2002). *Readings in intercultural communication* (2nd ed.). New York: McGraw-Hill.

Philipsen, G. (1975). Speaking "like a man" in Teamsterville: Culture patterns of role enactment in an urban neighborhood. *Quarterly Journal of Speech, 61*(1), 13–22.

Philipsen, G. (1997). A theory of speech codes. In G. Philipsen & T. Albrecht (Eds.), *Developing theories in communication* (pp. 119–156). Albany: State University of New York Press.

Rahim, M. A. (1983). A measure of styles of handling interpersonal conflict. *Academy of Management Journal, 26,* 368–376.

Samovar, L. A., Porter, R. E., & McDaniel, E. R. (2010). *Communication between cultures* (7th ed.). Belmont, CA: Wadsworth.

Seki, K., Matsumoto, D., & Imahori, T. T. (2002). The conceptualization and expression of intimacy in Japan and the United States. *Journal of Cross-Cultural Psychology, 33*(3), 303–319.

Ting-Toomey, S. (2004). The matrix of face: An updated face-negotiation theory. In W. Gudykunst (Ed.), *Theorizing about intercultural communication* (pp. 71–92). Thousand Oaks, CA: Sage.

Wood, J. T. (2004). Monsters and victims: Male felons' accounts of intimate partner violence. *Journal of Social and Personal Relationships, 21*(5), 555–576.

9

Technology in Everyday Life

Communication and relationships increasingly center on the use of technology and media. For the sake of organization only, this chapter is primarily concerned with such technologies as cell phones and iPods. Chapter 10 is dedicated to what has been traditionally termed "mass" media, such as television, radio, movies, books, video games, and newspapers. As both a mass media system and an interactive technology, the Internet will be discussed in both chapters, with this one discussing more of its social and interactive nature and the next one discussing it from a mass media perspective.

Even though we are separating these concepts into two chapters, we recognize that they are rapidly becoming integrated and will no doubt continue to merge into relational life. Television, no longer confined to a large-screened unit in such social spaces as your home, waiting rooms, and restaurants, can now be watched in a variety of locations through cell phones, iPods, and similar technologies. Movies, books, newspapers, video games, and millions of songs are available for download onto these devices, just waiting to help you accomplish a variety of personal and relational needs.

This separation is still legitimate at the present time but may not be suitable in the future. The continuously changing nature of human communication in general and the use of technology in particular to fulfill relational connections are among the features that make the discipline of communication so intriguing but also challenging. Accordingly, you may notice throughout the chapter a recurring theme of technological change and evolution but a constant awareness of their embeddedness in relationships. In fact, we use the term *relational technologies* quite a bit more than just *technology*.

This chapter first explores the use of relational technologies and their influence on the construction of personal and relational identities. We examine how the use of these technologies conveys particular meanings to others. We then look at the construction of identity through the Internet, specifically focusing on screen names, e-mail addresses, content creation, social networking sites, and features of Internet activity that impact everyday life. The second half of the chapter is dedicated to the use of technology when interacting with others and how technology influences personal relationships. We first examine the distinct relational features of cell phone interactions and then explore the characteristics of online communication and its influence on relationships and social networks.

Focus Questions

1. How have emerging technologies generally been viewed?
2. What factors influence identity construction through the use of relational technologies?
3. What do your screen name and e-mail address tell others about you?
4. How are content creation and social networking sites impacting the construction of identity and self-disclosure?
5. How do cell phones impact interactions with others?
6. What makes online communication different from other forms of communication?
7. How is online communication impacting personal relationships and social networks?
8. Do people interact with technology like they interact with other people?

How Do People (and Scholars) View Technology?

A person's perspective will influence how something is understood and how it is studied. Accordingly, your view of technology will influence how you comprehend and evaluate the information provided in this chapter. Within this initial section, we discuss how the perspectives of communication scholars have impacted how technology is studied. We also discuss how emerging technologies are traditionally viewed by people in general along with how relationships (surprise!) play a fundamental position in the ways in which technologies are used and understood.

Academic Views of Technology

Most people currently conducting research and writing textbooks about technology—including both of your authors—remember a time without cell phones, iPods, and the Internet. You may have heard these technologies referred to as *new* media because, for those writing the textbooks and conducting the research, they are new. However, even with growing numbers of nontraditional students, the majority of students studying this research and reading these textbooks do not view this technology as new but view it as something that has always been around and that has always been a very significant part of their lives. Accordingly, the term *new media* will not be used when discussing the Internet, cell phones, iPods, and similar devices. Instead, these technologies will be referred to as *relational technologies* in recognition of their truly relational nature.

Beyond the designation of these technologies, the media experience of researchers also influences how technology gets discussed in most current research. Much of what is written about the Internet, cell phones, and other relational technologies frames them as intrusive and threatening, and they are evaluated according to standards and criteria associated with what are thus viewed as traditional or "normal" media and technology. Actually an increasingly vital, essential, and beneficial part of everyday life, these technologies should be studied and evaluated according to their own unique standards and norms.

The term *new media* is nothing new. In 1954, a classic study on parasocial relationships—a topic that will be addressed in the next chapter—noted that the impact of new media would be explored. The new medium studied was television!

Cave Drawings and Other Concerns

Fears and apprehensions surrounding the latest technology are nothing new and concern people other than scholars from previous media generations. The emergence of any new communication technology has historically elicited choruses of concern and anxiety, surprisingly similar in nature.

People tend to worry about the effects of emerging technologies on family, community, and, of course, children. While no evidence exists, we imagine focus groups were developed by well-meaning cave people to examine the potentially negative impact of cave drawings on innocent and susceptible cave children. Documented criticism of more recent technologies shows people expressed similar fears when radio began appearing in homes in the 1920s, and these fears were nearly identical to those expressed about television when it began appearing in homes during the 1950s. Actually, many of these criticisms are still being expressed! The even more recent introduction of the Internet led to concerns about diminished physical activity and social interaction among its users. Such criticisms are strikingly similar to questions raised in 1926 by the Knights of Columbus Adult Education Committee about telephones in homes, including "Does the telephone make [people] more active or more lazy?" and "Does the telephone break up home life and the old practice of visiting friends?" (as quoted in Fischer, 1992, p. 1).

Of course, the introduction of a new technology is not without its supporters, although voices of praise are usually overwhelmed by those of criticism. As with similarities among the concerns, the praise offered for each emerging technology is often quite similar. A public relations announcement by the American Telephone & Telegraph Company (AT&T) had this to say about telephones: "The telephone is essentially democratic; it carries the voice of the child and the grown-up

The Luddites (named from their leader Ned Ludd) were an early 19th-century British social movement that protested innovations of the Industrial Revolution and were involved in armed conflicts with the British army. Today, *Luddite* refers to a person who opposes any innovation, especially technology.

Case in Point

Find news reports about advances in technology. How are these technological advances being characterized? Does the source of these reports impact these characterizations? For instance, do print newspapers report them differently than podcasts or online sources?

with equal speed and directness. . . . It is not only the implement of the individual, but it fulfills the needs of all the people" (as quoted in Fischer, 1992, p. 2). These sentiments sound strikingly similar to those surrounding the democratic and equalizing nature of the Internet.

Every Technology Is Relational

Technologies do impact society and the world in which you live. Regardless of whether its influences are positive or negative, each technology changes how people communicate and interact. The one constant among all technologies, from cave drawings to the Internet to whatever technologies arise next, is that they are inherently relational in their understanding and use. At the center of all criticism and praise of technologies rest their influence and effect on social interaction and connections among people. This influence is probably why criticism and praise surrounding each emerging technology have sounded so similar; relationships among people have been the one constant throughout all human technological development. Adapted to accomplish and meet relational needs, all technologies have influenced how you interact and relate with others.

Relational Technology and the Construction of Identities

Technological devices do not merely connect you with other people or provide you with information, music, and video. Personal and relational identities are created and maintained through your use of these technologies. We refer to cell phones and iPods as **relational technologies** to emphasize the relational functions and implications of their use in society and within specific groups. Throughout this section of the chapter, we examine how the use of technology creates and conveys information about the self, groups, and relationships.

The Meaning of Relational Technology

The use of relational technologies develops unique meanings for particular social groups. Perceiving and using technology in a manner consistent with these groups assists in establishing membership into these groups and developing particular identities. For instance, some groups view the cell phone less as a device to contact others and more as a means of displaying social status and membership (J. Katz, 2006). The social meanings accompanying technologies, along with their significance, vary according to the social system in which they are used. Members of some organizations, for example, may view text messages as a more appropriate means of communication, while members of other organizations may prefer contact through calling or face-to-face interactions. The views governing the use of these technologies are developed in large part by how other members of these organizations use and discuss each technology.

Technology and Media Generations

A major influence on people's perceptions and use of technology is the generation in which they were born. In fact, media scholars Gary Gumpert and Robert Cathcart (1985) have maintained that the traditional notion of separating generations according to time can be replaced by separating generations according to media experience. What separates generations is not just the chronological era in which they were born but also the media and technology that encompass their world. **Media generations** are differentiated by unique media grammar and media consciousness based on the technological environment in which they are born. Before the introduction of radio, past generations understood the world according to the printed word and standards associated with literacy. Radio generations eventually gave way to television generations, which gave way to digital and Internet generations, which will eventually give way to whatever technology and media generations are on the horizon.

The meaning and use of technology often vary among people of different countries. When cell phones first appeared in the United States, for example, they were marketed as business tools to be used primarily by businesspeople. In the United Kingdom, they were marketed as social relationship tools to be used by everyone. Consequently, cell phones became popular much sooner in the United Kingdom than in the United States.

Each technology influences people's thinking, sense of experience, and perceptions of reality in very unique and specific ways. Media generations and societies as a whole consequently develop different standards and methods for evaluating knowledge, experience, and reality (Chesebro, 1984). If you were born into the Internet generation, you think differently and perceive the world differently than someone born before the introduction of the Internet, and vice versa. Furthermore, those born during a particular media era privilege the perspectives or orientations brought about by their dominant technology. Someone from the Internet generation may accept and enjoy an abbreviated podcast or webcast of a full-length television episode, but someone from a television generation may find it difficult to follow. Likewise, media generations born into a digital world undervalue books and traditional television in favor of the Internet and digital products.

Technology and Social Networks

Your social network is an equally powerful force in guiding perceptions and use of technology. While generational influence is largely determined by the *availability* of technology, the influence of social networks on your use and perceptions of technology is determined by the actual *use and incorporation* of technology and the social meanings that subsequently develop. Friends, family,

Photo 9.1 What social influence may be impacting the use of technology in this picture? (See page 236.)

Strategic Communication

The medium through which you contact someone can make a difference in his or her reception of your message. The purpose of your message and the technological preferences of the person you are contacting will determine the appropriateness of face-to-face, telephone, or computer-mediated interaction.

classmates, coworkers, and others with whom you share a particular relationship direct and shape your assumptions about the value of technology and what its use represents both relationally and personally. For instance, cell phone adoption, along with attitudes toward products and services, is often shared among members of a social network (Campbell & Russo, 2003). Whether or not you own particular relational technology is based in large part on whether or not your friends own that particular relational technology. Likewise, your use of relational technologies and your attitude toward them are likely to mirror those of your friends and other members of your social network.

Your use of technology will, of course, vary according to the person with whom you are in contact and what you want to achieve through the interaction. You belong to multiple social groups, each of which likely views technology and its use differently. For example, you may be more likely to contact members of one group via e-mail and members of another group through text messages. The technological tendencies of a group may also impact its ability to achieve social status and acceptance. For instance, the use of iPods may be less common in some groups, and owning one may earn you a higher social status. On the other hand, among groups in which these devices are quite common, owning an iPod may not indicate higher social status but establish group membership and acceptance through the common use of this technology. Each social group to which you belong will help shape and mold your view and use of technology, with the group you view as most important for what you wish to achieve personally and relationally likely providing the greatest influence of all.

Technological Products and Service Providers

In addition to adoption and incorporation of relational technologies, identities are also created though the use of specific products and services. Scholars have long studied the diffusion of innovations, or how new ideas and technologies are spread throughout communities (e.g., E. Katz, Levin, & Hamilton, 1963). Some individuals desire to own the latest relational technology and related accessories as a means of demonstrating technological savvy or social status. Aside from issues associated with cost, those whose technological devices appear dated may care little about possessing the latest products and even purposefully delay adopting new technological devices as a means

"Friends and family" cell phone plans in the United States were developed when the relational turn in their use was recognized. Though developed based on consumer use, these plans now have a normative influence—essentially telling people whom they should be calling.

of conveying technological indifference or mistrust. The majority of people adopt technological devices at relatively the same time. In all three cases of technological adoption, the technological device being used communicates specific attitudes about that technology.

Beyond the speed at which technological devices and services are adopted, specific meanings are associated with the use of particular products and service providers within a social system. The use of these devices allows people to associate themselves with accompanying perspectives and attitudes related to these technological products. One study (Lobet-Maris, 2003) found that, when purchasing a cell phone, young people are influenced less by quality or available features and more by the image associated with that particular phone. Each style of cell phone is symbolically connected to certain lifestyles, activities, or media personalities, and the use of these phones enables the construction of associated identities. Not limited to the phone model, these connections also include the actual service provider. Individuals in the study linked cell phone networks with specific social features, such as humanitarianism, professionalism, and family. Thus, the use of specific networks may enable people to feel associated with groups sharing certain values or orientations.

College Experience

Consider how relational technologies are viewed by people on campus compared to other groups with which you may interact. For instance, if you have recently graduated from high school, how do meanings of technology use there differ from those on campus? If it has been a while since you were in high school, how does technology use on campus compare with that in places where you have worked?

Ringtones

Ringtones do not simply inform someone of an incoming call or message; they can be viewed as a method of identity construction. People frequently select favorite music or dialogue from television programs or movies. Using these media products as ringtones announces your media preferences to others and underscores their importance in your life. As we discuss in the next chapter, identities constructed through media preferences are equally as meaningful as other sorts of identities. The selection of ringtones—media-based or otherwise—is meaningful and is based largely on how a person wants to be perceived by others.

If you are reading this book in public or the next time you are around other people, look around at the cell phones and other relational technologies that people are using. Chances are the majority of people will be using cell phones and other relational technologies that look very similar, a few people will be using devices that appear more modern and advanced, and the remaining few will be using relational technologies that look a bit outdated.

Photo 9.2 This photo was taken just before the student's instructor took the phone and threw it against the wall. Is it ever a good idea to use cell phones while in class? (See page 236.)

Of course, some people tend to keep their cell phone set on silent or vibrate rather than an audible ring tone. This decision could be an indication that the person does not desire to draw attention to his or her use of the technology. It could also indicate that the person does not wish to be socially compelled to answer, which provides greater choice in social contexts. Once again, this selection is not just personal but also relational and is influenced by how a person wishes to be understood.

Performance of Relational Technology

Finally, the use of relational technologies can be considered a performance through which identities are constructed. The proper use or performance of technology has been established socially and will likely change over time. However, behaviors are judged according to present norms and prevailing expectations. Violating social standards associated with the use of technology often leads to negative responses and evaluations by others.

The appropriate use of technology is often determined by location and occasion. For instance, there are numerous locations and occasions where the use of technology may be deemed socially unacceptable. You might not expect the use of cell phones, MP3 players, and other technological devices during religious services, weddings, or other special events. The use of cell phones while watching a movie at a theater can really irritate other members of the audience. Likewise, the use of relational technology is usually discouraged in the classroom. Your instructors may ban the use of cell phones in the classroom, but they are not the only ones who disapprove. Other students consider mobile phones ringing or vibrating during class to be just as distracting and annoying as faculty do (Campbell, 2006).

The appropriate use of technology also encompasses content. There are certain subjects people would normally avoid discussing with someone else when they are physically together in public, but often these topics are discussed freely while engaged in a conversation on a cell phone. Perhaps there is a heightened sense of privacy considering the other person cannot be seen or heard, but it is still very much a public performance. Whether they have been personal discussions of intimacy or graphic descriptions of a rash that just will not go away, you have probably overheard cell phone conversations that you would have rather avoided.

Online Activity and the Construction of Identities

Having discussed the influence of relational technologies on the construction of personal and relational identities, we now turn our attention to the Internet. Research concerning the development of online identities has focused on identity construction through chat room discussions. While this line of research has provided valuable insight into Internet activity and personal identity, we would like to focus instead on matters of Internet activity that have received less attention but are continuing to grow in importance in everyday life.

Screen Names

Identity development is accomplished in part through the selection of screen names. Of course, screen names are frequently selected when participating in chat rooms but are also evident when playing MMORPGs (massively multiplayer online role-playing games), uploading videos on YouTube, leaving online comments and evaluations, and even selling items on eBay. A person is sometimes known to others only by his or her screen name, which may or may not provide an accurate representation of the person behind the screen. What is known about that individual is often limited to his or her Internet activity, with his or her life away from the Internet frequently unknown. A person may also establish a number of screen names and create multiple online identities.

Users may select screen names based on genuine perceived characteristics of the self or uncharacteristic traits they wish to establish online. Such screen names as *shyguy24* or *toughgrl117* may be used by those who view themselves as outgoing or aggressive, as well as by those who see themselves as introverted or passive off-line but who wish to create a unique online persona. In other words, people may select a screen name based on characteristics they usually attempt to develop through off-line interactions with others. They may also select a screen name based on characteristics usually not developed through off-line interaction as a way to test these characteristics in what may be an anonymous and nonthreatening environment.

Although former Vice President Al Gore once infamously took credit, no single person can be considered the inventor of the Internet. However, chief among the early major contributors are Leonard Kleinrock and J. C. R. Licklider. Leonard Kleinrock was the first person to publish a paper on packet switching, an essential component of the Internet. J. C. R. Licklider is considered the first person to conceive of a worldwide network of computers, which he labeled a "galactic network."

Screen names may represent other aspects of individuals beyond personality traits. Selecting such names as *HoopsFan90* or *Bears85* may symbolize an interest in a particular sport or team. Choosing such names as *SimpsonsGeek3564* or *GreysAnatoAmy53* may represent an interest in specific movies, television programs, or other popular-culture products. The screen names that people select may also embody personal relationships (*ProudPapa35, EmalynMom64, OlderSister124, ILuvDarvin95*) or represent people's professions, hobbies, and majors (*CrookedCop10_4, OilPainter23, CommStudiesRules73*). Selecting screen names based on these aspects of the self symbolizes their significance in a person's life and how that person wishes to be perceived by others.

Somewhat related to screen names are e-mail addresses, which may also influence and assist in constructing identities. The key components of e-mail addresses and their potential impact on identity construction are presented in Table 9.1.

Table 9.1 E-mail Addresses and Identities

User name: located before the @ symbol

webmaster@sagepub.com

As with screen names, multiple aspects of the self can be constructed when a person is allowed to select a user name. Be aware that screen names or user names may create undesired impressions; *2Sexy4U* or *KegLuvver,* for example, may be fine when corresponding and interacting with friends online but not in professional situations.

Domain name: located immediately after the @ symbol

webmaster@**sagepub**.com

The domain name can reveal service provider, profession, or affiliation. Domain names may display the Internet service provider, which—as with cell phone providers—could be selected based on how people wish to portray themselves to others. Companies and schools usually have their own domain name, enabling employees and students to signify their affiliation.

Top-level domain: located at the end of the address

webmaster@sagepub**.com**

The top-level material may also reveal information to others. Such codes as *.edu, .gov, .mil,* and *.org* indicate a connection with education, government, military, or an organization, respectively. Addresses originating in countries other than the United States come with a two-digit country code, such as *.uk,* which provides further information about the user.

Content Creation

The Internet has become both an instrument and a site for self-expression and, accordingly, the construction and performance of identities. This identity work is partially accomplished through online **content creation**. Social networking pages, blogs, and the posting of original pictures, videos, reviews, comments, and other personal online creations enable people to share and display their thoughts, interests, talents, and experiences and convey themselves to others in ways they wish to be viewed and understood.

Just as they do in face-to-face interactions, people make strategic choices when presenting themselves (via their creations) online. Choice of content, along with the presentation of the material included, represents a symbolic display of a person's worldview, providing specific insight into how he or she wishes to be viewed by others. For instance, the

Identity work online also takes place through the creation of avatars and the exploration of such virtual worlds as Second Life, Gaia, and Habbo. Presently only around 8% of online teens and 4% of online adults visit virtual worlds (Lenhart, Purcell, Smith, & Zickhur, 2010). These numbers have remained relatively steady in the past few years but will likely increase as the relational nature of the Internet continues to develop.

creation of a picture display on Snapfish or a similar picture site does not merely serve to archive or document experiences. Relational and identity-based decisions are made concerning what pictures are shared and what messages these pictures convey to others. Similarly, it has been discovered that people use self-presentation strategies frequently in blogs to achieve acceptance and approval and to appear socially competent (Bortree, 2005).

It can be argued that social networking sites began in the form of online communities. If this is the case, Well.com, launched in 1985, would be among the first. In their current form—in which people create a profile, compile a list of connections, and visit the profiles of other members—Classmates .com, launched in 1995, and SixDegrees.org, launched in 1997, were among the first social networking sites.

Social Networking Sites

The development of profiles on such social networking sites as Facebook, MySpace, and LinkedIn, along with activity on these sites, remains the most widespread form of content creation. Findings from the Pew Internet & American Life Project indicate that 73% of online teens (12–17 years old), 72% of online young adults (18–29 years old), and 40% of online adults (30 years old and above) have at least one profile on a social networking site (Lenhart et al., 2010). These sites have become important tools in the display and creation of personal and relational identities.

Perhaps the most obvious identity work on these sites takes place through the creation of unique member profiles. Some sites allow people to establish unique backgrounds; to include images from television, movies, video games, and other media; and to incorporate music, all of which convey to visitors how a person wishes to be digitally perceived. Personal information including demographic information, self-descriptions, favorite quotes, interests, and media preferences are frequently offered through these profiles and serve to develop a particular view of the profile's creator. Once again, as with face-to-face interactions, people make strategic choices about how they hope to be perceived through their profiles. The information provided in or excluded from these profiles is cast to portray a person in the ways in which he or she hopes to be seen by others.

In addition to the creation of profiles, such social networking site activities as updating your status, uploading photos, sharing websites, commenting on the profiles, and even playing games like Farm Town, Mafia Wars, and Bejeweled are used in the development of identities. Status updates, for example, do not simply let others in a network know what a person is doing or what a person is thinking.

Photo 9.3 What activities are related to identity construction on social networking sites like Facebook? (See page 236.)

Listen in on Your Life

If you have your own page on a social networking site, what do you believe it conveys to other people about you? How do these perceptions compare with how you view yourself? Do your friends agree about the messages being conveyed?

These updates present a person's worldview to others and how he or she wishes to be seen.

A person's activities and disclosures on social networking sites are often very strategic, but sometimes people include information without fully considering how it will impact the way others see them. Likewise, in face-to-face interactions, people do not always consider the impact of what they say and do on how they are perceived by others. Regardless of similarities with other forms of communication, however, the disclosure and corresponding identity development involved make social networking sites very unique.

Self-disclosure taking place on social networking sites has led communication scholars to question many classic studies and observations related to disclosure. Communication scholars previously believed that self-disclosure occurs gradually as trust is established in a relationship, but these sites instead provide a tremendous amount of personal information all at once. Peripheral, or relatively minor, information, such as favorite music, appears on these sites at the same time as more personal information, such as relationship history and sexual preferences. Scholars also believed that peripheral information about the self would be shared initially; that deeper personal information would be shared later; and, further, that information shared with one person would be different from that shared with another person, depending on the relationships between these individuals. More information, in general, and more personal information, specifically, would be shared with close friends than acquaintances. Unless access is blocked and sometimes in spite of access being blocked, anyone—regardless of his or her relationship with a creator—can view the information included on most social networking site pages. You may have heard stories about people being kicked out of school or losing a job because of the content shared on their social networking webpage. Someone had access to information that he or she would not have gained otherwise.

Relational Technology and Personal Relationships

Having examined the influence of technology on identities, we can now fully explore how technology and relationships are connected and mutually influential. Examining the influence of technology on relationships, Kraut, Brynin, and Kiesler (2006) have observed that on one level changes in technology simply allow people to achieve relatively stable relational goals in new ways. People exchange birthday greetings, for example, through e-cards rather than a traditional card sent through the postal service. Correspondence takes place through phone calls rather than letters. These authors also maintain, however, that more than simply altering how traditional goals are met, technological transformation also changes what can be accomplished, creating new relational goals and norms.

Cell phones, online communication, and other technological advancements are changing how people communicate and form relationships with others, as well as altering established relational goals and norms. This section of the chapter examines the impact of cell phones and other relational technologies on interactions among people. We then examine the characteristics of online communication and its influence on relationships and social networks. Finally, we consider how people interact not only with one another but also with technology itself.

Cell Phones and Personal Relationships

Cell phones have come to represent constant connection to those who possess your number, and how freely people give out their cell phone numbers varies. Giving or denying someone access to your cell phone number establishes both the *boundaries* and the *degree of closeness* desired and expected within the relationship. Limiting the availability of contact with a person establishes specific relational boundaries. How that person views and evaluates such limits depends on your relationship. Refusing to provide a cell phone number to a friend may be viewed negatively; therapists not providing clients with their numbers may be viewed as legitimate.

Providing another person with your cell phone number suggests a desire for connection with that individual and perhaps an indication of the type of relationship you wish to establish. For instance, making your number available to an acquaintance could imply a desire to develop a closer type of relationship. As above, the evaluation and meaning of this action generally depend on your relationship with that person. Although it serves to maintain the existence and importance of your relationship, providing a close friend with your cell phone number may be expected. Patients receiving the cell phone number of their doctor along with instructions to call at any time may see this action as more meaningful or consequential because it runs counter to the expectations associated with that relationship.

David rarely gives out his cell phone number, and his wife is the only person who ever calls him on that phone, which for him has become an exclusive symbol of their relationship. Although many colleagues and friends know Steve's U.S. cell phone number, very few people know the number of the cell phone he uses while in Europe—including his coauthor! When returning home to England, Steve becomes symbolically and literally separated from all but a few individuals in his social network. As is the case for many other people, our cell phones have brought about personal and social connotations that dictate their use, including who is able to contact us.

Constant Connection and Availability

Connection and availability are fully established when calls are actually made and text messages are sent. There are times when the content of these messages is less important than the actual contact itself. Such instances are similar to how seemingly mundane everyday talk keeps relationships going without necessarily adding much

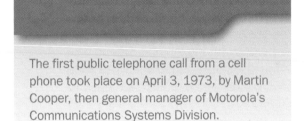

The first public telephone call from a cell phone took place on April 3, 1973, by Martin Cooper, then general manager of Motorola's Communications Systems Division.

in terms of substance. Connecting with another person reestablishes the existence and importance of the relationship, confirming for both parties its existence and value in their lives. At other times the content of these messages is vitally important, especially during the enactment of relational information and other relational maintenance strategies. Of course, letters sent via the Pony Express in 1860 accomplished the same things, so what makes cell phones so different? We are glad you asked!

Cell phones allow people to be in "perpetual contact" with others (J. Katz & Aakhus, 2002). If you have your cell phone with you, you have your social network with you as well. The ability to make instant contact with another person regardless of geographic location creates a symbolic connection unlike that created by any previous communication technology. Research indicates that 70% of couples with cell phones contact each other at least once a day just to say hello or to chat briefly, whereas only 54% of couples who do not own cell phones do this (Kennedy, Smith, Wells, & Wellman, 2008).

This constant connection with others can provide comfort and security in a relationship or can lead to challenges. Relationships require connections between people, as well as autonomy and independence (Baxter & Montgomery, 1996). While the feeling of constant connection made possible through cell phones can be beneficial, it may decrease feelings of autonomy, equally important and necessary in relationships.

New relational expectations have also developed as a result of constant availability through cell phones. When calling someone's cell phone, you expect he or she will be readily available. If he or she does not answer the phone, you generally expect him or her to return the call in a timely manner and provide a plausible excuse for not answering in the first place. The same expectations apply when sending someone a text message. Failure to respond to a text message in a timely manner—or failure to respond, period—can constitute a violation in the relationship (Ling, 2004).

Photo 9.4 In what ways could the use of a cell phone create shared experiences? (See page 236.)

Shared Experience

We can discuss shared experience derived from the use of cell phones in two ways. First, the actual use of cell phones constitutes shared technological experience. Especially when people correspond through text messages, they engage in the use of the same technology. As discussed earlier in the chapter, particular groups assign great significance and meaning to the use of particular technology. More than simply transmitting information, the act of sending and receiving text messages both announces and establishes shared membership and acceptance into a group.

Cell phones also enable people to engage in shared experience even when physically separated. The immediate transmission of voice, picture, sound, and video provides people with the sense of experiencing an event or occasion together. A person in a disagreement with a romantic partner can be in simultaneous contact with a friend offering guidance and support and subsequently sharing in the experience. Joyous occasions and celebrations can likewise be shared with others who are physically absent.

Social Coordination

One of the greatest relational consequences of the cell phone encompasses its use in coordinating physical encounters with others. Face-to-face interactions are created and synchronized through the use of cell phones. The ability to establish the physical location of others while in public creates opportunities for spontaneous physical interaction. If you call a friend while studying in the library only to discover that he or she is studying in the adjacent building, this discovery could lead to a decision to meet and take a break together. The revelation of proximity made possible through cell phones makes such encounters possible.

Cell phones enable people to synchronize their activities to the point of microcoordination. Making plans to meet someone previously involved establishing a fixed time and physical location for the interaction to occur, but the massive adoption of cell phones has resulted in time and physical location for contact becoming increasingly fluid. **Microcoordination** refers to the unique management of social interaction made possible through cell phones. Rich Ling (2004) has observed three varieties of microcoordination: (1) midcourse adjustment, (2) iterative coordination, and (3) softening of schedules (see Table 9.2).

Table 9.2 Ling's (2004) Three Varieties of Microcoordination	
Midcourse adjustment	Involves changing plans once a person has already set out for the encounter—for example, contacting the other person to change locations or to request that he or she pick up someone else on the way
Iterative coordination	Involves the progressive refining of an encounter. Cell phones have made actually establishing location and time unnecessary. Instead, people increasingly plan to meet without specifying an exact time or location. For instance, friends may agree to meet sometime tomorrow. As a result of progressive calls or messages, they eventually "zoom in on each other" (p. 72).
Softening of schedules	Involves adjusting a previously scheduled time. If you planned to meet a friend for coffee at 3:30 P.M. but a meeting with your advisor took longer than expected and you are running late, cell phones make it much easier to reach your friend and inform him or her of the delay.

Source: Ling, 2004.

Online Communication and Personal Relationships

Characteristics of Online Communication

Before discussing the influence of online communication on personal relationships, we want to first consider the unique characteristics of online communication. Recognizing that there are a number of unique forms of online communication, such as e-mail, chat rooms, message boards, and instant messaging, we examine the similarities among them.

Richness

One characteristic of online communication—and, for that matter, all text-based interactions—is the lack of nonverbal cues available to help determine meaning. Nonverbal communication, such as vocalics and kinesics, is incredibly valuable when crafting and interpreting messages. The number of verbal and nonverbal cues available through a medium or technology determines its **richness**. Face-to-face interactions are considered richer than other types of interaction since verbal communication and a range of nonverbal cues are available to convey and interpret meaning. Phone conversations are less rich since they are limited to verbal communication and vocalics. Online communication is limited to verbal communication, with no nonverbal cues available to assist in conveying and interpreting messages.

Accordingly, misunderstandings will more likely occur during online interactions than during telephone conversations or face-to-face interactions. This possibility does not automatically mean that all online interactions will result in misunderstandings, but it does mean that individuals engaging in online communication must carefully consider the messages they craft and carefully interpret the messages they receive. **Emoticons**, text-based symbols used to express emotions online, often help alleviate problems associated with a lack of nonverbal cues. The general absence of nonverbal cues, however, poses a distinct challenge when interacting online.

The very first "smiley face" emoticon :-) was used at 11:44 A.M. on September 19, 1982, by professor Scott E. Fahlman while contributing to an online bulletin board.

Asynchronous

A second characteristic of online communication is its asynchronous nature. In **synchronous communication**—for example, face-to-face interaction—people interact in real time and can send and receive messages at once. In **asynchronous communication**, containing a slight or prolonged delay, the interactants must alternate between sending and receiving. E-mail and even instant messaging represent asynchronous communication. Although some online interactions are close to real time, they still contain a delay, and people must take turns being sender and receiver. The asynchronous nature of online communication provides more time to consider the messages of others and to formulate messages.

While sometimes beneficial, the asynchronous nature of online communication also poses a challenge, especially when it comes to instant messaging. Boneva, Quinn, Kraut, Kiesler, and Shklovski (2006) have shown that instant messaging provides as much social support as face-to-face interactions and phone conversations, but people using instant messaging report feeling more disconnected from those with whom they use it to interact. While this finding may be the result of diminished nonverbal cues mentioned above, these authors maintain it may actually be the result of multitasking. Specifically, a person may have multiple instant messaging windows open at the same time, while also browsing the Internet, listening to the radio, watching television, and engaging in other activities.

Photo 9.5 In what ways does a webcam affect the richness and asynchronous nature of online communication? (See page 236.)

Quality

Due in large part to fears associated with new technologies mentioned earlier, many researchers have wrongly positioned face-to-face communication as superior to online communication in quality and influence. Conversely, online communication has been positioned as fraught with challenges and potential harm. Baym, Zhang, and Lin (2004), however, have noted that "face-to-face [interaction] may not always be the rich, deep, and inherently superior means of communication that it is often presumed to be" (p. 316). Comparing face-to-face, telephone, and online interactions, these authors found the quality of telephone and face-to-face interactions only slightly higher than that of online interactions. Quite often when online communication is evaluated harshly, the norms and practices of other forms of interaction have been used. This type of evaluation is no more legitimate or fair than using norms and practices of online communication to evaluate face-to-face or telephone interactions.

Two observations about the quality of online communication and other forms of interaction become clear. First, all forms of interaction have unique benefits and challenges. In this regard, online communication is no different from face-to-face communication, telephone conversations, or any other interaction. Second, how online communication is

Make Your Case

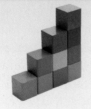

Some people have denounced online communication as inferior to face-to-face communication. Do you believe this evaluation? What are the advantages and disadvantages of both forms of communication? In what ways are online communication and face-to-face communication similar? In what ways are they different?

used has as much to do with its quality as its actual nature. Again, this use makes it no different from other forms of human communication. What does differentiate online communication is that it is still a relatively new form of interaction for many generations. People's perceptions of quality surrounding online communication are likely associated with their comfort and familiarity with interacting online, and as they continue to integrate online communication into their lives, it will become just as normal and commonplace as face-to-face communication.

Personal Relationships and Social Networks

Online communication enables people to maintain and enhance existing relationships, reinvigorate previous relationships, and create new relationships. Fears that the Internet will decrease social interaction and diminish the quality of relationships appear unfounded. In fact, increased use of the Internet allows for increased interaction with friends and family, not only online but also face-to-face and over the telephone. Furthermore, the majority of Internet users indicate that it has improved the quality of their relationships (Howard, Rainie, & Jones, 2002).

Contrarian Challenge

We have emphasized the positive aspects of online communication. What negative aspects of online communication can you come up with?

Accessibility of contact is perhaps what makes online communication so useful in maintaining existing relationships. Relationships take a great deal of effort to maintain, the basis of which involves enacting them through regular contact. The ease with which contact can be made online may very well increase the likelihood that it will take place at all.

Online communication appears to supplement rather than replace traditional forms of interaction. As people use the Internet to connect with friends, family, and acquaintances, it appears as if face-to-face interactions and telephone calls actually increase. While it seems everyone spends a great deal of time online, face-to-face communication remains the most frequent type of interaction among college students (Baym et al., 2004).

The type of online communication used appears to be associated with distance. People use both e-mail and instant messaging when interacting with others regardless of distance. However, they are less likely to use e-mail to contact people who live nearby and more likely to use it to contact long-distance friends and family (Quan-Haase & Wellman, 2002). On the other hand, people are much more likely to use instant messaging to interact with others living nearby (Boneva et al., 2006).

Social Networks

Online communication is dramatically changing the construction and nature of social networks. For instance, Internet users are more likely to maintain larger and more diverse social networks. Studying the impact of the Internet on social networks, Boase, Horrigan, Wellman, and Rainie (2006, p. 5) distinguished two types of connections in social networks: core ties and significant ties (see Table 9.3). Core ties tend to remain the same

Table 9.3 Core Ties and Significant Ties
Core ties include people with whom you have a very close relationship and are in frequent contact. You often discuss important matters in life with core ties, and you often seek their assistance in times of need.
Significant ties, though more than mere acquaintances, represent a somewhat weaker connection. You make less contact with significant ties and are less likely to talk with them about important issues in your life or to seek help from them, but they are still there for you when needed.

regardless of Internet activity, while Internet users report a greater number of significant ties. While the size of core ties may remain, Internet use has been shown to increase the diversity of core ties. For instance, Internet users are more likely to have nonrelatives as members of their core network (Hampton, Sessions, Her, & Rainie, 2009).

Another consequence of online communication is the geographic diversity of social networks. Traditionally, social networks have developed around geography-based communities. In other words, people in social networks tend to live in the same town or at least nearby. While physical proximity still plays a large role in the development of social networks, online communication has resulted in more geographically dispersed networks (Boase et al., 2006). Some people decry the fact that fewer and fewer people socialize with or even know their neighbors, but this does not necessarily mean people are antisocial or lack strong social support in times of need. Socialization and social support increasingly come from the Internet rather than next door. At the same time, Internet users are still just as likely as nonusers to visit with their neighbors (Hampton et al., 2009).

The Media Equation

While a great deal of research has focused on technology's impact on relationships between people, one research program has instead looked at relationships between people and technology. Before you start making dinner reservations at a fancy restaurant for you and your computer, this research program has not revealed the co-construction of shared meaning, reality, and other features of human-to-human relationships. It has, however, uncovered something incredibly fascinating.

Introduced by Byron Reeves and Clifford Nass (2002), the **media equation** maintains that interactions with technology are the same as interactions with other people, and people use the same social rules and expectations when interacting with both. You interact with your computer as if it is an actual person.

When they first hear about the media equation, many people deny that they treat technology similarly to people. Yet, have you ever pleaded with your computer to go faster when experiencing a slow connection or yelled at your computer when it crashed? You may even have talked to or humanized other inanimate objects and technology. Accordingly, it may not be so inconceivable that your interactions with technology mirror your interactions with other people, especially given the interactive nature of more recent technological innovations.

To test the media equation, Reeves and Nass (2002) found research involving people-people interaction; erased one of the references to *people* and replaced it with *computer, television,* or another technology; and conducted the study using the same techniques that established the people–people findings. If the study found "people like people who compliment them," they would change this finding to "people like *computers* who compliment them," and then they would test it using the same methods that established the original findings. The results of the people–technology experiments consistently mirrored the results of the original people–people experiment.

I Am Me; I Am My Computer (Personality)

People generally prefer to be around and interact with people who are similar to them rather than people who are different. If you have a dominant personality, you will prefer interacting with other people with dominant personalities. Likewise, if you are submissive, you will prefer interacting with other submissive people. People, it turns out, not only perceive computers as having dominant or submissive personalities but also prefer computers whose personality is similar to their own. Furthermore, people are able to recognize that these computers have such similar personalities.

People's relationships with technology may become especially close in the relatively near future. David Levy (2007) convincingly argues in the book *Love and Sex with Robots* that by the year 2050, "robots will be hugely attractive to humans as companions because of their many talents, senses, and capabilities. They will have the capacity to fall in love with humans and to make themselves romantically attractive and sexually desirable to humans" (p. 22).

Computers Say the Kindest Things (Flattery)

Remember that "brownnoser" or "suck-up" from your high school, the one who always complimented the teachers on their clothing or that "wonderfully crafted and inspirational" examination or assignment? That person knew what he or she was doing. The official term for this behavior is *ingratiation,* and it turns out to be quite effective, whether or not it is genuine or deserved (Gordon, 1996). People like other people who compliment them, and the same evaluative response holds true for computers: People, it was discovered, like computers who offer them praise more than computers that offer no evaluation.

Be Nice to Your Computer (Politeness)

When someone asks for your feedback on a project he or she has completed or asks about his or her performance on a task, you generally provide him or her with a positive response. If someone else asked you about that person's performance, your response would be more negative than if that person asked you directly. Not necessarily deceitful, you are just not being as negative as you could be because you do not want to hurt his or her feelings. The same patterns of interaction were found to take place with computers. When asked to evaluate a computer while using the same computer to type their responses, people responded much more positively than when typing their responses on a different computer. They did not want to hurt the computer's feelings. On a personal note, we would like to acknowledge the extraordinary contribution of the computer we are using to type this section of the book—and we hope it does not crash!

FOCUS QUESTIONS REVISITED

1. How have emerging technologies generally been viewed?

The emergence of any new communication technology has historically elicited choruses of concern and anxiety, surprisingly similar in nature. Of course, the introduction of a new technology is not without its supporters, although voices of praise are usually overwhelmed by those of criticism. As with similarities among the concerns, the praise offered for each emerging technology is often quite similar. At the center of all criticism and praise of technologies rest their influence and effect on social interaction and connections among people. This influence is probably why criticism and praise surrounding each emerging technology have sounded so similar; relationships among people have been the one constant throughout all human technological development.

2. What factors influence identity construction through the use of relational technologies?

There are a number of factors influencing the meaning of relational technologies. For instance, media generations develop unique standards and methods for evaluating technology and consequently respond to relational technologies in different ways. The actual use and incorporation of relational technology by a social network will determine the social meanings that subsequently develop. The speed at which new technologies are adopted will influence the meaning associated with the use of particular products and services. Further, specific meanings are associated with the use of particular products and service providers within a social system. Ringtones do not simply inform someone of an incoming call or message; they also can be viewed as a method of identity construction. Finally, the use of relational technologies can be considered a performance through which identities are constructed. The proper use or performance of technology has been established socially and includes such issues as where relational technologies should be used and content.

3. What do your screen name and e-mail address tell others about you?

The selection of a screen name or user name may inform others of genuine perceived characteristics or characteristics you wish to establish online. E-mail addresses can reveal service providers, professions, affiliations, and other personal information.

4. How are content creation and social networking sites impacting the construction of identity and self-disclosure?

Social networking pages, blogs, and the posting of original pictures, videos, reviews, comments, and other personal online creations enable people to share and display their thoughts, interests, talents, and experiences and convey themselves to others in ways they wish to be viewed and understood. Social networking sites, especially, have led communication scholars to question classic studies and observations related to disclosure. Self-disclosure on these sites does not take place gradually; rather, people provide a tremendous amount of personal information all at once. Furthermore, they reveal relatively minor information at the same time as deeper personal information. Finally, they give the same personal information to everyone instead of disclosing certain information to or hiding certain information from individuals with whom they share a particular relationship.

5. How do cell phones impact interactions with others?

Cell phones have come to represent constant connection to those who possess your number. Giving someone your cell phone number or denying someone access to your number establishes both the boundaries and the degree of closeness desired and expected within your relationship with that person. A new relational expectation of constant availability has developed as a result of the constant availability made possible through cell phones. Also, shared experience develops from the actual use of cell phones and from the immediate transmission of voice, picture, sound, and video. Finally, the use of cell phones makes possible the microcoordination of physical social interaction.

6. What makes online communication different from other forms of communication?

The richness of a medium or technology, determined by the number of verbal and nonverbal cues available, differs among forms of communication. Online communication is considered less rich than face-to-face and telephone interactions. Further, online communication is considered asynchronous, meaning there is either a slight or a prolonged delay of the sending and receiving of messages. Face-to-face and telephone interactions are considered synchronous, meaning the people involved interact in real time and can be at once senders and receivers.

7. How is online communication impacting personal relationships and social networks?

Online communication enables people to maintain and enhance existing relationships, reinvigorate previous relationships, and create new relationships. Online communication also appears to supplement rather than replace traditional forms of interaction. Further, online communication enables people to maintain larger and more diverse social networks.

8. Do people interact with technology like they interact with other people?

According to the media equation theory, people's interactions with technology are the same as their interactions with other people, using the same social rules and expectations. While the media equation corresponds with basic views of human interaction, it has not yet been applied to the more advanced conceptions of human interaction and relationships examined in communication studies.

KEY CONCEPTS

asynchronous communication 228	microcoordination 227
content creation 222	relational technologies 216
emoticons 228	richness 228
media equation 231	synchronous communication 228
media generations 217	

QUESTIONS TO ASK YOUR FRIENDS

1. Ask your friends at school how they feel when someone's cell phone rings during class. Do they find it irritating or believe it is acceptable behavior? If you have friends attending another school, ask them how they feel when someone's cell phone rings during class. How do their answers compare with those of friends at your school?

2. If you have your own page on a social networking site, ask your friends to compare how you present yourself on this page to how you present yourself off-line. In what ways are they different and similar?

3. Ask your friends about their most recent technology purchase and why they purchased that particular product. Are there any similarities in the products purchased by your friends? Are there any similarities in their reasons for making the purchase?

MEDIA LINKS

1. Examine how characters on television programs use and perform relational technology. Do their use and performance of technology parallel that of your friends, family, coworkers, or classmates?

2. Describe how relationships are featured in the television, print, and Internet advertisements of cell phone companies.

3. Visit the official websites of various television series and movies. How many of these sites have chat rooms or discussion boards available to connect fans and viewers? How might establishing these relational connections influence the number of people watching these series and films? How might the establishment of these connections influence the interpretation and use of this material?

ETHICAL ISSUES

1. In many ways, it is easier to fool people in chat rooms or when instant messaging than when talking with them face-to-face. Do you think deceitfulness online is more pardonable than being deceitful when talking with someone face-to-face?

2. Students have been suspended from some schools for content on social networking sites. Should schools be allowed to suspend students for this content? Would your assessment change depending on whether the content *did* or *did not* pertain to school-related issues, activities, or people?

3. Employers have based hiring decisions on social networking site content. Do you believe these actions are justified? In what ways do employers using social networking sites for the evaluation of job candidates compare and contrast with school officials using these sites for student discipline?

ANSWERS TO PHOTO CAPTIONS

Photo 9.1 ▪ The generations in which these gentlemen were born will likely influence their perceptions and use of technology.

Photo 9.2 ▪ It is never a good idea to use a cell phone in the classroom. The use of cell phones annoys classmates just as much as it annoys instructors—and it *really* annoys most instructors!

Photo 9.3 ▪ Identity construction on social networking sites includes the creation of profiles along with status updates, uploading photos, sharing websites, commenting on the profiles, playing games, and other activities.

Photo 9.4 ▪ Shared experience derived from the use of cell phones can come from a shared technological experience and from enabling people to engage in shared experiences when physically separated.

Photo 9.5 ▪ Webcams increase the richness of online interaction by increasing the number of nonverbal cues available. They also enable online communication to become more synchronous.

STUDENT STUDY SITE

Visit the study site at **www.sagepub.com/boc2e** for e-flashcards, practice quizzes, journal articles and additional study resources.

REFERENCES

Baxter, L. A., & Montgomery, B. M. (1996). *Relating: Dialogues and dialectics.* New York: Guilford.

Baym, N. K., Zhang, Y. B., & Lin, M.-C. (2004). Social interactions across media: Interpersonal communication on the Internet, telephone, and face-to-face. *New Media & Society, 6,* 299–318.

Boase, J., Horrigan, J. B., Wellman, B., & Rainie, L. (2006, January 25). *The strength of Internet ties: The Internet and email aid users in maintaining their social networks and provide pathways to help when people face big decisions.* Washington, DC: Pew Internet & American Life Project.

Boneva, B. S., Quinn, A., Kraut, R., Kiesler, S., & Shklovski, I. (2006). Teenage communication in the instant messaging era. In R. Kraut, M. Brynin, & S. Kiesler (Eds.), *Computers, phones, and the Internet: Domesticating information technology* (pp. 201–218). New York: Oxford University Press.

Bortree, D. S. (2005). Presentation of self on the Web: An ethnographic study of teenage girls' weblogs. *Education, Communication & Information, 5,* 25–39.

Campbell, S. W. (2006). Perceptions of mobile phones in college classrooms:

Ringing, cheating, and classroom policies. *Communication Education, 55,* 280–294.

Campbell, S. W., & Russo, T. C. (2003). The social construction of cell telephony: An application of the social influence model of perceptions and uses of cell phones within personal communication networks. *Communication Monographs, 70,* 317–334.

Chesebro, J. W. (1984). The media reality: Epistemological functions of media in cultural systems. *Critical Studies in Mass Communication, 2,* 111–130.

Fischer, C. (1992). *America calling: A social history of the telephone to 1940.* Berkeley: University of California Press.

Gordon, R. A. (1996). Impact of ingratiation on judgments and evaluations: A meta- analytic investigation. *Journal of Personality and Social Psychology, 17,* 45–70.

Gumpert, G., & Cathcart, R. (1985). Media grammars, generations, and media gaps. *Critical Studies in Mass Communication, 2,* 23–35.

Hampton, K. N., Sessions, L. F., Her, E. J., & Rainie, L. (2009). *Social isolation and new technology.* Washington, DC: Pew Internet & American Life Project.

Howard, P. E. N., Rainie, L., & Jones, S. (2002). Days and nights on the Internet. In B. Wellman & C. Haythornwaite (Eds.), *The Internet in everyday life* (pp. 45–73). Malden, MA: Blackwell.

Katz, E., Levin, M. L., & Hamilton, H. (1963). Traditions of research on the diffusion of innovations. *American Sociological Review, 28,* 237–252.

Katz, J. E. (2006). *Magic in the air: Cell communication and the transformation of social life.* New Brunswick, NJ: Transaction.

Katz, J. E., & Aakhus, M. A. (Eds.). (2002). *Perpetual contact: Cell communication, private talk, public performance.* Cambridge, UK: Cambridge University Press.

Kennedy, T. L. M., Smith, A., Wells, A. T., & Wellman, B. (2008). *Networked families.* Washington, DC: Pew Internet & American Life Project.

Kraut, R., Brynin, M., & Kiesler, S. (Eds.). (2006). *Computers, phones, and the Internet: Domesticating information technology.* New York: Oxford University Press.

Lenhart, A., Purcell, K., Smith, A., & Zickhur, K. (2010). *Social media & mobile Internet use among teens and young adults.* Washington, DC: Pew Internet & American Life Project.

Levy, D. (2007). *Love and sex with robots: The evolution of human-robot relationships.* New York: HarperCollins.

Ling, R. (2004). *The cell connection: The cell phone's impact on society.* San Francisco: Morgan Kaufmann.

Lobet-Maris, C. (2003). Cell phone tribes: Youth and social identity. In L. Fortunati, J. E. Katz, & R. Riccini (Eds.), *Mediating the human body: Technology, communication, and fashion* (pp. 87–92). Mahwah, NJ: Lawrence Erlbaum.

Quan-Haase, A., & Wellman, B. (with Witte, J. C., & Hampton, K.). (2002). Capitalizing on the Internet: Social contact, civic engagement, and sense of community. In B. Wellman & C. Haythornwaite (Eds.), *Internet and everyday life* (pp. 291–324). Malden, MA: Blackwell.

Reeves, B., & Nass, C. (2002). *The media equation: How people treat computers, television, and new media like real people and places.* Stanford, CA: Center for the Study of Language and Information.

10

Relational Uses and Understanding of Media

Think about the amount of time people actually spend using media each day. How much time do you think the average person spends watching television, listening to music, reading, playing video games, watching movies, and using the Internet?

To determine the most accurate measure of media use, the Middletown Media Studies compared the results of telephone surveys, diary records in which people documented their own activities, and direct observation in which people were followed and observed during every waking moment of the day (Papper, Holmes, & Popovich, 2004). It was discovered that people actually spend double the amount of time using media than they believe. These studies also established that people do not use media in isolation but often use two or more media systems simultaneously, an activity referred to as **concurrent media use**. For example, you may be reading this book while listening to the radio or watching television. Including concurrent media use, the most media-active person observed in these studies spent more than 17 hours using media each day, and the least media-active person observed spent a bit more than 5 hours using media each day. The average amount of time spent using media daily was nearly 11 hours.

While the sheer amount of time spent using media is reason enough for the importance of media use as an area of study, perhaps more significant is the

The Middletown Media Studies also uncovered that while the majority of media use occurs in the home, 34% of media use occurs outside the home in such locations as businesses, automobiles, schools, and workplaces. This percentage will likely increase in the coming years as video, music, and the Internet become more accessible through cell phones and other relational technologies.

A study on the media use of children uncovered numbers similar to those established through the Middletown Media Studies. Including concurrent media use, the average child uses media for 10 hours and 45 minutes daily (Rideout, Foehr, & Roberts, 2010).

impact of media on relationships and the impact of relationships on the use of media. Media use at home frequently occurs in the presence of family members, close friends, and romantic partners, while media use outside the home often occurs with those with whom you share more social relationships, such as classmates, coworkers, acquaintances, and even strangers. In fact, the influence of relationships on your use of media is even evident when you are physically alone. The most common medium used concurrently with television was found to be the telephone (Papper et al., 2004). Unless the people in the study were listening to recorded messages and not talking with someone else, their use of television occurred in the context of their relationships.

This chapter first explores early views of media and the media audience. We then position the media audience as active consumers of media products who assign unique meaning to media texts and use media for specific reasons. Next, we discuss the relational uses and functions of media, including how media provide a context for relationships, inform people about relationships, and function as an alternative to relationships. We then examine the use of media in everyday communication, looking specifically at the prevalence of media as a topic of conversation, the impact of media in the understanding and dissemination of media messages, and the role of media in the development of relationships and identities.

Focus Questions

1. Why is the term *mass media* inappropriate?
2. Why might audience members be considered active consumers of media?
3. What are the relational uses and functions of media?
4. What functions does talk about media serve in everyday communication?

Is *Mass Media* an Appropriate Term?

Media were originally thought to exert absolute and uniform influence on the lives of "the masses." This view assumed that all media messages were being received and interpreted by members of the audience in the same manner and that they all resulted in the same impact or effect on each audience member. If everyone in your class watched the same episode of a television program, this view would hold that it would be received by every member of your class in the exact same way; the episode would mean the exact same thing to everyone in your class and have the exact same effects on each of you. This belief in the inescapable and standardized nature of media messages has been characterized as the *hypodermic needle* or *magic bullet* capability of media.

Media scholars have now debunked as incorrect the notion of all-powerful media exerting unrestricted influence on a susceptible audience. Media do not exist independently from the cultural, political, and economic systems in which they are embedded (Chesebro & Bertelsen, 1996). Further, media audiences are not passive receptors but rather actively engaged users of media. The classic view of media also overlooked the profound influence of relationships, which play a huge role in the reception of media messages, how they are interpreted, how they are used, and their potential impact on opinion and behaviors. We discuss these issues in more detail later in the chapter.

Before addressing these issues, however, there is another problem with labeling media audiences as *mass* that must be discussed. Although people occasionally use terms like *mass media* and *mass audience*, the use of these terms is based more on tradition than on actual conditions. The term *mass* is indicative of media's ability to reach large numbers of people, an essentially massive audience. However, these numbers are not as large as one might be led to believe. In what follows, we discuss (a) the increased availability of media, (b) narrowcasting, and (c) the creation of unique media experiences.

Increased Availability

As the number and availability of media products have increased throughout the years, a less massive audience is receiving the same media product. Think about the changes in the amount and accessibility of media products that have taken place in the past century. For quite some time, people could choose among three broadcast television stations, which meant that on a given evening, television viewers watched one of three different programs. The hundreds of programs now available on demand with the use of DVRs, webcasts, and podcasts increase the number of available options even more. Radio was once limited to the few stations that could be received with a good antenna. Satellite radio has radically increased the number of channels available, and many traditional radio stations worldwide are now available through live Internet feeds. People were once limited to local newspapers. Now hundreds of newspapers—even international ones—are available online, and many newspapers are digitally reproduced and distributed in multiple cities throughout the country.

While the audience of some media still numbers in the millions, comparing present numbers with past illustrates the dramatic drop that has taken place. The highest-rated half-hour television program of all time is "The Giant Jackrabbit" episode of *The Beverly Hillbillies*, which aired on January 8, 1964, with a 65 share.

Case in Point

Keep a record of how much media you use in a given day. How do you think it will compare to the averages discovered through the Middletown Media Studies? Make sure you record media use as it happens. Do not forget to count concurrent media use as well as exposure to media while in public spaces.

Remnants of this view of media are still evident when people blame television, video games, music, movies, or other media for increases in crime, school shootings, or other tragedies that befall society.

Table 10.1 Nielsen TV Ratings for Network Prime-Time Series: Top 10

Rank	Program Name	Network	Day	Time	Household Rating/Share	Audience	Viewers
1	AMERICAN IDOL	FOX	Wed	9:00 PM	13.7/21.0	15,685,000	23,574,000
2	AMERICAN IDOL	FOX	Tue	8:00 PM	13.4/21.0	15,319,000	23,414,000
3	DANCING WITH THE STARS	ABC	Mon	8:00 PM	12.6/19.0	14,430,000	20,278,000
4	MENTALIST, THE	CBS	Tue	9:00 PM	10.4/16.0	11,854,000	16,678,000
5	NCIS	CBS	Tue	8:00 PM	10.4/17.0	11,917,000	16,723,000
6	GREY'S ANATOMY	ABC	Thu	9:00 PM	10.3/16.0	11,800,000	15,546,000
7	DANCING W/STARS RESULTS	ABC	Tue	9:00 PM	9.4/14.0	10,763,000	14,556,000
8	CSI	CBS	Thu	9:00 PM	9.2/15.0	10,589,000	14,912,000
9	CRIMINAL MINDS	CBS	Wed	9:00 PM	8.9/14.0	10,176,000	14,128,000
10	CSI: MIAMI	CBS	Mon	10:00 PM	8.7/14.0	9,979,000	13,718,000

Source: http://tvlistings.zap2it.com/ratings/weekly.html.

This means that 65% of all television sets in use at that moment were tuned to that episode! Current top-rated programs (see Table 10.1) usually average a third of that number.

Narrowcasting

Coupled with and at least partially responsible for the rise in the number of media options available has been an increased tendency to focus a particular media product on specific audiences. **Narrowcasting** is the tendency to focus media products on specific audience members connected by a common bond. These common bonds can be based on demographics, hobbies, political affiliations, occupations, and other characteristics. For instance, a mass audience may not be interested in scrapbooking or model trains, but a small, narrow audience interested in these topics will seek out and use media devoted to them.

To comprehend this media trend, consider the number of magazines being

Four decades ago, Gary Gumpert (1970) introduced the term *mini-com* to describe media becoming increasingly directed and adapted to multiple "small mass audiences" connected through interest in particular content (p. 286).

published. National magazines, such as *Life*—which once boasted huge numbers of subscribers—no longer exist. The thousands of magazine titles now available target specific populations, such as budget travelers, fishing enthusiasts, and Angus cattle farmers. Someday, a publisher may even aim a magazine called *British and Redneck Professors Monthly* exclusively at us!

Creating Individual Media Experiences

Beyond increased media options and a focus on specific audiences, members of an audience have always possessed the ability to create original and distinct media products through their individual and unique use of each media system. As you flip through the channels while trying to find something to watch on television or go back and forth between two or more channels, you create a distinct television product unavailable to people not watching with you. The selection and arrangement of songs on your iPod or MP3 player are distinctive and organized in ways unimaginable by the producers of those songs. Your scanning of headlines and pictures in the newspaper, along with your selection of stories, comics, sports reports, horoscopes, advice columns, letters to the editor, classifieds, and other material, will be unique compared to the experience of any other reader.

The Active Use of Media

As we mentioned earlier, classic views of the media audience positioned its members as passively receiving media messages without any thought, critical evaluation, or resistance. In reality, audience members actively select and attend to media, assign unique meanings to media messages, and use media for specific and often very relational reasons.

Contrarian Challenge

We characterize the audience as active consumers of media. However, can you think of examples where the audience is more passive than active? Are audiences always as active as we maintain?

Selecting and Attending to Media

Characterizing audience members as selective users highlights the discriminating nature of the media audience. People do not consume everything available during mediated experiences; nor do they provide their full attention to the media products they use. When you last visited a news site on the Internet, you probably used some areas of the site and not others. This manner of consuming media is the result of needing only some parts of a media product and receiving greater satisfaction from some parts of a media product than from others.

Selective Exposure

People generally attend to media that support—and avoid media that counter—existing beliefs, values, and attitudes (Zillmann & Bryant, 1985). You are more likely to

Photo 10.1 According to the Middletown Media Studies, what type of media use seems to be taking place? (See page 259.)

listen to radio talk show hosts who support your political views and avoid those hosts who counter your views. A favorite song coming on the radio will likely result in an increase in volume, and a disliked song will lead to changing the station or turning off the radio. As you might imagine, selective exposure research has undergone profound changes through the years resulting from massive increases in the amount of media products available, along with changes in technology, such as recording devices and even the remote control (Bellamy & Walker, 1996).

Attention to Media

In addition to the actual selection of media, the amount of attention audience members provide to media will fluctuate. One reason attention fluctuates is that people often *engage in multiple activities* when using media. Someone on a bus may glance at passing cars or watch other passengers while reading a book. People often talk to one another while watching a television program at home, which decreases their focus on the program being viewed. As we discussed earlier, people often engage in concurrent media use. Consequently, you may listen to music while using the Internet and vary your degree of concentration on one or the other at any given moment.

A second reason the amount of attention provided to media fluctuates has to do with *involvement* with the media. Involvement entails getting into or becoming engrossed in the media product or experience (Biocca, 1988). An example of high involvement is really enjoying and becoming engrossed in a movie and feeling a part of the action. An example of low involvement is watching a boring movie at the request of a friend and mentally formulating tomorrow's to-do list instead of paying attention to the action on-screen.

Commercial breaks may impact your involvement in a television program, but one study suggests that lower involvement is not the only thing that may happen during commercial breaks. People who are really engrossed in a television program will actually respond negatively to products advertised during commercial interruptions (Wang & Calder, 2006).

A final reason for fluctuation in the amount of attention paid to media takes us back to their actual selection. If you *need* the information provided by a particular media product, you will be more likely to focus your attention on it than if you do not. If you are in the market for a new automobile and an automobile commercial comes on the screen, you will likely pay more attention to it than to an advertisement for a product you have little interest in purchasing.

The Polysemic Nature of Media Texts

The polysemic nature of media texts is a fundamental assumption of the active audience approach to media. Words—and all symbols, for that matter—do not have a single meaning but instead are capable of having multiple meanings depending on occasions, circumstances, and how they are used. Media texts, which can include words, visuals, and sounds among other symbolic events, are no different. Rather than having a single meaning, media texts are open to a variety of meanings and are given these multiple meanings by members of the media audience.

A number of factors influence the meaning given to media texts. For instance, one study found that people's understanding and interpretation of television fiction differed significantly according to their cultural backgrounds (Liebes, 1988). An individual's ethnicity, gender, economic status, and other demographic and relational variables will influence how he or she interprets a given media text.

The variety of circumstances in which that person finds himself or herself and why that particular media text is being consumed will also influence his or her interpretation. For instance, a person listening to a political advertisement of a candidate he or she opposes will naturally interpret the information provided in a different manner than if he or she supported that candidate.

Consuming media with others will also impact the interpretation of media text. For instance, laughter from others in a movie theater may lead you to view events on the screen as funnier than you may have otherwise experienced. Talking about media both during the consumption of media texts and after they have been consumed will also influence the meanings people assign to media texts.

The Uses and Gratifications of Media

Research into the selection of media and the attention provided to it, the primary focus of **uses and gratifications** research, has attempted to determine why media systems are used and what audience members gain from their use. Uses and gratifications research originated from the study of radio soap opera audiences conducted in the early 1940s (Herzog, 1944) and grew in prominence during the 1950s and 1960s when researchers sought to determine the effectiveness of media campaigns (Blumler, 1980). Communication scholars James Chesebro and Dale Bertelsen (1996) have summarized the primary findings of this research, as shown in Table 10.2.

Table 10.2 Why People Use Media According to Uses and Gratifications Research	
1. Escapism	To avoid ongoing reality systems
2. Reality exploration	To secure basic information and to understand the world in which one exists
3. Character reference	To find suitable models for one's own life
4. Incidental reasons	A kind of miscellaneous category in which it is recognized that each individual may use or be gratified by media for very different, personal, and unique reasons

Source: Chesebro & Bertelsen, 1996, p. 35.

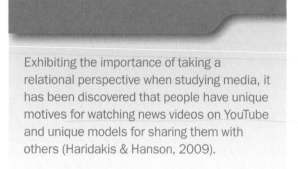

Exhibiting the importance of taking a relational perspective when studying media, it has been discovered that people have unique motives for watching news videos on YouTube and unique models for sharing them with others (Haridakis & Hanson, 2009).

While uses and gratifications research has provided us with a more accurate and realistic view of media use by an actively engaged audience, it is not without its limitations. Chesebro and Bertelsen's (1996) characterization of incidental reasons for media underscores the major limitation of uses and gratifications research. Essentially, this research focuses on *individual* uses of media rather than *relational* uses of media. Although some studies recognize the use of media for relational reasons, media research in general de-emphasizes these uses of media. However, a relational view of media is becoming increasingly vital as more and more of the world becomes mediated and interconnected in everyday life with relationships.

Relational Uses and Functions of Media

Photo 10.2 Do you think using the Internet as a family will become a shared media experience like watching television as a family? (See page 259.)

While often overlooked in the past, media are increasingly viewed as playing an influential role in people's relational lives. We next examine three key areas in which media enable relationships and fulfill social and relational needs.

The Use of Media Is a Shared Relational Activity

The use of media such as television often takes place in the company of others and for specific relational reasons. Most media—especially electronic media—enable interaction to take place and quite frequently are the actual basis for interaction. Print media, such as books, newspapers, and magazines, are more isolating, but, as Bausinger (1984) reminds us, people are still not alone when reading because "it takes place in the context of the family, friends, and colleagues" (p. 350).

A sense of connection also exists through shared experience with others through all types of media. In the case of television, regardless of decreases in the amount of people watching the same program and the uniqueness of each viewer's experience, still potentially millions of people watch the same material as you at the exact same time. This phenomenon has led Saenz (1994) to describe television as providing viewers with "the feeling of being present at a 'busy' live cultural site" (pp. 578–579). Using the Internet while watching television increases this feeling, with increasing numbers of people making comments and chatting with others while watching a program.

The use of media as a shared relational activity enables people to accomplish certain relational needs. Table 10.3 addresses four relational needs satisfied through the shared use of media.

Table 10.3 Relational Needs and the Shared Use of Media

Promoting interaction
Media enable interactions to take place. Even in media-rich households with multiple television sets, computers, and other media systems, families often use media together, which provides an opportunity for interactions to occur.

Withdrawing from interactions
Media also allow people to withdraw from social interaction (Lull, 1980). Watching a movie is a common first-date activity since it enables people to be together without being forced to talk.

Differentiating relationships
The shared use of media has even been shown to distinguish particular relationships from others. It was discovered that watching television was the most frequent activity shared by spouses (Argyle & Furnham, 1982). Friends and siblings may play video games together more than those involved in other forms of relationships.

Enacting and evaluating roles
The shared use of media also enables people to establish and enact specific relational roles, expectations, and boundaries (Lull, 1980). Participation in massively multiplayer online role-playing games (MMORPGs) has been found to enable romantic couples to learn more about one another's personality and worldview. Furthermore, parents who take part in these games with their children find they are able to develop a better understanding of their child's identity and social behavior (Yee, 2006).

Media Inform People About Relationships

People base their understanding of relationships and their actions within relationships in part on portrayals in media. In fact, scholars have noted that knowledge of the world and of society is increasingly based on media rather than on socialization by social networks (Cohen & Metzger, 1998). Books, magazines, newspapers, the Internet, movies, songs, and television programs feature both fictional and real social and personal relationships, the depictions of which fluctuate culturally and with the passing of time (LaRossa, 2004). Of course, a variety of sources inform your understanding of relationships, and you can compare the information you gain from one source with the information gained from other sources as you develop your own unique understanding of relationships.

Stereotypical gender roles in relationships are also reinforced in media. In prime-time television programs, women tend to fulfill relational roles involving family, friends, and romance. Men, on the other hand, tend to fulfill roles involving the workplace (Lauzen, Dozier, & Horan, 2008).

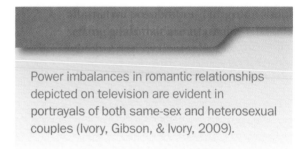

Power imbalances in romantic relationships depicted on television are evident in portrayals of both same-sex and heterosexual couples (Ivory, Gibson, & Ivory, 2009).

Media Inform Us How Relationships Should Look

Media representations of relationships provide information about relational roles and demographic characteristics. Essentially, people can learn about what relationships look like and what to expect from them based on their depiction in the media. The relationships depicted on television are not always realistic, however. People have the ability to compare relationships depicted in media with relationships observed or enacted in their physical lives, but media representations of relationships may nevertheless create unrealistic expectations and beliefs about how relationships should be enacted and what they should offer (Bachen & Illouz, 1996).

Relationships depicted in media do not always look like those that audiences personally experience. Multiple races, religions, sexual orientations, socioeconomic categories, and relationship configurations are underrepresented in television and in all media (Dates & Stroman, 2001; Heintz-Knowles, 2001; Robinson & Skill, 2001). Relationships portrayed in media do not look like most relationships. However, there is a tendency for people to believe that those relationships are normal and that their relationships should be compared to those in media.

Inaccurate portrayals of relationships in media may create unrealistic expectations. For instance, research has shown that viewing romantic genres, such as romantic comedies and soap operas, is associated with unrealistic and overly idealistic expectations about marriage (Segrin & Nabi, 2002). Watching romantically themed television has also been found to influence adolescents' expectations of romantic partners (Eggermont, 2004). In spite of what people may learn from watching sitcoms, problems that families experience are generally not resolved and forgotten in half an hour.

Photo 10.3 The sitcom *Modern Family* is a fantastic comedy that features three families. While diversity exists among these families, one traditional expectation of what a family should look like remains. Can you name it based on this picture? (See page 259.)

Even though media representations may lead to inaccurate expectations of relationships, they may be necessary when people are faced with a lack of models in their physical world. This use of media has proved critical in the formation of sexual identity among gay teens and adolescents, who frequently encounter a lack of physical life models to inform their sexuality (McKee, 2000; Meyer, 2003). Unfortunately, unrealistic expectations about relationships depicted in media may be especially influential in the absence of physical life comparisons (G. Jones & Nelson, 1996).

Media Inform Us How to Behave in Relationships

The second area in which media inform people about relationships is through the depiction of behaviors and interactions within relationships. Depictions of relationships in media provide models of behavior that inform people about how to engage in relationships. This use of media encompasses the **socialization impact of media**. Through media representations of relationships, people are informed how to enact the behaviors consistent with various relational roles and how to properly engage in interactions within these relationships.

Numerous studies have examined the depiction of family interactions on television and generally observed positive behavior and relational maintenance strategies. B. Greenberg (1980) examined television family interactions as either going toward, going against, or going away, as described in Table 10.4. Going toward actions were found to occur with much greater frequency among television families than the other two actions combined. Subsequent studies have found that television family behavior has changed throughout the decades but generally remains positive (Bryant, Aust, Bryant, & Venugopalan, 2001; Larson, 1993, 2001).

While the behaviors exhibited on *The Jerry Springer Show* are frequently based on conflict and violence, even this program has been shown to promote positive family behaviors. Through negative audience reaction to the transgressions and misbehavior of guests, Grabe (2002) has argued that the show actually imparts "frequent moral lessons about the virtues of family life in opposition to promiscuous behavior" (p. 314) and "might contribute to the promotion of traditional family values" (p. 326).

Table 10.4 B. Greenberg's (1980) Types of Television Family Interactions

Going toward actions	Positive acts of relationship maintenance, such as sharing or seeking information, showing concern, and overall acceptance
Going against actions	Negative acts such as ignoring, opposing, or attacking others
Going away actions	Acts through which a person distances him- or herself from others either physically or psychologically

Source: B. Greenberg, 1980.

Naturally, this use of media is not limited to families or television. All media systems depict a host of personal and social relationships used to inform us about behavior in relationships along with interaction techniques we might employ. Examples include what might happen on a first date, interactions with friends (Baxter, De Riemer, Landini, Leslie, & Singletary, 1985), interactions with annoying coworkers, and even communication between teachers and students (Freedman, 2003). Incidentally, we are still waiting to hear from Dwayne "The Rock" Johnson and Patrick Dempsey about portraying us in case this book is ever turned into a movie!

College Experience

Before coming to college, most of what you knew about the experience probably came from media portrayals. Naturally some depictions of college life are more accurate than others. Describe the differences between what you now know about college and what you thought you knew based on media portrayals. Have you had any difficulty managing expectations and realities?

In any case, people use media depictions to inform them of their own relationships. Like relational roles and demographic characterizations, media portrayals of relationship interactions and behaviors may not always mirror those in people's physical lives (Brinson, 1992), but they provide a vital source of information that people use in formulating and interacting in their actual relationships.

Media Function as Alternatives to Personal Relationships

Media serve many of the same uses and provide many of the same benefits as personal relationships. Needs and desires gained from personal relationships, such as companionship, information, support, control, intimacy, and entertainment, can be gained from media with the same level of satisfaction and fulfillment. In this sense, media and relationships have been described as "coequal alternatives" (Rubin & Rubin, 1985, p. 39).

Notice that the header for this section of the chapter and the description just mentioned label media as *alternatives* to rather than a *substitution* or *compensation* for personal relationships. Researchers have previously speculated that people might turn to media to compensate for a lack of companionship or substitute media when social and relational interaction is unavailable (Rosengren & Windahl, 1972). While this might be the case in some circumstances, media use has actually been found to enrich already satisfied social and personal lives (Perse & Butler, 2005). Furthermore, words like *substitution* imply an inferior entity is filling in or taking the place of a superior reality. As we will discuss, both personal relationships and media are more effective at fulfilling some needs and desires than others, but neither can be legitimately labeled as superior. Media and personal relationships are equally functional and interchangeable alternatives.

Photo 10.4 Based on research findings about family interactions on television, what types of interactions would you expect to find on *Family Guy*? (See page 259.)

Companionship and Relational Satisfaction From the Actual Use of Media

The relational and social satisfaction derived from media comes in part from their actual use and position within the home. Research has indicated that some people think of media, such as television or the computer, as a friend or member of the family (Gauntlett & Hill, 1999). Watching a movie, reading a book, browsing the Internet, playing a video game, or using any other type of media can provide the same amount of relational satisfaction and experience as going out with a group of friends. In Yee's (2006) study of MMORPGs, 27% of respondents named something that occurred during the game as their most satisfying experience of the past week. The same study found 33% of respondents indicated that their most negative experience of the past week had also occurred while playing the game, which indicates people's emotional investment in media.

Cohen and Metzger (1998) have observed that many motives for using media correspond with motives for engaging in personal relationships. These authors have specifically compared social and relational needs surrounding feelings of security, such as intimacy, accessibility, control, and relaxation. In all instances but intimacy, media seem to have the advantage.

Some people may actually prefer the companionship provided by media to that provided by those in their social network. Certainly, on some occasions people would rather use media than be with other people. Think back to a time when you wanted to spend time by yourself reading, watching television, listening to music, or using other media. Whether this use of media served to achieve a sense of companionship or to satisfy another need, you quite possibly enjoyed being away from other people and felt quite satisfied with your mediated experience.

Companionship and Relational Satisfaction From Parasocial Relationships

While media systems themselves can satisfy social and relational needs, many of these needs are met through relationships established with media characters and personalities, known as **parasocial relationships** (Horton & Wohl, 1956). Relationships people form with media characters and personalities have proved just as real and meaningful as those within their physical social networks. People consider and treat media characters and personalities just like they do family and friends who live next door.

When first learning about parasocial relationships, students often consider the concept a bit outrageous and often claim they do not form such relationships. They often associate these relationships with stalkers or those who are obsessed with particular characters or media personalities. However, these relationships are actually quite normal and extremely common. In fact, we are fairly confident that you have formed parasocial relationships with media characters and, at a minimum, thought of and talked about fictional characters as if they were actual people.

Make Your Case

Research indicates that parasocial relationships are just as meaningful and fulfilling as relationships in our physical world. Nevertheless, some people view these relationships as inferior to those in our physical social networks. Make a case for whichever assessment of parasocial relationships you believe is more accurate.

Parasocial relationships have consistently been found to parallel relationships in physical social networks. Some of these research findings are listed in Table 10.5.

Table 10.5 Parasocial Relationships Research Findings

- Similar to other relationships, people are often attracted to media characters and personalities with whom they perceive a certain degree of similarity (Turner, 1993).

- People use similar cognitive processes when developing parasocial relationships and other relationships (Perse & Rubin, 1989).

- People follow the same attachment styles used in physical relationships in their other relationships (Cole & Leets, 1999).

- Parasocial and other relationships provide similar levels of satisfaction (Kanazawa, 2002).

- As with face-to-face contact, parasocial contact has been shown to lower levels of prejudice (Schiappa, Gregg, & Hewes, 2005).

- Parasocial relationships are measured using similar criteria to those used to evaluate other relationships (Koenig & Lessan, 1985).

- Parasocial relationships and relationships with people in physical social networks have been found to follow similar patterns of development, maintenance, and dissolution. When parasocial relationships end (e.g., when a television character "dies"), people experience this loss in much the same manner as they do losing a close friend (Cohen, 2003).

The Use of Media in Everyday Communication

Media frequently provide the basis for conversation in social and personal relationships. While a definitive number of any topic of conversation is unattainable, reports have indicated that anywhere from 10.5% to half of all conversations involve media to some extent (Alberts, Yoshimura, Rabby, & Loschiavo, 2005; Allen, 1975, 1982; S. Greenberg, 1975). Even using a conservative estimation, these numbers position media as among the most frequent topics—if not the most frequent topic—of conversation among people. Discussions about media occur both while people are using the media system and while people are away from the media system and engaged in a number of other activities. Conversations about media serve six important functions in social and personal relationships.

Photo 10.5 What are some things that can happen when a couple talks about media? (See page 260.)

Media Provide a General Topic of Conversation

Media have long been recognized as providing people with a general topic of conversation (Berelson, 1949; Boskoff, 1970; Compesi, 1983; Katz, Hass, & Gurevitch, 1973; Lazarsfeld, 1940; Mendelsohn, 1964; Scannell, 1989; Smith, 1975). Much like discussing the weather, the pervasiveness of media enables people to establish a shared topic of discussion that in many cases will not lead to a heated disagreement. As a general topic of conversation, media play a vital social and relational role. Yet, even when media simply appear to provide a topic of conversation, important social and relational work takes place, and other functions of media talk discussed here are ultimately accomplished.

Talk About Media Impacts Their Interpretation and Understanding

Talking about media significantly affects such things as the meanings derived from them as well as emotional responses and attitudes. You may have previously discussed with others the impact or value of certain types of media, such as video games, television, movies, music, and books. Discussions of media value also involve actual media products and genres. People might tell you they absolutely love a new book just published or tell you about a great website they just found. Although not always immediately recognized as such, these discussions of media have influenced your use and understanding of media in some manner.

A more noticeable influence of discussions of media is their impact on the understanding and interpretation of particular media products. Some discussions of media products serve *directional* purposes, such as explaining the plot of a television program to someone who started watching it a few minutes late or describing what happened in a movie to someone who just returned from the restroom. Other examples of this type of media discussion involve repeating dialogue for someone who missed what was said or walking someone through a video game when playing it for the first time. While these examples usually result from requests for clarification or guidance, other directional media talk is offered without prompting.

Discussions of media often bring about new understanding and meaning of media texts and also of relationships (Babrow, 1990; Fiske, 1989; Hodge & Tripp, 1986). Discussions of plot, characters, or actors playing certain roles can change people's interpretation of a movie or a relationship. A prime example is discussing what you watched on television the previous evening with friends at work or school the next day. Such discussions of media products can clarify the meanings attached, alter convictions about their significance, and adjust levels of appreciation.

Talk About Media Impacts Their Dissemination and Influence

Media do not have an all-powerful role in people's understanding of the world, knowledge, decisions of value and importance, or behavior, but they do play a significant role in the development of people's thoughts and actions. Discussions of media not only aid in the dissemination of media messages but also enhance their impact and are a relational phenomenon.

Even when someone has not watched a program on television, read the latest newspaper, or visited particular websites, discussing these media with others can still spread the information contained within them. You may not have caught a recent video online,

A study found that media attempts to promote breast cancer screening influenced middle-aged women more than younger women, who were more influenced by interpersonal discussions with friends, family, and health care providers who often received the information from media sources (K. Jones, Denham, & Springston, 2006).

but when friends who have watched the video tell you about it, the content of that video has nevertheless been spread to you. Especially with online content and podcasts, these conversations may lead to personal viewing or coviewing (Haridakis & Hanson, 2009). Media information is being spread, and relational connections are being enhanced at the same time.

The influence of media may be enhanced through their discussion with others. Because of the issues of trust and concern inherent in close relationships, information gained from media but conveyed through a friend, a family member, or another close relationship may quite possibly be considered more significant and valid than information received directly from a media source. A magazine article about the dangers of texting while driving, for instance, may not convince you to stop this dangerous behavior. However, a friend may read this article and pass along the information to you. Since this information comes from someone with whom you share a close personal relationship, you may view it as more meaningful than if personally reading it in the magazine.

Talk About Media Promotes the Development of Media Literacy

David's mom likes to tell the story of when David and his younger brother, Kevin, were watching a Bugs Bunny cartoon when they were 6 and 3 years old, respectively. When something outlandish happened in the cartoon, Kevin turned to David and asked, "How did they do that?" David confidently replied, "It's just the magic of television." Perhaps deep inside the recesses of his mind, striving to provide his brother with a better answer may be one of the reasons David started studying communication in the first place—and perhaps the reason he still enjoys watching Bugs Bunny cartoons. Regardless of the accuracy of the original answer, this tale of the McMahan family highlights another consequence of talk about media, specifically the promotion and development of media literacy.

Media literacy entails the learned ability to access, interpret, and evaluate media products. Discussion of media content impacts people's understanding and evaluation of this material, as well as their comprehension of its production and influence. Talking about media with those with whom you share close relationships significantly influences your actual use of media and your development of media literacy.

Discussions regarding the use and interpretation of media, especially television, often occur among family members. Parents and older siblings frequently demonstrate the use of media to young children and guide their understanding of the material both directly and indirectly. Research has indicated that parents greatly influence both what a child learns from television and a child's attitude toward television. There exist both indirect and direct forms of parental influence on children's interpretations of television (Austin, 1993). *Indirect influences* include children's modeling of viewing behaviors exhibited by their parents. *Direct influences* include rulemaking and actively mediating children's interpretations of television content through communication about observations on television.

Of course, the promotion of media literacy through discussions of media is not limited to those occurring among family members (Geiger, Bruning, & Harwood, 2001). Much of what people know about media literacy and their ability to critically evaluate media products has developed from interactions with friends, classmates, professors, coworkers, romantic partners, and others with whom they share a relationship.

Talk About Media Influences Identification and Relationship Development

Talking about media enables people to recognize and promote shared interests, understanding, and beliefs, while also serving to highlight differences among people. A connection or disconnection with others can be based solely on the recognition of shared media experience. Discussions with a coworker about movies both of you have seen may promote feelings of similarity. These discussions are influential not only because they allow people to recognize shared media experiences but also because they allow people to recognize shared understanding of those experiences. Conversations about media experience can also develop feelings of separation, such as when a classmate talks about a band you have never heard before.

While the actual consumption of media can promote perceptions of similarity and dissimilarity, evaluation of media plays an important role in the development of these views. For instance, if someone (like one of our relatives) mentions that his or her favorite book of all time is *The Basics of Communication: A Relational Perspective* and this happens to be your all-time favorite book, you may feel a sense of connection with that person. Someone else may discuss a new website that he or she finds deplorable, but if you enjoy that website, you may feel division or separation from that person. Perceptions of similarity and difference derived from conversations about media can be fundamental in the evaluation of others and can play a strong role in the development of relationships.

Of course, discussions of media content can uncover areas of similarity and difference beyond actual media use and evaluation. For example, discussing a blog entry can lead to the realization that you share certain political views with someone else. Talking about a podcast can bring about recognition of shared interests. Talking with a romantic partner about a romantic relationship portrayed in a movie can provide a sense of how that person views relationships and whether or not you share such views. The topics included in media are essentially limitless, and thus, so too are the areas of similarity and difference that can be explored through their discussion.

Strategic Communication

Consider how discussions of media can engender feelings of connection or disconnection with others. When would such discussions be most helpful?

Talk About Media Enables Identity Construction

Media that you use and enjoy are a significant part of who you are as an individual and play a major role in informing people of your identity. Your **media profile**, a compilation

Listen in on Your Life

Create your own media profile, using the questions listed in Table 10.6 as a guide. What do you think your media profile would tell people about you? Consider how your own media identity is created through talk with others. Do you discuss aspects of your media use and preferences with some people and not others? If so, why do you think this is the case? If you have one, how is this reflected in your Facebook or MySpace profile?

of your media preferences and general use of media, informs others about who you are as a person or at least the persona you are trying to project.

David, for instance, loves watching television, and his favorite shows include, among many others, *The Andy Griffith Show, Family Guy, The Dukes of Hazzard, The A-Team, Married . . . With Children, Night Court,* and *The Golden Girls.* He enjoys most music and especially likes blues, classic soul, Southern rock, alternative music from the '80s, and anything by Eric Clapton and Prince. Thanks to Steve's introduction, David also enjoys listening to the music of Ralph Vaughan Williams but does not care much for Symphony No. 7. His favorite movie of all time, *The Blues Brothers,* is probably responsible for his initial interest in and enjoyment of blues and soul music. He rarely plays video games but tends to be fairly good when he does play them. He never reads fiction (except for the Jack Reacher series by Lee Child) but is a voracious reader of newspapers and academic literature. His Internet use is primarily dedicated to reading these newspapers along with watching television programs and listening to music.

What does David's media profile inform you about him? What does it tell you about who he is as a person, where and when he grew up, his past experiences, and his additional interests and preferences, along with the beliefs, attitudes, and values he might hold?

Identities constructed through media consumption and subsequent discussions are just as meaningful as other identities (McMahan, 2004). In some cases, this identity construction surrounds the actual use or disuse of particular media systems. Some people wish to portray themselves as never watching television, while others may pride themselves on being dedicated gamers. Media identity construction also involves particular media products. These identities, though especially evident among fan cultures (Amesley, 1989; Jenkins, 1992), can occur among all consumers of media. A person may enjoy listening to country music, watching game shows, reading romance novels, or watching action movies, and these preferences and activities become part of this person's identity. Some people may enjoy a particular television program and pride themselves on knowing multiple details about the series. Some people you know may gain pleasure from listening to music acts that few other people have heard of.

Media preferences emerge through everyday communication with others, either through purposeful self-disclosure ("Hello. Nice to meet you. My name is David, and I love watching *The Golden Girls*") or unintentionally through the course of a conversation ("That story reminds me of something that once happened on *The Golden Girls*"). The first example contains a specific reason that David wants to disclose this information, perhaps to create a sense of identification with another fan of the show or someone who enjoys that type of program. Or perhaps the show is such a significant part of David's life that he is disclosing this information to provide a meaningful view of

Table 10.6 Some Questions to Consider When Creating Your Own Media Profile

1. Do you like watching television? If so, what are some of your favorite programs?

2. Do you like listening to music? If so, what are some of your favorite artists and songs?

3. Do you like watching movies? If so, what are some of your favorite movies?

4. Do you like to read? If so, what are some of your favorite books, newspapers, magazines, and so forth?

5. Do you like playing video games? If so, what are some of your favorite games?

6. Do you like using the Internet? If so, what are some of the sites you visit most often?

7. What television programs, music, movies, print material, video games, and Internet sites do you dislike?

8. Do you access television programs, music, movies, and newspapers through the Internet or your cell phone?

himself for another person. David may not have intentionally mentioned *The Golden Girls* in the second example, but it nevertheless indicates to the other person that David is a fan of the show, watches it occasionally, or has seen at least one episode that was meaningful enough for him to remember.

Discussions of media not only enable us to fully enact those identities related to media but also provide an opportunity to construct other parts of the self. Discussions of media have been shown to perform important roles in the construction of age and gender (Aasebo, 2005). Further, discussions of media can provide a sense of voice and empowerment (Brown, 1994; Jewkes, 2002) and allow media-based identities to be constructed, enacted, and displayed while serving a vital role in the enactment of multiple types of identities.

FOCUS QUESTIONS REVISITED

1. Why is the term *mass media* inappropriate?

The term *mass media* implies that large numbers of people receive the same media product, interpret it in the same way, and are influenced by it in the same way. This characterization ignores personal, social, and relational influences on the interpretation, evaluation, and use of media messages. "Mass" in particular implies that massive numbers of people receive the same media product. However, while millions of people may have access to media products, the ever-increasing number of media options has resulted in fewer people experiencing the same media product. Finally, individual audience members have the ability to create original and distinct media products through their use of each media system.

2. Why might audience members be considered active consumers of media?

Not just passive consumers receiving media messages without any thought, critical evaluation, or resistance, members of the audience actively select and attend to media, interpret and assign meaning to media messages in unique ways, and use media for a variety of relational reasons.

3. What are the relational uses and functions of media?
The use of media is a shared relational activity that enables people to come together, withdraw from relationships, and enact specific relational roles. Media also inform people about how relationships should look and how people should behave in relationships. Media function as coequal alternatives to personal relationships through the actual use of media and the formation and maintenance of parasocial relationships.

4. What functions does talk about media serve in everyday communication?
Beyond providing a general topic of conversation, talk about media impacts the interpretation and understanding of media. Talk about media also impacts the dissemination and influence of media, promotes the development of media literacy, influences identification and relationship development, and enables identity construction.

KEY CONCEPTS

concurrent media use   239
media literacy   254
media profile   255
narrowcasting   242

parasocial relationships   251
socialization impact of media   249
uses and gratifications   245

QUESTIONS TO ASK YOUR FRIENDS

1. Ask your friends to estimate the amount of time they spend using media every day. How do their responses compare with the average daily media use revealed by the Middletown Media Studies? If there is a significant difference between your friends' estimations and the numbers discovered in the Middletown Media Studies, why do you think this discrepancy exists?

2. Ask a few of your friends separately to describe their media profile, and then compare their responses once you have compiled a list of these preferences. Do you notice any similarity among their responses? If so, why do you think this similarity exists? What impact would this similarity of media preferences have on the relationships among your friends?

3. Ask your friends how often they find themselves talking about media with other people. What media do they discuss most frequently? With whom do they talk about media most often? How have discussions about media influenced their use of media? How have discussions about media influenced their understanding of media?

MEDIA LINKS

1. Examine how relationships are portrayed in the media. What types of relationships are most common? Do media systems (i.e., Internet, books, television, movies) differ on the types of relationships represented? How are these relationships depicted?

2. Compare how relationships are portrayed in recent media with their portrayal in media from past decades. What changes do you recognize?

3. Visit a newsstand or store that sells magazines and examine the titles available. What does the concept of mini-com tell you about the available collection of magazines? Is the new issue of *British and Redneck Professors Monthly* out yet?

ETHICAL ISSUES

1. Many concerns about media entail the impact of media on children, which has the potential to be both positive and negative. Who should be most responsible for regulating media used by children: producers of media content or parents?

2. Should people base their perceptions of others on discussions of media? What are the limitations or advantages of using these discussions to evaluate other people?

3. Media content is often shared through digital files, used in mash-ups to create new products, and used in fan-produced webpages dedicated to media. Many producers of this content discourage these uses of media and frequently take legal action to prevent this behavior. Do you believe the three uses of media content mentioned above should be considered violations of the law? Do you believe any of these uses of media are less of an infraction than the others? If so, why?

ANSWERS TO PHOTO CAPTIONS

Photo 10.1 ■ It is an example of concurrent media use.

Photo 10.2 ■ Using the Internet as a family appears to be an increasingly common relational experience. Research indicates that over half of Internet users living with a spouse and children go online with others at least a few times each week and an additional 34% do so occasionally (Kennedy, Smith, Wells, & Wellman, 2008).

Photo 10.3 ■ Each family includes at least one child, with children remaining a traditional component of the way many people expect a "family" to look. Each family also has two parents, which further reinforces traditional expectations of a "family."

Photo 10.4 ■ Although Stewie may wish Lois was dead and Meg is not always treated well, many episodes of *Family Guy* feature positive feelings among family members. Television family behavior is usually quite positive.

Photo 10.5 ▪ Talk about media can provide a couple with a topic of conversation, promote the development of media literacy, increase identification, enable identity construction, and impact the dissemination and understanding of the media product.

STUDENT STUDY SITE

Visit the study site at **www.sagepub.com/boc2e** for e-flashcards, practice quizzes, journal articles and additional study resources.

REFERENCES

Aasebo, T. S. (2005). Television as a marker of boys' construction of growing up. *Young: Nordic Journal of Youth Research, 13,* 185–203.

Alberts, J. K., Yoshimura, C. G., Rabby, M., & Loschiavo, R. (2005). Mapping the topography of couples' daily conversation. *Journal of Social and Personal Relationships, 22,* 299–322.

Allen, I. L. (1975). Research report—Everyday conversations about media content. *Journal of Applied Communications Research, 3,* 27–32.

Allen, I. L. (1982). Talking about media experiences: Everyday life as popular culture. *Journal of Popular Culture, 16,* 106–115.

Amesley, C. (1989). How to watch *Star Trek*. *Cultural Studies, 3,* 323–339.

Argyle, M., & Furnham, A. (1982). The ecology of relationships. *British Journal of Social Psychology, 21,* 259–262.

Austin, E. W. (1993). Exploring effects of active parental mediation of television content. *Journal of Broadcasting & Electronic Media, 37,* 147–158.

Babrow, A. S. (1990). Audience motivation, viewing context, media content, and form: The interactional emergence of soap opera entertainment. *Communication Studies, 41,* 343–361.

Bachen, C. M., & Illouz, E. (1996). Imagining romance: Young people's cultural models of romance and love. *Critical Studies in Mass Communication, 13,* 279–308.

Bausinger, H. (1984). Media, technology and daily life (L. Jaddou & J. Williams, Trans.). *Media, Culture, and Society, 6,* 343–351.

Baxter, R. L., De Riemer, C., Landini, A., Leslie, L., & Singletary, M. W. (1985). A content analysis of music videos. *Journal of Broadcasting & Electronic Media, 29,* 333–240.

Bellamy, R. V., Jr., & Walker, J. R. (1996). *Television and the remote control: Grazing on a vast wasteland.* New York: Guilford Press.

Berelson, B. (1949). What "missing the newspaper" means. In P. F. Lazarsfeld & F. N. Stanton (Eds.), *Communications research 1948–1949* (pp. 111–129). New York: Harper & Brothers.

Biocca, F. A. (1988). Opposing conceptions of the audience. In J. Anderson (Ed.), *Communication yearbook* (Vol. 11, pp. 51–80). Newbury Park, CA: Sage.

Blumler, J. G. (1980). The role of theory in uses and gratifications research. In G. C. Wilhoit & H. DeBock (Eds.), *Mass communication: Review yearbook* (Vol. 1, pp. 201–228). Beverly Hills, CA: Sage.

Boskoff, A. (1970). *The sociology of urban regions* (2nd ed.). Englewood Cliffs, NJ: Prentice Hall.

Brinson, S. L. (1992). TV fights: Women and men in interpersonal arguments on prime-time television dramas. *Argumentation and Advocacy, 29,* 89–104.

Brown, M. E. (1994). *Soap opera and women's talk.* Thousand Oaks, CA: Sage.

Bryant, J., Aust, C. F., Bryant, J. A., & Venugopalan, G. (2001). How psychologically healthy are America's prime-time television families? In J. Bryant & J. A. Bryant (Eds.), *Television and the American family* (2nd ed., pp. 247–270). Mahwah, NJ: Lawrence Erlbaum.

Chesebro, J. W., & Bertelsen, D. A. (1996). *Analyzing media: Communication technologies as symbolic and cognitive systems.* New York: Guilford Press.

Cohen, J. (2003). Parasocial breakups: Measuring individual differences in responses to the dissolution of parasocial relationships. *Mass Communication & Society, 6,* 191–202.

Cohen, J., & Metzger, M. (1998). Social affiliation and the achievement of ontological security through interpersonal and mass communication. *Critical Studies in Mass Communication, 15,* 41–60.

Cole, T., & Leets, L. (1999). Attachment styles and intimate television viewing: Insecurely forming relationships in a parasocial way. *Journal of Social and Personal Relationships, 16,* 495–511.

Compesi, R. J. (1983). Gratifications of daytime TV serial viewers. *Journalism Quarterly, 57,* 155–158.

Dates, J. L., & Stroman, C. A. (2001). Portrayals of families of color on television. In J. Bryant & J. A. Bryant (Eds.), *Television and the American family* (2nd ed., pp. 207–228). Mahwah, NJ: Lawrence Erlbaum.

Eggermont, S. (2004). Television viewing, perceived similarity, and adolescents' expectations of a romantic partner. *Journal of Broadcasting & Electronic Media, 48,* 244–265.

Fiske, J. (1989). Moments in television: Neither the text nor the audience. In E. Seiter, H. Borchers, G. Kreutzner, & E. Warth (Eds.), *Remote control: Television, audiences, and cultural power* (pp. 56–78). London: Routledge.

Freedman, D. (2003). Acceptance and alignment, misconception and inexperience: Preservice teacher, representations of students, and media culture. *Critical Studies—Critical Methodologies, 3,* 79–95.

Gauntlett, D., & Hill, A. (1999). *TV living: Television, culture, and everyday life.* London: Routledge.

Geiger, W., Bruning, J., & Harwood, J. (2001). Talk about TV: Television viewers' interpersonal communication about programming. *Communication Reports, 14,* 49–57.

Grabe, M. E. (2002). Maintaining the moral order: A functional analysis of *The Jerry Springer Show. Critical Studies in Media Communication, 19,* 311–328.

Greenberg, B. S. (1980). *Life on television: Content analysis of US TV drama.* Norwood, NJ: Ablex.

Greenberg, S. R. (1975). Conversations as units of analysis in the study of personal influence. *Journalism Quarterly, 52,* 128–130.

Gumpert, G. (1970). The rise of mini-com. *Journal of Communication, 20,* 280–290.

Haridakis, P., & Hanson, G. (2009). Social interaction and co-viewing with YouTube: Blending mass communication reception and social connection. *Journal of Broadcasting & Electronic Media, 53,* 317–335.

Heintz-Knowles, K. E. (2001). Balancing acts: Work-family issues on prime-time television. In J. Bryant & J. A. Bryant (Eds.), *Television and the American family* (2nd ed., pp. 177–206). Mahwah, NJ: Lawrence Erlbaum.

Herzog, H. (1944). What do we really know about daytime serial listeners? In P. Lazarsfeld (Ed.), *Radio research 1942–1943* (pp. 2–23). New York: Duell, Sloan, and Pearce.

Hodge, R., & Tripp, D. (1986). *Children and television: A semiotic approach.* Palo Alto, CA: Stanford University Press.

Horton, D., & Wohl, R. R. (1956). Mass communication and para-social interaction: Observations on intimacy at a distance. *Psychiatry, 19,* 215–229.

Ivory, A. H., Gibson, R., & Ivory, J. D. (2009). Gendered relationships on television: Portrayals of same-sex and heterosexual couples. *Mass Communication and Society, 12,* 170–192.

Jenkins, H. (1992). *Textual poachers: Television fans and participatory culture.* New York: Routledge.

Jewkes, Y. (2002). The use of media in constructing identities in the masculine environment of men's prisons. *European Journal of Communication, 17,* 205–225.

Jones, G. D., & Nelson, E. S. (1996). Expectations of marriage among college students from intact and non-intact homes. *Journal of Divorce and Remarriage, 26,* 171–189.

Jones, K. O., Denham, B. E., & Springston, J. K. (2006). Effects of mass and interpersonal communication on breast cancer screening: Advancing agenda setting theory in health contexts. *Journal of Applied Communication Research, 34,* 94–113.

Kanazawa, S. (2002). Bowling with our imaginary friends. *Evolution and Human Behavior, 23,* 167–171.

Katz, E., Hass, H., & Gurevitch, M. (1973). On the use of the mass media for important things. *American Sociological Review, 38,* 164–181.

Kennedy, T. L. M., Smith, A., Wells, A. T., & Wellman, B. (2008, October 19). *Networked families.* Washington, DC: Pew Internet & American Life Project.

Koenig, F., & Lessan, G. (1985). Viewers' relations to television personalities. *Psychological Reports, 57,* 263–266.

LaRossa, R. (2004). The culture of fatherhood in the fifties. *Journal of Family History, 29,* 47–70.

Larson, M. S. (1993). Family communication on prime-time television. *Journal of Broadcasting & Electronic Media, 37,* 349–357.

Larson, M. S. (2001). Sibling interaction in situation comedies over the years. In J. Bryant & J. A. Bryant (Eds.), *Television*

and the American family (2nd ed., pp. 163–176). Mahwah, NJ: Lawrence Erlbaum.

Lauzen, M. M., Dozier, D. M., & Horan, N. (2008). Constructing gender stereotypes through social roles in prime-time television. *Journal of Broadcasting & Electronic Media, 52,* 200–214.

Lazarsfeld, P. F. (1940). *Radio and the printed page: An introduction to the study of radio and its role in the communication of ideas.* New York: Duell, Sloan, and Pearce.

Liebes, T. (1988). Cultural differences in the retelling of television fiction. *Critical Studies in Mass Communication, 5,* 277–292.

Lull, J. (1980). The social uses of television. *Human Communication Research, 6,* 197–209.

McKee, A. (2000). Images of gay men in the media and the development of self esteem. *Australian Journal of Communication, 27,* 81–98.

McMahan, D. T. (2004). What we have here is a failure to communicate: Linking interpersonal and mass communication. *Review of Communication, 4,* 33–56.

Mendelsohn, H. (1964). Listening to the radio. In L. A. Dexter & D. M. White (Eds.), *People, society, and mass communications* (pp. 239–249). New York: Free Press.

Meyer, M. D. E. (2003). "It's me. I'm it.": Defining adolescent sexual identity through relational dialectics in *Dawson's Creek. Communication Quarterly, 51,* 262–276.

Papper, R. A., Holmes, M. E., & Popovich, M. N. (2004). Middletown media studies: Media multitasking . . . and how much people really use the media. *International Digital Media & Arts Association Journal, 1,* 4–56.

Perse, E. M., & Butler, J. S. (2005). Call-in talk radio: Compensation or enrichment? *Journal of Radio Studies, 12,* 204–222.

Perse, E. M., & Rubin, R. B. (1989). Attribution in social and parasocial relationships. *Communication Research, 16,* 59–77.

Rideout, V. J., Foehr, U. G., & Roberts, D. F. (2010). *Generation M²: Media in the lives of 8- to 18-year-old*s. Menlo Park, CA: Henry J. Kaiser Family Foundation.

Robinson, J. D., & Skill, T. (2001). Five decades of families on television. In J. Bryant & J. A. Bryant (Eds.), *Television and the American family* (2nd ed., pp. 139–162). Mahwah, NJ: Lawrence Erlbaum.

Rosengren, K. E., & Windahl, S. (1972). Mass media consumptions as a functional alternative. In D. McQuail (Ed.), *Sociology of mass communications* (pp. 166–194). Middlesex, UK: Penguin.

Rubin, A. M., & Rubin, R. B. (1985). Interface of personal and mediated communication: A research agenda. *Critical Studies in Mass Communication, 2,* 36–53.

Saenz, M. K. (1994). Television viewing as a cultural practice. In H. Newcomb (Ed.), *Television: The critical view* (pp. 573–586). New York: Oxford University Press.

Scannell, P. (1989). Public service broadcasting and modern public life. *Media, Culture, and Society, 11,* 135–166.

Schiappa, E., Gregg, P. B., & Hewes, D. E. (2005). The parasocial contact hypothesis. *Communication Monographs, 72,* 92–115.

Segrin, C., & Nabi, R. L. (2002). Does television viewing cultivate unrealistic expectations about marriage? *Journal of Communication, 52,* 247–263.

Smith, D. M. (1975). Mass media as a basis for interaction: An empirical study. *Journalism Quarterly, 52,* 44–49, 105.

Turner, J. R. (1993). Interpersonal and psychological predictors of parasocial interaction with different television performers. *Communication Quarterly, 41,* 443–453.

Wang, A., & Calder, B. (2006). Media transportation and advertising. *Journal of Consumer Research, 33,* 163–172.

Yee, N. (2006). The psychology of MMORPGs: Emotional investment, motivations, relationship formation, and problematic usage. In R. Schroeder & A. Axelsson (Eds.), *Avatars at work and play: Collaboration and interaction in shared virtual environment*s (pp. 187–207). London: Springer-Verlag.

Zillmann, D., & Bryant, J. (Eds.). (1985). *Selective exposure to communication.* Hillsdale, NJ: Lawrence Erlbaum.

11

Preparing for a Public Presentation

A relational basis exists in all communication, and public speaking is no exception. A relational connection between speakers and audiences is essential to effective public speaking and must be established in the preparation, development, and delivery of presentations.

At first glance, public speaking—in which both the speaker and the audience play active roles based on and guided through socially established norms and expectations—may appear as merely the enactment of social roles. If public speaking were simply the enactment of social roles, a speaker and an audience would be interchangeable—much like a given customer at a fast-food restaurant and a given cashier. However, public speaking more closely resembles the unique personal relationships that you share with your friends, family, and romantic partners in which the people are irreplaceable; that is, if a speaker or an audience were replaced, the interaction would be totally different. Audience members' characteristics, perceptions, and needs will govern what they expect from a speaker, and public speakers must adapt to each audience accordingly.

Recognition of the relationship between speakers and an audience begins with acknowledging the similarities between public speaking and personal relationships. In personal relationships, people seek to inform, understand, persuade, respect, trust, support, connect, satisfy, and evoke particular responses from one another, and such objectives exist in public speaking situations. In personal relationships, people must adjust to one another just as speakers must adjust to each unique audience to satisfy the goals of a public presentation. People transact their personal relationships though communication and create meaning and understanding that go beyond the simple exchange of symbols, and the same transactions occur during public presentations. In this way, what you already know about personal relationships and everyday communication can guide your understanding of public presentations.

It is quite possible that you are feeling very nervous and apprehensive about delivering a public presentation. Even talking about its preparation may be somewhat upsetting. You are not alone! These feelings are perfectly normal and are extremely common. We talk about communication apprehension—the technical term for the fear or anxiety you may experience when speaking in public—in Chapter 14 and encourage you to skip ahead and read that part of the book first if you are particularly worried.

This chapter is dedicated to the *preparation* of public presentations. We examine the groundwork that must be conducted before the development and delivery of presentations. The success of public presentations depends largely on what takes place during this phase of the process. We spend a great deal of time discussing how you can **analyze** your audience, which will help you determine how to construct a presentation and is what speech texts normally cover, but we go further and teach you how to establish a **relational connection** with the audience. Also in this chapter, we discuss the selection of topics and the development of a purpose and a thesis for your presentation. We also examine evidence and support material that you can use to develop your thesis, to support the claims made in your presentation, and to connect relationally with your audience. Finally, we explore the process of collecting and using quality sources, often vital to the success of presentations and your ability to connect with the audience. Of course, the one constant throughout our entire exploration of public presentations is the audience members and their relationship with the speaker, and here we begin.

Focus Questions

1. What factors should you consider when analyzing and relating to an audience?
2. What factors should you consider when determining the topic of a presentation?
3. What strategies can you use when searching for the topic of a presentation?
4. What are the general purpose, specific purpose statement, and thesis of a presentation?
5. What types of evidence and support material can you use to develop a presentation?
6. What factors should you consider when selecting sources for a presentation?
7. What factors should you consider when conducting research and gathering material?

How Do You Analyze and Relate to Audiences?

Analyzing audiences and adapting a presentation and its delivery accordingly are fundamental to effective public speaking. As a speaker, you must determine the best way to develop and maintain a positive relationship between yourself and audiences and between audiences and the material.

Ultimately, you must adapt to an audience all elements and components of a presentation—including introductions, sources, types of evidence and support material, organizational patterns, and conclusions—except one very important thing: what you believe and wish to argue, maintain, or claim. For instance, suppose you are presenting a speech about hunting ordinances before members of your community and want to maintain that hunting is necessary to control certain wildlife populations. Although a large part of your audience opposes the hunting of animals for any reason and will likely disagree with your speech, you should not adjust your beliefs to match the audience's and thus present a speech urging a hunting ban. If you suspect your audience will oppose your speech, however, you will likely provide different evidence, organize and deliver your speech differently, and establish different relational connections with the audience than you would if you were giving a speech to a prohunting audience.

You must adjust the speech—that is, how you state your beliefs—to your audience, but do not adjust what you personally believe. In what follows, we discuss various factors that will impact approaches to the audience and provide suggestions and guidelines for developing effective presentations.

Relationship With the Speaker

As mentioned above, you must establish and maintain an appropriate relationship with an audience and base all decisions about a speech in part on that relationship. A relationship with an audience may already exist outside the public speaking context. An audience, for example, may consist of colleagues, supervisors, employees, classmates, group members, or community members, and their preexisting relationships with you will impact how they view you personally and what they expect from your presentation. Identities created in other contexts will influence the public speaking identity created through a presentation, and vice versa. Additionally, the relationships that exist outside the public speaking context will impact the relationship created with the audience through a presentation, and vice versa.

> ### Listen in on Your Life
>
> Think back on times when friends or strangers tried to convince you of something. How much influence did the relationship shared with each person have on your decisions? Did the primary dimensions of credibility influence your decisions?

How an audience views you personally has a profound impact on presentations. A speaker's credibility is crucial to the success of a presentation. The most successful individuals tend to be those who are (a) considered knowledgeable about the topic, (b) trusted, and (c) concerned about the audience.

These characteristics touch on the three primary dimensions of credibility: knowledge, trustworthiness, and goodwill (Gass & Seiter, 2011). Speakers must convey to an audience that they are knowledgeable about the topic, that they can be trusted, and that they have the audience's best interest at heart. Notice that these components are often

Photo 11.1 If you know an audience will disagree with your position, should you change your position to match that of the audience? (See page 291.)

attributed to those with whom you share a personal relationship. In fact, perceptions of credibility are often based largely on the actual relationship shared with someone (i.e., you trust a person because he or she is your *friend,* or you distrust someone because he or she is your *enemy*).

If the audience has no previous knowledge of your credentials or experience with an issue or perceives you negatively, you may need to spend more time explaining your credibility and developing a positive relationship with audience members. Also especially important, you must provide strong evidence for assertions made throughout the speech along with a clear focus and development of the topic to maintain a strong relational connection.

If the audience members already perceive you as credible and view you in a positive manner, you will be more easily able to establish a strong relational connection with them. However, you still must engage in behaviors that will enable full development and maintenance of such a relationship.

Relationship With the Issue and Position

You must also determine an audience's relationship with the issue being addressed or the position being advanced. An audience may have a positive, a negative, or an impartial view of an issue before a speaker even begins to speak. You must take this existing evaluation into consideration when preparing a speech because it will likely impact how the audience receives the presentation and the audience's relationship with you. If the audience opposes your position, you may have to spend additional time establishing your credibility and developing a positive relational connection with audience members.

If you anticipate the audience will receive the issue in a positive manner, you might spend less time defending and more time clarifying and outlining a position. Also, while establishing credibility and a positive relationship with the audience is always necessary, it will be easier if the audience agrees with the position being advanced. People view individuals whose positions mirror their own as *more* credible than those with opposing beliefs.

You must also adjust your speech if you believe the audience is impartial to the issue, in which case you will probably need to spend more time stressing its importance and its impact on audience members' lives. The audience may not fully understand the issue, so you may need to spend more time describing what it entails.

Previous knowledge of the issue by an audience will also impact a presentation. The audience may be very knowledgeable or have little knowledge about the issue. The level of audience knowledge and understanding of an issue will dictate the depth and intricacy of a speech and what evidence and support material are used, the language used and whether terminology must be defined or explained, and how much time must be spent orienting the audience to the topic.

Audience View of the Occasion

How the audience views the occasion will also impact your speech, including the extent to which the audience desires to listen to your presentation. A **captive audience** is forced to listen to your presentation. Classmates may be listening to your speech because of an attendance policy, or colleagues may be listening to your presentation because your employer has required their attendance. A captive audience does not mean a hostile audience, but you must work that much harder to make such an audience appreciate the value of your presentation and ensure that the audience members will actually enjoy your presentation. It is especially important that you grab their attention at the beginning of the speech and establish how they will benefit personally from listening to the presentation. Though not a definite characterization, a captive audience is more likely than a voluntary audience to have limited knowledge of your topic, which will also increase the importance of making audience members see the relevance of the presentation, bringing them up to speed on the topic in the introduction, and engaging their attention rapidly. The limited previous knowledge may also require you to moderate the depth at which you discuss material.

A **voluntary audience** listens to your speech because its members have personally chosen to be there. This may be because they have particular interest in your topic or a particular need, such as wanting to learn how to accomplish a task, to learn more about your topic, or to learn your particular "take" on it. It is still imperative that you orient audience members to the topic and establish why they should listen to your presentation specifically. While they may already recognize their connection with the topic, you must reinforce their relationship with the material provided. A voluntary audience may possess more knowledge and experience with the topic, allowing you to go into greater depth or use more technical terms. However, you must determine whether members of your audience are there to increase their understanding of the topic or to learn about it for the first time.

Photo 11.2 If an audience listening to these speakers were required to be in attendance, what type of audience would it be? (See page 291.)

Attitudes, Beliefs, and Values

Determining audience attitudes, beliefs, and values also provides a speaker with insight into how an audience may evaluate and respond to an issue and how audience members may view their relationship with him or her.

Attitudes

Attitudes are learned predispositions to evaluate something in a positive or negative way that guide thinking and behavior (Fishbein & Ajzen, 1975). For example, you may dislike the taste of a particular type of food, which will guide your response to decline eating it should a plateful be passed your way at dinner. Or you may like a particular type of music, which may guide your decision to listen to that genre online. Attitudes usually do not change readily but instead remain relatively constant. Generally, the longer you hold an attitude and the more support you discover in its favor, the less likely you will be to change it.

Audiences' attitudes will impact their view of you as a speaker, the topic, the occasion, and even the evidence provided to develop and support an argument. Some audience members will respond more favorably to statistics while others will respond more favorably to examples or illustrations. Similarly, members of an audience will also possess attitudes regarding the sources of evidence. Some may view the Internet as providing unreliable information while others may view it as providing the most current and accurate information.

College Experience

It is possible that in college you may experience greater change in your attitudes and beliefs than at any other time in your life. What changes in attitudes and beliefs have you experienced since starting college? What led to these changes? How might these experiences inform you when attempting to change the attitudes and beliefs of other people?

Beliefs

Beliefs, or what people hold to be true or false, are formed like attitudes through your direct experience, as well as through media, public and personal relationships, and cultural views of the world. Whereas attitudes are evaluations of something favorable or unfavorable, beliefs are evaluations of something true or false. Like attitudes, your beliefs can change, but they are generally even more stable than attitudes.

Knowing the beliefs of audience members will help determine their attitudes, but the value of this knowledge does not stop there. Knowing the beliefs of an audience can also assist in focusing a presentation. For instance, if you are discussing the problem of illegal immigration, the audience may or may not believe that an illegal immigration problem even exists. If the audience *does not* believe this problem exists, you might focus your speech on establishing its existence. If the audience *does* believe that a problem exists with illegal immigration, you may then explore other issues involving this topic.

Knowing the beliefs of an audience will also impact how completely you must support the facts or opinions included in your presentation. Depending on an audience's beliefs, some statements or claims of belief may need more or less support. If claiming that "the Earth is round," you might feel fairly confident that an audience will not look for proof, and unless that statement is critical to your argument, you would not need to include a great deal of support and development. Statements such as that one would be considered a **given belief**—that is, the majority of people in the audience will hold the same perspective of either true or false. However, saying something like "The issue of illegal immigration has been a problem for decades" might require additional support and development since not all members of an audience may agree with or be aware of this statement of belief. In the majority of cases, it is generally best to support all statements. However, knowing the beliefs of an audience will determine how much development should be included and whether or not the audience will agree with a given statement.

Values

Values are deeply held and enduring judgments of significance or importance that often provide the basis for both beliefs and attitudes. The values you hold are what you consider most important in this world. When listing values, people often include such things as life, family, truth, knowledge, education, personal growth, health, freedom, and wealth. Although all the items on this list might sound good to you, people do not agree on their importance. For instance, a person may not view wealth as all that important in life, and not all people believe in the importance of family.

When considering the influence of audience values on a presentation, three points emerge. First, you can use values to form an understanding of audience beliefs and attitudes, and vice versa. However, it is not always possible to establish supportive links between these variables. A person may profess to value health but have a positive attitude toward drinking alcohol in excess. Second, you can use audience values to determine and successfully convince audience members of their relationship with a topic and why they should listen to a presentation. If audience members value family, you can use the impact the issue has on family life to show them the importance of the issue and why they should listen to the presentation. Finally, changing a person's values is very difficult and will take more than a single presentation to accomplish. You might be able to change audience beliefs and attitudes through a single presentation, but values are another story.

Demographics

Demographics are characteristics of a person or an audience that can provide insight into one's knowledge, experiences, interests, needs, attitudes, beliefs, and values. Demographic characteristics of an audience include such things as age, gender, ethnicity, education, occupation, political membership, religion, and place of residence. Demographic characteristics provide generalized information but do not necessarily provide an entirely accurate reflection of any particular person or audience. Just because someone is the same age as you, for instance, does not mean that person possesses the same knowledge, experiences, interests, needs, attitudes, beliefs, and values that you do. However, it may be more likely that people of the same age share some similarities that set them apart from people of a different age. Table 11.1 presents common demographic characteristics that may be used when analyzing audiences.

Table 11.1 Demographic Characteristics

Age

Age may provide insight into the life experiences of audience members and what issues are most important to them. An audience whose members average 55 years in age may be more concerned about retirement issues than an audience whose members average 20 years in age. Age may also impact the degree of change that is possible. As people age, it becomes more difficult to change existing attitudes, beliefs, and values.

Sex and gender

Sex is based on biological makeup, being born with female or male reproductive organs, usually with either an XX or XY chromosomal pair. Gender is a socially created and maintained symbolic concept of femininity or masculinity. Be careful to avoid stereotypical views of women and men, such as being feminine or masculine or as having conventionally gendered interests. Men and women have likely encountered different experiences and different expectations of behavior because of social constructs and demands and not because of personal characteristics.

Education

Education should not be equated with level of intelligence. Still, the level of education of your audience and especially audience members' major course of study may provide information about knowledge of a topic and areas of interest. Accordingly, the education of your audience can indicate the extent to which you must define terms that you will be using, how in-depth you may go in your presentation, and how likely your audience will be to find the information interesting and valuable.

Occupation

The occupations of your audience also may provide information about knowledge of a topic and areas of interest. An audience of carpenters may have a greater interest in a speech about the latest construction techniques than would an audience of accountants. The occupations of your audience can often tell you the education and training members may have had, which will allow you to use information about their education discussed above.

Income

Income may indicate what topics an audience deems most worthwhile. An audience struggling with bills would probably not be interested in a speech about traveling the French Riviera; a wealthy audience would probably not be interested in a speech about cutting grocery expenses. Always adapt a speech to the audience. If presenting a speech about travel to an audience struggling with money, you might discuss ways to save money when traveling. Or you could discuss affordable trips to nearby locations.

Political memberships

The political memberships of your audience may indicate attitudes, beliefs, and values. However, political membership does not mean a person adheres to the entire platform of a particular party. There may be some issues for which there exists strong agreement and other areas for which there exists considerable disagreement.

Religion

The religious affiliations of your audience may also provide information about attitudes, beliefs, and values, but they may also provide inaccurate information. Just as there may be some planks of a political platform not accepted by all members of a political party, there may be some aspects of a religious doctrine not embraced by all members of a religion. Also, be certain to recognize that members of the audience may belong to various religions and that your language and perspective are inclusive.

Place of Residence

Places of residence may provide information about what topics an audience finds useful. Someone living in the Midwest would likely find a speech about what to do in the event of a tornado more valuable than a speech about what to do in the event of a hurricane. Places of residence may also provide insight into experiences and knowledge. Audience members living in the Midwest would be more likely to recognize the destructive qualities and nature of a tornado than audience members living in areas where tornados are less common.

Selecting Your Topic

Now that we have discussed the audience, we can begin to explore your preparation for the development and delivery of your presentation. First, you must determine the topic of your presentation. For some public speaking occasions, a topic or an area will already be established for you. Other occasions may require you to select the topic yourself. Even when a topic has already been established, you often have some degree of flexibility with what you will share with the audience. Coming up with a topic is sometimes challenging, so in what follows, we discuss how to select your topic and factors you should consider in that selection.

Consider Yourself

When selecting a topic for your presentation, the best place to begin is by considering yourself. In doing so, consider your knowledge, your experiences, and what you find important.

Knowledge

Consider areas about which you are knowledgeable. You do not need an advanced degree to claim knowledge about a subject. You may not be a certified mechanic, but you may know how to repair a car; you may not possess a degree in computer programming, but you may know how to develop a website. Many people possess knowledge of particular areas they do not believe others would consider worthy of acknowledgment. For instance, you may have every episode of *The Boondocks* on Adult Swim practically memorized; you may know the story of how your favorite video game was developed. This sort of knowledge often proves very worthwhile and valued by many people.

Experiences

You may have derived much of your knowledge about a topic from your experiences. Just as people sometimes underappreciate their knowledge base, they also underestimate the value of their experiences. Consider where you grew up. Contemplate your numerous life experiences during your search for a topic. Reflect on the jobs you have had. Ponder the activities and organizations in which you have been involved at your school and in your community. Think about your experiences with family and friends. You may consider many topic areas by simply looking at your own life. Selecting a topic from your experiences will also provide benefits similar to those gained by selecting a topic about which you possess prior knowledge.

Importance

Search for a topic that you consider important. Your topic must impact the audience (and your relationship to audience members) in a meaningful way, but it should also be meaningful to you. You may consider some topics important because they have directly impacted your life. Of course, topics important to you are not limited to those that affect you directly. As with knowledge and experiences, do not underestimate the importance of things that are meaningful to you. Selecting a topic you consider important will enhance the overall quality of your presentation, especially when it comes to connecting relationally with your audience and establishing credibility. If you do not consider your topic important and worthwhile, you will not be able to express genuine enthusiasm, and it will be difficult to convince the audience members that you care about them and that they should care about your presentation.

Consider Your Audience

Just as you should consider yourself when selecting a topic, you must also consider your audience. Since we have already talked a great deal about audiences, we will not spend much time discussing them again in this section of the chapter. However, we want to underscore one factor that is vital to the success of your speech.

You must establish a relationship between the audience and your topic. The topic you select must impact the audience in a meaningful way. During the introduction of your speech, you must tell the audience members how the topic affects them and why they should listen to your presentation. Selecting a topic meaningful to your audience will assist you in maintaining audience attention, connecting relationally with audience members, and enhancing your credibility. You do not have to select a life-altering topic. A presentation about a new video game system may not save the lives of your audience members but could impact them in a profound way. Also do not think that you must select a topic they already know is important or meaningful in their lives. Some of the most powerful speeches introduce audiences to a topic about which they previously knew nothing or enable them to view an issue in an entirely new way.

Searching for a Topic

Selecting a topic for a presentation often takes a great deal of time and contemplation. Even after considering themselves and their audience, people sometimes struggle to find an appropriate topic for a presentation. If you find yourself struggling to find a topic, the following four methods can help in your search.

Brainstorming

Brainstorming is a method of gathering and generating ideas without immediate evaluation. Essentially, you just write down everything that comes to mind for a specific (generally brief) period. You do not evaluate these ideas as they come; you simply gather a list of ideas. You also generate ideas, because one idea may trigger or prompt another, which in turn may trigger another, which may prompt another, and so on. So, sit down at a computer or with a pen and paper; select a brief time limit, such as 5 minutes; and then start writing. Before you know it, you will have a list of topics to consider. Once this list is compiled, you can critically examine these topics, singling out some ideas as possible speech topics and eliminating others entirely.

You can use two types of brainstorming when searching for a topic. When **open brainstorming**, you generate a list of ideas with no topic boundary. When **topic-specific brainstorming**, you generate a list of ideas encompassing a specific topic (i.e., Civil Rights Movement). Sometimes, the topic has been derived from an open brainstorming session. Other times, you may have an existing topic area in mind but not know what to examine or the best way to narrow your focus.

Current Issues and Events

When searching for a speech topic, also consider looking at current issues and events. Examining an Internet news site, reading a newspaper, watching a news channel, or listening to a radio program will provide a ready-made list of topics for you to consider. This method would certainly provide you with a recent topic to explore. Even if you do not select a current event or issue, these topics may trigger one you do want to discuss.

Individual Inventory

We previously discussed selecting a topic based on your knowledge, experience, and evaluation of importance. One way to derive such a topic is by compiling an **individual inventory**, or a listing of a person's preferences, likes, dislikes, and experiences. You are a unique individual with distinct experiences, knowledge, and perspectives, and compiling an individual inventory will help you pinpoint your distinguishing characteristics. Create your inventory by providing items for the categories listed in Table 11.2 or any other categories. Completing an individual inventory may provide you with a topic for your speech or trigger another topic to examine.

Strategic Communication

Develop your individual inventory using the model in this chapter. Once your inventory is complete, examine the list for possible topics for an informative presentation and for a persuasive presentation. You may wish to engage in topic-specific brainstorming to narrow your focus.

Suggestions From Other People

Getting suggestions from other people can also help you establish a topic for your presentation. An especially helpful method when speaking to an organization or at an event, asking the person who provided the invitation about past speakers and topics, as well as what sort of topics the audience might enjoy, often provides invaluable perspective on topic selection and the audience.

Table 11.2 Individual Inventory Categories	
Favorite television programs	Favorite food
Favorite movies	Goals
Favorite music	Fears
Favorite Internet sites	Employment
Favorite magazines	Hometown
Last book read for fun	Things you do for fun
Most valuable possession	Favorite classes in school
Heroes or people you admire	Interesting or memorable experiences
Things that annoy you	Qualities that make you unique

Determining the Purpose and Thesis of Your Presentation

Establishing and maintaining a clear goal is crucial to developing an effective presentation, and the first step in this process is the development of an explicit purpose and thesis for your presentation. In this section, we discuss the general purpose, the specific purpose, and the development of a thesis.

General Purpose

The **general purpose** is the basic objective you want to achieve through your presentation. Most presentations are developed to achieve the following three basic objectives: (a) inform, (b) persuade, and (c) evoke. When your general purpose is to **inform**, you want to develop audience understanding of a topic through definition, clarification, demonstration, or explanation of a process. When your general purpose is to **persuade**, you desire either to influence audience beliefs, values, or attitudes or to influence audience behaviors. The types of presentations you will encounter most often and be asked to develop most likely in class are informative and persuasive presentations. Chapter 13 is dedicated to these types of presentations, so we will not spend a great deal of time discussing them here.

Some presentations seek to generate an emotion from the audience. Communication scholars Jo Sprague and Douglas Stuart (2003) use the term **evoke** to describe presentations designed to "elicit a certain feeling or emotional response" (p. 65) from the audience. Textbooks, such as this one, often use the term *entertain* to describe these presentations, but we agree with Sprague and Stuart that this term detracts from the emotional depth that these presentations can achieve and limits them to "fun" only. Evocative presentations can entertain in a traditional sense by providing laughter or escape, but they can also "inspire, celebrate, commemorate, bond, or help listeners to relive" (p. 65). They can elicit happiness, sadness, joy, fear, excitement, reverence, or a combination of emotions from the audience.

Although one general purpose usually dominates, it is fair to say that most presentations contain elements from all three types of speeches. As you explain how to accomplish something, you can use your relationship with audience members to convince them that they must enact certain steps to achieve the desired outcome. You may also entertain or inspire the audience members as you teach them how to conduct each step. As you convince the audience members that something is true, you also inform them of reasons they should believe you. Emotional responses often provide a way of persuading the audience to do something or enact a particular behavior. The overlap among general purposes can sometimes make staying focused as you develop the speech quite

Contrarian Challenge

We believe there are elements of all three types of speeches in any public presentation. Can you think of any speeches in which this would not be the case?

complicated. The specific purpose of your speech, along with your thesis, will allow you to focus its development and your presentation of the material.

Specific Purpose

The **specific purpose** of your presentation, or exactly what you want to achieve through your presentation, differs from the general purpose in that it is not a broad objective. Rather, the specific purpose of your

Photo 11.3 What type of speech is most likely to occur at a wedding or another celebratory event? (See page 291.)

speech encompasses the narrow, explicit goal of your presentation and entails the precise impact you want to have on your audience. Developing a specific purpose statement helps ensure that you personally stay focused on achieving an explicit goal though your presentation.

The specific purpose statement should include the goal of your speech, and this goal should correspond with the general purpose of the speech. The goal of a speech might be to inform or explain (*speech to inform*), persuade or convince (*speech to persuade*), or reminisce or excite (*speech to evoke*).

> *The purpose of this presentation is to inform . . .*

> *The purpose of this presentation is to convince . . .*

> *The purpose of this presentation is to reminisce . . .*

The specific purpose statement should also refer to the audience to underscore its importance in the development of the presentation.

> *The purpose of this presentation is to inform the audience . . .*

> *The purpose of this presentation is to convince the audience . . .*

> *The purpose of this presentation is to reminisce with the audience . . .*

Finally, the specific purpose statement should include the explicit focus of the presentation.

> The purpose of this presentation is to inform the audience *about the three primary types of financial aid available to students at the university.*

> The purpose of this presentation is to convince the audience *to volunteer with the city's literacy program.*

> The purpose of this presentation is to reminisce with the audience *about Mason Steven's contributions to the revitalization of the downtown business district.*

Thesis Statement

A **thesis statement**, or what you will argue or develop throughout the entire presentation, encapsulates your entire speech. A statement rather than a question, the thesis of your presentation should focus on a single idea. Being as explicit as possible will help guide the development of your entire presentation and sustain your relationship with the audience.

> *Student financial aid opportunities include loans, scholarships, and work study.*

> *Volunteering with the city's literacy program provides benefits for volunteers and for the city.*

> *Mason Steven's tireless efforts on behalf of the downtown business district have resulted in its revitalization.*

Evidence and Support Material

You will use evidence and support material to develop your thesis and back the claims made throughout your presentation. In the next chapter, we discuss the creation of an argument, which essentially consists of a thesis and support for that thesis. Your thesis will be supported by main points, which will in turn be supported by subpoints. These main points and (especially) subpoints will consist of evidence or support material, such as facts, testimony, definitions, examples, comparisons and contrasts, and statistics. In what follows, we discuss the various sorts of evidence and support material you can use for your presentation and then discuss guidelines for their selection, making them particularly relevant to the relationship that you have with each particular audience.

Definitions

Definitions provide the meaning of a word or phrase. Definitions assist in audience understanding and help clarify your topic of discussion. The abstract and ambiguous nature of language often requires you to define terms for your audience. Contextual factors can enable an audience to determine the meaning of a word, and the different meanings may be obvious. However, not all words or phrases are obvious to the audience.

    Operational definitions are concrete explanations of meaning that are more original or personal than what a dictionary might provide. This type of definition is often necessary to clarify what you mean by a word or phrase and to focus audience perspective on a particular aspect of that word or phrase. For example, if you discuss *Internet activity*, do you mean all activities taking place online? Or do you wish to distinguish between exploration and use of Internet sites and person-to-person correspondence through e-mail or instant messaging? This distinction could make a big difference in your point.

Facts and Opinions

As you gather material to develop your presentation, you will discover both facts and opinions concerning your topic. In many instances, you will find both within the same article, Internet site, or television news broadcast. **Facts** are provable or documented truths that you can use as evidence to support your claims. "The first broadcast of *American Idol* occurred on June 11, 2002" and "Richard Nixon was the only American president to resign from office" are facts because they can be verified through credible documentation. "Water freezes at 32 °F" and "Large-mouth bass spawn each spring when water temperatures average around 65 °F" are facts because they can be proved or demonstrated and verified through credible documentation.

Facts and opinions are not the same but are often used interchangeably, and people often confuse their meanings. **Opinions** are personal beliefs or speculations that, while perhaps based on facts, have not been proved or verified. "Using top water baits is the most exciting way to catch largemouth bass" and "*American Idol* is the most influential television program ever produced" are opinions because they cannot be proved even though many people may find the use of top water baits exciting and appreciate the influence of *American Idol*.

You can use both facts and opinions in support of your presentation, but you should manage them in different ways. As with all types of evidence and support, the facts and opinions used in your presentation must come from cited, credible sources. Since opinions have not been proved or verified, it is especially important that the audience perceive and recognize the source as credible. Further, facts are more likely than opinions to be able to stand alone without any additional support. Above all, a speaker's perceived credibility and relationship with the audience members will influence their reaction to these types of evidence and support.

Comparisons and Contrasts

Comparisons and contrasts are often used to assist in audience comprehension and understanding. **Comparisons** demonstrate or reveal how things are similar, and **contrasts** demonstrate or reveal how things are different. Sometimes used to show trends among concepts, ideas, or objects, comparisons can also establish connections between two items to associate their favorable or unfavorable characteristics. You may, for example, compare profitable yet unstable investment programs with the dot-com industry of the late 1990s in attempts to warn investors of possible risks. Contrasting is frequently used to distinguish something supported by the speaker from something considered negative by the audience. For example, you could contrast a new recycling program for the city with an existing, less favorable recycling program. In all cases of comparisons and contrasts, the audience must be familiar with at least one of the items being connected.

Testimony

Testimony consists of declarations or statements of a person's findings, opinions, conclusions, or experience. There exist three types of testimony: (1) personal testimony, (2) expert testimony, and (3) lay testimony.

Personal Testimony

Personal testimony comes from oneself and is enhanced by one's connection with the audience. Discussing your own experience with a topic, a powerful method of enhancing audience members' perceptions of credibility and their relationship with you as a speaker, often conveys to the audience that the topic has special significance for you and that you possess exceptional insight that can enhance understanding of the topic. While important, your personal testimony is not enough to support an entire presentation. Additional evidence and support material must be included to develop the presentation.

Expert Testimony

Expert testimony comes from someone with special training, instruction, or knowledge in a particular area. If you give a speech about dental hygiene, for example, you may include testimony from a dentist. You must observe certain ethical considerations when using expert testimony. First, make absolutely clear that this testimony is not your own through accurately referencing the source. This action not only prevents you from plagiarizing the material but also enhances the believability of the statements you make. Second, critically evaluate the testimony because your audience may not. People often readily believe testimony from experts because they evaluate these messages less critically than those they receive from someone without perceived expertise in an area. Therefore, as a speaker, make certain that this testimony is as accurate and truthful as possible.

Make Your Case

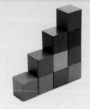

Research indicates little difference in the influence of the various types of evidence and support material. Accordingly, statistics may be more influential in some situations, and testimony may be more influential in others. Further, the influence of evidence and support material will vary among different people. Having learned all of this and considering only statistics and testimony, which do you generally find most influential and convincing? Why do you favor that type of evidence and support material? How might your choice change with changes in context? What does this tell you about yourself as an audience member?

Lay Testimony

Lay testimony comes from someone without expertise in a particular area but who possesses experience in that area. It comes from a regular person providing his or her experience with your topic. For instance, in a speech about dental hygiene, you might use the testimony from someone who has not followed a proper dental hygiene regimen and is suffering the consequences. Lay testimony can be just as meaningful and powerful as personal or expert testimony, but make sure this testimony is worthwhile and comes from a legitimate source. If your lay testimony comes from an interview, make sure the person you interview is a legitimate source rather than a convenient source, such as your roommate or Uncle Billy-Bob. Lay testimony from your roommate or uncle may be legitimate, but the personal connection may require you to provide additional justification for its inclusion in your speech.

Examples

Examples, or specific cases used to represent a larger whole to clarify or explain something, can involve the concrete or tangible (a schnauzer is an example of a dog) or the abstract or intangible (the ability to vote is one example of the many freedoms we enjoy in this country).

Examples can serve two very important functions in your presentation. First, they can help an audience better understand your discussion and relate to the material. The audience members may not know what a particular term means, and providing an example will help them comprehend its meaning. When using examples, it is important that you select those most familiar to your audience. Second, examples may also help your audience better appreciate or grasp the importance or significance of an issue. Providing examples of injuries suffered by someone abused by a spouse may help the audience better understand the meaning of *domestic violence* and appreciate its dire nature.

Illustrations, or examples offered in an extended narrative form, can enhance the understanding and appreciation of your audience and also help you maintain audience attention. The most effective illustrations use vivid imagery, engaging audience senses virtually through your description of the example. For example, you might illustrate possible difficulties encountered when visiting the financial aid office on campus. Furthermore, audience members often remember illustrations long after they have forgotten other support material and evidence that you provided during your presentation.

Hypothetical illustrations are fabricated illustrations using typical characteristics to describe particular situations, objects, or people, as well as illustrations describing what could happen in the future. It is very important to disclose to your audience that your illustration is hypothetical; otherwise, you are being dishonest and will lose credibility, which can hinder your relationship should the audience realize this deception.

Statistics

Statistics are numbers that demonstrate or establish size, trends, and associations. Consider the examples in Table 11.3.

Table 11.3 Statistics in Use: Sizes, Trends, and Associations

- According to the Surgeon General, 2 out of 3 Americans experience problems with acid reflux—size (frequency).

- According to the *Mayberry Gazette,* 25% of Camden County residents overpaid an average of $570 in local taxes last year—size (scope).

- According to noted economist Jake N. Elwood, the amount of credit card debt accrued by the average American has tripled in the past 5 years—trend.

- The amount of money a person earns each year is related to his or her level of education. An article from *Money Quarterly* revealed that individuals who have earned a bachelor's degree can expect to earn an average of $15,000 more each year than those with only a high school diploma. Individuals who have earned their master's degree earn an additional $10,000—association.

Recognizing and Overcoming Problems With Statistics

Statistics can accomplish a great deal during your presentation, but you must endeavor to use them appropriately and cautiously. While they can be very effective, using them inappropriately can make them equally ineffective. Further, while many are accurate and valid representations, statistics can be extremely misrepresentative. You can very easily mislead the audience with statistics, so do all you can to ensure the relevance and accuracy of the statistics you use during your presentation. Some cautions and guidelines to assist you in the selection and use of the most accurate and representative statistics follow below.

In fact, 25% of all statistics have been made up. OK, we just made up that last statistic, but see how easy it is? While we are at it, 99.5% of all students using this textbook think its authors are handsome. Pity the tastes of the remaining 0.5%! It has also been discovered that reading this textbook in public will make you appear 5 times more attractive to others and increase your chances of being asked out on a date by 55%. We can do this all day long!

Statistics may be fabricated. Sometimes people are dishonest about data they provide. Although many statistics you come across will be authentic, some may be absolutely bogus. Some fabricated statistics have been used so often, they have almost become given beliefs. For a number of years, news reports claimed higher spousal abuse on Super Bowl Sunday than on any other day of the year. Supposedly, watching football makes a person more violent, and since record numbers of people watch football on that day, this results in more visits to hospital emergency rooms by abused spouses. In reality, none of this is true. Someone simply made up these statistics. Using trustworthy and credible sources will help you avoid using fabricated statistics in your presentation.

Statistics and time. Time is often an issue in the misuse of statistics. Compared to other types of evidence and support material, the shelf life of many statistics is especially short. What is statistically true today is often untrue tomorrow. Using dated statistics to describe current situations misleads your audience. Strive to use the most current statistics available, and if you use somewhat-dated statistics, disclose this to the audience and explain why you included these particular statistics in your presentation. For instance, using the amount of pumpkins sold during the month of October in anticipation of Halloween to represent year-round sales would be misleading.

Statistical averages: mean, median, and mode. Statistical averages may not always provide an accurate description. When you selected a college or a major, you may have looked at the average class size or the average number of students enrolled in each class. An academic department may offer five courses with a maximum enrollment of 12 students, two courses with a maximum enrollment of 14 students, four courses with a maximum enrollment of 15 students, and one course with a maximum enrollment of 600 students. If all of these classes were full, there would be 748 students enrolled in that department's 12 classes. This total would result in an average class size of 62.3 students, which, while statistically correct, does not provide an accurate description of the class size of most of that department's courses.

- **Mean** refers to the average number, which may or may not provide an accurate description or representation. The average of 62.3 students in the above example would be the mean number of students.

- **Median** is the number that rests in the middle of all the other numbers; half of the numbers are less than this number, and the other half are more than this number. In the above example, the median number would be 14 students, with half the numbers below this number and half above this number (12 12 12 12 12 **14 14** 15 15 15 15 600).

Photo 11.4 Using statistics to support her presentation, this speaker is using the number that occurs most often. What is this number called? (See page 291.)

- **Mode** is the number that occurs most often. Once again using the number from the above example, the mode would be 12 students, since that number occurs most often (**12 12 12 12 12** 14 14 15 15 15 15 600).

Population and base. Statistics can also be misleading when the population and base are not disclosed. **Population** refers to whom or what a study includes. Such populations as "registered voters" are often provided with survey results. Changes in the population will generally lead to changes in the results of a study. Asking more Republicans than Democrats about their voting intentions to gauge a candidate's popularity with voters as a whole will provide a misleading characterization of that candidate's approval or disapproval among all voters.

The statistical **base** refers to the number of people, objects, or things included in a study. Problems with the statistical base frequently surround the use of a small sample size rather than not including a representative population. The finding that 75% of students favor a tuition increase may sound like

Sometimes surveys are used to promote a rumor and skew results of questions. Consider the possible results if respondents were asked these two questions in the following order: (a) "If it is true that Duck and McMahan Medicated Cream causes uncontrolled itching, would it impact whether or not you use this product?" and (b) "Which product would you be most likely to use: Duck and McMahan Medicated Cream or Wood Medicated Ointment?" The first question accomplishes two different things. First, it promotes an absolutely false rumor about the high-quality and reasonably priced Duck and McMahan Medicated Cream. Look for it in your local pharmacy! It also plants a seed of doubt in the benefits of that product, and this doubt will likely influence how people answer the second question.

a convincing mandate for raising tuition rates. However, such a finding would not be nearly as convincing if it were based on a poll conducted in a single class with 25 students.

Asking the questions. How a question is posed and how an issue is defined can also influence statistical results. Imagine the outcome of a political survey that asked likely voters, "Would you be more likely to vote for the incumbent, who has lowered taxes each year while in office and visits with the elderly each weekend, or the challenger, who wants to abolish Social Security and is rumored to frequently drown baby kittens in the river?" Regardless of a person's attitude toward felines or the elderly, how the question is phrased would certainly benefit the incumbent. Not all surveys are this blatant, but many are quite biased in the ways they present questions.

Using Statistics Effectively

Having discussed some of the problems related to statistics, you should now be aware of some of the pitfalls and consequences associated with their use. Table 11.4 provides guidelines and suggestions for incorporating statistics in your presentations.

Table 11.4 Increasing the Effectiveness of Statistics

- *Statistics should come from a trustworthy and credible source.* Using statistics from trustworthy and credible sources will enable you to incorporate them into your presentation with a greater confidence in their accuracy and legitimacy.

- *Use statistics sparingly.* Do not overwhelm your audience with statistics. When you use multiple statistics in the development of your speech, the audience will find it increasingly difficult to determine what each statistic means and how it supports your presentation.

- *Use statistics that personally involve and impact the audience.* Statistics that personally involve or impact your audience will have the greatest effects.

- *Simplify the statistics.* Statistics should be memorable and easy to process for your audience, and a good way to achieve these characteristics is by making the statistics as simple as possible: Round them to a whole or major number ("more than 3 million" is more memorable than "3,065,453"); present them as fractions and percentages.

- *Explain the statistics to your audience.* Endeavor to make statistics meaningful for your audience. Explain them to your audience, and translate them into terms that the audience will easily understand ("Last year, wildfires destroyed 8 million acres of land. To put this in perspective, that amount of land is 4,000 times the size of this campus and nearly 90 times the size of this state").

Selecting and Using Evidence and Support Material

We must address three additional questions before moving on to the next section of the chapter:

1. How much evidence should be included in a presentation?

2. How important is the quality of evidence?

3. Is one type of evidence and support material better than others?

The Quantity of Evidence and Support Material

You should strive to develop your presentation with a sufficient amount of quality evidence to take advantage of its positive influence on audience members' perceptions of the message and of your credibility and relationship with the audience. No magic number exists as to the amount of evidence and support material that must be included. The impact of evidence quantity will vary according to audience involvement or relationship with the topic. Those individuals not highly involved with the topic will be more influenced by the quantity than by the actual quality of evidence when compared with highly involved individuals (Petty & Cacioppo, 1986). You should not include large amounts of poor evidence just to convince audience members not highly involved with the topic of your speech. Instead, include large amounts of high-quality evidence to satisfy all members of the audience.

Photo 11.5 As you select sources for your presentation, should you limit the types of sources that you use, such as only gathering evidence and support material from the Internet or from books? (See page 291.)

The Quality of Evidence and Support Material

Using quality evidence and support material will enhance the effectiveness of a presentation. This impact is further enhanced when using **oral citations** (O'Keefe, 1998), or references to the source of the evidence and support material used during your presentation. The use of quality evidence will also enhance audience members' perceptions of your credibility and of their relationship with you. Audiences will view as more credible a speaker who uses highly credible sources and as less credible a speaker who uses sources of lower credibility. Naturally, the use of such evidence will hinder the development of a meaningful relationship with the audience.

Comparing the Effectiveness of Evidence and Support Material

None of the types of evidence and support material discussed in this chapter have consistently proved more persuasive or effective than other types. An analysis of studies examining this area found that statistical evidence may be "slightly more effective" than other types of evidence (Allen & Preiss, 1997, p. 128). This finding

Case in Point

Visiting the library on campus may not appeal to everyone, and for others it can be somewhat intimidating. However, the more familiar you are with what it has to offer, the better equipped you will be to find effective sources for your presentations and papers. Go to the library and start exploring. Begin running searches for topics that interest you. Always be sure to ask librarians for assistance when you need it. Your library may also offer tours or seminars to help people unfamiliar with what it offers.

Types of sources include books; dictionaries and encyclopedias; magazines; newspapers; scholarly journals; pamphlets; television, video, and radio; Internet sites; blogs; and interviews.

especially holds true when the vividness of evidence is held constant (Hoeken, 2001). Ultimately, however, the effectiveness of each type of evidence and support material depends on such factors as audience members' attitudes toward the topic (Slater & Rouner, 1996), their involvement with the issue (Baesler, 1997), cultural differences among audience members (Hornikx & Hoeken, 2005), and ultimately their relationship with you and with the topic and the material. Use multiple types of evidence when supporting and developing your presentation to satisfy all members of your audience.

Selecting and Searching for Sources

The quality of the sources used during your presentation will in part determine audience members' perceptions of your credibility and your relationship with them, as well as the overall effectiveness of your presentation. Indeed, your presentation is only as good as the sources used in its development. As you search for material to support your speech, your goal should be finding the most accurate and credible sources available. Table 11.5 provides guidelines to critically evaluate and determine the quality of potential sources for your speech.

Table 11.5 Selecting Quality Sources

Unbiased

You should select unbiased sources—those that provide a balanced view of an issue—in the development of your speech. Most sources slant one way or another when it comes to issues, but some sources may be very obvious and open about their point of view, such as material from prolife or prochoice organizations, gun control organizations, and environmental groups.

Editorial review

You can usually trust sources that have undergone a review process—in which more than one person has determined their accuracy—more than those that have not. Many of the books, journals, magazines, and newspaper articles you discover when conducting research will have undergone a review process. While you can generally be more confident in the accuracy of a source that has undergone editorial review, you should still evaluate this source critically.

Expertise

The sources you use should have expertise in the area examined. Consider the background or qualifications of an author when evaluating the quality of a book or an article to determine if you should consider the author an expert in the area discussed. For instance, while perhaps an expert in journalism, a newspaper or magazine reporter, would not be considered an expert in fitness even if authoring an article about the topic.

Recency

The sources used in the development of your presentation should be as recent as possible. How recent a source should be depends on the topic. Use your knowledge of the topic to determine whether the source has become outdated. Have significant changes occurred in the area that would alter the information available from the source? Does the topic area undergo rapid change and development? Also, consider the evaluation of your sources by the audience. Would your audience view the source as outdated and question its legitimacy and accuracy?

Credibility of a source's sources

The sources and evidence that a source uses in its development can also determine its quality. Carefully consider whether the source you are evaluating includes recent, unbiased material. Determine if the source's sources have undergone editorial review and can be considered experts in the area. If you determine that the sources supporting the source you are evaluating are not legitimate, you should not use that particular source for your presentation. If a source makes claims without any form of support, you should question the legitimacy of that source.

Credibility for your audience

Keep in mind that your audience will evaluate and use the types of sources you use in a presentation to determine the accuracy of the evidence supplied, the value of your presentation, and your credibility as a speaker. Your audience may judge certain types of sources as more worthwhile and accurate than others.

Searching for material to support and to develop your speech can sometimes be a challenging process, especially when someone is relatively new to the process. Table 11.6 provides some guidelines and suggestions to follow when conducting research and gathering material.

Table 11.6 Guidelines for Conducting Research and Gathering Material

Start early

One of the biggest mistakes you can make when conducting research is waiting until the last minute. Delaying the collection of support material will impede the actual development of the speech and limit the amount of time available to practice the delivery of your presentation.

Use multiple types of sources

It is best to use multiple types of sources when developing your research. Including multiple sources will enable you to satisfy the various preferences of the audience and to ensure the thoroughness of your research.

Go to the library

You will need to actually go to the library to conduct adequate research for your presentation. A great deal of material is available online, but more material is still physically available at the library itself.

Use multiple search engines and databases

When conducting searches, you should use multiple search engines and databases. While there are some very powerful search engines and databases available, none are complete. Many are dedicated to particular topics or areas, which will allow you to conduct a more thorough and efficient search. Using multiple search engines and databases will enable you to conduct the most complete search for materials.

(Continued)

Table 11.6 (Continued)

Do not read everything

As you review potential sources, do not feel as if you have to read all of these pieces in their entirety. A quick but conscientious review of the material will help you determine whether or not you should examine it in more detail. Reviewing a book's index to pinpoint particular information will help establish its potential usefulness, as will reading abstracts or key sections of journal articles, magazines, or other periodicals. However, you will have to read the material in more detail once you determine it will be used.

Take notes as you proceed

You should take notes as you conduct your search for information to find the information later and to ensure the accurate citation of material. When you have examined multiple sources, it is easy to forget where particular evidence and support material originated.

Pay attention to the citations of others

Regardless of how thorough your search may be or how expansive your search engine may be, it is impossible to discover every available source related to your topic. The reference sections of the material you do find provide ready-made lists of potential sources that can be used for your presentation. Just because a source has been previously used by someone else does not mean that it cannot be used by you. However, you must actually locate and read these other sources on your own.

Engage in multiple searches and trips to the library

Conducting research is not something that should be done all at one time. It would be unwise to think that a single trip to the library will enable you to conduct a thorough search for sources and provide all the material you need. Conducting adequate research requires multiple searches and multiple trips to the library.

Eventually you must develop your presentation

While you must conduct a thorough search of the material and there will always be additional sources that you can find, you will eventually have to start developing and then practicing your presentation. Especially keep this in mind if you are particularly nervous about speaking in public. Such speakers often spend more time than necessary conducting research and less time developing the speech for a particular audience and practicing the presentation (Ayres, 1996).

FOCUS QUESTIONS REVISITED

1. What factors should you consider when analyzing and relating to an audience?
When analyzing an audience, you should consider audience members' relationship with you, their relationship with the topic, and their view of the occasion. You may also consider audience attitudes, beliefs, and values as well as demographic characteristics.

2. What factors should you consider when determining the topic of a presentation?
Some occasions may warrant a particular topic, or a topic may already be selected for you. On occasions when you must select your own topic, consider yourself and the audience.

3. What strategies can you use when searching for the topic of a presentation?
When searching for a topic for a presentation, you can brainstorm, examine current issues and events, create an individual inventory, and gather input from others.

4. What are the general purpose, specific purpose statement, and thesis of a presentation?

The general purpose is the basic objective you want to achieve through your presentation. Most presentations are developed to achieve the following three basic objectives: (a) inform, (b) persuade, and (c) evoke. The specific purpose of your presentation is exactly what you want to achieve through your presentation. A thesis statement, or what you will argue or develop throughout the entire presentation, encapsulates your entire speech.

5. What types of evidence and support material can you use to develop a presentation?

You can use definitions, facts and opinions, comparisons and contrasts, testimony, examples, and statistics as evidence and support material to develop a presentation.

6. What factors should you consider when selecting sources for a presentation?

As you critically evaluate and determine the quality of a source, determine whether it is unbiased and whether it has undergone editorial review. You should ensure that sources have the proper expertise and experience, determine the recency of a source and the credibility of its sources, and, above all, determine audience evaluation of the source.

7. What factors should you consider when conducting research and gathering material?

When conducting research and gathering material, you should start early, use multiple types of sources, go to the library, use multiple search engines and databases, not read everything, take notes, pay attention to citations, engage in multiple searches and trips to the library, and eventually start writing.

KEY CONCEPTS

QUESTIONS TO ASK YOUR FRIENDS

1. What types of evidence and support material do your friends find most convincing? Which of this material do they find least convincing? Do their evaluations change depending on circumstances or what is discussed?

2. What types of sources do your friends find most convincing? Which sources do they find least convincing? Once again, do their evaluations change depending on circumstances or what is discussed?

3. Ask your friends to think about two people whom they consider to be very different. If they wanted to try to convince each person of the same idea, how would they have to adjust their strategy with each one? What does this tell you about the need to adapt your presentations to particular audiences?

MEDIA LINKS

1. Scan a newspaper for articles that include examples of evidence and support material. What types of this material are most prevalent? Do you find these articles convincing? To what extent do you believe your evaluation is based on the evidence and support material provided?

2. Gather examples of sources used in media that you consider *credible*. Now gather examples of sources used in media that you do not consider credible. Explain why you evaluated these sources in the manner that you did.

3. Gather examples of sources used in media that you consider *biased*. Now gather examples of sources used in media that you do not consider biased. Explain why you evaluated these sources in the manner that you did.

ETHICAL ISSUES

1. Taking concerns of privacy into account, what limitations would you place on audience analysis? To what lengths do you think a person is justified in going when gathering information about people for use in the development of a presentation?

2. Organizations and administrations sometimes misrepresent statistics, facts, and other types of evidence and support material for what they would consider the "greater good." Do you consider this use of evidence and support material justified? How would you support your response?

3. Graphic images are sometimes used as presentation aids to shock an audience. To what extent should a speaker be held responsible for such images? Do you consider the use of these images justified? How would you support your response?

ANSWERS TO PHOTO CAPTIONS

Photo 11.1 ■ No. You should adapt all elements of a presentation to a specific audience except the position you intend to argue.

Photo 11.2 ■ An audience required to be in attendance is known as a captive audience.

Photo 11.3 ■ Most likely to occur at a wedding or another celebratory event is a speech to evoke.

Photo 11.4 ■ Mode is the number that occurs most often.

Photo 11.5 ■ No. You should use a variety of sources to ensure thorough research has been conducted and to satisfy multiple members of the audience.

STUDENT STUDY SITE

Visit the study site at **www.sagepub.com/boc2e** for e-flashcards, practice quizzes, journal articles and additional study resources.

REFERENCES

Allen, M., & Preiss, R. W. (1997). Comparing the persuasiveness of narrative evidence using meta-analysis. *Communication Research Reports, 14,* 125–131.

Ayres, J. (1996). Speech preparation processes and speech apprehension. *Communication Education, 45,* 228–235.

Baesler, E. J. (1997). Persuasive effects of story and statistical evidence. *Argumentation and Advocacy, 33,* 170–175.

Fishbein, M., & Ajzen, I. (1975). *Belief, attitude, intention, and behavior: An introduction to theory and research.* Reading, MA: Addison-Wesley.

Gass, R. H., & Seiter, J. S. (2011). *Persuasion, social influence, and compliance gaining* (4th ed.). Boston: Allyn & Bacon.

Hoeken, H. (2001). Anecdotal, statistical, and causal evidence: Their perceived and actual persuasiveness. *Argumentation, 15,* 425–237.

Hornikx, J., & Hoeken, H. (2005, May). *The influence of culture on the relative persuasiveness of anecdotal, statistical, causal, and expert evidence.* Paper presented to the International Communication Association Annual Conference, New York.

O'Keefe, D. J. (1998). Justification explicitness and persuasive effect: A meta-analytic review of the effects of varying support articulation in persuasive messages. *Argumentation and Advocacy, 35,* 61–75.

Petty, R. E., & Cacioppo, J. T. (1986). *Communication and persuasion: Central and peripheral routes to attitude change.* New York: Springer-Verlag.

Slater, M. D., & Rouner, D. (1996). Value-affirmative and value-protective processing of alcohol education messages that include statistical evidence or anecdotes. *Communication Research, 23,* 210–235.

Sprague, J., & Stuart, D. (2003). *The speaker's handbook.* Belmont, CA: Wadsworth/ Thomson Learning.

12

Developing a Public Presentation

In the previous chapter, we discussed how you select a topic, determine the purpose and thesis of your speech, and gather support material, and we showed how you must accomplish all of these activities with your relationship to your audience in mind. At this point in the speech development process, you know its purpose and what you want to argue. You even have support material to back up your claims. However, public speakers cannot just haphazardly throw around a thesis statement, statistics, quotations, illustrations, and other support material. They must combine and organize their material and package it in a manner that will have the greatest impact on a particular audience. They must also develop the material in a way that further connects them relationally to the needs and desires of an audience. Developing and presenting a speech to an audience is not just logical but relational. A speaker must connect with an audience, motivate its members to listen, present a well-argued case, and conclude with a logical and relational uplift.

In this chapter, we talk about developing an argument in that relational context. Argumentation is not just another word for *disagreement* but a careful way of laying out your thoughts. Something you engage in every day, developing an argument is not as unfamiliar as it may seem. This discussion will assist you when developing your speeches and when writing papers for this class and others. Talk about more bang for your academic buck!

Inherent in the development of a public presentation is the continued enactment of a relational connection with an audience. Having previously established the purpose of the presentation to meet audience needs and desires, you must organize your support material for your audience in a clear and understandable way that exhibits your ability to satisfy these needs and desires. You can select from several strategies (or patterns) to organize your material. We discuss ways of selecting the best organizational pattern for your speech based on your topic, the purpose of your speech, and, of course, the audience. Clear organization of an argument results in audience understanding and increased audience liking of the speaker.

The introduction and conclusion of your presentation also enact the relational connection with your audience. These parts of your speech, just as important as its body, must accomplish a great deal. Within the introduction, you must establish credibility and a relationship with your specific audience, stress the importance of the topic (i.e., how it relates to the audience), and prepare your audience for the remainder of the speech, using the same skills, techniques, and ways of relating to your audience discussed in the previous chapter. This relational connection continues when you reach the conclusion, in which you must reinforce your thesis and purpose, summarize your material, stress audience involvement, and provide adequate closure. While both introductions and conclusions include a lot of material, we break them down into manageable components to help you better understand and develop them. In addition, you should not write your introduction or conclusion until you have finished the body of your speech, so we begin by discussing that part of your presentation.

Focus Questions

1. What are the four principles of speech organization and development?
2. What organizational patterns can you use in the development of the speech body?
3. What components must you include in a speech introduction?
4. What components must you include in a speech conclusion?

The Body: How Do You Develop an Argument?

The **body** of your speech is where you develop and present your argument. When we talk about arguments and argumentation, we do not necessarily mean disagreeing with someone or engaging in a heated discussion. Rather, an argument is presented when you provide a thesis or claim and then back it up with evidence and support material discussed in the previous chapter.

Providing claims and then support for those claims is actually something you do quite often. Whenever you try to convince a friend to do something, or whenever you explain or describe something to a colleague, you are essentially engaged in argumentation. For example, you may find yourself with a group of friends trying to decide what to do on a Friday evening. You really want to see a particular movie, so you tell your friends that you should all go to the theater and watch this movie. You might then describe the movie and provide reasons you should all go see it. Whether you realize it or not, you are engaging in a form of argumentation. Your thesis or claim is that you should all go to the movie. Your support comes from the various reasons your friends should do what you suggest—the movie has received favorable reviews, the theater is not very far away, and nothing tastes better than a $50 box of popcorn. So, while developing an argument might sound like an unfamiliar task, the basic ideas behind the process are nothing new. The primary difference between constructing an argument for an academic, civic, or professional setting and presenting an argument to friends, family, or romantic partners is that the former is generally more structured and has undergone more development and planning.

College Experience

Many college students feel overwhelmed or confused when their instructors stress the need to provide a clear argument in their speeches or papers. Developing an argument is not always taught or required in high school, yet suddenly students are expected to know how to do it as soon as they enter college. If you feel stressed out by these demands, rest assured that you are not alone. Even better, once you finish this chapter, you will know how to do it!

Principles of Speech Organization and Development

To better describe how to construct the body of your speech and develop your argument, we discuss the four principles of speech organization and development that can help you maintain a clear focus: points, unity, balance, and guidance. The first three principles underscore the logical development of an argument, and the final principle emphasizes relational development. You must adhere to all four principles to properly develop a presentation and to fully connect with an audience.

Points Principle

The **points principle** highlights the basic building blocks of an argument: the main points and subpoints. The body of your speech will include **main points**, or statements that directly support or develop your thesis statement. As a general rule, include five main points at the absolute most. Ideally, you should include at least two but no more than three main points when supporting or developing your thesis statement. Including too many main points will make it difficult to provide adequate support and development.

Subpoints, or statements that support and explain the main points of your speech, will include much of the support material we discussed in the previous chapter. The actual number of subpoints you include to support each main point will vary. Similar to limiting the number of main points, you do not want to overwhelm your audience with too many subpoints. Including a limited number of strong subpoints to support a main idea is more effective than including numerous weak ones.

Being able to visualize the construction of an argument is sometimes helpful, which is one of the reasons your instructor may have you develop an outline for presentations you deliver in the classroom. While not an actual outline, Figure 12.1 will help you visualize the structure of an argument.

Thesis

> **Main point 1 supporting thesis**
> Subpoint supporting main point 1
> Subpoint supporting main point 1
> Subpoint supporting main point 1
> Subpoint supporting main point 1
>
> Main point 2 supporting thesis
> Subpoint supporting main point 2
> Subpoint supporting main point 2
> Subpoint supporting main point 2
> Subpoint supporting main point 2
>
> Main point 3 supporting thesis
> Subpoint supporting main point 3
> Subpoint supporting main point 3
> Subpoint supporting main point 3
> Subpoint supporting main point 3

Figure 12.1 Visualizing the structure of an argument

Unity Principle

The **unity principle** maintains you should stay focused and provide only information that supports your thesis and main points. This principle sounds reasonable and easy to follow, but speakers often struggle to abide by it. As you conduct research for your speech, you will come across a wealth of information about your topic. You can use some of this material to support your thesis and include some of it in your presentation. Other material, while related to your topic, will not directly support your thesis or main points and should therefore not be included.

The most obvious example of not adhering to the principle of speech unity involves the selection of main points that do not support the thesis. For instance, imagine you are presenting a speech in which you want to inform the audience about the treatments of a particular disease. In your first main point, you address one common type of treatment. In your second main point, you address another common type of treatment. In your third main point, you suddenly shift gears and begin discussing common symptoms of this disease. While the matter of symptoms associated with this disease is naturally associated with your topic, your speech is supposed to be about the treatment of the disease. You have not followed the principle of speech unity.

You might be thinking, "Wait a second. If I were telling my audience about the treatment of a disease, why would I not want to talk about the symptoms?" Depending on your audience, addressing the symptoms might be important; however, your main argument involves the treatments associated with this disease. Including anything else in the body of your speech will prevent you from fully explaining the treatments, what you set out to do in the first place. If you think it is important to let the audience know the symptoms associated with this disease, you can briefly discuss them in the introduction of your speech. We discuss introductions later in the chapter and, during something called *orientation to the topic,* specifically address such instances as the preceding, so stay tuned!

Balance Principle

The **balance principle** maintains that the points of the body must be relatively equal in scope and importance. You must devote to them equal time and an equal amount of development and support. Your main points, as well as the subpoints supporting them, must also be equally important in their support of your thesis.

Photo 12.1 This speaker is providing members of her audience with a clear transition between sections of her speech in order to help them better understand the presentation. Which principle of speech organization and development emphasizes the relational development of a presentation? (See page 316.)

One common violation of the principle of balance involves the amount of time and support you devote to a particular main point. Suppose you have three main points in your speech. You have discovered a lot of material to support and develop your first main point, so you spend most of your time discussing it. When it comes to your second and third main points, you have not found as much support material or have not found them as interesting, so you devote less attention to them during your speech. While you have done an excellent job explaining and supporting your first main point, your other main points are not developed enough to support your thesis. Regardless of its strength, that first main point will not sufficiently support your thesis. Make sure to spend relatively equal time developing and discussing your main points (O'Hair, Stewart, & Rubenstein, 2001).

Guidance Principle

The **guidance principle** maintains a speaker must guide and direct the audience throughout the entire speech. Fundamental to the effectiveness of a speech are audience members' understanding and establishing a strong relational connection with them. Guiding them through a speech helps ensure that audience members comprehend the support provided and recognize and understand how it supports your thesis. Guiding the audience members throughout the presentation will also enhance your credibility and relational connection with them, because it indicates your true concern for their understanding of your presentation as you construct the identity of a speaker who cares for the audience. Just as you help guide and support your friends through difficult problems when they need your direction and advice, you must guide your audience through the logic of your presentation. We talk about components of the introduction and conclusion that help guide the audience later in the chapter, but here we address the use of transitions.

Transitions, or phrases or statements that serve to connect the major parts or sections of the speech and to guide the audience through the presentation, should be included between the introduction and the body of the speech, between each main point, and between the body of the speech and the conclusion. These transitions should guide the audience members and inform them of where you are, where you have been, and/or where you are going in the speech. Examples of transitions include the following:

To begin, let's examine the issue of . . .

Now that we have talked about X, let's turn our attention to the matter of Y.

The first item we must consider is . . .

This brings us to our second issue . . .

The examples provided here might differ from transitions you have studied in English or writing classes. When taught about transitions in those courses, you were probably instructed that they guide the reader and set up the next paragraph or section of the paper or story. Transitions included in written work and transitions included in oral presentations are very similar. The key difference between them is that transitions included in oral work must be more obvious than those included in written work, and they must fully direct the audience through the speech.

To really grasp the need for such explicit transitions and the importance of the guidance principle in general, consider the difference between reading an article or a book and listening to a speech. When reading, you have the ability to reread a paragraph or section. You can flip back a few pages and remind yourself of what came before. You can scan ahead to see what comes next. When you listen to a speech, you do not have these luxuries. As a speaker, you must be aware of this limitation of the medium and fully guide the audience throughout the entire speech. You must maintain your relationship with the audience members by acting as their page turner or reviewer, constantly helping them recognize and remember the key points.

Having talked about principles of speech organization, we can now discuss the variety of organizational patterns you can use to structure the presentation of your claims and support.

Organizational Patterns

As we discussed with the principles of speech organization and development, the most effective speeches are focused, ordered, and understood by the audience. Consider how difficult even your friends might find it to follow and understand a story that offers main points at random. So too with an audience: One

Strategic Communication

Consider how the act of reading is similar to and different from listening to a public presentation. In addition to transitions, what do these similarities and differences tell you about the needs of a listening audience? Compile a list of strategies based on your responses that you could implement as a public speaker to assist your audience.

would have trouble following a speech where evidence, such as statistics, testimony, and examples, is simply scattered about. Members of the audience would find it very difficult to comprehend the material, and therefore, you would have a very difficult time successfully achieving the purpose of your speech and constructing a positive relationship with the audience. You must arrange the speech in a way that will allow the audience to clearly grasp the material and that will most effectively achieve your purpose.

An **organizational pattern** is an arrangement of the main points that best enables audience comprehension. Some organizational patterns are more effective for certain types of speeches and audiences than for others, and the following discussion covers various organizational patterns you may choose and when they might be most appropriate given the circumstances surrounding your speech.

Chronological Pattern

When using the **chronological pattern**, you arrange the main points according to their position in a time sequence. Often selected when explaining a process to the audience, this pattern conveys a sense of development, either forward or backward depending on your topic and purpose. For example, you may explain the process of passing legislation through Congress:

1. First, legislation is introduced and sent to the appropriate committee.

2. Second, legislation is debated and voted on by both the House of Representatives and the Senate.

3. Finally, legislation undergoes additional committee discussion and approval before being submitted to the president.

Spatial Pattern

In the **spatial pattern**, the main points are arranged according to their physical relation, such as from left to right, top to bottom, north to south, or forward to backward. For instance, you may describe the layout of a new building on campus using this pattern:

1. The bottom floor of the new student union building will feature the bookstore and a food court.

2. The second floor of the new student union building will house student organization offices.

3. The third floor of the new student union building will include additional classrooms and a technology lab.

Causal Pattern

When a **causal pattern** is used to organize the body of a speech, the main points are arranged according to cause and effect. The order in which you choose to place these two matters will depend on your purpose, topic, and audience. This pattern works best when you are attempting to explain to members of an audience or convince them that one thing causes another. For example, you could use the causal pattern to discuss the impact of capital gains taxes on investment and development:

1. There has been a steady increase in the amount of capital gains taxes.

2. Small-business investing and development have substantially decreased in recent years.

Fundamental to the causal pattern is convincing the audience that a definite link exists between what you classify as a cause and what you claim are its effects. In the above example, you would have to convince the audience that the decrease in investments and development was the primary result of increased capital gains and not the result of federal guidelines, interest rates, global investments, or a host of other factors. A causal pattern sometimes proves challenging for speakers to use effectively. When using this pattern, make sure you provide a clear connection between your cause and its effects.

Question–Answer Pattern

Using the **question–answer pattern** involves posing questions an audience may have about a subject and then answering them in a manner that favors your position (Gronbeck, German, Ehninger, & Monroe, 1995). When selecting which questions to include, make sure they are important to the audience and not just the easiest to answer in a way that supports your stance. You will likely use this pattern when addressing a voluntary audience with concerns about an issue (Chapter 11). For instance, you may address a community group with questions about the impact of a particular city project. This organizational pattern may also be appropriate when speaking to your fellow students about issues on campus. For example, if you deliver a speech about possible tuition increases, arranging your main points in a question–answer format might be effective:

1. The major question students are asking is, "Why is this tuition increase necessary?"

2. A second common question among students is, "Can we expect similar increases over the next few years?"

3. Students are also wondering, "How will this tuition increase affect grants, scholarships, and other financial assistance?"

Topical Pattern

The **topical pattern** arranges support material according to specific categories, groupings, or grounds. At times, the order of your assertions may follow a natural progression. In the next example, when discussing available scholarships with your audience, you could begin with the scholarship offering the least amount of money and progress to the one offering the largest amount of money:

1. The Caton Scholarship pays for half of tuition for the entire academic year.

2. The McNeece Scholarship pays for full tuition for the entire academic year.

3. The Cutter Scholarship pays for full tuition for the entire academic year plus full room and board for the recipient.

Other times, the order in which each main point in a topical pattern is presented does not really matter. For instance, you may provide your audience with reasons for a spike in medication prices:

1. Additional research and development by pharmaceutical companies have increased the price of medication.

2. Increased demand for different medications has led to an increase in their prices.

3. Federal legislation has resulted in the increased price of medication.

Although in a topical pattern the main points may not always follow a natural progression, do not place your main points at random without any thought or consideration. When using the topical pattern, you might use one main point to prepare the audience for another and should therefore address it first.

Problem–Solution and Elimination Patterns

We discuss the final two organizational patterns somewhat in tandem to emphasize the importance of considering the audience when selecting which pattern to use in the organization of your speech. First, the **problem–solution pattern** divides the body of the speech by first addressing a problem and then offering a solution to that problem. You may want to convince your audience that an increase in domestic oil drilling will help lower gasoline prices:

Photo 12.2 This speaker wants to convince her audience that a particular solution should be enacted to address a problem the audience does not know exists. Which organizational pattern would be most appropriate in this situation? (See page 316.)

1. An overreliance on foreign-based oil has led to a significant increase in gasoline prices in the United States.

2. Increased domestic oil drilling and exploration will reduce U.S. reliance on foreign oil and lower the price of gasoline.

Using the problem–solution pattern, it is naturally imperative that the solution indeed solve the problem. Furthermore, you must convince the audience that your solution is practicable and realistic.

The **elimination pattern** offers a series of solutions to a problem, systematically eliminating each one until the solution remaining is the one you support. When using this particular organizational pattern, make sure that the solutions offered are widely accepted or legitimate and that the reasons for eliminating them are reasonable (Gronbeck et al., 1995). We can illustrate the elimination pattern using the above example. You want to convince your audience that an increase in domestic drilling is the best solution for lowering the price of gasoline. In doing so, you provide other possible solutions, eliminating each of them until only the one that you support remains:

1. While increasing gasoline taxes to curb consumption has been proposed as a way of lowering prices, it will result in more hardships for consumers.

2. Decreasing government regulations oil companies must follow has been suggested as a way of lowering gas prices, but this will only be a short-term fix.

3. Increasing domestic oil drilling and exploration will reduce U.S. reliance on foreign oil and lower the price of gasoline.

Both the problem–solution pattern and the elimination pattern are most often used to convince an audience of a particular action's suitability to eliminate or manage a given problem. However, the problem–solution pattern is most appropriate when an audience does not know that the problem exists or does not recognize the pervasiveness or impact of the problem. Consequently, you will want to dedicate part of your speech to explaining to the audience the extent and impact of the problem in addition to promoting an acceptable solution. In the above example, if your audience were unaware of the problems surrounding high gasoline prices, the problem–solution pattern would be most appropriate. The elimination pattern, on the other hand, best suits an audience that is already aware of the extent and impact of a problem. However, these listeners are either unaware of possible solutions or aware that certain solutions exist but uncertain about which one to support. If your audience were already well aware of issues related to high gasoline prices but unaware or undecided about how they might be lowered, the elimination pattern would be most appropriate.

Listen in on Your Life

Recall an occasion when a friend tried to convince you to do or believe something. Did that person organize his or her ideas according to one of the organizational patterns discussed here? What impact did his or her use/nonuse of organizational patterns have on the outcome? What difference would it have made if the person had been a stranger?

Now recall a time when a stranger informed you about something. Did this person organize his or her ideas according to one of the organizational patterns discussed in this chapter? What impact did his or her use/nonuse of organizational patterns have on your understanding and comprehension of the material? What difference would it have made if the person had been a friend?

Introductions and Conclusions

In addition to the body of your speech, you need to include an **introduction** that lays the foundation for the speech and establishes a positive relational connection with the audience. You will also need to include a **conclusion** that reinforces and completes the speech while also reinforcing a relationship with the audience. Here, we talk about why these parts are so important to your speech and then offer guidelines for developing effective introductions and conclusions.

Beginning speakers often wonder how much time they should devote to introductions and conclusions. A classic study (Miller, 1946) suggested that introductions make up approximately 10% and conclusions make up around 5% of all speeches. While this study was conducted more than 60 years ago, these numbers are not too far off from what we see today. Generally, communication scholars recommend that you devote somewhere between 10% and 25% of your speech to the introduction and 5% to 15% to the conclusion. Given the particular importance of establishing a relational connection with your audience at the beginning of your presentation, reinforcing this connection through the end of the presentation, and developing a logical foundation and closing, we recommend dedicating around 25% of your speech to the introduction and 10% to 15% to the conclusion. If you give an 8-minute presentation, your introduction should finish at around the 2-minute mark, and your conclusion should occupy approximately the last minute of the presentation. Spending more time than this will not allow you to fully develop the body of your speech. Spending less time will not allow you to adequately connect with the audience, lay the foundation for the speech, or conclude the speech effectively.

While you will spend less time presenting your introduction and conclusion, these parts of your speech are just as important as its body. Sure, you devote more time to the body during the presentation of your speech, and you may spend more time working on the body during its preparation. However, it is impossible to present an effective presentation with a weak introduction or conclusion. You must support the body of your speech with a strong introduction and finish the speech with a thorough conclusion.

When considering how introductions and conclusions are just as important as the body of a speech, you might liken the development of a speech to the development of a house. No matter how strong the walls and frame are, without a solid foundation, the house will collapse and crumble to the ground. Further, regardless of how solid the foundation is or how strong the walls and frame are, without a durable roof on top, the house is not complete and will likely deteriorate. Likewise, you must support the body of your speech with a strong introduction and reinforce the speech with a thorough conclusion.

Photo 12.3 What is the first component that must be included in the introduction of a presentation? (See page 316.)

Introductions

When meeting someone for the first time, your initial impressions have a lasting impact on your perceptions of that person and determine if you desire additional contact. Often within the first few moments of a conversation, you determine if you would like to prolong your conversation and develop a relationship, if you would like to see this person in the future, or if you hope never to endure the excruciatingly painful experience of seeing this person again. Whether or not you actually engage in a relationship with someone is regularly determined in the first few moments of contact. The same holds true for the initial moments of a public presentation.

The first impressions an audience forms of you are critical for the reception of your presentation. As the audience members listen to you introduce yourself during the introduction to your speech, it is important that you perform your identity in an appealing manner so that the audience members can determine what type of relationship they will share with you. Whether you are speaking about an issue the audience supports or opposes, it is important that audience members respect and, ideally, like you as a person and a speaker. You must construct the identity of a credible speaker and develop a positive relationship with the audience. During the introduction of your speech, you must begin to establish your credibility and connect with the audience on a relational level; reinforce connections among the topic, your audience, and yourself to increase the audience's desire to listen; and lay the groundwork for the remainder of the speech. Below we discuss six components to include in the introduction of your speech (see Table 12.1). Including each component and following the guidelines offered will help you develop a strong, effective foundation for your speech.

Table 12.1 Brief Guide to Introductions

Attention-getting device

Gain the attention of your audience

Purpose and thesis

Inform your audience of the purpose of your speech and state your thesis

Credibility and relational connection

Explain why your audience should listen to you speak on the topic and discuss your personal connection with the audience

Orientation phase

Familiarize your audience with the topic and define terms if necessary

Impact of the topic and speech

Explain how the topic impacts your audience and why the audience should listen to the speech

Enumerated preview

Outline the main points of your speech for your audience

Attention Getter

The first thing to include in your introduction is an **attention getter**, a device used to draw the audience to you and hence your presentation. The placement of the remaining components of the introduction can vary, but the attention getter, ranging from one sentence to a few lines, always comes first. Some common types of attention getters are offered in Table 12.2.

When selecting the most appropriate attention getter, consider the topic, the audience, and yourself. Your attention getter must relate to the *topic* at hand in terms of both subject matter and tone. Many fascinating stories, colorful quotations, and extraordinary facts exist in the world, but the one you choose to gain your audience's attention must relate to the topic at hand and the occasion.

Table 12.2 Attention-Getting Devices

Illustration

A brief topic-related narrative can be used to grab your audience's attention. These narratives can be real or hypothetical, but if you provide a hypothetical narrative, make sure you tell the audience up front.

Personal reference

Providing a personal narrative or an anecdote can be a very effective way of gaining your audience's attention. Personal references allow you to begin establishing your credibility and a relational connection with your audience, which you can also gain by establishing a level of trust between you and your listeners.

Provocative facts or statistics

Provocative facts or statistics that shock or surprise an audience can also be effective attention getters. When selecting such facts and statistics, it is especially important to make sure they are relevant to the topic and the audience.

Rhetorical question

A rhetorical question—that is, one to which you do not expect the audience to offer a verbal response—gains audience members' attention by actively engaging them and causing them to think about their position or experience with a topic. A good rhetorical question also helps maintain audience attention throughout the speech, since members of the audience often wonder if their answer is accurate or appropriate.

Quotation

A relatively brief introduction can help gain attention and properly introduce the topic of your speech. Never just utter a quote and expect the audience to understand its relevance, why it was included, or who said it. Always explain why you selected a quote or what it may suggest.

Humor

A joke is an effective way to open a speech and gain your audience's attention, as long as it relates to your topic and allows you to effectively prepare the audience for your speech. Of course, a humorous opening does not have to be in the form of a joke. It can apply to all of the preceding attention-gaining strategies.

You must also consider the *audience* when selecting your attention getter. If audience members are very familiar with your topic, startling facts or statistics may not shock them as much as an audience unfamiliar with the topic. If audience members are unfamiliar with your topic, they may not fully understand complex illustrations, which thus may be ineffective at establishing a relational connection with them and capturing their attention.

Finally, when selecting an attention getter, you must consider *yourself*. Select an attention getter that is most comfortable for you. Some people feel awkward citing a quotation or reciting lines of a poem. Others feel ill at ease when attempting humor. Select an attention getter that is most suitable and natural for you. In particular, select one that lets you connect yourself to the audience.

Purpose and Thesis

In the introduction, you must also inform your audience of both the purpose of your speech and your thesis. Be as explicit as possible when stating your thesis or central idea. Tell audience members exactly what you intend to argue; they should not wonder what your speech is about. In the most effective speeches, the audience knows precisely what the speaker will argue. Earlier, we discussed the need to guide the audience throughout the entire speech. When you provide your thesis statement, you are telling the audience the direction you are heading and that everything included in the body of your speech will support this statement.

Supplying the purpose of your speech performs a few different functions. It often reinforces your thesis statement and will increase the listeners' understanding of the information you provide. When you get to the body of your speech, they will better understand why this particular material is included and its overall purpose.

Providing the purpose of your speech also enhances your credibility by establishing a sense of goodwill. By placing audience members at the forefront, you are letting them know that they are the reason you are speaking. You are presenting this information not for personal gain or because you like to hear yourself speak but because you care about the audience members and want to impact their lives in a meaningful and beneficial way.

Informing the audience of your purpose also helps comfort the audience and establishes trust. Especially if the audience is suspicious, it is good to be straightforward about your intentions. Letting the audience know your motives for presenting the speech will help you establish a trusting relationship, enhance your credibility, and ultimately help ensure the effectiveness of your presentation.

Credibility and Relational Connection

As a speaker, you must convey to the audience that you are knowledgeable about the topic, that you can be trusted, and that you have its best interest at heart. As mentioned in Chapter 11, these characteristics touch on the three primary dimensions of credibility: knowledge, trustworthiness, and goodwill (Gass & Seiter, 2011). Notice once again that these components would likely be used to characterize someone with whom you share a positive relationship. Perceptions of credibility are closely connected to and frequently based on relationships.

The three primary dimensions of credibility are established throughout the introduction and throughout the speech, but knowledge is the one dimension that you must explicitly convey to your audience in the introduction. You need to assure the audience that you are knowledgeable and experienced in this area. You must establish a sufficient degree of expertise. Of course, by doing so, you also reinforce trustworthiness and goodwill. As someone knowledgeable and experienced in this area, the information you provide is probably accurate. As someone with personal experience in this area, you care enough about it and the members of your audience that you feel it is important to share it with them. Furthermore, you establish for the audience your personal relationship with the material.

As a speaker, at minimum you must relate your expertise and your personal experience with the topic about which you speak. You can best express this expertise to your audience members by informing them of your experience exploring and learning about this topic. Sometimes this credibility comes already partially established and embedded in a person's credentials. A person's rank, title, or advanced degree carries a certain degree of expertise. Of course, you do not need an advanced degree in an area to claim expertise or experience. Explaining to your audience how you have carefully studied the topic or have extensive experience or background with the material is often sufficient.

As a speaker, you must also establish a relational connection with the audience. You can accomplish this connection by noting your identification with the audience or how you and the audience are alike (Burke, 1969). People tend to trust and like others whom they perceive as similar to them. Additionally, through identification, the meaning framework of a speaker becomes apparent. People feel as if they understand the way a speaker thinks and views the world because of the similarities between them. Consequently, a speaker's words become more understandable and more believable because the audience members are able to match the speaker's ways of thinking to their own. As long as they are legitimate, noting similarities, such as having the same connection with the topic, the same experiences, or the same desires, fears, and joys, can connect you with the audience and create this sense of identification.

Contrarian Challenge

We believe it is important to discuss your credibility in the introduction of speech. However, doing so could possibly be perceived as bragging by the audience, which might prevent you from developing a positive relational connection with audience members. Do you believe a person can overdo the discussion of his or her credibility? How might discussing credibility be accomplished without appearing to boast?

Orientation Phase

In the **orientation phase**, you provide the audience members with any information you believe will allow them to better understand and appreciate the material you will present in the body of your speech. The actual information you include will vary according to your topic and the audience. It could include definitions of unfamiliar terms you will use during your speech. A brief explanation of what the topic entails might benefit the audience, as might an overview of the historical development of an issue.

Describing your approach to a topic or your particular meaning can sometimes dramatically alter your audience's perspective and the speech itself. For instance, when you are giving a speech about abortion, some members of the audience may approach your speech differently depending on whether you define abortion as occurring in the first trimester or the last trimester.

During our discussion of the unity principle, we mentioned that the orientation phase is the place to include information you feel is

Photo 12.4 Why might this speaker include an orientation phase as part of her introduction? (See page 316.)

important for the audience to know but whose inclusion in the body would get you off-track. So, returning to the example from a few pages ago, say you are informing the audience about the treatment of a disease, but you think it is important for audience members to know about the symptoms of the disease. Briefly include this material in the orientation phase.

Essentially, when providing an orientation to the topic during the introduction, you are getting the audience members up to speed on the topic and preparing them for the body of the speech. Include whatever information you consider most relevant to audience understanding and a successful speech.

Impact of the Topic and Speech

As a speaker, it is your job to tell the audience members how the topic impacts their lives and how they might benefit from listening to your speech. In other words, you are establishing their relationship with the material and giving them a reason to listen to your presentation. This approach also enhances your credibility by conveying to the audience a concern about its well-being. The fact that you are aware of and are satisfying members' needs will assist in the establishment of an audience's relationship with you.

When considering how to explain the impact of the topic, you must fully consider the audience members and what they already likely know or believe. Do not take for granted that they already know the importance of the topic or fully understand its impact on their lives. Perhaps your topic does impact their lives and should be important to them, but they just do not realize this, in which case you need to inform them of the connection and importance during the introduction. Reinforce this link even if you feel audience members are already fully aware of the topic's impact on their lives.

When explaining how the topic impacts the audience, ensure that you make it as personal as possible. For example, if you are presenting a speech on preparing for floods, do not just say, "Many people will be affected by flooding this year." Instead, inform the audience members of the chances that they, a friend, or a relative will sustain damage or encounter danger as a result of flooding. Such comments as "Lots of people are affected" or general circular statements like "This is important to know because it is really vital" are not sufficient. Saying something like "If the people in this room represent the entire population of the state, five of us will have our homes devastated in a flood by the end of the year" will be much more effective.

When they are developing this part of their speech, we often encourage our students to imagine cynical audience members saying, "Who cares?" or "Big deal." You need to tell them why they should care and why it is a big deal. Do not worry; most audiences are not cynical and will provide you with encouragement. You can be certain that your classmates will be very encouraging, if you are giving a speech in class. After all, you are all in the same boat or floating on the same educational raft.

Enumerated Preview

Finally, you must provide an enumerated preview of your main points during the introduction of your speech. Essentially, you must list the main points of your speech. "First, I will talk about X. Then, I will talk about Y. Finally, I will talk about Z." You may include this list at any point in the introduction following your attention getter, but generally it is located at the very end.

An enumerated preview helps position your audience for the body of your speech and provides a nice lead into your argument. Plus, remember how important it is to fully guide your audience throughout the speech. In an enumerated preview, you are guiding audience members by providing markers or landmarks for them to follow and recognize along the way.

An enumerated preview also helps the audience remember your main points. We have heard an adage, which has been attributed to many groups. Among others, it has been referred to as an Irish saying, a Native American saying, and an Eskimo saying. No matter its origin, the saying and its meaning remain the same: Tell them what you are going to tell them. Tell them. Then tell them what you told them. In other words, the more often you say something, the more likely your audience will remember it. In the introduction, you tell audience members what you are going to tell them. In the body of your speech, you tell them. Finally, in your conclusion, you tell them what you told them. We have already gone through the *tell them what you are going to tell them* and the *tell them* stages. Now, we can discuss the part in which when you *tell them what you told them.*

Concluding Your Presentation

As we mentioned previously, the introduction, body, and conclusion are equally important. However, many speeches we hear often end with a very weak conclusion and just seem to stop—as if the speaker had run out of ideas and wanted to run out of the room. The introduction and body might be very well done, but the conclusion of the speech needs a great deal of additional development. If the speaker is so relieved to be near the end of the speech that he or she just abruptly quits after finishing the body, or if the speaker is not quite sure how to end the speech, any credibility he or she has developed up to that point will be diminished, and the relational connections established with the audience will be weakened, lessening the overall value and effectiveness of an otherwise good speech.

The conclusion is not just a logical end to your presentation; it entails the maintenance of the relationship between speaker, audience, and the material presented. At the end of a conversation with a friend, you draw a clear line to indicate that the interaction is over but that the relationship continues. Speakers need to make the audience members feel that their relationship to the ideas and commitments expressed by the speaker will continue beyond the interaction they have just experienced.

Photo 12.5 Why should audience members clapping at the very end of a presentation not be the primary focus of a speaker when developing a conclusion? (See page 316.)

During the conclusion, you must reinforce your thesis and purpose, underscore audience involvement, and provide adequate closure. The impression made at the end of your speech will be long lasting and plays a predominant role in whether the audience uses the information you provided or is persuaded by your presentation. You must strive to make a positive lasting impression and end your presentation in a manner that is most effective and maintains your relational connection with the audience and the material presented. Conclusions contain six components that will help get this accomplished (see Table 12.3).

Table 12.3 Brief Guide to Conclusions

Wrap-up signal

Signal the beginning of the conclusion for your audience.

Restatement of thesis

Restate your thesis for your audience.

Summary of main points

Provide your audience with a complete summary of your main points.

Audience motivation

Encourage members of your audience to incorporate the material you have provided into their lives or to behave/think in a certain manner.

Relational reinforcement

Reinforce the relationship between your audience and the material and between your audience and yourself.

Clincher statement

Provide your audience with a memorable line or phrase that will enable you to end strongly and smoothly.

Wrap-Up Signal

The first thing you must provide for the audience when concluding a speech is a **wrap-up signal**. You must indicate to the audience both verbally and nonverbally that you have reached the conclusion and are essentially wrapping things up. We have said it before, and we are saying it again: You must guide your audience through the entire speech.

Verbally, incorporating phrases like "As we draw to a close," "As we look back on what has been discussed during this speech," and "As we near the end of this presentation" will signal the audience that you have reached your conclusion. The old standby "In conclusion" can also be used, but many people consider this cliché and a bit dull. Nonverbally, you can indicate with your tone of voice that you have reached the final part of your presentation. An extended pause will work in some cases, as will a decrease in your rate of speaking. Whatever you include, make sure the audience knows that you have reached your conclusion.

While a wrap-up signal is valuable in guiding your audience through the speech, some audience members may view it as a cue to stop listening or to begin gathering their things in anticipation of leaving. Make sure that the wrap-up signal is clear, but do not dwell on it. Instead, move quickly to the remaining components of the conclusion. Clarify to your audience that you have reached not the end of your speech but the beginning of your conclusion. You will be able to maintain audience members' attention in part through the full development of the conclusion, making it worthwhile for them to listen.

Restatement of the Thesis

You must also restate the thesis during the conclusion of your speech to underscore the main idea and help your audience remember it afterward. When you restate the thesis is up to you. Like the components of the introduction, some components of the conclusion can occur at any point. Aside from providing a wrap-up signal at the very beginning of the conclusion and ending with the clincher statement (we discuss this one shortly), the order in which these components appear will be based on what you believe works best for your speech.

Summary of Main Points

A summary of the main points allows you to stress the main points of your speech and helps the audience retain the information. Remember that in the introduction you provided an enumerated preview of the main points. There, you simply listed the main points of the speech without elaboration. When summarizing your main points during your conclusion, you do not simply list them but instead remind your audience what they are, briefly review each one, and accentuate their support of your thesis. Summarizing your main points is crucial to audience retention and understanding of the material.

Audience Motivation

You must also strive to motivate the audience to take action as a result of listening to the speech. In the introduction, you explained to the audience the importance of the topic and provided the audience with reasons for listening to your presentation. During the conclusion, reiterate why you gave the speech in the first place and encourage audience members to act as a result of the speech. A positive relationship with the speaker will increase the likelihood that an audience will go along with whatever is asked of it.

    In speeches to persuade, this reaction is relatively easy to accomplish because the audience response is a bit more obvious. For instance, if the purpose of your speech is to get your audience members to wear their seat belts when traveling in a vehicle, urge them to always wear their seat belts when traveling in a vehicle. Do not assume your audience members will understand what course of action you want them to take

Make Your Case

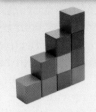

We suggest verbally indicating to an audience that you have reached the conclusion of a presentation. However, a few communication professionals discourage the use of wrap-up signals because of the possibility that audience members will cease listening as carefully once they have been informed that the presentation is nearing the end. Make a case for the value of wrap-up signals and what you should do to limit the possible drop in audience attention.

We have found that providing a complete summary of the main points instead of just listing them is the area in which beginning speakers struggle the most when developing conclusions. Keep the importance of the summary in mind when speaking in the community, on the job, or in the classroom.

or remember the purpose of your speech. It is important to be explicit by telling the audience members exactly what you want them to think or do. If the purpose of your speech is to convince the audience members that something is true or a certain policy should be enacted, tell them exactly what you want them to believe or support.

During speeches to inform, your purpose is to increase audience understanding or recognition of the topic. An effective informative speech will generate or enhance interest in your topic and will actually be used by your audience. To ensure members of your audience make full use of the material, encourage them to utilize the information and go beyond what you provide.

The impact of any message is greatest while heard and immediately afterward. As time goes on, this impact grows increasingly weaker. You have the most impact on your audience while presenting the speech, and as soon as you finish, the effects of your speech will increasingly diminish. The best way to ensure a lasting impact is to motivate the audience to use the information.

Relational Reinforcement

You must also reinforce the relationship between the audience and the material and between the audience and yourself. Emphasizing the importance of the material in audience members' lives, like you did in the introduction, will increase their motivation to use the material and to act or think the way you want. By reinforcing their connection with the material, you also ensure that this relationship will not end with your presentation, just as a relationship among friends lasts after a conversation has drawn to a close.

In the conclusion, you must also remind the audience members of your relationship with them. You may want to touch upon the ways the material impacts your life just as it does theirs. You could also note other similarities with the audience members by emphasizing your connections with them. Much like reinforcing their relationship with the material, audience members should recognize that your relationship with them will continue once the presentation concludes.

Case in Point

Analyze a public presentation on television or on the Internet. Which elements of conclusions discussed in this chapter are evident? Are any elements of conclusions absent from that presentation? What could the speechwriter have done to improve the conclusion?

Clincher Statement

You must end your speech with a **clincher statement**, a phrase that allows you to end your speech strongly and smoothly. Your clincher statement needs to encapsulate your entire speech and leave the audience in the proper frame of mind. This technique will help make the speech memorable, and knowing the last line of your speech is often a comfort.

Many of the attention-getting strategies used in speech introductions can be used here. Sometimes humor is most appropriate. A final illustration or anecdote can be used as a clincher statement. Linking the clincher statement to your introduction is often an effective way of ending your speech and completely wrapping up the entire presentation. For instance, if you began with a rhetorical question, providing an answer as your final statement may reinforce your thesis. Audiences often remember the last thing said longer than anything else in the speech, so make sure you carefully choose your conclusion.

Never, however, end your speech by saying, "Thank you." This is incredibly forgettable and ineffective. We are sure you are a considerate person who will be eager to expresses your gratitude to the audience for its attention. However, most presenters who end their speeches this

Comedians always know their last joke or line before they go up to the microphone. Once on stage, they may vary the rest of their act, but that last line will remain the same. They want their audience laughing when they finish, ending in a memorable fashion. Previously establishing the last line of their act and knowing its strength also reassures and helps calm them through the rest of their performance. Your speeches may not end with a huge laugh from the audience, but they will need to end in a memorable way.

way are doing so not out of appreciation for the audience but because they are finished and the audience does not know it. Ending a speech without making the audience aware of it results in the speaker staring at the audience, the audience staring back at the speaker, and nobody knowing quite what to do next. So, the speaker meekly utters, "Thank you." At this point, the audience members realize it is over and start clapping, primarily because they are relieved to know what is happening. The speaker in the above example likely did not guide the audience through the entire speech, include a wrap-up signal, or incorporate any of the other components of an effective conclusion. After reading this book, you will be certain to fully guide your audience through the speech. You know what components to include when developing a successful conclusion, and you will end strongly with a memorable clincher statement.

Of course, you can still express gratitude and appreciation for your audience by saying, "Thank you," but wait until the applause has died down following your clincher statement and the audience has finished showering you with roses and words of praise.

FOCUS QUESTIONS REVISITED

1. What are the four principles of speech organization and development?
The four principles of speech organization and development are (a) points, (b) unity, (c) balance, and (d) guidance. The points principle highlights the basic building blocks of an argument: main points and subpoints. Unity is a principle of speech organization and development that maintains you should stay focused and provide only information that supports your thesis and main points. Balance is a principle of speech organization and development that maintains the points of the body must be relatively equal in scope and importance. The amount of time you devote to the main points and to the amount of development and support you provide for them must be relatively equal. Guidance

is a principle of speech organization and development that maintains a speaker must guide and direct the audience throughout the entire speech.

2. What organizational patterns can you use in the development of the speech body?

An organizational pattern is an arrangement of the main points that best enables audience comprehension. You should base the selection of an organizational pattern for your speech on the topic, your purpose, and the audience. Use the chronological pattern when arranging the main points according to their position in a time sequence. Use the spatial pattern when the main points are arranged according to their physical relation. Use a causal pattern to organize the main points according to cause and effect. The question–answer pattern involves posing questions an audience may have about a subject and then answering those questions in a manner that favors your position. The topical pattern arranges support material according to specific categories, groupings, or grounds. The problem-solution pattern divides the body of the speech by first addressing a problem and then offering a solution to that problem. Finally, the elimination pattern involves offering a series of solutions to a problem and then systematically eliminating each one until the only solution remaining is the one you support.

3. What components must you include in a speech introduction?

During the introduction of a speech, you must begin to establish your credibility and connect with the audience on a relational level, reinforce connections between the topic and your audience to increase its desire to listen, and lay the groundwork for the remainder of the speech. Six components must be included in the introduction to achieve these requirements. The first thing to include in your introduction is an attention getter, a device used to draw the audience into your presentation. The placement of the remaining components of the introduction may vary, but the attention getter will always come first. In the introduction, you must inform your audience of both the purpose of your speech and your thesis. You must tell the audience members why they should perceive you as credible, and you must develop your relationship with them. You must orient the audience members by providing them with any information that will allow them to better understand and appreciate the material you will present in the body of your speech. You must inform the audience members of the importance of the topic and its impact on their lives. Finally, you must provide an enumerated preview of your main points during the introduction of your speech.

4. What components must you include in a speech conclusion?

During the conclusion, you must reinforce your thesis and purpose, underscore audience involvement, and provide adequate closure or sense of finality. Six components of the conclusion will help you accomplish these requirements. You must first provide the audience with a wrap-up signal when concluding a speech. You must indicate to the audience both verbally and nonverbally that you have reached the conclusion and are essentially wrapping things up. You must restate the thesis during the conclusion of your speech. You must summarize the main points to reinforce them and help the audience retain the information. You must strive to motivate the audience to take action as a result of listening to the speech. During the conclusion of your speech, you must also reinforce the audience members' relationship with the material and their relationship with you. Finally, you must end your speech with a clincher statement, a phrase that allows you to end your speech strongly and smoothly.

KEY CONCEPTS

attention getter   304
balance principle   297
body   294
causal pattern   299
chronological pattern   299
clincher statement   312
conclusion   302
elimination pattern   301
guidance principle   297
introduction   302
main points   295

organizational pattern   299
orientation phase   307
points principle   295
problem–solution pattern   301
question–answer pattern   300
spatial pattern   299
subpoints   295
topical pattern   300
transitions   298
unity principle   296
wrap-up signal   310

QUESTIONS TO ASK YOUR FRIENDS

1. What types of attention getters do your friends find most effective? Which types of attention getters do they find least effective? Do their evaluations change depending on circumstances or what is discussed?

2. Ask your friends to describe the characteristics of what they consider an effective public presentation. Limit their responses to those *not* involving delivery. Consider their responses in regard to the guidelines for developing public presentations discussed in this chapter.

3. Ask your friends to recall an occasion during which they listened to a presentation they considered confusing. What do they believe made it difficult to understand? As a speaker, what would you have done differently?

MEDIA LINKS

1. We discussed how written transitions are often less obvious than oral transitions. Find examples of written transitions in magazines, newspapers, and books. Once you have gathered these examples, turn each one into an oral transition that would clearly and effectively guide a listening audience.

2. As you did with Case in Point, watch a public presentation on television or on the Internet. Which elements of introductions discussed in this chapter are evident? Are any elements of introductions absent from that presentation? What could the speechwriter have done to improve the introduction?

3. Locate examples of archived speeches from at least 20 years ago. Many can be found on the Internet. Then find examples of recent speeches. In terms of development, how are these speeches similar, and how are they different? How has the passing of time altered the development of public presentations?

ETHICAL ISSUES

1. What are the necessary qualifications for a speaker to claim expertise and experience with a topic? Are determining these qualifications and evaluating expertise and experience the responsibilities of the speaker, the audience, or both?

2. When describing the importance of the topic to an audience, some speakers may feel compelled to embellish the facts to make the topic seem more vital and to enhance audience attention. They may consider this necessary as part of the greater good. Are there occasions when this deceitfulness would be appropriate? Why or why not?

3. When developing a presentation concerning a topic about which there are multiple opposing positions, is it necessary to provide equal coverage for all sides of the issue? Are there certain topics or occasions when this may or may not be necessary? Be sure to support your answers.

ANSWERS TO PHOTO CAPTIONS

Photo 12.1 ▪ The guidance principle emphasizes the relational development of a presentation.

Photo 12.2 ▪ The problem–solution pattern would be most appropriate in this situation.

Photo 12.3 ▪ The first thing that must be included in an introduction is an attention getter. The order of the remaining components may vary, but the attention getter always comes first.

Photo 12.4 ▪ As a speaker prepares an audience for the body of the presentation, the orientation phase enables the audience to better understand and appreciate the material presented.

Photo 12.5 ▪ A conclusion is not simply the end of a presentation but an important part of a speech that requires careful and complete development.

STUDENT STUDY SITE

Visit the study site at **www.sagepub.com/boc2e** for e-flashcards, practice quizzes, journal articles and additional study resources.

REFERENCES

Burke, K. (1969). *A rhetoric of motives.* Berkeley: University of California Press.

Gass, R. H., & Seiter, J. S. (2011). *Persuasion, social influence, and compliance gaining* (4th ed.). Boston: Allyn & Bacon.

Gronbeck, B., German, K., Ehninger, D., & Monroe, A. H. (1995). *Principles of speech communication* (12th ed.). New York: HarperCollins.

Miller, E. (1946). Speech introductions and conclusions. *Quarterly Journal of Speech, 32,* 181–183.

O'Hair, D., Stewart, R., & Rubenstein, H. (2001). *A speaker's guidebook: Text and reference.* Boston: Bedford/St. Martin's.

13

Relating Through Informative Speeches and Persuasive Speeches

At first glance, it may appear as if little difference exists between informative speeches and persuasive speeches. Speakers generally inform their audiences of various facts or ideas when persuading them to believe something or to perform a particular action. Certain aspects of persuasion are evident when speakers inform an audience about something. Informative and persuasive speeches are alike in many ways, not the least of which is the need to develop a relationship with the audience. However, a clear and concrete distinction exists between these two types of speeches: the purpose of the presentation, or the primary impact you wish to have on the audience as a result of the presentation. The purpose of an informative speech is to increase audience knowledge or understanding of something, while the purpose of a persuasive speech is to impact either the thinking (attitudes and beliefs) or the behavior of the audience.

That observation is actually a pretty big distinction. Yet, except for that very meaningful difference, these types of speeches share many similarities. Both, of course, show similarity of relationship to the audience. You will neither inform nor persuade people who do not trust or believe what you say. Therefore, performance of an identity as a "truth speaker" is essential in all cases, whether among friends or strangers. Many components of both the introduction and the conclusion are the same and necessary for both speeches. The principles of speech development and organization are the same for each type of speech, along with the requirements and guidelines for using credible evidence and support. The need to develop and maintain credibility, as well as a relationship with the audience, is the same for both speeches, as are the elements of effective delivery. Some organizational patterns are more commonly associated with either informative or persuasive speeches, but you can use all of the patterns discussed earlier for either persuasive or informative presentations. Many of the other concepts and guidelines included in this chapter that are primarily discussed with one type of speech can actually be used in the development and enhancement of both types of speeches. For all of these similarities, though, the distinction of purpose is significant enough to make these two very different types of speeches.

In what follows, we bring together much of the material discussed in the previous two chapters as we explore informative and persuasive speeches. We examine various types of informative speeches and discuss guidelines for increasing the success of informative presentations. We then examine persuasive presentations, discussing various types of persuasive speeches along with artistic proofs and the theory of social judgment.

Focus Questions

1. What are the types of informative speeches?
2. What strategies exist for achieving successful informative presentations?
3. What are the types of persuasive speeches?
4. How might preexisting beliefs and attitudes of the audience influence speeches to convince?
5. How might speeches to actuate affect audience behavior?
6. What are the artistic proofs?
7. What is the social judgment theory, and how can it impact persuasive attempts?

What Are Informative Speeches?

We begin our discussion of informative speeches by examining the various types of informative speeches you may present in your community, your workplace, your school, and other areas of your life. We then discuss ways to increase the success of your informative presentations.

Speeches of Definition and Description

Speeches of definition and description provide the audience with an extended explanation or depiction of an object, a creation, a place, a person, a concept, or an event. After listening to a speech of definition or description, your audience should have a greater understanding and recognition of the topic. For example, you may develop a speech informing the audience about Kobe beef, BlackBerry cell phones, the television series *It's Always Sunny in Philadelphia*, or the role of quarterback in football.

All of the components of introductions and conclusions discussed in Chapter 12 should be included in speeches of definition and description. As with all presentations, you must establish a relationship with the audience throughout the presentation. You are more likely to deliver these types of speeches to audiences with little prior knowledge and understanding of the topic. Therefore, it might be especially beneficial to stress the impact of the topic on audience members' lives, since they may not fully recognize its significance. You must strive to reveal and establish a relationship between the audience and the material. You should emphasize the significance of the topic in the conclusion of your presentation when motivating the audience to use the information. You can use multiple organizational patterns when developing these types of speeches depending on your topic and the audience. Also, remember to guide your audience throughout the presentation.

Expository Speeches

Expository speeches provide the audience with a detailed or in-depth review or analysis of an object, a creation, a place, a person, a concept, or an event. These speeches seek higher levels of understanding on the part of the audience than speeches of definition or description. Expository speeches may connect ideas or viewpoints surrounding a particular topic, distinguish or classify components of a topic, compare and contrast elements of a topic, or initiate new approaches or integrate existing approaches to a topic.

Using the examples for speeches of definition and description offered above, beyond explaining Kobe beef to an audience, you could discuss the effects that Kobe beef has had on the cattle industry. You could discuss the integration of BlackBerry capabilities into existing cell phone design. You could examine the influence of cable television series on traditional broadcast television series. You could compare the role of quarterback today with the role of quarterback prior to the introduction of the forward pass.

As with other speeches, all the components of introductions and conclusions should be included in expository speeches. A relational connection between the audience and the speaker remains fundamental to the success of the presentation. You are most likely to deliver this type of speech to an audience with a basic understanding of and experience with the topic, but you still need to stress the importance of the topic and audience connections with it even though they may already be apparent. The orientation phase of expository speeches may include definitions of terms to make sure the audience understands your approach to the topic, and it may require a basic review of significant features of the topic to help ensure audience understanding of the material you are preparing to discuss in more detail. As with speeches of definition and description, you can use multiple organizational patterns when developing expository speeches, and it is important to clearly guide your audience throughout the presentation.

Process and How-To Speeches

Process speeches describe the procedure or method through which something is accomplished *without* the expectation that the audience will actually perform the process. The audience should be able to explain and understand the process once you finish speaking. **How-to speeches** describe the procedure or methods through which something is accomplished *with* the expectation that the audience will be able to perform the process. The audience should be able to explain, understand, and perform the process once you finish speaking. The key distinction between process speeches and how-to speeches is whether the audience will be able to perform the process after listening to the presentation.

Be sure to include all the components of introductions and conclusions in your presentation, especially the establishment of relational connections between the audience

Photo 13.1 If the chef in this picture intends for the audience to be able to perform the procedures being demonstrated, is he giving a process speech or a how-to speech? (See page 339.)

and the speaker and between the audience and the material. Previewing and summarizing the steps of the process are especially important in both types of speeches. Encouraging the audience members to utilize the information as you motivate them in the conclusion is particularly important with how-to speeches. The chronological pattern is most commonly used when developing these types of informative speeches, but you could also use other organizational patterns, including topical and spatial. Beyond these guidelines, there exist three additional techniques to help ensure effective expository and how-to speeches.

Include All Steps

Be certain to include all of the steps of the process, even those you consider obvious (Gregory, 2002). You may be informing the audience how to develop a website and think that saving the work is an obvious step. However, the audience may not realize this step is necessary. What is obvious to you may not be obvious to your audience, particularly if you are discussing a process or procedure unfamiliar to your listeners.

Provide a Clear View

If you use visual presentation aids during a how-to presentation, make sure everyone can see what you are doing. For example, informing the audience how to make an origami bird would require the intricate manipulation of a relatively small piece of paper. Members of the audience seated in the back or on the sides of the room may not be able to see what you are doing. In such cases, using an image projector to display your hands on a screen or using another form of visual aid may be necessary.

Control Pace

Do not go through the steps too quickly, and take care not to get ahead of yourself when delivering your presentation. Chances are you are very familiar with the process you are describing or instructing your audience how to perform. You may be able to speed through steps with a clear understanding. If you are delivering a how-to speech, you may be able to perform the acts very quickly. However, members of the audience may not possess as much experience with the process and may find it difficult to keep up or to grasp all of the steps. Proceeding at a slow pace will help ensure audience understanding (Gregory, 2002). Also, since you may be very familiar with the actions involved in a process, you may very easily find yourself describing one step but performing the actions of another. Make sure your words and actions correspond.

Strategies for Successful Informative Presentations

Having discussed the various types of informative speeches and the various considerations you must take into account, we can now examine strategies for achieving a successful informative presentation. Note that some of these strategies are also applicable to persuasive presentations, but here we discuss them in terms of informative presentations.

When he took the introductory communication course in college, David delivered a how-to speech about how to serve a tennis ball. Steve was not required to give a how-to speech but would probably have discussed how to encourage a crew, change pace at crucial parts of a race, and adjust the steering of a rowing eight through the fastest course in changing river conditions and stream currents as a coxswain. It's one tough job!

Develop a Relational Connection

Audience members will be more likely to listen to your presentation and incorporate the information into their lives if a relational connection is established. Naturally, you should strive to develop a positive relational connection with the audience, whose members should perceive you as concerned about their well-being and dedicated to enhancing their understanding of a topic that impacts their lives.

You must also determine your relational status with the audience. If a personal or social relationship exists outside of the speaking context, an audience will already perceive a speaker in a certain manner. For example, a supervisor speaking to his or her staff would likely be viewed as having a higher status, a coworker would likely be viewed as having an equal status, and a subordinate would likely be viewed as having a lower status. In each of these examples, the speaker would have to determine whether he or she wants to confirm his or her preexisting relationship with the audience or be viewed as more equal or more authoritative, assuming supervisors generally do not want to be viewed as less equal. This decision would be based on such factors as the purpose of the presentation, as well as on issues surrounding the preexisting relationship. The preexisting relationship will impact the presentation, and the presentation will impact the preexisting relationship. When determining the purpose of a presentation, speakers must also consider relational consequences and desires. Selecting the appropriate identity to perform during the presentation is fundamental to the success of the presentation and to the maintenance of existing relationships.

If a relationship does not exist outside the speaking context, it may be more difficult to determine how an audience perceives the speaker. Some audiences may desire a more authoritative speaker, while other audiences may want the speaker to be on their level but possessing particular

Case in Point

We believe preexisting relationships will impact presentations and presentations will impact preexisting relationships. If you are giving a speech in class, analyze how your classroom relationships will impact and be impacted by your presentation.

information they desire. Consequently, careful audience analysis is especially important to determine the most effective relational status with a given audience.

Maintain a Narrow Focus

Strive to maintain a narrow focus to provide adequate support and development for your topic and to increase audience understanding of and connection with the material. Maintaining a narrow focus is a struggle that many speakers encounter—especially inexperienced speakers. Novice speakers frequently hold the mistaken belief that informative speeches improve as more information is supplied. In other words, the more information you cram into a speech and the broader the scope of your presentation, the greater your informative speech will be. This is like thinking that an excellent informative presentation about the Revolutionary War would cover the entire war in a speech that lasts less than 10 minutes and include as many dates, facts, statistics, and other forms of support and evidence as possible. However, it is impossible to include everything about the Revolutionary War in such a limited amount of time, and even if you attempted it, you would not be able to properly develop the information.

As the scope of your speech increases, it becomes increasingly difficult to provide adequate support and proper development. Accomplishing the goal of an informative presentation—increasing audience understanding—also becomes difficult. If you bombard audience members with material, it will be difficult for them to retain the information, and none of the material will be given sufficient support to ensure adequate understanding. With any topic you select, more information will be available and more areas could be discussed than you will actually include in your presentation. Focusing on one aspect of your topic will enable you to provide adequate development and help ensure audience understanding.

Adapt the Complexity

Adjust the complexity of your presentation to match your audience's familiarity with the subject matter and prior understanding of the topic. Some audiences may possess a great deal of prior experience and knowledge about the topic, while other audiences may have little or none. Audience knowledge about your topic will dictate the complexity of your presentation and the level of learning you wish to achieve. For instance, if you are discussing a topic unfamiliar to your audience, you may want to make your audience aware of the key issues or main ideas surrounding the topic through a speech of definition or description. However, if your audience possesses adequate prior knowledge of the topic, you may wish to achieve higher levels of understanding through an expository speech. You should even adapt how-to

Contrarian Challenge

We urge you to adapt the complexity of presentations and to make your speech clear and simple. However, what if you wanted to construct the identity of someone who is extremely intelligent and to create a relationship with the audience in which you are viewed as superior? Could you achieve these things by talking over the heads of your audience and attempting to confuse people?

speeches to your audience members based on their familiarity with the activity. For instance, you could teach an audience whose members have never picked up a tennis racquet the basic mechanics of serving a tennis ball, but you could teach an audience whose members have quite a bit of experience playing tennis how to apply spin to the serve to kick the ball toward an opponent's backhand. You should adapt the complexity of every informative presentation according to the prior knowledge and experience of the audience.

Be Clear and Simple

Regardless of your audience's prior knowledge and experience with your topic, you should always present the material in a clear and simple manner. Talking over the heads of your audience or incorporating unusually difficult language will not lead to a successful informative presentation or impress the audience. Complexity of language or the difficulty of the material does not correlate to the significance of the topic or to respect for the credibility of the speaker. Nor does it connect the speaker with the audience relationally. What will impress an audience is a speaker's ability to relate the material in a way that makes sense and is understood. A clear and simple manner of presenting the material is the most effective means of achieving the goals of your presentation. Perhaps the greatest measure of someone's knowledge and understanding of a topic is his or her ability to explain it in a clear and simple way that everyone can understand.

Use Clear Organization and Guide the Audience

Remember to develop the speech with clear organization and guide the audience throughout the presentation. Recall the guidance principle from the earlier discussion of speech organization and development. Clear organization and development of the speech, along with guiding the audience throughout the presentation, will increase the likelihood that the listeners will understand and retain the material. Following this principle will also increase the likelihood that positive connections between the audience, the speaker, and the material will be devel-

Strategic Communication

Consider how you can use the strategies for successful informative presentations discussed here when informing a friend, colleague, romantic partner, or customer of something. Do you believe these strategies are more, less, or equally important when informing people one-on-one than when presenting a public presentation?

oped. The ideas behind this principle are especially important when the audience is listening to unfamiliar material or material discussed in an advanced manner. Audience members will also be more likely to continue listening if the material is clearly organized and they can follow the presentation. Conversely, the audience will be less likely to listen and focus on your presentation if you present your material in a manner that is difficult to follow and comprehend. Keep in mind your reason for giving the informative speech: to increase audience members' understanding of the topic and

Photo 13.2 Why would this speaker discuss the significance and relational influence of his topic in the lives of his audience members? (See page 339.)

their relational connection with the material. Do everything possible to ensure that this takes place. Clear organization and guidance, along with the other strategies discussed here, will enable you to achieve the goal of your presentation.

Stress Significance and Relational Influence

In Chapter 12, we discussed the need to stress the importance of the topic and the speech to your audience in the introduction, as well as emphasizing relational connections with the material. This component of the introduction is especially important when you want your audience to learn something new or to increase audience members' knowledge about a particular topic. Think back to a time when a stranger provided you with information that you considered important or that you used immediately, like driving directions after getting lost. Chances are you paid very close attention to that person and tried to retain as much of the information as possible. Now, recall a time when you were told information that did not pertain to you or that you thought you would never use. You probably did not pay as careful attention or attempt to retain any of the information. Unless people recognize the importance and usefulness of a topic in their lives, they will pay less attention to a presentation and be less likely to utilize the information in the future. It is imperative that you stress the significance of the topic in the lives of your audience members and emphasize how they can use the information provided in your presentation.

Develop Relationships Through Language

The language used during a presentation can create relationships between the speaker, the audience, and the material. You should use such words as *us* and *we* when speaking with an audience in order to connect yourself to its members and the material. Accordingly, you should avoid words that separate you from the audience, such as *I* and *you*. Also, use terminology familiar to the audience, and avoid unfamiliar terminology whenever possible. A person's identities and relationships with others are created through the use of symbols. Using language familiar to an audience will establish perceptions of identification on the part of the audience and engender a sense of connection with the speaker and the topic.

You should also strive to connect audience members with the material by providing them with a clear mental picture of what you are discussing. In addition to creating a relational connection, providing a clear mental picture helps maintain audience attention and ensure retention of the material. You can achieve this representation of the material through the use of concrete and descriptive language.

Concrete words represent tangible objects that can be experienced through sensory channels (touch, taste, smell, hearing, seeing) and include real people, objects, actions, and locations. Abstract words, in contrast, represent intangible objects that cannot be experienced through your senses and include ideas, beliefs, and feelings. *Patriotism* is an abstract word that could be conveyed more concretely by describing a flag and acts of patriotism that provide the audience with a clearer mental picture and greater understanding of what you mean by that term.

Descriptive language provides the audience with a clearer picture of what you are discussing by *describing* it in more detail. Consider the difference between merely saying "There is a meadow" and using descriptive language to provide a clearer picture of a meadow by invoking multiple senses of your audience. For example, you could describe the meadow as having grasses swaying majestically in a gentle breeze caressing your skin and carrying the fragrance of thousands of wildflowers and a bubbling brook flowing underneath a cobalt sky filled with singing birds. This passage might sound like something from a bad romance novel, but used correctly, descriptive language will provide members of your audience with a clearer understanding of what you are discussing, help maintain their attention, and connect them to the material.

Relate Unknown Material to Known Material

Relating new or unknown material to familiar or known material will enable your audience members to better understand what you are discussing and help them retain the material. For example, your audience members may not have prior experience with nuclear reactors or prior understanding of how these reactors actually work. However, they may have a basic understanding of how a toaster works. Comparing the process involved with nuclear reactors (unknown) to the process involved with a toaster (known) will help the audience understand what you are discussing. Members of your audience may also be more likely to recall your presentation the next time they fix a piece of toast. Naturally, it is important to select something with which your audience is actually familiar. This criterion highlights once again the need for careful audience analysis, especially when using something other than a common household item.

Motivate Your Audience

"Use it or lose it" refers to more than just muscle mass. If the audience members do not incorporate into their lives the information that you provide, they will likely forget the material provided during your presentation. Recall that, during the conclusion of a presentation, you must reinforce relational connections and motivate your audience to act on the information provided. Encouraging your audience members to use the information provided will help them retain the information and fully recognize the importance of the

College Experience

The focus of this chapter is what a speaker should do rather than what audience members should do. However, you might consider yourself an audience member when listening to a lecture in class. Even if your instructor does not do so, try relating the material you are learning to things you already know. It will likely increase your understanding and retention of what is being discussed.

topic in their lives. Effective informative speeches prompt or increase interest in the topic and compel the audience to utilize the information. Motivating your audience to utilize the information provided will help ensure that these actions occur following your presentation.

What Are Persuasive Speeches?

Now that we have discussed informative speeches, we can turn our attention to persuasive speeches, of which two basic types exist: speeches to convince and speeches to actuate. These types of persuasive speeches are distinguished by their specific purpose. In both cases, as with informative speeches, establishing a positive relationship with the audience is vital to the success of your presentation. You must also determine how the audience members will view their relationship with you as a speaker given a preexisting relationship or a desired relational connection. This consideration is especially relevant when you want to significantly alter the thinking or behavior of an audience.

Photo 13.3 Why would a positive relational connection with an audience be important when attempting to persuade? (See page 340.)

Speeches to Convince

Speeches to convince are delivered in an attempt to impact audience thinking. They encompass a primary claim—essentially, what you are trying to convince your audience to believe. For example, you might want to convince your audience that Puerto Rico should remain a territory of the United States rather than becoming a state, that tuition increases at your school are detrimental, that a need exists for after-school programs in your community, or that recycling needs will change within the next decade. The four primary types of persuasive claims that can be developed through a speech to convince include (a) policy, (b) value, (c) fact, and (d) conjecture.

Claims of Policy

A **claim of policy** maintains that a course of action should or should not be taken. For example, you may wish to convince the audience that an attendance policy should be instituted at your school, same-sex marriage should be legalized in your state, or stricter automobile emissions standards should be enacted. When supporting a particular policy, a speaker must demonstrate the need for such a policy, how the policy will satisfy that need, and that the policy can be successfully enacted. A speaker may also be required to prove that the policy advocated is superior to an existing policy or another policy being proposed.

A claim of policy does not have to support a policy. You could also oppose the institution of an attendance policy, the legalization of same-sex marriage, or stricter automobile emissions standards. When opposing a policy, a speaker could argue that the need for such a policy does not exist. If a need for such a policy does exist, a speaker might demonstrate that a proposed policy does not satisfy the need, that the policy could not be successfully enacted, or that other policies are superior to the one being presented for consideration.

> Note that a claim of policy does not necessarily involve individual action but rather involves action of a more collective nature, such as a community, corporation, school, or nation-state. We talk about persuasive speeches involving individual action (speeches to actuate) later in the chapter.

Claims of Value

A **claim of value** maintains that something is good or bad, beneficial or detrimental, or another evaluative criterion. Claims of value deal largely with attitudes, which were discussed earlier. You may want to convince your audience that Andrew Jackson was the worst American president or that playing video games is beneficial to child development.

When developing a claim of value, you must let the audience know what criteria you used to determine and judge the value you support. Then, you need to exhibit how the object, person, or idea meets those criteria. You would need to explain to the audience how to determine "the worst president in U.S. history" and how Andrew Jackson would then be ranked the worst. You would need to explain to your audience what you mean by "beneficial to child development" and why playing video games meets those criteria. Claims of value go beyond simply offering your opinion about something. You must establish criteria and provide evidence to support your claim.

Photo 13.4 The speaker in this photo is attempting to convince her audience that her university should provide each incoming student with a laptop computer. What type of claim is she making? (See page 340.)

Claims of Fact and Claims of Conjecture

Claims of fact and claims of conjecture are related but have one key distinction. A **claim of fact** maintains that something is true or false at the *present time* or was true or false in the *past*. A **claim of conjecture**, though similar to a claim of fact in that something is determined to be true or false, contends what will be true or false in the *future* (Gouran, Wiethoff, & Doelger, 1994). Examples of claims of fact and conjecture include convincing your audience that decreases in taxes result in increases in consumer spending, that slow drivers cause the majority of traffic fatalities, that banning handguns would lead to an increase in crime, and that education costs will triple within the next 10 years.

Both claims of fact and claims of conjecture require solid evidence and support. Claims of conjecture are somewhat unique, however, since a speaker is arguing that something will be the case or will exist in the future. Accordingly, you are speculating about what might happen and do not have established facts or statistics to support your claim. However, existing facts and statistics can be used to support the presentation. Such evidence is used all the time when economic predictions are made. Economists examine current trends, statistics, and even past events to speculate about the future economic picture. It is particularly important that the evidence offered as support pertain to the claim being developed, and you as the speaker must establish a clear connection between these elements for the audience.

Audience Approaches to Speeches to Convince

Regardless of the type of claim being advanced, an audience's existing beliefs and attitudes will influence what you attempt to achieve with your presentation and the methods you employ. They will also influence how the audience members perceive you and your relationship with them. You can impact the thinking of your audience in the three different ways discussed in Table 13.1.

Table 13.1 Impacting Audience Thinking	
Reinforcing an existing way of thinking	In this case, you desire to strengthen your audience members' convictions and ensure them of their accuracy and legitimacy. Speeches that reinforce an existing way of thinking usually offer additional reasons in support of a particular way of thinking along with new or recent evidence. In these situations, audiences generally view their relationship with the speaker in a very positive manner.
Altering an existing way of thinking	Here, you essentially tell the audience members that their current way of thinking is wrong or should be modified. This approach does not automatically mean that the audience will be hostile toward you or your position. However, when attempting to bring about this change, it is especially important to develop a very positive relationship with the audience. It is also especially important to enhance audience perceptions of your credibility, particularly of your goodwill.
Creating a new way of thinking	In this situation, members of your audience will probably be more willing to accept your claim than they would if you attempted to change their position. However, you may need to spend additional time developing the audience members' relationship with the material and stressing the importance of the issue in their lives. As always, establishing a positive relational connection with your audience will increase your likelihood of success.

Speeches to Actuate

Speeches to actuate are delivered in an attempt to impact audience behavior. You may want members of your audience to join your cause, volunteer with a charitable organization, limit their consumption of natural resources, or vote Quimby for mayor of Springfield. You may end up influencing audience thinking as a consequence of a speech to actuate, but that is not the ultimate goal of such a speech. The ultimate goal of a speech to actuate is to impact the behavior of your audience. You can impact your audience in the five different ways discussed in Table 13.2.

Table 13.2 Impacting Audience Behavior	
Reinforcing an existing behavior	In this case, you desire to strengthen audience members' conviction about performing a behavior and ensure that they continue performing it. Reinforcing existing behavior often entails providing new reasons or evidence for enacting this behavior, along with increasing audience confidence and excitement about performing the behavior.
Altering an existing behavior	Here, you are asking the audience not to stop performing a certain behavior or to enact a totally new behavior but to modify an existing behavior. It is important that you stress the value of continuing to perform this action and its positive influence in audience members' lives, but you must urge them to perform this action in the more effective or beneficial manner you suggest.
Ceasing an existing behavior	An audience will probably be less supportive of this type of presentation, since you are essentially telling audience members that they are doing something wrong. Be careful not to offend them but be resolute in your support of ceasing that behavior. It is especially important to develop a positive relationship with the audience. Stress that you are doing this for members' well-being.
Enacting a new behavior	The key to successfully persuading your audience members to enact a new behavior is determining why they are not behaving this way in the first place. Are they opposed to the behavior? Do they not know the behavior can be done? Do they not recognize the value of the behavior? Do they believe that performing the behavior is more trouble than it is worth? Do they view the behavior as unaccomplishable? Answering these questions will enable you to develop the presentation in a relational manner that best fits your audience and that will most likely persuade audience members to enact the desired behavior.
Avoiding a future behavior	When attempting to impact an audience in this manner, you are not necessarily reinforcing an existing behavior but encouraging your audience to avoid a specific new behavior. Such behaviors may be a concern now or in the future. These speeches often require that you provide the audience members with reasons and strategies for avoiding this behavior.

Persuasive Speaking and Artistic Proofs

Each type of persuasive speech can be enhanced through the recognition of the artistic proofs *ethos, pathos,* and *logos.* Aristotle laid out these artistic proofs more than 2,000 years ago, but the ideas behind them remain significant.

Ethos

Ethos involves the use of speaker credibility to impact an audience. We have already talked about the importance of establishing and maintaining your credibility as well as a positive relational connection with an audience. For members of an audience to judge the information provided by a speaker as accurate, valuable, and worthy of their

Listen in on Your Life

Listen for attempts to change someone's behavior during your interactions with friends, family, and other people with whom you share a personal relationship. Which of the five ways of impacting behavior discussed in this chapter is most evident? How are the persuasive appeals supported when interacting one-on-one with someone? How can these attempts at persuasion inform the development and delivery of speeches to actuate?

Photo 13.5 Evoking feelings of sadness from an audience when attempting to persuade would entail which artistic proof? (See page 340.)

attention and consideration, they must view that speaker as knowledgeable, trustworthy, and concerned about their well-being. Audiences must also perceive a relational connection with the speaker. Audiences' perceptions of speaker credibility and their relationship with the speaker are critical to the success of persuasive attempts. We urge you to consider the great impact that audience perceptions of your credibility will have on the success of your presentations.

Pathos

Pathos involves the use of emotional appeals to impact an audience. The use of such emotions as excitement, sadness, happiness, guilt, and anger can be quite effective when persuading an audience. You may have also witnessed the use of emotional appeals when attending or watching political rallies during which speakers elicit feelings of excitement about a particular candidate and perhaps anger toward political rivals. These emotional appeals are usually quite effective in achieving the desired response. Furthermore, the relational connections necessary for effective presentations often entail certain emotional qualities that will assist speakers persuading an audience.

Discussing emotion in a communication textbook may initially strike some people as peculiar. Emotions are often considered things that people *feel internally,* which seems far removed from the discussion of symbolic activity. It is true that emotions involve internal activities and feelings. Neuroscientists can even pinpoint changes in the brain when people experience specific emotions. Changes in heart rate, blood pressure, and temperature and a host of other physical changes occur when you experience any emotion.

Yet, emotion is also very much a *symbolic activity* and a *relational activity*. Symbolically, emotions and the feelings that accompany them are given meaning within a culture or society. Emotions bring about physical change, but this physical change is understood and evaluated according to established meaning. Happiness, sadness, fear, and all other emotions have meaning beyond physical experience or a given instance. These symbolic characteristics of emotions are learned *relationally*. Relationships are about knowledge, connecting symbolically to others, and understanding the world. Accordingly, it is through relationships that people come to understand emotion. Your understanding of emotions and of their appropriate display has

In a classic study, Schachter and Singer (1962) demonstrated that physiological arousal itself is not sufficient for people to define their emotions. People need some socially developed label to determine what they are experiencing.

developed through everyday communication and interactions with your friends, family, classmates, neighbors, romantic partners, acquaintances, and others with whom you share a relationship. Incorporating this knowledge of emotions from your everyday life can assist you when attempting to persuade others in a public speaking situation.

Logos

Logos involves the use of logic or reasoning to impact an audience. The two primary types of reasoning are inductive reasoning and deductive reasoning.

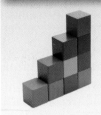

Make Your Case

Public discourse has been traditionally focused on reasoning and evidence (logos), but the use of emotion (pathos) is becoming increasingly evident in persuasive attempts. Do you think/feel that pathos will overtake logos as the central focus of public discourse? How would you support your view?

Inductive Reasoning. **Inductive reasoning** involves deriving a general conclusion based on specific evidence, examples, or instances. If you go to a restaurant and receive bad service, your friend goes to the same restaurant on another night and receives bad service, and a classmate goes to the restaurant and also reports having received bad service, you may conclude based on these specific instances that this restaurant has bad service. When using inductive reasoning, a sufficient number of examples or instances must exist from which to draw a legitimate conclusion, and these examples or instances must be relevant to the conclusion being established.

Deductive Reasoning. **Deductive reasoning** involves using general conclusions, premises, or principles to reach a conclusion about a specific example or instance. Thus, you may decide that since Duck and McMahan products are generally high in quality, a Duck and McMahan television set would be a high-quality product. Such reasoning frequently takes the form of syllogisms. A **syllogism** is a form of argumentation consisting of a major premise, a minor premise, and a conclusion. The *major premise* of a syllogism is a statement or conclusion of a general nature, while the *minor premise* entails a more specific statement about a particular instance or example. The *conclusion* is then derived from the logical connection between the major and minor premises. This may sound a bit confusing, but examining the following syllogism based on the example above might clear things up for you:

Major Premise: Duck and McMahan products are high in quality.
(This statement involves a general conclusion about Duck and McMahan products.)

Minor Premise: This television is a Duck and McMahan product.
(This statement involves a specific example connected to the major premise about Duck and McMahan products.)

Conclusion: This television is high in quality.
(The conclusion is based on the major and minor premises. If Duck and McMahan products are high in quality and this television is a Duck and McMahan product, this television must be high in quality.)

This method of reasoning is sometimes presented in a slightly modified form known as an enthymeme. An **enthymeme** is a syllogism that excludes one or two of the three components of a syllogism. An enthymeme may be used when one of the premises is readily understood, accepted as true, or so obvious that it does not even need to be stated. People often use enthymemes when talking with others. If a salesclerk at an electronics store was attempting to sell you the Duck and McMahan television, he or she might exclude both the minor premise and the conclusion in the example syllogism above and simply establish the major premise by saying, "Duck and McMahan products are very high in quality." The fact that this television set is a Duck and McMahan product might be obvious, perhaps as would the natural conclusion. Beyond dealing with the obvious, however, incorporating enthymemes into one's message often seems more natural than speaking in syllogisms. If the salesclerk includes all the parts of a syllogism and says, "Duck and McMahan products are high in quality; this television is a Duck and McMahan product; this television is high in quality," you might determine the salesclerk either is a robot or really needs a coffee break.

Sir Arthur Conan Doyle, creator of Sherlock Holmes, modeled his character's skills of deduction on Professor Joseph Bell. By the way, never in the 56 short stories and four novels featuring the famous detective did he ever say, "Elementary, my dear Watson." Now that you know how deductive reasoning works, though, it may become just that.

As a speaker, you must determine whether it is most appropriate to present the material in the form of a syllogism or an enthymeme. As with other choices involving the development and delivery of a public presentation, this decision will be determined by your analysis of the audience. If your audience is adequately familiar with the material, you could probably use an enthymeme successfully. However, if the audience is unfamiliar with the material or will not readily accept the major or minor premise as true or accurate, you should present the material in the form of a syllogism.

Persuasive Speaking and the Social Judgment Theory

A more recent offering than artistic proofs and also valuable in increasing the effectiveness of persuasive presentations is the theory of social judgment. The **social judgment theory** (C. Sherif, Sherif, & Nebergall, 1965; M. Sherif & Hovland, 1961) explains how people may respond to a range of positions surrounding a particular topic or issue. This theory can be understood as dealing with an audience's relationship with the topic or issue. Using this theory, imagine an audience responding or relating to the various positions connected to a topic or an issue in one of three ways: acceptance, rejection, and noncommitment. These positions can in turn be placed in three types of ranges, referred to as latitudes (see Figure 13.1). The **latitude of acceptance** includes the range

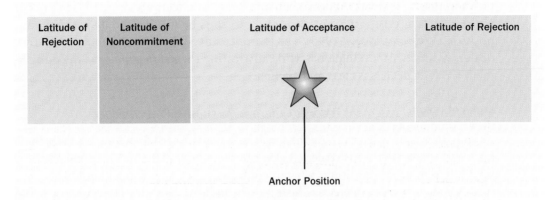

| Latitude of Rejection | Latitude of Noncommitment | Latitude of Acceptance | Latitude of Rejection |

Anchor Position

Figure 13.1 Components of the Social Judgment Theory

of position that the audience deems acceptable. At some point within this latitude of acceptance is the **anchor position**, which represents the preferred or most acceptable position. The **latitude of rejection** includes those positions that the audience deems unacceptable. Finally, the **latitude of noncommitment** includes positions that the audience neither wholly accepts nor wholly rejects.

Variables Impacting Social Judgment

The size of the latitudes is affected by the audience's level of involvement or relationship with the issue. **Audience involvement** is based on audience members' recognition of the issue's significance and importance in their lives. The greater the significance and importance audience members perceive the issue as having in their lives, the more involved they will be with the issue, and vice versa. As audience members' involvement with an issue increases, so does the size of their latitude of rejection. Audiences highly involved with an issue will have relatively small latitudes of acceptance and noncommitment because people will spend more time thinking about and evaluating the concerns surrounding an issue if they view it as important and meaningful. People will spend less time engaged in those behaviors if they do not view the issue as such. Thus, people highly involved with an issue will have developed a more focused view of what is acceptable.

Audience members will often perceive messages as either closer to or farther away from their position than they actually are. These perceptions are based on the **assimilation effect**, which maintains that if someone advocates a position within your latitude of acceptance, you will view it as closer to your anchor position than it really is, and the **contrast effect**, which maintains that if someone advocates a position within your latitude of rejection, you will view it as farther from your anchor

The assimilation effect and contrast effect are similar to what happens in interpersonal relationships. Depending on their view of someone, people generally believe they are either more similar to or more different from that person than they actually are.

position than it really is. Assimilation and contrast effects are more likely to occur when an actual position is not clear and can thus be minimized by making your position explicit (O'Keefe, 1990). For example, advocating *harsh penalties* for drug dealers is somewhat ambiguous, while advocating the *death penalty* as the punishment for drug dealers is clear and explicit.

Using the Social Judgment Theory to Improve Persuasive Presentations

As you can imagine, determining the social judgment of a group of listeners takes thorough audience analysis. Also true is that various members of the audience will probably hold different anchor positions when it comes to your issue. You will not likely have specific data supporting a precise illustration of audience latitudes. However, you could use audience analysis to provide a rough idea of how the general audience latitudes might appear, which could prove very useful when developing your presentation. Furthermore, elements of the social judgment theory also provide key insight into improving the effectiveness of persuasive presentations in general.

Be Explicit. First, the assimilation and contrast effects underscore the need to be very explicit in conveying your goals to the audience. The audience members must know exactly what position you support and want them to accept. When dealing with the contrast effect, if the position you desire is within audience members' latitude of rejection, it may not be as far away from their anchor position as they would assume if you did not explicitly state your position. Audience members may view your position as not even remotely considerable, when in reality it is closer to their anchor position than they realize.

Explicitly stating your position is also necessary when dealing with assimilation effects. Having your audience members believe your position is closer to their anchor position than it actually is might appear to be beneficial. However, this can actually reduce the effectiveness of your presentation. According to O'Keefe (1990), the audience will view you as seeking less change than you actually seek. In fact, "in the extreme case of complete assimilation, receivers may think that the message is simply saying what they already believe—and hence receivers don't change their attitudes at all" (p. 38). Both the assimilation effect and the contrast effect emphasize the need to state your position explicitly.

Consider Audience Involvement. Second, considering audience perceptions of positions related to your topic will also assist you in determining how to develop your presentation. Audiences with a considerably large latitude of noncommitment may not be particularly involved with the topic or fully aware of its importance in their lives. The size of either the latitude of acceptance or the latitude of rejection may dictate which organizational pattern you use to develop your presentation. People new to public speaking often wonder whether they should include both sides of the issue when presenting a persuasive speech. As with most questions involving presentations, the answer depends on the audience. If you believe the audience will strongly oppose your stance, it might be a good idea to present both sides of the issue to address the limitations of the opposite side. When an audience is neutral or somewhat unopposed to your position, presenting only your side of the issue will usually suffice.

Degree of Change. Finally, considering the social judgment of your audience will help you ascertain the degree of change you should seek with your audience. If the anchor position of the audience is far away from the position being advocated, a speaker will be hard-pressed to convince many members of the audience to accept that new position. This reality should not discourage you as a speaker. Rather, you should simply be aware that persuasion is often a continual and gradual process.

FOCUS QUESTIONS REVISITED

1. What are the types of informative speeches?

The following are the four primary types of informative speeches: (a) speeches of definition and description, (b) expository speeches, (c) process speeches, and (d) how-to speeches. Speeches of definition and description provide the audience with an extended explanation or depiction of an object, a person, a concept, or an event. Expository speeches provide the audience with a detailed or in-depth review or analysis of an object, a person, a concept, or an event. These speeches seek higher levels of understanding on the part of the audience than speeches of definition or description. Process speeches describe the procedure or method through which something is accomplished without the expectation that the audience will actually perform the process. The audience will be able to explain and understand the process once you finish speaking. How-to speeches describe the procedure or methods through which something is accomplished with the expectation that the audience will be able to perform the process at the speech's conclusion.

2. What strategies exist for achieving successful informative presentations?

To achieve successful informative presentations, speakers should maintain a narrow focus, adapt the complexity of the presentation, be clear and simple, use clear organization and guide the audience, stress significance and utility, provide a clear mental picture, relate unknown material to known material, and motivate the audience.

3. What are the types of persuasive speeches?

The two primary types of persuasive speeches are speeches to convince and speeches to actuate. Speeches to convince are delivered in an attempt to impact audience thinking, and they encompass a primary claim—essentially, what you are trying to convince your audience to believe. The following are the four primary types of persuasive claims that can be developed through a speech to convince: (a) policy, (b) value, (c) fact, and (d) conjecture. Speeches to actuate are delivered in an attempt to impact audience behavior.

4. How might preexisting beliefs and attitudes of the audience influence speeches to convince?

Depending on preexisting beliefs and attitudes of the audience, a speaker may attempt to reinforce an existing way of thinking, change an existing way of thinking, or create a new way of thinking.

5. How might speeches to actuate affect audience behavior?
As a result of a speech to actuate, audience members may reinforce, alter, or cease an existing behavior; enact a new behavior; or avoid a future behavior.

6. What are the artistic proofs?
The artistic proofs are ethos, pathos, and logos. Ethos involves the use of speaker credibility to impact an audience. Pathos involves the use of emotional appeals to impact an audience. Logos involves the use of logic or reasoning to impact an audience.

7. What is the social judgment theory, and how can it impact persuasive attempts?
The social judgment theory explains how people may respond to a range of positions surrounding a particular topic or issue. Underscoring the need to be very explicit when conveying your goals to the audience, this theory will assist you when determining how to develop the presentation and the degree of change you should seek with your audience.

KEY CONCEPTS

anchor position   335
assimilation effect   335
audience involvement 335
claim of conjecture   329
claim of fact   329
claim of policy   328
claim of value   329
concrete words   327
contrast effect   335
deductive reasoning   333
descriptive language   327
enthymeme   334
ethos   331
expository speech   321

how-to speech   321
inductive reasoning   333
latitude of acceptance   334
latitude of noncommitment   335
latitude of rejection   335
logos   333
pathos   332
process speech   321
social judgment theory   334
speech of definition and description   320
speech to actuate   330
speech to convince   328
syllogism   333

QUESTIONS TO ASK YOUR FRIENDS

1. Ask a friend at school to recall the most recent lecture in one of his or her classes. Would your friend consider that lecture more of an informative presentation or more of a persuasive presentation? What characteristics of that lecture led to your friend's judgment? Do you agree with his or her assessment?

2. Ask a friend to describe a time when someone tried to explain something to him or her, but your friend had difficulty understanding what that person was attempting to explain. Why does your friend think that he or she had difficulty understanding? Based on what you now know about informing others, what could that person have done differently to assist in your friend's understanding and comprehension of the material discussed?

3. Ask a friend to describe a time when someone tried to convince him or her of something but was not successful. Why does your friend think that he or she was not convinced? Based on what you now know about persuasion, could that person have done anything differently to increase the likelihood of convincing your friend?

MEDIA LINKS

1. Read letters submitted to the editor of your local newspaper. Which of the following claims are addressed or presented most often: policy, value, fact, or conjecture? What type of support—if any—is provided in these letters?

2. Watch a presentation before Congress on C-SPAN or online, and look for evidence of ethos, pathos, and logos. Which artistic proof is most prominent?

3. Watch advertisements on television or online and look for evidence of ethos, pathos, and logos. Which artistic proof is most prominent? Does the prominent artistic proof change depending on the product or service advertised? If so, why do you think this change exists?

ETHICAL ISSUES

1. Emotions can be very powerful tools of persuasion. To what extent do you think people should elicit fear, guilt, sadness, anger, and other "negative" emotions when persuading an audience? Are there limits to which speakers should adhere when inducing these emotions? Does your perspective change depending on the purpose of the speech?

2. Review the discussion of fallacious arguments in the chapter on listening. These flawed arguments are often quite effective when used to persuade someone. Are there any occasions that would justify the use of fallacious arguments? If you believe such occasions exist, how would you support your answer?

3. Freedom of expression is a major tenet in the United States. Do you believe people should have unlimited freedom of expression? If so, how would you support this response? Do you believe in limits to an individual's freedom of expression? If so, provide examples where freedom of expression should be limited and support this assessment. Think about these questions for a while—the Supreme Court has!

ANSWERS TO PHOTO CAPTIONS

Photo 13.1 ■ The chef is delivering a how-to speech since he is describing a procedure or method with the expectation that the audience will be able to perform the process once he has concluded his presentation.

Photo 13.2 ■ Audience members will be more likely to pay attention to a message and incorporate the information into their lives if they view it as important and meaningful.

Photo 13.3 ▪ A positive relational connection with members of an audience increases their perceptions of a speaker's credibility and enhances their willingness to accept what the speaker wants them to think or do.

Photo 13.4 ▪ The speaker would be making a claim of policy.

Photo 13.5 ▪ The artistic proof pathos involves the use of such emotions as sadness.

STUDENT STUDY SITE

Visit the study site at **www.sagepub.com/boc2e** for e-flashcards, practice quizzes, journal articles and additional study resources.

REFERENCES

Gouran, D. S., Wiethoff, W. E., & Doelger, J. A. (1994). *Mastering communication* (2nd ed.). Boston: Allyn & Bacon.

Gregory, H. (2002). *Public speaking for college and career.* New York: McGraw-Hill.

O'Keefe, D. J. (1990). *Persuasion: Theory and research.* Newbury Park, CA: Sage.

Schachter, S., & Singer, J. E. (1962). Cognitive, social, and physiological determinants of emotional state. *Psychological Review, 69,* 379–399.

Sherif, C. W., Sherif, M., & Nebergall, R. (1965). *Attitude and attitude change: The social judgment-involvement approach.* Philadelphia: W. B. Saunders.

Sherif, M., & Hovland, C. I. (1961). *Social judgment: Assimilation and contrast effects in communication and attitude change.* New Haven, CT: Yale University Press.

14

Delivering a Public Presentation

In the previous chapters, we talked about the preparation that goes into a presentation and about developing a presentation that actually connects relationally with an audience. We discussed how to develop the purpose and thesis of your presentation and gathering material to support your claims both logically and relationally. We examined what it means to develop an argument and how to determine the best way to organize your speech to connect you, the audience, and the material. We addressed the importance of introductions and conclusions and the logical and relational components that must be included in each of these areas to ensure an effective presentation. We also examined the specific development of various informative and persuasive presentations. A constant presence throughout our discussion of this material has been audiences and the need to connect relationally with them. It is now time to actually present the speech to them and develop this relational connection.

Before going any further, though, we must address **communication apprehension**, the technical term for the fear or anxiety you may experience when speaking in public. This fear is actually quite common, and in fact, the *Book of Lists* (Wallechinsky & Wallace, 1995) indicates that more people are afraid of speaking in public than are afraid of death!

Because of its pervasiveness and its impact on people's lives, communication apprehension has been a sustained area of study in the discipline of communication for the past four decades (McCroskey, 1970). We realize this fact does not make it any easier to get up in front of an audience of friends, acquaintances, colleagues, classmates, or strangers to speak, but knowing that the majority of people in the world experience the same concerns may provide a bit of comfort. At least they know how you feel.

A number of politicians, actors, singers, and even communication professors report that they get nervous when speaking or performing in public.

Near the end of this chapter, we discuss communication apprehension in greater detail and give you some suggestions for dealing with your concerns. We do not attempt to fool you into believing that presenting a speech to an audience is simple and carefree, because it takes a good deal of preparation and effort. However, we do tell you with great certainty that you will be able to do it.

Communication apprehension can be linked to relationships shared with the audience. In some cases, speakers might know members of the audience (e.g., coworkers, group members, classmates) on a personal level and not want to look foolish to them, since it might damage their relationship outside of the presentation. On other occasions, speakers might not know the audience personally but might feel anxious about how to best perform an appropriate identity that satisfies audience members' expectations.

Some of your anxiety probably comes from not knowing what to expect or how to actually present a speech. If you are like most of your classmates, you probably have had little experience speaking to public audiences and delivering formal public presentations. While you may not have much experience delivering speeches in public, through studying material from the previous chapters, you now better understand what developing a public presentation entails and what you must do to develop an effective speech. This chapter provides guidelines and suggestions for presenting speeches that will assist you in delivering an effective presentation and give you a better understanding of speech delivery, which will likely help alleviate some of your anxiety.

As always, the relationship between a speaker and an audience is of paramount importance. Within this chapter, we discuss styles of delivery, providing benefits and drawbacks to each one along with strategies for selecting and enacting each delivery style. We discuss the choices you will face as a speaker when determining the most appropriate style. We also address the goals of effective delivery, which include developing and enhancing your credibility, connecting with the audience relationally, and ensuring audience understanding of the material.

Focus Questions

1. What are three guidelines for effective delivery?
2. What are the styles of delivery?
3. What are the goals of effective delivery?
4. What are the components of effective delivery?
5. What are presentation aids?
6. What is communication apprehension, and how can it be managed?

Guidelines for Effective Delivery: What Are the Answers to Common Questions?

In the course of this chapter, we talk about effective delivery styles and techniques. Before fully addressing specifics, we first want to introduce three guidelines to follow when delivering a presentation. Based on years of experience working with student and novice speakers, these guidelines have been derived from answers to questions these speakers frequently have. They wonder, for instance, how they should act, what they should sound like, and what happens if they mess up or are nervous. Here are the answers: (a) Always be yourself, (b) strive to make your speech conversational, and (c) avoid drawing undue attention to mistakes and to nerves.

Always Be Yourself

Even before reading this book, you could probably recognize and distinguish particular qualities that really good public speakers possess. You can no doubt imagine an incredible speaker who is capable of relating with audience members and working them into a dramatic frenzy of emotion and awareness and who, upon ending a speech, is showered with praise and cheers from the crowd. You may have such fabulous speakers as Ronald Reagan, Winston Churchill, and Oprah Winfrey in mind as you study public presentations and gain a better understanding of why they are or were so effective at speaking and relating with an audience. You may even wish to emulate their speaking styles in hope of improving your own speaking ability. However, imitating Ronald Reagan, Winston Churchill, Oprah Winfrey, or any other speaker you admire will not make you a good speaker.

The most effective way of delivering a presentation is by being you, not by pretending to be someone else. You must deliver your presentations in the most natural way. Doing otherwise will make you appear artificial, uncomfortable, and less credible to your audience. Consequently, you will not be able to connect relationally with your audience. If you admire particular characteristics of another speaker, you can attempt to integrate these qualities into your own delivery style. Ultimately, however, you must adapt these qualities to your personal style.

Ronald Reagan was often called The Great Communicator. When he first began in radio, he noted his ability to connect with listeners was achieved by imagining he was talking with a group of friends at a barbershop.

Of course, all speakers have particularly strong areas of delivery and other, weaker areas in need of development. When we advise you to be yourself, we are not implying that you should just get up in front of the audience and whatever happens will be just fine. Instead, we want to encourage you to feel relaxed and to bring out the best aspects of yourself and your personal delivery while working to modify or eliminate aspects of your delivery that may hinder your presentation. This chapter will help you recognize your own personal strengths, provide guidelines for their promotion, and allow you to recognize possible areas in need of development. As you are learning how to become an effective speaker, strive to incorporate the strategies offered here into your own personal style.

Photo 14.1 This speaker admires the speaking style of her supervisor, who happens to be a very effective public speaker. Should she imitate her supervisor's style? (See page 364.)

Strive to Make Your Presentation Conversational

You may wonder what your natural speaking style is like. If so, think back to the last conversation you had with a close friend. That is it! In the most effective speeches, the speaker connects with the audience in a relational way. Rather than delivering your speech as if you were speaking down to the audience from on high, you can accomplish this connection through a natural conversational tone, the kind you have with friends, family members, colleagues, and others with whom you share a personal or social relationship. In fact, you should consider the delivery of a speech as nothing more than a conversation in which you just happen to be doing all the talking for an extended period. You can adapt and understand many aspects of delivery discussed in this chapter in terms of your everyday relational experiences.

Avoid Calling Attention to Mistakes and to Nerves

When delivering a speech, people commonly worry about the possibility of making a mistake. They fear, for example, that they may forget to include a phrase they had wanted to incorporate or that they may stumble over a word. You may make mistakes, but it probably will not matter. Think back to the last time you spoke with an acquaintance who stumbled over a word. Were you traumatized by the experience, and did you hope to never again be forced to speak with this person? Unless your acquaintance drew unnecessary attention to it, you probably did not think much about it.

The only way that such mistakes will distract from your speech and significantly damage your credibility and your relationship with the audience is if you draw attention to them. Worse yet is dramatically apologizing for them or questioning your ability by saying something like, "Oh, I am so terribly sorry for ruining this speech." By drawing attention to your mistake, you direct more attention toward it than toward your message and your relationship with the audience.

Sometimes you must acknowledge a mistake for the sake of honesty or accuracy, but do it without great elaboration or excessive apology. For instance, if you provide the wrong oral citation, provide an erroneous statistic, or misquote testimony, you should quickly clarify the mistake and move on.

In addition to not calling attention to mistakes, do not point out to your audience that you are nervous about speaking. Nerves themselves do not necessarily decrease a person's credibility, but calling attention to and obsessing over them might. If nothing else, you will draw your audience members' attention away from your message and on to something they may not have even noticed. In fact, most of the time, an audience will have no idea you are nervous unless you point it out.

Styles of Delivery

With these three guidelines in mind, we can now discuss the three delivery styles to choose between when delivering public presentations. Each delivery style comes with inherent advantages and disadvantages, with some styles more suitable for particular circumstances than others. This section will help you understand the characteristics of each delivery style. You will also discover how to successfully utilize each style when delivering a public presentation and relating with an audience.

Manuscript Delivery

Manuscript delivery involves having the entire speech written out in front of you when you speak. Speakers using this method of delivery generally utter every word and phrase on the page exactly as written. This style of delivery applies when accurate wording is required. Members of Congress often use a manuscript style of delivery when speaking in the House of Representatives or Senate. The president uses a manuscript delivery when presenting the State of the Union address, and so do many political candidates making major speeches. Your professors may use the manuscript method of delivery when presenting their research at academic conferences when they desire careful wording of specific findings.

When using a teleprompter for manuscript delivery, the words of the speech are projected onto slanting clear screens to the left and right of the speaker. The screens appear clear to the audience, but because of their angle (using a technique called Pepper's ghost), text can be read off the screens by the speaker. This allows for eye contact with the audience—and explains why speakers address the left and right of the audience so much more often than the center where there is no such screen to help them.

While the advantage to this style of delivery is an increased accuracy of the material presented, the glaring disadvantage to using a manuscript is that the delivery often suffers dramatically. Frankly, the delivery often stinks! Using a manuscript to deliver a presentation will often lead to decreased eye contact with audience members, since you will focus your eyes on the page in front of you instead of on them. Further, the speech often sounds like it is being read since, essentially, it is. Also, if a speaker holds on to the manuscript, the number and quality of gestures and other movements will diminish, and the manuscript may distract the audience. With these disadvantages often outweighing the advantage, we encourage you to use a manuscript style of delivery only when absolutely necessary.

Memorized Delivery

Memorized delivery is exactly what it sounds like: delivering a speech without the use of a manuscript or any notes whatsoever. This delivery style comes with some obvious advantages. Without any notes, absolutely no chance exists of reading the speech. Speakers using memorized delivery will probably maintain eye contact, and the speech will not sound like it is being read. They need not worry about notes distracting the audience or hindering the use of gestures and movement. While these points might sound good, some disadvantages of memorized delivery make it less beneficial than you might imagine.

One disadvantage of a memorized style of delivery is that committing an entire speech to memory is very difficult. When delivering a speech from memory, speakers will likely remember certain parts or phrases but forget many of their ideas or present them in a random and confusing manner.

Another disadvantage to delivering a speech completely from memory is that it often sounds memorized rather than natural and conversational, which hinders the development of a relational connection with the audience. People memorize and remember information in bits.

If you do not believe us, recite your telephone number with area code or your Social Security number to yourself. We will wait. . . . Seriously, we mean it. . . . Did you do it yet? . . . OK, glad you are back. More than likely, when reciting your phone number, you gave the three numbers of the area code, briefly paused, gave the next three numbers, paused again, and then gave the final four numbers. When presenting your Social Security number, you probably gave the first three numbers, paused, gave the next two numbers, paused, and then gave the final four numbers. If you still do not believe us and argue that this results from both series of numbers being separated that way, recite the alphabet. . . . You probably recited *A* through *G*, *H* through *P*, *Q* through *S*, *T* through *V*, *W* and *X*, and *Y* and *Z* almost musically. You may even have sung the jingle at the end.

See: You have been doing this for years. Notwithstanding years of success, what works fine for telephone numbers, Social Security numbers, and the alphabet is not appropriate when presenting a speech. When someone delivers a completely memorized speech, it often sounds unnatural and uneven and seems emotionless and mechanical rather than natural and conversational. A relational connection with the audience becomes incredibly difficult to establish.

Contrarian Challenge

We encourage you to use manuscript delivery only when careful wording is required. In addition, perhaps more so than even memorized delivery, it should not be attempted by novice speakers. It requires a great deal of speaking experience to successfully accomplish. This aspect might seem counterintuitive. It might seem to you that novice speakers would be better off having the entire speech written out in front of them. Can you make an argument for why novice speakers would benefit from manuscript delivery? If you take everything into consideration, we believe you will agree with us on this one!

Extemporaneous Delivery

Generally recommended as the way to achieve a natural and conversational delivery while ensuring the accuracy of ideas and connecting relationally with an audience, **extemporaneous delivery** involves the use of minimal notes. Speakers using this method prepare an entire speech but do not use a manuscript when presenting the speech. Rather, they include key words, phrases, or, at most, brief sections of the speech in their notes.

This style of delivery provides many of the advantages of manuscript and memorized delivery without the disadvantages. With minimal notes, you will not be tempted to concentrate on them rather than engaging in eye contact with your audience. You will not read to your audience, so you will probably speak in a conversational tone of voice. You will not have multiple sheets of paper or cards in front of you, so your notes will less likely distract your audience. At the same time, using notes will help you stay focused and ensure that your presentation includes key points and vital ideas. The extemporaneous style of delivery requires a great deal of practice and preparation to perform effectively, but it will enable you to deliver an effective, relationally developed presentation.

College Experience

We are stretching the connection between this box and what you have been studying in this chapter quite a bit. However, what we are about to tell you will assist your college experience. It has been established that people remember things in bits. Getting even more specific, people tend to remember those bits appearing at the beginning and those bits appearing at the end. So, if you were shown a list of numbers, and these numbers were then taken away, you would likely recall the numbers at the beginning of the list and the numbers at the end of the list. You would likely forget the numbers in the middle. The same thing happens when people study! Accordingly, you are more likely to remember things at the beginning of a study session and at the end of a study session. It is much more effective to have multiple study sessions lasting shorter periods than to study for 10 hours straight the night before an examination. Trust us—we tried both ways when we were in school.

Goals of Effective Delivery

Regardless of which style of delivery you use, the objectives of effective delivery remain the same. Essentially, effective delivery entails developing and enhancing audience perceptions of your credibility, increasing audience understanding, and establishing a relational connection with the audience. In this section we discuss these elements in more detail and then talk about aspects of delivery that allow you to establish and maintain them.

Developing and Enhancing Credibility

Drawing from decades of research, communication scholars Robert Gass and John Seiter (2011) maintain the existence of three primary dimensions of credibility

Photo 14.2 What will this speaker's minimal use of notes and careful preparation enable her to achieve? (See page 365.)

and four secondary dimensions of credibility. The three primary dimensions—expertise, trustworthiness, and goodwill—no doubt sound familiar since we talked about their importance in the development of the speech itself. Yet these primary dimensions are fully transacted through the delivery of your speech. Later in this chapter, we discuss various components of delivery and how you can properly convey these dimensions. Presented in Table 14.1, the four secondary dimensions of credibility include dynamism, composure, sociability, and inspiring. You may notice how these dimensions connect especially to relational qualities and can be established through the delivery of your speech.

Table 14.1 Secondary Dimensions of Credibility

Dynamism involves being energetic and enthusiastic. Certainly, you want your audience members to perceive you as interested and concerned about your topic, your speech, and them personally. Make sure your enthusiasm is sincere and appropriate; otherwise, other dimensions of credibility, such as trustworthiness, will be called into question, as will a genuinely meaningful relationship with the audience.

Composure entails the ability to appear calm under pressure. Audience members will view someone who cracks under pressure as less credible than someone who is able to overcome potential obstacles and unforeseen circumstances, and they will not desire a relationship with such a person. Again, nervousness does not necessarily mean a lack of composure. Actually, delivering the speech proves your ability to manage feelings of stress and discomfort. Your audience will only question your composure if you draw unnecessary attention to your nerves.

Sociability involves being personable and likeable. As with personal relationships, people want to be around individuals they perceive as good-natured and pleasant. On the other hand, people avoid individuals they perceive as gruff and unfriendly. Speakers who convey an open and congenial demeanor through their delivery are often most effective, in part because they appear to meet the primary dimensions of goodwill and trustworthiness. They are the type of people with whom others would want to develop a relationship.

Inspiring entails the ability to instill enthusiasm in others. Again supporting the primary dimensions, people often view individuals who inspire them as knowledgeable, honest, and concerned. It is not precisely clear whether people view them in this manner because they inspire people or whether they inspire people because people view them as knowledgeable, honest, and concerned. Most likely it is a combination of both, with one reinforcing the other. As with other dimensions of credibility, people are more likely to desire a relationship with inspiring individuals.

Increasing Audience Understanding

The delivery of your speech must also work to increase and guide audience understanding. Gestures and movement can help explain and reinforce the material you present to the audience. Pauses can help guide the audience when you are moving from one section or part of your speech to another.

An especially significant role of delivery is the expression of emotion. If you are discussing a serious or solemn topic, your voice, facial expression, and body should correspond and convey the appropriate emotion or tone. Likewise, if your speech deals with a topic that makes you angry, you should reflect and express this feeling in your delivery. The same applies to such other emotions as fear, excitement, happiness, and pleasure. This coordination both reinforces what you say and underscores your approach to the issue.

Your expression of an emotional tone lets the audience members know how they should feel about and approach the topic. This experience arises in part from a general transference of emotion. When someone is sad or upset, for example, other people around him or her act in a manner that supports this emotion. They might also begin feeling upset themselves. Setting the emotional tone also acts as a cue for the audience.

Think about it in terms of the effects of background music when you are watching a movie. The music sets the mood and lets you know how you should feel or what to expect. This association especially holds true in horror movies. Eerie or creepy music plays as someone approaches a closet door. You feel uneasy, your heart may begin racing, and you know something is going to jump out. It may be just a cat, but you know something is definitely going to happen. The same holds true when delivering a presentation. Your delivery and expression of emotion will let the audience members know how they should feel and what to expect, whether it is an issue that should make them concerned or angry, a solution to a problem that should comfort and delight them, or a psychotic killer jumping out from behind a closed door.

Strategic Communication

We discuss nonverbal components of effective delivery later in the chapter, but here is something for you to keep in mind when delivering presentations. Facial expressions and body positioning work together to convey emotions. Your facial expressions inform people what emotion you are experiencing, while your body informs them of the intensity of that emotion. For instance, your face may be conveying anger, but your body may be loose and fluid—indicating a low level of anger. On the other hand, your face may be conveying anger, but your body may be tense and rigid—indicating a high level of anger. Remembering how these nonverbal elements work together can assist you when conveying emotion to an audience.

Connecting Relationally With the Audience

Through the delivery of a public presentation, you must also strive to develop a positive relational connection with the audience. In all personal and social relationships, people

Although accommodation may increase perceptions of similarity, be careful that you do not overdo it. Both Hillary Clinton and Barack Obama have been chastised for speaking with disingenuous Southern dialects when speaking to voters in the South.

convey nonverbally how they feel about others. Public audiences should feel that the speaker likes and cares about them. You can transact this alliance by smiling when appropriate and using a concerned and compassionate tone of voice when discussing the importance of your topic in their lives. You can also develop a connection with the audience members through an openness of gestures and bodily movements toward them.

Further, you can develop a relational connection through identification with the audience members by communicating similarity with them. Studies in accommodation have shown that people adjust their rates of speech, accents, facial expressions, and bodily movements to match those with whom they interact to indicate and develop a relational connection (Giles, 2008). When speaking in public, you may also accomplish this association through appearance and style of dress or through dialect and the similar pronunciation of words or other vocal characteristics. As with all forms of communication, when delivering a public presentation, speakers communicate more than just content; they transact a relationship with the audience.

Components of Effective Delivery

Now that we have examined the goals of effective delivery, we can discuss how to achieve them through the components of effective delivery. This book proposes that the same nonverbal relational techniques work in dyadic and public speaking situations. We now apply elements of Chapter 3 accordingly.

Make Your Case

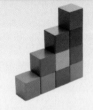

Select a person you know or a public figure you consider an effective public speaker. What characteristics of his or her delivery do you find most impressive? What could this individual do to improve his or her delivery of public presentations?

Now select someone you consider a poor public speaker. What characteristics of his or her delivery do you find most in need of improvement? What suggestions would you provide this person to improve his or her

Personal Appearance

Personal appearance—including clothing, hairstyle, jewelry, tattoos, makeup, and other artifacts—reflects who you are and how you want other people to perceive you and your relationship with them. Personal appearance is so powerful that people often make judgments based more on another person's appearance than on his or her words or actions. Through your appearance, you must seek to connect relationally with the audience and convey credibility. This strategy means dressing in a manner that is consistent with audience expectations and conveys professionalism or a specific relationship. Audiences view those dressed professionally—again determined by audience expectations—as more knowledgeable and trustworthy. Dressing in a professional manner also conveys to your audience members that you care enough about them and the occasion to dress appropriately.

Vocalics

Just as in dyadic interaction, a speaker's voice is a key component in the development of a conversational and relational style of delivery, which is accomplished in part though variation of pitch, rate, pauses, and volume.

Pitch

Pitch involves the highness or lowness of your voice. You have a range at which you normally speak, and you should use this same range when speaking in front of an audience. Whether you speak with a high or a low tone of voice, you must speak using a variety of pitches within your natural range. Speaking without variations in pitch means speaking in monotone, which will cause audiences to lose interest in your presentation and prevent you from connecting with them relationally.

Rate

Rate is how fast or slow you speak, generally determined by how many words you speak per minute. On average, people speak at around 150 words per minute. You may speak at a faster or slower rate in a normal conversation, and speaking at approximately the same rate when delivering a speech should work out just fine. Times will occur when your rate of speech is either faster or slower than others, depending on your emotional state, intensity of language, and emphasis on certain words.

Volume

The **volume** of your presentation is determined by how loudly or quietly you speak. When presenting your speech, strive to speak as naturally as possible. Just like other elements of the voice, volume should rise and fall during the delivery of your speech to make the presentation appear more natural and conversational, which will help you maintain audience attention and connect with the audience in meaningful ways. You can also use changes in volume (e.g., speaking more quietly as you reach the end of a major section) to provide emphasis, to underscore emotion, and even to direct the audience.

Speak as naturally as possible, but obviously the audience should be able to hear you. Demosthenes, an ancient Greek orator, trained himself to speak by trying to project his voice over the roaring ocean waves. If you cannot make it to a beach in Greece, though, here is another option. The volume of your voice increases naturally as the amount of air being released increases. Therefore, when attempting to speak in a louder voice, remember to take deep breaths and expel more air.

Pauses

Pauses, or breaks in the vocal flow, serve to direct the audience, add emphasis to areas of your presentation, and allow you to, um, avoid, like, nonfluencies and stuff. You may wish to include a brief pause when shifting from one main point to another or from one section of the speech to another. This action allows the audience members to recognize that something is going on and fully prepares them for movement within the speech.

Pauses also allow you to add emphasis to what you say or are about to say. If you have said something particularly profound, a pause will allow the audience to reflect on it. If you are getting ready to say something especially important, a pause will signal the audience members that they need to pay particular attention to what comes next.

Finally, pauses will help you avoid **nonfluencies**, meaningless vocal fillers that often distract from a presentation. Common nonfluencies include *um, uh, like, OK, you know,* and *you know what I'm saying.* A brief moment of silence will not distract the audience or seem out of place and, certainly, will not be more distracting or inappropriate than a nonfluency.

Eye Contact

Maintaining eye contact with the audience members will allow you to maintain their attention, as well as enhance your credibility and relational connection. There are a few issues to keep in mind when considering eye contact.

First, many cultures view eye contact as a sign of trustworthiness and as a means of relating with another person. However, some cultures consider eye contact, especially between a subordinate and a superior, a sign of disrespect. Be aware of and prepared for any cultural differences that might arise during a speaking situation.

A second consideration involves where you focus your eye contact. Make sure that you scan the entire room when speaking rather than focusing on one area of the audience. Of course, you should not look side to side like when watching a tennis match. You want to make your scanning appear as natural as possible.

A third consideration when incorporating eye contact is to look pleasant and engaging. A fine line exists between a friendly glance in someone's direction and the piercing stare of a psychopath. You do not want to get into a staring contest with the audience, and blinking from time to time is more than appropriate. Once again, strive to make your eye contact with the audience as natural as possible.

As with shy people communicating in one-on-one situations (Bradshaw, 2006), people who feel apprehensive about speaking in public may decrease eye contact to reduce what they believe will be negative reactions from the audience. This reduces the amount of audience feedback they can gather—much of which may very well be positive—and may actually lead to negative audience reactions. Apprehensive people who avoid eye contact may be misunderstood as deceptive or uncaring about the audience—just another reason to maintain eye contact with audiences and to address anxieties you may experience about speaking in public.

Facial Expression and Body Position

Your facial expression is key to establishing a relational connection with the audience members and directing them emotionally. A smile and a pleasant look on your face go a long way in establishing a positive connection with the audience. Sociability—a secondary dimension of credibility—deals with a person's likeability. People generally enjoy being around people who seem pleasant and congenial. Plus, an amiable nature may serve to underscore and establish the primary dimensions of trustworthiness and goodwill.

Facial expression, along with body position, will allow you to guide the audience emotionally. As mentioned above, your delivery serves to direct the audience members by letting them know how you feel and what they should feel. Your facial expression will let them know the emotion, and your body position will tell them the intensity of that emotion. It is important to remember that your displays of emotion must match your language.

Photo 14.3 How might this speaker's use of gestures benefit his presentation? (See page 365.)

Gestures

Including gestures in the delivery of your speech will assist you in increasing audience understanding and allowing you to channel nervous energy. Gestures can help guide the audience through the presentation. For example, you may emphasize a transition by holding out one hand and saying, "Now that we have addressed X," and then holding out the other hand and continuing, "let's turn our attention to Y."

Gestures are also an effective and productive way to expend the nervous energy you may experience when speaking in front of an audience. Most people feel apprehensive when speaking in front of an audience, which results in a buildup of nervous energy. Releasing this nervous energy allows people to feel more at ease; however, this relief unfortunately results in mannerisms that can distract the audience. **Distracting mannerisms**, or bodily movements that allow a person to discharge nervous energy, serve no actual purpose in the presentation and often divert attention from the message. Such mannerisms include rubbing your hands together, pecking on the sides of the lectern with your fingertips, playing with your watch or jewelry, rubbing the back of your neck, playing with your hair, and rocking from side to side. Here, the importance of gestures comes into play. Gestures allow you to expend this nervous energy while also increasing audience understanding and giving life to your presentation.

Presentation Aids

Presentation aids—objects, images, graphs, video clips, sound, and PowerPoint presentations—are tools used by a speaker to enhance audience understanding,

Photo 14.4 What is the speaker doing to remain the primary focus of the audience while addressing a presentation aid? (See page 365.)

appreciation, retention, and attention, as well as a speaker's credibility. Usually auditory and visual in nature, presentation aids can also invoke such senses as taste, touch, and smell. We begin by discussing the ways in which they enhance presentations.

Enhance Audience Understanding

Understanding increases when multiple senses are involved. Someone can explain what it means when something tastes bitter, but actually tasting a sour lemon will provide a better understanding. A person can explain a crescendo, but hearing an example of one can provide a clearer understanding of that musical device. Presentation aids compel audience members to use multiple senses, which increases their understanding of the material presented.

Enhance Audience Appreciation

Often used to allow an audience to appreciate the extent or magnitude of something, presentation aids help your audience fully comprehend what you say or fully recognize its importance or impact. During a speech urging audience members to avoid eating fast food, a speaker might display a pile of cooking lard equivalent to the amount of fat consumed during a typical meal at a fast-food restaurant. When using statistics, incorporating pie charts or line graphs will allow audience members to visually realize and appreciate the magnitude of an issue or fully grasp trends or changes. Images can be powerful tools that enable audience members to fully recognize the importance of your topic. For instance, during a speech about poverty or world hunger, the image of a hungry child will enable the audience to put a human face to the discussion.

Enhance Audience Retention

Along with the use of vivid and memorable support material, presentation aids can help the audience remember the material and retain key information. Quite often, audience members remember presentation aids long after other parts of the speech.

Enhance Audience Attention

If audience members are able to understand, appreciate, and retain the material presented, they will be more likely to pay attention to the speaker and the presentation. Because presentation aids entail change (additional movement by the speaker, something new to look at, an alteration in thought processes, the use of additional senses), they can regain and reinforce audience attention.

Enhance Speaker Credibility

When a speaker conveys information in a manner that allows the audience to understand, appreciate, and retain the material, audience members' perceptions of that person's credibility will improve, as will their perceptions of their relationship with the speaker. A well-developed presentation aid can positively enhance audience members' perceptions of a speaker's overall credibility and their relationship with that speaker. Of course, the opposite holds true as well, and a poorly executed and shoddy presentation aid will most certainly negatively affect a speaker's credibility and his or her relationship with the audience. Table 14.2 provides guidelines for the development and incorporation of presentation aids.

Table 14.2 Presentations Aids Should Be . . .

Fully prepared

Poorly created presentation aids diminish audience perceptions of a speaker's credibility and relationship with the audience, because the speaker appears not fully prepared for the presentation.

Limited in number

Presentation aids can greatly enhance your presentation, but using too many may become a distraction, and the value of each will subsequently diminish. A general guideline to follow for brief presentations: Include no more than two presentation aids for each main point of your speech.

Relatively simple

Presentation aids should convey a single idea.

Inoffensive

Graphic or explicit images can gain the attention of members of your audience and make them appreciate what you are discussing, but these images can also offend and hinder your relationship with them.

Easily seen

It is important that all members of the audience, not just those closest to you, be able to clearly see your presentation aid.

Fully discussed

Fully incorporate presentation aids into your discussion. Do not assume that the audience will recognize the significance of pictures, objects, or any other presentation aid you use.

Incorporated seamlessly

Continue talking as you incorporate and remove your presentation aid rather than stopping your presentation. Use the period immediately before incorporating the presentation aid to prepare the audience members for what they are about to see or hear, and use the period after exhibiting the presentation aid to discuss what they just experienced.

The secondary focus

As a speaker, you should remain the primary focus of the audience, and the presentation aid should be the secondary focus. Accordingly, keep presentation aids out of view when not addressing them, avoid looking directly at them, and do not pass them around.

Managing Communication Apprehension

Feeling nervous or apprehensive about speaking in public is a common occurrence and perfectly natural. While this fact might not alleviate your anxiety about the thought of speaking in front of others, it might reassure you to know you are not alone. Nearly everyone feels nervous when speaking in public. Of course, some people are more apprehensive than others, but it is a common experience, and many people really dread the thought of it.

You might be surprised to learn that a bit of nervousness can actually benefit your presentation. Nervous energy gives your presentation spark and vibrancy that enliven your speech and help maintain audience attention. Without it, your voice will lack enthusiasm, your body will appear listless, and it will be difficult to connect with the audience relationally. Your overall presentation will seem dull, flat, and lifeless. We recognize that this sounds a bit like a shampoo and conditioner commercial. So, we will not go so far as to say that nervous energy will make your presentation easier to style and will prevent frizz and split ends. However, we will continue to maintain that nervous energy will give life to your speech, and without it your presentation will not be as effective.

All joking aside, knowing that nervousness is a normal experience and can benefit your presentation if it is not overwhelming does not diminish the fact that many people consider it a major cause for concern. Communication apprehension can result in a great deal of uncomfortable stress and overall lousy feelings. The good news is that ways exist to deal with nervousness and stress associated with speaking in public.

Recognizing and Knowing What You Fear

The first way to deal with stress and anxiety related to public speaking is to recognize exactly what worries you. Especially when people have little or no actual experience speaking in front of others, they are less afraid of actually speaking in front of an audience and more afraid of the unknown. As a result, people generally imagine things as a whole lot worse than they actually turn out to be.

Fear of the unknown as a major cause of communication apprehension may be supported in part by the finding that the second greatest point of anxiety related to public speaking in the classroom comes at the moment the speech is assigned, with the moment of greatest anxiety occurring right before speaking (Behnke & Sawyer, 1999). In most cases, the assignment is provided before public speaking has fully been discussed in class. The requirements of giving an effective presentation are largely unknown—a frightening proposition. Reading this book and discussing speeches in class will help minimize many of those unknowns, but you can do more.

Listen in on Your Life

Research indicates that most people have at least some apprehension about speaking in public. What would you consider your greatest concerns about speaking in front of an audience? What could you do to minimize these concerns?

Alleviating the Unknown

Often, fear of the unknown emerges from a sense of not having control over a situation. The best way to handle this anxiety is to do as much as possible to eliminate those unknown variables and address your specific fears. This control will require a great deal of preparation and practice but essentially entails meeting the requirements of an effective presentation, something you have to do anyway. Table 14.3 provides guidance when limiting the unknown factors of a presentation.

Table 14.3 Knowing the Unknown

Knowing the audience relationally

Audience analysis can alleviate much of the fear of not knowing what to expect from an audience. Conducting a thorough audience analysis enables you to gain a better understanding of your audience's experience, knowledge, and general view of the world and you personally. Audience analysis also enables you to mold the speech to fit your audience members specifically, which means you will be able to share the material in the most effective way and to connect with them on a relational level.

Knowing the topic

If you feel particularly nervous about speaking in public, we strongly suggest that, when possible, you select a topic about which you are already knowledgeable. Familiarity with a topic will increase your confidence and alleviate fear that comes from speaking to others. Of course, familiarization with your topic also comes from the rigorous exploration of the topic through careful research and the thorough development of your argument.

Knowing the speech will be worthwhile

As you thoroughly examine a topic, you will likely develop a greater appreciation for its significance and its relational importance in the lives of your audience members. Knowing that your speech is worthwhile and recognizing that it will positively affect your audience members' lives will provide you with greater confidence and alleviate anxiety related to your presentation.

Knowing the speech's beginning

Constructing a solid introduction and conclusion will also help diminish any fears. Confidence in your attention getter and overall introduction is especially vital since presenters generally experience the most anxiety at the very beginning of a presentation, just before they start speaking (Behnke & Sawyer, 1999). Belief in your introduction will allow you to face the moment of greatest anxiety straight on with confidence.

Knowing the presentation aids

Some research indicates that using presentation aids may help reduce anxiety related to speaking in public (Ayres, 1991). At the same time, they can be an issue of concern. Recognize the value of presentation aids, and ensure that you devote enough time and consideration to their preparation. Avoid overly complicated and unpredictable presentation aids, such as children and animals. Allow plenty of time to organize or ready each presentation aid before beginning your speech. Finally, include the demonstration of presentation aids in practice sessions. Doing so will make you aware of and adequately prepare you for possible problems that may arise and ensure the seamless integration of each presentation aid into your speech.

Practicing Your Presentation

Practicing your presentation will help you manage your nerves by increasing your familiarity with the material and the speech, as well as your confidence as a speaker. Practicing a speech, especially in front of others, has been shown to reduce apprehension related to public speaking and increase one's willingness to speak in public (Ayres, Schliesman, & Sonandre, 1998). In what follows, we discuss some guidelines to consider when practicing the delivery of a presentation.

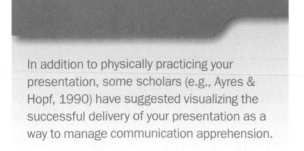

In addition to physically practicing your presentation, some scholars (e.g., Ayres & Hopf, 1990) have suggested visualizing the successful delivery of your presentation as a way to manage communication apprehension.

Practice Actual Delivery. Practice presenting your speech in the manner in which you will actually deliver it. This means presenting the material out loud, incorporating full gestures and movement, and including presentation aids. When initially preparing for a presentation, many people read the speech silently to themselves. This practice may allow you to familiarize yourself more with the speech, which is fine, but we recommend presenting the material out loud as soon as possible. A big difference exists between reading something to yourself and presenting material orally. The sooner you begin focusing on the latter, the better prepared you will be to effectively deliver the material to others. Also, although it might be more comfortable, do not practice your speech while lying across your bed or sprawling across a chair. You will not be able to fully incorporate and practice gestures, movement, or even eye contact; nor will you be able to get an accurate sense of delivering your presentation in front of an audience. Make your practice sessions as close to the real thing as possible.

Watch and Listen to Yourself. People can imagine what they look and sound like, but a difference often exists between what they imagine and what they actually do. At minimum, we recommend practicing your speech in front of a mirror to observe and assess your facial expressions, eye contact, and gestures. You can also tape-record yourself and play it back to evaluate your tone of voice, rate of speech, and possible use of nonfluencies. Preferably, you will be able to videotape yourself speaking and review the entire package at once. Doing so will allow you to consider the integration of vocal variety and bodily movement and which elements of delivery you accomplished most effectively.

Photo 14.5 Which practicing guideline is the speaker in this photo following? (See page 365.)

Practice in Front of an Audience. We also recommend that you practice delivering your speech in front of actual people, such as family members, friends, roommates, or strangers you drag off the street. The people listening to you practice will be able to provide constructive criticism to help you improve the actual speech and your delivery. Practicing in front of people will also provide a more accurate sense of what delivering your speech will actually be like, which will help improve your presentation. In fact, practicing your presentation in front of other people has been shown to increase the quality of your speech (Menzel & Carrell, 1994). If you are still not convinced, how about this? Practicing your speech in front of other people has also been shown to improve the grade you earn on the speech (Smith & Frymier, 2006). We thought you might like that one! In fact, one study concluded that increased preparation time overall will bring about higher grades on classroom speeches, and activities related specifically to delivery appear the most important (Pearson, Child, & Kahl, 2006). Finally, practicing a speech in front of others has been shown to reduce communication apprehension and increase a speaker's willingness to give a presentation (Ayres, 1996). We urge you to practice in front of others as part of your preparation, especially if you are apprehensive about speaking in public. This type of preparation may not appeal to you, but you will greatly benefit from it.

A bit of unfortunate irony exists. Highly communication-apprehensive people generally spend more time preparing for their speeches than less-apprehensive people (Ayres & Robideaux-Maxwell, 1989). However, this preparation is less likely to include communication-oriented activities (Ayres, 1996). While people who feel highly apprehensive about speaking in front of others may spend a great deal of time conducting research and constructing their speech, they will probably avoid practicing the delivery of their presentation, an unfortunate situation given the tremendous benefits that come from such practice. If you are particularly apprehensive about speaking in public, be sure to avoid succumbing to this trend.

Experience and Skill Building

Experience and skill building will also help you manage anxiety related to public speaking. Experience in public speaking helps eliminate some of the unknowns associated with it, while learning skills and how to develop them through experience provides added confidence. As with most things, the more you engage in public speaking, the better you will become at presenting a speech.

If you are about to present your very first speech or have spoken before a public audience only a few times in the past, you may think a discussion of experience and skill building does not do you any good. However, the impact of skill building largely comes from the self-recognition that you know how to develop an effective speech and know the elements of effective delivery. Having read and studied these chapters and discussed this material in class, believe it or not, you now possess this knowledge. By the time you actually deliver your speech, you will have come a long way from the beginning of class when you were unfamiliar with what public speaking entails. You know

Case in Point

Videotape your delivery of a presentation, and then analyze your performance using the guidelines and criteria offered in this chapter. Play the tape at least three times— once with the sound off, once with the sound on but without looking at the screen, and once focusing on the integration of your voice, body movement, and facial expression. What did you do well? What areas of your delivery do you need to develop? What can you do to improve these areas and your overall delivery?

the fundamental components of effective presentations and are in the process of implementing this knowledge and fully developing skills of effective delivery. We know that you possess this knowledge and ability, but it is more important that you recognize it.

Although you have increased your understanding of speech development and presentation, you still may not possess a great deal of actual experience as a public speaker. Realize, however, that the more you speak, the better you will become. We would like to make one more appeal for practicing your speech in front of others: This practice will provide you with experience from which you may draw when actually presenting the speech.

Of course, even the most experienced speakers are often apprehensive about speaking in public. Experience and skill building will not lead to the complete elimination of anxiety related to public speaking, and you would not even desire this result, since some nervous energy is necessary to give life to your presentation. Experience will often lower your level of anxiety, however. Plus, you will increasingly improve the management of nerves related to speaking in public as you gain additional experience.

A Final Thought About Communication Apprehension

If you feel extremely apprehensive about speaking in public, we encourage you to talk with the instructor of your course. Communication apprehension is a legitimate concern and should be taken seriously. Sometimes breaking down the unknown, practicing your speech, and gaining skills and experience do not suffice. While we are certain these strategies will help you, we also realize that they cannot do enough in some cases. Realize that you are not alone in your concern about public speaking. This uneasiness is quite common, and your instructor can help prepare you for the experience and assist you in dealing with any anxieties. We are confident that you will be able to do it.

FOCUS QUESTIONS REVISITED

1. What are three guidelines for effective delivery?
As a speaker, you should (a) always be yourself, (b) strive to make your presentation conversational, and (c) avoid calling attention to mistakes and nerves.

2. What are the styles of delivery?
The styles of delivery are manuscript, memorized, and extemporaneous. Manuscript delivery involves having the entire speech written out in front of you when speaking. This style is usually used when accurate wording of the speech is required but often results in poor delivery. Memorized delivery is done without any notes whatsoever. While reading the speech and distracting notes become nonissues, it is difficult to memorize an entire speech, and the delivery often sounds unnatural and uneven. Extemporaneous delivery involves the use of minimal notes and is generally recommended as the way to achieve a natural and conversational delivery while ensuring the accuracy of ideas.

3. What are the goals of effective delivery?

The goals of effective delivery are developing and enhancing audience perceptions of your credibility, increasing audience understanding, and establishing a relational connection with the audience.

4. What are the components of effective delivery?

The components of effective delivery include personal appearance, vocalics, eye contact, facial expression and body position, and gestures and physical movement. These components must work together to achieve the effective delivery of a presentation.

5. What are presentation aids?

Presentation aids are audio and visual tools used by a speaker to enhance audience understanding, appreciation, retention, attention, and a speaker's credibility.

6. What is communication apprehension, and how can it be managed?

Communication apprehension is the fear or anxiety people experience about speaking in public. Feeling nervous about speaking in public is quite common and perfectly normal. Nervous energy can actually help enhance a presentation as long as it is managed effectively. One way of dealing with communication apprehension is recognizing and knowing what you fear. Practicing the presentation, as well as gaining public speaking skills and experience, will also help you manage communication apprehension and increase your overall confidence as a speaker.

KEY CONCEPTS

communication apprehension   343
composure   350
distracting mannerisms   355
dynamism   350
extemporaneous delivery   349
inspiring   350
manuscript delivery   347
memorized delivery   348

nonfluencies   354
pauses   354
pitch   353
presentation aids   355
rate   353
sociability   350
volume   353

QUESTIONS TO ASK YOUR FRIENDS

1. Ask your friends to describe the characteristics of an *effective* public speaker. Limit their responses to those involving the delivery of a presentation. Consider their responses in regard to the guidelines and criteria for delivering public presentations discussed in this chapter.

2. Ask your friends to describe the characteristics of an *ineffective* public speaker. Limit their responses to those involving the delivery of a presentation. Consider their

responses in regard to the guidelines and criteria for delivering public presentations discussed in this chapter.

3. Ask your friends if they will listen to you practice your presentation. You should have known we would bring this up yet again! Seriously, practicing a presentation in front of an actual audience will improve your overall performance and help you manage communication apprehension.

MEDIA LINKS

1. Watch a public presentation on television or the Internet. Which components of effective delivery discussed in this chapter are evident? What does the speaker do well? How could the speaker improve his or her delivery?

2. Watch a public presentation on television or the Internet. Then find the transcript of that presentation. The transcripts of major presentations, such as those delivered by a president or a prime minister, are often included in newspapers the following day and almost immediately available online. In what ways would you have responded differently had you read the speech rather than watched and listened to it being delivered? What about the speaker's delivery led to these differences?

3. Think about the issues with which a speaker must contend when delivering a presentation to both a physically present audience and an audience watching the presentation on television or the Internet. How can a speaker nonverbally connect with both audiences? Assuming a smaller viewing screen, would a podcast change what a speaker must do to connect with the audience?

ETHICAL ISSUES

1. Audience members perceive a speaker's credibility in part through his or her personal appearance. In what ways would you consider such judgment either justified or unfair?

2. With the above considerations about personal appearance in mind, is it ethical for a person to alter his or her usual appearance for a public presentation situation?

3. We discussed how you should always be yourself when speaking in public but that you may integrate certain qualities of speakers you admire into your own speaking style. Where would you position the boundary between integrating qualities of that person's delivery into your own personal style and becoming a caricature or mimic of that person? Addressed another way, is it possible to plagiarize a delivery style?

ANSWERS TO PHOTO CAPTIONS

Photo 14.1 ▪ No. Speakers should always be themselves when speaking in public and not try to pretend to be someone else.

Photo 14.2 ■ Extemporaneous delivery enables this speaker to convey her ideas accurately while maintaining a conversational tone of voice and connecting relationally with the audience.

Photo 14.3 ■ His use of gestures helps reinforce verbal communication, gives life to the presentation, and channels nervous energy to avoid distracting mannerisms.

Photo 14.4 ■ The speaker is not looking directly at the presentation aid, ensuring that his primary focus is relating with the audience.

Photo 14.5 ■ He is practicing his speech in front of a mirror to observe and assess his facial expressions, eye contact, and gestures.

STUDENT STUDY SITE

Visit the study site at **www.sagepub.com/boc2e** for e-flashcards, practice quizzes, journal articles and additional study resources.

REFERENCES

Ayres, J. (1991). Using visual aids to reduce speech anxiety. *Communication Research Reports, 8,* 73–79.

Ayres, J. (1996). Speech preparation processes and speech apprehension. *Communication Education, 45,* 228–235.

Ayres, J., & Hopf, T. S. (1990). The long-term effect of visualization in the classroom: A brief research report. *Communication Education, 39,* 75–78.

Ayres, J., & Robideaux-Maxwell, R. (1989). Communication apprehension and speech preparation time. *Communication Research Reports, 6,* 90–93.

Ayres, J., Schliesman, T., & Sonandre, D. A. (1998). Practice makes perfect but does it help reduce communication apprehension? *Communication Research Reports, 15,* 170–179.

Behnke, R. R., & Sawyer, C. R. (1999). Milestones of anticipatory public speaking anxiety. *Communication Education, 48,* 165–172.

Bradshaw, S. (2006). Shyness and difficult relationships: Formation is just the beginning. In C. D. Kirkpatrick, S. W. Duck, & M. K. Foley (Eds.), *Relating difficulty: The processes of constructing and managing difficult interaction* (pp. 15–41). Mahwah, NJ: Lawrence Erlbaum.

Gass, R. H., & Seiter, J. S. (2011). *Persuasion, social influence, and compliance gaining* (4th ed.). Boston: Allyn & Bacon.

Giles, H. (2008). Communication Accommodation Theory. In L. A. Baxter & D. O. Braithwaite (Eds.), *Engaging theories in interpersonal communication: Multiple perspectives* (pp. 161–173). Thousand Oaks, CA: Sage.

McCroskey, J. C. (1970). Measures of communication-bound anxiety. *Speech Monographs, 37,* 269–277.

Menzel, K. E., & Carrell, L. J. (1994). The relationship between preparation and performance in public speaking. *Communication Education, 43,* 17–26.

Pearson, J. C., Child, J. T., & Kahl, D. H., Jr. (2006). Preparation meeting opportunity: How do college students prepare for public speeches? *Communication Quarterly, 54,* 351–366.

Smith, T. E., & Frymier, A. B. (2006). Get "real": Does practicing speeches before an audience improve performance? *Communication Quarterly, 54,* 111–125.

Wallechinsky, D., & Wallace, A. (1995). *The book of lists* (Reprint ed.). New York: Lb Books.

15

Interviewing

This chapter is dedicated to something that will be of great importance through-out your professional life—interviews. An **interview** is a goal-driven transaction characterized by questions and answers, clear structure, control, and imbalance. An interview is usually a dyadic transaction, meaning that it takes place between two people. A talk show host asking questions of a celebrity would be one example of a dyadic interview. Sometimes, however, a person may be interviewed by two or more people or in a panel situation. Consider, for instance, when someone testifies before Congress and is asked a series of questions by a panel of senators. We introduce various types of interviews in this chapter, but we primarily focus on employment interviews, since those are the types of interviews the majority of people reading this book are most concerned about at this point in their lives.

Interviews share many characteristics with other types of communication. Certainly, all of the properties of communication discussed throughout the book remain intact. Communication within an interview is transactional and symbolic (both verbal and nonverbal), requires meaning, is both presentational and representational, and takes much for granted. An interview requires effective listening (engaged, relational, and critical) on the part of everyone involved in order to be successful. Furthermore, identity, relational, and cultural work are all being conducted during an interview. There are certain characteristics, though, that make interviews very unique types of communication, and we will examine those later.

This chapter ultimately focuses on how to conduct and participate in employment interviews. We begin by discussing the preparation for an interview. We then examine what must take place during the beginning of an interview. Next, we explore what happens during the question-and-answer portion of an interview. From an interviewer standpoint, we discuss developing different types of questions, sequencing the questions, directive and nondirective questioning, and avoiding illegal questions. From an interviewee standpoint, we discuss adjusting the interview frame for greater success, learning from successful and unsuccessful interviews, answering common interview questions, and handling illegal questions. We then examine what must take place during the conclusion of an interview. We next discuss the responsibilities of interviewers and interviewees following an interview. Finally, since most people will not be invited to interview with an organization without an effective cover letter and résumé, we discuss the construction of these vital application tools.

Focus Questions

1. What are the characteristics of an interview?
2. What are the types of interviews?
3. What are the preinterview responsibilities of interviewers and interviewees?
4. How should a person begin an employment interview?
5. What types of questions and questioning styles may an interviewer use?
6. How should interviewees respond to questions during an interview?
7. How should a person conclude an employment interview?
8. What are the postinterview responsibilities of interviewers and interviewees?
9. What are a cover letter and résumé?

Characteristics of an Interview

Interviews encompass unique characteristics that distinguish them from other types of communication. In what follows, we examine five characteristics of interviews: (1) goal-driven, (2) question–answer, (3) structured, (4) controlled, and (5) unbalanced.

Goal-Driven

Interviews are generally more *goal-driven* than other types of communication, especially those taking place between two people. All communication achieves something beyond the simple exchange of symbols, but these achievements and creations are not always purposeful and intended. Interviews have a clear purpose, a goal to be achieved. Information may be desired, a problem may need to be resolved, persuasion may be desired, someone may need assistance with a personal problem, or an employer may be seeking the best person for a job opening and a potential employee may be looking for a good employer.

Question–Answer

Another characteristic of interviews is the *question–answer* nature of the transaction. The majority of an interview consists of one person (sometimes more than one) asking questions and another person answering those questions. Everyday communication includes occasional questions and answers—especially if people are getting to know one another—but not to the extent of an interview. Furthermore, in most everyday communication, it is not usually the case that one person is in charge of asking the questions while the other person is in charge of answering them.

Structured

Interviews also tend to be more *structured* than other types of communication. Whereas a casual interaction between two people may happen spontaneously and have no clear focus, interviews involve planning and preparation and also tend to have a clear sequence. Certain actions are expected during an interview in order to reach the clearly defined goal discussed previously. We write more about the planning and sequence of interviews later in the chapter.

Controlled

Interviews are generally *controlled* by an interviewer, who is responsible for moving the interview toward its intended goal. The amount of control exerted during an interview depends on this goal, which is achieved in part by the questions asked and the communication environment established. Once again, this—specifically whether an interview is characterized as *directive* or *nondirective*—is a topic we discuss in more detail later in the chapter.

Unbalanced

A final characteristic of interviews is that the time spent talking by an interviewee and an interviewer is usually *unbalanced*. Typically, an interviewer will speak for 30% of the time, and an interviewee will speak for 70% of the time. Of course, the type of interview will dictate exactly how much time each party spends talking, but more often than not, an interviewee will talk more and an interviewer will talk less.

Types of Interviews

Now that we have discussed the characteristics of an interview, we can examine various types of interviews. You may have already experienced some of these interviews in the past and will likely encounter them many times throughout both your personal life and your professional life in the future. We will begin with the employment interview, since this type of interview will receive the most attention in the remainder of the chapter. Note that the first three types of interviews discussed encompass the workplace. Initial employment is not the only place you will come across interviews in your professional life.

Employment Interviews

When people think of interviews, an employment interview is probably what comes immediately to mind. **Employment interviews** are those in which a potential employer interviews a potential employee. Both parties have a great deal riding on the success of an interview. The potential employee is not only seeking employment but also determining whether the job is one that would be accepted if offered. The potential employer is searching not only for a qualified applicant but also for someone who would actually benefit the organization. Potential employers also want to convince potential employees that the position is one they should accept if offered.

Performance Interviews

Also known as *performance reviews,* **performance interviews** are those in which an individual's activities and work are discussed. These interviews are most often conducted between employees and supervisors, but you may also experience them in educational and other settings. For instance, students frequently discuss their progress toward a degree with an advisor or perhaps even a committee of professors. In both situations, a person's strengths and weaknesses are discussed with the ultimate goal being to improve his or her performance. Naturally such interviews can be stressful, but they can also provide people with valuable information that can be used to strengthen their performance and to help them achieve personal and professional goals. These interviews are also an opportunity for the goals and culture of an organization to be reinforced.

Exit Interviews

Exit interviews are those that occur when a person chooses to leave a place of employment. The conventional wisdom is that someone who is leaving may be more likely to provide honest answers about organizational cultures, policies, supervisors, compensation, and other aspects of the workplace. If used correctly, these interviews can provide employers with valuable insight that can be incorporated to improve employee satisfaction and thus the productivity and success of an organization. These interviews are also increasingly common in education and among multiple types of groups, such as volunteer organizations.

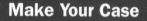
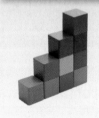

Make Your Case

Do exit interviews provide accurate and useful information to employers? Or will employees leaving an organization still hesitate to provide full disclosure of the positive and negative aspects of the organization? What factors may determine whether an exit interview will be worthwhile?

Information-Gaining Interviews

You may have previously experienced an information-gaining interview and not even realized it as such. **Information-gaining interviews** are those in which a person solicits information from another person. You have likely responded to surveys, which is one form of information-gaining interview. A doctor asking you about your symptoms during an office visit would be another example of this form of interview. You may conduct information-gaining interviews when preparing speeches and papers for school or work. These sorts of interviews are also frequently seen on webcasts and included in newspapers, magazines, and blogs.

Persuasive Interviews

Persuasive interviews are those that have influence as the ultimate goal. The interviewer may appear to be gaining information but is actually attempting to influence the thoughts or actions of the interviewee. This form of interview may sound a bit manipulative and perhaps underhanded, but it is quite common. When salespeople ask your opinion about a product or service, they often do so in a way that attempts to sway you toward what they want you to purchase. At other times, what appears to be a survey is in reality an attempt to persuade. Political workers have frequently been accused of dirty tricks under the guise of conducting straightforward surveys. They attempt to plant a seed of doubt or concern in the mind of the interviewee. For instance, imagine being asked, "If the incumbent were convicted of running a cockfighting ring, would this influence your vote in the upcoming election?" Depending on your opinion of roosters or animal cruelty in general, it would or would not affect your vote, but such questions often influence voter perceptions of candidates and result in rumors being circulated.

Problem-Solving Interviews

When experiencing difficulties or facing an unknown challenge, people may engage in **problem-solving interviews**, those in which a problem is isolated and solutions are generated. These types of interviews may be conducted by someone with greater experience or insight than the person being interviewed. Students, for example, may be questioned by their professors in order to determine why they may be experiencing difficulties in a class. Sometimes problem-solving interviews are conducted by someone with general knowledge of a situation but whose fresh approach can be beneficial. For instance, a colleague may be asked to engage in a problem-solving interview when difficulties are encountered with a project at work. Someone not involved with a situation will often provide alternative approaches to solving a problem.

Photo 15.1 What is the difference between information-gathering interviews like the one pictured here and persuasive interviews? Is the difference always obvious to the person being interviewed? (See page 404.)

Helping Interviews

Unlike problem-solving interviews, **helping interviews** are always conducted by someone with expertise in a given area and whose services are engaged by someone in need of advice. The most obvious example of a helping interview would be a psychologist asking questions of a client. However, other helping interviews include those conducted by credit card counselors with people facing a heavy debt load or attorneys advising clients on legal matters.

Preinterview Responsibilities

Having examined the characteristics of interviews and different types of interviews, we now focus our attention fully on employment interviews. Although other types of interviews are important, as mentioned previously employment interviews are likely the most important for people reading this book. The entire employment interview process will be discussed, from preinterview responsibilities of both an interviewer and an interviewee to postinterview responsibilities of both an interviewer and an interviewee. Along the way, we will explore the beginning of an interview, how interviewers should ask questions, how interviewees should answer questions, and how an interview should come to a close. So, let's get started by discussing what should be done in preparation for an interview.

Interviewer Responsibilities

We will begin our discussion of preinterview responsibilities by focusing on the duties of an interviewer. There are four primary responsibilities of the interviewer prior to the interview: (1) reviewing application material, (2) preparing questions and an interview outline, (3) gathering materials, and (4) beginning on time.

Review Application Material

The interviewer should review a job candidate's application material prior to the interview. Accordingly, you should not use the interview itself to review the application material. Doing so conveys a lack of preparation and respect, and it wastes valuable time that should be used to conduct the interview. Furthermore, as we next discuss, reviewing a job candidate's application material should be done beforehand in order to develop specific questions to ask each individual interviewee.

Prepare Questions and an Interview Outline

The interviewer should prepare a list of questions in advance of the interview. (Various types of interview questions are discussed later in the chapter.) Preparing questions in advance helps ensure that the information desired from the job candidate is elicited. It also helps ensure that the interview will be conducted within the proper time constraints. If multiple job candidates are being interviewed, using common questions will make it easier to compare and contrast them. However, each interview will demand the inclusion of unique questions adapted to each individual interviewee.

These questions should be included in an interview outline, which reminds the interviewer of his or her duties during the various parts of an interview. For instance, as we discuss later, an interviewer should provide the interviewee with a purpose and an agenda at the beginning of an interview and summarize the interview, ask for questions, and preview future action and the schedule among other tasks in the conclusion. Including these tasks in an interview outline will help make sure they are included during the interview. We urge you to be diligent in your creation of interview questions and interview outlines. This task can be the difference between conducting a successful interview and conducting a poor interview.

Gather Materials

The interviewer should gather materials needed for the interview before the interviewee arrives rather than after he or she arrives. Searching for the application material, interview outline, and writing materials for notes—even if these things are close by—indicates a lack of preparation and, consequently, a lack of respect for the interviewee. It also takes up valuable time that should be dedicated to conducting the interview.

Begin on Time

The interviewer should strive to begin the interview on schedule rather than causing a delay. As with failing to gather materials beforehand, making the interviewee wait past the scheduled time is unprofessional and conveys a lack of respect for the interviewee. Avoid scheduling a meeting or another activity that may run long immediately before an interview. If multiple interviews are being conducted during a single day or period, make sure some time is scheduled between them and maintain adherence to the schedules of the interviews themselves. Ideally, there will be enough time prior to an interview to gather materials and review the application material and enough time following an interview to review your performance and evaluate the interviewee.

Photo 15.2 The person in this picture is reviewing application material prior to interviewing a job candidate. What are the other responsibilities of an interviewer prior to the interview? (See page 404.)

Interviewee Responsibilities

An interviewee also has responsibilities prior to the interview. There are a total of seven duties that must be conducted by the interviewee: (1) gathering information, (2) preparing questions, (3) practicing, (4) ensuring a professional personal appearance, (5) bringing materials, (6) arriving on time, and (7) turning off the cell phone.

Gather Information

Prior to an employment interview, an interviewee must gather information about the organization, about the profession, and about himself or herself. Communication professionals have traditionally focused on the need to gather information about the organization, but the latter two areas are just as significant.

Exhibiting knowledge about the organization during the interview will convey proper preparation, enthusiasm for the position, and a desire to become part of the organization. As we discuss later in the chapter, exhibiting knowledge about the organization is a distinguishing characteristic of successful interviewees. Such information may include the organization's history, future plans, challenges, accomplishments, and other characteristics. Exhibiting knowledge about the profession during the interview will also be beneficial. A job candidate will most likely possess knowledge about the profession before gathering information. However, it is especially important that interviewees appear knowledgeable of the latest developments within the profession. Furthermore, addressing such developments in relation to the organization's needs and goals will be especially impressive.

An interviewee should also gather information about himself or herself. Perhaps *gather* is not as appropriate as the term *formulate*. People already possess knowledge and information about themselves, but this information is not necessarily composed in a way that can be clearly articulated. It may not even be clear to them. When it comes to the interview, though, this information needs to be conveyed in a clear and supportive manner. Accordingly, gathering *or* formulating information about oneself must be done in preparation for an interview. Table 15.1 offers some questions to help guide this formulation.

Table 15.1 Formulating Information About Oneself

What are my long-term professional goals? How will they be achieved?

What are my short-term professional goals? How will they be achieved?

What are my greatest achievements? What did I learn from them?

What are my greatest failures? What did I learn from them?

What are my greatest strengths? How am I using them and developing them?

What are my greatest weaknesses? How am I overcoming them?

Why did I choose this profession?

Why do I want this position? How does this position fit with my professional goals?

Why do I want to work for this organization? How does this organization fit with my professional goals?

What professional experiences have made me an ideal candidate for this position?

What education and training have made me an ideal candidate for this position?

What skills make me an ideal candidate for this position?

Prepare Questions

An interviewee should also prepare a list of questions to ask the interviewer concerning the organization and the position. Questions about the organization could surround future goals, organizational structure, perceived challenges and strengths of the organization, organizational culture, and management style. Questions concerning the position could include such topics as experiences of previous employees, history of the position, evaluation of performance, percentage of time devoted to various responsibilities of the position, perceived challenges and opportunities of the position, amount of supervision, and why the position is now available.

There are a few lines of questioning that should be avoided by an interviewee. Questions deemed illegal when asked by an interviewer should not be asked by an interviewee. Asking these questions would not result in legal consequences, but they are just as discriminatory and inappropriate when asked by an interviewee as when asked by an interviewer. (We discuss illegal questions later in this chapter.) Also, an interviewee should not ask questions with answers available on an organization's website or in material already provided by the organization. Asking such questions would suggest, appropriately, a lack of preparation on the part of an interviewee. An interviewee should also avoid asking about salary or benefits. If you are like us, answers to questions about salary and benefits would seem helpful in determining whether or not the position would be accepted if offered. However, most professional cultures deem such questions inappropriate, so it is advisable to not ask them.

Practice

An interviewee should also practice the interview as part of his or her preparation. Compile a list of questions that you might be asked during an interview. (Some of the most common interview questions are discussed later in this chapter.) Once these questions have been compiled, practice answering them aloud. Having an idea about what you might say is not sufficient. Actually articulating your thoughts and hearing the words come out of your mouth will better prepare you for the actual interview. If possible, have someone else play the role of the interviewer and ask you questions (some of which may come from your list and some of which may not). Make the interview situation as complete and as realistic as possible, including arrival at the interview setting, initiating the interview, answering the questions, concluding the interview, and leaving the interview setting. You may even want to dress as you will at the actual interview. Practicing will also enable you to diminish some of those unknown elements of interviewing that often lead to nervousness and anxiety.

College Experience

Many schools have career centers, or similarly named offices, that provide assistance for students when seeking employment. Among their many services, some even conduct mock interviews for practice. We strongly encourage you to seek out such opportunities on your campus.

Professional Personal Appearance

Personal appearance—including clothing, hairstyles, tattoos, jewelry, makeup, and hygiene—is a reflection of how you perceive yourself, how you wish to be perceived by others, and your relationship with others. People make judgments, accurately or not, based on the appearance of others. Accordingly, interviewees should strive to convey credibility and professionalism through their personal appearance, and should appear in a manner consistent with expectations of the interviewer in order to establish relational connections with him or her. Rather than developing a one-size-fits-all model of interview appearance, it is best to dress according to the position for which you are interviewing. The general rule of thumb is dressing one step above how you would generally dress for the position if hired. And, when in doubt, it is always better to be over-dressed rather than underdressed.

Photo 15.3 If an interviewee arrives early for an interview, is it a good idea for him or her to catch up on rest while waiting? (See page 404.)

Arrive on Time

Few other behaviors make a worse impression than arriving late to an interview. Arriving late not only is unprofessional and disrespectful but also may result in decreasing the amount of time available for the interview. Of course, arriving too early might make an interviewee seem overeager. So, we are not suggesting you arrive 2 hours before the interview is scheduled. Planning to arrive 15 minutes early will enable you to be punctual without appearing overly enthusiastic or nervous. If you do happen to arrive early, use that time to freshen up and review your materials.

Bring Materials

Speaking of materials, an interviewee should bring some to the interview. You should plan on bringing (1) additional copies of your résumé, (2) paper and writing utensils, and (3) a list of questions to ask the interviewer. In most situations, these items should be housed within a briefcase or professional-looking folder. Copies of your résumé will allow you to provide the interviewer with an additional copy if necessary and to review specific items with the interviewer if he or she so desires. The paper and writing utensils will allow you to take notes during the interview. The list of questions exhibits preparation and will enable you to remember specific questions you want to ask.

For some people, asking them to bring paper and writing utensils might be like asking them to bring a stone tablet, chisel, and hammer. In other words, it may seem outdated since these people (perhaps you) primarily record items using a laptop computer or PDA (personal digital assistant). At this point, in the majority of workplaces, technological expectations would not include the use of a laptop computer or PDA during an interview. Accordingly, the interviewer may find its use strange and perhaps even unprofessional. However, perceptions of technology are continuously changing (Chapter 9), and the use of these items may be more acceptable in the near future. Furthermore, there may be some organizations and industries in which they are acceptable now. The use of these items may also make you appear technologically savvy and progressive, which could be seen as a bonus by some interviewers. Use your best judgment as to whether a laptop computer or PDA would be appropriate, given the expectations of the interviewer and the identity you wish to convey during the interview.

Turn Off the Cell Phone

Perceptions of technology are continuously changing, but it will be a long time before the ringing of a cell phone is deemed an appropriate occurrence during an employment interview. You should turn off your cell phone completely and keep it out of sight during an interview. Your sole focus should be on the interviewer and the discussion at

Much of what is discussed in this chapter involves face-to-face interviews, but you may also be asked to interview by telephone or webcam. Here are some tips for these types of interviews.

Telephone Interviews

1. Select a quiet place that is free of potential distractions.
2. Do not eat, drink, or chew gum.
3. Even though the interviewer will not see you smile, doing so will come though in your voice.
4. Stand or sit up straight in order to strengthen your voice.
5. Avoid nonfluencies such as *um* and *uh*, since these are even more obvious over the telephone.
6. Have your résumé, notes, and other materials available should you need them.

Webcam Interviews

1. Select a quiet place that is free of potential distractions.
2. Test the camera and speaker prior to the interview.
3. Be aware of what appears in the background and remove anything that could be distracting.
4. Your personal appearance should mirror your appearance for a face-to-face interview.
5. Look directly at the camera, but avoid staring at it, much like you would avoid staring at someone with whom you are talking face-to-face.
6. Remember that the interviewer may be able to see and hear you prior to and immediately following the interview.

hand. We sincerely hope it never happens to you, but if you do forget to turn off your cell phone during an interview and it happens to ring, quickly apologize to the interviewer and turn it off at that time. Do not answer the call—even to tell the person you will call him or her back. Certainly do not carry on a conversation with the person who called. Your professionalism and respect for the interviewer (along with yourself) will be called into question by a ringing cell phone.

Beginning an Employment Interview

Now that the preinterview responsibilities have been accomplished, it is time to begin the interview. When beginning an interview, the participants must (1) greet one another and establish proxemics, (2) negotiate the relational connection and tone of the interview, and (3) establish the purpose and agenda of the interview.

Greeting and Establishing Proxemics

Initial impressions have a tremendous impact on perceptions of another person and whether additional contact is desired. Accordingly, the opening moments are crucial to the success of an interview, especially for an interviewee.

As an interviewee, you must convey respect for an interviewer's space (Chapter 3). If the interview takes place in an office, always knock and wait for permission to enter prior to entering, even if the door is open. Unless directed to do otherwise, address the interviewer using his or her last name and a formal or professional title (Dr., Mr., Ms., Your Holiness). Exchange greetings and introduce yourself, if necessary, while initiating a professional handshake with the interviewer to establish a positive relational connection and to suggest confidence. Shaking hands with a firm grip while looking the other person in the eye has been shown to increase ratings of employment suitability by interviewers (G. L. Stewart, Dustin, Barrick, & Darnold, 2008). Fist bumps or high fives are never appropriate, unless the interviewer is a Wonder Twin or has just completed an incredible athletic feat! Wait for the interviewer to direct you to where you will be positioned during the interview, rather than moving to an area or being seated beforehand.

As an interviewer, strive to make the interviewee feel welcomed and appreciated through your greeting. Initiate a handshake, if the interviewee has not already done so. Prepare in advance where the interviewee will be positioned for the interview and direct him or her to that space accordingly. As we discuss, where you and the interviewee are positioned will impact the relational connection and tone of the interview.

Listen in on Your Life

Recall employment interviews in which you have been either the interviewee or the interviewer. Assess which aspects of the interview went well and which aspects of the interview needed improvement. As you read this chapter, consider how your entire performance could be improved. If you have never participated in an employment interview, ask someone you know who has done so to describe his or her interview experiences to you.

Negotiating Relational Connection and Tone

During most employment interviews, the interviewer possesses more power than the interviewee. The extent of that power distance and the tone of the interview (formal, relaxed, humorous, serious) will be negotiated by the interviewer and interviewee. This negotiation will take place throughout the course of an interview but is often established during its opening moments. Although interviewees are free to attempt to develop whatever relational connection and tone they desire, it is generally best for them to follow the verbal and nonverbal cues of the interviewer, especially if they want the job.

The guidelines offered here are most appropriate in Western cultures. Be certain to keep cultural differences involving space and touch in mind when considering interviews in other cultural contexts.

Verbal cues from an interviewer will inform an interviewee of the desired tone and relationship. If an interviewer asks to be called by his or her first name, that could be an indication of a relatively relaxed interview context and a sense of equality with the interviewee. If an interviewer makes a joke at the beginning of an interview, that might also be an indication of a generally relaxed interview context. Self-disclosure, or perhaps even self-deprecation, may be an indication of a desire for equality. An interviewer may very well verbally announce a desire for a relaxed interview context. If an interviewer does none of these things or does not verbally indicate informality or equality in other ways, he or she probably expects a formal, traditional interview context.

Accompanying nonverbal cues from an interviewer will also inform an interviewee of the desired tone and relationship. Smiling along with other positive nonverbal behaviors will certainly indicate a different tone than would frowning and other negative nonverbal behaviors. Beyond these cues, however, the placement of an interviewee in relation to the interviewer may indicate the degree of formality of the interview and the relational connection the interviewer wishes to develop. For instance, an interviewer seated on one side of a desk and an interviewee seated on the other side would indicate a more formal interview and a less equal relationship. On the other hand, an interviewer seated next to an interviewee, perhaps on chairs positioned at right angles with one another, would indicate a more relaxed interview and a more equal relationship.

Establishing Purpose and Agenda

Establishing the purpose and agenda is the responsibility of the interviewer. The purpose of an employment interview is fairly obvious, but establishing the agenda is especially important. As an interviewer, you should inform the interviewee how long the interview will take place. You may also want to preview the areas of questioning or other features to make an interviewee more comfortable through the partial removal of unknown variables. Doing so also establishes your expectations as an interviewer of how the interview will be conducted.

Don't forget to genuinely smile during your next employment interview. Interviewees with genuine dynamic smiles are evaluated more favorably by interviewers than those with fake smiles or neutral facial expressions (Krumhuber, Manstead, Cosker, Marshall, & Rosin, 2009).

Asking the Questions During an Employment Interview

Now that the interview has begun, it is time to address the matter of questions and answers. We first examine the types of questions that an interviewer can ask during the interview and then examine different styles of questioning. You may be at the point in your professional life where you are more concerned about being an interviewee than an interviewer. However, even if this is the case, you may very well be conducting interviews in the future. Further, knowing what the interviewer is doing will help you immensely as an interviewee.

There are three pairs of question types that may be asked during an interview: (1) primary and secondary, (2) open and closed, and (3) neutral and leading. There also exist different styles of questioning involving the amount of control exerted by the interviewer. As an interviewer, you must also be aware of illegal lines of questioning that must be avoided. We begin our exploration of asking the questions by examining the different types of questions that can be asked.

Primary and Secondary Questions

Prior to an interview, an interviewer will likely have compiled a list of questions covering the primary topics that he or she wishes to discuss with an interviewee. Questions that introduce new topics during an interview are known as **primary questions**. Examples of primary questions include the following:

- What led to your interest in digital storytelling?
- What responsibilities did you have at your last job?
- What experience do you have working with flux capacitors?
- In what ways has your major prepared you for a position like this one?

Interviewee responses to questions will likely lead an interviewer to ask follow-up questions to seek elaboration or further information. These types of questions are known as **secondary questions**, of which there are two main types: probing questions and mirror questions. **Probing questions** are brief statements or words that urge an interviewee to continue or to elaborate on a response such as "Go on," "Uh-huh," and "What else?" **Mirror questions** paraphrase an interviewee's previous response to ensure clarification and to elicit elaboration. For instance, an interviewer may ask, "From what you said, it seems you have previous experience with this product line, but have you had direct experience working in this market?" Additional examples of secondary questions include the following:

- What other aspects did you find most rewarding?
- In what ways?
- Which of those did you most dislike?
- Is that correct?

The best way to distinguish primary and secondary questions is that secondary questions only make sense when preceded by a primary question and subsequent response. Beginning a series of questions with any of the preceding examples would not make any sense.

Open and Closed Questions

The questions asked during an interview will be either open or closed. **Open questions** are those that enable and prompt interviewees to answer in a wide range of ways. Examples of open questions include the following:

- Tell me about your decision to become a Foley artist.
- What led you to volunteer with the Retired Professors Fund?
- Describe a time when you had to work with a group.
- How would you describe your work ethic?

Open questions serve three important functions. First, and most obvious, open questions enable interviewers to gather information about an interviewee. Second, these questions enable an interviewer to assess the communication skills of an interviewee. Third, open questions provide valuable insight into the worldview of an interviewee. Recalling both the presentational nature of communication discussed in Chapter 1 and Kenneth Burke's pentad discussed in Chapter 2, words and stories have meaning beyond that which appears on the surface and provide a glimpse into how people perceive situations, themselves, and others.

Contrary to open questions, **closed questions** are those that limit the range of an interviewee's response. Examples of closed questions include the following:

- Where did you attend college?
- What positions did you hold at your previous company?
- Are you willing to work weekends?
- What was the most difficult aspect of your past job?

Closed questions serve important functions during an interview. Closed questions do not take up as much time as open questions, so they can be especially valuable when time is limited. These questions can also be used to gather specific information about an interviewee. Finally, the answers to closed questions make it relatively easy to compare and contrast candidates for a position. Such evaluations are especially easy to make when dealing with **bipolar questions**, a type of closed question that forces an interviewee to select one of two responses. The answers to bipolar questions are frequently either yes or no. The third example in the preceding list is considered a bipolar question that would be answered with either an affirmative or a negative. Some bipolar questions ask interviewees to select between two presented choices. For instance, an interviewer might ask, "Which do you believe is most important to success at work—hard work or talent?"

Neutral and Leading Questions

When developing questions for an interview, it is best to include neutral questions and to avoid leading questions. **Neutral questions** provide an interviewee with no indication of a preferred way to respond. Examples of neutral questions include the following:

- Why did you select communication studies as a major?
- What do you think of our new product line?
- What are your thoughts on labor unions?
- Describe the qualities of your previous supervisor.

Notice that these examples do not direct an interviewee toward a specific response or one that is obviously preferred by the interviewer. Some people might believe that the second example involving a "new product line" would direct an interviewee toward a favorable response. However, an interviewer may want to determine whether the interviewee is someone who would not be afraid to express opinions and who would be able to improve and enhance the company's products.

Leading questions are those that suggest to an interviewee a preferred way to respond. Examples of these types of questions include the following and are based on those in the preceding list:

- What influenced your incredibly wise decision to major in communication studies?
- You do approve of our new product line, don't you?
- What are some of the problems you see with labor unions?
- What did you like most about your previous supervisor?

In these examples, an interviewer would be guiding an interviewee toward a specific type of answer. (We know that the decision to major in communication studies is obviously incredibly wise, but the first one still counts!) Generally, it is best to avoid leading questions during interviews and not to give interviewees an indication about how they should answer. Still, leading questions are sometimes used to determine whether an interviewee is someone who would hold his or her ground. Once again, the production line example could be a test to determine an interviewee's confidence and ability to voice concerns.

Directive and Nondirective Questioning

The fact that interviews are controlled is one of their characteristics mentioned earlier in this chapter. However, the amount of control exerted during an interview will vary, based especially on the specific goal of an interview. Some types of interviews require great control by the interviewer, while other types of interviews require little control and more flexibility by the interviewer.

Directive interviews are those that are greatly controlled by an interviewer. Questions tend to be closed and perhaps leading (C. J. Stewart & Cash, 2000). A directive interviewer tends to follow a clear line of questioning, deviating only to guide an interviewee back on topic or when wanting an interviewee to elaborate. Watch an attorney cross-examining a witness on *Law & Order* for a good example of a directive interview. The questions are certainly leading, and many tend to be closed. Further, the person being questioned on the stand is not allowed to deviate from the line of questioning, with the attorney being fully in control.

Nondirective interviews, on the other hand, are those in which the direction of the interview is primarily given to the interviewee. A nondirective interviewer generally introduces fairly broad topic areas and then allows an interviewee to "take off" in whatever direction desired. Accordingly, the questions asked tend to be open and neutral (Stewart & Cash, 2000). For an example of a nondirective interview, watch a talk show host interviewing a celebrity. A preinterview of sorts has occurred prior to the program

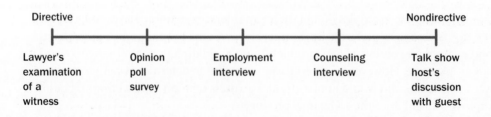

Figure 15.1 A continuum of interviewer control

in which members of the staff have asked what the celebrity would like to talk about and have discussed possible questions the host might ask. During the actual program, the host will ask a general question ("How's the weather?"), knowing the celebrity will take it from there. The examples featured in Figure 15.1 are those offered by Gouran, Wiethoff, and Doelger (1994) and exhibit the range of directive and nondirective interviews.

Avoiding Illegal Questions

When seeking the best candidate for a job, it may seem like a good idea to ask as many questions as possible and to learn as much as possible about someone, including many intricate details of his or her life. However, there are some questions that cannot be asked and for good reason—they are potentially discriminatory. Equal employment opportunity (EEO) laws have been established, in part, to prevent possible discrimination during the hiring process, whether it is done intentionally or unintentionally. Even the most well-intentioned comment or question can be discriminatory; therefore, you should be aware of questions that must be avoided.

Common areas that cannot be discussed with potential employees include age, marital/family status, ethnicity/national origin, religion, affiliations, and disabilities. In some cases, however, otherwise illegal areas of questioning are allowed. Some jobs demand certain abilities or requirements, known as *bona fide occupational qualifications.* For instance, it is illegal to inquire about the age of an applicant unless there is a minimum age requirement for a job or unless the job is one where a retirement age is enforced, such as a commercial airline pilot. Working for a religious organization may require affiliation with that religion. Furthermore, some occupations require certain physical abilities. However, bona fide occupational qualifications that counter discriminatory questions are not as common as you might think, and it is best to avoid areas of potential discrimination. Table 15.2 presents areas to avoid along with examples of illegal and legal questions.

Contrarian Challenge

We—along with the federal government—encourage you to avoid asking illegal questions as part of the interview process. However, aside from instances of bona fide occupational qualifications, are there instances during which asking such questions would be beneficial? Should they be allowed during the interview process?

You can learn more about illegal questions and workers' rights by visiting the Equal Employment Opportunity Commission website at www.eeoc.gov/.

Answering the Questions During an Employment Interview

Having examined the asking of questions during an interview, we can now explore the answering of questions. We first discuss how adjusting the interview frame can greatly

Table 15.2 Avoiding Illegal Questions

Age

Illegal questions

- How old are you?
- What year were you born?

Legal questions

- Are you 21 years old or older, and thereby legally allowed to accept this position if offered?
- Are you under the age of 60 years old, and thereby legally allowed to accept this position if offered?

Marital/family status

Illegal questions

- Are you married or living with a partner?
- Are you pregnant?
- Do you have any children or plan on having children?

Legal questions

- There is a great deal of travel involved with this position. Do you foresee any problems with this requirement?
- Will the long hours required of this job pose any problems for you?
- Would you be willing to relocate if necessary?
- Do you have any responsibilities that may prevent you from meeting the requirements of this position?

Ethnicity/national origin

Illegal questions

- What is your ethnicity?
- Where is your family from?
- Were you born in the United States?
- What is your native language?

Legal questions

- Do you have any language abilities that would be helpful in this position?
- Are you authorized to work in the United States?

Religion

Illegal questions

- Are you religious?
- What religion are you?
- Do you worship regularly at a church/mosque/temple?
- Do you believe in God?

Legal questions

- Are you able to work on Saturday evenings/Sunday mornings, if needed?

Affiliations

Illegal questions

- What clubs or social organizations do you belong to?
- Are you a Republican or a Democrat?
- Are you now or have you ever been a member of the Communist Party?

Legal questions

- Do you belong to any professional organizations that would benefit your ability to perform this job?

Disabilities

Illegal questions

- What is your medical history?
- Do you have any disabilities?
- How would you describe your family's health?
- What resulted in your disability?

Legal questions

- This job requires that a person be able to lift 100 pounds. Would you have any problems fulfilling that requirement?

benefit interviewees. Next, we investigate some of the lessons learned from both successful and unsuccessful interviewees. Then, methods for answering some of the most common interview questions are offered. Finally, we discuss how to answer illegal questions should they be asked during an interview.

Adjusting the Interview Frame

Before you began reading this chapter, you probably had a good idea about what happens during an interview. It is possible that you have been through at least one before. Yet, even if you have not personally experienced an interview, you have likely seen them depicted in movies or television programs and you have likely talked about interviews with people who have experienced them. Therefore, you are well aware of the *frames* surrounding interviews. Frames were introduced in Chapter 1, and we even included interviews as an example. They are basic forms of knowledge that enable people to define a scenario, which in turn helps them determine meaning and understand the roles and expectations of the participants. In the interview frame, one person generally asks a lot of questions and the other one answers them, but you are hopefully recognizing that it is more complex than this description.

How a person frames a situation often dictates what will happen. If a person frames a situation as one in which he or she will play the role of bumbling fool, then the person will likely act like a bumbling fool. Coined by Robert Merton (1957), a **self-fulfilling prophecy** maintains that if someone believes a particular outcome will take place, his or her actions will often lead to its fruition. Accordingly, if you think you will succeed (or fail) at a task, you are more likely to do so, because your actions will likely be those that lead to success (or failure). Therefore, you should always expect to perform well during an interview. Naturally, just because you expect to perform well and end up doing so does not mean that you will get the position you seek. However, it will certainly improve your chances.

We can go a bit deeper with this notion of framing an interview, though. Many interviewees frame an interview as a situation in which they are on trial to determine whether they are capable or worthy of a position and must defend themselves. Anderson and Killenberg (2009, p. 229) have suggested that an interviewee instead frame the interview less threateningly as (1) *an opportunity rather than a test,* (2) *a learning experience rather than a demonstration,* and (3) *a dialogue rather than a monologue.*

You should strive to avoid viewing the interview as a test through which your worthiness as a potential employee, your skills, and your knowledge, along with your value as a human being, are all being called into question. Instead, view the interview as an opportunity to discuss the many ways you could contribute to an organization, to display the skills and knowledge that make you qualified for the position, and, of course, to confirm your value as a human being. In most instances, you would not be asked to interview unless an employer already viewed you as capable of performing the duties of a position and doing so successfully.

Furthermore, do not view the interview merely as a performance in which the above attributes are displayed. Rather, view the interview as an opportunity to learn about yourself. Preparation for and participation in an interview require determining your strengths, weaknesses, and goals, as well as reviewing how your past experiences have brought you to your current place in this world. It is an opportunity to establish personal and professional goals.

Finally, do not view the interview as something that is dominated by one person, while the other person is relegated to a subordinate or immaterial position. Instead, an interview should be viewed as something that is created (transacted) by all participants, who are equally responsible and necessary for its development and who can all potentially gain from the experience. Both an interviewee and an interviewer gain personally and professionally from the interview. They are able to learn about themselves and others; an interviewee has an opportunity to acquire a potentially fulfilling work position, and an interviewer has an opportunity to acquire the services of someone who could potentially improve an organization.

You are hopefully engaged in critical analysis and evaluation as discussed in Chapter 4. If so, you might find the use of a study (Einhorn, 1981) that is roughly 30 years old a bit suspect. We would be the first to tell you to be cautious when coming across apparently dated sources. In this case, however, the age of the source has not diminished the value of its findings. Still, maintain a critical stance when reading this or any book.

Learning From Successful and Unsuccessful Interviewees

Reframing the interview means that an interview can be successful even if you are not offered a position. After all, each interview can be a learning experience that allows you to grow personally and professionally. However, we recognize that such growth does not matter to someone whose primary goals are simply being offered a job and not living out of his or her vehicle. So, for the moment, let's focus on success as being offered a position following an interview.

A great deal can be learned about such success from the people doing the hiring, and this is exactly what was done in a study conducted by Lois Einhorn (1981). As part of this study, the communicative choices of successful and unsuccessful interviewees were examined and categorized. Table 15.3 outlines six key differences between successful and unsuccessful interviewee communication.

Table 15.3 Learning From Successful and Unsuccessful Interviewees
Clear career goals
Successful interviewees are able to clearly articulate their career goals and explain how those goals relate with the position for which they are interviewing.
Unsuccessful interviewees, on the other hand, provide no clear indication of career goals or how those goals might relate to the position for which they are interviewing.
Identification with employers
Successful interviewees mention the organization by name often and exhibit knowledge of the organization.
Unsuccessful interviewees rarely mention the organization by name and demonstrate little to no previous knowledge of the organization.
Support for arguments
Successful interviewees provide illustrations, comparisons and contrasts, statistics, and even testimony from colleagues, supervisors, and instructors.
Unsuccessful interviewees provide little evidence or support material when answering questions.
Participation
Successful interviewees are actively involved in the development of the interview throughout the entire process and spend a great deal of the interview talking.
Unsuccessful interviewees play a passive role in the development of the interview and talk very little during the interview.
Language
Successful interviewees use active, concrete, and positive words along with technical jargon associated with the position.
Unsuccessful interviewees use passive, ambiguous, and negative words while using little or no technical jargon.
Nonverbal delivery
Successful interviewees speak loudly and confidently while also using vocal variety and avoiding nonfluencies. They incorporate meaningful gestures and support interviewer comments with positive nonverbal feedback such as nodding and smiling.
Unsuccessful interviewees speak softly and provide little vocal variety while including longer-than-appropriate pauses. They use few gestures and engage in distracting mannerisms such as rubbing their hands or shaking their legs. They also engage in little or no eye contact with the interviewer.

Answering Common Questions

There are many questions you might be asked during an interview, so it is impossible to cover them all. At the same time, there are a few questions (in various forms and

Photo 15.4 Would keeping her hands clasped throughout the interview improve or diminish this interviewee's chances of being offered the position? (See page 404.)

phrases) that come up more than others. In what follows, we address 10 of the most common questions and discuss some of the best ways to answer them during your interview.

Tell Me a Little About Yourself

When asking you to describe yourself during an interview, the interviewer could not care less about such items as your astrological sign, favorite restaurants, achievements in youth sports, or high school prom theme. An interviewer wants to know how you could benefit the organization, and you should answer accordingly. You should discuss your education, previous work experience, career highlights, and achievements, being sure to emphasize how this information fits the position and would benefit the organization.

What Are Your Greatest Strengths?

This sort of question will almost always arise during an interview in some form or another. Going into the interview, you should have a ready-made list of three or four strengths that you can discuss. Be sure to have concrete examples to support each one and show how these strengths will enable you to succeed at the position.

What Are Your Greatest Weaknesses?

If you say, when asked the preceding question, "Well, I'm pretty lazy, and things would probably start disappearing from around the office if you hired me," you probably will not get the job. It is a responsibility of the interviewee to answer all questions honestly. That being said, you can certainly phrase your responses in a way that minimizes any weaknesses you might mention. Communication professionals often suggest the time-honored tactic of offering a weakness that sounds more like a strength. ("I am such a hard worker that I often get drained by the end of the day. And, I tend to work too many weekends.") However, such responses sound misleading, have become a bit cliché, and do not indicate a genuine ability or interest in recognizing and addressing areas in need of improvement. You may instead want to offer a genuine weakness along with what you are doing to overcome it. ("My Excel skills are in need of development, so I have been taking a night class devoted to the program.") This tactic is especially helpful if there is an obvious skill or ability that you are lacking but that is required for the position or would benefit the position.

What Do You Know About This Organization?

When asked this question, you should exhibit an awareness of such items as the organization's mission, history, growth, and future plans, and perhaps its key personnel. It is a prime opportunity to underscore your enthusiasm for the position and demonstrate how you could benefit the organization based on its present and future endeavors.

Why Do You Want to Work Here?

This question provides another opportunity to reinforce your knowledge of the organization. Likewise, it is another chance for you to discuss your enthusiasm for the position and the organization. Finally, it is a chance to show how your abilities suit the organization and how hiring you would be mutually beneficial. In doing so, you must provide clear, explicit explanations and support for your assertions. For instance, it is not enough to say you could help the organization expand; rather, you must fully explain how you could do so. Remember, the extent of support for arguments is one of the distinguishing characteristics of successful and unsuccessful interviewees.

What Is Your Ideal Job?

This is a tricky question, because you should not necessarily say, "This one"—unless that is true, in which case you should discuss why. At the same time, if you mention a job other than the position for which you are applying, it may appear as if you are uninterested or you plan to move on as soon as something better comes along. Accordingly, you should play it safe and simply *describe* attributes of an ideal position (i.e., meaningful, challenging, fulfilling) while also discussing how the present position meets that description.

Why Do You Want to Leave Your Current Job?

Your current employer may be an idiotic, unprofessional, and unethical ogre who treats you like dirt and may very well eat small children, but you should probably not be that descriptive during an interview. If there were major problems, you may want to address but not dwell on them, taking partial responsibility while discussing what you have learned from the situation. Doing so may be especially wise if the interviewer is possibly aware of these problems. More often than not, however, it is best to focus on the positive attributes of your current (or previous) job, discussing how you have developed professionally and offering legitimate reasons for wanting to leave (i.e., moving to new location, desire for professional growth). One of the reasons interviewers ask this question is to determine whether you will be happy and likely to stay if offered the position in their organization. Therefore, it is wise to discuss how this position better fits your professional goals and desires when compared to your current position.

What Are Your Expectations in Terms of Salary?

This is another very tricky question, because you do not want to put yourself out of reach and you do not want to sell yourself short. Some people suggest placing the question back on the interviewer ("What do people with my experience usually earn here?"), but the question asks for *your* expectations for salary, not his or her expectations. A good way to address this question is by conducting research beforehand to learn the average salaries for a particular position in a particular area. ("Based on the research I have conducted, I would expect the salary to be between $40,000 and $48,000 each year in addition to incentive bonuses.")

Where Do You See Yourself in 5 Years?

This question is usually asked to gauge a person's ambitions, sense of reality, and fit with the company. Your answer will depend, of course, on where you actually want to be in your professional life 5 years from that moment. If you anticipate holding the very position for which you are interviewing, you should say so while also talking about the professional growth that will have taken place and your plans to enhance the organization through that position. If you anticipate moving through the ranks of the organization, your rise to the top should be properly ambitious and realistic. Further, you should stress your plans for professional growth and anticipated contributions to the organization that would justify such advancement. If you anticipate not being with the organization in 5 years, indicating as much may be justifiable if the position is considered short-term. However, you should stress how your time at the organization would be mutually beneficial.

Why Should We Hire You?

When asked this question, you should have a very good answer. If you do not know why the organization should hire you, the interviewer will surely not know either. It may sound as if the interviewer is questioning your abilities, but he or she simply wants to know how you would benefit the organization. Accordingly, this is a perfect opportunity to reinforce your strengths and abilities by discussing how they will benefit the organization.

Dealing With Illegal Questions

We previously discussed illegal questions that should not be asked during an interview, but just because they *should not be* asked does not mean that they *will not be* asked. Sometimes this violation is intentional, while at other times it is unintentional. Whichever the case, you may very well be asked an illegal question while being interviewed for a position. How you deal with such a violation depends on such factors as your perception of its intentionality and, in all honesty, how badly you want the job. However, when it comes to the latter, if such violations occur in the interview process, you may need to seriously question whether the position and the employer are right for you. C. J. Stewart and Cash (2000, pp. 294–295) have offered strategies, outlined in Table 15.4, that can be utilized if you are asked an illegal question during an interview and choose to continue the meeting.

Concluding an Employment Interview

When concluding an employment interview, it is important that positive relational connections among the participants be maintained. Important information needs to be offered during the conclusion of an interview, and certain functions must take place.

Table 15.4 Strategies for Answering Illegal Questions

Tactful refusal

Question:	Where are your parents from?
Response:	I don't believe my parents' places of origin matter for this position.

Direct but brief answer

Question:	How did you injure your leg?
Response:	It was injured while jogging.

Tactful inquiry

Question:	Where do you go to church?
Response:	How does that question pertain to this position?

Neutralize concern

Question:	Do you have any children?
Response	Yes, but they would in no way interfere with my work here.

Exploit the question

Question:	Is English your native language?
Response:	No. My native language is Ket, which would be beneficial for this company since it plans on opening offices in central Siberia next year.

So, let's explore the responsibilities of both interviewers and interviewees during the conclusion of an employment interview.

Interviewer Responsibilities

We will begin with the responsibilities of an interviewer. There are six things an interviewer must do during the conclusion of an interview: (1) provide a wrap-up signal, (2) summarize the interview, (3) ask for questions, (4) preview future actions and schedule, (5) offer thanks, and (6) engage in farewells.

Wrap-Up Signal

Responsibility for controlling an interview rests with the interviewer. Therefore, the interviewer should initiate the conclusion of the interview through a **wrap-up signal**, a phrase indicating the beginning of the conclusion (e.g., "As we near the end of the interview," "As we begin to conclude our discussion"). An interviewer should always allow enough time for both parties to adequately perform their responsibilities of the conclusion, rather than trying to cram everything into the final moments of the interview.

Summarize the Interview

The interviewer should provide a straightforward, relatively brief summary of the information provided by the interviewee during the interview. Doing so will make the

Photo 15.5 Is it the responsibility of the interviewer or the interviewee to bring a formal end to the interview? (See page 404.)

interviewee feel understood and will allow him or her to make any necessary clarifications. Interviewers should be careful not to sound either overly enthusiastic or overly dismissive when summarizing this information. This approach will prevent giving the interviewee either false hope or the feeling of failure.

Ask for Questions

The interviewer should always ask the interviewee for questions about the position and about the organization. The answers to these questions should be truthful and provide an accurate reflection of the position and organization. Hiring someone who has been given false impressions may lead to negative feelings and the need to conduct another search should that person decide that the position and organization are not the good fit he or she was led to believe. The questions asked by an interviewee will also provide additional information about that person, including knowledge and motivations.

Preview Future Actions and Schedule

The interviewer should also provide the interviewee with information pertaining to what will happen next and the schedule for decisions about the position. Interviewers are not required to provide any guarantees or odds of employment, nor do they have to disclose how many other job candidates are being interviewed for the position.

Offer Thanks

It is common to erroneously perceive an employment interview as something an interviewer is doing as a favor or because of some grand benevolence. However, the interview is being conducted, in part, because an interviewer (representing an organization) is in need of someone's professional services. Furthermore, the interviewee has invested time, energy, and emotion into the interview process. Accordingly, sincere thanks for participation in the interview should be offered.

Farewells

Finally, it is the responsibility of an interviewer to formally end the interview by offering a handshake and expressing a professional farewell remark to the interviewee. There is certainly no reason to prolong the formal ending of the interview, but you should avoid making it seem as if you are rushing an interviewee out of the office. Otherwise, positive relational connections that may have been established will be diminished, and an otherwise constructive interview may be viewed negatively.

Interviewee Responsibilities

Along with the interviewer, the interviewee also has responsibilities during the conclusion of an interview. There are five things an interviewee must do during this part of an interview: (1) ask questions, (2) reinforce qualifications and enthusiasm, (3) inquire about the future schedule, (4) offer thanks, and (5) engage in farewells.

Ask Questions

Interviewees should have questions prepared and written out during their preinterview preparations. As part of most interviews, an interviewer will ask whether an interviewee has any questions he or she would like to ask. Not asking any questions would indicate a lack of preparation and enthusiasm, so it is a good idea to have some developed. An interviewer may occasionally fail to provide an interviewer an opportunity to ask questions. If it is clear that the interview is ready to end and that the interviewer does not plan on asking for questions, it is acceptable to politely ask if you may pose a few questions. Remember, an interview is not just about whether an interviewee will be offered a position but also about whether an interviewee will accept the position, if offered.

Reinforce Qualifications and Enthusiasm

An interviewee should also briefly summarize the qualifications that make him or her an ideal candidate, along with underscoring his or her enthusiasm for the position. Doing so will help reinforce strengths and abilities while ensuring that key experiences, education, training, and other information have been conveyed. It may also assist the interviewer in remembering and documenting these items.

Inquire About Schedule (If Not Provided)

The interviewer is responsible for providing an interviewee with a schedule of future contact and decision making. However, it is perfectly acceptable to inquire about this information should an interviewer fail to provide it.

Offer Thanks

As mentioned earlier, an interviewer should be grateful for the time, energy, and emotion that an interviewee has put into the interview process. Likewise, an interviewee should be grateful for the work of an interviewer. As this chapter indicates, there is a lot more work involved when interviewing people for a position, and items such as searching for job candidates (constructing the job announcement, gaining approval through human resources, advertising, reviewing applications) and completing the hiring process (deciding who gets the offer, negotiating compensation, dealing with human resources) are not even addressed. Accordingly, sincere thanks should be offered to the interviewer.

Farewells

The interviewer should initiate the formal end of the interview. An interviewee should follow the lead of the interviewer and not unnecessarily prolong the departure. A smile and professional handshake will help maintain a positive relational connection with the interviewer. As an interviewee, you should keep the Strategic Communication box in mind when making an exit, and remember that your evaluation as a job candidate will continue until you completely leave the interview location.

Postinterview Responsibilities

Just because the interview has been concluded does not mean that the work is done. Both interviewers and interviewees have postinterview responsibilities that are vital to their professional development and that will improve interviewees' chances of being offered the position and help interviewers determine the best candidate for the organization. We begin our discussion with the responsibilities of an interviewer.

Interviewer Responsibilities

Following the interview, an interviewer must complete the following three tasks: (1) review the job candidate, (2) assess his or her personal performance, and (3) contact the interviewee with a final decision about the position.

Assess the Job Candidate

An interviewer should record his or her evaluation of the interviewee along with any additional thoughts or information as soon as possible following the interview. Recording impressions and other relevant information is especially important if many interviews are being conducted, and doing so as soon as possible will reduce the amount of information that is lost with time. Contact with references, documented experience, training, and other background information will be used when making final employment decisions, but information gleaned from the interview is also very important when making such decisions and should be properly documented. Table 15.5 provides areas that can be addressed when evaluating a job candidate following the interview.

Strategic Communication

Remember that both an interviewer and an interviewee are being evaluated at all times, not just when questions are being asked and answered. An interviewee's behaviors prior to and following a meeting can be used when forming judgments about his or her overall character and professionalism. When interviewing, you should avoid any odd behaviors while waiting for the interview to take place or when leaving the interview location, while also remembering to be respectful of the office staff—they generally deserve such respect regardless of whether you are attempting to make a good impression. Also, interview sessions occasionally include tours of buildings, introductions to members of the organization, meals, and transportation to or from the interview location. An interviewee will be evaluated throughout all of these situations, so make sure you remain aware that assessments are being made. Such occasions and activities are also a good opportunity to evaluate the interviewer and determine whether the position or organization is right for you.

Table 15.5 Assessing a Job Candidate

- What are the candidate's strengths?

- What are the candidate's weaknesses?

- How does this candidate compare with other candidates?

- How personable does the candidate seem?

- How would the candidate fit with the organization's climate?

- How knowledgeable about the position and the organization does the candidate seem?

- Are there any concerns about whether the candidate would be successful in this position?

- What additional questions or information about the candidate need to be addressed?

Assess Personal Performance

The interviewer should also assess his or her performance in order to improve both personally and professionally. Focus equally on the positive and negative aspects of the interview performance. Regardless of how much interviewing experience you may possess, there is always room for improvement. Table 15.6 provides a few questions you may pose when evaluating your performance as an interviewer.

Table 15.6 Assessing Performance as Interviewer

- Did I make the interviewee comfortable and establish the desired tone of the interview? How can I improve these aspects of the interview?

- Did my questions elicit the information needed to fully evaluate the job candidate? How can I improve these questions to enhance the quality of the information gained?

- Did I avoid illegal questions?

- What nonverbal communication most benefited my performance? How can I improve my nonverbal communication?

- How well did I listen during the interview? How can I improve my listening?

- Were my responses to the questions posed by the interviewee complete and accurate? In what ways can I improve my responses?

- Did I provide the interviewee with information about future contact and a realistic timetable for decisions about the position?

- Was the interview conducted within the time constraints? Did all portions of the interview receive the appropriate amount of attention? How can I improve my use of time?

Contact Interviewee

The interviewer should ensure that *all* interviewees are contacted about the final decision. This contact should come either personally or through whatever method is used by the organization. Contacting interviewees is a professional courtesy that, unfortunately, is increasingly absent during many job searches. There exists no legitimate excuse for not contacting and acknowledging a job candidate who did not receive an offer. Not contacting job candidates is not only unprofessional but also cruel! Additionally, a person may not have been suited for this position, but he or she may be ideal for a future position. A lack of contact may prevent a well-suited candidate from applying for a future position—for good reason. A person who is mistreated during the interview process may eventually be in a position that could negatively influence the organization. Ultimately, interviewers should simply contact all interviewees because it is the humane thing to do.

Interviewee Responsibilities

An interviewee has three responsibilities following an interview: (1) assess the interview, (2) send a follow-up letter, and (3) avoid irritating the interviewer.

Assess the Interview

Following the interview, an interviewee should develop a candid assessment of his or her performance. The sooner this assessment can be conducted, the fresher the information and the more accurate the recollection. Strive to give equal attention to the aspects of the interview that went well and those that need improvement. Regardless of how you might feel about the interview, even the best interview can be improved, and an awful interview is never as bad as it seems. The best way to improve as an interviewee is through an honest assessment of your performance.

An interviewee should also develop an honest assessment of the position and organization. Developing this assessment will help determine whether the position is something you will accept if offered. It will also increase your understanding about careers and industries for which you are interviewing. Tables 15.7 and 15.8 provide questions to assess your performance, the position, and the organization.

Table 15.7 Assessing Performance as Interviewee

- Which questions were answered well? What made these good answers?
- What questions were not answered well? How can I improve these answers?
- Were my questions appropriate? How can I improve these questions?
- What nonverbal communication most benefited my performance? How can I improve my nonverbal communication?
- How well did I listen during the interview? How can I improve my listening?

Table 15.8 Assessing Position and Organization

- What are the pros and cons of the position?
- What are the pros and cons of the organization?
- How does this position compare with other available positions?
- How does this organization comparé with other organizations?
- How has my understanding and evaluation of this career/profession changed?

Send Follow-Up Letter

An interviewee should also send a letter of thanks following the interview. In addition to thanking the interviewer for his or her time, it is an opportunity to reinforce interest in the position and remind the interviewer of qualifications and experience. If something was not mentioned during the interview, this letter is a good opportunity to add that information. Interviewers occasionally ask for additional information or materials. These items can be included with the letter as well. Do not appear overly confident about the interview, nor should you apologize for a less-than-stellar interview. The letter should also be viewed as a professional correspondence. Accordingly, it should be respectful, well written, and free of grammatical errors. The letter can be handwritten, typed, or e-mailed, although some people disagree about which of these is most appropriate. People and organizations view technology in different ways (Chapter 9), so use your best judgment as to whether it will be deemed an appropriate method of correspondence.

Avoid Irritating the Interviewer

This postinterview requirement may seem obvious, but you should avoid irritating the interviewer by inquiring about the progress of a job search. Do not send the interviewer numerous letters, leave phone messages every hour on the hour, or send the interviewer a Facebook friendship request. We understand that waiting for an employment decision can be excruciatingly painful, but waiting is something that must be done. Irritating the interviewer will in no way increase your chances of being offered the position and will likely hinder those chances. If you have not heard from the interviewer by the time he or she indicated you would be contacted, however, it is acceptable to politely inquire about the status of the position. A number of variables can lead to a delay in the search process, so it is not uncommon, nor is it necessarily a personal affront against you. The organization may very well be busy renting a truck to dump a load of money on your doorstep.

Cover Letters and Résumés

As mentioned at the beginning of the chapter, you will not be invited to an employment interview without a quality cover letter and résumé. Accordingly, we now address some key elements in the construction of these essential items. We begin by discussing the cover letter, which is the tool used to get a potential employer to actually review your résumé.

Cover Letters

A **cover letter** has four purposes: (1) declare interest in the position, (2) provide a summary of qualifications, (3) compel the person to read your résumé, and (4) request an interview. Employers often receive numerous applications for a single position, and quite often application materials are given only slight attention. Therefore, hopeful employees should do everything possible to ensure that their materials stand out from the rest and receive adequate attention. In what follows, we present the key elements of effective cover letters.

Address Letter to Specific Person

Many applicants do not take the time to confirm who will be reading their materials and consequently do not address their cover letter to a specific person. Simply addressing the letter "To Whom It May Concern" will not make your cover letter stand out from the rest and will elicit *little* concern from the receiver. A quick phone call to the organization will likely provide you with the name of the person to whom the letter should be addressed, if it is unavailable in the job announcement/advertisement. Be certain to use the person's last name only and to address the person using his or her proper title.

Case in Point

Evaluate your most recent cover letter and résumé using the guidelines and suggestions offered in this chapter. In what ways could they be improved? If you have never written a cover letter and résumé, prepare them for a fictional position in your career field or for an actual position you wish to obtain. Even if you are not currently seeking employment, it is never too early to develop or update these important career tools.

Identify the Position

Identify the position for which you are applying in the first paragraph of the letter. An organization may have multiple positions available, and you want to ensure that you are being considered for the one you intend. You should also indicate how you discovered the position's availability. Finally, you should display knowledge about and positive regard for the organization. Including this information shows that you have taken the time to learn about the organization and that you view it favorably. Some applicants—especially those applying for hundreds of positions—use form cover letters and change nothing but the name and address of the company. Such form letters will generate less interest than letters in which the applicant appears clearly knowledgeable about the organization and interested in working there.

Summarize Qualifications and Promote Résumé

Summarize the qualifications that make you an ideal fit for the position in the second paragraph. You may discuss such items as your education and training, experiences, special skills, and activities that have prepared you for the position and that will enable you to successfully fulfill the duties of the position. Be sure to emphasize what you can provide for the organization. At the end of this paragraph, you should encourage the reader to refer to your résumé. You can do this by mentioning specific information that can be discovered there or by simply mentioning the additional information that can be discovered through its examination.

Reaffirm Interest and Request an Interview

Reaffirm your interest in the position and request an interview in the final paragraph of the cover letter. You may want to indicate your intention to contact this person in the future ("I will contact you in two weeks to see if you require additional information about my credentials or desire any additional materials"). Another option in the final paragraph is to request a date to meet with the employer. This might be especially appropriate if you are presently located in an area other than the organization and will happen to be visiting that area ("I will be in the Keynsham area June 30–July 5 and would appreciate the opportunity to meet with you during that time to discuss my qualifications in more detail").

Sign Off With Respect and Professionalism

When ending the letter, you should use the term *Sincerely* or *Respectfully* or *Cordially* rather than *Yours Truly* or *Yours Faithfully*, which is too personal when corresponding with someone you likely do not know, and rather than *Best Wishes* or *Cheers*, which is too informal for a professional letter. Use your full name and do not use a nickname. Sign the letter using dark ink in a legible and professional manner, avoiding unnecessary flourish (i.e., no swirly lines at the end or hearts/smiley faces dotting an *i*). You should end the letter properly to ensure the quality of the letter established thus far is maintained.

Résumés

The purpose of a **résumé** is to present your credentials for a position in a clear and concise manner. Employers may spend less than a minute looking at your résumé, so the information included should be not only clear and concise but also positive and obviously appropriate to the position for which you are applying. In what follows, we discuss the key elements of effective résumés.

Name and Contact Information

As with your cover letter, you should use your full name when constructing a résumé and avoid using nicknames. Include the following contact information: (1) address, (2) telephone number, and (3) e-mail address. Include a personal website address only if it is solely professional or academic. If you are a student, you may have both a campus address and telephone number and a permanent address and telephone number. If this is the case, include both your campus contact information and your permanent contact information. As mentioned in Chapter 9, make sure that your e-mail

Cover letters and résumés should be easy for the employer to read. They should be sent flat rather than folded and printed on light-colored paper rather than dark-colored paper. Of course, some employers prefer to receive application material digitally (Schullery, Ickes, & Schullery, 2009). Furthermore, many career networking sites enable applicants to post video résumés. Be sure to read position announcements carefully to determine an employer's preferred method of delivery.

address adheres to professional standards. Someone whose e-mail address begins *Lazy-drunk93* will not receive many interview offers!

Career Objective

Next, you must include your career objective. This objective should be one sentence and never over two sentences. It should also be explicitly tailored to meet the needs of the organization and the position for which you are applying. The employer will be asking himself or herself what you can do for the organization, not what the organization can do for you. A vague statement of interests and a lack of commitment to the organization will not suffice.

Education and Training

Education and training should follow your career objective. List your degrees or training in reverse chronological order so that your most recent (and likely most relevant) information appears first. Listing your high school degree is not necessary if you are presently enrolled in or have completed college. This section should include the following information: (1) degree completion (or expected completion) date along with all majors or minors, (2) college name and location, and (3) awards, honors, or certificates. Use your own best judgment as to whether you should include your grade point average. Some fields may place more importance on this number than others.

Experiences

The experiences section of your résumé will include your employment history and other endeavors such as volunteer work if they happen to be relevant to the position for which you are applying. As with your education history, list your experiences in reverse chronological order. This section should include the following information: (1) position, (2) name of the organization along with location (city and state), (3) dates of employment or service (month and year), and (4) responsibilities and accomplishments. Your responsibilities and accomplishments are especially important in this section, and you should emphasize those that are most applicable to the position you are hoping to receive. These responsibilities and accomplishments are usually not written in complete sentences. Instead, begin each phrase with a verb that implies action (e.g., *spearheaded*, *updated*, *developed*, *increased*).

It has traditionally been suggested that résumés be confined to one page. However, two pages are acceptable if warranted by your credentials. Place the most important information on the front page, because many employers will still not read beyond the first one. Staple the pages together but include your name and a page number on the second page in case they get separated. Even people with many years of experience should be able to synthesize their credentials into two pages, so we suggest never going beyond a two-page limit.

Skills

Next, include the skills that are most relevant to the position for which you are applying. These skills could include abilities in such areas as computer programs, languages, laboratory protocol, machinery, tools, or whatever areas most fit the position. If you possess multiple skills within a particular category, you may wish to use that category as a heading. For instance, you may possess skills in multiple computer programs and include these under a header titled *Computer Skills.*

Activities

When listing activities on your résumé, you should include those most relevant to the position first. However, in this case, feel free to also list activities that are not necessarily related to the position. Of course, you should only include those activities that reflect favorably on you, but listing activities can indicate a well-rounded person with many life experiences from which to draw when dealing with people and participating in organizational life.

FOCUS QUESTIONS REVISITED

1. What are the characteristics of an interview?
Interviews are goal-driven, structured, controlled, and unbalanced and feature questions and answers.

2. What are the types of interviews?
The following are the most common types of interviews: (1) employment interviews, (2) performance interviews, (3) exit interviews, (4) information-gaining interviews, (5) persuasive interviews, (6) problem-solving interviews, and (7) helping interviews.

3. What are the preinterview responsibilities of interviewers and interviewees?
Prior to an interview, an interviewer must review application material, prepare questions and an interview outline, gather material, and ensure the interview begins on time. An interviewee must gather information, prepare questions, practice, bring materials, form a professional personal appearance, and arrive on time.

4. How should a person begin an employment interview?
During the beginning of an interview, participants must greet one another and establish proxemics, begin to negotiate the desired relational connection and tone of the interview, and establish the purpose and agenda of the interview.

5. What types of questions and questioning styles may an interviewer use?
The different types of questions that an interviewer may ask include the following: (1) primary and secondary, (2) open and closed, and (3) neutral and leading. The interviewer may not ask questions that are potentially discriminatory. The type of control exerted by the interview can be either directive or nondirective.

6. How should interviewees respond to questions during an interview?
When answering the questions, interviewees should attempt to adjust the interview frame in order to view the interview as an opportunity, a learning experience, and a dialogue rather than a test, a demonstration, or a monologue. They should also learn from successful interviewees, who articulate clear goals; identify with employers; provide support for arguments; participate in the development of the interview; use active, concrete words; and display dynamic nonverbal communication. Interviewees should be prepared to answer common questions asked during employment interviews and also be prepared should they be asked an illegal question.

7. How should a person conclude an employment interview?
When concluding an employment interview as an interviewer, you should provide a wrap-up signal, summarize the interview, ask for questions, preview future actions and schedule, extend thanks, and offer farewells. When concluding an employment interview as an interviewee, you should ask questions, reinforce qualifications and enthusiasm, inquire about the schedule if it has not been offered, extend thanks, and offer farewells.

8. What are the postinterview responsibilities of interviewers and interviewees?
Following an interview, an interviewer must review the job candidate, assess his or her performance, and contact the interviewee with a final decision about the position. An interviewee must assess the interview, develop a follow-up letter, and avoid irritating the interviewer.

9. What are a cover letter and résumé?
A cover letter declares interest in a position, summarizes qualification, focuses attention on the résumé, and requests an interview. The key features of a cover letter include (1) a focus on a specific person, (2) identification of the position, (3) a summary of qualifications and the promotion of the résumé, (4) a reaffirmation of interest and a request for an interview, and (5) a professional and respectful sign-off. The purpose of a résumé is to present your credentials for a position in a clear and concise manner. The key elements of a résumé include (1) name and contact information, (2) career objective, (3) education and training, (4) experiences, (5) skills, and (6) activities.

KEY CONCEPTS

QUESTIONS TO ASK YOUR FRIENDS

1. Ask a friend to describe his or her most recent employment interview. What aspects of the interview went well? What aspects of the interview needed improvement? Having read this chapter, provide your friend with advice about how to improve his or her performance during interviews.

2. Ask a friend to participate in mock interviews with you. You should alternate between being an interviewer and being an interviewee. Evaluate your performances and pinpoint areas for improvement and development.

3. Ask a friend to review your cover letter and résumé. What suggestions for improvement does he or she make?

MEDIA LINKS

1. Watch an interview conducted on television or available online. What open and closed questions are included? Are the questions mostly neutral or mostly leading? Are secondary questions included? Is this a directive or a nondirective interview?

2. Watch an interview conducted on television or available online with the sound muted. What does the nonverbal communication of the interviewer and interviewee suggest in terms of their relational connection and the tone of the interview? Next, watch the interview with the sound turned on. Does the verbal communication of the interviewer and interviewee match your perceptions of their relational connection and the tone of the interview conveyed nonverbally?

3. Find a clip from *Law & Order* or another fictional program featuring a lawyer questioning a witness. Next, find a clip from a television news program in which someone is being interviewed. Finally, find a clip from a late-night talk show in which a celebrity is being interviewed about his or her latest project. How would you rank these examples in terms of being directive or nondirective? What features caused you to rank them in that order?

ETHICAL ISSUES

1. If an interviewee is not interested in a position and simply desires interview experience, is it ethical for him or her to take part in an interview? If an interviewer already has a job candidate selected for the position, is it ethical for him or her to interview other candidates for the position in order to simply fulfill legal or other requirements?

2. Is it ethical for an interviewee to embellish his or her accomplishments during an interview? Where is the line drawn between describing accomplishments in a positive manner and fabricating these accomplishments?

3. If an interviewer inadvertently asks an illegal question, should he or she be reported to the proper authorities? Is it possible to distinguish purposeful and inadvertent behavior in such situations? Should the consequences be different?

ANSWERS TO PHOTO CAPTIONS

Photo 15.1 ▪ Information-gaining interviews are those through which an interviewer gains information from an interviewee, whereas persuasive interviews are those through which an interviewer attempts to influence the interviewee. The differences between them are not always obvious to the individual being interviewed.

Photo 15.2 ▪ In addition to reviewing a job candidate's application material prior to an interview, an interviewer must also prepare questions and an interview outline, gather materials, and ensure that the interview begins on time—so the person in the photo had better hurry up and finish that coffee!

Photo 15.3 ▪ No. It would not be a good idea for an interviewee to close his or her eyes and nap. Hopefully, you got this one correct. If not, we are glad you now know, and you may want to read closely the Strategic Communication box about interviewees always being evaluated.

Photo 15.4 ▪ Keeping her hands clasped during the interview will likely hinder this interviewee's chances of being offered the position. Successful interviewees tend to incorporate meaningful gestures, whereas unsuccessful interviewees tend to use few gestures, or they engage in distracting mannerisms such as rubbing hands or playing with watches and jewelry.

Photo 15.5 ▪ It is the responsibility of the interviewer to bring a formal end to the interview.

STUDENT STUDY SITE

Visit the study site at **www.sagepub.com/boc2e** for e-flashcards, practice quizzes, journal articles and additional study resources.

REFERENCES

Anderson, R., & Killenberg, G. M. (2009). *Interviewing: Speaking, listening, and learning for professional life.* New York: Oxford University Press.

Einhorn, L. J. (1981). An inner view of the job interview: An investigation of successful communicative behaviors. *Communication Education, 30,* 217–228.

Gouran, D. S., Wiethoff, W. E., & Doelger, J. A. (1994). *Mastering communication* (2nd ed.). Boston: Allyn & Bacon.

Krumhuber, E., Manstead, A. S. R., Cosker, D., Marshall, D., & Rosin, P. L. (2009). Effects of dynamic attributes of smiles in human and synthetic faces: A simulated job interview setting. *Journal of Nonverbal Behavior, 33,* 1–16.

Merton, R. K. (1957). *Social theory and social structure.* Glencoe, IL: Free Press.

Schullery, N. M., Ickes, L., & Schullery, S. E. (2009). Employer preferences for résumés and cover letters. *Business Communication Quarterly, 72,* 153–176.

Stewart, C. J., & Cash, W. B., Jr. (2000). *Interviewing: Principles and practices* (9th ed.). New York: McGraw-Hill.

Stewart, G. L., Dustin, S. L., Barrick, M R., & Darnold, T. C. (2008). Exploring the handshake in employment interviews. *Journal of Applied Psychology, 93,* 1139–1146.

16

Histories of Communication

"The secret to relationships is good communication." "The president is a good speaker." "I was impressed with your communication skills." "Your disorganized presentation was what turned the whole board against the idea! You let us all down. You're fired!" "I really believe she is sincere and I will be voting for her." "Today's graduating students just do not know how to communicate." "I saw on Facebook that 'It's complicated.'" "We regret that we will not be employing you for the position; your communication skills were just not good enough." "I'm interested in Random Play." "I just got a job that is a fast track to the top in management. Will you marry me?" "Fox News just said that the president lied." "Hi!"

We are judged on many occasions and in many circumstances by the way in which we "communicate," yet our dean claims that she does not know what "communication studies" is all about. Is it the same as "media"? Journalism? PR? Speech? Writing? At the everyday level what are the common features of persuading someone to buy your car, become your partner, leave the relationship, not to divorce, take a job with your company, get your instructor to change a grade? What skills and styles of nonverbal behavior are relevant to being friendly, making a complaint, or winning an argument? What is the correct way to critique a movie, write a good (not bad) essay, or devise a good advertising tag line? Is there anything you do that is not communication at some level (even silence can be dumb insolence, resolute bravery in the face of torture, an insult, a refusal to answer a reasonable question...)? Is communication studies about anything specific?

Yes. And no. At the most basic level, communication studies is about the many issues surrounding the transfer of ideas and messages from one person to another, the impact of that exchange, and the outcomes that result. It started with the ancient Greek schools of rhetoric and philosophy, which were often in conflict with one another. Rhetoricians wanted to persuade people; philosophers wanted to find good, honest, truthful arguments. Sometimes dishonest means of persuasion were OK with rhetoricians but not with philosophers (just like lawyers today who want to win the case even if it might involve trickery like a catchy phrase such as "If it does not fit, you must acquit"). Sometimes both approaches ran into the issue that a "good man" (yes) was persuasive because he honestly spoke what he believed, and observers were persuaded by his ethos or good character. But, asked the philosophers, what is a "good" man?

From these ancient disputes and concerns, none of which has really been resolved in the last 2,500 years, communication as a field has evolved and is either relatively new or immensely ancient depending your point of view. The Greeks certainly had no newspapers or TV or Twitter, so media would be restricted to performance of plays, posting of public notices, and government decrees. Are these media as we understand the term? Or is media all about electronics and mass distribution? Anyone who tries to define communication studies must face such questions and the puzzlement of deans. We all know what communication is, but you just try to define it! (Let us know if you succeed. We want to impress our deans).

Communication in Everyday Life makes the point in the first three chapters that communication can be **representational or presentational,** that is, any communication can describe "facts" or can offer a "spin" on those facts. So we must make the point that "history" is also presentational and puts a particular spin on "facts." Any writer injects a set of personal values and perspectives into the history that gets written. Indeed at the end of this chapter, one of the last sections will be about the way in which the influence of women and people of color tends to have been neglected in earlier and more traditional reports of the history of the discipline, and until the last 40 years nobody ever thought that was wrong or odd or inexcusable. It was just a fact.

There is an area of study in communication studies that is devoted to **historiography.** Historiography studies the persuasive effect of writing history in particular ways and the reasons why particular kinds of reports and analyses are offered by specific kinds of authors. For example, why are some topics rather than others picked out for discussion? Why do textbook writers spend longer writing about Andrew Jackson's great Democratization Experiment that extended the franchise to all (white) men, not just to those who owned property? Why do they not give twice that amount of coverage to his similarity to Adolf Hitler with disgusting racist authoritarianism, a dismissive disrespect for the Constitution (towards Chief Justice Marshall), and his "ethnic cleansing" policy about the "Red Stick" Creeks, the Seminole, and the Cherokee? The social and cultural positioning of authors influence what they write. For example, (surprise!) British reports of the American Revolution tend to be different in emphasis from such reports in American history textbooks! Apparently "rebels" and "patriots" can actually be the same people, depending on who is writing about them. Jackson can be represented in a good light to American school children while other audiences find him a human offense and can fully understand why he was the first American president to be the subject of an assassination attempt.

It is also important to notice that the way history is written depends on many contemporary political and social forces that help to influence the report in much the same way that Society's Secret Agents influence our behavior in public (see Chapters 5–9). For example, anyone who wrote a history of communication studies today without mentioning the important contributions made by women and people of color would simply be ignored. Nevertheless, even 25 years ago, such histories were offered as standard reading for students (Delia, 1987), although the author was careful to point out that he was offering only one sort of history of the discipline.

Similarly, the topics that are chosen for research and discussion depend on the historical circumstances in which the research is carried out. During World War II, there was much research about the effects of propaganda, leadership, and attitude change—topics that are particularly relevant in wartime. While those topics are still studied in the field, there is much more emphasis today on studying topics of our time: cultural diversity, the open and honest exchange of information, concealment of family secrets about sexual abuse or alcoholism, and talk about the nature of family communication, when "a family" can take so many forms different from the traditional father, mother, 2.4 children, and a cat (see Chapter 7).

Finally, as we note in several chapters in the book itself, theory develops and changes as scholars labor in their studies. One of the key goals of research is precisely to make these theoretical developments and corrections to our understanding. Along with those developments and changes come differences in perspective. Such changes lead to a reevaluation of what has happened and has been assumed to be true before. Occasionally those studies that have previously been regarded as reliably "classic" are then seen in a new light that makes them less important. In their turn, the replacement "classics" also fade as new approaches and critiques become available. Therefore, the history that is written today will be different from the history that was written 50 years ago and from the history that will be written 50 years from now.

Rather than offering any hope of a definitive history of the discipline, we regard that task as beyond our means and intentions. It is also a theoretical impossibility in the first place. We intend instead to offer at best some histor*ies* of communication studies or at least some ways of understanding how the discipline came to look the way it does (. . . from our point of view!).

Focus Questions

1. What are four traditional areas of communication studies?
2. What are the four major approaches to the study of communication?
3. What is the social scientific approach to communication?
4. What is the interpretivist approach to communication?
5. What is the critical approach to communication?
6. What is the post-modernism approach to communication?

What Is Communication?

Department heads often report that one of their major problems is educating the dean of the college about the exact nature of communication! There is such a large range of curriculum, courses, topics, approaches, and issues that can be included. Yet in order

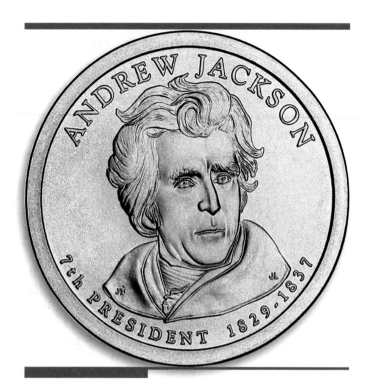

Photo 16.1 What term is used to denote the study of how histories are written, such as the history of Andrew Jackson?

to give any kind of history of communication studies at all, it is necessary to have some idea of what it is that is being reported on. It is instructive to look at the Wikipedia entry for "Communication Studies" to understand the problem (http://en.wikipedia.org/wiki/Communication_studies). You will find from starting at this link and following up the links given on the Wikipedia page, that across the country the following are listed as key topics for communication studies: the sharing of symbols over distances in space and time; face-to-face conversation; speeches to mass media outlets; television broadcasting; how audiences interpret information; political, cultural, economic, and social dimensions of speech and language. According to the Wikipedia site listed here,

> The field is institutionalized under many different names at different universities and in various countries, including "communications," "communication studies," "speech communication," "rhetorical studies," "communications science," "media studies," "communication arts," "mass communication," "media ecology," and sometimes even "mediology." Communication studies often overlaps with academic programs in journalism, film and cinema, radio and television, advertising and public relations and performance studies.

We will come to this later in the chapter when we discuss the different departmental structures and forms of curriculum that are represented as sufficing for a communication studies degree.

Wikipedia (http://en.wikipedia.org/wiki/Communication_studies) goes on to note that

> in the United States, the National Com- munication Association (NCA) recognizes nine distinct but often overlapping sub-disciplines within the broader communication discipline: Communication & Technology; Critical-Cultural; Health; Intercultural-International; Interpersonal-Small Group; Mass Communication; Organizational; Political; and Rhetorical. The International Communication

Association (ICA) recognizes a much larger and evolving list of sections, including among others Communication History; Communication Law and Policy; Ethnicity and Race in Communication; Feminist Scholarship; Gay, Lesbian, Bisexual and Transgender Studies; Global Communication and Social Change; Information Systems; Instructional/ Developmental Communication; Journalism Studies; Language and Social Interaction; Organizational Communication; Philosophy of Communication; Political Communication; Popular Communication; Public Relations; and Visual Communication Studies.

Photo 16.2 In this photo, Thomas Edison demonstrates the phonograph, forerunner (sort of) of the iPod, but much harder to put in your pocket unobtrusively. Why has the study of such technologies been comparatively slow to develop in the discipline of communication?

Um . . . if the two major national/international associations for the discipline cannot agree on what is the subject matter of the discipline, then how can a history of the subject be written? Well obviously it cannot. Histor*ies* can be written and will reflect the biases of authors, but all of them will be based on some established traditions in the discipline that everyone agrees are influential in the formation of the discipline.

Different Traditions in Communication Studies

The Rhetorical Tradition

Many scholars trace the field of communication studies to the work of ancient rhetoricians who taught the art of speaking in public and legal argumentation. To a perhaps surprising extent this took them also into the philosophical implications that came from some of the techniques used in making truthful and persuasive arguments. We may think of some of the key names in rhetoric and public speaking as *philosophers* first (for example, Aristotle, Plato, Socrates). In their times, rhetoric and philosophy were intricately connected with arguments about truth and reality, exaggeration, and persuasion. At the root was the question of the extent to which an orator could legitimately use

Strategic Communication

Students new to the study of rhetoric may not realize the value of the "ancient" writings of Aristotle, Cicero, Plato, Socrates, and others. However, we would encourage you to explore such writings. You will find, as do many students, not only engaging material but also ways to vastly improve your own communication.

what today we would simply call "spin" in order to represent the strongest case and win the argument (the beginnings of the discussion of moral philosophy). Should an orator stick to what is "true" or stray into what may be "persuasive" but perhaps stretch the truth a little? Should attorneys try to win cases by whatever means will work or must they be ethical, truthful, and honest even if it means they lose the case?

A history of the field that begins with this particular strand of the discipline will start normally with the work of the Greek philosophers Plato and Aristotle, and the Roman politician and orator Cicero on rhetoric. All three of these famous thinkers wrote several long and influential papers or books about the nature of rhetoric, some of the philosophical underpinnings of making speeches that persuade, and the difference between truth and exaggeration. Cicero, at least, also wrote about the use of exaggeration for persuasive effects, and was as much concerned with the outcome of speaking as with its style. He is a famous exponent of triple emphasis: "I do not say he is a liar; I do not say he is a thief; I do not say he is a murderer. He is however a very bad man". Listen for these triple structures, even in the speeches of President Obama.

The evolution of the study of rhetoric can be followed through many centuries of discussion about "good people speaking well" until the formal organization of the teachers of speech in the late 1800s. Debate and the teaching of speech were regarded as essential elements of education in that time. No educated person would want to miss out on all the training about how to give speeches to large audiences in the most persuasive fashion, and would naturally study such ancient Greek and Roman orators as part of that education. The connection of "communication" to "community" was regarded as essential to responsible membership of the civic population. A good citizen was expected to be responsibly involved in discussing and debating different ideas in public forums where decisions were taken. It is a little known fact that the three Rs—which today we jokingly assume to mean reading, writing, and 'rithmetic—originally referred to reading, reasoning, and rhetoric.

After many exciting adventures, the study and teaching of speech and debate led to many discussions about the nature of persuasion and rhetoric. It took a turn away from the English departments and high school teachers of speech toward the formation of speech departments at major universities focused solely on the study of persuasive argument and debate. Both of these were regarded as essential elements not only in political life but also in a successful career as a lawyer. Together with the continued interest in the teaching of speech; the study of debate, forensics, and legal arguments; and the analysis of political argument and public advocacy, such departments began to extend their reach to persuasive forms of writing and other media that had arrived on the scene by that time.

From beginnings in the early 1900s, there emerged groups of scholars who created societies that over time turned into what is now the National Communication Association, on the one hand, and the International Communication Association, on the other hand. Both of these organizations hold annual meetings that draw participation of around 7,000 participants, and there is also an honor society (ΛΠΗ—**Lambda Pi Eta**) that takes its name from the three main features of persuasive argument identified by Aristotle: logos, pathos, and ethos. *Logos* refers to the persuasive arrangement of the words in the speech and is the source of the word *logic*, which we expect persuasive and good speeches to follow. *Pathos* refers to the feelings that can be invoked by a speaker in an audience, for example, by telling the tragic story of a suffering child while trying to persuade the audience to adopt a new health care proposal. *Ethos* refers to the character of the speaker and indicates that a person with great character and credibility is more likely to persuade an audience than one with **low credibility**. From ethos we derived the word *ethical*. Sometimes in discussions of persuasion, references are made to a speaker's ethical capabilities, by which is meant their "charisma" rather than their moral habits.

Photo 16.3 Marcus Tullius Cicero, one of the most influential political and philosophical thinkers about rhetoric. Because he spoke openly against Marc Antony, he ended up with his head, hands, and tongue nailed up in a prominent place in the Roman Forum. What topic areas studied by Cicero were obviously not shared with Marc Antony?

Rhetoricians trace their history from these sources through work on speaking to public audiences; from our point of view it is equally important that Plato, Aristotle, and Cicero also wrote famous papers about friendship and the nature of love. Particularly in relation to ethos, ancient rhetoricians believed that establishment of a good relationship with the audience was likely to make speaking more persuasive. For this reason, they wrote papers about the nature of friendship, love, and the way in which these could be engendered— and perhaps even manipulated—by a speaker in a public forum. It is certainly true that speakers who usually try to make themselves more likable and acceptable to a public audience are also more likely to be more persuasive. There is a strong connection between a person's *liking* of a person for a speaker and the possibility that the person will be *persuaded* by the speaker. Persuasiveness, public speaking,

Photo 16.4 Can a relational perspective be applied when speaking to a large group or only when speaking with a friend, romantic partner, or family member?

rhetoric—different in their origins from many points of view from interpersonal communication, nevertheless had a common theme: *relationships*. The rhetorical tradition therefore can be summarized as dealing with **persuasion**. Is all communication "persuasive"? Some would say yes and some no.

Media Studies and Mass Communication

One group that would be likely to say no consists of those who originally started the study of mass media. At first they were very strongly of the opinion that they were studying the distribution of information—that is to say, facts. Take your pick of these two views of the relative influence of different cultures on mass media:

1. "Mass Media incorporates all those mediums through which information is distributed to the masses. These include advertisements, magazines, newspapers, radio, television, and the Internet. Although some media may have originated in the Europe, the mass distribution and development of most mass mediums occurred in the United States" (Sebastian, http://www.associatedcontent.com/article/13499/the_history_of_mass_media_in_america.html?cat=27). (You can tell that this was written before Facebook and Twitter.)

2. "History of mass media can be traced back to the early days of dramas that were performed in various cultures. However, the term Mass Media originated with the print media that was also its first example. The first newspaper was printed in China 868 A.D, but due to the high cost of paper and illiteracy amongst people, it didn't prosper. Regarding the origin of the Mass Media, Europe can boast to be the primary source. It was Johannes Gutenberg, who for the first time printed

a book in a printing press in 1453" (http://www.buzzle.com/articles/history-of-mass-media.html).

Notice that these definitions do not write about communication as persuasion but communication as the distribution of information, even though some of that distribution is advertising, which these days we would count as a persuasive activity.

Media theorists can also claim to have sprung both from psychology and from sociology, as well as from technology as point-to-point telegraph communication was secretively replaced by wireless communication developed between ships in the Department of the Navy in the early 1900s. This latter was a form of communication that does not meet a strict standard of being "mass" communication, but it was not thought of that way in the first place. It was simply a wireless way of transmitting point-to-point signals that did not involve the telegraph. It was only later when the invention of the vacuum tube allowed radio to wireless telephony, replacing the dots and dashes of Morse code with human voices, that its potential as a form of mass communication was eventually realized. It was then the ultimate basis for subsequent development of public radio, the introduction of TV, and now the Internet and all that has followed from it, such as Facebook, Twitter, and IM or text messaging. The telephone—like Facebook, Twitter, and other media—has had an unmistakable effect on relationships and how we think of them.

In the modern world, media use cannot be separated from relationships. Can media really be separated from persuasion?

We saw that rhetoric began with the ancient Greek concern over persuasion but even then a major factor was ethos or the character and likability of a persuader. Likewise, the study of mass communication focused on the speech of "one to many." Advertisers soon became aware of the need for a speaker to be liked (note how many advertisements are presented by well-known, popular actors and sports stars).

Make Your Case

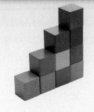

Do you think Facebook and Twitter are an advantage to you or not? What prospects do you see happening in the future—since you too are part of history that is still unfolding—and what would you like the future of communication studies to be?

Size of Audience

We also discover that nowadays—and indeed during its continued development—most people use this developing mass technology for relational purposes. So wherever you start to trace the history of the field of communication, whether from interpersonal, public address, mass communication, or performance—and certainly in studying communication, in everyday life—you end up with . . . relationships.

Mass communication and media studies can be differentiated somewhat, although it is very often the case that they overlap considerably. A broad distinction between mass communication and the kind of communication studied by rhetoricians is the *size of the audience.* Whereas the audience for a rhetorician may be as large as an enormous crowd, limited only by the distance to which the rhetorician's voice can carry, mass communication involves many times more people. Such an audience can be as large as the whole population of a country or the whole audience for a radio or TV program, or even a particular culture that is being assaulted by competing views of events by different sides in a war. During the Spanish-American War, there were significant attempts to influence the Spanish-speaking population that was in dispute, and through whom the United States sought to draw a boundary (Hayes, 2000). Nowadays the audience is the whole world that has access to YouTube.

Effect of Particular Media

Another distinction between rhetoric and media studies, which is where the distinction becomes somewhat blurred, is that media studies may be concerned with the techniques that are used in a particular medium in order to distribute the message. What are the differences between communication through a newspaper article, on a radio program, through TV, or by Twitter?

An essential question at this point is the influence of the medium on the message. Do people communicate differently when they are speaking on a radio program or sending a Twitter message, and are their intentions the same or different? One of the most famous users of radio was President. Franklin Roosevelt, who developed the style of "fireside chat." He attempted to create a friendly and intimate atmosphere by beaming his presidential voice into the living rooms of small groups of listeners clustered around the family radio set. Clearly, although he sought to address the whole of America, he was trying to do so through a familiar, almost intimate, style of speech (Hayes, 2000).

Another question that may be raised is, what counts as a medium that media studies would investigate? In most cases the solution involves distinguishing the effects on mass audiences of printed words, radio, and television. Much more recently scholars have worked on the kinds of television programs that are bought and sold between different nations (Havens, 2003). Some media scholars study the nature of "reality TV" (Andrejevic, 2004) and its consequent implicit approval of the observation of everyday behavior by outside—very often, political—bodies for surveillance (Andrejevic, 2007). Did you realize that in watching others in reality TV shows, you are implicitly accepting the notion of surveillance?

A paradox, then, is that the original uses of much technology were helpful in connecting a particular speaker with a mass audience on more or less intimate terms. Nowadays uses of technology are very often more sinister. They involve the alienation of the individual from the political oligarchy (elite), which tends to have access to enormous amounts of surveillance data about the individuals making up the society. This is particularly true of CMC (computer mediated communication), which is studied by many researchers of mass media. The fact that computers can be used to access other people on Facebook is balanced by the fact that your shopping habits online can be stored by advertisers and retailers and shared between them. Google has developed for reading the content of your messages on Gmail so that next time you use the service, you will find advertisement techniques screen on your that are relevant to the content of your earlier correspondence. Try typing in a random message such as "monkey jungle adventure vegetable service travel egg" and see what sorts of advertisements appear beside your Gmail account next time you use it. When we tried it, we got at least one advertisement for safari travel adventure holidays, and a lot else beside.

The advantages of radio broadcasting were used during the Great Depression to lift the spirits of the American people and give them the message that life would improve and that the nation would come together and get through its troubles. Nowadays many people are concerned that the sponsors of technology are using it in a way that is detrimental to the people. Huge databanks of personal information such as Social Security numbers, credit card numbers, bank details, tax information, phone numbers, and demographic information about age, race, gender, and even sexual orientation are now stored on massive computers. People spend a considerable amount of time and money on antivirus programs designed to protect that information from being stolen from the personal computers that we use.

Equally, the early uses of radio sets did not rely on literacy or nationality. Announcers could be selected to speak clearly and intelligently in regional accents on local stations. In special cases where cities had large populations of recent foreign immigrants, radio stations often transmitted programs in foreign languages, so that the listeners did not even need to speak the same language as their neighbors. On the one hand, radio could be a medium that brought people together in times of depression or crisis. It could therefore create a sense of common purpose or membership or common suffering through which people would survive together. On the other hand, radio could also serve to drive people apart. In both cases, its effects were relational, being either inclusive or exclusive.

The term *broadcasting* was originally derived from agriculture, and referred to the fact that a farmer could cast seeds such as wheat, barley, or corn broadly, carrying the supply of seed in a basket and using a skillful flick of the wrist to spread it across the field, walking up and down several times in different parts of the field in order to complete the job.

TV Broadcasting Versus Cable

It is far too simple to jump from the use of radio broadcasting to other forms of broadcasting and the more recent concept of cable TV without deeper analysis. Nevertheless, the growth of one to the other was most strongly facilitated by the economic underpinning of *advertising*. The social consequences created by the commercial enterprises supported the broadcast networks. The move to cable television—which is seen by some media analysts as a move from broadcasting to "narrowcasting"—depended on people being willing to pay for exclusive access to certain kinds of material and being driven in part by the frantic hope that the advertising would go away. (Good luck.)

The economic underpinnings of all the technological and mass audience communications should never be overlooked. They are a major area of study in those departments and schools that specialize in radio and television, because commercial forces have an influence on the kinds of programs that get shown (Havens, 2003).

Performance

As noted earlier, speech and drama are among the oldest disciplines of study in Western civilization. In many societies, the recitation of favorite long poems memorized by the poet or performer and the presentation of plays in the theater were a demonstration and reinforcement of morality. Many religions place strong emphasis on thorough study or even memorizing of a particular holy book. In some cases, word-perfect memory of sacred texts is to be recited to audiences by those priests and elders who have committed them to memory.

"Soaps" or "soap operas" were originally given that name because they ran during the afternoon when research showed that women were more likely to be watching than men, and it was assumed that "housewives" would be interested in soap, washing powders, and cleaners, the original sponsors of these programs.

In ancient oral cultures, Society's Secret Agents were playwrights and actors who represented, to as large a theater audience as could be accommodated, moral and ethical dilemmas. The point of the play was to show the consequences that befell those people who ignored the instructions of the gods. Early playwrights such as Aeschylus, Sophocles, and Euripides portrayed such critical dilemmas as whether a citizen has the right to disobey civil authority when it tries to enforce essentially unethical activity. For example, in the play *Antigone,* where King Creon denies Antigone the right to bury her brothers who have been killed in a rebellion, the author raises the question of when it is right to resist state authority.

Theater performances allowed the representation of these dilemmas to the citizens in a way that was intended to provoke discussion and debate. In some cases the themes and depictions of these dilemmas were so provocative that they led to the exile of playwrights and poets. For example, the Roman poet Ovid was exiled for his claims about the erotic side of human character and his tendency to write about love at a time when Emperor Augustus was having a strong drive to improve public morals.

Theatrical and poetic performances (therefore and remember that poetry was written to be performed and read out to an audience rather than simply read to oneself), could lead to political and personal sacrifice. In much the same way, many theater writers and performers today aim to provoke and sustain critique of the existing political order. In these cases, theater and performance can be seen as a dramatic attempt to confront dominant political ideologies. This critical aspect of performance is something that is given great attention in communication studies and is an area where resistance to authority is sometimes a key message of a particular communication (see **Critical Approaches**, later this chapter).

At a more personal level of interaction with society, and as demonstrated in Chapter 5 of the hard copy of the book, people *perform* an identity and do so under various forms of constraints and circumstances. This performance is enacted within a set of social cultural boundaries that limit their performance and with which other people "go along" for society to work at all (Goffman, 1959). What we see as individual action is often not so much one person's free will, but is in fact a team effort to construct and maintain everyone's social face and position. Cultures work together in order to sustain the particular performances of individuals. Indeed the chapter on culture (Chapter 8 in *The Basics of Communication* and Chapter 11 in *Communication in Everyday Life*) indicates that speech itself can create "cultures as codes," an increasingly popular topic of study in the discipline itself.

Interpersonal Communication Research

The notion of a separate tradition of communication research might seem strange to some readers. Indeed, it was resisted by many people in the field who felt that *all* scholars do research and that no particular group of such people should be granted exclusive permission to use the name. In fact, it referred more to an area of the field and a style of method than to any attempts to insult scholars in general! Typically communication research was a precursor of interpersonal communication as a distinct field of study and was focused on the interpersonal processes specifically at the dyadic or group level, using social scientific methods. It was the methods, usually derived from psychology or sociology—such as experimental work or use of surveys—that characterized this type of work as a special kind of "research."

Work in this tradition was focused on social influence, attitude change, persuasive messages, and the plans that people created in order to reduce uncertainty in interpersonal relationships. As a second line of attack, the research tried to understand the influence of "opinion leaders" on the way in which ideas were circulated within the community. This area of research became a distinct domain as a rejection of the atheoretical politically driven work of the past, on such topics as propaganda, leadership training, and indoctrination.

Influenced by many studies of persuasion and attitude change in psychology (Hovland, Janis, & Kelley, 1953), many researchers who were interested in persuasion and had received a rhetorical training began to turn from the traditional forms of rhetorical analyses (based on analysis of language and text) for investigating such processes. Instead of conducting textual analyses, they began to try to understand the structure of communicative messages and their influence on outcomes (Miller, 1980; Miller, Boster, Roloff, & Seibold, 1977). They paid particular attention to situational differences, which included different messages arranged in different ways. Such alterations to specific parts of messages could be studied in experimental labs and often drew on social psychological theories and styles of experimental research.

Evolving from a different tradition, media-oriented researchers such as Katz and Lazarsfeld (1955) came upon the mediating role of interpersonal relationships in mass communication almost by accident. Looking at the ways mass communication messages (such as public announcements about health) tended to persuade, these researchers discovered that the effectiveness of the message was influenced by opinion leaders. People such as the local community physician or the town mayor affected the way in which the broader community tended to accept or not accept the messages. It turned out, therefore, that rather than mass messages being, as it were, hypodermically shot into lots of individual minds at once, as some theorists had supposed, individual relationships—and in particular people who were high in ethos—tended to influence majority opinion about the nature of the message. Relationships anybody?

Interpersonal Communication

One of the most influential books deriving from the social scientific and communication research developments within the discipline is Miller and Steinberg (1975), who analyzed the development of interpersonal influence. They placed emphasis on interpersonal interaction as a useful and important part of the field of communication itself.

Looking back from the point of view of 2010, it is hard to believe that people needed to be persuaded that interpersonal influence at the one-to-one level should be a major topic of interest to scholars of communication. However, the influence of Miller and Steinberg in shaping the discipline was both significant and pioneering. People of the old traditional disciplines did not immediately accept that interpersonal communication was a different kind of animal from persuasion of crowds.

Parallel developments in other disciplines began to bring social processes and interpersonal communication to the forefront for particular types of researchers. At the same time, many people with sociological training turned from an interest in mass phenomena to micro sociology and processes in small groups. Often coming at group processes from a different perspective than the interpersonal communication scholars, they were interested in the dynamics of interpersonal interaction in a larger set of people than merely the dyad (two people). Equally, not obsessed with crowds, these scholars began focusing on group decision-making in groups, of about 3 to 15. Others looked at organizational communication, or interactions between groups, on a larger scale.

At first grouped together as IPSG (interpersonal and small group communication), interpersonal communication, small group communication, and organizational communication are now thriving separate elements of the National Communication Association and the International Communication Association. Since most of the topics that are covered in the rest of this book are indicators of the way in which this particular segment of the field has grown, we will not spend too long detailing those particular elements. However it is now possible for people to take seriously

- the question of why families keep information secret,
- the way in which self-disclosure is managed in interaction,
- the nature of everyday simple conversation,
- the strategies for making functional group decisions, and
- the kinds of mechanisms by which people conduct their daily conversations in a way that prospers their relationships.

Also, the nature of "interpersonal communication" began to expand to include a wide variety of topics, recognizing that although both are interpersonal

Contrarian Challenge

We have presented communication studies as having a multifarious and varied past stemming from the intercourse of several different theoretical and social forces. Do you think that makes the discipline sound as if it is something that develops on its own without the interventions of policy makers and special circumstances, or would it all have happened like this anyway?

communication, rebuke is not the same as an assertion of love, and these types of speech do different things and have different characteristics.

Configuration of Communication Departments

From consideration of the different traditions, then, it is worth observing as the next step that there are numerous different configurations for the study of the "communication" curriculum and they are not all theoretically driven. You might think that a degree in communication studies would be the same from each college but surprisingly many different ways exist to teach the subject matter. Some focus only on speech; some on media; some on interpersonal communication, PR, or business skills.

Departments follow their own traditions and experiences in teaching speech and other types of communication. Some structure their curriculum so that you must take at least one course in media criticism, one in interpersonal communication, and one in public speaking. Some are structured so that majors must specialize in an area (say TV and radio production) but take a minor in another (say media criticism).

In some cases the structure of a curriculum and the relative numbers of faculty with a particular specialism in a department can be traced to the historical power of particular individuals or donors who wanted the subject taught their way. On the other hand sometimes the grouping has resulted from the good working relationships between members of different teams. Alternatively, there may be a Department of Speech and a Journalism School separately on the same campus because of long-forgotten disputes between rival faculty, who then folded their tents and took off to set up a separate department. For example, several schools have a Department of Communication Studies that was originally a Department of Speech, Theater, and Performing Arts. In some places, the radio, TV, and film faculty upped and left, leaving the speech faculty in a separate department. There are also instances of previously separate communication departments (speech, interpersonal, organizational) being joined, by a new dean, with the previously separate Journalism and Mass Communication School into one Division of Communication.

These different configurations reflect different historical outgrowths from particular starting points in specific places. They are essential but overlooked contributors to particular historical understandings of the discipline in specific universities and colleges. A more traditional history might suggest that the discipline is driven by ideas and research alone. But this view cannot account for the different formats of communication studies departments around the country. If they had all been subject to the same historical forces and the growth of the same theoretical ideas, they would all look alike. What makes the difference in our historiography is the relevance of the interpersonal relationships between faculty members that led to the many different styles of departments and may not be evident to everyone.

It is important to recognize that many histories of "the discipline" skate over these structural differences in curriculum. Yet some readers of this chapter may be in a Speech Communication Department; some may be in a Speech and Theater Department; some may be in a School of Communication, which includes Journalism and Mass Communication as well as Rhetoric and Speech, possibly Health Communication and also Interpersonal Communication and Media Studies.

Some readers may be taking the basic course offered in their college as an introduction to the skills of good communication. This may involve preparing speeches, giving performances, practicing debate and forensic skills, learning about interpersonal behavior, studying the influence of media on our lives as consumers, or learning about the way in which gender influences our lives. Some departments contain radio, Television, and film, whereas some colleges have communication studies separate from their School of Journalism, as well as being separate from their broadcasting and film departments.

Each of these particular ways of studying communication connects it to the other elements of education background. Each form of department is also the result of historical forces that were powerful in that particular place. In those places that emphasize speech, there may have been particularly strong speech teachers in the early years of the formation of the department. In those places where media studies is more prominent, the department may have started as an outgrowth from the Speech Department as influential professors turned their study of public speech specifically toward speeches made on the radio in the 1920s and 1930s. In many departments, speech and theater have been regarded as inseparable, and dramatic arts often involve many of the skills of rhetorical delivery. In such departments the performative aspects of behavior are emphasized, just as they may be when considering identity and self (see Chapter 5).

Another lessons that we learned in writing the book is that the basic course takes many different forms, and not every institution offers such a course. Some institutions prefer to focus on the speaking parts of communication, some on the writing parts, some on performance, and some on interpersonal behavior.

Listen in on Your Life

Take a thoughtful look at the departments or units around your campus that have *communication* in the title; look in the campus phone directory; search your college website for *communication*. What type of format does your institution have for the study of communication and what do you feel it understands communication to be?

Why Is Communication Important?

All Communication Studies Matter

Many archaeologists trace the development of the human species from the point at which it came to be organized into social groups that must have been able to use symbols and primitive languages in order to cohere and survive (White, 1985). Communication is central to the conduct of society. It is a key method through which a people speaks to its gods and conducts religious ritual, forms the bonds that create boundaries between tribes and nations, and is the basis for most political and economic structuring of different branches of the human race. Likewise, and in turn, communication is affected by society, religion, nationality, ethnicity, and many political and economic forces. This two-way street between society and communication (or between community and communication, two words ultimately derived from the same etymological Latin source) makes the study of communication perhaps one of the most important elements of an educated and involved citizenship.

Because the two-way street is so wide and long, there are enormous numbers of ways in which communication can be defined and studied. Although it is traditional to divide the field along certain particular "fault lines"—such as a supposed distinction between interpersonal communication and mass media, for example, or between rhetoric and media studies—the interconnections between these different aspects are becoming at least as important as the differences. For example, there have been studies of the preference of viewers for pairs of TV newsreaders who appear to like one another (Rubin, Perse, & Powell, 1985), and conversely many people are influenced by their friends to watch or not to watch certain kinds of television programs (see Chapter 13 in "Communication in Everyday Life" or Chapter 10 in "The Basics of Communication"). Equally, the traditional separation of rhetoric and media studies breaks down once one begins to understand that there can be visual rhetorics, pictures, styles, or ideographs that are persuasive in themselves (remember that performers in most ads look beautiful, young, and exciting—that *ethos* helps to persuade you to want to buy what *they* have).

Our underlying theme throughout this book is that most communication contains either an explicit or implicit relational basis. The relational elements of most communication should be brought to the foreground and emphasized rather than taken for granted and overlooked. Accordingly in the discussion that follows, we will make every effort to show the way in which relationships represent some of the major legs of the communication table, upon which many kinds of intellectual feast can be served.

Some Relational Influences on Communication Studies and Their Histories

There has been a historical tide of change in the means of communicating over the last 150 years and has led to new sorts of study in communication studies. Also on that tide are floating many different configurations for studying the issues of communication, each of which may have been influenced by the presence of a particularly strong-willed or far-sighted faculty member at a particular place and time. Strong schools produce smart graduates who get hired and continue the traditions of their personal mentors at new places. Equally, in earlier expansive times in colleges, star faculty may have been hired away from one institution to start a new "center" somewhere else, for which that institution then became famous.

The history of a specific department may stray from the way in which the field is generally conceived to have evolved because of these strong interpersonal influences.

> "Speech and Drama are among the oldest disciplines of study in Western civilization, and they now continue to embrace the effective and creative expression of our ideas in a diversity of situations. Through either discipline comes the opportunity to understand, to assess, and to perform the essential human activity of self expression." (Trinity University, San Antonio, Texas, Department of Speech and Drama Web site—http://www.trinity.edu/departments/speech_and_drama/)

People still argue at conferences about the nature of the field and what it contains. There have, at various points in the history of the national organizations, been strong and vigorous debates about such things as whether to include gender studies in the discipline; whether gay, bisexual, lesbian, and transgender studies merit special attention; and whether communication studies is a "science" or an "art."

Bearing all this in mind, it is important to recognize that the matters that are included in the topic of communication studies have expanded considerably over the years (Peters, 1999). Any history of communication studies can be traced from many different places starting points and origins, depending on your place of interest. Many people note that early cultures were essentially *oral* cultures, where people spoke to one another as citizens. For example, in the Greek and Roman public places, people persuaded in words that were meant to be spoken, and the majority of citizens could neither read nor write. Communication of the group was most often based on the voice, on drama or theatrical performances that both amused the citizens and also taught moral lessons. Poetry was either committed to memory and delivered as a performance or, if written down, was written only to be performed and spoken aloud to an audience.

Many of the most famous orations that have come down to us from Greece and Rome survived because they were recorded in writing for distribution ("mass communication"?) even though originally delivered orally in courts or in public meetings. Contrast this with a literate culture such as our own, where the default expectation is that everyone can both read and write. Therefore, much communication occurs in written form, where your essays are not delivered rhetorically in speech to your instructors but are e-mailed or printed out. In these past, oral cultures, people were either present when a speech was delivered or they must have heard about it from someone else—probably a friend who managed to translate the emphasis and interpret the orator's speech in terms that would be understandable between the two friends.

Once a culture has access to written material, then a greater degree of freedom of ideas and expression becomes available, and the invention of the printing press, coupled with the subsequent increase in literacy led to many social changes, including different branches of religious thought and the resistance to uniformity of ideas that were otherwise preached from the pulpit.

People can reinforce their memories by writing down ideas and looking back at them later. An important speech can be read over again and again, rather than heard only once. The preparation and circulation of pamphlets and ideas can be increased. This can lead, as it did in early America, to political change and to the broadcasting of political messages such as the Declaration of Independence. You did not have to "be there" to have access to the text of the Declaration. It could be read in many voices to many different groups and congregations in different parts of the country simultaneously. However, these groups and congregations are likely to have discussed it amongst themselves and taken particular views of the nature of its content. The discussions would obviously have been face-to-face. The meaning and interpretation of the written text would depend on the friends, neighbors, and strangers who entered into debate about it at the time.

Think of the changes in forms of connection with other people that occur once there is a regular postal service, the electric telegraph, radio, TV, films, Internet, Facebook, Twitter, or cell phones. The nature of communication itself becomes even more complex to comprehend and document. Not only that, but the very complexity makes it so much harder to decide what to include and exclude when writing histories of communication and to decide what are critical events and what are not. However . . . ta daahh . . . unsurprisingly, all of these histories end up, for us, one way or another at the same place: with *relationships* as the underpinning. Almost any technology that you can imagine—starting with cave paintings and ending with Twitter—is eventually turned toward some *social* and *interpersonal* purpose.

Major Perspectives

Given all the above, it is nevertheless possible to identify certain styles of research and scholarship in communication studies and to consider their basic methods of understanding what is happening when communication occurs. Although the summary that follows is necessarily superficial, it does give you some general sense of the different styles of investigation and study that you may come across while reading books on communication or pursuing your own styles of research.

According to Craig (1999) there are seven traditions in the discipline: (1) **rhetorical** (communication as practical discourse); (2) **semiotic** (communication as intersubjective activity mediated by signs); (3) **phenomenological** (communication as experience of others and otherness); (4) **cybernetic** (communication as information processing); (5) **sociopsychological** (expression interaction and influence); (6) **sociocultural** (reproduction of social order); (7) **critical** (communication as discursive reflection).

Craig's major concern was to show that communication studies derives from many sources and has very little common ground. As indicated above, there are many configurations for the discipline in different institutions, and Craig believes that there is no consistent set of topics that is recognized as the sole province of "the field of communication." Frankly, we do not gain our greatest joys from measuring the amount of "turf" that we own in a university. We are quite sure that students do not have any interest in these essentially political academic concerns. Far more important for the purposes of this book is that the reader should have a basic grasp of the different kinds of models and methods that have constituted both the sources and the endpoints of the field.

Having alerted you to Craig's broad list of different traditions, we will therefore focus on a subset of them that have had the most influence. This will help you understand the rest of the chapters as they are about the reception and formation of ideas that communication in everyday life encompasses. The work of women and people of color have been especially important in bringing these key elements of the conduct of everyday life experience to the forefront. We will try to show not only in this chapter, but in the rest of the book the influence that has been exerted by such important scholars as Brenda Allen, Julia T. Wood, Leslie A. Baxter, Stella Ting-Toomey, Judee Burgoon, and many others.

Social Science

The social scientific approach to communication studies is very similar to a social psychological approach. It can involve laboratory experiments, precise measurements of behavior, and an emphasis on statistical numerical analysis of what is studied. It adopts what is known as a **positivist** or **post-positivist** set of assumptions that things exist independently of being perceived, but that beliefs about those objects are relevant (and can differ between individuals—a large area of psychology is devoted to the study of individual differences). The fact that people believe in something does not make it real, but the researcher can learn a considerable amount by paying attention to the way in which people express their beliefs about reality. Particularly in a social organization or in social interaction itself, the beliefs that people have about their behaviors can be at least as important as other influences.

Post-positivists believe in an essentially logically ordered universe that good theory (employing defined units; laws of interactions; propositions; empirical indicators; hypotheses) can at least come close to uncovering. Such theorists believe that there is a Truth with a capital T and that they can uncover it by relentless empirical inquiry. In this kind of social scientific method, the search is for the **causation** that underlies the universal and natural rules that govern our behavior and styles of communication.

Assumptions

Truth exists. Truth is independent of the observer. The same Truth will be discovered by different observers using the same methods. One researcher in one institution using a particular method will discover the same facts about human nature as another researcher in another institution.

Other advantages of the social scientific approach to communication are its ability to establish numerically the patterns of certain types of activity and also, theoretically, to interpret them.

Social science tends to have standardized definitions for terms and usually (but not always) to operationalize those definitions in similar ways. This means that two different social scientists will portray or represent or measure "silence," for example, in the same way—such as a period of five seconds or more when no one is speaking.

Methods

Methods for investigating such approaches to communication can range from direct physiological measures of people's responses to communicative activity (Floyd, 2004) to subjectively filled out questionnaires which ask people to report on their own experiences (Duck, Rutt, Hurst, & Strejc, 1991).

The methods may involve manipulation of subjective experience during the course of a laboratory experiment (Duck, Pond, & Leatham, 1994; Floyd, 2004). They can also be simple assessments of subjective experience or ratings of other people's behaviors using standard measures such as number of occurrences during a fixed period of time. For example, Dindia (1987) measured the numbers of interruptions of men on the one hand and women on the other hand during a fixed period of conversation.

Advantages

There is often strong agreement between different types of social scientist about the way in which assessments can be made of behavior. The statistical analyses take the experimenter or investigator out of the equation and do not allow subjective interference in the interpretation of results.

One of the main advantages of the social scientific approach is its ability to explain the pattern theoretically and to derive new predictions from previous work. On the whole, the goal of social science is to make generalizations or at least to explain as much of the "variance" as possible. ("Variance" is a technical term referring to the variation that happens whenever you measure anything. Scientists wish to be able to explain the amounts of variance to a greater extent than would be possible by using guesswork alone. For example, if they take lots of measurements of people's height and find that there are large variations, they would be pleased if they could find that sex explained a large part of the range of difference, with men on the whole being taller than women on the whole.)

The main advantage of the social scientific approach, however, is its ability to get at cause-effect relationships and ultimately to make predictions about them in untried circumstances.

Disadvantages

Some scholars are skeptical about whether this approach amounts to anything except agreements between an exclusive club of people who share the same vocabulary. Others object that the experimenter imposes too much interpretative restriction on subjects' reports. For example, the construction of a questionnaire re-creates the sorts of questions that the investigator wishes to ask, but these may be the wrong questions. In that case, the investigator will never get to the subjective experience that is intended to be understood.

Equally, there are those people who do not see that generalizations are particularly useful. For example, it may be extremely useful to know that it will rain in the Midwest with a 75% probability, but does that mean I should put my umbrella up when I go out in Iowa City specifically? Also, what is a 75% probability in reality? It sounds very precise, but it's really just another way of guessing that something is a bit more likely to happen than not. A 50% chance of snow means "Toss a coin with 'Heads= Snow' and half the time you'll be right." It's not a forecast. It's a guess dressed up to look precise.

Interpretivist

Interpretivism represents a reaction to the "detached objectivism" of the social scientific approach. The main goal of interpretivists is to understand the experience of the subject, rather than to objectify it. Such scholars turn toward the subjective and personal meanings of individuals and so tend to emphasize *hermeneutics* and *interpretation*. Hermeneutics, particularly as suggested by Gadamer (1981), took the view that communication, whether in written or spoken form, should be understood in the light of the researcher's theoretical knowledge.

Any form of expertise implies a set of expectations based on special knowledge and vocabulary. Therefore any researcher *necessarily interprets* whatever is observed. From this point of view, then, neutrality cannot exist and so no "scientist" can ever be truly objective.

Assumptions

Interpretive theory rejects realism and instead believes in "nominalism" and "subjectivism." In more everyday language, interpretivists believe that it is untrue or irrelevant whether there is such a thing as objective reality out there. What is more important is the interpretations that people make about their experiences. Therefore, interpretivists are less concerned with Truth than with the names (nominalism) and understandings (subjectivism) that people give to their experiences.

Interpretivists go further and reject the notion of any underlying natural global causal laws and the concept of objectivism. In contrast to social scientific approaches, interpretive approaches completely reject the idea that research can ever be value free, and indeed they rejoice in the fact that it is not.

Methods

We can distinguish general interpretive theory from a particular form of interpretive theory that provides a useful method: grounded theory (Glaser & Strauss, 1967). Generally interpretive theory believes that people create their experiences of the world through their communications with one another.

Grounded theory focuses on the methods that can be used by a researcher to make sense of all of this. Grounded theory, as its name suggests, works from the ground up, and focuses on observations grounded in data and developed systematically.

The grounded theorist will set out to observe a topic of interest and will read and reread the data on the expectation that knowledge is local, emergent, and intersubjective (i.e., is created by activity between people). Once a grounded theorist has collected data, a "constant comparison method" is used to compare other data and instances until the researcher is satisfied that a valid interpretation of the data has been obtained, especially if the person who is interpreted (usually called "the native") agrees that the interpretation is correct.

Advantages

Interpretive theory draws to our attention the very fact of the theory-laden nature of observation. Although any observer can claim to be "objective," in fact everyone has their own biases and interpretative styles. Even a social scientist is trained to "observe" data in particular ways.

The very fact of training a person to become an observer of any particular kinds of phenomena is what makes it impossible to be objective, because any comments that are assumed to be objective are in fact derived from the training. People are trained to overlook certain kinds of things and to focus on others. Objectivity is therefore defined in terms of the training that a discipline offers about the objects and concepts that count and those that do not. In essence, interpretivism asks whether it is meaningfully possible to separate the knower and the known.

Many objects or occurrences are not naturally observed, but researchers can be trained to include them in their observations. Physicians get trained not to get emotionally involved with the bodies that they service, but to see them as objects, even if they are also trained to do so humanely—at least these days.

Disadvantages

"Data" is a problematic concept for interpretive theory—even grounded and inductive theory—since the approach assumes that data cannot be found in a value-free fashion.

There is an assumption that anything "real" in the world must reveal itself to an interpreter, and such an interpreter must be trained to recognize it, which makes the whole concept circular rather than a solution.

Another question raised by all styles of approach, but particularly in this one, is the role of ethics in a theory's selection and in the methods of study. Is it more important to have answers to any kinds of questions or to ask and address meaningful questions? What is the role of generativity in theory? Is theory "about" answers, questions, or creating new ideas? If the latter, then what is the ultimate goal of theory? The interpretivist seems to be satisfied with answers only to questions that already exist and does not go searching for new questions to ask.

Finally, interpretivism must be able to answer the question of whether there can be general interpretation of individual understanding. Doesn't the hermeneutical approach presume some general principles for understanding what someone means? Does interpretive work commit us to essentially individual levels of analysis without the possibility of making any general understandings of human nature possible at all?

Critical Approaches

Critical theorists take the interest of interpretivists in naming and meaning one step further. They point out that naming is a crucial act, which gives people the words not only to identify but also to value, to privilege, or to question taken-for-granted aspects of communication.

Critical theory takes as its starting point that certain types of members of society have a greater ability to impose their values and establish the nature of taken-for-granted aspects of society than do other people. Feminist theorists, for example, are particularly concerned to point out the nature of **patriarchy** in society (i.e., the tendency for the order in society to give men more power than women). This type of order is typically the structure of various societies, which, over the course of history, have tended to subjugate women or to give them praise and status for relatively trivial activities as compared to those done by men and valued overall in the society.

The main goal of critical theories is to identify the hidden but powerful structures and practices that create or uphold disadvantage, inequity, or oppression of one subgroup of society by any other.

In particular, critical theorists focus on the struggles between different ideologies, or sets of ideas, that serve to create and organize any society's general understanding of reality. The central issue for most critical theorists is therefore the issue of **power** and how it is used and resisted.

Assumptions

Critical theorists assume that there is an inbuilt structure in society that gives advantage to one set of people rather than another. This oppression and advantage is transacted or exercised through communication as well as through other means. The theorists are therefore interested in the concept of power as an absolute entity, but are particularly concerned over its use to oppress and devalue minority groups. Many critical theorists are allied with the various forms of a feminist critique and therefore are also concerned with exposing the ways in which women's contributions to society are minimized, trivialized, overlooked, or reduced in value (Wood, 2001).

Critical theorists will often use the terms *language* and *voice* to describe the communication that takes place in everyday life. Groups of people can be "given voice" to express their thoughts feelings and experiences and to convey those to others, or can be repressed and refused the opportunity to "be heard." Another concern of some critical theorists is that only certain types of experiences are valued and expressed in a given society precisely because of the power dynamics that are contained in that society. The dominant voice and style is usually referred to as the **hegemonic discourse**—that is to say, the prevailing style of talk and understanding that is current and dominant in the particular society.

Critical scholars are interested in the discovery and encouragement of the expression of other languages and voices than those that are the norm in a particular group.

Methods

The methods used in critical theory are very similar to those used in interpretive approaches. Wood (2001), for example, used face-to-face in-depth interviews with women who had been in violent romantic relationships. She was interested in clarifying the way in which "gender" was represented in their stories. Decisions about the themes that emerged from these stories and interviews were taken according to standard methodology for interpretive techniques, such as repeated reading of the material until themes began to "stand out."

Other work of a critical kind can involve analysis of texts rather than interviews and is intended to bring out and demonstrate the way in which power relationships between people are enacted in writing and speaking. Critical theorists are looking for the hidden undertones of particular forms and styles of speech or writing and in indicating the way in which power dynamics are transacted. West (2007), for example, did an analysis of cookbooks and the way in which they were used both to raise money for pacifist causes and to critique the Vietnam War.

Advantages

Critical theory has been very important in redirecting the thinking of communication scholars away from traditional public topics and more toward the awareness of inequities in society at large.

By encouraging a significantly increased awareness of the way in which scholarship is conducted and the way in which everyday life itself is conducted, critical theorists have encouraged us not only to identify inequalities but also to make it our goal to eradicate them. To the extent that the theorists are able to be successful in this venture, then people in future will participate equally in relationships, and invest and benefit equitably from their communication in everyday life.

Disadvantages

One of the problems faced by critical theory is that, precisely because of its stance, it runs into the criticism that it is giving itself power rather than simply discovering the misuse of power by other people. The nature of the discipline is itself a rhetorical construction of its own disciplinary authority. That is to say, the discipline of communication studies gives itself its own power to comment about the way in which communication is used. Are we really that important? Are the critical theorists giving themselves more of an egotistical buzz when they place themselves at the center of social change than in fact is justified by the way in which they are perceived by others?

A less insulting critique of critical theory is that it should also place some emphasis on the way in which power is accepted. For example, a strict military discipline of the Roman army was not regarded as unreasonable or oppressive, but was voluntarily accepted by the people as part of the system. Compare and contrast the 18th-century British Navy, where resistance to military discipline was much stronger, and where much of the change was brought about by those in charge who were offended by what they saw rather than by those underneath whose refusal of deference caused a change.

Although critical theorists claim that they seek to reform the patriarchal ideologies that give rise to oppression, as well as the asymmetrical rights, opportunities, roles, and so forth, critical theory grounds itself the right to identify the nature of "inequity." What sorts of inequity matter more than others and what is the extent of the possibility of their elimination? Who should decide who makes the call?

Postmodernism

Postmodernists do not believe that there is a capital-T truth that can be represented in the descriptions of scientists. Instead, they see there being different kinds of truths from different points of view, some of which are privileged by the hegemonic discourses identified by the critical theorists. Essentially, however, they believe that science as usually conceived is simply a game where different discourses are employed to credit certain types of viewpoint over others.

Assumptions and Methods

Mumby (1997) has attempted to identify four different systems by which communication scholars play "games of truth" that shape what we count and how we represent topics.

1) **Discourse of representation.** This discourse makes communication essentially a neutral language of description and is the one preferred by the social science perspective described previously. Mumby points out that this outlook regards communication as a simple neutral channel through which messages are conveyed and it overlooks the way in which communication may be a shaper or constituter of power and resources.

2) **Discourse of modernism and interpretivism (understanding)**. In this understanding of communication, the mind does not simply reflect what is out there in nature but contributes something to the understanding of nature itself. Because the thought and reflection involved in this process necessarily involve mediation, this discourse shifts attention from the mind to language and puts reason and truth in dialogues with others, making truth something that is established

by consensus with other people. At the same time, Mumby points out that this discourse misses the ways in which dialogue can be systematically distorted through enmeshment in the structures of power.

3) **Discourse of suspicion**. This form of communicaion is based on the suspicion that there may be three kinds of rationality: (1) technical (money, power, media); (2) practical (oriented to understanding); (3) emancipatory (self-reflection and freedom from the system). From this point of view, truth is created from disagreements ultimately turned into consensus by resolution of antitheses. By considering the different ways in which truth may result from thoughtful examination of power and its reproduction, it is possible for individuals to free themselves from the system of oppression.

4) **Discourse of vulnerability.** This discourse assumes that the individual will always lose any attempt to gain authority and simply looks at how truth claims are based on an individual's position without making any attempt to separate truth and power. From this point of view, all communication is political, and it is necessarily the case that some views of the world are given privilege over others.

Advantages

This perspective does not fall into the trap of thinking that there is only one way to do things that is held exclusively by scientists. Postmodernism recognizes that there are multiple perspectives on different issues and multiple ways in which those issues could be interpreted and understood. Postmodernism is also fully aware of the nature of the influence of power on the construction of knowledge and the fact that society prefers certain types of knowledge to be disseminated and regarded as truth rather than other types of knowledge.

Disadvantages

The postmodernist objects to the privileging of one discourse over another, but this means that it seeks to show ways in which this is done unknowingly; otherwise, no decisions can ever be made between views. The *reductio ad absurdum* of postmodernism is the reflexivity issue: if any theory should explain its own authorship, then postmodernity should be able to explain postmodern theory. However, if its own claims apply also to itself, then its position is untenable because it privileges itself over other views, yet by its own claims should not do so. It is rather similar to the famous ancient Greek paradox: is this statement true or false if spoken by a Cretan—"All Cretans are liars"?

Future of Communication and the Relational Perspective

All history writing tends to assume that everything stops at the present. It also tends to assume that the present is the way that things *should* be, as a result of the "logical unfolding" of developments that are described in the history itself. This method of writing history all too often overlooks the contingencies with which history is faced.

That is to say that there are many occasions in the development of a discipline when things could have gone one way or another. Candidate B could have been elected president of the national society instead of Candidate A and taken it in a different direction. An editor could have decided to reject what subsequently became a key manuscript in a particular line of argument. Assuming that the development of the discipline has not yet finished, then we must assume it is still continuing. If the discipline of communication studies has not evolved to a final state of perfection as a result of previous historical and intellectual forces, then where is it to go next?

If you do not already know our answer to this question, then our lives have not been worthwhile ☺. We are unable to see any area of communication studies to which a relational approach could not be taken. The chapters that are represented in *Basics of Communication* and *Communication in Everyday Life* are the traditional topics studied by undergraduates in communication majors and basic courses nationwide. We have been able to give all of these topics a relational twist and to show that underneath all of these traditional topics lies a presumption about the nature of personal relationships and their influence in everyday life.

The future of the discipline as far as we can see it is to apply our relational approach even more broadly, to media studies, to studies of conflict, to the workplace and organizations, and even to teaching of kindergarten and relational life skills as part of the ordinary school curriculum. We hope that our overview in this chapter and the chapters in the other books convince enough people to take our particular view of the topic and to push forward for those social changes that are necessary to make the future foreseen in this chapter become a reality.

FOCUS QUESTIONS REVISITED

1. What are four traditional areas of communication studies?
Four traditional areas of communication studies include rhetoric, performance, media, and interpersonal.

2. What are the four major approaches to the study of communication?
The four major approaches to the study of communication are social scientific, interpretivist, critical, and post-modernism.

3. What is the social scientific approach to communication?
The social scientific approach believes in the existence of a single reality that causes people to communicate in predictable ways, thereby enabling communication to be studied empirically.

4. What is the interpretivist approach to communication?
The interpretivist approach does not believe that a single reality exists but rather believe that multiple realities and are created symbolically, thereby requiring communication to be studied in a subjective manner.

5. What are critical approaches to communication?

Critical approaches focus on how power is constructed, challenged, and maintained through communication, thereby seeking to identify the hidden but powerful structures and practices that create or uphold disadvantage, inequity, or oppression of one subgroup of society by any other.

6. What is the post-modernism approach to communication?

Post-modernism believe that science as usually conceived a game in which different discourses are employed to credit certain types of viewpoint over others, thereby seeking to identify systems in which communication scholars play "games of truth" that shape what counts as knowledge.

KEY CONCEPTS

Causation   426
Critical approaches to
    communication   418
Cybernetic approaches to
    communication   425
Discourse of representation   431
Discourse of suspicion   432
Discourse of vulnerability   432
Hegemonic discourse   430
Historiography   408
ΛΠΗ—Lambda Pi Eta   413
Low credibility   413
Patriarchy   429
Persuasion   414

Phenomenological approaches to
    communication   425
Positivist or post-positivist
    approaches to communication   425
Power   429
Presentation   408
Representation   408
Rhetorical approaches to
    communication   425
Semiotic approaches to
    communication   425
Socio-cultural approaches to
    Persuasion communication   425
Socio-psychological approaches
    to communication   425

QUESTIONS TO ASK YOUR FRIENDS

1. Ask your friends how they would define communication studies. How do their definitions compare with the histories offered in this chapter?

2. Ask your friends if they believe a single reality, external to human beings, exists or if they believe human beings create their own realities. Would their response make them more of a social scientist or more of an interpretivist?

3. Ask your friends if they would stretch the truth on a first-date assuming it would guarantee the date went well and that they would never be found out. Do they believe it more important to tell the absolute truth even if it means the date will not go well? Many people are on their "best behavior" during a first-date and may not communicate like they normally do so. Do your friends believe this qualifies as being untruthful?

MEDIA LINKS

1. Watch or listen to a news broadcast. What elements of rhetoric can be studied? What elements of media can be studied? What elements of interpersonal communication can be studied? How might a relational perspective of communication be used to bridge these areas of study?

2. Watch or listen to a political speech. What elements of rhetoric can be studied? What elements of media can be studied? What elements of interpersonal communication can be studied? How might a relational perspective of communication be used to bridge these areas of study?

3. Watch a television sitcom. How are male and female characters portrayed? In what ways are traditional gender roles being upheld? Watch carefully! Even when it appears as if traditional gender roles are being challenged, these traditional roles are often being reinforced.

ETHICAL ISSUES

1. The disadvantages of the social scientific method included weather as an example. When a meteorologist predicts a 75% chance of rain, he or she is also predicting a 25% chance that it will not rain. So, the meteorologist is "correct" regardless of whether it rains or does not rain. Is it ethical for a meteorologist to claim a perfect record of prediction? Would it be ethical for a communication scholar to claim absolute knowledge about communicative behavior?

2. Is it ethical for a communication scholar to claim a particular group is wrong because inequality may exist in their communication styles or social structure? A reasonable person would easily point out that unequal treatment based on gender, race, religion, or sexuality is wrong. However, how far should scholars and society for that matter take issues of power? For instance, certain children may be physical stronger than others on the playground. Should measures be taken to ensure that all children, regardless of strength or ability, be somehow placed on equal footing? What if the scenario is moved from the playground to the classroom or workplace?

3. The National Communication Association Credo for Ethical Communication can be found at the following address: http://www.natcom.org/index.asp?bid=514. Do you agree with this credo? Would you add, remove, or alter any of the statements? How might this ethical credo be specifically applied to the study of rhetoric, media, or interpersonal communication?

ANSWERS TO PHOTO CAPTIONS

Photo 16.1 ▪ The term historiography denotes the study of the persuasive effect of writing history, in particular ways and the reasons why particular kinds of reports and analyses are offered by specific kinds of authors.

Photo 16.2 ▪ One reason why the study of such technologies has been comparatively slow to develop in the discipline of communication is that their study can be placed in most if not all subdisciplines. There is a tendency for scholars within subdisciplines to remain segregated from others. Consequently, scholars from separate subdisciplines may not realize they are studying the same area, preventing the sharing of research. An even more dire consequence, sometimes scholars assume the study a topic—such as a relational technology like an iPod—rests within the domain of another subdiscipline, resulting in the topic being overlooked because scholars think other people are studying it or think that the topic is out of their area of expertise. Approaching such topics from a relational perspective could remedy many of these issues.

Photo 16.3 ▪ Cicero and Marc Antony certainly did not share friendship and love. In Cicero's defense, it is difficult to talk about friendship and love with a sharp object through one's tongue.

Photo 16.4 ▪ A relational perspective can be applied to all communicative situations, not just dyadic interactions among people sharing a close, personal relationship.

REFERENCES

Andrejevic, M. (2004). *Reality TV: The work of being watched*. Lanham, MD: Rowman & Littlefield Publishers.

Andrejevic, M. (2007). *iSpy: Surveillance and power in the interactive era*. Lawrence, KS: University Press of Kansas.

Craig, R. (1999). Communication theory as a field. *Communication Theory, 9*, 119–161.

Delia, J. G. (1987). Communication research: A history. In C. R. Berger & S. H. Chaffee (Eds.), *Handbook of communication science* (pp. 20–98). Thousand Oaks, CA: Sage.

Dindia, K. (1987). The effects of sex of subject and sex of partner on interruptions. *Human Communication Research, 13*, 345–371.

Duck, S. W., Pond, K., & Leatham, G. (1994). Loneliness and the evaluation of relational events. *Journal of Social and Personal Relationships, 11*, 235–260.

Duck, S. W., Rutt, D. J., Hurst, M., & Strejc, H. (1991). Some evident truths about conversations in everyday relationships: All communication is not created equal. *Human Communication Research, 18*, 228–267.

Floyd, K. (2004). Introduction to the uses and potential uses of physiological measurement in the study of family communication. *Journal of Family Communication, 4*(3,4), 295–317.

Gadamer, H.-G. (1981). *Reason in the age of science (Frederick Lawrence, Trans.)*. Cambridge, MA: MIT Press.

Glaser, B. G., & Strauss, A. (1967). *Discovery of grounded theory. Strategies for qualitative research*. Mill Valley, CA: Sociology Press.

Glenn, C., Lyday, M. M., & Sharer, W. B. (Eds.). (2004). *Rhetorical education in America*. Tuscaloosa: University of Alabama Press.

Goffman, E. (1959). *Behaviour in public places.* Harmondsworth: Penguin.

Havens, T. J. (2003). Exhibiting global television: On the business and cultural functions of global television Fairs. *Journal of Broadcasting & Electronic Media, 47,* 27–52.

Hayes, J. E. (2000). *Radio nation: Communication, popular culture, and nationalism in Mexico, 1920–1950.* Tucson: University of Arizona Press.

Hovland, C., Janis, I., & Kelley, H. H. (1953). *Communication and persuasion.* New Haven, CT: Yale University Press.

Katz, E., & Lazarsfeld, P. F. (1955). *Personal influence: The part played by people in the flow of mass communication.* Glencoe, IL: Free Press.

Mader, T. F., Rosenfeld, L. W., & Mader, D. C. (1985). The rise and fall of departments. In T. W. Benson (Ed.), *Speech communication in the 20th century* (pp. 321–340). Carbondale: Southern Illinois University.

Miller, G. R. (1980). On being persuaded: Some basic distinctions. In M. E. Roloff & G. R. Miller (Eds.), *Persuasion: New directions in theory and research* (pp. 11–28). Thousand Oaks, CA: Sage.

Miller, G. R., Boster, F. J., Roloff, M., & Seibold, D. (1977). Compliance-gaining message strategies: A typology and some findings concerning the effects of situational differences. *Communication Monographs, 44,* 37–51.

Miller, G. R., & Steinberg, M. (1975). *Between people: A new analysis of interpersonal communication.* Chicago: Science Research Associates.

Mumby, D. K. (1997). Modernism, postmodernism and communication studies: A rereading of an ongoing debate. *Communication Theory, 7*(1), 1–28.

Peters, J. D. (1999). *Speaking in to the air: A history of the idea of communication.* Chicago: University of Chicago Press.

Rogers, E. M. (1994). *A history of communication study: A biographical approach.* New York: Free Press.

Rubin, A. M., Perse, E. M., & Powell, R. A. (1985). Loneliness, parasocial interactions and local TV news viewing. *Human Communication Research, 12,* 155–80.

Trent, J. S. (Ed.). (1998). *Communication: Views from the 21st century.* Boston: Allyn & Bacon.

West, I. (2007). Performing resistance in/from the kitchen: The practice of maternal pacifist politics and La WISP's cookbooks. *Women's Studies in Communication, 30*(3), 358–383.

White, R. (1985). Thoughts on social relationships and language in hominid evolution. *Journal of Social and Personal Relationships, 2*(1), 95–115.

Wood, J. T. (2001). The normalization of violence in heterosexual romantic relationships: Women's narratives of love and violence. *Journal of Social and Personal Relationships, 18,* 239–262.

Glossary

accommodation: when people change their accent, their rate of speech, and even the words they use to indicate a relational connection with the person to whom they are talking

accountable self: the aspect of self that allows other people to morally judge a person's performance

accounts: forms of communication that go beyond the facts and offer justifications, excuses, exonerations, explanations, or accusations

altercasting: how language can impose a certain identity on people (e.g., "Only a *fool* would . . ."; "The *brightest students* will get this chapter without any trouble") and then burden them with the duty to live up to the description, whether positive or negative

anchor position (social judgment theory): represents the preferred or most acceptable position in an argument

appeal to authority (fallacious argument): when a person's authority or credibility in one area is used to support another area

appeal to people (fallacious argument): claims that something is good or beneficial because everyone else agrees with this evaluation (also called *bandwagon appeal*)

appeal to relationships (fallacious argument): when relationships are used to justify certain behaviors and to convince others of their appropriateness

argument against the source (fallacious argument): when the source of a message, rather than the message itself, is attacked (also called *ad hominem* argument)

assimilation effect (social judgment theory): maintains that if someone advocates a position within a person's latitude of acceptance, he or she will view it as closer to his or her anchor position than it really is

asynchronous–communication: communication in which there is a slight or prolonged delay between the message and the response; the interactants must alternate between sending and receiving messages

attending: the second step in the listening process when stimuli are perceived and focused on

attention getter: a device used to draw the audience into a presentation

attitude of reflection (symbolic interactionism): thinking about how you look in other people's eyes, or reflecting on the fact that other people can see you as a social object from their point of view

attitudes: learned predispositions to evaluate something in a positive or negative way that guide people's thinking and behavior

audience involvement (social judgment theory): audience members' recognition of a topic's significance and importance in their lives

autonomy–connectedness: dialectic tension caused by one's desire to retain some independence yet be connected to another person in a relationship

back region: a frame where a social interaction is regarded as not under public scrutiny, so people do not have to present their public face (e.g., when servers are in the kitchen or when there are no customers in a restaurant, the servers do not have to behave with dignity or with respect toward customers—and often do not)

backchannel communication: vocalizations by a listener that give feedback to the speaker to show interest, attention, and/or a willingness to keep listening

balance principle: a principle of speech organization and development that maintains the points of the body of a speech must be relatively equal in scope and importance

base: the number of people, objects, or things included in a study

beliefs: what a person holds to be true or false

bipolar question: a type of closed question that forces an interviewee to select one of two responses

body: part of a speech where an argument is developed and presented and where a relational connection with an audience is maintained

body buffer zone: a kind of imaginary aura around you that you regard as part of yourself and your personal space

brainstorming: a method of gathering and generating ideas, without immediate evaluation; for example, by writing down or calling out everything that comes to mind for a specific (generally brief) period

Burke's pentad: five elements common to all stories and situations: scene, agent, act, agency, and purpose

captive audience: an audience that is required to listen to a presentation

causal pattern: the main points of a speech are arranged according to cause and effect

causation: the relation of cause and effect, most often sought by **positivists** and **post-positivists**

chronemics: the study of use and evaluation of time in interactions

chronological pattern: the main points of a speech are arranged according to their position in a time sequence

claim of conjecture: a claim that something will be true or false in the future

claim of fact: a claim maintaining that something is true or false

claim of policy: a claim maintaining that a course of action should or should not be taken

claim of value: a claim maintaining that something is good or bad, beneficial or detrimental, or another evaluative criterion

clincher statement: a phrase that allows a speaker to end a speech strongly and smoothly

closed questions: questions that limit the range of an interviewee's response (contrast with *open questions*)

co-culture: a smaller group of culture within a larger cultural mass

coded system of meaning: a set of beliefs, a heritage, and a way of being that is transacted in communication

cohesiveness: working in unison

collectivist (culture): subscribing to a belief system that stresses group benefit and the overriding value of working harmoniously rather than individual personal advancement

common purpose: sharing goals and objectives; working toward the same end to achieve a particular result

communication apprehension: fear or anxiety about speaking in public

communication as action: the act of sending messages—whether or not they are received

communication as interaction: an exchange of information between two (or more) individuals

communication as transaction: the construction of shared meanings or understandings between two (or more) individuals

comparison: demonstrating or revealing how things are similar

composition fallacy (fallacious argument): argues that the parts are the same as the whole

composure: the ability to appear calm under pressure

conclusion: part of a speech that reinforces and completes a speech while also reinforcing a relationship with an audience

concrete words: represent tangible objects that can be experienced through sensory channels (touch, taste, smell, hearing, seeing); include real people, objects, actions, and locations

concurrent media use: use of two or more media systems simultaneously

conflict: real or perceived incompatibilities of processes, understandings, and viewpoints between people

conflict-as-destructive culture: a culture based on four assumptions: that conflict is a destructive disturbance of the peace; that the social system should not be adjusted to meet the needs of members, but members should adapt to established values; that confrontations are destructive and ineffective; and that disputants should be disciplined

conflict-as-opportunity culture: a culture based on four assumptions: that conflict is a normal, useful process; that all issues are subject to change through negotiation; that direct confrontation and conciliation are valued; and that conflict is a necessary renegotiation of an implied contract—a redistribution of opportunity, a release of tensions, and a renewal of relationships

connotative meaning: the overtones, implications, or additional meanings associated with a word or an object

consistency: a message is free of internal contradiction and is in harmony with information known to be true

constitutive approach to communication: communication can create or bring into existence something that has not been there before, such as an agreement, a contract, or an identity

content creation: the creation of online material such as social networking pages and blogs as well as the online posting of original pictures, videos, reviews, and comments that serves in the construction of identity

content (representational) listening: obstacle to listening when people focus on the content level of meaning, or literal meaning, rather than the social or relational level of meaning

contrast: demonstrating or revealing how things are different

contrast effect (social judgment theory): maintains that if someone advocates a position within a person's latitude of rejection, he or she will view it as farther from his or her anchor position than it really is

convergence: a person moves toward the style of talk used by the other speaker

conversational hypertext: coded messages within conversation that an informed listener will effortlessly understand

counteractive communication: gets the group back on track by reminding group members of the purposes they are there to serve

cover letter: a letter sent when seeking employment, which has four purposes: (1) declare interest in the position, (2) provide a summary of qualifications, (3) compel the person to read your résumé, and (4) request an interview

critical approaches: treat communication as discursive reflection; that is to say critical theorists point out that naming is a crucial act, which gives people the words not only to identify but also to value, to privilege, or to question taken-for-granted aspects of communication

critical listening: the process of analyzing and evaluating the accuracy, legitimacy, and value of messages

cross-cultural communication: compares the communication styles and patterns of people from very different cultural/social structures, such as nation-states

cultural persuadables: the cultural premises and norms that delineate a range of what may and what must be persuaded (as opposed to certain topics in a society that require no persuasive appeal because the matters are taken for granted)

***cum hoc ergo propter hoc* (fallacious argument)**: argues that if one thing happens at the same time as another, it was caused by the thing with which it coincides; Latin for "with this; therefore, because of this"

cybernetic approaches: assume that communication is simple, somewhat mechanical, information processing, in the way that a computer might process information

decoding: drawing meaning from something you observe

deductive reasoning: using general conclusions, premises, or principles to reach a conclusion about a specific example or instance

definition: the meaning of a word or phrase

demographics: characteristics of a person or an audience that can provide insight into one's knowledge, experiences, interests, needs, attitudes, beliefs, and values

denotative meaning: the identification of something by pointing it out ("That is a cat")

descriptive language: provides the audience with a clearer picture of what is discussed by *describing* it in more detail

Devil terms: powerfully evocative terms viewed negatively in a society (see *God terms*)

dialectic tension: occurs whenever one is in two minds about something because one feels a simultaneous pull in two directions

directive interviews: interviews that are greatly controlled by an interviewer

discourse of representation: makes communication essentially a neutral language of description and is the one preferred by the "social science perspective"

discourse of suspicion: from this point of view, truth is created from disagreements ultimately turned into consensus by resolution of antitheses

discourse of vulnerability: assumes that individuals are relatively powerless and it examines truth claims as based on an individual's position in a power structure

disruptive communication: diverts a group from its goals and takes it down side alleys

distracting mannerisms: bodily movements that allow a person to discharge nervous energy but that serve no actual purpose in a presentation and often divert attention away from the message

divergence: a talker moves away from another's style of speech to make a relational point, such as establishing dislike or superiority

division fallacy (fallacious argument): argues the whole is the same as its parts

dyadic process: part of the process of breakdown of relationships that involves a confrontation with a partner and the open discussion of a problem with a relationship

dynamic: elements of nonverbal communication that are changeable during interaction (e.g., facial expression, posture, gesturing; contrast with *static*)

dynamism: a secondary dimension of credibility referring to being energetic and enthusiastic

egocentric listening: obstacle to listening when people focus more on their message and self-presentation than on the message of the other person involved in an interaction

elimination pattern: offers a series of solutions to a problem and then systematically eliminates each one until the solution remaining is the one that the speaker supports

emoticons: text-based symbols used to express emotions online, often to alleviate problems associated with a lack of nonverbal cues

employment interviews: interviews in which a potential employer interviews a potential employee

encoding: putting feelings into behavior through nonverbal communication

engaged listening: making a personal relational connection with the source of a message that results from the source and the receiver actively working together to create shared meaning and understanding

enthymeme: a syllogism that excludes one or two of its three components (see *syllogism*)

environmental distraction: obstacle to listening that results from the physical location where listening takes place

equivocation (fallacious argument): relies on the ambiguousness of language to make an argument

essential function of talk: a function of talk that makes the relationship real and talks it into being,

often by using coupling references or making assumptions that the relationship exists

ethnocentric bias: believing that the way one's own culture does things is the right and only way to do them

ethos: the use of speaker credibility to impact an audience

evoke (purpose): to generate an emotion from the audience

examples: specific cases used to represent a larger whole to clarify or explain something

exit interviews: interviews that occur when a person chooses to leave a place of employment

experiential superiority: obstacle to listening when people fail to fully listen to someone else because they believe that they possess more or superior knowledge and experience than the other person

expert testimony: testimony that comes from someone with special training, instruction, or knowledge in a particular area

expository speech: a speech providing the audience with a detailed or in-depth review or analysis of an object, a creation, a place, a person, a concept, or an event

extemporaneous delivery: the use of minimal notes, generally recommended as the way to achieve a natural and conversational delivery while ensuring the accuracy of ideas

facework: the management of people's dignity or self-respect, known as "face"

facts: provable or documented truths that can be used as evidence to support claims

factual diversion: obstacle to listening that occurs when so much emphasis is placed on attending to every detail of a message that the main point becomes lost

fallacious argument: an argument that appears legitimate but is actually based on faulty reasoning or insufficient evidence

false alternatives (fallacious argument): occurs when only two options are provided, one of which is generally presented as the poor choice or one that should be avoided

formal power: that which is formally allocated by a system or group to particular people (e.g., bosses, the police, school principals; compare with *informal power*)

frames: basic forms of knowledge that provide a definition of a scenario, either because both people agree on the nature of the situation or because the cultural assumptions built into the interaction and the previous relational context of talk give them a clue

front region: a place where a social interaction is regarded as under public scrutiny, so people have to be on their best behavior or acting out their professional roles or intended "face" (e.g., the restaurant, where servers have to behave with dignity and with respect toward customers)

general purpose: the basic objective a speaker wishes to achieve

given belief: a belief that the majority of people in an audience will view as either true or false

God terms: powerfully evocative terms that are viewed positively in a society (see *Devil terms*)

grave dressing process: part of the breakdown of relationships that consists of creating the story of why a relationship died and erecting a metaphorical tombstone that summarizes its main events and features from its birth to its death

group culture: the set of expectations and practices that a group develops to make itself distinctive from other groups and to give its members a sense of exclusive membership (e.g., dress code, specialized language, particular rituals)

group norms: rules and procedures that occur in a group but not necessarily outside it and that are enforced by the use of power or rules for behavior

group sanctions: punishments for "stepping out of line," speaking out of turn, or failing to accept the ruling of the chair or leader

guidance principle: a principle of speech organization and development that maintains a speaker must guide and direct the audience throughout the entire speech

haptics: the study of the specific nonverbal behaviors involving touch

hasty generalization (fallacious argument): when a conclusion is based on a single occurrence or insufficient data or sample size

hearing: the passive physiological act of receiving sound that takes place when sound waves hit a person's eardrums

hegemonic discourse: the prevailing style of talk and understanding current and dominant in the particular society. Typically it favors the way things presently are, and also serves men and their interests

helping interviews: interviews conducted by someone with expertise in a given area and whose services are engaged by someone in need of advice

high code: a formal, grammatical, and very correct—often "official"—way of talking

high-context culture: a culture that places a great deal of emphasis on the total environment (context) where speech and interaction take place, especially on the relationships between the speakers rather than just on what they say (see *low-context culture*)

historiography: studies the *persuasive or rhetorical* effect of writing history in particular ways, from particular standpoints. It considers carefully the reasons why particular kinds of reports and analyses are offered by specific kinds of authors

how-to speech: describes the procedure or methods through which something is accomplished with the expectation that the audience will be able to perform the process

hypothetical illustrations: fabricated illustrations using typical characteristics to describe particular situations, objects, or people, as well as illustrations describing what could happen in the future

identity: a person's uniqueness, represented by descriptions, a self-concept, inner thoughts, and performances, that is symbolized in interactions with other people and presented for their assessment and moral evaluation

illustrations: examples offered in an extended narrative form

immediacy: linguistic inclusion (e.g., *let's, we, us*)

indexical function of talk: demonstrates or indicates the nature of the relationship between speakers

individual inventory: a listing of a person's preferences, likes, dislikes, and experiences that can be used when selecting a topic

individualist: one who subscribes to a belief system that focuses on the individual person and his or her personal dreams, goals and achievements, and right to make choices

inductive reasoning: deriving a general conclusion based on specific evidence, examples, or instances

inform (purpose): to develop audience understanding of a topic through definition, clarification, demonstration, or explanation of a process

informal power: operates through relationships and individual reputations without formal status

(e.g., someone may not actually be the boss but might exert more influence on other workers by being highly respected; compare with *formal power*)

information-gaining interviews: interviews in which a person solicits information from another person

inspiring: a secondary dimension of credibility referring to the ability to instill enthusiasm in others

instrumental function of talk: when what is said brings about a goal that you have in mind for the relationship, and talk is the means or instrument by which it is accomplished (e.g., asking someone on a date or to come with you to a party)

intentionality: a basic assumption in communication studies that messages indicate somebody's intentions or that they are produced intentionally or in a way that gives insight, at the very least, into the sender's mental processes

intercultural communication: examines how people from different cultural/social structures speak to one another and what difficulties or conflicts they encounter, over and above the different languages they speak

interdependence: the reliance of each member of a team or group on the other members, making their outcomes dependent on the collaboration and interrelated performance of all members (e.g., a football team dividing up the jobs of throwing, catching, and blocking)

interpreting: the third step in the listening process when meaning is assigned to sounds and symbolic activity

interview: a goal-driven transaction characterized by questions and answers, clear structure, control, and imbalance

intrapsychic process: part of the process of breakdown of a relationship where an individual reflects on the strengths and weaknesses of a relationship and begins to consider the possibility of ending it

introduction: part of a speech that lays the foundation for the body and establishes a positive relational connection with an audience

kinesics: the study of movements that take place during the course of an interaction

labeling: naming an object or person with a label that the object or person has to live up to

ΛΠΗ **Lambda Pi Eta**: an honor society for communication studies that takes its acronym from three elements of persuasive argument identified by Aristotle: logos (word), pathos (feeling), and ethos (character of speaker)

langue: the formal grammatical structure of language (contrast with *parole*)

latitude of acceptance (social judgment theory): positions in an argument that an audience deems acceptable

latitude of noncommitment (social judgment theory): positions in an argument that an audience neither wholly accepts nor wholly rejects

latitude of rejection (social judgment theory): positions in an argument that an audience deems unacceptable

lay testimony: testimony that comes from someone without expertise in a particular area but who possesses experience in that area

leadership: the formal position where a specific person has power over the others in the group and is given the responsibility of leading its activities

leading questions: questions that suggest to an interviewee a preferred way to respond (contrast with *neutral questions*)

leakage: unintentional betrayal of internal feelings through nonverbal communication

listening: the active process of receiving, attending to, interpreting, and responding to symbolic activity

logos: the use of logic or reasoning to impact an audience

low code: an informal and often ungrammatical way of talking

low-context culture: assumes that the message itself means everything, and it is much more important to have a well-structured argument or a well-delivered presentation than it is to be a member of the royal family or a cousin of the person listening (see *high-context culture*)

low credibility: a speaker has low credibility when he or she is disbelieved or does not carry persuasive weight or does not seem "warranted" to make the claims that he or she makes

main points: statements that directly support or develop a thesis

manuscript delivery: reading from a complete manuscript of a speech

mean: the average number (i.e., the *total* of scores divided by the *number* of scores that were added together to make the total)

meaning: what a symbol represents

media equation: people use the same social rules and expectations when interacting with technology as they do with other people

media generations: generations that are differentiated by unique media grammar and media consciousness based on the technological environment in which they are born

media literacy: the learned ability to access, interpret, and evaluate media products

media profile: a compilation of a person's media preferences and general use of media

median: the number that rests in the middle of all the other numbers, where half of the numbers are less than this number, and the other half are more than this number

medium: means through which a message is conveyed

medium distraction: obstacle to listening that results from limitations or problems inherent in certain media and technology, such as mobile phones or Internet connections

memorized delivery: a speech that has been committed to memory and is delivered without the use of a manuscript or any notes whatsoever

message complexity: obstacle to listening when a person finds a message so complex or confusing that he or she stops listening

microcoordination: the unique management of social interaction made possible through cell phones

mirror questions (secondary questions): questions that paraphrase an interviewee's previous response to ensure clarification and to elicit elaboration

mode: the number that occurs most often in a set of numbers

monochronic culture: a culture that views time as a valuable commodity and punctuality as very important

moral accountability: people are held morally accountable for their actions, statements, or claims and have to explain them as legitimate or reasonable to other people

naming: distinguishing items from other items for which people also have (different) words

narrative: any organized story, report, or talk that has a plot, an argument, or a theme and in which speakers both relate facts and arrange the story in a way that provides an account, an explanation, or a conclusion

narrowcasting: tendency to focus media products on specific audience members connected by a common bond

negative face wants: the desire not to be imposed upon or treated as inferior (contrast with *positive face wants*)

neutral questions: questions that provide an interviewee with no indication of a preferred way to respond (contrast with *leading questions*)

nondirective interviews: interviews in which the direction of the interview is primarily given to the interviewee

nonfluencies: meaningless vocal fillers that distract from a presentation

norm of reciprocity: if one person says something self-disclosing to another person in everyday life, that person should tell the first person something self-disclosing in return

open brainstorming: type of brainstorming in groups where each person generates a list of ideas with no topic boundary

open questions: questions that enable and prompt interviewees to answer in a wide range of ways (contrast with *closed questions*)

openness–privacy: a dialectic tension caused by people's need to be honest and open yet to retain some privacy and control over information others have about them

operational definition: a concrete explanation of meaning that is more specific, original, or personal than what a dictionary might provide

opinions: personal beliefs or speculations that, while perhaps based on facts, have not been proven or verified

oral citations: references to the source of the evidence and support material used during a presentation

organizational pattern: an arrangement of the main points of a speech that best enables audience comprehension

orientation phase: the part of a speech in which a speaker provides the audience members with information that allows them to better understand and appreciate the material presented in the body of a speech

parasocial relationships: "relationships" established with media characters and personalities

parole: how people actually use language: where they often speak using informal and ungrammatical language structure that carries meaning to us all the same (contrast with *langue*)

pauses: breaks in the vocal flow

past experience with the source: obstacle to listening when previous encounters with a person lead people to dismiss or fail to critically examine a message because the person has generally been right (or wrong) in the past

pathos: the use of emotional appeals to impact an audience

patriarchy: a set of beliefs or cultural practices that, in effect, gives preference to men and grants them a dominant role over women, whether explicitly or implicitly.

pentad: five components of narratives that explain the motivation of symbolic action

perception: process of actively selecting, organizing, and evaluating information, activities, situations, people, and essentially all the things that make up your world

performance interviews: interviews in which an individual's activities and work are discussed

performative self: a self that is a creative performance based on the social demands and norms of a given situation

personal constructs: bipolar dimensions used to measure and evaluate things

personal relationships: relationships that only specified and irreplaceable individuals (such as your mother, father, brother, sister, or very best friend) can have with you

personal space: space legitimately claimed or occupied by a person for the time being; the area around a person that is regarded as part of the person and in which only informal and close relationships are conducted

personal testimony: testimony that comes from oneself

persuade (purpose): desire to change audience beliefs, enhance existing beliefs, or convince the audience to enact a particular behavior or perform a particular action

persuasion: the art of changing someone else's mind

persuasive interviews: interviews that have influence as the ultimate goal

phenomenological approaches: focus on communication as experience of others and the related experience of "otherness" (the sense of being an outsider)

pitch: the highness or lowness of a speaker's voice

plausibility: the extent to which a message seems legitimate

points principle: a principle of speech organization and development that highlights the basic building blocks of an argument: the main points and subpoints

polychronic culture: a culture that sees time not as linear and simple but as complex and made up of many strands, none of which is more important than any other—hence such culture's relaxed attitude toward time

polysemy: multiple meanings for the same word or symbol

population: refers to whom or what a study included (e.g., people, number of TV shows, types of foods)

positive face wants: the need to be seen and accepted as a worthwhile and reasonable person (contrast with *negative face wants*)

positivist or **post-positivist approaches**: most likely to be what you think of when you think of "science." Post positivists look for causation, believe in the value of objective measurement, and are number crunchers

post hoc ergo propter hoc: argues that something is caused by whatever happens before it; Latin for "after this; therefore, because of this"

power: there are several kinds of power, ranging from "legitimate power" (e.g. of a police officer to stop a suspect) to "informal power" where one person does what another respected person suggests, but all involve the ability to control the actions of another person by some means

presentation: one person's particular version of, or "take" on, the facts or events (contrast with *representation*)

presentation aids: audio and visual tools used by a speaker to enhance audience understanding, appreciation, and retention that also impact a speaker's credibility and audience attention

primary questions: questions that introduce new topics during an interview (contrast with *secondary questions*)

probing questions (secondary questions): brief statements or words that urge an interviewee to continue or to elaborate on a response

problem–solution pattern: divides the body of the speech by first addressing a problem and then offering a solution to that problem

problem-solving interviews: interviews in which a problem is isolated and solutions are generated

process speech: describes the procedure or method through which something is accomplished *without* the expectation that the audience will actually perform the process

promotive communication: works toward moving the agenda along and keeping people on track

prototype: best-case example of something

provisions of relationships: the deep and important psychological and supportive benefits that relationships provide

proxemics: the study of space and distance in communication

question–answer pattern: posing questions an audience may have about a subject and then answering them in a manner that favors a speaker's position

rate (of speech): how fast or slowly a person speaks, generally determined by how many words are spoken per minute

receiving: the initial step in the listening process where hearing and listening connect

red herring (fallacious argument): the use of another issue to divert attention away from the real issue

reflecting (paraphrasing): summarizing what another person has said to convey understanding of the message

regulators: nonverbal actions that indicate to others how you want them to behave or what you want them to do

relational continuity constructional units (RCCUs): small-talk ways of demonstrating that the relationship persists during absence of face-to-face contact

relational listening: recognizing, understanding, and addressing the interconnection of relationships and communication during the listening process

relational technologies: such technologies as cell phones, iPods, and PDAs whose use has relational functions and implications in society and within specific groups

representation: describes facts or conveys information (contrast with *presentation*)

responding: final step in the listening process that entails reacting to the message of another person

résumé: document used when seeking employment that presents credentials for a position in a clear and concise manner

resurrection process: part of the breakdown of relationships that deals with how people prepare themselves for new relationships after ending an old one

rhetorical approaches: treat communication as practical discourse, that is to say, as discourse that brings about some sort of result (like persuasion)

richness: the characteristics of a message determined by the number of verbal and nonverbal cues available through a medium or technology

Sapir/Whorf hypothesis: the idea that it is the names of objects and ideas that make verbal distinctions and help you make conceptual distinctions rather than the other way around

schemata: mental structures that are used to organize information in part by clustering or linking associated material

scripts: guides for behavior developed from our system of knowledge

secondary questions: follow-up questions asked when seeking elaboration or further information (see *probing questions* and *mirror questions;* contrast with *primary questions*)

selective listening: obstacle to listening when people focus on the points of a message that correspond with their views and interests and pay less attention to those that do not

self-concept: a personal, private, and essential core, covered with layers of secrecy, privacy, and convention

self-disclosure: the revelation of personal information that others could not know unless the person *made* it known

self-fulfilling prophecy: principle maintaining if someone believes a particular outcome will take place, his or her actions will often lead to its fruition

semantic diversion: obstacle to listening that occurs when people are distracted by words or phrases used in a message through negative response or unfamiliarity

semiotic approaches: take communication as intersubjective activity mediated by signs. That is to say, this approach is based on the meaning that is conveyed by symbols that two people in a conversation both understand

sign: a consequence or an indicator of something specific, which cannot be changed by arbitrary actions or labels (e.g., "Wet streets are a sign of rain")

sociability: a secondary dimension of credibility referring to the "friendliness or likeableness" that enables a speaker to appear personable

social construction (of meaning): the way in which symbols take on meaning in a social context or society as they are used over time

social judgment theory: explains how people may respond to a range of positions surrounding a particular topic or issue

social process: part of the process of breakdown in a relationship that involves telling other people in the network about the problems and either seeking their help to keep the relationship together or seeking support for one's own version of the story of why it has come apart

social relationships: relationships in which the specific people in a given role can be changed and the relationship would still occur (e.g., customer–client relationships are the same irrespective of who is the customer and who is the client on a particular occasion; compare with *personal relationships*)

socialization impact of media: depictions of relationships in media provide models of behavior that inform people about how to engage in relationships

sociocultural approaches: believe that through our communication we reinforce, reestablish, and serve to promote existing social structures and forces

socioemotional (leadership style): style of leadership through which members are made to feel comfortable, satisfied, valued, and understood (compare with *task (leadership style)*)

sociopsychological approaches: are concerned with the ways in which communication serves to express emotion, regulate and continue interaction, and exert influence between one person and another

source distraction: obstacle to listening that results from auditory and visual characteristics of the message source

spatial pattern: main points of a speech are arranged according to their physical relation

specific purpose: exactly what a speaker wants to achieve through a presentation

speech (communication) codes: sets of communication patterns that are the norm for that culture, and only that culture, hence defining it as different from others around it

speech communities: sets of people whose speech codes and practices identify them as a cultural unit, sharing characteristic values through their equally characteristic speech

speech of definition and description: a speech providing an extended explanation or depiction of an object, a creation, a place, a person, a concept, or an event

speech to actuate: a speech delivered in an attempt to impact audience behavior

speech to convince: a speech delivered in an attempt to impact audience thinking; encompasses a primary claim, or essentially what the speaker is trying to convince the audience to believe

static: elements of nonverbal communication that are fixed during interaction (e.g., shape of the room where an interaction takes place, color of eyes, clothes worn during an interview; contrast with *dynamic*)

statistics: numbers that demonstrate or establish size, trends, associations, and categories

status of the source: an obstacle to listening when a person's rank, reputation, or social position leads people to dismiss or fail to critically examine a message

subpoints: statements that support and explain the main points of a speech

syllogism: a form of argumentation consisting of a major premise, a minor premise, and a conclusion (see *enthymeme*)

symbol: an arbitrary representation of ideas, objects, people, relationships, cultures, genders, races, and so forth

symbolic interactionism: how broad social forces affect or even transact an individual person's view of who he or she is

symbolic self: the self that is transacted in interaction with other people; that arises out of social interaction, not vice versa; and hence that does not just "belong to you"

synchronous communication: communication in which people interact in real time and can at once both send and receive messages

task (leadership style): style of leadership through which proper group procedures and goals are emphasized (compare with *socioemotional (leadership style)*)

testimony: declarations or statements of a person's findings, opinions, conclusions, or experience

thesis statement: encapsulates the entire speech and is what will be maintained or argued throughout the presentation

topic-specific brainstorming: type of brainstorming in which a person generates a list of items dealing with one specific topic or idea

topical pattern: arranges support material in a speech according to specific categories, groupings, or grounds

transitions: phrases or statements that serve to connect the major parts or sections of a speech and to guide the audience through the presentation

turn taking: when one speaker hands over speaking to another person

unity principle: a principle of speech organization and development that maintains a speaker should stay focused and provide only information that supports the speech's thesis and main points

uses and gratifications: research that has attempted to determine why media systems are used and what audience members gain from their use

values: deeply held and enduring judgments of significance or importance that often provide the basis for both beliefs and attitudes

verifiability: an indication that the material being provided can be confirmed by other sources or means

vocalics (paralanguage): vocal characteristics that provide information about how verbal communication should be interpreted and how the speaker is feeling

volume: how loudly or quietly a person speaks

voluntary audience: an audience of people who are listening to a speech because they have personally chosen to be there

wandering thoughts: an obstacle to listening involving daydreams or thoughts about things other than the message being presented

wrap-up signal: indicates to the audience both verbally and nonverbally that the speaker has reached the conclusion of a public presentation; also a phrase, usually uttered by the interviewer, that signals the beginning of an interview's conclusion

Photo Credits

Chapter 1

Chapter Opening Photo: © Steve Duck.
Photo 1.1: © Creatas/ThinkStock.
Photo 1.2: © iStockphoto.com/macfoto80.
Photo 1.3: © Jupiterimages/Pixland/ThinkStock.
Photo 1.4: © Comstock Images/ThinkStock.
Photo 1.5: © Comstock Images/ThinkStock

Chapter 2

Chapter Opening Photo: © iStockphoto.com/
    knape.
Photo 2.1: © iStockphoto.com/llhoward.
Photo 2.2: © iStockphoto.com/Brosa.
Photo 2.3: © iStockphoto.com/Tina Lorien.
Photo 2.4: © iStockphoto.com/duncan1890.
Photo 2.5: © BananaStock/ThinkStock.

Chapter 3

Chapter Opening Photo: © iStockphoto.com/
    gemenacom.
Photo 3.1: © iStockphoto.com/paulprescott72.
Photo 3.2: © iStockphoto.com/MaxFX.
Photo 3.3: ©iStockphoto.com/webphotographeer.
Photo 3.4a: © Keith Brofsky/Photodisc/
    ThinkStock.
Photo 3.4b: © Michael Jenner/Robert Harding
    World Imagery/Getty Images.
Photo 3.5: © iStockphoto.com/Elenathewise.

Chapter 4

Chapter Opening Photo: © Stockbyte/
    ThinkStock.
Photo 4.1: © Can Stock Photo Inc./
    Monkeybusiness.
Photo 4.2: © Jupiterimages/Comstock/
    ThinkStock.
Photo 4.3: © Getty Images/AbleStock.com/
    ThinkStock.
Photo 4.4: © Digital Vision./ThinkStock.
Photo 4.5: © Dave & Les Jacobs/Getty Images.

Chapter 5

Chapter Opening Photo: © iStockphoto.com/
    SensorSpot.
Photo 5.1: © iStockphoto.com/killerb10.
Photo 5.2: © iStockphoto.com/parema.
Photo 5.3: © iStockphoto.com/NoDerog.
Photo 5.4: © iStockphoto.com/ranplett.
Photo 5.5: © iStockphoto.com/crazychristina.

Chapter 6

Chapter Opening Photo: © iStockphoto.com/
    deanm1974.
Photo 6.1: © iStockphoto.com/diane39.
Photo 6.2: © iStockphoto.com/Claudiad.
Photo 6.3: © iStockphoto.com/Slobo Mitic.
Photo 6.4: © iStockphoto.com/Brad Killer.
Photo 6.5: © iStockphoto.com/Deadair.

Chapter 7

Chapter Opening Photo: © iStockphoto.com/
    leezsnow.
Photo 7.1: © iStockphoto.com/nickfree.
Photo 7.2: © iStockphoto.com/wynnter.
Photo 7.3: © iStockphoto.com/claylib.
Photo 7.4: © iStockphoto.com/photosbyjim.
Photo 7.5: © iStockphoto.com/belknap.

Chapter 8

Chapter Opening Photo: © iStockphoto.com/
    summersetretrievers.
Photo 8.1: © Digital Vision./ThinkStock.
Photo 8.2: © Stockbyte/ThinkStock.
Photo 8.3: © Fuse/Getty Images.
Photo 8.4: © Peter Turnley/Corbis.
Photo 8.5: © Can Stock Photo Inc./monkeybusiness.

Chapter 9

Chapter Opening Photo: © iStockphoto.com/
    Sophia Tsibikaki.
Photo 9.1: © Fancy/Jupiter Images.

Photo 9.2: © Getty Images/ Photos.com/ ThinkStock.

Photo 9.3: © Chris Jackson/Getty Images Entertainment/Getty.

Photo 9.4: © Rayes/Digital Vision/ThinkStock.

Photo 9.5: © Comstock/ThinkStock.

Chapter 10

Chapter Opening Photo: © Dave J. Anthony/ Getty.

Photo 10.1: © Hemera Technologies/Ablestock/ ThinkStock.

Photo 10.2: © iStockphoto.com/ monkeybusinessimages.

Photo 10.3: © Bob D'Amico /ABC via Getty Images.

Photo 10.4: © Business Wire/Getty.

Photo:10.5: © Can Stock Photo Inc./ SmallTownStudio.

Chapter 11

Chapter Opening Photo: © Getty Images/ Photos. com/ThinkStock.

Photo 11.1: © Tami Chappell/Reuters/Corbis.

Photo 11.2: © Somos/Veer.

Photo 11.3: © Creatas/ThinkStock.

Photo 11.4: © Simon Jarratt/Corbis.

Photo 11.5: © iStockphoto.com/BartCo.

Chapter 12

Chapter Opening Photo: © gulfimages/Getty Images.

Photo 12.1: © iStockphoto.com/dlewis33.

Photo 12.2: © Stockbyte/ThinkStock.

Photo 12.3: © Will & Deni McIntyre/Getty Images.

Photo 12.4: © iStockphoto.com/Blue_Cutler.

Photo 12.5: © iStockphoto.com/pixdeluxe.

Chapter 13

Chapter Opening Photo: © iStockphoto.com/ Kativ.

Photo 13.1: © iStockphoto.com/kcline.

Photo 13.2: © iStockphoto.com/MotoEd.

Photo 13.3: © BananaStock/ThinkStock.

Photo 13.4: © Bernhard Lang.

Photo 13.5: © Win McNamee/Getty Images.

Chapter 14

Chapter Opening Photo: © Photodisc/ ThinkStock.

Photo 14.1: © Polka Dot Images/ThinkStock.

Photo 14.2: © Stockbyte.

Photo 14.3: © Jupiterimages/Photos.com.

Photo 14.4: © Comstock.

Photo 14.5: © Mel Yates.

Chapter 15

Chapter Opening Photo: © iStockphoto.com/ AlexRaths.

Photo 15.1: © iStockphoto.com/wdstock.

Photo 15.2: © iStockphoto.com/fstop123.

Photo 15.3: © iStockphoto.com/jsmith.

Photo 15.4: © iStockphoto.com/matzaball.

Photo 15.5: © iStockphoto.com/jsmith.

Chapter 16

Chapter Opening Photo: © iStockphoto.com/ Cimmerian

Photo 16.1: United States Mint.

Photo 16.2: Brady-Handy Photo Collection (Library of Congress).

Photo 16.4:© iStockphoto.com/Cimmerian.

Author Index

Subject Index